SHADOW OF THE HEGEMON

ORSON SCOTT CARD

TOR®
A TOM DOHERTY ASSOCIATES BOOK
NEW YORK

SHADOW OF THE HEGEMON

A Tor Book
Published by Tom Doherty Associates, LLC
175 Fifth Avenue
New York, NY 10010

www.tor-forge.com

ISBN 978-0-8125-6595-9
Library of Congress Catalog Card Number: 00-031678

First Edition: January 2001
First Mass Market Edition: December 2001

Printed in the United States of America

20 19 18 17 16 15 14 13 12

Praise for *Shadow of the Hegemon*

"This fine follow-up to *Ender's Shadow* features that novel's hero, Bean (now a young man), wrestling with Card's trademark: superbly real moral and ethical dilemmas. . . . The complexity and serious treatment of the book's young protagonists will attract many sophisticated YA readers, while Card's impeccable prose, fast pacing, and political intrigue will appeal to adult fans of spy novels, thrillers, and science fiction."

—*Publishers Weekly* (starred review)

"As are all Card's books, this one is strangely moving. Although *Shadow of the Hegemon* has the bones of a simple thriller, Card's ability to evoke character—especially the character of children essentially raised by each other while continually under siege—makes these books seem not like fiction but like family stories, tales of what our relatives endured in a world too close to our own."

—*San Jose Mercury News*

"The author's graceful storytelling and engaging cast of youthful characters add an extra dimension to an already gripping story of children caught up in world-shaking events."

—*Library Journal*

"The novels of Orson Scott Card's Ender series are an intriguing combination of action, military and political strategy, elaborate war games, and psychology."

—*USA Today*

"Bean comes out mostly, though not entirely, from Ender's shadow in this fast-paced, stand-alone sequel to *Ender's Shadow*, which picks up a year later after the Battle School kids have all been returned to Earth."

—*Locus*

Praise for *Ender's Shadow*

"Card is always at his best, as here, when he's writing about children: an absorbing, near-flawless performance that, while fully intelligible, should send everyone scurrying to reread the original."

—*Kirkus Reviews*

"As always, everyone will be struck by the power of Card's children, always more and less than human, perfect yet struggling, tragic yet hopeful, wondrous and strange." —*Publishers Weekly* (starred review)

"The author's superb storytelling and his genuine insight into the moral dilemmas that lead good people to commit questionable actions make this title a priority for most libraries." —*Library Journal*

"[*Ender's Shadow* is] a strong, encouraging, enlightening story that reads as brave and as bright as the young adult novels since Heinlein, but with enough depth, breadth, and Dickensian squalor to stand proudly alongside any mainstream novel on your shelf."

—*The San Diego Union-Tribune*

"An excellent addition to the series, which will leave readers panting for the next installment." —*Kliatt*

Praise for Orson Scott Card

"Card's prose is powerful here, as is his consideration of mystical and quasi-religious themes. Though billed as the final Ender novel, this story leaves enough mysteries unexplored to justify another entry; and Card fans should find that possibility, like this novel, very welcome indeed."

—*Publishers Weekly* (starred review) on *Children of the Mind*

"Orson Scott Card, one of our best writers, understands that to imagine the Other is one of the best ways to explore our hidden selves."

—*The Columbus Dispatch*

"An undeniable heavyweight . . . This book combines Card's quirky style with his hard ethical dilemmas and sharply drawn portraits."

—New York *Daily News* on *Ender's Game*

"Card has taken the venerable SF concepts of a superman and an interstellar war against aliens, and, with superb characterization, pacing, and language, combines them into a seamless story of compelling power."

—*Booklist* on *Ender's Game*

"This book provides a harrowing look at the price we pay for trying to mold our posterity in our own aggressive image of what we believe is right."

—*The Christian Science Monitor* on *Ender's Game*

Tor Books by Orson Scott Card

Empire
The Folk of the Fringe
Future on Fire (editor)
Future on Ice (editor)
Hart's Hope
Hidden Empire
Invasive Procedures
(with Aaron Johnston)
Keeper of Dreams
The Lost Gate
Lovelock
(with Kathryn Kidd)
Pastwatch: The Redemption of Christopher Columbus
Saints
Songmaster
Treason
The Worthing Saga
Wyrms

Ender

Ender's Game
Speaker for the Dead
Xenocide
Children of the Mind
Ender's Shadow
Shadow of the Hegemon
Shadow Puppets
Shadow of the Giant
First Meetings: In the Enderverse
A War of Gifts
Ender in Exile

The Tales of Alvin Maker

Seventh Son
Red Prophet
Prentice Alvin
Alvin Journeyman
Heartfire
The Crystal City

Homecoming

The Memory of Earth
The Call of Earth
The Ships of Earth
Earthfall
Earthborn

Women of Genesis

Sarah
Rebekah
Rachel & Leah

Short Fiction

Maps in a Mirror: The Short Fiction of Orson Scott Card (hardcover)
Maps in a Mirror, Volume 1: The Changed Man (paperback)
Maps in a Mirror, Volume 2: Flux (paperback)
Maps in a Mirror, Volume 3: Cruel Miracles (paperback)
Maps in a Mirror, Volume 4: Monkey Sonatas (paperback)

TO CHARLES BENJAMIN CARD

YOU ARE ALWAYS LIGHT TO US,

YOU SEE THROUGH ALL THE SHADOWS,

AND WE HEAR YOUR STRONG VOICE

SINGING IN OUR DREAMS.

CONTENTS

Part One

VOLUNTEERS

1

Petra

To: Chamrajnagar%sacredriver@ifcom.gov
From: Locke%espinoza@polnet.gov
Re: What are you doing to protect the children?

Dear Admiral Chamrajnagar,
I was given your idname by a mutual friend who once worked for you but now is a glorified dispatcher—I'm sure you know whom I mean. I realize that your primary responsibility now is not so much military as logistical, and your thoughts are turned to space rather than the political situation on Earth. After all, you decisively defeated the nationalist forces led by your predecessor in the League War, and that issue seems settled. The I.F. remains

independent and for that we are all grateful.

What no one seems to understand is that peace on Earth is merely a temporary illusion. Not only is Russia's long-pent expansionism still a driving force, but also many other nations have aggressive designs on their neighbors. The forces of the Strategos are being disbanded, the Hegemony is rapidly losing all authority, and Earth is poised on the edge of cataclysm.

The most powerful resource of any nation in the wars to come will be the children trained in Battle, Tactical, and Command School. While it is perfectly appropriate for these children to serve their native countries in future wars, it is inevitable that at least some nations that lack such I.F.-certified geniuses or who believe that rivals have more-gifted commanders will inevitably take preemptive action, either to secure that enemy resource for their own use or, in any event, to deny the enemy the use of that resource. In short, these children are in grave danger of being kidnapped or killed.

I recognize that you have a hands-off policy toward events on Earth, but it was the I.F. that identified these children and trained them, thus making them targets. Whatever happens to these children, the I.F. has ultimate responsibility. It would go a long way toward protecting them if you were to issue an order placing these children under Fleet protection, warning any nation or group attempting to harm or interfere with them that they would face swift and harsh military retribution. Far from regarding this as interference in Earthside affairs, most nations would welcome this action, and, for whatever it is worth, you would have my complete support in all public forums.

I hope you will act immediately. There is no time to waste.

Respectfully,
Locke

Nothing looked right in Armenia when Petra Arkanian returned home. The mountains were dramatic, of course, but they had not really been part of her childhood experience. It was not until she got to Maralik that she began to see things that should mean something to her. Her father had met her in Yerevan while her mother remained at home with her eleven-year-old brother and the new baby—obviously conceived even before the population restrictions were relaxed when the war ended. They had no doubt watched Petra on television. Now, as the flivver took Petra and her father along the narrow streets, he began apologizing. "It won't seem much to you, Pet, after seeing the world."

"They didn't show us the world much, Papa. There were no windows in Battle School."

"I mean, the spaceport, and the capital, all the important people and wonderful buildings . . ."

"I'm not disappointed, Papa." She had to lie in order to reassure him. It was as if he had given her Maralik as a gift, and now was unsure whether she liked it. She didn't know yet whether she would like it or not. She hadn't liked Battle School, but she got used to it. There was no getting used to Eros, but she had endured it. How could she dislike a place like this, with open sky and people wandering wherever they wanted?

Yet she *was* disappointed. For all her memories of Maralik were the memories of a five-year-old, looking up at tall buildings, across wide streets where large vehicles loomed and fled at alarming speeds. Now she was much older, beginning to come into her womanly height, and the cars were smaller, the streets downright narrow, and the buildings—designed to survive the next earthquake, as the old buildings had not—were squat. Not ugly—there was grace in them, given the eclectic styles that were somehow blended here, Turkish and Russian, Spanish and Riviera, and, most incredibly, Japanese. It was a marvel to see how they were still unified by the choice of colors, the closeness to the street, the almost uniform height as all strained against the legal maximums.

She knew of all this because she had read about it on Eros as she and the other children sat out the League War. She had seen pictures on the nets. But nothing had prepared her for the fact that she had left here as a five-year-old and now was returning at fourteen.

"What?" she said. For Father had spoken and she hadn't understood him.

"I asked if you wanted to stop for a candy before we went home, the way we used to."

Candy. How could she have forgotten the word for candy?

Easily, that's how. The only other Armenian in Battle School had been three years ahead of her and graduated to Tactical School, so they overlapped only for a few months. She had been seven when she got from Ground School to Battle School, and he was ten, leaving without ever having commanded an army. Was it any wonder that he didn't want to jabber in Armenian to a little kid from home? So in effect she had gone without speaking Armenian for nine years. And the Armenian she had spoken then was a five-year-old's language. It was so hard to speak it now, and harder still to understand it.

How could she tell Father that it would help her greatly if he would speak to her in Fleet Common—English, in effect? He spoke it, of course—he and Mother had made a point of speaking English at home when she was little, so she would not be handicapped linguistically if she was taken into Battle School. In fact, as she thought about it, that was part of her problem. How often had Father actually called candy by the Armenian word? Whenever he let her walk with him through town and they stopped for candy, he would make her ask for it in English, and call each piece by its English name. It was absurd, really—why would she need to know, in Battle School, the English names of Armenian candies?

"What are you laughing for?"

"I seem to have lost my taste for candy while I was in space, Father. Though for old times' sake, I hope you'll have time to walk through town with me again. You won't be as tall as you were the last time."

"No, nor will your hand be as small in mine." He laughed, too. "We've been robbed of years that would be precious now, to have in memory."

"Yes," said Petra. "But I was where I needed to be."

Or was I? I'm the one who broke first. I passed all the tests, until the test that mattered, and there I broke first. Ender comforted me by telling me he relied on me most and pushed me hardest, but he pushed us all and relied upon us all and I'm the one who broke. No one ever spoke of it; perhaps here on Earth not one living soul knew of it. But the others who had fought with her knew it. Until that moment when she fell asleep in the midst of combat, she had been one of the best. After that, though she never broke again, Ender also never trusted her again. The others watched over her, so that if she suddenly stopped commanding her ships, they could step in. She was sure that one of them had been designated, but never asked who. Dink? Bean? Bean, yes—whether Ender assigned him to do it or not, she knew Bean would be watching, ready to take over. She was not reliable. They did not trust her. She did not trust herself.

Yet she would keep that secret from her family, as she kept it in talking to the prime minister and the press, to the Armenian military and the schoolchildren who had been assembled to meet the great Armenian hero of the Formic War. Armenia needed a hero. She was the only candidate out of this war. They had shown her how the online textbooks already listed her among the ten greatest Armenians of all time. Her picture, her biography, and quotations from Colonel Graff, from Major Anderson, from Mazer Rackham.

And from Ender Wiggin. "It was Petra who first stood up for me at risk to herself. It was Petra who trained me when no one else would. I owe everything

I accomplished to her. And in the final campaign, in battle after battle she was the commander I relied upon."

Ender could not have known how those words would hurt. No doubt he meant to reassure her that he did rely upon her. But because she knew the truth, his words sounded like pity to her. They sounded like a kindly lie.

And now she was home. Nowhere on Earth was she so much a stranger as here, because she ought to feel at home here, but she could not, for no one knew her here. They knew a bright little girl who was sent off amid tearful good-byes and brave words of love. They knew a hero who returned with the halo of victory around her every word and gesture. But they did not know and would never know the girl who broke under the strain and in the midst of battle simply . . . fell asleep. While her ships were lost, while real men died, she slept because her body could stay awake no more. That girl would remain hidden from all eyes.

And from all eyes would be hidden also the girl who watched every move of the boys around her, evaluating their abilities, guessing at their intentions, determined to take any advantage she could get, refusing to bow to any of them. Here she was supposed to become a child again—an older one, but a child nonetheless. A dependent.

After nine years of fierce watchfulness, it would be restful to turn over her life to others, wouldn't it?

"Your mother wanted to come. But she was afraid to come." He chuckled as if this were amusing. "Do you understand?"

"No," said Petra.

"Not afraid of you," said Father. "Of her firstborn daughter she could never be afraid. But the cameras.

The politicians. The crowds. She is a woman of the kitchen. Not a woman of the market. Do you understand?"

She understood the Armenian easily enough, if that's what he was asking, because he had caught on, he was speaking in simple language and separating his words a little so she would not get lost in the stream of conversation. She was grateful for this, but also embarrassed that it was so obvious she needed such help.

What she did not understand was a fear of crowds that could keep a mother from coming to meet her daughter after nine years.

Petra knew that it was not the crowds or the cameras that Mother was afraid of. It was Petra herself. The lost five-year-old who would never be five again, who had had her first period with the help of a Fleet nurse, whose mother had never bent over her homework with her, or taught her how to cook. No, wait. She had baked pies with her mother. She had helped roll out the dough. Thinking back, she could see that her mother had not actually let her do anything that mattered. But to Petra it had seemed that she was the one baking. That her mother trusted her.

That turned her thoughts to the way Ender had coddled her at the end, pretending to trust her as before but actually keeping control.

And because that was an unbearable thought, Petra looked out the window of the flivver. "Are we in the part of town where I used to play?"

"Not yet," said Father. "But nearly. Maralik is still not such a large town."

"It all seems new to me," said Petra.

"But it isn't. It never changes. Only the architecture. There are Armenians all over the world, but only because they were forced to leave to save their lives. By nature, Armenians stay at home. The hills are the womb, and we have no desire to be born." He chuckled at his joke.

Had he always chuckled like that? It sounded to Petra less like amusement than like nervousness. Mother was not the only one afraid of her.

At last the flivver reached home. And here at last she recognized where she was. It was small and shabby compared to what she had remembered, but in truth she had not even thought of the place in many years. It stopped haunting her dreams by the time she was ten. But now, coming home again, it all returned to her, the tears she had shed in those first weeks and months in Ground School, and again when she left Earth and went up to Battle School. This was what she had yearned for, and at last she was here again, she had it back . . . and knew that she no longer needed it, no longer really wanted it. The nervous man in the car beside her was not the tall god who had led her through the streets of Maralik so proudly. And the woman waiting inside the house would not be the goddess from whom came warm food and a cool hand on her forehead when she was sick.

But she had nowhere else to go.

Her mother was standing at the window as Petra emerged from the flivver. Father palmed the scanner to accept the charges. Petra raised a hand and gave a small wave to her mother, a shy smile that quickly grew into a grin. Her mother smiled back and gave her own small wave in reply. Petra took her father's hand and walked with him to the house.

The door opened as they approached. It was Stefan, her brother. She would not have known him from her memories of a two-year-old, still creased with baby fat. And he, of course, did not know her at all. He beamed the way the children from the school group had beamed at her, thrilled to meet a celebrity but not really aware of her as a person. He was her brother, though, and so she hugged him and he hugged her back. "You're really Petra!" he said.

"You're really Stefan!" she answered. Then she turned to her mother. She was still standing at the window, looking out.

"Mother?"

The woman turned, tears streaking her cheeks. "I'm so glad to see you, Petra," she said.

But she made no move to come to Petra, or even to reach out to her.

"But you're still looking for the little girl who left nine years ago," said Petra.

Mother burst into tears, and now she reached out her arms and Petra strode to her, to be enfolded in her embrace. "You're a woman now," said Mother. "I don't know you, but I love you."

"I love you too, Mother," said Petra. And was pleased to realize that it was true.

They had about an hour, the four of them—five, once the baby woke up. Petra shunted aside their questions—"Oh, everything about me has already been published or broadcast. It's *you* that I want to hear about"—and learned that her father was still editing textbooks and supervising translations, and her mother was still the shepherd of the neighborhood, watching out for everyone, bringing food when someone was sick, taking care of children while parents ran errands, and providing lunch for any child who showed up. "I remember once that Mother and I had lunch alone, just the two of us," Stefan joked. "We didn't know what to say, and there was so much food left over."

"It was already that way when I was little," Petra said. "I remember being so proud of how the other kids loved my mother. And so jealous of the way she loved them!"

"Never as much as I loved my own girl and boy," said Mother. "But I do love children, I admit it, every one of them is precious in the sight of God, every one of them is welcome in my house."

"Oh, I've known a few you wouldn't love," said Petra.

"Maybe," said Mother, not wishing to argue, but plainly not believing that there could be such a child.

The baby gurgled and Mother lifted her shirt to tuck the baby to her breast.

"Did I slurp so noisily?" asked Petra.

"Not really," said Mother.

"Oh, tell the truth," said Father. "She woke the neighbors."

"So I was a glutton."

"No, merely a barbarian," said Father. "No table manners."

Petra decided to ask the delicate question boldly and have done with it. "The baby was born only a month after the population restrictions were lifted."

Father and Mother looked at each other, Mother with a beatific expression, Father with a wince. "Yes, well, we missed you. We wanted another little girl."

"You would have lost your job," said Petra.

"Not right away," said Father.

"Armenian officials have always been a little slow about enforcing those laws," said Mother.

"But eventually, you could have lost everything."

"No," said Mother. "When you left, we lost half of everything. Children are everything. The rest is . . . nothing."

Stefan laughed. "Except when I'm hungry. Food is something!"

"You're always hungry," said Father.

"Food is always something," said Stefan.

They laughed, but Petra could see that Stefan had had no illusions about what the birth of this child would have meant. "It's a good thing we won the war."

"Better than losing it," said Stefan.

"It's nice to have the baby and obey the law, too," said Mother.

"But you didn't get your little girl."

"No," said Father. "We got our David."

"We didn't need a little girl after all," said Mother. "We got you back."

Not really, thought Petra. And not for long. Four years, maybe fewer, and I'll be off to university. And you won't miss me by then, because you'll know that I'm not the little girl you love, just this bloody-handed veteran of a nasty military school that turned out to have real battles to fight.

After the first hour, neighbors and cousins and friends from Father's work began dropping by, and it was not until after midnight that Father had to announce that tomorrow was not a national holiday and he needed to have *some* sleep before work. It took yet another hour to shoo everyone out of the house, and by then all Petra wanted was to curl up in bed and hide from the world for at least a week.

But by the end of the next day, she knew she had to get out of the house. She didn't fit into the routines. Mother loved her, yes, but her life centered around the baby and the neighborhood, and while she kept trying to engage Petra in conversation, Petra could see that she was a distraction, that it would be a relief for Mother when Petra went to school during the day as Stefan did, returning only at the scheduled time. Petra understood, and that night announced that she wanted to register for school and begin class the next day.

"Actually," said Father, "the people from the I.F. said that you could probably go right on to university."

"I'm fourteen," said Petra. "And there are serious gaps in my education."

"She never even heard of Dog," said Stefan.

"What?" said Father. "What dog?"

"Dog," said Stefan. "The zip orchestra. You know."

"Very famous group," said Mother. "If you heard them, you'd take the car in for major repairs."

"Oh, *that* Dog," said Father. "I hardly think that's the education Petra was talking about."

"Actually, it is," said Petra.

"It's like she's from another planet," said Stefan. "Last night I realized she never heard of *anybody*."

"I *am* from another planet. Or, properly speaking, asteroid."

"Of course," said Mother. "You need to join your generation."

Petra smiled, but inwardly she winced. Her generation? She had no generation, except the few thousand kids who had once been in Battle School, and now were scattered over the surface of the Earth, trying to find out where they belonged in a world at peace.

School would not be easy, Petra soon discovered. There were no courses in military history and military strategy. The mathematics was pathetic compared to what she had mastered in Battle School, but with literature and grammar she was downright backward: Her knowledge of Armenian was indeed childish, and while she was fluent in the version of English spoken in Battle School—including the slang that the kids used there—she had little knowledge of the rules of grammar and no understanding at all of the mixed Armenian and English slang that the kids used with each other at school.

Everyone was very nice to her, of course—the most popular girls immediately took possession of her, and the teachers treated her like a celebrity. Petra allowed herself to be led around and shown everything, and studied the chatter of her new friends very carefully, so she could learn the slang and hear how school English and Armenian were nuanced. She knew that soon enough the popular girls would tire of her—especially when they realized how bluntly outspoken Petra was, a trait that she had no intention of changing. Petra was quite used to the fact that people who cared about the social hierarchy usually ended up hating her and, if they were wise, fearing her, since pretensions didn't last long in her presence. She would find her real friends over the next few weeks—if, in fact, there were any here who would value her for what she was. It didn't matter. All the friendships here, all the social concerns, seemed so trivial to her. There was nothing at stake here, except each student's own social life and academic future, and what did that matter? Petra's previous schooling had all been conducted in the shadow of war, with the fate of humanity riding on the outcome of her studies and the quality of her skills. Now, what did it matter? She would read Armenian literature because she wanted to learn Armenian, not because she thought it actually mattered what some expatriate like Saroyan thought about the lives of children in a long-lost era of a far-off country.

The only part of school that she truly loved was physical education. To have sky over her head as she ran, to have the track lie flat before her, to be able to run and run for the sheer joy of it and without a clock ticking out her allotted time for aerobic exercise—such a luxury. She could not compete, physically, with most of the other girls. It would take time for her body to reconstruct itself for high gravity, for despite the great pains that the I.F. went to to make sure that soldiers' bodies did not deteriorate too much during long months and years in space, nothing trained you for living on a planet's surface except living there. But Petra didn't care that she was one of the last to complete every race, that she couldn't leap even the lowest hurdle. It felt good simply to run freely, and her weakness gave her goals to meet. She would be competitive soon enough. That was one of the aspects of her innate personality that had taken her to Battle School in the first place—that she had no particular interest in competition because she always started from the assumption that, if it mattered, she would find a way to win.

And so she settled in to her new life. Within weeks she was fluent in Armenian and had mastered the local slang. As she had expected, the popular girls dropped her in about the same amount of time, and a few weeks later, the brainy girls had cooled toward her as well. It was among the rebels and misfits that she found her friends, and soon she had a circle of confidants and co-conspirators that she called her "jeesh," Battle School slang for close friends, a private army. Not that she was the commander or anything, but they were all loyal to each other and amused at the antics of the teachers and the other students, and when a school counselor called her in to tell her that the administration was growing concerned about the fact that Petra seemed to be associating with an antisocial element in school, she knew that she was truly at home in Maralik.

Then one day she came home from school to find the front door locked. She carried no house key—no one did in their neighborhood because no one locked up, or even, in good weather, closed their doors. She could hear the baby crying inside the house, so instead of making her mother come to the front door to let her in, she walked around back and came into the kitchen to find that her mother was tied to a chair, gagged, her eyes wide and frantic with fear.

Before Petra had time to react, a hypostick was slapped against her arm and, without ever seeing who had done it, she slipped into darkness.

2

Bean

To: Locke%espinoza@polnet.gov
From: Chamrajnagar%%@ifcom.gov
Re: Do not write to me again

Mr. Peter Wiggin,
Did you really think I would not have the resources to know who you are? You may be the author of the "Locke Proposal," giving you a reputation as a peacemaker, but you are also partly responsible for the world's present instability by your jingoist use of your sister's identity as Demosthenes. I have no illusions about your motives.

It is outrageous of you to suggest that I jeopardize the neutrality of the International Fleet in order to take control of children who have completed their military service with the I.F. If you attempt to manipulate public opinion to force me to do so, I will expose your identity as both Locke and Demosthenes.

I have changed my idname and have informed our mutual friend that he is not to attempt to relay communication between you and me again. The only comfort you are entitled to take from my letter is this: The I.F. will not interfere with those trying to assert hegemony over other nations and peoples—not even you.

Chamrajnagar

The disappearance of Petra Arkanian from her home in Armenia was worldwide news. The headlines were full of accusations hurled by Armenia against Turkey, Azerbaijan, and every other Turkish-speaking nation, and the stiff or fiery denials and counter-accusations that came in reply. There were the tearful interviews with her mother, the only witness, who was sure the kidnappers were Azerbaijani. "I know the language, I know the accent, and that's who took my little girl!"

Bean was with his family on the second day of their vacation at the beach on the island of Ithaca, but this was Petra, and he read the nets and watched the vids avidly, along with his brother, Nikolai. They both reached the same conclusion right away. "It wasn't any of the Turkish nations," Nikolai announced to their parents. "That's obvious."

Father, who had been working in government for many years, agreed. "Real Turks would have made sure to speak only Russian."

"Or Armenian," said Nikolai.

"No Turk speaks Armenian," said Mother. She was right, of course, since real Turks would never deign to learn it, and those in Turkish countries who did speak Armenian were, by definition, not really Turks and would never be trusted with a delicate assignment like kidnapping a military genius.

"So who was it?" said Father. "Agents provocateurs, trying to start a war?"

"My bet is on the Armenian government," said Nikolai. "Put her in charge of their military."

"Why kidnap her when they could employ her openly?" asked Father.

"Taking her out of school openly," said Nikolai, "would be an announcement of Armenia's military intentions. It might provoke preemptive actions by surrounding Turkey or Azerbaijan."

There was superficial plausibility in what Nikolai was saying, but Bean knew better. He had already foreseen this possibility back when all the militarily gifted children were still in space. At that time the main danger had come from the Polemarch, and Bean wrote an anonymous letter to a couple of opinion leaders on Earth, Locke and Demosthenes, urging them to get all the Battle School children back to Earth so they couldn't be seized or killed by the Polemarch's forces in the League War. The warning had worked, but now that the League War was over, too many governments had begun to think and act complacently, as if the world now had peace instead of a fragile ceasefire. Bean's original analysis still held. It was Russia that was behind the Polemarch's coup attempt in the League War, and it was likely to be Russia that was behind the kidnapping of Petra Arkanian.

Still, he didn't have any hard evidence of this and knew of no way to get it—now that he wasn't inside a Fleet installation, he had no access to military computer systems. So he kept his skepticism to himself, and made a joke out of it. "I don't know, Nikolai," he said. "Since staging this kidnapping is having an even more destabilizing effect, I'd have to say that *if* she was taken by her own government, it proves they really *really* need her, because it was a deeply dumb thing to do."

"If they're *not* dumb," said Father, "who did it?"

"Somebody who's ambitious to fight and win wars and smart enough to know they need a brilliant commander," said Bean. "And either big enough or invisible enough or far enough away from Armenia not to care about the consequences of kidnapping her. In fact, I'll bet that whoever took her would be perfectly delighted if war broke out in the Caucasus."

"So you think it's some large and powerful nation close by?" asked Father. Of course, there was only one large and powerful nation close to Armenia.

"Could be, but there's no telling," said Bean. "Anybody who needs a commander like Petra wants a world in turmoil. Enough turmoil, and anybody might emerge on top. Plenty of sides to play off against each other." And now that Bean had said it, he began to believe it. Just because Russia was the most aggressive nation before the League War didn't mean that other nations weren't going to get into the game.

"In a world in chaos," said Nikolai, "the army with the best commander wins."

"If you want to find the kidnapper, look for the

country that talks most about peace and conciliation," said Bean, playing with the idea and saying whatever came to mind.

"You're too cynical," said Nikolai. "Some who talk about peace and conciliation merely want peace and conciliation."

"You watch—the nations that offer to arbitrate are the ones that think they should rule the world, and this is just one more move in the game."

Father laughed. "Don't read too much into *that*," he said. "Most of the nations that are always offering to arbitrate are trying to recover lost status, not gain new power. France. America. Japan. They're always meddling just because they used to have the power to back it up and they haven't caught on yet that they don't anymore."

Bean smiled. "You never know, do you, Papa. The very fact that you dismiss the possibility that they could be the kidnappers makes me regard them as all the more likely candidates."

Nikolai laughed and agreed.

"That's the problem with having two Battle School graduates in the house," said Father. "You think because you understand military thinking that you understand political thinking, too."

"It's all maneuver and avoiding battle until you have overwhelming superiority," said Bean.

"But it's also about the will to power," said Father. "And even if individuals in America and France and Japan have the will to power, the people don't. Their leaders will never get them moving. You have to look at nations on the make. Aggressive peoples who think they have a grievance, who think they're undervalued. Belligerent, snappish."

"A whole nation of belligerent, snappish people?" asked Nikolai.

"Sounds like Athens," said Bean.

"A nation that takes that attitude toward other nations," said Father. "Several self-consciously Islamic nations have the character to make such a play, but they'd never kidnap a Christian girl to lead their armies."

"They might kidnap her to prevent her own nation from using her," said Nikolai. "Which brings us back to Armenia's neighbors."

"It's an interesting puzzle," said Bean, "which we can figure out later, after we get to wherever we're going."

Father and Nikolai looked at him as if he were crazy. "Going?" asked Father.

It was Mother who understood. "They're kidnapping Battle School graduates. Not just that, but a member of Ender's team from the actual battles."

"And one of the best," said Bean.

Father was skeptical. "One incident doesn't make a pattern."

"Let's not wait to see who's next," said Mother. "I'd rather feel silly later for overreacting than grieve because we dismissed the possibility."

"Give it a few days," said Father. "It will all blow over."

"We've already given it six hours," said Bean. "If the kidnappers are patient, they won't strike again for months. But if they're impatient, they're already in motion against all their other targets. For all we know, the only reason Nikolai and I aren't in the bag already is because we threw off their plans by going on vacation."

"Or else," said Nikolai, "our being here on this island gives them the perfect opportunity."

"Father," said Mother, "why don't you call for some protection?"

Father hesitated.

Bean understood why. The political game was a delicate one, and anything Father did right now could have repercussions throughout his career. "You won't be perceived as asking for special privileges for yourself," said Bean. "Nikolai and I are a precious national resource. I believe the prime minister is on record as saying that several times. Letting Athens know where we are and suggesting they protect us and get us out of here is a good idea."

Father got on the cellphone.

He got only a System Busy response.

"That's it," said Bean. "There's no way the phone system can be too busy here on Ithaca. We need a boat."

"An airplane," said Mother.

"A boat," said Nikolai. "And not a rental. They're probably waiting for us to put ourselves in their hands, so there won't be a struggle."

"Several of the nearby houses have boats," said Father. "But we don't know these people."

"They know *us,*" said Nikolai. "Especially Bean. We *are* war heroes, you know."

"But any house around here could be the very one from which they're watching us," said Father. "*If* they're watching us. We can't trust anybody."

"Let's get in our bathing suits," said Bean, "and walk to the beach and then wander as far as we can before we cut inland and find somebody with a boat."

Since no one had a better plan, they put it into action at once. Within two minutes they were out the door, carrying no wallets or purses, though Father and Mother slipped a few identification papers and credit cards into their suits. Bean and Nikolai laughed and teased each other as usual, and Mother and Father held hands and talked quietly, smiling at their sons . . . as usual. No sign of alarm. Nothing to cause anyone watching to spring into action.

They were only about a quarter mile up the beach when they heard an explosion—loud, as if it were close, and the shockwave made them stumble. Mother fell. Father helped her up as Bean and Nikolai looked back.

"Maybe it's not our house," said Nikolai.

"Let's not go back and check," said Bean.

They began to jog up the beach, matching their speed to Mother, who was limping a little from having skinned one knee and twisted the other when she fell. "Go on ahead," she said.

"Mother," said Nikolai, "taking you is the same as taking us, because we'd do whatever they wanted to get you back."

"They don't want to take us," said Bean. "Petra they wanted to use. Me they want dead."

"No," said Mother.

"He's right," said Father. "You don't blow up a house in order to kidnap the occupants."

"But we don't know it was our house!" Mother insisted.

"Mother," said Bean. "It's basic strategy. Any resource you can't get control of, you destroy so your enemy can't have it."

"What enemy?" Mother said. "Greece has no enemies!"

"When somebody wants to rule the world," said Nikolai, "eventually everyone is his enemy."

"I think we should run faster," said Mother.

They did.

As they ran, Bean thought through what Mother had said. Nikolai's answer was right, of course, but Bean couldn't help but wonder: Greece might have no enemies, but *I* have. Somewhere in this world, Achilles is alive. Supposedly he's in custody, a prisoner because he is mentally ill, because he has murdered again and again. Graff promised that he would never be set free. But Graff was court-martialed—exonerated, yes, but retired from the military. He's now Minister of Colonization, no longer in a position to keep his promise about Achilles. And if there's one thing Achilles wants, it's me, dead.

Kidnapping Petra, that's something Achilles would think of. And if he was in a position to cause *that* to happen—if some government or group was listening to him—then it would have been a simple enough matter for him to get the same people to kill Bean.

Or would Achilles insist on being there in person?

Probably not. Achilles was not a sadist. He killed with his own hands when he needed to, but would never put himself at risk. Killing from a distance would actually be preferable. Using other hands to do his work.

Who else would want Bean dead? Any other enemy would seek to capture him. His test scores from Battle School were a matter of public record since Graff's trial. The military in every nation knew that he was the kid who in many ways had topped Ender himself. He would be the one most desired. He would also be the one most feared, if he were on the other side in a war. Any of them might kill him if they knew they couldn't take him. But they would try to take him first. Only Achilles would prefer his death.

But he said nothing of this to his family. His fears about Achilles would sound too paranoid. He wasn't sure whether he believed them himself. And yet, as he ran along the beach with his family, he grew more certain with every step that whoever had kidnapped Petra was in some way under Achilles' influence.

They heard the rotors of helicopters before they saw them, and Nikolai's reaction was instantaneous. "Inland now!" he shouted. They scrambled for the nearest wooden stairway leading up the cliff from the beach.

They were only halfway up before the choppers came into view. There was no point in trying to hide. One of the choppers set down on the beach below them, the other on the bluff above.

"Down is easier than up," said Father. "And the choppers do have Greek military insignia."

What Bean didn't point out, because everyone knew it, was that Greece was part of the New Warsaw Pact, and it was quite possible that Greek military craft might be acting under Russian command.

In silence they walked back down the stairs. Hope and despair and fear tugged at them by turns.

The soldiers who spilled out of the chopper were wearing Greek Army uniforms.

"At least they're not trying to pretend they're Turks," said Nikolai.

"But how would the Greek Army know to come rescue us?" said Mother. "The explosion was only a few minutes ago."

The answer came quickly enough, once they got to the beach. A colonel who Father knew slightly came to meet them, saluting them. No, saluting Bean, with the respect due to a veteran of the Formic War.

"I bring you greetings from General Thrakos," said the colonel. "He would have come himself, but there was no time to waste when the warning came."

"Colonel Dekanos, we think our sons might be in danger," said Father.

"We realized that the moment word came of the kidnapping of Petra Arkanian," said Dekanos. "But you weren't at home and it took a few hours to find out where you were."

"We heard an explosion," said Mother.

"If you had been inside the house," said Dekanos, "you'd be as dead as the people in the surrounding houses. The army is securing the area. Fifteen choppers were sent up to search for you—we hoped—or, if you were dead, the perpetrators. I have already reported to Athens that you are alive and well."

"They were jamming the cellphone," said Father.

"Whoever did this has a very effective organization," said Dekanos. "Nine other children, it turns out, were taken within hours of Petra Arkanian."

"Who?" demanded Bean.

"I don't know the names yet," said Dekanos. "Only the count."

"Were any of the others simply killed?" asked Bean.

"No," said Dekanos. "Not that I've heard, anyway."

"Then why did they blow up our house?" Mother demanded.

"If we knew why," said Dekanos, "we'd know who. And vice versa."

They were belted into their seats. The chopper rose from the beach—but not very high. By now the other choppers were ranged around them and above them. Flying escort.

"Ground troops are continuing the search for the perpetrators," said Dekanos. "But your survival is our highest priority."

"We appreciate that," said Mother.

But Bean was not all that appreciative. The Greek military would, of course, put them in hiding and protect them carefully. But no matter what they did, the one thing they could not do was conceal the knowledge of his location from the Greek government itself. And the Greek government had been part of the Russia-dominated Warsaw Pact for generations now, since before the Formic War. Therefore Achilles—if it was Achilles, if it was Russia he worked for, if, if—would be able to find out where they were. Bean knew that it was not enough for him to be in protection. He had to be in true concealment, where no government could find him, where no one but himself would know who he was.

The trouble was, he was not only still a child, he was a famous child. Between his youth and his celebrity, it would be almost impossible for him to move unnoticed through the world. He would have to have help. So for the time being, he had to remain in military custody and simply hope that it would take him less time to get away than it would take Achilles to get to him.

If it was Achilles.

3

Message in a Bottle

To: Carlotta%agape@vatican.net/orders/sisters/ind
From: Graff%pilgrimage@colmin.gov
Re: Danger

I have no idea where you are and that's good, because I believe you are in grave danger, and the harder it is to find you, the better.

Since I'm no longer with the I.F., I'm not kept abreast of things there. But the news is full of the kidnapping of most of the children who served with Ender in Command School. That could have been done by anybody, there is no shortage of nations or groups that might conceive and carry out such a project. What you may not know is that there was no attempt to kidnap one of them. From a friend of mine I have learned that the beach house in Ithaca where Bean and his family were vacationing was simply blown up—with so much force that the neighboring houses were also flattened and everyone in them killed. Bean and his family had already escaped and are under the protection of the Greek military. Supposedly this is a secret, in hopes that the assassins will think they succeeded, but in fact, like most governments, Greece leaks like a colander, and the assassins probably already know more than I do about where Bean is.

There is only one person on Earth who would prefer Bean dead.

That means that the people who got Achilles out of that mental hospital are not just using him—he is making, or at least influencing, their decisions to fit his private agenda. The danger to you is grave. The danger to Bean, more so. He must go into deep hiding, and he cannot go alone. To save his life and yours, the only thing I can think of is to get both of you off planet. We are within months of launching our first colony ships. If I am the only one to know your real identities, we can keep

```
you safe until launch. But we must get
Bean out of Greece as quickly as possi-
ble. Are you with me?

Do not tell me where you are. We will
work out how to meet.
```

How stupid did they think she was?

It took Petra only about half an hour to realize that these people weren't Turkish. Not that she was some kind of expert on language, but they'd be babbling along and every now and then out would pop a word of Russian. She didn't understand Russian either, except for a few loan words in Armenian, and Azerbaijani had loan words like that, too, but the thing is, when you say a Russian loan word in Armenian, you give it an Armenian pronunciation. These clowns would switch to an easy, native-sounding Russian accent when they hit those words. She would have to have been a gibbon in the slow-learner class not to realize that the Turkish pose was just that, a pose.

So when she decided she'd learned all she could with her eyes closed, listening, she spoke up in Fleet Common. "Aren't we across the Caucasus yet? When do I get to pee?"

Someone said an expletive.

"No, pee," she answered. She opened her eyes and blinked. She was on the floor of some ground vehicle. She started to sit up.

A man pushed her back down with his foot.

"Oh, that's clever. Keep me out of sight as we coast along the tarmac, but how will you get me into the airplane without anyone seeing? You want me to come out walking and acting normal so nobody gets all excited, right?"

"You'll act that way when we tell you to or we'll kill you," said the man with the heavy foot.

"If you had the authority to kill me, I'd be dead back in Maralik." She started to rise again. Again the foot pushed her back down.

"Listen carefully," she said. "I've been kidnapped because somebody wants me to plan a war for them. That means I'm going to be meeting with the top brass. They're not stupid enough to think they'll get anything decent from me without my willing cooperation. That's why they wouldn't let you kill my mother. So when I tell them that I won't do anything for them until I have your balls in a paper bag, how long do you think it will take them to decide what's more important to them? My brain or your balls?"

"We *do* have the authority to kill you."

It took her only moments to decide why such authority might have been given to morons like these. "Only if I'm in imminent danger of being rescued. Then they'd rather have me dead than let somebody else get the use of me. Let's see you make a case for *that* here on the runway at the Gyuniri airport."

A different rude word this time.

Somebody spurted out a sentence of Russian. She caught the gist of it from the intonation and the bitter laughter afterward. "They warned you she was a genius."

Genius, hell. If she was so smart, why hadn't she anticipated the possibility that somebody would make a grab for the kids who won the war? And it had to be kids, not just her, because she was too far down the list for somebody outside Armenia to make her their only choice. When the front door was locked, she should have run for the cops instead of puttering around to the back door. And that was another stupid thing they did, locking the front door. In Russia you had to lock your doors, they probably thought that was normal. They should have done better research. Not that it helped her now, of course. Except that she knew they weren't all that careful and they weren't all that bright. Anybody can kidnap someone who's taking no precautions.

"So Russia makes her play for world domination, is that it?" she asked.

"Shut up," said the man in the seat in front of her.

"I don't speak Russian, you know, and I won't learn."

"You don't have to," said a woman.

"Isn't that ironic?" said Petra. "Russia plans to take over the world, but they have to speak English to do it."

The foot on her belly pressed down harder.

"Remember your balls in a bag," she said.

A moment, and then the foot let up.

She sat up, and this time no one pushed her down.

"Untape me so I can get myself up on the seat. Come on! My arms hurt in this position! Haven't you learned anything since the days of the KGB? Unconscious people don't have to have their circulation cut off. Fourteen-year-old Armenian girls can probably be overpowered quite easily by big strong Russian goons."

By now the tape was off and she was sitting beside Heavy-foot and a guy who never looked at her, just kept watching out the left window, then the right, then the left again. "So this is Gyuniri airport?"

"What, you don't recognize it?"

"I've never been here before. When would I? I've only taken two airplane trips in my life, one out of Yerevan when I was five, and the other coming back, nine years later."

"She knew it was Gyuniri because it's the closest

airport that doesn't fly commercial jets," said the woman. She spoke without any tone in her voice—not contempt, not deference. Just . . . flat.

"Whose bright idea was this? Because captive generals don't strategize all that well."

"First, why in the world do you think anyone would tell us?" said the woman. "Second, why don't you shut up and find things out when they matter?"

"Because I'm a cheerful, talkative extrovert who likes to make friends," said Petra.

"You're a bossy, nosy introvert who likes to piss people off," said the woman.

"Oh, you actually did some research."

"No, just observation." So she did have a sense of humor. Maybe.

"You'd better just pray you can get over the Caucasus before you have to answer to the Armenian Air Force."

Heavy-foot made a derisory noise, proving that he didn't recognize irony when he heard it.

"Of course, you'll probably have only a small plane, and we'll probably fly out over the Black Sea. Which means that I.F. satellites will know exactly where I am."

"You're not I.F. personnel anymore," said the woman.

"Meaning they don't care what happens to you," said Heavy-foot.

By now they had pulled to a stop beside a small plane. "A jet, I'm impressed," said Petra. "Does it have any weaponry? Or is it just wired with explosives so that if the Armenian Air Force does start to force you down, you can blow me up and the whole plane with me?"

"Do we have to tie you again?" asked the woman.

"That would look really good to the people in the control tower."

"Get her out," said the woman.

Stupidly, the men on both sides of her opened their doors and got out, leaving her a choice of exits. So she chose Heavy-foot because she knew he was stupid, whereas the other man was anyone's guess. And, yes, he truly was stupid, because he held her by only one arm as he used his other hand to close the door. So she lurched to one side as if she had stumbled, drawing him off balance, and then, still using his grip to support her weight, she did a double kick, one in the groin and one in the knee. She landed solidly both times, and he let go of her very nicely before falling to the ground, writhing, one hand clutching his crotch and the other trying to slide his kneecap back around to the front of his knee.

Did they think she'd forgotten all her hand-to-hand unarmed combat training? Hadn't she warned him that she'd have his balls in a bag?

She made a good run for it, and she was feeling pretty good about how much speed she had picked up during her months of running at school, until she realized that they weren't following her. And that meant they knew they didn't have to.

No sooner had she noticed this than she felt something sharp pierce the skin over her right shoulder blade. She had time to slow down but not to stop before she collapsed into unconsciousness again.

—

This time they kept her drugged until they reached their destination, and since she never saw any scenery except the walls of what seemed to be an underground bunker, she had no guesses about where they might have taken her. Somewhere in Russia, that's all. And from the soreness of the bruises on her arms and legs and neck and the scrapes on her knees and palms and nose, she guessed that they hadn't been too careful with her. The price she paid for being a bossy, nosy introvert. Or maybe it was the part about pissing people off.

She lay on her bunk until a doctor came in and treated her scrapes with a special no-anesthetic blend of alcohol and acid, or so it seemed. "Was that just in case it didn't hurt enough?" she asked.

The doctor didn't answer. Apparently they had warned the woman what happened to those who spoke to her.

"The guy I kicked in the balls, did they have to amputate them?"

Still no answer. Not even a trace of amusement. Could this possibly be the one educated person in Russia who didn't speak Common?

Meals were brought to her, lights went on and off, but no one came to speak to her and she was not allowed out of her room. She heard nothing through the heavy doors, and it became clear that her punishment for her misbehavior on the trip was going to be solitary confinement for a while.

She resolved not to beg for mercy. Indeed, once it became clear to her that she was in isolation, she accepted it and isolated herself still further, neither speaking nor responding to the people who came and went. They never tried to speak to her, either, so the silence of her world was complete.

They did not understand how self-contained she was. How her mind could show her more than mere reality ever could. She could recall memories by the sheaf, by the bale. Whole conversations. And then new versions of those conversations, in which she was actually able to say the clever things that she only really thought of later.

She could even relive every moment of the battles on Eros. Especially the battle where she fell asleep in the middle. How tired she was. How she struggled frantically to stay awake. How she could feel her mind being so sluggish that she began to forget where she was, and why, and even who she was.

To escape from this endlessly repeating scene, she tried to think of other things. Her parents, her little brother. She could remember everything they had said and done since she returned, but after a while the only memories that mattered to her were the early ones from before Battle School. Memories she had suppressed for nine years, as best she could. All the promises of the family life that was lost to her. The good-bye when her mother wept and let her go. Her father's hand as he led her to the car. That hand had always meant that she was safe, before. But this time that hand led her to a place where she never felt safe again. She knew she had chosen to go—but she was only a child, and she knew that this was what was expected of her. That she should not succumb to the temptation to run to her weeping mother and cling to her and say no, I won't do it, let someone else become a soldier, I want to stay here and bake with Mama and play mother to my own little dolls. Not go off into space where I can learn how to kill strange and terrible creatures—and, by the way, humans as well, who trusted me and then I fell . . . a . . . sleep.

Being alone with her memories was not all that happy for her.

She tried fasting, simply ignoring the food they brought her, the liquids too, nothing by mouth. She expected someone to speak to her then, to cajole. But no. The doctor came in, slapped an injection into her arm, and when she woke up her hand was sore where the IV had been and she realized that there was no point in refusing to eat.

She hadn't thought to keep a calendar at first, but after the IV she did keep a calendar on her own body, pressing a fingernail into her wrist until it bled. Seven days on the left wrist, then switch to the right, and all she had to remember in her head was the number of weeks.

Except she didn't bother going for three. She realized that they were going to outwait her because, after all, they had the others they had kidnapped, and no doubt some of them were cooperating, so it was perfectly all right with them if she stayed in her cell and got farther and farther behind so that when she finally did emerge, she'd be the worst of them at whatever it was they were doing.

Fine, what did she care? She was never going to help them anyway.

But if she was to have any chance to get free of these people and this place, she had to be out of this room and into a place where she could earn enough trust to be able to get free.

Trust. They'd expect her to lie, they'd expect her to plot. Therefore she had to be as convincing as possible. Her long time in solitary was a help, of course—everyone knew that isolation caused untold mental pressures. Another thing that helped was that it was undoubtedly known to them by now, from the other children, that she was the first one who broke under pressure during the battles on Eros. So they would be predisposed to believe a breakdown now.

She began to cry. It wasn't hard. There were plenty of real tears pent up in her. But she shaped those emotions, made it into a whimpering cry that went on and on and on. Her nose filled with mucus, but she did not blow it. Her eyes streamed with tears but she did not wipe them. Her pillow got soaked with tears and covered with snot but she did not evade the wet place. Instead she rolled her hair right through it as she turned over, did it again and again until her hair was matted with mucus and her face stiff with it. She made sure her crying did not get more desperate—let no one think she was trying to get attention. She toyed with the idea of falling silent when anyone came into the room, but decided against it—she figured it would be more convincing to be oblivious to other people's coming and going.

It worked. Someone came in after a day of this and slapped her with another injection. And this time when she woke up, she was in a hospital bed with a window that showed a cloudless northern sky. And sitting by her bed was Dink Meeker.

"Ho Dink," she said.

"Ho Petra. You pasted these conchos over real good."

"One does what one can for the cause," she said. "Who else?"

"You're the last to come out of solitary. They got the whole team from Eros, Petra. Except Ender, of course. And Bean."

"He's not in solitary?"

"No, they didn't keep it a secret who was still in the box. We thought you made a pretty fine showing."

"Who was second-longest?"

"Nobody cares. We were all out in the first week. You lasted five."

So it had been two and a half weeks before she started her calendar.

"Because I'm the stupid one."

" 'Stubborn' is the right word."

"Know where we are?"

"Russia."

"I meant where in Russia."

"Far from any borders, they assure us."

"What are our resources?"

"Very thick walls. No tools. Constant observation. They weigh our bodily wastes, I'm not kidding."

"What have they got us doing?"

"Like a really dumbed-down Battle School. We put up with it for a long time till Fly Molo finally gave up and when one of the teachers was quoting one of Von Clausewitz's stupider generalizations, Fly continued the quotation, sentence after sentence, paragraph after paragraph, and the rest of us joined in as best we could—I mean, nobody has a memory like Fly, but we do OK—and they finally got the idea that we could teach the stupid classes to them. So now it's just . . . war games."

"Again? You think they're going to spring it on us later that the games are real?"

"No, this is just planning stuff. Strategy for a war between Russia and Turkmenistan. Russia and an alliance between Turkmenistan, Kazakhstan, Azerbaijan, and Turkey. War with the United States and Canada. War with the old NATO alliance except Germany. War with Germany. On and on. China. India. Really stupid stuff, too, like between Brazil and Peru, which makes no sense but maybe they were testing our compliance or something."

"All this in five weeks?"

"Three weeks of kuso classes, and then two weeks of war games. When we finish our plan, see, they run it on the computer to show us how it went. Someday they're going to catch on that the only way to do this that isn't a waste of time is to have one of us making the plan for the opponent as well."

"My guess is you just told them."

"I've told them before but they're hard to persuade. Typical military types. Makes you understand why the whole concept of Battle School was developed in the first place. If the war had been up to adults, there'd be Buggers at every breakfast table in the world by now."

"But they *are* listening?"

"I think they record it all and play it back at slow speeds to see if we're passing messages subvocally."

Petra smiled.

"So why did you finally decide to cooperate?" he asked.

She shrugged. "I don't think I decided."

"Hey, they don't pull you out of the room until you express really sincere interest in being a good, compliant little kid."

She shook her head. "I don't think I did that."

"Yeah, well, whatever you did, you were the last of Ender's jeesh to break, kid."

A short buzzer sounded.

"Time's up," said Dink. He got up, leaned over, kissed her brow, and left the room.

—

Six weeks later, Petra was actually enjoying the life. By complying with the kids' demands, their captors had finally come up with some decent equipment.

Software that allowed them very realistic head-to-head strategic and tactical wargaming. Access to the nets so they could do decent research into terrains and capabilities so their wargaming had some realism—though they knew every message they sent was censored, because of the number of messages that were rejected for one obscure reason or another. They enjoyed each other's company, exercised together, and by all appearances seemed to be completely happy and compliant Russian commanders.

Yet Petra knew, as they all knew, that every one of them was faking. Holding back. Making dumb mistakes which, if they were made in combat, would lead to gaps that a clever enemy could exploit. Maybe their captors realized this, and maybe they didn't. At least it made them all feel better, though they never spoke of it. But since they were all doing it, and cooperating by not exposing those weaknesses by exploiting them in the games, they could only assume that everyone felt the same about it.

They chatted comfortably about a lot of things—their disdain for their captors, memories of Ground School, Battle School, Command School. And, of course, Ender. He was out of the reach of these bastards, so they made sure to mention him a lot, to talk about how the I.F. was bound to use him to counter all these foolish plans the Russians were making. They knew they were blowing smoke, that the I.F. wouldn't do anything, they even said so. But still, Ender was there, the ultimate trump card.

Till the day one of the erstwhile teachers told them that a colony ship had gone, with Ender and his sister Valentine aboard.

"I didn't even know he had a sister," said Hot Soup.

No one said anything, but they all knew that this was impossible. They had all known Ender had a sister. But . . . whatever Hot Soup was doing, they'd play along and see what the game was.

"No matter what they tell us, one thing we know," said Hot Soup. "Wiggin is still with us."

Again, they weren't sure what he meant by this. After the briefest pause, though, Shen clapped his hand to his chest and cried out, "In our hearts forever."

"Yes," said Hot Soup. "Ender is in our hearts."

Just the tiniest extra emphasis on the name "Ender."

But he had said Wiggin before.

And before that, he had called attention to the fact that they all knew Ender had a sister. They also knew that Ender had a brother. Back on Eros, while Ender was in bed recovering from his breakdown after finding out the battles had been real, Mazer Rackham had told them some things about Ender. And Bean had told them more, as they were trapped together while the League War played itself out. They had listened as Bean expounded on what Ender's brother and sister meant to him, that the reason Ender had been born at all during the days of the two-child law was because his brother and sister were so brilliant, but the brother was too dangerously aggressive and the sister too passively compliant. How Bean knew all this he wouldn't tell, but the information was indelibly planted in their memories, tied as it was with those tense days after their victory over the Formics and before the defeat of the Polemarch in his attempt to take over the I.F.

So when Hot Soup said "Wiggin is still with us," he had not been referring to Ender or Valentine, because they most assuredly were not "with us."

Peter, that was the brother's name. Peter Wiggin.

Hot Soup was telling them that he was one whose mind was perhaps as brilliant as Ender's, and he was still on Earth. Maybe, if they could somehow contact him on the outside, he would ally himself with his brother's battle companions. Maybe he could find a way to get them free.

The game now was to find some way to communicate with him.

Sending email would be pointless—the last thing they needed to do was have their captors see a bunch of email addressed to every possible variant of Peter Wiggin's name at every single mailnet that they could think of. And sure enough, by that evening Alai was telling them some tall tale about a genie in a bottle that had washed up on the shore. Everyone listened with feigned interest, but they knew the real story had been stated right at the beginning, when Alai said, "The fisherman thought maybe the bottle had a message from some castaway, but when he popped the cork, a cloud of smoke came out and . . ." and they got it. What they had to do was send a message in a bottle, a message that would go indiscriminately to everyone everywhere, but which could only be understood by Ender's brother, Peter.

But as she thought about it, Petra realized that with all these other brilliant brains working to reach Peter Wiggin, she might as well work on an alternative plan. Peter Wiggin was not the only one outside who might help them. There was Bean. And while Bean was almost certainly in hiding, so that he would have far less freedom of action than Peter Wiggin, that didn't mean they couldn't still find him.

She thought about it for a week in every spare moment, rejecting idea after idea.

Then she thought of one that might get past the censors.

She worked out the text of her message very carefully in her head, making sure that it was phrased and worded exactly right. Then, with that memorized, she figured the binary code of each letter in standard two-byte format, and memorized that. Then she started the really hard stuff. All done in her head, so nothing was ever committed to paper or typed into the computer, where a keystroke monitor could report to their captors whatever she wrote.

In the meantime, she found a complex black-and-white drawing of a dragon on a netsite somewhere in Japan and saved it as a small file. When she finally had the message fully encoded in her mind, it took only a few minutes of fiddling with the drawing and she was done. She added it as part of her signature on every letter she sent. She spent so little time on it that she did not think it would look to her captors like anything more than a harmless whim. If they asked, she could say she added the picture in memory of Ender's Dragon Army in Battle School.

Of course, it wasn't just a picture of a dragon anymore. Now there was a little poem under it.

```
Share this dragon.
If you do,
lucky end for
them and you.
```

She would tell them, if they asked, that the words were just an ironic joke. If they didn't believe her, they would strip off the picture and she'd have to find another way.

She sent it on every letter from then on. Including to the other kids. She got it back from them on messages after that, so they had picked up on what she was doing and were helping. Whether their captors were actually letting it leave the building or not, she had no way of knowing—at first. Finally, though, she started getting it back on messages from outside. A single glance told her that she had succeeded—her coded message was still embedded in the picture. It hadn't been stripped out.

Now it was just a question of whether Bean would see it and look at it closely enough to realize that there was a mystery to solve.

4

Custody

To: Graff%pilgrimage@colmin.gov
From: Chamrajnagar%Jawaharlal@ifcom.gov
Re: Quandary

You know better than anyone how vital it is to maintain the independence of the Fleet from the machinations of politicians. That was my reason for rejecting "Locke's" suggestion. But in the event I was wrong. Nothing jeopardizes Fleet independence more than the prospect of one nation becoming dominant, especially if, as seems likely, the particular nation is one that has already shown a disposition to take over the I.F. and use it for nationalist purposes.

I'm afraid I was rather harsh with Locke. I dare not write to him directly, because, while Locke would be reliable, one can never know what Demosthenes would do with an official letter of apology from the Polemarch. Therefore please arrange for him to be notified that my threat is rescinded and I wish him well.

I do learn from my mistakes. Since one of Wiggin's companions remains outside the control of the aggressor, prudence dictates that young Delphiki be protected. Since you are Earthside and I am not, I give you brevet command over an IFM contingent and any other resources you need, orders forthcoming through level 6 backchannels (of course). I give you specific instructions not to tell me or anyone else of the steps you have taken to protect Delphiki or his family. There is to be no record in the I.F. system or that of any government.

By the way, trust no one in the Hegemony. I always knew they were a nest of careerists, but recent experience shows that the careerist is now being replaced by worse: the ideologue rampant.

Act swiftly. It appears that we are either on the verge of a new war, or the League War never quite ended after all.

How many days can you stay closed in, surrounded by guards, before you start to feel like a prisoner? Bean never felt claustrophobic in Battle School. Not even on Eros, where the low ceilings of the Buggers' tunnels teetered over them like a car slipping off its jack. Not like this, closed up with his family, pacing the four-room apartment. Well, not actually pacing it. He just *felt* like pacing it, and instead sat still, controlling himself, trying to think of some way to get control of his own life.

Being under someone else's protection was bad enough—he had never liked that, though it had happened before, when Poke protected him on the streets of Rotterdam, and then when Sister Carlotta saved him from certain death by taking him in and sending him to Battle School. But both those times, there were things he could do to make sure everything went right. This was different. He knew something was going to go wrong, and there was nothing he could do about it.

The soldiers guarding this apartment, surrounding the building, they were all good, loyal men, Bean had no reason to doubt that. They weren't going to betray him. Probably. And the bureaucracy that was keeping his location a secret—no doubt it would just be an honest oversight, not a conscious betrayal, that would give his address to his enemies.

And in the meantime, Bean could only wait, pinned down by his protectors. They were the web, holding him in place for the spider. And there wasn't a thing he could say to change this situation. If Greece were fighting a war, they'd set Bean and Nikolai to work, making plans, charting strategies. But when it came to a matter of security, they were just children, to be protected and taken care of. It would do no good for Bean to explain that his best protection was to get out of here, get off completely on his own, make a life for himself on the streets of some city where he could be nameless and faceless and lost and safe. Because they looked at him and saw nothing but a little kid. And who listens to little kids?

Little kids have to be taken care of.

By adults who don't have it in their power to keep those little kids safe.

He wanted to throw something through the window and jump down after it.

Instead he sat still. He read books. He signed on to the nets using one of his many names and cruised around, looking for whatever dribbles of information oozed through the military security systems of every nation, hoping for something to tell him where Petra and Fly Molo and Vlad and Dumper were being held. Some country that was showing signs of a little more cockiness because they thought they had the winning hand now. Or a country that was acting more cautious and methodical because finally somebody with a brain was running their strategy.

But it was pointless, because he knew he wasn't going to find it this way. The real information never got onto the net until it was too late to do anything about it. Somebody knew. The facts he needed to find his way to his friends were available in a dozen sites—he knew that, *knew* it, because that's the way it always was, the historians would find it and wonder for a thousand pages at a time: Why didn't anybody notice? Why didn't anybody put it together? Because the people who had the information were too dim to know what they had, and the people who could have understood it were locked in an apartment in an abandoned resort that even tourists didn't want to come to anymore.

The worst thing was that even Mother and Father were getting on his nerves. After a childhood with no parents, the best thing that had ever happened to him was when Sister Carlotta's research found his biological parents. The war ended, and when all the other kids got to go home to their families, Bean wasn't left over. He got to go home to his family, too. He had no childhood memories of them, of course. But Nikolai had, and Nikolai let Bean borrow them as if they were his own.

They were good people, his mother and his father. They never made him feel as if he were an intruder, a stranger, even a visitor. It was as if he had always belonged with them. They liked him. They loved him. It was a strange, exhilarating feeling to be with people who didn't want anything from you except your happiness, who were glad just to have you around.

But when you're already going crazy from confinement, it doesn't matter how much you like somebody, how much you love them, how grateful you are for their kindness to you. They will make you nuts. Everything they do grates on you like a bad song that won't get out of your head. You just want to scream at them to *shut. Up.* But you don't, because you love them and you know that you're probably driving them crazy too and as long as there's no hope of release you've got to keep things calm . . .

And then finally there comes a knock on the door and you open it up and you realize that something different is finally going to happen.

It was Colonel Graff and Sister Carlotta at the door. Graff in a suit now, and Sister Carlotta in an extravagant auburn wig that made her look really stupid but also kind of pretty. The whole family recognized them at once, except that Nikolai had never met Sister Carlotta. But when Bean and his family got up to greet them, Graff held up a hand to stop them and Carlotta put her finger to her lips. They came inside and closed the door after them and beckoned the family to gather in the bathroom.

It was a tight fit, the six of them in there. Father and Mother ended up standing in the shower while Graff hung a tiny machine from the overhead light. Once it was in place and the red light began blinking, Graff spoke softly.

"Hi," he said. "We came to get you out of this place."

"Why all the precautions in here?" asked Father.

"Because part of the security system here is to listen in on everything said in this apartment."

"To protect us, they spy on us?" asked Mother.

"Of course they do," said Father.

"Since anything we say here might leak into the system," said Graff, "and would most certainly leak right back out of the system, I brought this little machine, which hears every sound we make and produces countersounds that nullify them so we pretty much can't be heard."

"Pretty much?" asked Bean.

"That's why we won't go into any details," said Graff. "I'll tell you only this much. I'm the Minister of Colonization, and we have a ship that leaves in a few months. Just time enough to get you off Earth, up to the ISL, and over to Eros for the launch."

But even as he said it, he was shaking his head, and Sister Carlotta was grinning and shaking *her* head, too, so that they would know that this was all a lie. A cover story.

"Bean and I have been in space before, Mother," said Nikolai, playing along. "It's not so bad."

"It's what we fought the war for," Bean chimed in. "The Formics wanted Earth because it was just like the worlds they already lived on. So now that they're gone, we get *their* worlds, which should be good for us. It's only fair, don't you think?"

Of course their parents both understood what was happening, but Bean knew Mother well enough by now that he wasn't surprised that she had to ask a completely useless and dangerous question just to be sure.

"But we're not really . . ." she began. Then Father's hand gently covered her mouth.

"It's the only way to keep us safe," Father said. "Once we're going at lightspeed, it'll seem like a couple of years to us, while decades pass on Earth. By the time we reach the other planet, everybody who wants us dead will be dead themselves."

"Like Joseph and Mary taking Jesus into Egypt," said Mother.

"Exactly," said Father.

"Except they got to go back to Nazareth."

"If Earth destroys itself in some stupid war," said Father, "it won't matter to us anymore, because we'll be part of a new world. Be happy about this, Elena. It means we can stay together." Then he kissed her.

"Time to go, Mr. and Mrs. Delphiki. Bring thc boys, please." Graff reached up and yanked the damper from the ceiling light.

The soldiers who waited for them in the hall wore the uniform of the I.F. Not a Greek uniform was in sight. And these young men were armed to the teeth. As they walked briskly to the stairs—no elevators, no doors that might suddenly open to leave them trapped in a box for an enemy to toss in a grenade or a few thousand projectiles—Bean watched the way the soldier in the lead watched everything, checked every corner, the light under every door in the hall, so that nothing could surprise him. Bean also saw how the man's body moved inside his clothes, with a kind of contained strength that made his clothes seem like Kleenex, he could rip through the fabric just by tugging at it a little, because nothing could hold him in except his own self-control. It was like his sweat was pure testosterone. This was what a man was supposed to be. This was a *soldier.*

I was never a soldier, thought Bean. He tried to imagine himself the way he had been in Battle School, strapping on cut-down flash-suit pieces that never fit him right. He always looked like somebody's pet monkey dressed up as a human for the joke of it. Like a toddler who got clothes out of his big brother's dresser. The man in front of him, that's what Bean wanted to be when he grew up. But try as he might, he could never imagine himself actually being big. No, not even being full size. He would always be looking up at the world. He might be male, he might be human, or at least humanesque, but he would never be manly. No one would ever look at him and say, Now, *that's* a *man.*

Then again, this soldier had never given orders that changed the course of history. Looking great in a uniform wasn't the only way to earn your place in the world.

Down the stairs, three flights, and then a pause for just a moment well back from the emergency exit while two of the soldiers came out and watched for the signal from the men in the I.F. chopper waiting thirty meters away. The signal came. Graff and Sister Carlotta led the way, still at a brisk walk. They looked neither left nor right, just focused on the helicopter. They got in, sat down, buckled up, and the chopper tilted and rose from the grass and flew low out over the water.

Mother was all for demanding to know the real plan, but again Graff cut off all discussion with a cheerful bellow of "Let's wait to discuss this until we can do it without shouting!"

Mother didn't like it. None of them did. But there was Sister Carlotta smiling her best nun smile, like a sort of Virgin-in-training. How could they help but trust her?

Five minutes in the air and then they set down on the deck of a submarine. It was a big one, with the stars and stripes of the United States, and it occurred to Bean that since they didn't know what country had kidnapped the other kids, how could they be sure they weren't just walking into the hands of their enemies?

But once they got down inside the ship, they could see that while the crew was in U.S. uniforms, the only people carrying weapons were the I.F. soldiers who had brought them and a half-dozen more who had been waiting for them with the sub. Since power came from the barrel of a gun, and the only guns on the ship were under Graff's command, Bean's mind was eased a little.

"If you try to tell us that we can't talk *here*," Mother began—but to her consternation Graff again held up a hand, and Sister Carlotta again made a shushing gesture as Graff beckoned them to follow their lead soldier through the narrow corridors of the sub.

Finally the six of them were packed once more into a tiny space—this time the executive officer's cabin—and once again they waited while Graff hung his noise damper and turned it on. When the light started blinking, Mother was the first to speak.

"I'm trying to figure out how we can tell we aren't being kidnapped just like the others," she said dryly.

"You got it," said Graff. "They were all taken by a group of terrorist nuns, aided by fat old bureaucrats."

"He's joking," said Father, trying to soothe Mother's immediate wrath.

"I know he's joking. I just don't think it's funny. After all we've been through, and then we're supposed to go along without a word, without a question, just . . . *trusting*."

"Sorry," said Graff. "But you were already trusting the Greek government back where you were. You've got to trust somebody, so why not us?"

"At least the Greek Army explained things to us and pretended we had a right to make some decisions," said Mother.

They didn't explain things to me and Nikolai, Bean wanted to say.

"Come, children, no bickering," said Sister Carlotta. "The plan is very simple. The Greek Army continues to guard that apartment building as if you were still inside it, taking meals in and doing laundry. This fools no one, probably, but it makes the Greek government feel like they're part of the program. In the meantime, four passengers answering your description but flying under assumed names are taken to Eros, where they embark on the first colony ship, and only then, when the ship is launched, is an announcement made that for their protection, the Delphiki family have opted for permanent emigration and a new life in a new world."

"And where are we really?" asked Father.

"I don't know," said Graff very simply.

"And neither do I," said Sister Carlotta.

Bean's family looked at them in disbelief.

"I guess that means we won't be staying in the sub,"

said Nikolai, "because then you'd absolutely know where we are."

"It's a double blind," said Bean. "They're splitting us up. I'll go one way, you'll go another."

"Absolutely not," said Father.

"We've had enough of a divided family," said Mother.

"It's the only way," said Bean. "I knew it already. I . . . want it that way."

"You want to leave us?" said Mother.

"It's me they want to kill," said Bean.

"We don't know that!" said Mother.

"But we're pretty sure," said Bean. "If I'm not with you, then even if you're found, they'll probably leave you alone."

"And if we're divided," said Nikolai, "it changes the profile of what they're looking for. Not a mother and father and two boys. Now it's a mother and father and one boy. And a grandma and her grandchild." Nikolai grinned at Sister Carlotta.

"I was rather hoping to be taken for an aunt," she said.

"You talk as if you already know the plan!" said Mother.

"It was obvious," said Nikolai. "From the moment they told us the cover story in the bathroom. Why else would Colonel Graff bring Sister Carlotta?"

"It wasn't obvious to me," said Mother.

"Or to me," said Father. "But that's what happens when your sons are both brilliant military minds."

"How long?" Mother demanded. "When will it end? When do we get to have Bean back with us?"

"I don't know," said Graff.

"He can't know, Mother," said Bean. "Not until we know who did the kidnappings and why. When we know what the threat actually is, then we can judge when we've taken sufficient countermeasures to make it safe for us to come partway out of hiding."

Mother suddenly burst into tears. "And you *want* this, Julian?"

Bean put his arms around her. Not because he felt any personal need to do it, but because he knew she needed that gesture from him. Living with a family for a year had not given him the full complement of normal human emotional responses, but at least it had made him more aware of what they ought to be. And he did have one normal reaction—he felt a little guilty that he could only fake what Mother needed, instead of having it come from the heart. But such gestures never came from the heart, for Bean. It was a language he had learned too late for it to come naturally to him. He would always speak the language of the heart with an awkward foreign accent.

The truth was that even though he loved his family, he was eager to get to a place where he could get to work making the contacts he needed to get the information that would let him find his friends. Except for Ender, he was the only one from Ender's jeesh who was outside and free. They needed him, and he'd wasted enough time already.

So he held his mother, and she clung to him, and she shed many tears. He also embraced his father, but more briefly; and he and Nikolai only punched each other's arms. All foreign gestures to Bean, but they knew he meant to mean them, and took them as if they were real.

The sub was fast. They weren't very long at sea before they reached a crowded port—Salonika, Bean assumed, though it could have been any other cargo port on the Aegean. The sub never actually entered the harbor. Instead, it surfaced between two ships moving in a parallel track toward the harbor. Mother, Father, Nikolai, and Graff were transferred to a freighter along with two of the soldiers, who were now in civilian clothes, as if that could conceal the soldierly way they acted. Bean and Carlotta stayed behind. Neither group would know where the other was. There would be no effort to contact each other. That had been another hard realization for Mother. "Why can't we write?"

"Nothing is easier to track than email," said Father. "Even if we use disguised online identities, if someone finds us, and we're writing regularly to Julian, then they'll see the pattern and track him down."

Mother understood it then. With her head, if not her heart.

Down inside the sub, Bean and Sister Carlotta sat down at a tiny table in the mess.

"Well?" said Bean.

"Well," said Sister Carlotta.

"Where are *we* going?" asked Bean.

"I have no idea," said Sister Carlotta. "They'll transfer us to another ship at another port, and we'll get off, and I have these false identities that we're supposed to use, but I really have no idea where we should go from there."

"We have to keep moving. No more than a few weeks in any one place," said Bean. "And I have to get on the nets with new identities every time we move, so no one can track the pattern."

"Do you seriously think someone will catalogue all the email in the entire world and follow up on all the ones that move around?" asked Sister Carlotta.

"Yes," said Bean. "They probably already do, so it's just a matter of running a search."

"But that's billions of e-mails a day."

"That's why it takes so many clerks to check all the email addresses on the file cards in the central switchboard," said Bean. He grinned at Sister Carlotta.

She did not grin back. "You really are a snotty and disrespectful little boy," she said.

"You're really leaving it up to me to decide where we go?"

"Not at all. I'm merely waiting to make a decision until we both agree."

"Oh, now, *that's* a cheap excuse to stay down here in this sub with all these great-looking men."

"Your level of banter has become even more crude than it was when you lived on the streets of Rotterdam," she said, coolly analytical.

"It's the war," said Bean. "It . . . it changes a man."

She couldn't keep a straight face any longer. Even though her laugh was only a single bark, and her smile lasted only a moment longer, it was enough. She still liked him. And he, to his surprise, still liked her, even though it had been years since he lived with her while she educated him to a level where Battle School would take him. He was surprised because, at the time he lived with her, he had never let himself realize that he liked her. After Poke's death, he hadn't been willing to admit to himself that he liked anybody. But now he knew the truth. He liked Sister Carlotta just fine.

Of course, she would probably get on his nerves after a while, too, just like his parents had. But at least when that happened, they could pick up and move. There wouldn't be soldiers keeping them indoors and away from the windows.

And if it ever became truly annoying, Bean could leave and strike out on his own. He'd never say that to

Sister Carlotta, because it would only worry her. Besides, she was bound to know it already. She had all the test data. And those tests had been designed to tell everything about a person. Why, she probably knew him better than he knew himself.

Of course, *he* knew that back when he took the tests, there was hardly an honest answer on any of the psychological tests. He had already read enough psychology by the time he took them that he knew exactly what answers were needed to show the profile that would probably get him into Battle School. So in fact she didn't know him from those tests at all.

But then, he didn't have any idea what his real answers would have been, then or now. So it isn't as if he knew himself any better.

And because she had observed him, and she was wise in her own way, she probably *did* know him better than he knew himself.

What a laugh, though. To think that one human being could ever really know another. You could get used to each other, get so habituated that you could speak their words right along with them, but you never knew why other people said what they said or did what they did, because they never even knew themselves. Nobody understands anybody.

And yet somehow we live together, mostly in peace, and get things done with a high enough success rate that people keep trying. Human beings get married and a lot of the marriages work, and they have children and most of them grow up to be decent people, and they have schools and businesses and factories and farms that have results at some level of acceptability—all without having a clue what's going on inside anybody's head.

Muddling through, that's what human beings do.

That was the part of being human that Bean hated the most.

5

Ambition

To: Locke%espinoza@polnet.gov
From: Graff%%@colmin.gov
Re: Correction

I have been asked to relay a message that a threat of exposure has been rescinded, with apologies. Nor should you be alarmed that your identity is widely known. Your identity was penetrated at my direction several years ago, and while multiple persons then under my command were made aware of who you are, it is a group that has neither reason nor disposition to violate confidentiality. The only exception has now been chastened by circumstance. On a personal level, let me say that I have no doubt of your capacity to achieve your ambition. I can only hope that, in the event of success, you will choose to emulate Washington, MacArthur, or Augustus rather than Napoleon, Alexander, or Hitler.

Colmin

Now and then Peter was almost overwhelmed by a desire to tell somebody what was actually happening in his life. He never succumbed to the desire, of course, since to tell it would be to undo it. But especially now that Valentine had gone, it was almost unbearable to sit there reading a personal letter from the Minister of Colonization and not shout for the other students in the library to come and see.

When he and Valentine had first broken through and placed essays or, in Valentine's case, diatribes on some of the major political nets, they had done a little hugging and laughing and jumping around. But it never took long for Valentine to remember how much she loathed half the positions she was forced to espouse in her Demosthenes persona, and her resulting gloom would calm him down as well. Peter missed her, of course, but he did not miss the arguments, the whining about having to be the bad guy. She could never see how the Demosthenes persona was the interesting one, the most fun to work with. Well, when he was done with it he'd give it back to her—long before she got to whatever planet it was that she and Ender were heading for. She'd know by then that even at his most outrageous, Demosthenes was a catalyst, making things happen.

Valentine. Stupid to choose Ender and exile over Peter and *life*. Stupid to get so angry over the obvious necessity of keeping Ender off planet. For his own protection, Peter told her, and hadn't events proven it? If he'd come home as Valentine originally wanted, he'd be a captive somewhere, or dead, depending on whether his captors had been able to get him to cooperate. I was right, Valentine, as I've always been right about everything. But you'd rather be nice than right, you'd rather be liked than powerful, and you'd rather be in exile with the brother who worships you than share power with the brother who made you influential.

Ender was already gone, Valentine. When they took him away to Battle School, he was never coming home—not the precious little Enderpoo that you adored and petted and watched over like a little mommy playing with a doll. They were going to make a soldier out of him, a killer—did you even *look* at the video they showed during Graff's court-martial?—and if something named Andrew Wiggin came home, it would *not* be the Ender you sentimentalized to the point of nausea. He'd be a damaged, broken, useless soldier whose war was finished. Pushing to have him sent off to a colony was the kindest thing I could have done for our erstwhile brother. Nothing would have been sadder than having his biography include the ruin that his life would have become here on Earth, even if nobody bothered to kidnap him. Like Alexander, he'll go out with a flash of brilliant light and live forever in glory, instead of withering away and dying in miserable obscurity, getting trotted out for parades now and then. I was the kind one!

Good riddance to both of you. You would have been drags on my boat, thorns in my side, pains in my ass.

But it would have been fun to show Valentine the letter from Graff—Graff himself! Even though he hid his private access code, even though he was condescending in his urging Peter to emulate the nice guys of history—as if anybody ever *planned* to create an ephemeral empire like Napoleon's or Hitler's—the fact was that even knowing that Locke, far from being some elder statesman speaking anonymously from retirement, was just an underage college student, Graff still thought Peter was worth talking to. Still worth giving advice to, because Graff knew that Peter Wiggin mattered now and would matter in the future. Damn right, Graff!

Damn right, everybody! Ender Wiggin may have saved your asses against the Buggers, but I'm the one who's going to save humanity's collective rectum from its own colostomy. Because human beings have always been more dangerous to the survival of the human race than anything else except the complete destruction of planet Earth, and now we're taking steps to evade even that by spreading our seed—including little Enderseed himself—to other worlds. Does Graff have any idea how hard I worked to make his little Ministry of Colonization come into existence in the first place? Has anybody bothered to track the history of the good ideas that have actually become law to see how many times the trail leads back to Locke?

They actually consulted with me when they were deciding whether to offer you the title of Colmin with which you so affectedly sign your emails. Bet you didn't know *that,* Mr. Minister. Without *me,* you might have been signing your letters with stupid good-luck dragon pictures like half the morons on the net these days.

And for a few minutes it just about killed him that nobody could know about this letter except himself and Graff.

And then . . .

The moment passed. His breathing returned to normal. His wiser self prevailed. It's better not to be distracted by the interference of personal fame. In due course his name would be revealed, he'd take his place in a position of authority instead of mere influence. For now, anonymity would do.

He saved the message from Graff, and then sat there staring at the display.

His hand was trembling.

He looked at it as if it were someone else's hand. What in the world is *that* about, he wondered. Am I such a celebrity hound that getting a letter from a top Hegemony official makes me shake like a teenager at a pop concert?

No. The cool realist took over. He was not trembling out of excitement. That, as always, was transitory, already gone.

He was trembling out of fear.

Because somebody was assembling a team of strategists. The top kids from the Battle School program. The ones they chose to fight the final battle to save humanity. Somebody had them and meant to use them. And sooner or later, that somebody would be Peter's rival, head to head with him, and Peter would have to outthink not only that rival, but also the kids he had managed to bend to his will.

Peter hadn't made it into Battle School. He didn't have what it took. For one reason or another, he was cut from the program without ever leaving home. So *every* kid who went to Battle School was more likely to make a good strategist and tactician than Peter Wiggin, and Peter's principal rival for hegemony had collected around himself the very best of them all.

Except for Ender, of course. Ender, whom I *could* have brought home if I had pulled the right strings and manipulated public opinion the other way. Ender, who was the best of all and might have been standing by my side. But no, I sent him away. For his own damn good. For his own *safety*. And now here I am, facing the struggle that my whole life has been devoted to, and all I've got to face the best of the Battle School is . . . me.

His hand trembled. So what? He'd be crazy *not* to be just a little bit afraid.

But when that moron Chamrajnagar threatened to expose him and bring the whole thing crashing down, just because he was too stupid to see how Demosthenes was necessary in order to bring about results that Locke's persona could never reach for—he had spent weeks in hell over that. Watching as the Battle School kids were kidnapped. Unable to do anything, to say anything pertinent. Oh, he answered letters that some people sent, he did enough investigating to satisfy himself that only Russia had the resources to bring it off. But he dared not use Demosthenes to demand that the I.F. be investigated for its failure to protect these children. Demosthenes could only make some routine suppositions about how it was bound to be the Warsaw Pact that had taken the kids—but of course everyone expected Demosthenes to say that, he was a well-known russophobe, it meant nothing. All because some shortsighted, stupid, self-serving admiral had decided to interfere with the one person on Earth who seemed to care about trying to keep the world from another visit from Attila the Hun. He wanted to scream at

Chamrajnagar: I'm the one who writes essays while the other guy kidnaps children, but because you know who I am and you have no clue who *he* is, you reach out to stop *me*? That was about as bright as the pinheads who handed the government of Germany to Hitler because they thought he would be "useful" to them.

Now Chamrajnagar had relented. Sent a cowardly apology through someone else so he could avoid letting Peter have a letter with his signature on it. Too late anyway. The damage was done. Chamrajnagar had not only done nothing, he had kept Peter from doing anything, and now Peter faced a chess game where his side of the board had nothing but pawns, and the other player had a double complement of knights, rooks, and bishops.

So Peter's hand trembled. And he sometimes caught himself wishing that he weren't in this thing so utterly, absolutely alone. Did Napoleon, in his tent alone, wonder what the hell he was doing, betting everything, over and over again, on the ability of his army to do the impossible? Didn't Alexander, once in a while, wish there were someone else he could trust to make a decision or two?

Peter's lip curled in self-contempt. Napoleon? Alexander? It was the other guy who had a stableful of steeds like that to ride. While I have had it certified by the Battle School testing program that I am about as militarily talented as, say, John F. Kennedy, that U.S. President who lost his PT boat through carelessness and got a medal for it because his father had money and political pull, and then became President and made an unbroken string of stupid moves that never hurt him much politically because the press loved him so much.

That's me. I can manipulate the press. I can paint public opinion, nudge and pull and poke and inject things into it, but when it comes to war—and it will come to war—I'm going to look about as clever as the French when the blitzkrieg rolled through.

Peter looked around the reading room. Not much of a library. Not much of a school. But because he entered college early, being a certifiably gifted pupil, and not caring a whit about his formal education, he had gone to the hometown branch of the state university. For the first time he found himself envying the other students who were studying there. All they had to worry about was the next test, or keeping their scholarship, or their dating life.

I could have a life like theirs.

Right. He'd have to kill himself if he ever came to care what some teacher thought of an essay he wrote, or what some girl thought about the clothes he wore, or whether one soccer team could beat another.

He closed his eyes and leaned back in his chair. All this self-doubt was pointless. He knew he would never stop until he was forced to stop. From childhood on, he knew that the world was his to change, if he found the right levers to pull. Other children bought the stupid idea that they had to wait until they grew up to do anything important. Peter knew better from the start. *He* could never have been fooled the way Ender was into thinking he was playing a game. For Peter, the only game worth playing was the real world. The only reason Ender was fooled was because he let other people shape reality for him. That had never been Peter's problem.

Except that all Peter's influence on the real world had been possible only because he could hide behind the anonymity of the net. He had created a persona—

two personas—that could change the world because nobody knew they were children and therefore ignorable. But when it came to armies and navies clashing in the real world, the influence of political thinkers receded. Unless, like Winston Churchill, they were recognized as being so wise and so right that when the crisis came, the reins of real power were put in their hands. That was fine for Winston—old, fat, and full of booze as he was, people still took him seriously. But as far as anyone who saw Peter Wiggin could know, he was still a kid.

Still, Winston Churchill had been the inspiration for Peter's plan. Make Locke seem so prescient, so right about everything, that when war began, public fear of the enemy and public trust in Locke would overwhelm their disdain for youth and allow Peter to reveal the face behind the mask and, like Winston, take his place as leader of the good guys.

Well, he had miscalculated. He had not guessed that Chamrajnagar already knew who he was. Peter wrote to him as the first step in a public campaign to get the Battle School children under the protection of the Fleet. Not so that they would actually be removed from their home countries—he never expected any government to allow *that*—but so that, when someone moved against them, it would be widely known that Locke had sounded the warning. But Chamrajnagar had forced Peter to keep Locke silent, so no one knew that Locke had foreseen the kidnappings but Chamrajnagar and Graff. The opportunity had been missed.

Peter wouldn't give up. There was some way to get back on track. And sitting there in the library in Greensboro, North Carolina, leaning back in a chair with his eyes closed like any other weary student, he'd think of it.

They rousted Ender's jeesh out of bed at 0400 and assembled them in the dining room. No one explained anything, and they were forbidden to talk. So they waited for five minutes, ten, twenty. Petra knew that the others were bound to be thinking the same things she was thinking: The Russians had caught on that they were sabotaging their own battle plans. Or maybe somebody had noticed the coded message in the dragon picture. Whatever it was, it wasn't going to be nice.

Thirty minutes after they were rousted, the door opened. Two soldiers came in and stood at attention. And then, to Petra's utter surprise, in walked . . . a kid. No older than they were. Twelve? Thirteen? Yet the soldiers were treating him with respect. And the kid himself moved with the easy confidence of authority. He was in charge here. And he loved it.

Had Petra seen him before? She didn't think so. Yet he looked at them as if he knew them. Well, of course he did—if he had authority here, he had no doubt been observing them for the weeks they'd been in captivity.

A child in charge. Had to be a Battle School kid—why else would a government give such power to somebody so young? From his age they had to be contemporaries. But she couldn't place him. And her memory was very, very good.

"Don't worry," said the boy. "The reason you don't know me is that I came to Battle School late, and I was only there a little while before you all left for Tactical. But I know *you*." He grinned. "Or is there someone here who *did* know me when I came in? Don't worry, I'll be studying the vid later. Looking for that little shock of recognition. Because if any of you did know me, well, then I'll know something more about you. I'll know that I saw you once before, silhouetted in the dark, walking away from me, leaving me for dead."

With that, Petra knew who he was. Knew because Crazy Tom had told them about it—how Bean had set a trap for this boy that he knew in Rotterdam, and with the help of four other kids had hung him up in an air shaft until he confessed to a dozen murders or so. They left him there, gave the recording to the teachers, and told them where he was. Achilles.

The only member of Ender's jeesh who had been with Bean that day was Crazy Tom. Bean had never talked about it, and no one asked. It made Bean a figure of mystery, that he had come from a life so dark and frightening that it was peopled with monsters like Achilles. What none of them had ever expected was to find Achilles, not in a mental institution or a prison, but here in Russia with soldiers under his command and themselves as his prisoners.

When Achilles studied the vids, it was possible that Crazy Tom would show recognition. And when he told his story, he would no doubt see recognition on all their faces. She had no idea what this meant, but she knew it couldn't be good. One thing was certain—she wasn't going to let Crazy Tom face the consequences alone.

"We all know who you are," said Petra. "You're Achilles. And nobody left you for dead, the way Bean told it. They left you for the teachers. To arrest and send you back to Earth. To a mental institution, no doubt. Bean even showed us your picture. If anybody recognized you, it was from that."

Achilles turned to her and smiled. "Bean would never tell that story. He would never show my picture."

"Then you don't know Bean," said Petra. She hoped the others would realize that admitting they heard it from Crazy Tom would be dangerous to him. Probably fatal, with this oomay in charge of the triggers. Bean wasn't here, so naming him as the source made sense.

"Oh, yes, you're quite the team," said Achilles. "Passing signals to each other, sabotaging the plans you submit, thinking we'll be too stupid to notice. Did you really think we'd set you to work on *real* plans before we turned you?"

As usual, Petra couldn't shut up. But she didn't really want to, either. "Trying to see which of us felt like outsiders, so you could turn them?" she said. "What a joke—there *were* no outsiders in Ender's jeesh. The only outsider here is you."

In fact, though, she knew perfectly well that Carn Carby, Shen, Vlad, and Fly Molo felt like outsiders, for various reasons. She felt like one herself. Her words were designed only to urge them all to maintain solidarity.

"So now you divide us up and start working on us," said Petra. "Achilles, we know your moves before you make them."

"You really can't hurt my pride," said Achilles. "Because I don't have any. All I care about is uniting humanity under one government. Russia is the only nation, the only *people* who have the will to greatness and the power to back it up. You're here because some of you might be useful in that effort. If we think you have what it takes, we'll invite you to join us. The rest of you, we'll just keep on ice till the war is over. The real losers, well, we'll send you home and hope your home government uses you against us." He grinned. "Come on, don't look so grim. You know you were going crazy back home. You didn't even know those people. You left them when you were so little you still got shit on your fingers when you wiped your ass. What did they know about you? What did you know about them? That they let you go. Me, I didn't have any families, Battle School just meant three meals a day. But you, they took away everything from you. You don't owe them anything. What you've got is your mind. Your talent. You've been tagged for greatness. You won their war with the Buggers for them. And they sent you home so your parents could go back to *raising* you?"

Nobody said anything. Petra was sure they all had as much contempt for his spiel as she did. He knew nothing about them. He'd never be able to divide them. He'd never win their loyalty. They knew too much about him. And they didn't like being held against their will.

He knew it, too. Petra saw it in his eyes, the rage dancing there as he realized that they had nothing but contempt for him.

At least he could see *her* contempt, because he zeroed in on her, took a few steps closer, smiling ever more kindly.

"Petra, it's so nice to meet you," he said. "The girl who tested so aggressive they had to check your DNA to make sure you weren't really a boy."

Petra felt the blood drain from her face. Nobody was supposed to know about that. It was a test the psychiatrists in Ground School had ordered when they decided her contempt for them was a symptom of dysfunction instead of what they deserved for asking her such stupid questions. It wasn't even supposed to be in her file. But apparently a record existed somewhere. Which was, of course, the message Achilles intended to get across to them: He knew everything. And, as a side benefit, it would start the others wondering just how piffed up she was.

"Ten of you. Only two missing from the glorious victory. Ender, the great one, the genius, the keeper of the holy grail—he's off founding a colony somewhere. We'll all be in our fifties by the time he gets there, and he'll still be a little kid. We're going to make history. He *is* history." Achilles smirked at his pun.

But Petra knew that mocking Ender wasn't going to play with this group. Achilles no doubt assumed that the ten of them were also-rans, runners-up, the ones who wanted to have Ender's job and had to sit there and watch him do it. He assumed that they were all burning with envy—because he would have been eaten alive with it. But he was wrong. He didn't understand them at all. They *missed* Ender. They were Ender's jeesh. And this yelda actually thought that he could forge them into a team the way Ender had.

"And then there's Bean," Achilles went on. "The youngest of you, the one whose test scores made you all look like halfwits. He could teach the rest of you classes in how to lead armies—except you probably wouldn't understand him, he's such a genius. Where *could* he be? Anybody miss him?"

Nobody answered. This time, though, Petra knew that the silence hid a different set of feelings. There had been some resentment of Bean. Not because of his brilliance, or at least no one admitted resenting him for that. What annoyed them was the way he just assumed he knew better than anyone. And that awkward time before Ender arrived on Eros, when Bean was the acting commander of the jeesh, that was hard on some of them, taking orders from the youngest of them. So maybe Achilles had guessed right about that.

Except that nobody was proud of those feelings, and bringing them out in the open didn't exactly make them love Achilles. Of course, it might be shame he was trying to provoke. Achilles might be smarter than they thought.

Probably not. He was so out of his league in trying to scope this group of military prodigies that he might as well be wearing a clown suit and throwing water balloons for all the respect he was going to get.

"Ah, yes, Bean," said Achilles. "I'm sorry to inform you that he's dead."

This was apparently too much for Crazy Tom, who yawned and said, "No he's not."

Achilles looked amused. "You think you know more about it than I do?"

"We've been on the nets," said Shen. "We'd know."

"You've been away from your desks since 2200. How do you know what's been happening while you slept?" Achilles glanced at his watch. "Oops, you're right. Bean *is* still alive right now. And for another fifteen minutes or so. Then . . . whoosh! A nice little rocket straight to his little bedroom to blow him up right on his little bed. We didn't even have to buy his location from the Greek military. Our friends there gave us the information for free."

Petra's heart sank. If Achilles could arrange for them to be kidnapped, he could certainly arrange for Bean to be killed. Killing was always easier than taking someone alive.

Did Bean already notice the message in the dragon, decode it, and pass along the information? Because if he's dead, there's no one else who'll be able to do it.

Immediately she was ashamed that the news of Bean's death made her think first of herself. But it didn't mean she didn't care about the kid. It meant that she trusted him so much that she had pinned all her hopes on him. If he died, those hopes died with him. It was not indecent of her to think of that.

To say it out loud, *that* would be indecent. But you can't help the thoughts that come to mind.

Maybe Achilles was lying. Or maybe Bean would survive, or get away. And if he died, maybe he'd already decoded the message. Maybe he hadn't. There was nothing Petra could do to change the outcome.

"What, no tears?" said Achilles. "And here I thought you were such close friends. I guess that was all hero-hype." He chuckled. "Well, I'm done with you for now." He turned to a soldier by the door. "Travel time."

The soldier left. They heard a few words of Russian and at once sixteen soldiers came in and divided up, one pair to each of the kids.

"You're being separated now," said Achilles. "Wouldn't want anyone to start thinking of a rescue operation. You can still email each other. We want your creative synergy to continue. After all, you're the finest little military minds that humanity was able to squeeze out in its hour of need. We're all really proud of you, and we look forward to seeing your finest work in the near future."

One of the kids farted loudly.

Achilles only grinned, winked at Petra, and left.

Ten minutes later they were all in separate vehicles, being driven away to points unknown, somewhere in the vast reaches of the largest country on the face of the Earth.

Part Two

ALLIANCES

6

Code

To: Graff%pilgrimage@colmin.gov
From: Konstan%Briseis@helstrat.gov
Re: Leak

Your Excellency, I write to you myself because I was most vociferously opposing to your plan to take young Julian Delphiki from our protection. I was wrong as we learnt from the missile assault on former apartment today leaving two soldiers dead. We are follow your previous advice by public release that Julian was killed in attack. His room was target in late night and he would die instead of soldiers sleeping there. Penetration of our system very deep, obviously. We trust no one now. You

```
were just in time and I regret my mak-
ing of delay. My pride in Hellene mil-
itary made me blind. You see I speak
Common a little after all, no more
bluffing between me and true friend to
Greece. Because of you and not me a
great national resource is not destroy.
```

If Bean had to be in hiding, there were worse places he could be than Araraquara. The town, named for a species of parrot, had been kept as something of a museum piece, with cobbled streets and old buildings. They weren't particularly beautiful old buildings or picturesque houses—even the cathedral was rather dull, and not particularly ancient, having been finished in the twentieth century. Still, there was the sense of a quieter way of life that had once been common in Brasil. The growth that had turned nearby Ribeirão Preto into a sprawling metropolis had pretty much passed Araraquara by. And even though the people were modern enough—you heard as much Common on the streets as Portuguese these days—Bean felt at home here in a way that he had never felt in Greece, where the desire to be fully European and fully Greek at the same time distorted public life and public spaces.

"It won't do to feel too much at home," said Sister Carlotta. "We can't stay anywhere for long."

"Achilles is the devil," said Bean. "Not God. He can't reach everywhere. He can't find us without some kind of evidence."

"He doesn't have to reach everywhere," said Sister Carlotta. "Only where we are."

"His hate for us makes him blind," said Bean.

"His fear makes him unnaturally alert."

Bean grinned—it was an old game between them. "It might not be Achilles who took the other kids."

"It might not be gravity that holds us to Earth," said Sister Carlotta, "but rather an unknown force with identical properties."

Then she grinned, too.

Sister Carlotta was a good traveling companion. She had a sense of humor. She understood his jokes and he enjoyed hers. But most of all, she liked to spend hours and hours without saying a thing, doing her work while he did his own. When they did talk, they were evolving a kind of oblique language where they both already knew everything that mattered so they only had to refer to it and the other would understand. Not that this implied they were kindred spirits or deeply attuned. It's just that their lives only touched at a few key points—they were in hiding, they were cut off from friends and family, and the same enemy wanted them dead. There was no one to gossip about because they knew no one. There was no chat because they had no interests beyond the projects at hand: trying to figure out where the other kids were being held, trying to determine what nation Achilles was serving (which would no doubt soon be serving him), and trying to understand the shape the world was taking so they could interfere with it, perhaps bending the course of history to a better end.

That was Sister Carlotta's goal, at least, and Bean was willing to take part in it, given that the same research required for the first two projects was identical to the research required for the last. He wasn't sure that he cared about the shape of history in the future.

He said that to Sister Carlotta once, and she only

smiled. "Is it the world outside yourself you don't care about," she said, "or the future as a whole, including your own?"

"Why should I care about narrowing down which things in particular I don't care about?"

"Because if you didn't care about your own future, you wouldn't care whether you were alive to see it, and you wouldn't be going through all this nonsense to stay alive."

"I'm a mammal," said Bean. "I try to live forever whether I actually want to or not."

"You're a child of God, so you care what happens to his children whether you admit it to yourself or not."

It was not her glib response that bothered him, because he expected it—he had provoked it, really, no doubt (he told himself) because he liked the reassurance that *if* there was a God, then Bean mattered to him. No, what bothered him was the momentary darkness that passed across her face. A fleeting expression, barely revealed, which he would not have noticed had he not known her face so well, and had darkness so rarely been expressed on it.

Something that I said made her feel sad. And yet it was a sadness that she wants to conceal from me. What did I say? That I'm a mammal? She's used to my gibes about her religion. That I might not want to live forever? Perhaps she worries that I'm depressed. That I try to live forever, despite my desires? Perhaps she fears that I'll die young. Well, that was why they were in Araraquara—to prevent his early death. And hers, too, for that matter. He had no doubt, though, that if a gun were pointed at him, she would leap in front of him to take the bullet. He did not understand why. He would not do the same for her, or for anyone. He would try to warn her, or pull her out of the way, or interfere with the shooter, whatever he could do that left them both a reasonable chance of survival. But he would not deliberately die to save her.

Maybe it was a thing that women did. Or maybe that grown-ups did for children. To give your life to save someone else. To weigh your own survival and decide that it mattered less to you than the survival of another. Bean could not fathom how anyone could feel that way. Shouldn't the irrational mammal take over, and force them to act for their own survival? Bean had never tried to suppress his own survival instinct, but he doubted that he could even if he tried. But then, maybe older people were more willing to part with their lives, having already spent the bulk of their starting capital. Of course, it made sense for parents to sacrifice themselves for the sake of their children, particularly parents too old to make more babies. But Sister Carlotta had never had children. And Bean was not the only one that she would die for. She would leap out to take a bullet for a stranger. She valued her own life less than anyone's. And that made her utterly alien to him.

Survival, not of the fittest, but of myself—that is the purpose at the core of my being. That is the reason, ultimately, that I do all the things that I've done. There have been moments when I felt compassion—when, alone of Ender's jeesh, I knowingly sent men to their certain deaths, I felt a deep sorrow for them. But I sent them, and they went. Would I, in their place, have gone as they did, obeying an order? Dying to save unknown future generations who would never know their names?

Bean doubted it.

He would gladly serve humanity if it happened also to serve himself. Fighting the Formics alongside Ender and the other kids, that made sense because saving humanity included saving Bean. And if by managing to stay alive somewhere in the world, he was also a thorn in the side of Achilles, making him less cautious, less wise, and therefore easier to defeat—well, it was a pleasant bonus that Bean's pursuit of his own survival happened also to give the human race a chance to defeat the monster. And since the best way to survive would be to find Achilles and kill him first, he might turn out to be one of the great benefactors of human history. Though now that he thought about it, he couldn't remember a single assassin who was remembered as a hero. Brutus, perhaps. His reputation had had its ups and downs. Most assassins, though, were despised by history. Probably because successful assassins tended to be those whose target was not particularly dangerous to anyone. By the time everyone agreed that a particular monster was well worth assassinating, the monster had far too much power and paranoia to leave any possibility of an assassination actually being carried out.

He got nowhere when he tried to discuss it with Sister Carlotta.

"I can't argue with you so I don't know why you bother. I only know that I won't help you plot his assassination."

"You don't consider it self-defense?" said Bean. "What is this, one of those stupid vids where the hero can never actually kill a bad guy who isn't actually pointing a gun at him right that very moment?"

"It's my faith in Christ," said Carlotta. "Love your enemy, do good to those who hate you."

"Well, where does that leave us? The nicest thing we could do for Achilles would be to post our address on the nets and wait for him to send someone to kill us."

"Don't be absurd," said Carlotta. "Christ said be

good to your enemies. It wouldn't be good for Achilles to find us, because then he'd kill us and have even more murders to answer for before the judgment bar of God. The best thing we can do for Achilles is to keep him from killing us. And if we love him, we'll stop him from ruling the world while we're at it, since power like that would only compound his opportunities to sin."

"Why don't we love the hundreds and thousands and millions of people who'll die in the wars he's planning to launch?"

"We do love them," said Carlotta. "But you're confused the way so many people are, who don't understand the perspective of God. You keep thinking that death is the most terrible thing that can happen to a person, but to God, death just means you're coming home a few moments ahead of schedule. To God, the dreadful outcome of a human life is when that person embraces sin and rejects the joy that God offers. So of all the millions who might die in a war, each individual life is tragic only if it ends in sin."

"So why are you going to such trouble to keep *me* alive?" asked Bean, thinking he knew the answer.

"You want me to say something that will weaken my case," said Carlotta. "Like telling you that I'm human and so I want to prevent your death right now because I love you. And that's true, I have no children but you're as close as I come to having any, and I would be stricken to the soul if you died at the hands of that twisted boy. But in truth, Julian Delphiki, the reason I work so hard to prevent your death is because, if you died today, you would probably go to hell."

To his surprise, Bean was stung by this. He understood enough of what Carlotta believed that he could have predicted this attitude, but the fact that she put it into words still hurt. "I'm not going to repent and get baptized, so I'm bound to go to hell, therefore no matter when I die I'm doomed," he said.

"Nonsense. Our understanding of doctrine is not perfect, and no matter what the popes have said, I don't believe for a moment that God is going to damn for eternity the billions of children he allowed to be born and die without baptism. No, I think you're likely to go to hell because, despite all your brilliance, you are still quite amoral. Sometime before you die, I pray most earnestly that you will learn that there are higher laws that transcend mere survival, and higher causes to serve. When you give yourself to such a great cause, my dear boy, *then* I will not fear your death, because I know that a just God will forgive you for the oversight of not having recognized the truth of Christianity during your lifetime."

"You really are a heretic," said Bean. "None of those doctrines would pass muster with any priest."

"They don't even pass muster with me," said Carlotta. "But I don't know a soul who doesn't maintain two separate lists of doctrines—the ones that they *believe* that they believe; and the ones that they actually try to live by. I'm simply one of the rare ones who knows the difference. You, my boy, are not."

"Because I don't believe in any doctrines."

"That," said Carlotta with exaggerated smugness, "is proof positive of my assertion. You are so convinced that you believe only what you believe that you believe, that you remain utterly blind to what you *really* believe without believing you believe it."

"You were born in the wrong century," said Bean. "You could make Thomas Aquinas tear out his hair. Nietzsche and Derrida would accuse you of obfuscation. Only the Inquisition would know what to do with you—toast you nice and brown."

"Don't tell me you've actually read Nietzsche and Derrida. Or Aquinas, for that matter."

"You don't have to eat the entire turd to know that it's not a crab cake."

"You arrogant impossible boy."

"But Geppetta, I'm *not* a real boy."

"You're certainly not a puppet, or not *my* puppet, anyway. Go outside and play now, I'm busy."

Sending him outside was not a punishment, however. Sister Carlotta knew that. From the moment they got their desks linked to the nets, they had both spent most of every day indoors, gathering information. Carlotta, whose identity was shielded by the firewalls in the Vatican computer system, was able to continue all her old relationships and thus had access to all her best sources, taking care only to avoid saying where she was or even what time zone she was in. Bean, however, had to create a new identity from scratch, hiding behind a double blind of mail servers specializing in anonymity, and even then he kept no identity for longer than a week. He formed no relationships and therefore could develop no sources. When he needed specific information, he had to ask Carlotta to help him find it, and then she had to determine whether it was something she might legitimately ask, or whether it was something that might be a clue that she had Bean with her. Most of the time she decided she dared not ask. So Bean was crippled in his research. Still, they shared what information they could, and despite his disadvantages, there was one advantage that remained to him: The mind looking at his data was his own. The mind that had scored higher than anyone else on the Battle School tests.

Unfortunately, Truth did not care much about such credentials. It refused to give up and reveal itself just because it realized you were bound to find it eventually.

Bean could only take so many hours of frustration before he had to get up and go outside. It wasn't just to get away from his work, however. "The climate agrees with me," he told Sister Carlotta on their second day, when, dripping with sweat, he headed for his third shower since waking. "I was born to live with heat and humidity."

At first she had insisted on going everywhere with him. But after a few days he was able to persuade her of several things. First, he looked old enough not to be accompanied by his grandmother everywhere he went—"Avó Carlotta" was what he called her here, their cover story. Second, she would be no protection for him anyway, since she had no weapons and no defensive skills. Third, he was the one who knew how to live on the streets, and even though Araraquara was hardly the kind of dangerous place that Rotterdam had been when he was younger, he had already mapped in his mind a hundred different escape routes and hiding places, just by reflex. When Carlotta realized that she would need his protection a lot more than he would need hers, she relented and allowed him to go out alone, as long as he did his best to remain inconspicuous.

"I can't stop people from noticing the foreign boy."

"You don't look that foreign," she said. "Mediterranean body types are common here. Just try not to speak a lot. Always look like you have an errand but never like you're in a hurry. But then, it was you who taught *me* that that was how to avoid attracting attention."

And so here he was today, weeks after they arrived in Brasil, wandering the streets of Araraquara and wondering what great cause might make his life worthwhile in Carlotta's eyes. For despite all her faith, it was *her* approval, not God's, that seemed like it might be worth striving for, as long as it didn't interfere with his project of staying alive. Was it enough to be a thorn in Achilles' side? Enough to look for ways to oppose him? Or was there something else he should be doing?

At the crest of one of Araraquara's many hills there was a sorvete shop run by a Japanese-Brazilian family. The family had been in business there for centuries, as their sign proclaimed, and Bean was both amused and moved by this, in light of what Carlotta had said. For this family, making flavored frozen desserts to eat from a cone or cup was the great cause that gave them continuity through the ages. What could be more trivial than that? And yet Bean came here, again and again, because their recipes were, in fact, delicious, and when he thought about how many other people for these past two or three hundred years must have paused and taken a moment's pleasure in the sweet and delicate flavors, in the feel of the smooth sorvete in their mouths, he could not disdain that cause. They offered something that was genuinely good, and people's lives were better because they offered it. It was not a noble cause that would get written up in the histories. But it was not nothing, either. A person could do worse than spend some large percentage of his life in a cause like that.

Bean wasn't even sure what it meant to give himself to a cause. Did that mean turning over his decision-making to someone else? What an absurd idea. In all likelihood there was no one smarter than him on Earth, and though that did not mean he was incapable of error, it certainly meant he'd have to be a fool to turn over his decisions to someone even *more* likely to be wrong.

Why he was wasting time on Carlotta's sentiment-ridden philosophy of life he didn't know. Doubtless that was one of his mistakes—the emotional human aspect of his mentality overriding the inhumanly aloof brilliance that, to his chagrin, only sometimes controlled his thinking.

The sorvete cup was empty. Apparently he had eaten it all without noticing. He hoped his mouth had enjoyed every taste of it, because the eating was done by reflex while he thought his thoughts.

Bean discarded the cup and went his way. A bicyclist passed him. Bean saw how the cyclist's whole body bounced and rattled and vibrated from the cobblestones. *That* is human life, thought Bean. So bounced around that we can never see anything straight.

Supper was beans and rice and stringy beef in the pensão's public dining room. He and Carlotta ate together in near silence, listening to other people's conversations and the clanking and clinking of dishes and silverware. Any real conversation between them would doubtless leak some memorable bit of information that might raise questions and attract attention. Like, why did a woman who talked like a nun have a grandson? Why did this child who looked to be six talk like a philosophy professor half the time? So they ate in silence except for conversations about the weather.

After supper, as always, they each signed on to the nets to check their mail. Carlotta's mail was interesting and real. All of Bean's correspondents, this week anyway, thought he was a woman named Lettie who was working on her dissertation and needed information, but who had no time for a personal life and so rebuffed with alacrity any attempt at friendly and personal conversation. But so far, there was no way to find Achilles' signature in any nation's behavior. While most countries simply did not have the resources to kidnap Ender's jeesh in such a short time, of those that did have the resources, there was not one that Bean could rule out because they lacked the arrogance or aggressiveness or contempt for law to do it. Why, it could even have been done by Brasil itself—for all he knew, his former companions from the Formic War might be imprisoned somewhere in Araraquara. They might hear in the early morning the rumble of the very garbage truck that picked up the sorvete cup that he threw away today.

"I don't know why people spread these things," said Carlotta.

"What?" asked Bean, grateful for the break from the eye-blearing work he was doing.

"Oh, these stupid superstitious good-luck dragons. There must be a dozen different dragon pictures now."

"Oh, é," said Bean. "They're everywhere, I just don't notice them anymore. Why dragons, anyway?"

"I think this is the oldest of them. At least it's the one I saw first, with the little poem," said Carlotta. "If Dante were writing today, I'm sure there'd be a special place in his hell for people who start these things."

"What poem?"

" 'Share this dragon,' " Carlotta recited. " 'If you do, lucky end for them and you.' "

"Oh, yeah, dragons always bring a lucky end. I mean, what does that poem actually *say*? That you'll die lucky? That it'll be lucky for you to end?"

Carlotta chuckled.

Bored with his correspondence, Bean kept the nonsense going. "Dragons aren't always lucky. They had to discontinue Dragon Army in Battle School, it was so unlucky. Till they revived it for Ender, and no doubt they gave it to him because people thought it was bad luck and they were trying to stack everything against him."

Then a thought passed through his mind, ever so briefly, but it woke him from his lethargy.

"Forward me that picture."

"I bet you already have it on a dozen letters."

"I don't want to search. Send me that one."

"You're still that Lettie person? Haven't you been that one for two weeks now?"

"Five days."

It took a few minutes for the message to be routed to him, but when it finally showed up in his mail, he looked closely at the image.

"Why in the world are you paying attention to this?" asked Carlotta.

He looked up to see her watching him.

"I don't know. Why are you paying attention to the way I'm paying attention to it?" He grinned at her.

"Because you think it matters. I may not be as smart as you are about most things, but I'm very much smarter than you are about you. I know when you're intrigued."

"Just the juxtaposition of the image of a dragon with the word 'end.' Endings really aren't considered all that lucky. Why wouldn't the person write 'luck will come' or 'lucky fate' or something else? Why 'lucky end'?"

"Why not?"

"End. Ender. Ender's army was Dragon."

"Now, that's a little far-fetched."

"Look at the drawing," said Bean. "Right in the middle, where the bitmap is so complicated—there's one line that's damaged. The dots don't line up at all. It's virtually random."

"It just looks like noise to me."

"If you were being held captive but you had computer access, only every bit of mail you sent out was scrutinized, how would you send a message?" asked Bean.

"You don't think this could be a message from—do you?"

"I have no idea. But now that I've thought of it, it's worth looking at, don't you think?"

By now Bean had pasted the dragon image into a graphics program and was studying that line of pixels. "Yes, this is random, the whole line. Doesn't belong here, and it's not just noise because the rest of the image is still completely intact except for this other line that's partly broken. Noise would be randomly distributed."

"See what it is, then," said Carlotta. "You're the genius, I'm the nun."

Soon Bean had the two lines isolated in a separate file and was studying the information as raw code. Viewed as one-byte or two-byte text code, there was nothing that remotely resembled language, but of course it couldn't, could it, or it would never have got out. So *if* it was a message, then it had to be in some kind of code.

For the next few hours Bean wrote programs to help him manipulate the data contained in those lines. He tried mathematical schemes and graphic reinterpretations, but in truth he knew all along that it wouldn't be anything that complex. Because whoever created it would have had to do it without the aid of a computer. It had to be something relatively simple, designed only to keep a cursory examination from revealing what it was.

And so he kept coming back to ways of reinterpreting the binary code as text. Soon enough he came upon a scheme that seemed promising. Two-byte text code, but shifted right by one position for each character, except when the right shift would make it correspond with two actual bytes in memory, in which case double shift. That way a real character would never show up if someone looked at the file with an ordinary view program.

When he used that method on the one line, it came up as text characters only, which was not likely to happen by chance. But the other line came up random-seeming garbage.

So he left-shifted the other line, and it, too, became nothing but text characters.

"I'm in," he said. "And it *is* a message."

"What does it say?"

"I haven't the faintest idea."

Carlotta got up and came to look over his shoulder. "It's not even language. It doesn't divide into words."

"That's deliberate," said Bean. "If it divided into words it would look like a message and invite decoding. The easy way that any amateur can decode language is by checking word lengths and the frequency of appearance of certain letter patterns. In Common, you look for letter groupings that could be 'a' and 'the' and 'and,' that sort of thing."

"And you don't even know what language it's in."

"No, but it's bound to be Common, because they know they're sending it to somebody who doesn't have a key. So it has to be decodable, and that means Common."

"So they're making it easy and hard at the same time?"

"Yes. Easy for me, hard for everyone else."

"Oh, come now. You think this was written to you?"

"Ender. Dragon. I was *in* Dragon Army, unlike most of them. And whom else would they be writing to? I'm outside, they're in. They know that everyone is there but me. And I'm the only person that they'd know they could reach without tipping their hand to everybody else."

"What, did you have some private code?"

"Not really, but what we have is common experience, the slang of Battle School, things like that. You'll see. When I crack it, it'll be because I recognize a word that nobody else would recognize."

"*If* it's from them."

"It is," said Bean. "It's what I'd do. Get word out. This picture is like a virus. It goes everywhere and gets its code into a million places, but nobody knows it's a code because it looks like something that most people think they already understand. It's a fad, not a message. Except to me."

"Almost thou persuadest me," said Carlotta.

"I'll crack it before I go to bed."

"You're too little to drink that much coffee. It'll give you an aneurysm."

She went back to her own mail.

Since the words weren't separated, Bean had to look for other patterns that might give things away. There were no obvious repeated two-letter or three-letter patterns that didn't lead to obvious dead ends. That didn't surprise him. If he had been composing such a message, he would have dropped out all the articles and conjunctions and prepositions and pronouns that he possibly could. Not only that, but most of the words were probably deliberately misspelled to avoid repetitive patterns. But some words would be spelled correctly, and they would be designed to be unrecognizable to most people who weren't from the Battle School culture.

There were only two places where the same character was apparently doubled, one in each line. That might just be the result of one word ending with the same letter that began another, but Bean doubted it. Nothing would be left to chance in this message. So he wrote a little program that would take the doubled letters in one word and, beginning with "aa," show him what the surrounding letters might be to see if anything looked plausible to him. And he started with the doubled letters in the shorter line, because that pair was surrounded by another pair, in a 1221 pattern.

The obvious failures, like "xddx" and "pffp," took no time, but he had to investigate all the variants on "abba" and "adda" and "deed" and "effe" to see what they did to the message. Some were promising and he saved them for later exploration.

"Why is it in Greek now?" asked Carlotta.

She was looking over his shoulder again. He hadn't heard her get up and come over behind him.

"I converted the original message to Greek characters so that I wouldn't get distracted by trying to read meanings into letters I hadn't decoded yet. The ones I'm actually working on are in Roman letters."

At that moment, his program showed the letters "iggi."

"Piggies," said Sister Carlotta.

"Maybe, but it doesn't flag anything for me." He started cycling through the dictionary matches with "iggi," but none of them did any better than "piggies" had.

"Does it have to be a word?" said Carlotta.

"Well, if it's a number, then this is a dead end," said Bean.

"No, I mean, why not a name?"

Bean saw it at once. "How blind can I be." He plugged the letters *w* and *n* to the positions before and after "iggi" and then spread the results through the whole message, making the program show hyphens for the undeciphered letters. The two lines now read

```
--n——g--n--n--n--i--n--g
-n-n-wiggin-
```

"That doesn't look right for Common," said Carlotta. "There should be a lot more *i*'s than that."

"I'm assuming that the message deliberately leaves out letters as much as possible, especially vowels, so it won't look like Common."

"So how will you know when you've decoded it?"

"When it makes sense."

"It's bedtime. I know, you're not sleeping till you've solved it." He barely noticed that she moved away from behind him. He was busy trying the other doubled letter. This time he had a more complicated job, because the letters before and after the double pair were different. It meant far more combinations to try, and being able to eliminate *g, i, n,* and *w* didn't speed up the process all that much.

Again, there were quite a few readings that he saved—more than before—but nothing rang a bell until he got to "jees." The word that Ender's companions in the final battle used for themselves. "Jeesh."

Could it be? It was definitely a word that might be used as a flag.

```
h-n-jeesh-g-en-s-ns-n--si--n--s-g
-n-n-wiggin--
```

If those twenty-seven letters were right, then he had only thirty left to solve. He rubbed his eyes, sighed, and set to work.

—

It was noon when the smell of oranges woke him. Sister Carlotta was peeling a mexerica orange. "People are eating these things on the street and spitting the pulp on the sidewalk. You can't chew it up enough to swallow it. But the juice is the best orange you'll ever taste in your life."

Bean got out of bed and took the segment she offered him. She was right. She handed him a bowl to spit the pulp into. "Good breakfast," said Bean.

"Lunch," she said. She held up a paper. "I take it you consider this to be a solution?"

It was what he had printed out before going to bed.

```
hlpndrjeeshtgdrenrusbnstun6rmysiz40ntrys-
btg
bnfndwigginptr
```

"Oh," said Bean. "I didn't print out the one with the word breaks." Putting another mexerica segment in his mouth, Bean padded on bare feet to the computer, called up the right file, and printed it. He brought it back, handed it to Carlotta, spat out pulp, and took his own mexerica from her shopping bag and began peeling.

"Bean," she said. "I'm a normal mortal. I get 'help' and is this 'Ender'?"

Bean took the paper from her.

```
hlp ndr jeesh tgdr en rus bns tun 6 rmy
            siz 40 n try sbtg
            bn fnd wiggin ptr
```

"The vowels are left out as much as possible, and there are other misspellings. But what the first line says is, 'Help. Ender's jeesh is together in Russia—' "

"T-g-d-r is 'together'? And 'in' is spelled like French?"

"Exactly," said Bean. "I understood it and it doesn't look like Common." He went on interpreting. "The next part was confusing for a long time, until I realized that the 6 and the 40 were numbers. I got almost all the other letters before I realized that. The thing is, the numbers matter, but there's no way to guess them from context. So the next few words are designed to give a context to the numbers. It says 'Bean's toon was 6'—that's because Ender divided Dragon Army into five toons instead of the normal four, but then he gave me a sort of ad hoc toon, and if you added it to the count, it was number six. Only who would know that except for somebody from Battle School? So only somebody like me would get the number. Same thing with the next one. 'Army size 40.' Everyone in Battle School knew that there were forty soldiers in every army. Unless you counted the commander, in which case it was forty-one, but see, it doesn't matter, because that digit is trivial."

"How do you know that?"

"Because the next letter is *n*. For 'north.' The message is telling their location. They know they're in

Russia. And because they can apparently see the sun or at least shadows on the wall, and they know the date, they can calculate their latitude, more or less. Six-four-zero north. Sixty-four north."

"Unless it means something else."

"No, the message is meant to be obvious."

"To you."

"Yes, to me. The rest of that line is 'try sabotage.' I think that means that they're trying to screw up whatever the Russians are trying to make them do. So they're pretending to go along but really gumming up the works. Very smart to get that on record. The fact that Graff was court-martialed after winning the Formic War suggests that they'd better get it on record that they were *not* collaborating with the enemy—in case the other side wins."

"But Russia isn't at war with anybody."

"The Polemarch was Russian, and Warsaw Pact troops were at the heart of his side in the League War. You've got to remember, Russia was the country that was most on the make before the Formics came and started tearing up real estate and forced humanity to unite under the Hegemon and create the International Fleet. They have always felt cheated out of their destiny, and now that the Formics are gone, it makes sense that they'd be eager to get back on the fast track. They don't think of themselves as bad guys, they think of themselves as the only people with the will and the resources to unite the world for real, permanently. They think they're doing a good thing."

"People always do."

"Not always. But yes, to wage war you have to be able to sell your own people on the idea that either you're fighting in self-defense, or you're fighting because you deserve to win, or you're fighting in order to save other people. The Russian people respond to an altruistic sales pitch as easily as anybody else."

"So what about the second line?"

" 'Bean find Wiggin Peter.' They're suggesting that I look for Ender's older brother. He didn't go off on the colony ship with Ender and Valentine. And he's been a player, under the net identity of Locke. And I suppose he's running Demosthenes, too, now that Valentine is gone."

"You knew about that?"

"I knew a lot of things," said Bean. "But the main thing is that they're right. Achilles is hunting for me and he's hunting for you, and he's got all the rest of Ender's jeesh, but he doesn't even know Ender's brother exists and he wouldn't care if he did. But you know and I know that Peter Wiggin would have been in Battle School except for a little character flaw. And for all we know, that character flaw may be exactly what he needs to be a good match against Achilles."

"Or it may be exactly the flaw that makes it so a victory for Peter is no better than a victory for Achilles, in terms of the amount of suffering in the world."

"Well, we won't know until we find him, will we?" said Bean.

"To find him, Bean, you'd have to reveal who you are."

"Yes," said Bean. "Isn't this exciting?" He did an exaggerated wriggle like a little kid being taken to the zoo.

"This is your life you're playing with."

"You're the one who wanted me to find a cause."

"Peter Wiggin isn't a cause, he's dangerous. You haven't heard what Graff had to say about him."

"On the contrary," said Bean. "How do you think I learned about him?"

"But he might be no better than Achilles!"

"I know of several ways already that he's better than Achilles. First, he's not trying to kill us. Second, he's already got a huge network of contacts with people all over the world, some of whom know he's as young as he is but most of whom have no idea. Third, he's ambitious just like Achilles is, only Achilles has already assembled almost all of the children who were tagged as the most brilliant military commanders in the world, while Peter Wiggin will have only one. Me. Do you think he's dumb enough not to use me?"

"*Use* you. That's the operative word here, Bean."

"Well, aren't *you* being used in *your* cause?"

"By God, not by Peter Wiggin."

"I'll bet Peter Wiggin sends a lot clearer messages than God does," said Bean. "And if I don't like what he's doing, I can always quit."

"With someone like Peter, you can't always quit."

"He can't make me think of what I don't want to think about. Unless he's a remarkably stupid genius, he'll know that."

"I wonder if Achilles knows that, as he's trying to squeeze brilliance out of the other children."

"Exactly. Between Peter Wiggin and Achilles, what are the odds that Wiggin could be worse?"

"Oh, it's hard to imagine how that could be."

"So let's start thinking of a way to contact Locke without giving away our identity and our location."

"I'm going to need more mexerica oranges before we leave Brasil," said Carlotta.

Only then did he notice that the two of them had already blown through the whole bagful. "Me too," he said.

As she left, the empty bag in hand, she paused at the door. "You did very well with that message, Julian Delphiki."

"Thanks, Grandma Carlotta."

She left smiling.

Bean held up the message and scanned it again. The only part of the message that he hadn't fully interpreted for her was the last word. He didn't think "ptr" meant Peter. That would have been redundant. "Wiggin" was enough to identify him. No, the "ptr" at the end was a signature. This message was from Petra. She could have tried to write directly to Peter Wiggin. But she had written to Bean, coding it in a way that Peter would never have understood.

She's relying on me.

Bean knew how the others in Ender's jeesh had resented him. Not a lot, but a little. When they were all in Command School on Eros, before Ender arrived, the military had made Bean the acting commander in all their test battles, even though he was the youngest of them all, even younger than Ender. He knew he'd done a good job, and won their respect. But they never liked taking orders from him and were undisguisedly happy when Ender arrived and Bean was dropped back to be one of them. Nobody ever said, "Good job, Bean," or "Hey, you did OK." Except Petra.

She had done for him on Eros the same thing that Nikolai had done for him in Battle School—provided him with a kind word now and then. He was sure that neither Nikolai nor Petra ever realized how important their casual generosity had been to him. But he remembered that when he needed a friend, the two of them had been there for him. Nikolai had turned out, by the workings of not-entirely-coincidental fate, to be his brother. Did that make Petra his sister?

It was Petra who reached out to him now. She trusted him to recognize the message, decode it, and act on it.

There were files in the Battle School record system that said that Bean was not human, and he knew that Graff at least sometimes felt that way because he had overheard those words from his own lips. He knew that Carlotta loved him but she loved Jesus more and anyway, she was old and thought of him as a child. He could rely on her, but she did not rely on him.

In his Earthside life before Battle School, the only friend Bean had ever had was a girl named Poke, and Achilles had murdered her long before. Murdered her only moments after Bean left her, and moments before he realized his mistake and rushed back to warn her and instead found her body floating in the Rhine. She died trying to save Bean, and she died because Bean couldn't be relied upon to take as much care to save her.

Petra's message meant that maybe he had another friend who needed him after all. And this time, he would not turn his back. This time it was his turn to save his friend, or die trying. How's that for a cause, Sister Carlotta?

7

Going Public

To:Demosthenes%Tecumseh@free america.org, Locke%erasmus@polnet.gov
From: dontbother@firewall.set
Re: Achilles heel

Dear Peter Wiggin,
A message smuggled to me from the kidnapped children confirms they are (or were, at the time of sending) together, in Russia near the sixty-fourth parallel, doing their best to sabotage those trying to exploit their military talents. Since they will doubtless be separated and moved frequently, the exact location is unimportant, and I am quite sure you already knew Russia was the only country with both the ambition and

the means to acquire all the members of Ender's jeesh.

I'm sure you recognize the impossibility of releasing these children through military intervention—at the slightest sign of a plausible effort to extract them, they will be killed in order to deprive an enemy of such assets. But it might be possible to persuade either the Russian government or some if not all of those holding the individual children that releasing them is in Russia's best interest. This might be accomplished by exposing the individual who is almost certainly behind this audacious action, and your two identities are uniquely situated to accuse him in a way that will be taken seriously.

Therefore I suggest that you do a bit of research into a break-in at a high-security institution for the criminally insane in Belgium during the League War. Three guards were killed and the inmates were released. All but one were recaptured quickly. The one who got away was once a student at Battle School. He is behind the kidnapping. When it is revealed that this psychopath has control of these children, it will cause grave misgivings inside the Russian command system. It will also give them a scapegoat if they decide to return the children.

Don't bother trying to trace this email identity. It already never existed. If you can't figure out who I am and how to contact me from the research you're about to do, then we don't have much to talk about anyway.

Peter's heart sank when he opened the letter to Demosthenes and saw that it had also been sent to Locke. The salutation "Dear Peter Wiggin" only confirmed it—someone besides the office of the Polemarch had broken his identities. He expected the worst—some kind of blackmail or a demand that he support this or that cause.

To his surprise, the message was nothing of the kind. It came from someone who claimed to have received a message from the kidnapped kids—and gave him a tantalizing path to follow. Of course he immediately searched the news archives and found the break-in at a high-security mental hospital near Genk. Finding the name of the inmate who got away was much harder, requiring that, as Demosthenes, he ask for help from a law enforcement contact in Germany, and then, as Locke, for additional help from a friend in the Anti-Sabotage Committee in the Office of the Hegemon.

It yielded a name that made Peter laugh, since it was in the subject line of the email that prompted this search. Achilles, pronounced "ah-SHEEL" in the French manner. An orphan rescued from the streets of Rotterdam by, of all things, a Catholic nun working for the procurement section of the Battle School. He was given surgery to correct a crippled leg, then taken up to Battle School, where he lasted only a few days before being exposed as a serial killer by some of the other students, though in fact he had not killed anyone in the Battle School.

The list of his victims was interesting. He had a pattern of killing anyone who had ever made him feel or seem helpless or vulnerable. Including the doctor who had repaired his leg. Apparently he wasn't much for gratitude.

Putting together the information, Peter could see that his unknown correspondent was right. If in fact this sicko was running the operation that was using these kids for military planning, it was almost certain that the Russian officers working with him did not know his criminal record. Whatever agency liberated Achilles from the mental hospital would not have shared that information with the military who were expected to work with him. There would be outrage that would be heard at the highest levels of the Russian government.

And even if the government did not act to get rid of Achilles and release the kids, the Russian Army jealously guarded its independence from the rest of the government, especially the intelligence-and-dirty-jobs agencies. There was a good chance that some of these children might "escape" before the government acted—indeed, such unauthorized actions might force the government to make it official and pretend that the "early releases" had been authorized.

It was always possible, of course, that Achilles would kill one or more of the kids as soon as he was exposed. At least Peter would not have to face those particular children in battle. And now that he knew something about Achilles, Peter was in a much better position to face him in a head-to-head struggle.

Achilles killed with his own hands. Since that was a very stupid thing to do, and Achilles did not test stupid, it had to be an irresistible compulsion. People with irresistible compulsions could be terrifying enemies—but they could also be beaten.

For the first time in weeks, Peter felt a glimmer of hope. This was how his work as Locke and Demosthenes paid off—people with certain kinds of secret information that they wanted to make public found ways to hand it to Peter without his even having to ask for it. Much of his power came from this disorganized network of informants. It never bothered his pride that he was being "used" by this anonymous correspondent. As far as Peter was concerned, they were using each other. And besides, Peter had earned the right to get such helpful gifts.

Still, Peter always looked gift horses in the mouth. As either Locke or Demosthenes, he emailed friends and contacts in various government agencies, trying to get confirmation of various aspects of the story he was preparing to write. Could the break-in at the mental institution have been carried out by Russian agents? Did satellite surveillance show any kind of activity near the sixty-fourth parallel that might correspond with the arrival or departure of the ten kidnapped kids? Was anything known about the whereabouts of Achilles that would contradict the idea of his being in control of the whole kidnap operation?

It took a couple of days to get the story right. He tried it first as a column by Demosthenes, but he soon realized that since Demosthenes was constantly putting out warnings about Russian plots, he might not be taken very seriously. It had to be Locke who published this. And that would be dangerous, because up to now Locke had been scrupulous about not seeming to take sides against Russia. That would now make it more likely that his exposure of Achilles would be taken seriously—but it ran a grave risk of costing Locke some of his best contacts in Russia. No matter how much a Russian might despise what his government was doing, the devotion to Mother Russia ran deep. There was a line you couldn't cross. For more than a few of his contacts there, publishing this piece would cross that line.

Until he hit upon the obvious solution. Before submitting the piece to *International Aspects,* he would send copies to his Russian contacts to give a heads-up on what was coming. Of course the exposé would fly through the Russian military. It was possible that the repercussions would begin even before his column officially appeared. And his contacts would know he wasn't trying to hurt Russia—he was giving them a chance to clean house, or at least put a spin on the story before it ran.

It wasn't a long story, but it named names and opened doors that other reporters could follow up on. And they *would* follow up. From the first paragraph, it was dynamite.

> The mastermind behind the kidnapping of Ender's "jeesh" is a serial killer named Achilles. He was taken from a mental institution during the League War in order to bring his dark genius to bear on Russian military strategy. He has repeatedly murdered with his own hands, and now ten brilliant children who once saved the world are completely at his mercy. What were the Russians thinking when they gave power to this psychopath? Or was Achilles' bloody record concealed even from them?

There it was—in the first paragraph, right along with the accusation, Locke was generously providing the spin that would allow the Russian government and military to extricate themselves from this mess.

It took twenty minutes to send the individual messages to all his Russian contacts. In each message, he warned them that they had only about six hours before he had to turn in his column to the editor at *International Aspects*. *IA*'s fact-checkers would add another hour or two to the delay, but they would find complete confirmation of everything.

Peter pushed SEND, SEND, SEND.

Then he settled down to pore over the data to figure out how it revealed to him the identity of his correspondent. Another mental patient? Hardly likely—they were all brought back into confinement. An employee of the mental hospital? Impossible for someone like that to find out who was behind Locke and Demosthenes. Someone in law enforcement? More likely—but few names of investigators were offered in the news stories. Besides, how could he know *which* of the investigators had tipped him off? No, his correspondent had promised, in effect, a unique solution. Something in the data would tell him *exactly* who his informant was, and exactly how to reach him. Emailing investigators indiscriminately would serve only to risk exposing Peter with no guarantee that any of the people he contacted would be the right one.

The one thing that did not happen as he searched for his correspondent's identity was any kind of response from any of his Russian friends. If the story had been wrong, or if the Russian military had already known about Achilles' history and wanted to cover it up, he would have been getting constant emails urging him not to run the story, then demanding, and finally threatening him. So the fact that no one wrote him at all served as all the confirmation he needed from the Russian end.

As Demosthenes, he was anti-Russian. As Locke, he was reasonable and fair to all nations. As Peter, though, he was envious of the Russian sense of national identity, the cohesiveness of Russians when they felt their country was in danger. If Americans had ever had such powerful bonds, they had expired long before Peter was born. To be Russian was the most powerful part of a person's identity. To be American was about as important as being a Rotarian—very important if you were elected to high office, but barely noticeable in most citizens' sense of who they were. That was why Peter never planned his future with America in mind. Americans expected to get their way, but they had no passion for anything. Demosthenes could stir up anger and resentment, but it amounted to spitefulness, not purpose. Peter would have to root himself elsewhere. Too bad Russia wasn't available to him. It was a nation that had a vast will to greatness, coupled with the most extraordinary run of stupid leadership in history, with the possible exception of the kings of Spain. And Achilles had got there first.

Six hours after sending the article to his Russian contacts, he pushed SEND once more, submitting it to his editor. As he expected, three minutes later he got a response.

```
You're sure?
```

To which Peter replied, "Check it. My sources confirm."

Then he went to bed.

And woke up almost before he had gone to sleep. He couldn't have closed his book, and then his eyes, for more than a couple of minutes before he realized that he had been looking in the wrong direction for his informant. It wasn't one of the investigators who tipped him off. It was someone connected to the I.F. at the highest level, someone who knew that Peter Wiggin was Locke and Demosthenes. But not Graff or Chamrajnagar—they would not have left hints about who they really were. Someone else, someone in whom they confided, perhaps.

But no one from the I.F. had turned up in the information about Achilles' escape. Except for the nun who found Achilles in the first place.

He reread the message. Could this have come from a nun? Possibly, but why would she be sending the information so anonymously? And why would the kidnapped children smuggle a message to her?

Had she recruited one of them?

Peter got out of bed and padded to his desk, where he called up the information on all the kidnapped children. Every one of them came to Battle School through the normal testing process; none had been found by the nun, and so none of them would have any reason to smuggle a message to her.

What other connection could there be? Achilles was an orphan on the streets of Rotterdam when Sister Carlotta identified him as having military talent—he couldn't have had any family connections. Unless he was like that Greek kid from Ender's jeesh who was killed in a missile attack a few weeks ago, the supposed orphan whose real family was identified while he was in Battle School.

Orphan. Killed in a missile attack. What was his name? Julian Delphiki. Called Bean. A name he picked up when he was an orphan . . . where?

Rotterdam. Just like Achilles.

It was not a stretch to imagine that Sister Carlotta found both Bean and Achilles. Bean was one of Ender's companions on Eros during the last battle. He was the only one who, instead of being kidnapped, had been killed. Everyone assumed it was because he was so heavily protected by the Greek military that the would-be kidnappers gave up and settled for keeping rival powers from using him. But what if there was never any intention to kidnap him, because Achilles already knew him and, more to the point, Bean knew too much about Achilles?

And what if Bean was not dead at all? What if he was living in hiding, protected by the widespread belief that he was dead? It was absolutely believable that the captive kids would choose him to receive their smuggled message, since he was the only one of their group, besides Ender himself, who wasn't in captivity with them. And who else would have such a powerful motive to work to get them out, along with the proven mental ability to think of a strategy like the one the informant had laid out in his letter?

A house of cards, that's what he was building, one leap after another—but each intuitive jump felt absolutely right. That letter was written by Bean. Julian Delphiki. And how would Peter contact him? Bean could be anywhere, and there was no hope of contacting him since anybody who knew he was alive would be all the more certain to pretend that he was dead and refuse to accept a message for him.

Again, the solution should be obvious from the data, and it was. Sister Carlotta.

Peter had a contact in the Vatican—a sparring partner in the wars of ideas that flared up now and then among those who frequented the discussions of international relations on the nets. It was already morning in Rome, though barely. But if anyone was at his desk early in Italy, it would be a hardworking monk attached to the Vatican foreign-affairs office.

Sure enough, an answer came back within fifteen minutes.

> Sister Carlotta's location is protected. Messages can be forwarded. I will not read what you send via me. (You can't work here if you don't know how to keep your eyes closed.)

Peter composed his message to Bean and sent it—to Sister Carlotta. If anyone knew how to reach Julian Delphiki in hiding, it would be the nun who had first found him. It was the only possible solution to the challenge his informant had given him.

Finally he went back to bed, knowing that he wouldn't sleep long—he'd undoubtedly keep waking through the night and checking the nets to see the reaction to his column.

What if no one cared? What if nothing happened? What if he had fatally compromised the Locke persona, and for no gain?

As he lay in bed, pretending to himself that he might sleep, he could hear his parents snoring in their room across the hall. It was both strange and comforting to hear them. Strange that he could be worrying about whether something he had written might *not* cause an international incident, and yet he was still living in his parents' house, their only child left at home. Comforting because it was a sound he had known since infancy, that comforting assurance that they were alive, they were close by, and the fact that he could hear them meant that when monsters leapt from the dark corners of the room, they would hear him screaming.

The monsters had taken on different faces over the years, and hid in corners of rooms far from his own, but that noise from his parents' bedroom was proof that the world had not ended yet.

Peter wasn't sure why, but he knew that the letter he had just sent to Julian Delphiki, via Sister Carlotta, via his friend in the Vatican, would put an end to his long idyll, playing at world affairs while having his mother do his laundry. He was finally putting himself into play, not as the cool and distant commentator Locke or the hot-blooded demagogue Demosthenes, both of them electronic constructs, but as Peter Wiggin, a young man of flesh and blood, who could be caught, who could be harmed, who could be killed.

If anything should have kept him awake, it was that thought. But instead he felt relieved. Relaxed. The long waiting was almost over. He fell asleep and did not wake until his mother called him to breakfast.

His father was reading a newsprint at breakfast. "What's the headline, Dad?" asked Peter.

"They're saying that the Russians kidnapped those kids. And put them under the control of a known murderer. Hard to believe, but they seem to know all about this Achilles guy. Got busted out of a mental hospital in Belgium. Crazy world we live in. Could have been Ender." He shook his head.

Peter could see how his mother froze for just a moment at the mention of Ender's name. Yes, yes, Mother, I know he's the child of your heart and you grieve every time you hear his name. And you ache for your beloved daughter Valentine who has left Earth and will never return, not in your lifetime. But you still have your firstborn with you, your brilliant and good-looking son Peter, who is bound to produce brilliant and beautiful grandchildren for you someday, along with a few other things like, oh, who knows, maybe bringing peace to Earth by unifying it under one government? Will that console you just a little bit?

Not likely.

"The killer's name is . . . Achilles?"

"No last name. Like some kind of pop singer or something."

Peter cringed inside. Not because of what his father had said, but because Peter had come *this* close to correcting his father's pronunciation of "Achilles." Since Peter couldn't be sure that any of the rags mentioned the French pronunciation of Achilles' name, how would he explain knowing the correct pronunciation to Father?

"Has Russia denied it, of course?" asked Peter.

Father scanned the newsprint again. "Nothing about it in this story," he said.

"Cool," said Peter. "Maybe that means it's true."

"If it was true," said Father, "they *would* deny it. That's the way Russians are."

As if Father knew anything at all about the "way Russians are."

Got to move out, thought Peter, and live on my own. I'm in college. I'm trying to spring ten prisoners from custody a third of the way around the world. Maybe I should use some of the money I've been earning as a columnist to pay rent.

Maybe I should do it right away, so that if Achilles finds out who I am and comes to kill me, I won't bring danger down on my family.

Only Peter knew even as he formed this thought that there was another, darker thought hidden deep inside himself: Maybe if I get out of here, they'll blow up the house when I'm not there, the way they must have done with Julian Delphiki. Then they'll think I'm dead and I'll be safe for a while.

No, I don't wish for my parents to die! What kind of monster would wish for that? I don't want that.

But one thing Peter never did was lie to himself, or at least not for long. He didn't wish for his parents to die, certainly not violently in an attack aimed at him. But he knew that if it did happen, he'd prefer not to be with them at the time. Better, of course, if no one was home. But . . . me first.

Ah yes. *That* was what Valentine hated about him. Peter had almost forgotten. *That's* why Ender was the son that everyone loved. Sure, Ender wiped out a whole species of aliens, not to mention offing a kid in a bathroom in Battle School. But he wasn't *selfish* like Peter.

"You aren't eating, Peter," said Mother.

"Sorry," said Peter. "I'm getting some test results back today, and I was brooding I guess."

"What subject?" asked Mother.

"World history," said Peter.

"Isn't it strange to realize that when they write history books in the future, your brother's name will always be mentioned?" said Mother.

"Not strange," said Peter. "That's just one of the perks you get when you save the world."

Behind his jocularity, though, he made a much grimmer promise to his mother. Before you die, Mother, you'll see that while Ender's name shows up in a chapter or two, it will be impossible to discuss this century or the next without mentioning my name on almost every page.

"Got to run," said Father. "Good luck with the test."

"Already took the test, Dad. I'm just getting the grade today."

"That's what I meant. Good luck on the grade."

"Thanks," said Peter.

He went back to eating while Mother walked Father to the door so they could kiss good-bye.

I'll have that someday, thought Peter. Someone who'll kiss me good-bye at the door. Or maybe just someone to put a blindfold over my head before they shoot me. Depending on how things turn out.

8

Bread Van

To:Demosthenes%Tecumseh@freeamerica.org
From: unready%cincinnatus@anon.set
Re: satrep

Satellite reports from date Delphiki family killed: Nine vehicles simultaneous departure from northern Russia location, 64 latitude. Encrypted destination list attached. Genuine dispersal? Decoy? What's our best strategy, my friend? Eliminate or rescue? Are they children or weapons of mass destruction? Hard to know. Why did that bastard Locke get Ender Wiggin sent away? We could use that boy now I think. As for why only nine, not ten vehicles: Maybe one is dead or sick. Maybe one has turned. Maybe two have turned and were sent together. All guesswork. I only see raw satdat, not intelnetcom reports. If you have other sources on that, feed some back to me?

Custer

Petra knew that loneliness was the tool they were using against her. Don't let the girl talk to any human at all, then when one shows up she'll be so grateful she'll blurt confessions, she'll believe lies, she'll make friends with her worst enemy.

Weird how you can know exactly what the enemy is doing to you and it still works. Like a play her parents took her to her second week back home after the war. It had a four-year-old girl on the stage asking her mother why her father wasn't home yet. The mother is trying to find a way to tell her that the father was killed by an Azerbaijani terrorist bomb—a secondary bomb that went off to kill people trying to rescue survivors of the first, smaller blast. Her father died as a hero, trying to save a child trapped in the wreckage even after the police shouted at him to stay away, there was probably going to be a second blast. The mother finally tells the child.

The little girl stamps her foot angrily and says, "He's *my* papa! Not that little boy's papa!" And the mother says, "That little boy's mama and papa weren't there to help him. Your father did what he hoped somebody else would do for you, if he couldn't be there for you." And the little girl starts to cry and says, "Now he isn't ever going to be there for me. And I don't want somebody else. I want my papa."

Petra sat there watching this play, knowing exactly how cynical it was. Use a child, play on the yearning for family, tie it to nobility and heroism, make the villains the ancestral enemy, and make the child say childishly innocent things while crying. A computer could have written it. But it still worked. Petra cried like a baby, just like the rest of the audience.

That's what isolation was doing to her and she knew it. Whatever they were hoping for, it would probably work. Because human beings are just machines, Petra knew that, machines that do what you want them to do, if you only know the levers to pull. And no matter how complex people might seem, if you just cut them off from the network of people who give shape to their personality, the communities that form their identity, they'll be reduced to that set of levers. Doesn't matter how hard they resist, or how well they know they're being manipulated. Eventually, if you take the time, you can play them like a piano, every note right where you expect it.

Even me, thought Petra.

All alone, day after day. Working on the computer, getting assignments by mail from people who gave no hint of personality. Sending messages to the others in Ender's jeesh, but knowing that their letters, too, were being censored of all personal references. Just data getting transferred back and forth. No netsearches now. She had to file her request and wait for an answer filtered through the people who controlled her. All alone.

She tried sleeping too much, but apparently they drugged her water—they got her so hopped up she couldn't sleep at all. So she stopped trying to play passive resistance games. Just went along, becoming the machine they wanted her to be, pretending to herself that by only pretending to be a machine, she wouldn't actually become one, but knowing at the same time that whatever people pretend to be, they become.

And then comes the day when the door opens and somebody walks in.

Vlad.

He was from Dragon Army. Younger than Petra, and a good guy, but she didn't know him all that well. The bond between them, though, was a big one: Vlad was the only other kid in Ender's jeesh who broke the way Petra did, had to be pulled out of the battles for a day. Everybody was kind to them but they both knew—it made them the weak ones. Objects of pity. They all got the same medals and commendations, but Petra knew that their medals meant less than the others, their commendations were empty, because they were the ones who hadn't cut it while the others did. Not that Petra had ever talked about it with Vlad. She just knew that he knew the same things she knew, because he had been down the same long dark tunnel.

And here he was.

"Ho, Petra," he said.

"Ho, Vlad," she answered. She liked hearing her own voice. It still worked. Liked hearing his, too.

"I guess I'm the new instrument of torture they're using on you," said Vlad.

He said it with a smile. That told Petra that he wanted it to seem like a joke. Which told her that it wasn't really a joke at all.

"Really?" she said. "Traditionally, you're simply supposed to kiss me and let someone else do the torture."

"It's not really torture. It's the way out."

"Out of what?"

"Out of prison. It's not what you think, Petra. The hegemony is breaking up, there's going to be war. The question is whether it drives the world down into chaos or leads to one nation ruling all the others. And if it's one nation, which nation should it be?"

"Let me guess. Paraguay."

"Close," said Vlad. He grinned. "I know, it's easier for me. I'm from Belarus, we make a big deal about being a separate country, but in our hearts, we don't mind the thought of Russia being the country that comes out on top. Nobody outside of Belarus gives a lobster tit about how we're not really Russians. So sure, I wasn't hard to talk into it. And you're Armenian, and they spent a lot of years being oppressed by Russia in the old Communist days. But Petra, just how Armenian are you? What's really good for Armenia anyway? That's what I'm supposed to say to you, anyway. To get you to see that Armenia benefits if Russia comes out on top. No more sabotage. Really help us get ready for the real war. You cooperate, and Armenia gets a special place in the new order. You get to bring in your whole country. That's not nothing, Petra. And if you don't help, that doesn't do a thing for anybody. Doesn't help you. Doesn't help Armenia. Nobody ever knows what a hero you were."

"Sounds like a death threat."

"Sounds like a threat of loneliness and obscurity. You weren't born to be nobody, Petra. You were born to shine. This is a chance to be a hero again. I know you think you don't care, but come on, admit it—it was great being Ender's jeesh."

"And now we're what's-his-name's jeesh. He'll really share the glory with us," said Petra.

"Why not? He's still the boss, he doesn't mind having heroes serve under him."

"Vlad, he'll make sure nobody knows any of us existed, and he'll kill us when he's done with us." She hadn't meant to speak so honestly. She knew it would get back to Achilles. She knew it would guarantee that her prophecy would come true. But there it was—the lever worked. She was so grateful to have a friend there, even one who had obviously been coopted, that she couldn't help but blurt.

"Well, Petra, what can I say? I told them, you're the tough one. I told you what's on offer. Think about it. There's no hurry. You've got plenty of time to decide."

"You're going?"

"That's the rule," said Vlad. "You say no, I go. Sorry."

He got up.

She watched him go out the door. She wanted to say something clever and brave. She wanted some name to call him to make him feel bad for throwing in his lot with Achilles. But she knew that anything she said would be used against her one way or another. Anything she said would reveal another lever to the lever-pullers. What she'd already said was bad enough.

So she kept her silence and watched the door close and lay there on her bed until her computer beeped and she went to it and there was another assignment and she went to work and solved it and sabotaged it just like usual and thought, This is going rather well after all, I didn't break or anything.

And then she went to bed and cried herself to sleep. For a few minutes, though, just before she slept, she felt that Vlad was her truest, dearest friend and she would have done anything for him, just to have him back in the room with her.

Then that feeling passed and she had one last fleeting thought: If they were really all that smart, they would have known that I'd feel like that, right that moment; and Vlad would have come in and I would have leapt from my bed and thrown my arms around him and told him yes, I'll do it, I'll work with you, thank you for coming to me like that, Vlad, thank you.

Only they missed their chance.

As Ender had once said, most victories came from instantly exploiting your enemy's stupid mistakes, and not from any particular brilliance in your own plan. Achilles was very clever. But not perfect. Not all-knowing. He may not win. I may even get out of here without dying.

Peaceful at last, she fell asleep.

—

They woke her in darkness.

"Get up."

No greeting. She couldn't see who it was. She could hear footsteps outside her door. Boots. Soldiers?

She remembered talking to Vlad. Rejecting his offer. He said there was no hurry; she had plenty of time to decide. But here they were, rousting her in the middle of the night. To do what?

Nobody was laying a hand on her. She dressed in darkness—they didn't hurry her. If this was supposed to be some sort of torture session or interrogation they wouldn't wait for her to dress, they'd make sure she was as uncomfortable, as off-balance as possible.

She didn't want to ask questions, because that would seem weak. But then, *not* asking questions was passive.

"Where are we going now?"

No answer. That was a bad sign. Or was it? All she knew about these things was from the few fictional war vids she'd seen in Battle School and a few spy movies in Armenia. None of it ever seemed believable to her, yet here she was in a real spy-movie situation and her only source of information about what to expect was those stupid fictional vids and movies. What happened to her superior reasoning ability? The talents that got her into Battle School in the first place? Apparently those only worked when you thought you were playing games in school. In the real world, fear sets in and you fall back on lame made-up stories written by people who had no idea how things like this really worked.

Except that the people doing these things to her had also seen the same dumb vids and movies, so how did she know they weren't modeling *their* actions and attitudes and even their words on what they'd seen in the movies? It's not like anybody had a training course on how to look tough and mean when you were rousting a pubescent girl in the middle of the night. She tried to imagine the instruction manual. *If she is going to be transported to another location, tell her to hurry, she's keeping everyone waiting. If she's going to be tortured, make snide comments about how you hope she got plenty of rest. If she is going to be drugged, tell her that it won't hurt a bit, but laugh snidely so she'll think you're lying. If she is going to be executed, say nothing.*

Oh, this is good, she told herself. Talk yourself into fearing the absolute worst. Make sure you're as close to a state of panic as possible.

"I've got to pee," she said.

No answer.

"I can do it here. I can do it in my clothes. I can do it naked. I can do it in my clothes or naked wherever we're going. I can dribble it along the way. I can write my name in the snow. It's harder for girls, it requires a lot more athletic activity, but we can do it."

Still no answer.

"Or you can let me go to the bathroom."

"All right," he said.

"Which?"

"Bathroom." He walked out the door.

She followed him. Sure enough, there were soldiers out there. Ten of them. She stopped in front of one burly soldier and looked up at his face. "It's a good thing they brought *you*. If it had just been those other guys, I would have made my stand and fought to the death. But with you here, I had no choice but to give myself up. Good work, soldier."

She turned and walked on toward the bathroom. Wondering if she had seen just the faintest hint of a smile on that soldier's face. *That* wasn't in the movie script, was it? Oh, wait. The hero was supposed to have a smart mouth. She was right in character. Only now she understood that all those clever remarks that heroes made were designed to conceal their raw fear. Insouciant heroes aren't brave or relaxed. They're just trying not to embarrass themselves in the moments before they die.

She got to the bathroom and of course he came right in with her. But she'd been in Battle School and if she'd had a shy bladder she would have died of urea poisoning long ago. She dropped trou, sat on the john, and let go. The guy was out the door long before she was ready to flush.

There was a window. There were ceiling air ducts. But she was in the middle of nowhere and it's not like she had anywhere she could run. How did they do this in the vids? Oh, yeah. A friend would have already placed a weapon in some concealed location and the hero would find it, assemble it, and come out firing. That's what was wrong with this whole situation. No friends.

She flushed, rearranged her clothing, washed her hands, and walked back out to her friendly escorts.

They walked her outside to a convoy, of sorts. There were two black limousines and four escort vehicles. She saw two girls about her size and hair color get into the back of each of the limos. Petra, by contrast, was kept close to the building, under the eaves, until she was at the back of a bakery van. She climbed in. None of her guards came with her. There were two men in the back of the van, but they were in civilian clothes.

"What am I, bread?" she asked.

"We understand your need to feel that you're in control of the situation through humor," said one of the men.

"What, a psychiatrist? This is worse than torture. What happened to the Geneva convention?"

The psychiatrist smiled. "You're going home, Petra."

"To God? Or Armenia?"

"At this moment, neither. The situation is still . . . flexible."

"I'd say it's flexible, if I'm going home to a place where I've never been before."

"Loyalties have not yet been sorted out. The branch of government that kidnapped you and the other children was acting without the knowledge of the army or the elected government—"

"Or so they say," said Petra.

"You understand my situation perfectly."

"So who are you loyal to?"

"Russia."

"Isn't that what they'll all say?"

"Not the ones who turned our foreign policy and military strategy over to a homicidal maniac child."

"Are those three equal accusations?" asked Petra. "Because *I'm* guilty of being a child. And homicide, too, in some people's opinion."

"Killing Buggers was not homicide."

"I suppose it was insecticide."

The psychiatrist looked baffled. Apparently he didn't know Common well enough to understand a wordplay that nine-year-olds thought was endlessly funny in Battle School.

The van began to move.

"Where are we going, since it's not home?"

"We're going into hiding to keep you out of the hands of this monster child until the breadth of this conspiracy can be discovered and the conspirators arrested."

"Or vice versa," said Petra.

The psychiatrist looked baffled again. But then he understood. "I suppose that's possible. But then, I'm not an important man. How would they know to look for me?"

"You're important enough that you have soldiers who obey you."

"They're not obeying me. We're all obeying someone else."

"And who is that?"

"If, through some misfortune, you were retaken by Achilles and his sponsors, you won't be able to answer that question."

"Besides, you'd all be dead before they could get to me, so your names wouldn't matter anyway, right?"

He looked at her searchingly. "You seem cynical about this. We *are* risking our lives to save you."

"You're risking *my* life, too."

He nodded slowly. "Do you want to return to your prison?"

"I just want you to be aware that being kidnapped a second time isn't exactly the same thing as being set free. You're so sure that you're smart enough and your people are loyal enough to bring this off. But if you're wrong, I could get killed. So yes, you're taking risks—but so am I, and nobody asked me."

"I ask you now."

"Let me out of the van right here," said Petra. "I'll take my chances alone."

"No," said the psychiatrist.

"I see. So I *am* still a prisoner."

"You are in protective custody."

"But I am a certified strategic and tactical genius," said Petra, "and you're not. So why are you in charge of *me*?"

He had no answer.

"I'll tell you why," said Petra. "Because this is not about saving the little children who were stolen away by the evil wicked child. This is about saving Mother Russia a lot of embarrassment. So it isn't enough for me to be safe. You have to return me to Armenia under just the right circumstances, with just the right spin, that the faction of the Russian government that you serve will be exonerated of all guilt."

"We are not guilty."

"My point is not that you're lying about that, but that you regard that as a much higher priority than saving me. Because I assure you, riding along in this van, I fully expect to be retaken by Achilles and his . . . what did you call them? Sponsors."

"And why do you suppose that this will happen?"

"Does it matter why?"

"You're the genius," said the psychiatrist. "Apparently you have already seen some flaw in our plan."

"The flaw is obvious. Far too many people know about it. The decoy limousines, and soldiers, the escorts. You're sure that not one of those people is a plant? Because if *any* of them is reporting to Achilles' sponsors, then they already know which vehicle really has me in it, and where it's going."

"They don't know where it's going."

"They do if the driver is the one who was planted by the other side."

"The driver doesn't know where we're going."

"He's just going around in circles?"

"He knows the first rendezvous point, that's all."

Petra shook her head. "I knew you were stupid, because you became a talk-therapy shrink, which is like being a minister of a religion in which you get to be God."

The psychiatrist turned red. Petra liked that. He was stupid, and he didn't like hearing it, but he definitely needed to hear it because he clearly had built his whole life around the idea that he was smart, and now that he was playing with live ammunition, thinking he was smart was going to get him killed.

"I suppose you're right, that the driver *does* know where we're going *first,* even if he doesn't know where we plan to go from the first rendezvous." The psychiatrist shrugged elaborately. "But that can't be helped. You have to trust *someone.*"

"And you decided to trust this driver because . . . ?"

The psychiatrist looked away.

Petra looked at the other man. "You're talkative."

"I am think," said the man in halting Common, "you make Battle School teachers crazy with talk."

"Ah," said Petra. "*You're* the brains of the outfit."

The man looked puzzled, but also offended—he wasn't sure how he had been insulted, since he probably didn't know the word *outfit,* but he knew an insult had been intended.

"Petra Arkanian," said the psychiatrist, "since you're right that I don't know the driver all that well, tell me what I should have done. You have a better plan than trusting him?"

"Of course," said Petra. "You tell him the rendezvous point, plan with him very carefully how he'll drive there."

"I did that," said the psychiatrist.

"I know," said Petra. "Then, at the last minute, just as you're loading me into the van, you take the wheel and make him ride in one of the limousines. And then you drive to a different place entirely. Or better yet, you take me to the nearest town and turn me loose and let me take care of myself."

Again, the psychiatrist looked away. Petra was amused at how transparent his body language was. You'd think a shrink would know how to conceal his own tells.

"These people who kidnapped you," said the psychiatrist, "they are a tiny minority, even within the intelligence organizations they work for. They can't be everywhere."

Petra shook her head. "You're a Russian, you were taught Russian history, and you actually believe that the intelligence service can't be everywhere and hear everything? What, did you spend your entire childhood watching American vids?"

The psychiatrist had had enough. Putting on his finest medical airs, he delivered his ultimate put-down. "And you're a child who never learned decent respect. You may be brilliant in your native abilities, but that doesn't mean you understand a political situation you know nothing about."

"Ah," said Petra. "The you're-just-a-child, you-don't-have-as-much-experience argument."

"Naming it doesn't mean it's untrue."

"I'm sure you understand the nuances of political speeches and maneuvers. But this is a military operation."

"It is a political operation," the psychiatrist corrected her. "No shooting."

Again, Petra was stunned at the man's ignorance. "Shooting is what happens when military operations fail to achieve their purposes through maneuver. *Any* operation that's intended to physically deprive the enemy of a valued asset is military."

"This operation is about freeing an ungrateful little girl and sending her home to her mama and papa," said the psychiatrist.

"You want me to be grateful? Open the door and let me out."

"The discussion is over," said the psychiatrist. "You can shut up now."

"Is that how you end your sessions with your patients?"

"I never said I was a psychiatrist," said the psychiatrist.

"Psychiatry was your education," said Petra. "And I know you had a practice for a while, because *real* people don't talk like shrinks when they're trying to reassure a frightened child. Just because you got involved in politics and changed careers doesn't mean you aren't still the kind of bonehead who goes to witch-doctor school and thinks he's a scientist."

The man's fury was barely contained. Petra enjoyed the momentary thrill of fear that ran through her. Would he slap her? Not likely. As a psychiatrist, he would probably fall back on his one limitless resource—professional arrogance.

"Laymen usually sneer at sciences they don't understand," said the psychiatrist.

"That," said Petra, "is precisely my point. When it comes to military operations, you're a complete novice. A layman. A bonehead. And I'm the expert. And you're too stupid to listen to me even now."

"Everything is going smoothly," said the psychiatrist. "And you'll feel very foolish and apologize as you thank me when you get on the plane to return to Armenia."

Petra only smiled tightly. "You didn't even look in the cab of this delivery van to make sure it was the same driver before we drove off."

"Someone else would have noticed if the driver changed," said the psychiatrist. But Petra could tell she had finally made him uneasy.

"Oh, yes, I forgot, we trust your fellow conspirators to see all and miss nothing, because, after all, *they* aren't psychiatrists."

"I'm a psychologist," he said.

"Ouch," said Petra. "That must have hurt, to admit you're only half-educated."

The psychologist turned away from her. What was the term the shrinks in Ground School used for that behavior—avoidance? Denial? She almost asked him, but decided to leave well enough alone.

And people thought she couldn't control her tongue.

They rode for a while in bristling silence.

But the things she said must have been working on him, nagging at him. Because after a while he got up and walked to the front and opened the door between the cargo area and the cab.

A deafening gunshot rang through the closed interior, and the psychiatrist fell back. Petra felt hot brains and stinging bits of bone spatter her face and arms. The man across from her started reaching for a weapon under his coat, but he was shot twice and slumped over dead without touching it.

The door from the cab opened the rest of the way. It was Achilles standing there, holding the gun in his hand. He said something.

"I can't hear you," said Petra. "I can't even hear my own voice."

Achilles shrugged. Speaking louder and mouthing the words carefully, he tried again. She refused to look at him.

"I'm not going to try to listen to you," she said, "while I still have his blood all over me."

Achilles set down the gun—far out of her reach—and pulled off his shirt. Bare-chested, he handed it to her, and when she refused to take it, he started wiping her face with it until she snatched it out of his hands and did the job herself.

The ringing in her ears was fading, too. "I'm surprised you didn't wait to kill them until you'd had a chance to tell them how smart you are," said Petra.

"I didn't need to," said Achilles. "You already told them how dumb they were."

"Oh, you were listening?"

"Of course the compartment back here was wired for sound," said Achilles. "And video."

"You didn't have to kill them," said Petra.

"That guy was going for his gun," said Achilles.

"Only after his friend was dead."

"Come now," said Achilles. "I thought Ender's whole method was the preemptive use of ultimate force. I only do what I learned from your hero."

"I'm surprised you did this one yourself," said Petra.

"What do you mean, 'this one'?" said Achilles.

"I assumed you were stopping the other rescues, too."

"You forget," said Achilles, "I've already had months to evaluate you. Why keep the others, when I can have the best?"

"Are you flirting with me?" She said it with as much disdain as she could muster. Those words usually worked to shut down a boy who was being smug. But he only laughed.

"I don't flirt," he said.

"I forgot," said Petra. "You shoot first, and then flirting isn't necessary."

That got to him a little—made him pause a moment, brought the slightest hint of a quickening of breath. It occurred to Petra that her mouth was indeed going to get her killed. She had never actually seen someone get shot before, except in movies and vids. Just because she thought of herself as the protagonist of this biographical vid she was trapped in didn't mean she was safe. For all she knew, Achilles meant to kill her, too.

Or did he? Could he have really meant that she was the only one of the team he was keeping? Vlad would be so disappointed.

"How did you happen to choose me?" she asked, changing the subject.

"Like I said, you're the best."

"That is such kuso," said Petra. "The exercises I did for you weren't any better than anyone else's."

"Oh, those battle plans, those were just to keep you

busy while the real tests were going on. Or rather, to make you think you were keeping *us* busy."

"What was this real test, then, since I supposedly succeeded at it better than anyone else?"

"Your little dragon drawing," said Achilles.

She could feel the blood drain from her face. He saw it and laughed.

"Don't worry," said Achilles. "You won't be punished. That was the test, to see which of you would succeed in getting a message outside."

"And my prize is staying with you?" She said it with all the disgust she could put in her voice.

"Your prize," said Achilles, "is staying alive."

She felt sick at heart. "Even you wouldn't kill all the others, for no reason."

"If they're killed, there's a reason. If there's a reason, they'll be killed. No, we suspected that your dragon drawing would have *some* meaning to someone. But we couldn't find a code in it."

"There wasn't a code in it," said Petra.

"Oh yes there was," said Achilles. "You somehow encoded it in such a way that someone was able to recognize it and decode it. I know this because the news stories that suddenly appeared, triggering this whole crisis, had some specific information that was more or less correct. One of the messages you guys tried to send must have gotten through. So we went back over every email sent by every one of you, and the only thing that couldn't be accounted for was your dragon clip art."

"If you can read a message in that," said Petra, "then you're smarter than I am."

"On the contrary," said Achilles. "You're smarter than I am, at least about strategy and tactics—like evading the enemy while keeping in close communication with allies. Well, not all *that* close, since it took them so long to publish the information you sent."

"You bet on the wrong horse," said Petra. "It wasn't a message, and therefore however they got the news it must have come from one of the other guys."

Achilles only laughed. "You're a stubborn liar, aren't you?"

"I'm not lying when I tell you that if I have to keep riding with these corpses in this compartment, I'm going to get sick."

He smiled. "Vomit away."

"So your pathology includes a weird need to hang around with the dead," said Petra. "You'd better be careful—you know where that leads. First you'll start dating them, and then one day you'll bring a dead person home to meet your mother and father. Oops. I forgot, you're an orphan."

"So I brought them to show *you.*"

"Why did you wait so long to shoot them?" asked Petra.

"I wanted it set up just right. So I could shoot the one while he was standing in the doorway. So his body would block any returning fire from the other guy. And besides, I was also enjoying the way you took them apart. You know, arguing with them like you did. Sounded like you hate shrinks almost as much as I do. And you were never even committed to a mental institution. I would have applauded several of your best bon mots, only I might have been overheard."

"Who's driving this van?" asked Petra, ignoring his flattery.

"Not me," said Achilles. "Are you?"

"How long are you planning to keep me imprisoned?" asked Petra.

"As long as it takes."

"As long as it takes to do what?"

"Conquer the world together, you and I. Isn't that romantic? Or, well, it *will* be romantic, when it happens."

"It will never be romantic," said Petra. "Nor will I help you conquer your dandruff problem, let alone the world."

"Oh, you'll cooperate," said Achilles. "I'll kill the other members of Ender's jeesh, one by one, until you give in."

"You don't have them," said Petra. "And you don't know where they are. They're safe from you."

Achilles grinned mock-sheepishly. "There's just no fooling Genius Girl, is there? But, you see, they're bound to surface somewhere, and when they do, they'll die. I don't forget."

"That's one way to conquer the world," said Petra. "Kill everybody one by one until you're the only one left."

"Your first job," said Achilles, "is to decode that message you sent out."

"What message?"

Achilles picked up his gun and pointed it at her.

"Kill me and you'll always wonder if I really sent out a message at all," said Petra.

"But at least I won't have to listen to your smug voice lying to me," said Achilles. "That would almost be a consolation."

"You seem to be forgetting that I wasn't a volunteer on this expedition. If you don't like listening to me, let me go."

"You're so sure of yourself," said Achilles. "But I know you better than you know yourself."

"And what is it you think you know about me?" asked Petra.

"I know that you'll eventually give in and help me,"

"Well, I know *you* better than you know yourself, too," said Petra.

"Oh, really?"

"I know that eventually you'll kill me. Because you always do. So let's just skip all the boring stuff in between. Kill me now. End the suspense."

"No," said Achilles. "Things like that are much better as a surprise. Don't you think? At least, that's the way God always did it."

"Why am I even talking to you?" asked Petra.

"Because you're so lonely after being in solitary for all these months that you'd do anything for human company. Even talk to *me.*"

She hated that he was probably right. "Human company—apparently you're under the delusion that you qualify."

"Oh, you're mean," said Achilles, laughing. "Look, I'm bleeding."

"You've got blood on your hands, all right."

"And you've got it all over your face," said Achilles. "Come on, it'll be fun."

"And here I thought nothing would ever be more tedious than solitary confinement."

"You're the best, Petra," said Achilles. "Except for one."

"Bean," said Petra.

"Ender," said Achilles. "Bean is nothing. Bean is dead."

Petra said nothing.

Achilles looked at her searchingly. "No smart remarks?"

"Bean is dead and you're alive," said Petra. "There's no justice."

The van slowed down and stopped.

"There," said Achilles. "Our lively conversation made the time *fly* by."

Fly. She heard an airplane overhead. Landing or taking off?

"Where are we flying?" she asked.

"Who says we're flying anywhere?"

"I think we're flying out of the country," said Petra, speaking the ideas as they came to her. "I think you realized that you were going to lose your cushy job here in Russia, and you're sneaking out of the country."

"You're really very good. You keep setting a new standard for cleverness," said Achilles.

"And you keep setting a new standard for failure."

He hesitated a moment, then went on as if she hadn't spoken. "They're going to pit the other kids against me," he said. "You already know them. You know their weaknesses. Whoever I'm up against, you're going to advise me."

"Never."

"We're in this together," said Achilles. "I'm a nice guy. You'll like me, eventually."

"Oh, I know," said Petra. "What's not to like?"

"Your message," said Achilles. "You wrote it to Bean, didn't you?"

"What message?" said Petra.

"That's why you don't believe he's dead."

"I believe he's dead," said Petra. But she knew her earlier hesitation had given her away.

"Or else you wonder—if he got your message before I had him killed, why did it take so long after he died to have it hit the news? And here's the obvious answer, Pet. Somebody else figured it out. Somebody else decoded it. And that really pisses me off. So don't tell me what the message said. I'm going to decode it myself. It can't be that hard."

"Downright easy," said Petra. "After all, I'm dumb enough to end up as your prisoner. So dumb, in fact, that I never sent anybody a message."

"When I do decode it, though, I hope it won't say anything disparaging about me. Because then I'd have to beat the shit out of you."

"You're right," said Petra. "You *are* a charmer."

Fifteen minutes later, they were on a small private jet, flying south by southeast. It was a luxurious vehicle, for its size, and Petra wondered if it belonged to one of the intelligence services or to some faction in the military or maybe to some crime lord. Or maybe all three at once.

She wanted to study Achilles, watch his face, his body language. But she didn't want him to see her showing interest in him. So she looked out the window, wondering as she did so whether she wasn't just doing the same thing the dead psychologist had done—looking away to avoid facing bitter truth.

When the chime announced that they could unbelt themselves, Petra got up and headed for the bathroom. It was small, but compared to commercial airplane toilets it was downright commodious. And it had cloth towels and real soap.

She did her best with a damp towel to wipe blood and body matter from her clothes. She had to keep wearing the dirty clothing but she could at least get rid of the visible chunks. The towel was so foul by the time she finished the job that she tossed it and got a fresh one to start in on her face and hands. She scrubbed until her face was red and raw, but she got it all off. She even soaped her hair and washed it as best she could in the tiny sink. It was hard to rinse, pouring one cup of water at a time over her head.

The whole time, she kept thinking of the fact that

the psychiatrist's last minutes were spent listening to her tell him how stupid he was and point out the worthlessness of his life's work. And yes, she was right, as his death proved, but that didn't change the fact that however impure his motives might have been, he *was* trying to save her from Achilles. He had given his life in that effort, however badly planned it might have been. All the other rescues went off smoothly, and they were probably just as badly planned as hers. So much depended on chance. Everybody was stupid about some things. Petra was stupid about the things she said to people who had power over her. Goading them. Daring them to punish her. She did it even though she knew it was stupid. And wasn't it even stupider to do something stupid that you *know* is stupid?

What did he call her? An ungrateful little girl.

He tagged me, all right.

As bad as she felt about his death, as horrified over what she had seen, as frightened as she was to be in Achilles' control, as lonely as she had been for these past weeks, she still couldn't figure out a way to cry about it. Because deeper than all these feelings was something even stronger. Her mind kept thinking of ways to get word to someone about where she was. She had done it once, she could do it again, right? She might feel bad, she might be a miserable specimen of human life, she might be in the midst of a traumatic childhood experience, but she was *not* going to submit to Achilles for one moment longer than she had to.

The plane lurched suddenly, throwing her against the toilet. She half-fell onto it—there wasn't room to fall down all the way—but she couldn't get up because the plane had gone into a steep dive, and for a few moments she found herself gasping as the oxygen-rich air was replaced by cold upper-level air that left her dizzy.

The hull was breached. They've shot us down.

And for all that she had an indomitable will to live, she couldn't help but think: Good for them. Kill Achilles now, and no matter who else is on the plane, it'll be a great day for humanity.

But the plane soon leveled out, and the air was breathable before she blacked out. They must not have been very high when it happened.

She opened the bathroom door and stepped back into the main cabin.

The side door was partway open. And standing a couple of meters back from it was Achilles, the wind whipping at his hair and clothes. He was posing, as if he knew just how fine a figure he cut, standing there on the brink of death.

She approached him, glancing at the door to make sure she stayed well back from it, and to see how high they were. Not very, compared to cruising altitude, but higher than any building or bridge or dam. Anyone who fell from this plane would die.

Could she get behind him and push?

He smiled broadly when she got near.

"What happened?" she shouted over the noise of the wind.

"It occurred to me," he yelled back, "that I made a mistake bringing you with me."

He opened the door on purpose. He opened it for her.

Just as she began to step back, his hand lashed out and seized her by the wrist.

The intensity of his eyes was startling. He didn't look crazy. He looked . . . fascinated. Almost as if he found her amazingly beautiful. But of course it wasn't *her.* It was his power over her that fascinated him. It was himself that he loved so intensely.

She didn't try to pull away. Instead, she twisted her wrist so that she also gripped him.

"Come on, let's jump together," she shouted. "That would be the most romantic thing we could do."

He leaned close. "And miss out on all the history we're going to make together?" he said. Then he laughed. "Oh, I see, you thought I was going to throw you out of the plane. No, Pet, I took hold of you so that I could anchor you while you close the door. Wouldn't want the wind to suck you out, would we?"

"I have a better idea," said Petra. "I'll be the anchor, you close the door."

"But the anchor has to be the stronger, heavier one," said Achilles. "And that's me."

"Let's just leave it open, then," said Petra.

"Can't fly all the way to Kabul with the door open."

What did it mean, his telling her their destination? Did it mean that he trusted her a little? Or that it didn't matter what she knew, since he had decided she was going to die?

Then it occurred to her that if he wanted her dead, she would die. It was that simple. So why worry about it? If he wanted to kill her by pushing her out the door, how was that different from a bullet in the brain? Dead was dead. And if he didn't plan to kill her, the door needed to be closed, and having him serve as anchor was the second-best plan.

"Isn't there somebody in the crew who can do this?" she asked.

"There's just the pilot," said Achilles. "Can *you* land a plane?"

She shook her head.

"So he stays in the cockpit, and we close the door."

"I don't mean to be a nag," said Petra, "but opening the door was a really stupid thing to do."

He grinned at her.

Holding tight to his wrist, she slid along the wall toward the door. It was only partially open, the kind of door that worked by sliding up. So she didn't have to reach very far out of the plane. Still, the cold wind snatched at her arm and made it very hard to get a grip on the door handle to pull it down into place. And even when she got it down into position, she simply didn't have the strength to overcome the wind resistance and pull it snug.

Achilles saw this, and now that the door wasn't open enough for anyone to fall out and the wind could no longer suck anybody out, he let go of her and of the bulkhead and joined her in pulling at the handle.

If I push instead of pulling, thought Petra, the wind will help me, and maybe we'll both get sucked right out.

Do it, she told herself. Do it. Kill him. Even if you die doing it, it's worth it. This is Hitler, Stalin, Genghis, Attila all rolled into one.

But it might not work. He might not get sucked out. She might die alone, pointlessly. No, she would have to find a way to destroy him later, when she could be sure it would work.

At another level, she knew that she simply wasn't ready to die. No matter how convenient it might be for the rest of humanity, no matter how richly Achilles deserved to die, she would not be his executioner, not now, not if she had to give her own life to kill him. If that made her a selfish coward, so be it.

They pulled and pulled and finally, with a whoosh, the door passed the threshold of wind resistance and locked nicely into place. Achilles pulled the lever that locked it.

"Traveling with you is always such an adventure," said Petra.

"No need to shout," said Achilles. "I can hear you just fine."

"Why can't you just run with the bulls at Pamplona, like any normal self-destructive person?" asked Petra.

He ignored her gibe. "I must value you more than I thought." He said it as if it took him rather by surprise.

"You mean you still have a spark of humility? You might actually need someone else?"

Again he ignored her words. "You look better without blood all over your face."

"But I'll never be as pretty as you."

"Here's my rule about guns," said Achilles. "When people are getting shot, always stand behind the shooter. It's a lot less messy there."

"Unless people are shooting back."

Achilles laughed. "Pet, I *never* use a gun when someone might shoot back."

"And you're so well-mannered, you always open a door for a lady."

His smile faded. "Sometimes I get these impulses," he said. "But they're not irresistible."

"Too bad. And here you had such a good insanity defense going."

His eyes blazed for a moment. Then he went back to his seat.

She cursed herself. Goading him like this, how is it different from jumping out of the airplane?

Then again, maybe it was the fact that she spoke to him without cringing that made him value her.

Fool, she said to herself. You are not equipped to understand this boy—you're not insane enough. Don't try to guess why he does what he does, or how he feels about you or anybody or anything. Study him so you can learn how he makes his plans, what he's likely to do, so that someday you can defeat him. But don't ever try to understand. If you can't even understand yourself, what hope do you have of comprehending somebody as deformed as Achilles?

They did not land in Kabul. They landed in Tashkent, refueled, and then went over the Himalayas to New Delhi.

So he lied to her about their destination. He hadn't trusted her after all. But as long as he refrained from killing her, she could endure a little mistrust.

9

Communing with the Dead

To: Carlotta%agape@vatican.net/orders/sisters/ind
From: Locke%erasmus@polnet.gov
Re: An answer for your dead friend

If you know who I really am, and you have contact with a certain person purported to be dead, please inform that person that I have done my best to fulfill expectations. I believe further collaboration is possible, but not through intermediaries. If you have no idea what I'm talking about, then please inform me of that, as well, so I can begin my search again.

Bean came home to find that Sister Carlotta had packed their bags.

"Moving day?" he asked.

They had agreed that either one of them could decide that it was time to move on, without having to defend the decision. It was the only way to be sure of acting on any unconscious cues that someone was closing in on them. They didn't want to spend their last moments of life listening to each other say, "I knew we should have left three days ago!" "Well why didn't you say so?" "Because I didn't have a *reason.*"

"We have two hours till the flight."

"Wait a minute," said Bean. "You decide we're going, I decide the destination." That was how they'd decided to keep their movements random.

She handed him the printout of an email. It was from Locke. "Greensboro, North Carolina, in the U.S.," she said.

"Perhaps I'm not decoding this right," said Bean, "but I don't see an invitation to visit him."

"He doesn't want intermediaries," said Carlotta. "We can't trust his email to be untraced."

Bean took a match and burned the email in the sink. Then he crumbled the ashes and washed them down the drain. "What about Petra?"

"Still no word. Nine of Ender's jeesh released. The Russians are simply saying that Petra's place of captivity has not yet been discovered."

"Kuso," said Bean.

"I know," said Carlotta, "but what can we do if they won't tell us? I'm afraid she's dead, Bean. You've got to realize that's the likeliest reason for them to stonewall."

Bean knew it, but didn't believe it. "You don't know Petra," he said.

"You don't know Russia," said Carlotta.

"Most people are decent in every country," said Bean.

"Achilles is enough to tip the balance wherever he goes."

Bean nodded. "Rationally, I have to agree with you. Irrationally, I expect to see her again someday."

"If I didn't know you so well, I might interpret that as a sign of your faith in the resurrection."

Bean picked up his suitcase. "Am I bigger, or is this smaller?"

"The case is the same size," said Carlotta.

"I think I'm growing."

"Of course you're growing. Look at your pants."

"I'm still wearing them," said Bean.

"More to the point, look at your ankles."

"Oh." There was more ankle showing than when he bought them.

Bean had never seen a child grow up, but it bothered him that in the weeks they had been in Araraquara, he had grown at least five centimeters. If this was puberty, where were the other changes that were supposed to go along with it?

"We'll buy you new clothes in Greensboro," said Sister Carlotta.

Greensboro. "Ender's home town."

"He only visited there once. His family moved there after he left for Battle School."

"Oh, é. He grew up in the big city, like me."

Sister Carlotta gave one bark of a laugh. "Not at all like you."

"Because he didn't have to fight off other children just to eat?"

"Plenty to eat," said Sister Carlotta. "Yet he did his first killing there all the same."

"You just won't let go of that, will you?" said Bean.

"When you had Achilles in your power, *you* didn't kill him."

Bean didn't like hearing himself compared to Ender that way. Not when it showed Ender at a disadvantage. "Sister Carlotta, we'd have a whole lot less difficulty right now if I *had* killed him."

"You showed mercy. You turned the other cheek. You gave him a chance to make something worthwhile out of his life."

"I made sure he'd get committed to a mental institution."

"Are you so determined to believe in your own lack of virtue?"

"Yes," said Bean. "I prefer truth to lies."

"There," said Carlotta. "Yet another virtue to add to my list."

Bean laughed in spite of himself. "I'm glad you like me," he said.

"Are you afraid to meet him?"

"Who?"

"Ender's brother."

"Not afraid," said Bean.

"How *do* you feel, then?"

"Skeptical," said Bean.

"He showed humility in that email," said Sister Carlotta. "He wasn't sure that he'd figured things out exactly right."

"Oh, there's a thought. The humble Hegemon."

"He's not Hegemon yet," said Carlotta.

"He got nine of Ender's jeesh released, just by publishing a column. He has influence. He has ambition. And now to learn he has humility—well, it's just too much for me."

"Laugh all you want. Let's go out and find a cab."

There was no last-minute business to take care of. They had paid cash for everything, owed nothing. They could walk away.

They lived on money drawn from accounts Graff had set up for them. There was nothing about the account Bean was using now to tag it as belonging to Julian Delphiki. It held his military salary, including his combat and retirement bonuses. The I.F. had given all of Ender's jeesh very large trust funds that they couldn't touch till they came of age. The saved-up pay and bonuses were just to tide them over during their childhood. Graff had assured him that he would not run out of money while he was in hiding.

Sister Carlotta's money came from the Vatican. One person there knew what she was doing. She, too, would have money enough for her needs. Neither of them had the temperament to exploit the situation. They spent little, Sister Carlotta because she wanted nothing more, Bean because he knew that any kind of flamboyance or excess would mark him in people's memories. He always had to seem to be a child running errands for his grandmother, not an undersized war hero cashing in on his back pay.

Their passports caused them no problems, either. Again, Graff had been able to pull strings for them. Given the way they looked—both of Mediterranean ancestry—they carried passports from Catalonia. Carlotta knew Barcelona well, and Catalan was her childhood language. She barely spoke it now, but no matter—hardly anyone did. And no one would be surprised that her grandson couldn't speak the language at all. Besides, how many Catalans would they meet in their travels? Who would try to test their story? If someone got too nosy, they'd simply move on to some other city, some other country.

They landed in Miami, then Atlanta, then Greensboro. They were exhausted and slept the night at an airport hotel. The next day, they logged in and printed out guides to the county bus system. It was a fairly modern system, enclosed and electric, but the map made no sense to Bean.

"Why don't any of the buses go through here?" he asked.

"That's where the rich people live," said Sister Carlotta.

"They make them all live together in one place?"

"They feel safer," said Carlotta. "And by living close together, they have a better chance of their children marrying into other rich families."

"But why don't they want buses?"

"They ride in individual vehicles. They can afford the fees. It gives them more freedom to choose their own schedule. And it shows everyone just how rich they are."

"It's still stupid," said Bean. "Look how far the buses have to go out of their way."

"The rich people didn't want their streets to be enclosed in order to hold a bus system."

"So what?" asked Bean.

Sister Carlotta laughed. "Bean, isn't there plenty of stupidity in the military, too?"

"But in the long run, the guy who wins battles gets to make the decisions."

"Well, these rich people won the economic battles. Or their grandparents did. So now they get their way most of the time."

"Sometimes I feel like I don't know anything."

"You've lived half your life in a tube in space, and before that you lived on the streets of Rotterdam."

"I've lived in Greece with my family and in Araraquara, too. I should have figured this out."

"That was Greece. And Brazil. This is America."

"So money rules in America, but not those other places?"

"No, Bean. Money rules almost everywhere. But different cultures have different ways of displaying it. In Araraquara, for instance, they made sure that the tram lines ran out to the rich neighborhoods. Why? So the servants could come to work. In America, they're more afraid of criminals coming to steal, so the sign of wealth is to make sure that the only way to reach them is by private car or on foot."

"Sometimes I miss Battle School."

"That's because in Battle School, you were one of the very richest in the only coin that mattered there."

Bean thought about that. As soon as the other kids realized that, young and small as he was, he could outperform them in every class, it gave him a kind of power. Everyone knew who he was. Even those who mocked him had to give him a grudging respect. But . . . "I didn't always get my way."

"Graff told me some of the outrageous things you did," said Carlotta. "Climbing through the air ducts to eavesdrop. Breaking into the computer system."

"But they caught me."

"Not as soon as they'd like to have caught you. And were you punished? No. Why? Because you were rich."

"Money and talent aren't the same thing."

"That's because you can inherit money that was earned by your ancestors," said Sister Carlotta. "And everybody recognizes the value of money, while only select groups recognize the value of talent."

"So where does Peter live?"

She had the addresses of all the Wiggin families. There weren't many—the more common spelling had an *s* at the end. "But I don't think this will help us," said Carlotta. "We don't want to meet him at home."

"Why not?"

"Because we don't know whether his parents are aware of what he's doing or not. Graff was pretty sure they don't know. If two foreigners come calling, they're going to start to wonder what their son is doing on the nets."

"Where, then?"

"He could be in secondary school. But given his intelligence, I'd bet on his being in college." She was accessing more information as she spoke. "Colleges colleges colleges. Lots of them in town. The biggest first, the better for him to disappear in . . ."

"Why would he need to disappear? Nobody knows who he is."

"But he doesn't want anyone to realize that he spends no time on his schoolwork. He has to look like an ordinary kid his age. He should be spending all his free time with friends. Or with girls. Or with friends looking for girls. Or with friends trying to distract themselves from the fact that they can't find any girls."

"For a nun, you seem to know a lot about this."

"I wasn't born a nun."

"But you were born a girl."

"And no one is a better observer of the folkways of the adolescent male than the adolescent female."

"What makes you think he doesn't do all those things?"

"Being Locke and Demosthenes is a fulltime job."

"So why do you think he's in college at all?"

"Because his parents would be upset if he stayed home all day, reading and writing email."

Bean wouldn't know about what might make parents upset. He'd only known his parents since the end of the war, and they'd never found anything serious to criticize about him. Or maybe they never felt like he was really theirs. They didn't criticize Nikolai much, either. But . . . more than they did Bean. There simply hadn't been enough time together for them to feel as comfortable, as parental, with their new son Julian.

"I wonder how my parents are doing."

"If anything was wrong, we would have heard," said Carlotta.

"I know," said Bean. "That doesn't mean I can't wonder."

She didn't answer, just kept working her desk, bringing new pages into the display. "Here he is," she said. "A nonresident student. No address. Just email and a campus box."

"What about his class schedule?" asked Bean.

"They don't post that."

Bean laughed. "And that's supposed to be a problem?"

"No, Bean, you aren't going to crack their system. I can't think of a better way for you to attract attention than to trip some trap and get a mole to follow you home."

"I don't get followed by moles."

"You never see the ones that follow you."

"It's just a college, not some intelligence service."

"Sometimes people with the least that is worth stealing are the most concerned with giving the appearance of having great treasures hidden away."

"Is that from the Bible?"

"No, it's from observation."

"So what do we do?"

"Your voice is too young," said Sister Carlotta. "I'll work the phone."

She talked her way to the head registrar of the university. "He was a very nice boy to carry all my things after the wheel broke on my cart, and if these keys are his I want to get them back to him right away, before he worries. . . . No I will not drop them in the mail, how would that be 'right away'? Nor will I leave them with you, they might not be his, and *then* what would I do? If they *are* his keys, he will be very glad you told me where his classes are, and if they aren't his keys, then what harm will it cause? . . . All right, I'll wait."

Sister Carlotta lay back on the bed. Bean laughed at her. "How did a nun get so good at lying?"

She held down the MUTE button. "It isn't lying to tell a bureaucrat whatever story it takes to get him to do his job properly."

"But if he does his job properly, he won't give you any information about Peter."

"If he does his job properly, he'll understand the purpose of the rules and therefore know when it is appropriate to make exceptions."

"People who understand the purpose of the rules don't become bureaucrats," said Bean. "That's something we learned really fast in Battle School."

"Exactly," said Carlotta. "So I have to tell him the story that will help him overcome his handicap." Abruptly she refocused her attention on the phone. "Oh, how very nice. Well, that's fine. I'll see him there."

She hung up the phone and laughed. "Well, after all that, the registrar emailed him. His desk was connected, he admitted that he *had* lost his keys, and he wants to meet the nice old lady at Yum-Yum."

"What is *that*?" asked Bean.

"I haven't the slightest idea, but the way she said it, I figured that if I were an old lady living near campus, I'd already know." She was already deep in the city directory. "Oh, it's a restaurant near campus. Well, this is it. Let's go meet the boy who would be king."

"Wait a minute," said Bean. "We can't go straight there."

"Why not?"

"We have to get some keys."

Sister Carlotta looked at him like he was crazy. "I made up the bit about the keys, Bean."

"The registrar knows that you're meeting Peter Wiggin to give him back his keys. What if he happens to be going to Yum-Yum right now for lunch? And he sees us meet Peter, and nobody gives anybody any keys?"

"We don't have a lot of time."

"OK, I have a better idea. Just act flustered and tell him that in your hurry to get there to meet him, you forgot to *bring* the keys, so he should come back to the house with you."

"You have a talent for this, Bean."

"Deception is second nature to me."

The bus was on time and moved briskly, this being an off-peak time, and soon they were on campus. Bean was better at translating maps into real terrain, so he led the way to Yum-Yum.

The place looked like a dive. Or rather, it was trying to look like a dive from an earlier era. Only it really *was* rundown and under-maintained, so it was a dive trying to look like a nice restaurant decorated to look like a dive. Very complicated and ironic, Bean decided, remembering what Father used to say about a neighborhood restaurant near their house on Crete: Abandon lunch, all ye who enter here.

The food looked like common-people's restaurant food everywhere—more about delivering fats and sweets than about flavor or nutrition. Bean wasn't picky, though. There were foods he liked better than others, and he knew something of the difference between fine cuisine and plain fare, but after the streets of Rotterdam and years of dried and processed food in space, anything that delivered the calories and nutrients was fine with him. But he made the mistake of going for the ice cream. He had just come from Araraquara, where the sorvete was memorable, and the American stuff was too fatty, the flavors too syrupy. "Mmmm, deliciosa," said Bean.

"Fecha a boquinha, menino," she answered. "E não fala português aqui."

"I didn't want to critique the ice cream in a language they'd understand."

"Doesn't the memory of starvation make you more patient?"

"Does everything have to be a moral question?"

"I wrote my dissertation on Aquinas and Tillich," said Sister Carlotta. "All questions are philosophical."

"In which case, all answers are unintelligible."

"And you're not even in grad school yet."

A tall young man slid onto the bench beside Bean. "Sorry I'm late," he said. "You got my keys?"

"I feel so foolish," said Sister Carlotta. "I came all the way here and then I realized I left them back home. Let me buy you some ice cream and then you can walk home with me and get them."

Bean looked up at Peter's face in profile. The resemblance to Ender was plain, but not close enough that anyone could ever mistake one for the other.

So this is the kid who brokered the ceasefire that ended the League War. The kid who wants to be Hegemon. Good looking, but not movie-star handsome—people would like him, but still trust him. Bean had studied the vids of Hitler and Stalin. The difference was palpable—Stalin never had to get elected; Hitler did. Even with that stupid mustache, you could see it in Hitler's eyes, that ability to see into you, that sense that whatever he said, wherever he looked, he was speaking to you, looking at you, that he cared about you. But Stalin, he looked like the liar that he was. Peter was definitely in the charismatic category. Like Hitler.

Perhaps an unfair comparison, but those who coveted power invited such thoughts. And the worst was seeing the way Sister Carlotta played to him. True, she was acting a part, but when she spoke to him, when that gaze was fixed on her, she preened a little, she warmed to him. Not so much that she'd behave foolishly, but she was aware of him with a heightened intensity that Bean didn't like. Peter had the seducer's gift. Dangerous.

"I'll walk home with you," said Peter. "I'm not hungry. Have you already paid?"

"Of course," said Sister Carlotta. "This is my grandson, by the way. Delfino."

Peter turned to notice Bean for the first time—though Bean was quite sure Peter had sized him up thoroughly before he sat down. "Cute kid," he said. "How old is he? Does he go to school yet?"

"I'm little," said Bean cheerfully, "but at least I'm not a yelda."

"All those vids of Battle School life," said Peter. "Even little kids are picking up that stupid polyglot slang."

"Now, children, you must get along, I insist on it." Sister Carlotta led the way to the door. "My grandson is visiting this country for the first time, young man, so he doesn't understand American banter."

"Yes I do," said Bean, trying to sound like a petulant child and finding it quite easy, since he really was annoyed.

"He speaks English pretty well. But you better hold his hand crossing this street, the campus trams zoom through here like Daytona."

Bean rolled his eyes and submitted to having Carlotta hold his hand across the street. Peter was obviously trying to provoke him, but why? Surely he wasn't so shallow as to think humiliating Bean would give him some advantage. Maybe he took pleasure in making other people feel small.

Finally, though, they were away from campus and had taken enough twists and turns to make sure they weren't being followed.

"So you're the great Julian Delphiki," said Peter.

"And you're Locke. They're touting you for Hegemon when Sakata's term is over. Too bad you're only virtual."

"I'm thinking of going public soon," said Peter.

"Ah, that's why you got the plastic surgery to make you so pretty," said Bean.

"This old face?" said Peter. "I only wear it when I don't care how I look."

"Boys," said Sister Carlotta. "*Must* you display like baby chimps?"

Peter laughed easily. "Come on, Mom, we was just playin'. Can't we still go to the movies?"

"Off to bed without supper, the lot of you," said Sister Carlotta.

Bean had had enough of this. "Where's Petra?" he demanded.

Peter looked at him as if he were insane. "*I* don't have her."

"You have sources," said Bean. "You know more than you're telling me."

"You know more than you're telling me, too," said Peter. "I thought we were working on trusting each other, and *then* we open the floodgates of wisdom."

"Is she dead?" said Bean, not willing to be deflected.

Peter looked at his watch. "At this moment. I don't know."

Bean stopped walking. Disgusted, he turned to Sister Carlotta. "We wasted a trip," he said. "And risked our lives for nothing."

"Are you sure?" said Sister Carlotta.

Bean looked back at Peter, who seemed genuinely bemused. "He wants to be Hegemon," said Bean, "but he's nothing." Bean walked away. He had memorized the route, of course, and knew how to get to the bus station without Sister Carlotta's help. Figuring out the bus route would distract him from the bitter disappointment of finding out that Peter was a game-playing fool.

No one called after him, and he did not look back.

Bean took, not the bus to the hotel, but the one that passed nearest the neighborhood school that Peter and Valentine probably attended. What if Ender had actually grown up here, had attended schools in this town instead of the city? His whole life might have been shaped differently. Maybe Ender's first killing would never have happened—maybe there would have been no bully like the boy Stilson, who ambushed Ender with his gang and paid for it with his life. And if Ender had not proved his brutal efficiency in combat, his determination to win without scruple or hesitation, would he have been taken into the Battle School program?

Bean had been there for Ender's second killing, which was pretty much the same situation as the first. Ender—alone, outnumbered, surrounded—talking his way into single combat and then destroying his enemy so no will to fight would remain. There were military strategists who taught that principle of warfare. But Ender had known it instinctively, at the age of five.

I knew things at that age, thought Bean. And younger, too. Not how to kill—that was beyond me, I was too small. But how to live. That was hard.

For me it was hard, but not for Ender. Bean walked through the neighborhoods of modest old houses and even more modest new ones—but to him they were all miracles. Not that he hadn't had plenty of chances, living with his family in Greece after the war, to see how most children grew up. How much of a child's character came from the place he grew up, the people, the family, the friends? How much was born in him? Could a harsh place like Rotterdam make a military genius out of a child? Could a gentler place like Greensboro keep a child's genius from surfacing?

I had more native talent for war than Ender had. But he was still the better commander. Was it because Ender grew up where he never worried about finding another meal, where people praised him and protected him? I grew up where if I found a scrap of food I had to worry that another street kid might kill me for it. Shouldn't that have made me the one who fought most desperately, and Ender the one who held back?

It wasn't the place. Two people in identical situations would never make exactly the same choices. Ender is who he is, and I am who I am. It was in him to destroy the Formics. It was in me to stay alive.

So what's in me now? I'm a commander without an army. I have a mission to perform, but no knowledge of how to perform it. Petra, if she's still alive, is in desperate peril, and she counts on me to free her. The others are all free. She alone remains hidden. What has Achilles done to her? I will not have Petra end like Poke.

There it was. The difference between Ender and Bean. Ender came out of his bitterest battle of childhood undefeated. He had done what was required. But Bean had not even realized the danger his friend Poke was in until too late. If he had seen in time how immediate her peril was, he could have warned her, helped her. Saved her. Instead, her body was tossed into the Rhine, to be found bobbing like so much garbage among the wharves.

And it was happening again.

Bean stood in front of the Wiggin house. Ender had never seen it, and no pictures of it had been shown at the court of inquiry. But it was exactly what Bean had expected. A tree in the front yard, with wooden slats nailed into the trunk to form a ladder to the platform in a high crotch of the tree. A tidy, well-tended garden. A place of peace and refuge. Something Ender never had. Peter and Valentine lived here, though.

Where is Petra's garden? For that matter, where is mine?

Bean knew he was being unreasonable. If Ender had come back to Earth, he too would no doubt be in hiding—if Achilles or someone else hadn't simply killed him straight off. And even as things stood, he couldn't help but wonder if Ender might not prefer to be living as Bean was, on Earth, in hiding, than where he was now, in space, bound for another world and a life of permanent exile from the world of his birth.

A woman came out of the front door of the house. Mrs. Wiggin?

"Are you lost?" she asked.

Bean realized that in his disappointment—no, call it despair—he had forgotten his vigilance. This house might be watched. Even if it was not, Mrs. Wiggin herself might remember him, this young boy who appeared in front of her house during school hours.

"Is this where Ender Wiggin's family lives?"

A cloud passed across her face, just momentarily, but Bean saw how her expression saddened before her smile could be put back. "Yes, it is," she said. "But he didn't grow up here and we don't give tours."

For reasons Bean could not understand, on impulse he said, "I was with him. In the last battle. I fought under him."

Her smile changed again, away from mere courtesy and kindness, toward something like warmth and pain. "Ah," she said. "A veteran." And then the warmth faded and was replaced by worry. "I know all the faces of Ender's companions in that last battle. You're the one who's dead. Julian Delphiki."

Just like that, his cover was blown—and he had done it to himself, by telling her that he was in Ender's jeesh. What was he thinking? There were only eleven of them. "Obviously, there's someone who wants to kill me," he said. "If you tell anyone I came here, it will help him do it."

"I won't tell. But it was careless of you to come here."

"I had to see," said Bean, wondering if that was anything like a true explanation.

She didn't wonder. "That's absurd," she said. "You wouldn't risk your life to come here without a reason." And then it came together in her mind. "Peter's not home right now."

"I know," Bean said. "I was just with him at the university." And then he realized—there was no reason for her to think he was coming to see Peter, unless she had some idea of what Peter was doing. "You know," he said.

She closed her eyes, realizing now what she had confessed. "Either we are both very great fools," she said, "or we must have trusted each other at once, to let our guard down so readily."

"We're only fools if the other can't be trusted," said Bean.

"We'll find out, won't we?" Then she smiled. "No use leaving you standing out here on the street, for people to wonder why a child your size is not in school."

He followed her up the walkway to the front door. Bean was walking up to a door that Ender must have longed to see. But he never came home. Like Bonzo, the other casualty of the war. Bonzo, killed; Ender, missing in action; and now Bean coming up the walk to Ender's home. Only this was no sentimental visit with a grieving family. It was a different war now, but war it was, and she had another son at risk these days.

She was not supposed to know what he was doing. Wasn't that the whole point of Peter's having to camouflage his activities by pretending to be a student?

She made him a sandwich without even asking, as if she simply assumed that a child would be hungry. It was, of all things, that plain American cliché, peanut butter on white bread. Had she made such sandwiches for Ender?

"I miss him," said Bean, because he knew that would make her like him.

"If he had been here," said Mrs. Wiggin, "he probably would have been killed. When I read what . . . *Locke* . . . wrote about that boy from Rotterdam, I couldn't imagine he would have let Ender live. You knew him, too, didn't you. What's his name?"

"Achilles," said Bean.

"You're in hiding," she said. "But you seem so young."

"I travel with a nun named Sister Carlotta," said Bean. "We claim we're grandmother and grandson."

"I'm glad you're not alone."

"Neither is Ender."

Tears came to her eyes. "I suppose he needed Valentine more than we did."

On impulse—again, an instinctive act instead of a calculated decision—Bean reached out and set his hand in hers. She smiled at him.

The moment passed. Bean realized again how dangerous it was to be here. What if this house was under surveillance? The I.F. knew about Peter—what if they were observing the house?

"I should go," said Bean.

"I'm glad you came by," she said. "I must have wanted very much to talk to someone who knew Ender without being envious of him."

"We were all envious," said Bean. "But we also knew he was the best of us."

"Why else would you envy him, if you didn't think he was better?"

Bean laughed. "Well, when you envy somebody, you tell yourself he isn't really better after all."

"So . . . did the other children envy his abilities?" asked Mrs. Wiggin. "Or only the recognition he received?"

Bean didn't like the question, but then remembered who it was that was asking. "I should turn that question back on you. Did Peter envy his abilities? Or only the recognition?"

She stood there, considering whether to answer or not. Bean knew that family loyalty worked against her saying anything. "I'm not just idly asking," Bean said. "I don't know how much you know about what Peter's doing . . ."

"We read everything he publishes," said Mrs. Wiggin. "And then we're very careful to act as if we hadn't a clue what's going on in the world."

"I'm trying to decide whether to throw in with Peter," said Bean. "And I have no way of knowing what to make of him. How much to trust him."

"I wish I could help you," said Mrs. Wiggin. "Peter marches to a different drummer. I've never really caught the rhythm."

"Don't you like him?" asked Bean, knowing he was too blunt, but knowing also that he wasn't going to get many chances like this, to talk to the mother of a potential ally—or rival.

"I love him," said Mrs. Wiggin. "He doesn't show us much of himself. But that's only fair—we never showed our children much of ourselves, either."

"Why not?" asked Bean. He was thinking of the openness of his mother and father, the way they knew Nikolai, and Nikolai knew them. It had left him almost gasping, the unguardedness of their conversations with each other. Clearly the Wiggin household did not have that custom.

"It's very complicated," said Mrs. Wiggin.

"Meaning that you think it's none of my business."

"On the contrary, I know it's very much your business." She sighed and sat back down. "Come on, let's not pretend this is only a doorstep conversation. You came here to find out about Peter. The easy answer is simply to tell you that we don't know a thing. He never tells anyone anything they want to know, unless it would be useful to him for them to know it."

"But the hard answer?"

"We've been hiding from our children, almost from the start," said Mrs. Wiggin. "We can hardly be surprised or resentful when they learned at a very early age to be secretive."

"What were you hiding?"

"We don't tell our children, and I should tell you?" But she answered her own question at once. "If Valentine and Ender were here, I think we *would* talk to them. I even tried to explain some of this to Valentine before she left to join Ender in . . . space. I did a very bad job, because I had never put it in words before. Let me just . . . let me start by saying . . . we were going to have a third child anyway, even if the I.F. hadn't asked us to."

Where Bean had grown up, the population laws hadn't meant much—the street children of Rotterdam were all extra people and knew perfectly well that by law not one of them should have been born, but when you're starving, it's hard to care much about whether you're going to get into the finest schools. Still, when the laws were repealed, he read about them and knew the significance of their decision to have a third child. "Why would you do that?" asked Bean. "It would hurt all your children. It would end your careers."

"We were very careful not to *have* careers," said Mrs. Wiggin. "Not careers that we'd hate to give up.

What we had was only jobs. You see, we're religious people."

"There are lots of religious people in the world."

"But not in America," said Mrs. Wiggin. "Not the kind of fanatic that does something so selfish and anti-social as to have more than two children, just because of some misguided religious ideas. And when Peter tested so high as a toddler, and they started monitoring him—well, that was a disaster for us. We had hoped to be . . . unobtrusive. To disappear. We're very bright people, you know."

"I wondered why the parents of such geniuses didn't have noted careers of their own," said Bean. "Or at least some kind of standing in the intellectual community."

"Intellectual community," said Mrs. Wiggin scornfully. "America's intellectual community has never been very bright. Or honest. They're all sheep, following whatever the intellectual fashion of the decade happens to be. Demanding that everyone follow their dicta in lockstep. Everyone has to be open-minded and tolerant of the things they believe, but God forbid they should ever concede, even for a moment, that someone who disagrees with them might have some fingerhold on truth."

She sounded bitter.

"I sound bitter," she said.

"You've lived your life," said Bean. "So you think you're smarter than the smart people."

She recoiled a bit. "Well, that's the kind of comment that explains why we never discuss our faith with anyone."

"I didn't mean it as an attack," said Bean. "I think I'm smarter than anybody I've ever met, because I am.

I'd have to be dumber than I am not to know it. You really believe in your religion, and you resent the fact that you had to hide it from others. That's all I was saying."

"Not religion, reli*gions,*" she said. "My husband and I don't even share the same doctrine. Having a large family in obedience to God, that was about the only thing we agreed on. And even at that, we both had elaborate intellectual justifications for our decision to defy the law. For one thing, we didn't think it would hurt our children at all. We meant to raise them in faith, as believers."

"So why didn't you?"

"Because we're cowards after all," said Mrs. Wiggin. "With the I.F. watching, we would have had constant interference. They would have intervened to make sure we didn't teach our children anything that would prevent them from fulfilling the role that Ender and you ended up fulfilling. That's when we started hiding our faith. Not really from our children, just from the Battle School people. We were so relieved when Peter's monitor was taken away. And then Valentine's. We thought we were done. We were going to move to a place where we wouldn't be so badly treated, and have a third child, and a fourth, as many as we could have before they arrested us. But then they came to us and requisitioned a third child. So we didn't have to move. You see? We were lazy and frightened. If the Battle School was going to give us a cover to allow us to have one more child, then why not?"

"But then they took Ender."

"And by the time they took him, it was too late. To raise Peter and Valentine in our faith. If you don't teach children when they're little, it's never really inside them. You have to hope they'll come to it later, on their own. It can't come from the parents, if you don't begin when they're little."

"Indoctrinating them."

"That's what parenting is," said Mrs. Wiggin. "Indoctrinating your children in the social patterns that you want them to live by. The intellectuals have no qualms about using the schools to indoctrinate our children in *their* foolishness."

"I wasn't trying to provoke you," said Bean.

"And yet you use words that imply criticism."

"Sorry," said Bean.

"You're still a child," said Mrs. Wiggin. "No matter how bright you are, you still absorb a lot of the attitudes of the ruling class. I don't like it, but there you are. When they took Ender away, and we finally could live without constant scrutiny of every word that we said to our children, we realized that Peter was already completely indoctrinated in the foolishness of the schools. He would never have gone along with our earlier plan. He would have denounced us. We would have lost him. So do you cast off your firstborn child in order to give birth to a fourth or fifth or sixth? Peter seemed sometimes not to have any conscience at all. If ever anyone needed to believe in God, it was Peter, and he didn't."

"He probably wouldn't have anyway," said Bean.

"You don't know him," said Mrs. Wiggin. "He lives by pride. If we had made him proud of being a secret believer, he would have been valiant in that struggle. Instead he's . . . not."

"So you never even tried to convert him to your beliefs?" asked Bean.

"Which ones?" asked Mrs. Wiggin. "*We* had always thought that the big struggle in our family would be over which religion to teach them, his or mine. Instead we had to watch over Peter and find ways to help him find . . . decency. No, something much more important than that. Integrity. Honor. We monitored him the way that the Battle School had monitored all three of them. It took all our patience to keep our hands off when he forced Valentine to become Demosthenes. It was so contrary to her spirit. But we soon saw that it was not changing her—that her nobility of heart was, if anything, stronger through resistance to Peter's control."

"You didn't try to simply block him from what he was doing?"

She laughed harshly. "Oh, now, you're supposed to be the smart one. Could someone have blocked *you*? And Peter failed to get into Battle School because he was *too* ambitious, too rebellious, too unlikely to fulfill assignments and follow orders. *We* were supposed to influence him by forbidding him or blocking him?"

"No, I can see you couldn't," said Bean. "But you did nothing at all?"

"We taught him as best we could," said Mrs. Wiggin. "Comments at meals. We could see how he tuned us out, how he despised our opinions. It didn't help that we were trying so hard to conceal that we knew everything he'd written as Locke; our conversations really were . . . abstract. Boring, I suppose. And we didn't have those intellectual credentials. Why should he respect us? But he *heard* our ideas. Of what nobility is. Goodness and honor. And whether he believed us at some level or simply found such things within himself, we've seen him grow. So . . . you ask me if you can trust him, and I can't answer, because . . . trust him to do what? To act as you want him to? Never. To act according to some predictable pattern? I should laugh. But we've seen signs of honor. We've seen him do things that were very hard, but that seemed to be not just for show, but because he really believed in what he was doing. Of course, he might have simply been doing things that would make Locke seem virtuous and admirable. How can we know, when we can't ask him?"

"So you can't talk to him about what matters to you, because you know he'll despise you, and he can't talk to you about what matters to him, because you've never shown him that you actually have the understanding to grasp what he's thinking."

Tears sprang to her eyes and glistened there. "Sometimes I miss Valentine so much. She was so breathtakingly honest and good."

"So she told you she was Demosthenes?"

"No," said Mrs. Wiggin. "She was wise enough to know that if she didn't keep Peter's secret, it would split the family apart forever. No, she kept that hidden from us. But she made sure we knew just what kind of person Peter was. And about everything else in her life, everything Peter left for her to decide for herself, she told us that, and she listened to us, too, she cared what we thought."

"So you told her what you believe?"

"We didn't tell her about our faith," said Mrs. Wiggin. "But we taught her the results of that faith. We did the best we could."

"I'm sure you did," said Bean.

"I'm not stupid," said Mrs. Wiggin. "I know you despise us, just as we know Peter despises us."

"I don't," said Bean.

"I've been lied to enough to recognize it when you do it."

"I don't despise you for . . . I don't despise you at all," said Bean. "But you have to see that the way you all hide from each other, Peter growing up in a family where nobody tells anybody anything that matters—that doesn't make me really optimistic about ever being able to trust him. I'm about to put my life in his hands. And now I find out that in his whole life, he's never had an honest relationship with anybody."

Her eyes grew cold and distant then. "I see that I've provided you with useful information. Perhaps you should go now."

"I'm not judging you," said Bean.

"Don't be absurd, of course you are," said Mrs. Wiggin.

"I'm not condemning you, then."

"Don't make me laugh. You condemn us, and you know what? I agree with you. I condemn us too. We set out to do God's will, and we've ended up damaging the one child we have left to us. He's grimly determined to make his mark in the world. But what sort of mark will it be?"

"An indelible one," said Bean. "If Achilles doesn't destroy him first."

"We did some things right," said Mrs. Wiggin. "We gave him the freedom to test his own abilities. We could have stopped him from publishing, you know. He thinks he outsmarted us, but only because we played incredibly dumb. How many parents would have let their teenage son meddle in world affairs? When he wrote against . . . against letting Ender come home—you don't know how hard it was for me not to claw his arrogant little eyes out. . . ."

For the first time, he saw something of the rage and frustration she must have been going through. He thought: This is how Peter's mother feels about him. Maybe orphanhood wasn't such a drawback.

"But I didn't, did I?" said Mrs. Wiggin.

"Didn't what?"

"Didn't stop him. And he turned out to be right. Because if Ender were here on Earth, he'd either be dead, or he would have been one of the kidnapped children, or he'd be in hiding like you. But I still . . . Ender is his brother, and he exiled him from Earth forever. And I couldn't help but remember the terrible threats he made when Ender was still little, and lived with us. He told Ender and Valentine then that someday he would kill Ender, and pretend that it was an accident."

"Ender's not dead."

"My husband and I have wondered, in the dark nights when we try to make sense of what has happened to our family, to all our dreams, we've wondered if Peter got Ender exiled because he loved him and knew the dangers he'd face if he returned to Earth. Or if he exiled him because he feared that if Ender came home Peter would kill him, just as he threatened to—so then, exiling Ender could be viewed as a sort of, I don't know, an elementary kind of self-control. Still, a very selfish thing, but still showing a sort of vague respect for decency. That would be progress."

"Or maybe none of the above."

"Or maybe we're all guided by God in this, and God has brought you here."

"So Sister Carlotta says."

"She might be right."

"I don't much care either way," said Bean. "If there is a God, I think he's pretty lousy at his job."

"Or you don't understand what his job is."

"Believe me, Sister Carlotta is the nunnish equivalent of a Jesuit. Let's not even get into trading sophistries, I've been trained by an expert and, as you say, you're not in practice."

"Julian Delphiki," said Mrs. Wiggin, "I knew when I saw you out on the front sidewalk that I not only could, I *must* tell you things that I have spoken of to no one but my husband, and I've even said things that I've never said to him. I've told you things that Peter never imagined that I knew or thought or saw or felt. If you have a low opinion of my mothering, please keep in mind that whatever you know, you know because I told you, and I told you because I think that someday Peter's future may depend on your knowing what he's going to do, or how to help him. Or—Peter's future as a decent human being might depend on his helping *you.* So I bared my heart to you. For Peter's sake. And I face your scorn, Julian Delphiki, for Peter's sake as well. So don't fault my love for my son. Whether he thinks he cares or not, he grew up with parents who love him and have done everything we could for him. Including lie to him about what we believe, what we know, so that he can move through his world like Alexander, boldly reaching for the ends of the earth, with the complete freedom that comes from having parents who are too stupid to stop you. Until you've had a child of your own and sacrificed for that child and twisted your life into a pretzel, into a knot for him, don't you dare to judge me and what I've done."

"I'm not judging you," said Bean. "Truly I'm not. As you said, I'm just trying to understand Peter."

"Well, do you know what I think?" said Mrs. Wiggin. "I think you've been asking all the wrong questions. 'Can I trust him?' " She mimicked him scornfully. "Whether you trust somebody or distrust him has a lot more to do with the kind of person *you* are than the kind of person he is. The real question you ought to be asking is, Do you really want Peter Wiggin to rule the world? Because if you help him, and he somehow lives through all this, that's where it will lead. He won't stop until he achieves that. And he'll burn up your future along with anybody else's, if it will help him reach that goal. So ask yourself, will the world be a better place with Peter Wiggin as Hegemon? And not some benign ceremonial figurehead like the ineffectual toad who holds that office now. I mean Peter Wiggin as the Hegemon who reshapes this world into whatever form he wants it to have."

"But you're assuming that I care whether the world is a better place," said Bean. "What if all I care about is my own survival or advancement? Then the only question that would matter is, Can I use Peter to advance my own plans?"

She laughed and shook her head. "Do *you* believe that about yourself? Well, you *are* a child."

"Pardon me, but did I ever pretend to be anything else?"

"You pretend," said Mrs. Wiggin, "to be a person of such enormous value that you can speak of 'allying' with Peter Wiggin as if you brought armies with you."

"I don't bring armies," said Bean, "but I bring victory for whatever army he gives me."

"Would Ender have been like you, if he had come home? Arrogant? Aloof?"

"Not at all," said Bean. "But I never killed anybody."

"Except Buggers," said Mrs. Wiggin.

"Why are we at war with each other?" said Bean.

"I've told you everything about my son, about my family, and you've given me nothing back. Except your . . . sneer."

"I'm not sneering," said Bean. "I like you."

"Oh, thank you very much."

"I can see in you the mother of Ender Wiggin," said Bean. "You understand Peter the way Ender understood his soldiers. The way Ender understood his enemies. And you're bold enough to act instantly when the opportunity presents itself. I show up on your doorstep, and you give me all this. No, ma'am, I don't despise you at all. And you know what I think? I think that, perhaps without even realizing it yourself, you believe in Peter completely. You want him to succeed. You think he should rule the world. And you've told me all this, not because I'm such a nice little boy, but because you think that by telling me, you'll help Peter move that much closer toward ultimate victory."

She shook her head. "Not everybody thinks like a soldier."

"Hardly anyone does," said Bean. "Precious few soldiers, for that matter."

"Let me tell you something, Julian Delphiki. You didn't have a mother and father, so you need to be told. You know what I dread most? That Peter will pursue these ambitions of his so relentlessly that he'll never have a life."

"Conquering the world isn't a life?" asked Bean.

"Alexander the Great," said Mrs. Wiggin. "He haunts my nightmares for Peter. All his conquests, his victories, his grand achievements—they were the acts of an adolescent boy. By the time he got around to marrying, to having a child, it was too late. He died in the midst of it. And he probably wouldn't have done a very good job of it either. He was already too powerful before he even tried to find love. That's what I fear for Peter."

"Love? That's what this all comes down to?"

"No, not just love. I'm talking about the cycle of life. I'm talking about finding some alien creature and deciding to marry her and stay with her forever, no matter whether you even like each other or not a few years down the road. And why will you do this? So you can make babies together, and try to keep them alive and teach them what they need to know so that someday *they'll* have babies, and keep the whole thing going. And you'll never draw a secure breath until you have grandchildren, a double handful of them, because then you know that your line won't die out, your influence will continue. Selfish, isn't it? Only it's not selfish, it's what life is for. It's the only thing that brings happiness, ever, to anyone. All the other things—victories, achievements, honors, causes—they bring only momentary flashes of pleasure. But binding yourself to another person and to the children you make together, that's life. And you can't do it if your life is centered on your ambitions. You'll never be happy. It will never be enough, even if you rule the world."

"Are you telling me? Or telling Peter?" asked Bean.

"I'm telling you what I truly want for Peter," said Mrs. Wiggin. "But if you're a tenth as smart as you think you are, you'll get that for yourself. Or you'll never have real joy in this life."

"Excuse me if I'm missing something here," said Bean, "but as far as I can tell, marrying and having children has brought you nothing but grief. You've lost Ender, you've lost Valentine, and you spent your life pissed off at Peter or fretting about him."

"Yes," she said. "Now you're getting it."

"Where's the joy? That's what I'm not getting."

"The grief *is* the joy," said Mrs. Wiggin. "I have someone to grieve for. Whom do you have?"

Such was the intensity of their conversation that Bean had no barrier in place to block what she said. It stirred something inside him. All the memories of people that he'd loved—despite the fact that he refused to love anyone. Poke. Nikolai. Sister Carlotta. Ender. His parents, when he finally met them. "I have someone to grieve for," said Bean.

"You think you do," said Mrs. Wiggin. "Everyone thinks they do, until they take a child into their heart. Only then do you know what it is to be a hostage to love. To have someone else's life matter more than your own."

"Maybe I know more than you think," said Bean.

"Maybe you know nothing at all," said Mrs. Wiggin.

They faced each other across the table, a loud silence between them. Bean wasn't even sure they'd been quarreling. Despite the heat of their exchange, he couldn't help but feel that he'd just been given a strong dose of the faith that she and her husband shared with each other.

Or maybe it really was objective truth, and he simply couldn't grasp it because he wasn't married.

And never would be. If there was ever anyone whose life virtually guaranteed that he'd be a terrible father, it was Bean. Without ever exactly saying it aloud, he'd always known that he would never marry, never have children.

But her words had this much effect: For the first time in his life, he found himself almost wishing that it were not so.

In that silence, Bean heard the front door open, and Peter's and Sister Carlotta's voices. At once Bean and Mrs. Wiggin rose to their feet, feeling and looking guilty, as if they had been caught in some kind of clandestine rendezvous. Which, in a way, they had.

"Mother, I've met a traveler," said Peter when he came into the room.

Bean heard the beginning of Peter's lie like a blow

to the face—for Bean knew that the person Peter was lying to knew his story was false, and yet would lie in return by pretending to believe.

This time, though, the lie could be nipped in the bud.

"Sister Carlotta," said Mrs. Wiggin. "I've heard so much about you from young Julian here. He says you are the world's only Jesuit nun."

Peter and Sister Carlotta looked at Bean in bafflement. What was he doing there? He almost laughed at their consternation, in part because he couldn't have answered that question himself.

"He came here like a pilgrim to a shrine," said Mrs. Wiggin. "And he very bravely told me who he really is. Peter, you must be very careful not to tell anyone that this is one of Ender's companions. Julian Delphiki. He wasn't killed in that explosion, after all. Isn't that wonderful? We must make him welcome here, for Ender's sake, but he's still in danger, so it has to be our secret who he is."

"Of course, Mother," said Peter. He looked at Bean, but his eyes betrayed nothing of what he was feeling. Like the cold eyes of a rhinoceros, unreadable, yet with enormous danger behind them all the same.

Sister Carlotta, though, was obviously appalled. "After all our security precautions," she said, "and you just blurt it out? And this house is bound to be watched."

"We had a good conversation," said Bean. "That's not possible in the midst of lies."

"It's my life you were risking here, too, you know," said Carlotta.

Mrs. Wiggin touched her arm. "Do stay here with us, won't you? We have room in our house for visitors."

"We can't," said Bean. "She's right. Coming here at

all has compromised us both. We'll probably want to fly out of Greensboro first thing in the morning."

He glanced at Sister Carlotta, knowing that she would understand that he was really saying they should leave by train that night. Or by bus the day after tomorrow. Or rent an apartment under assumed names and stay here for a week. The lying had begun again, for safety's sake.

"At least stay for dinner?" asked Mrs. Wiggin. "And meet my husband? I think he'll be just as intrigued as I was to meet a boy who is so famously dead."

Bean saw Peter's eyes glaze over. He understood why—to Peter, a dinner with his parents would be an excruciating social exercise during which nothing important could be said. Wouldn't all your lives be simpler if you could just tell each other the truth? But Mrs. Wiggin had said that Peter needed to feel that he was on his own. If he knew that his parents knew of his secret activities, that would infantilize him, apparently. Though if he were really the sort of man that could rule the world, surely he could deal with knowing that his parents were in on his secrets.

Not my decision. I gave my word.

"We'd be glad to," said Bean. "Though there's a danger of having your house blown up because we're in it."

"Then we'll eat out," said Mrs. Wiggin. "See how simple things can be? If something's going to be blown up, let it be a restaurant. They carry insurance for that sort of thing."

Bean laughed. But Peter didn't. Because, Bean realized, Peter doesn't know how much she knows, and therefore he thinks her comment was idiocy instead of irony.

"Not Italian food," said Sister Carlotta.

"Oh, of course not," said Mrs. Wiggin. "I don't know of a decent Italian restaurant in Greensboro."

With that, the conversation turned to safe and meaningless topics. Bean took a certain relish in watching how Peter squirmed at the utter waste of time that such chitchat represented. I know more about your mother than you do, thought Bean. I have more respect for her.

But you're the one she loves.

Bean was annoyed to notice the envy in his own heart. Nobody's immune from those petty human emotions, he knew that. But somehow he had to learn how to distinguish between true observations and what his envy told him. Peter had to learn the same. The trust that Bean had given so easily to Mrs. Wiggin would have to be earned step by step between him and Peter. Why?

Because he and Peter were so alike. Because he and Peter were natural rivals. Because he and Peter could so easily be deadly enemies.

As I am a second Ender in his eyes, is he a second Achilles in mine? If there were no Achilles in the world, would I think of Peter as the evil I must destroy?

And if we do defeat Achilles together, will we then have to turn and fight each other, undoing all our triumphs, destroying everything we've built?

10

Brothers in Arms

To: RusFriend%BabaYaga@MosPub.net
From: VladDragon%slavnet.com
Re: allegiance

Let's make one thing clear. I never "joined" with Achilles. From all I could see, Achilles was speaking for Mother Russia. It was Mother Russia that I agreed to serve, and that is a decision I did not and do not regret. I believe the artificial divisions among the peoples of Greater Slavia serve only to keep any of us from achieving our potential in the world. In the chaos that has resulted from the exposure of Achilles' true nature, I would be glad of any opportunity to serve.

The things I learned in Battle School could well make a difference to the future of our people. If my link with Achilles makes it impossible for me to be of service, so be it. But it would be a shame if we all suffered from that last act of sabotage by a psychopath. It is precisely now that I am most needed. Mother Russia will find no more loyal son than this one.

For Peter, the dinner at Leblon with his parents and Bean and Carlotta consisted of long periods of excruciating boredom interrupted by short passages of sheer panic. Nothing that anyone was saying mattered in the slightest. Because Bean was passing himself off as little more than a tourist visiting Ender's shrine, all anyone could talk about was Ender Ender Ender. But inevitably the conversation would skirt topics that were highly sensitive, things that might give away what Peter was really doing and the role that Bean might end up playing.

The worst was when Sister Carlotta—who, nun or not, clearly knew how to be a malicious bitch when she wanted to—began probing Peter about his studies at UNCG, even though she knew perfectly well that his schoolwork there was merely a cover for far more important matters. "I'm just surprised, I suppose, that you spend your time on a regular course of study when clearly you have abilities that should be used on a broader stage," she said.

"I need the degree, just like anyone else," said Peter, writhing inside.

"But why not study things that will prepare you to play a role on the great stage of world affairs?"

Ironically, it was Bean who rescued him. "Come now, Grandmother," he said. "A man of Peter Wiggin's ability is ready to do anything he wants, whenever he wants. Formal study is just busywork to him anyway. He's only doing it to prove to other people that he's able to live by the rules when he needs to. Right, Peter?"

"Close enough," Peter said. "I'm even less interested in my studies than you all are, and you shouldn't be interested in them at all."

"Well, if you hate it so much, why are we paying for tuition?" asked Father.

"We're not," Mother reminded him. "Peter has such a nice scholarship that they're paying *him* to attend there."

"Not getting their money's worth, though, are they?" said Father.

"They're getting what they want," said Bean. "For the rest of his life, whatever Peter here accomplishes, it will be mentioned that he studied at UNCG. He'll be a walking advertisement for them. I'd call that a pretty good return on investment, wouldn't you?"

The kid had mastered the kind of language Father understood—Peter had to credit Bean with knowing his audience when he spoke. Still, it annoyed Peter that Bean had so easily sussed what kind of idiots his parents were, and how easily they could be pandered to. It was as if, by pulling Peter's conversational irons out of the fire, Bean was rubbing it in about Peter's still being a child living at home, while Bean was out dealing with life more directly. It made Peter chafe all the more.

Only at the end of the dinner, as they left the Brazilian restaurant and headed for the Market/Holden station, did Bean drop his bombshell. "You know that since we've compromised ourselves here, we have to go back into hiding at once." Peter's parents made little noises of sympathy, and then Bean said, "What I was wondering was, why doesn't Peter go with us? Get out of Greensboro for a while? Would you like to, Peter? Do you have a passport?"

"No, he doesn't," said Mother, at exactly the same moment that Peter said, "Of course I do."

"You do?" asked Mother.

"Just in case," said Peter. He didn't add: I have six passports from four countries, as a matter of fact, and ten different bank identities with funds from my writing gigs socked away.

"But you're in the middle of a semester," said Father.

"I can take a leave whenever I want," said Peter. "It sounds interesting. Where are you going?"

"We don't know," said Bean. "We don't decide until the last minute. But we can email you and tell you where we are."

"Campus email addresses aren't secure," said Father helpfully.

"No email is really secure, is it?" asked Mother.

"It will be a coded message," said Bean. "Of course."

"It doesn't sound very sensible to me," said Father. "Peter may think his studies are just busywork, but in fact you have to have that degree just to get started in life. You need to stick to something long term and finish it, Peter. If your transcript shows that you did your education in fits and starts, that won't look good to the best companies."

"What career do you think I'm going to pursue?" Peter asked, annoyed. "Some kind of corporate dull bob?"

"I really hate it when you use that ersatz Battle School slang," said Father. "You didn't go there, and it makes you sound like some kind of teenage wannabe."

"I don't know about that," said Bean, before Peter could blow up. "I *was* there, and I think that stuff is just part of the language. I mean, the word 'wannabe' was once slang, wasn't it? It can grow into the language just by people using it."

"It makes him sound like a kid," said Father, but it was just a parting shot, Father's pathetic need to have the last word.

Peter said nothing. But he wasn't grateful to Bean for taking his side. On the contrary, the kid really pissed him off. It's like Bean thought he could come into Peter's life and intervene between him and his parents like some kind of savior. It diminished Peter in his own eyes. None of the people who wrote to him or read his work as Locke or Demosthenes ever condescended to him, because they didn't know he was a kid. But the way Bean was acting was a warning of things to come. If Peter did come out under his real name, he would immediately have to start dealing with condescension. People who had once trembled at the idea of coming under Demosthenes' scrutiny, people who had once eagerly sought Locke's imprimatur, would now poo-poo anything Peter wrote, saying, Of course a child would think that way, or, more kindly but no less devastatingly, When he has more experience, he'll come to see that. . . . Adults were always saying things like that. As if experience actually had some correlation with increased wisdom; as if most of the stupidity in the world were not propounded by adults.

Besides, Peter couldn't help but feel that Bean was

enjoying it, that he loved having Peter at such a disadvantage. Why *had* the little weasel gone to his house? To come home and find Bean sitting there talking to his mother, that was like catching a burglar in the act. He hadn't liked Bean from the beginning—especially not after the petulant way he walked off just because Peter didn't immediately answer the question he was asking. Admittedly, Peter *had* been teasing him a little, and there was an element of condescension about it—toying with the little kid before telling him what he wanted to know. But Bean's retaliation had gone way overboard. Especially this miserable dinner.

And yet . . .

Bean was the real thing. The best that Battle School had produced. Peter could use him. Peter might actually even need him, precisely because he could not yet afford to come out publicly as himself. Bean had the credibility despite his size and age, because he'd fought the fight. He could actually do things instead of having to pull strings in the background or try to manipulate government decisions by influencing public opinion. If Peter could secure some kind of working alliance with him, it might go a long way toward compensating for his impotence. If only Bean weren't so insufferably smug.

Can't let my personal feelings interfere with the work at hand.

"Tell you what," Peter said. "Mom and Dad, you've got stuff to do tomorrow, but my first class isn't till noon. Why don't I go with these two wherever they're spending the night and talk through the possibility of maybe taking a field trip with them."

"I don't want you just taking off and leaving your mother to worry about what's happening to you," said Father. "I think it's very clear to all of us that young

Mr. Delphiki here is a trouble magnet, and I think your mother has lost enough children without having to worry about something even worse happening to you."

It made Peter cringe the way Father always talked as if it were only Mother who would be worried, only Mother who cared what happened to him. And if it was true—who could tell, with Father?—that was even worse. Either Father didn't care what happened to Peter, or he did care but was such a git that he couldn't admit it.

"I won't leave town without checking in with Mommy," said Peter.

"You don't need to be sarcastic," said Father.

"Dear," said Mother, "Peter isn't five, to be rebuked in front of company." Which, of course, made him seem to be maybe six years old. Thanks so much for helping, Mom.

"Aren't families complicated?" said Sister Carlotta.

Oh, thanks, thou holy bitch, said Peter silently. You and Bean are the ones who complicated the situation, and now you make smug little comments about how much better it is for unconnected people like you. Well, these parents are my *cover*. I didn't pick them, but I have to use them. And for you to mock my situation only shows your ignorance. And, probably, your envy, seeing how you are never going to have children or even get laid in your whole life, Mrs. Jesus.

"Poor Peter has the worst of both worlds," said Mother. "He's the oldest, so he was always held to a higher standard, and yet he's the last of our children left at home, which means he also gets babied more than he can bear. It's so awful, the fact that parents are mere human beings and constantly make mistakes. I think sometimes Peter wishes he had been raised by robots."

Which made Peter want to slide right down into the

sidewalk and spend the rest of his life as an invisible patch of concrete. I converse with spies and military officers, with political leaders and power brokers—and my mother still has the power to humiliate me at will!

"Do what you want," said Father. "It's not like you're a minor. We can't stop you."

"We could never stop him from doing what he wanted even when he *was* a minor," said Mother.

Damn right, thought Peter.

"The curse of having children who are smarter than you," said Father, "is that they think their superior rational process is enough to compensate for their lack of experience."

If I were a little brat like Bean, that comment would have been the last straw. I would have walked away and not come home for a week, if ever. But I'm not a child and I can control my personal resentments and do what's expedient. I'm not going to throw off my camouflage out of pique.

At the same time, I can't be faulted, can I, for wondering if there's any chance that my father might have a stroke and go permanently mute.

They were at the station. With a round of goodbyes, Father and Mother took the bus north toward home, and Peter got on an eastbound bus with Bean and Carlotta.

And, as Peter expected, they got off at the first stop and crossed over to catch the westbound bus. They really made a religion out of paranoia.

Even when they got back to the airport hotel, they did not enter the building. Instead they walked through the shopping mall that had once been a parking garage back when people drove cars to the airport. "Even if they bug the mall," said Bean, "I doubt they can afford the manpower to listen to everything people say."

"If they're bugging your room," said Peter, "that means they're already on to you."

"Hotels routinely bug their rooms," said Bean. "To catch vandals and criminals in the act. It's a computer scan, but nothing stops the employees from listening in."

"This is America," said Peter.

"You spend way too much time thinking about global affairs," said Bean. "If you ever do have to go underground, you won't have a clue how to survive."

"You're the one who invited me to join you in hiding," said Peter. "What was that nonsense about? I'm not going anywhere. I have too much work to do."

"Ah, yes," said Bean. "Pulling the world's strings from behind a curtain. The trouble is, the world is about to move from politics to war, and your strings are going to be snipped."

"It's still politics."

"But the decisions are made on the battlefield, not in the conference rooms."

"I know," said Peter. "That's why we should work together."

"I can't think why," said Bean. "The one thing I asked you for—information about where Petra is—you tried to sell me instead of just giving it to me. Doesn't sound like you want an ally. Sounds like you want a customer."

"Boys," said Sister Carlotta. "Bickering isn't how this is going to work."

"If it's going to work," said Peter, "it's going to work however Bean and I make it work. Between us."

Sister Carlotta stopped cold, grabbed Peter's shoulder, and drew him close. "Get this straight right now, you arrogant twit. You're not the only brilliant person in the world, and you're far from being the only one who thinks he pulls all the strings. Until you have the courage to come out from behind the veil of these ersatz personalities, you don't have much to offer those of us who are working in the real world."

"Don't ever touch me like that again," said Peter.

"Oh, the personage is sacred?" said Sister Carlotta. "You really do live on Planet Peter, don't you?"

Bean interrupted before Peter could answer the bitch. "Look, we gave you everything we had on Ender's jeesh, no strings attached."

"And I used it. I got most of them out, and pretty damn fast, too."

"But not the one who sent the message," said Bean. "I want Petra."

"And I want world peace," said Peter. "You think too small."

"I may think too small for you," said Bean, "but you think too small for me. Playing your little computer games, juggling stories back and forth—well, my friend trusted me and asked me for help. She was trapped with a psychopathic killer and she doesn't have anyone but me who cares a rat's ass what happens to her."

"She has her family," murmured Sister Carlotta. Peter was pleased to learn that she corrected Bean, too. An all-purpose bitch.

"You want to save the world, but you're going to have to do it one battle at a time, one country at a time. And you need people like me, who get our hands dirty," said Bean.

"Oh, spare me your delusions," said Peter. "You're a little boy in hiding."

"I'm a general who's between armies," said Bean. "If I weren't, you wouldn't be talking to me."

"And you want an army so you can go rescue Petra," said Peter.

"So she's alive?"

"How would I know?"

"I don't know how you'd know. But you know more than you're telling me, and if you don't give me what you have, right now, you arrogant oomay, I'm done with you, I'll leave you here playing your little net games, and go find somebody who's not afraid to come out of Mama's house and take some risks."

Peter was almost blind with rage.

For a moment.

And then he calmed himself, forced himself to stand outside the situation. What was Bean showing him? That he cared more for personal loyalty than for longterm strategy. That was dangerous, but not fatal. And it gave Peter leverage, knowing what Bean cared about more than personal advancement.

"What I know about Petra," said Peter, "is that when Achilles disappeared, so did she. My sources inside Russia tell me that the only liberation team that was interfered with was the one rescuing her. The driver, a bodyguard, and the team leader were shot dead. There was no evidence that Petra was injured, though they know she was present for one of the killings."

"How do they know?" asked Bean.

"The spatter pattern from a head shot had been blocked in a silhouette about her size on the inside wall of the van. She was covered with the man's blood. But there was no blood from her body."

"They know more than that."

"A small private jet, which once belonged to a crimelord but was confiscated and used by the intelligence service that sponsored Achilles, took off from a nearby airfield and flew, after a refueling stop, to India. One of the airport maintenance personnel said that it looked to him like a honeymoon trip. Just the pilot and the young couple. But no luggage."

"So he has her with him," said Bean.

"In India," said Sister Carlotta.

"And my sources in India have gone silent," said Peter.

"Dead?" asked Bean.

"No, just careful," said Peter. "The most populous country on Earth. Ancient enmities. A chip on the national shoulder from being treated like a second-class country by everyone."

"The Polemarch is an Indian," said Bean.

"And there's reason to believe he's been passing I.F. data to the Indian military," said Peter. "Nothing that can be proved, but Chamrajnagar is not as disinterested as he pretends to be."

"So you think Achilles may be just what India wants to help them launch a war."

"No," said Peter. "I think India may be just what Achilles wants to help him launch an empire. Petra is what *they* want to help them launch a war."

"So Petra is the passport Achilles used to get into a position of power in India."

"That would be my guess," said Peter. "That's all I know, and all I guess. But I can also tell you that your chance of getting in and rescuing her is nil."

"Pardon me," said Bean, "but you don't know what I'm capable of doing."

"When it comes to intelligence-gathering," said Peter, "the Indians aren't in the same league as the Russians. I don't think your paranoia is needed anymore.

Achilles isn't in a position to do anything to you right now."

"Just because Achilles is in India," said Bean, "doesn't mean that he's limited to knowing only what the Indian intelligence service can find out for him."

"The agency that's been helping him in Russia is being taken over and probably will be shut down," said Peter.

"I know Achilles," said Bean, "and I can promise you—if he really is in India, working for them, then it is absolutely certain that he has already betrayed them and has connections and fallback positions in at least three other places. And at least one of them will have an intelligence service with excellent world-wide reach. If you make the mistake of thinking Achilles is limited by borders and loyalties, he'll destroy you."

Peter looked down at Bean. He wanted to say, I already knew all that. But it would be a lie if he said that. He hadn't known that about Achilles, except in the abstract sense that he tried never to underestimate an opponent. Bean's knowledge of Achilles was better than his. "Thank you," said Peter. "I wasn't taking that into account."

"I know," said Bean ungraciously. "It's one of the reasons I think you're headed for failure. You think you know more than you actually know."

"But I listen," said Peter. "And I learn. Do you?"

Sister Carlotta laughed. "I do believe that the two most arrogant boys in the world have finally met, and they don't much like what they see."

Peter did not even glance at her, and neither did Bean. "Actually," said Peter, "I *do* like what I see."

"I wish I could say the same," said Bean.

"Let's keep walking," said Peter. "We've been standing in one place too long."

"At least he's picking up on our paranoia," said Sister Carlotta.

"Where will India make its move?" asked Peter. "The obvious thing would be war with Pakistan."

"Again?" said Bean. "Pakistan would be an indigestible lump. It would block India from further expansion, just trying to get the Muslims under control. A terrorist war that would make the old struggle with the Sikhs look like a child's birthday party."

"But they can't move anywhere else as long as they have Pakistan poised to plunge a dagger in their back," said Peter.

Bean grinned. "Burma? But is it worth taking?"

"It's on the way to more valuable prizes, if China doesn't object," said Peter. "But are you just ignoring the Pakistan problem?"

"Molotov and Ribbentrop," said Bean.

The men who negotiated the nonaggression pact between Russia and Germany in the 1930s that divided Poland between them and freed Germany to launch World War II. "I think it will have to be deeper than that," said Peter. "I think, at some level, an alliance."

"What if India offers Pakistan a free hand against Iran? It can go for the oil. India is free to move east. To scoop up the countries that have long been under her cultural influence. Burma. Thailand. Not Muslim countries, so Pakistan's conscience is clear."

"Is China going to sit and watch?" asked Peter.

"They might if India tosses them Vietnam," said Bean. "The world is ripe to be divided up among the great powers. India wants to be one. With Achilles directing their strategy, with Chamrajnagar feeding them information, with Petra to command their armies, they can play on the big stage. And then, when Pakistan has exhausted itself fighting Iran . . ."

The inevitable betrayal. If Pakistan didn't strike first. "That's too far down the line to predict now," said Peter.

"But it's the way Achilles thinks," said Bean. "Two betrayals ahead. He was using Russia, but maybe he already had this deal with India in place. Why not? In the long run, the whole world is the tail, and India is the dog."

More important than Bean's particular conclusions was the fact that Bean had a good eye. He lacked detailed intelligence, of course—how would he get that?—but he saw the big picture. He thought the way a global strategist had to think.

He was worth talking to.

"Well, Bean," said Peter, "here's my problem. I think I can get you in position to help block Achilles. But I can't trust you not to do something stupid."

"I won't mount a rescue operation for Petra until I know it will succeed."

"That's a foolish thing to say. You never *know* a military operation will succeed. And that's not what worries me. I'm sure if you mounted a rescue, it would be a well-planned and well-executed one."

"So what worries you about me?" asked Bean.

"That you're making the assumption that Petra wants to be rescued."

"She does," said Bean.

"Achilles seduces people," said Peter. "I've read his files, his history. This kid has a golden voice, apparently. He makes people trust him—even people who know he's a snake. They think, He won't betray *me,* because we have such a special closeness."

"And then he kills them. I know that," said Bean.

"But does Petra? *She* hasn't read his file. *She* didn't know him on the streets of Rotterdam. She didn't even know him in the brief time he was in Battle School."

"She knows him now," said Bean.

"You're sure of that?" asked Peter.

"But I'll promise you—I won't try to rescue her until I've been in communication with her."

Peter mulled this over for a moment. "She might betray you."

"No," said Bean.

"Trusting people will get you killed," said Peter. "I don't want you to bring me down with you."

"You have it backward," said Bean. "I don't trust anybody, except to do what they think is necessary. What they think they have to do. But I know Petra, and I know the kind of thing she'll think she has to do. It's *me* I'm trusting, not her."

"And he can't bring you down," said Sister Carlotta, "because you're not up."

Peter looked at her, making little effort to conceal his contempt. "I am where I am," he said. "And it's not down."

"Locke is where Locke is," said Carlotta. "And Demosthenes. But Peter Wiggin is nowhere. Peter Wiggin is nothing."

"What's your problem?" Peter demanded. "Is it bothering you that your little puppet here might actually be cutting a few of the strings you pull?"

"There are no strings," said Carlotta. "And you're too stupid, apparently, to realize that *I'm* the one who believes in what you're doing, not Bean. He couldn't care less who rules the world. But I do. Arrogant and condescending as you are, I've already made up my mind that if anybody's going to stop Achilles, it's you.

But you're fatally weakened by the fact that you are ripe to be blackmailed by the threat of exposure. Chamrajnagar knows who you are. He's feeding information to India. Do you really think for one moment that Achilles won't find out—and soon, if not already—exactly who is behind Locke? The one who got him booted out of Russia? Do you really think he isn't already working on plans to kill you?"

Peter blushed with shame. To have this nun tell him what he should have realized by himself was humiliating. But she was right—he wasn't used to thinking of physical danger.

"That's why we wanted you to come with us," said Bean.

"Your cover is already blown," said Sister Carlotta.

"The moment I go public as a kid," said Peter Wiggin, "most of my sources will dry up."

"No," said Sister Carlotta. "It all depends on *how* you come out."

"Do you think I haven't thought this through a thousand times?" said Peter. "Until I'm old enough . . ."

"No," said Sister Carlotta. "Think for a minute, Peter. National governments have just gone through a nasty little scuffle over ten *children* that they want to have command their armies. You're the older brother of the greatest of them all. Your youth is an asset. And if you control the way the information comes out, instead of having somebody else expose you . . ."

"It will be a momentary scandal," said Peter. "No matter how my identity comes out, there'll be a flurry of commentary on it, and then I'll be old news—only I'll have been fired from most of my writing gigs. People won't return my calls or answer my mail. I really *will* be a college student then."

"That sounds like something you decided years

ago," said Sister Carlotta, "and haven't looked at with fresh eyes since then."

"Since this seems to be tell-Peter-he's-stupid day, let's hear *your* plan."

Sister Carlotta grinned at Bean. "Well, I was wrong. He actually *can* listen to other people."

"I told you," said Bean.

Peter suspected that this little exchange was designed merely to make him think Bean was on his side. "Just tell me your plan and skip the sucking-up phase."

"The term of the current Hegemon will end in about eight months," said Sister Carlotta. "Let's get several influential people to start floating the name of Locke as the replacement."

"That's your plan? The office of Hegemon is worthless."

"Wrong," said Sister Carlotta, "and wrong. The office is not worthless—eventually you'll have to have it in order to make you the legitimate leader of the world against the threat posed by Achilles. But that's later. Right now, we float the name of Locke, not so you'll get the office, but so that you can have an excuse to publicly announce, as Locke, that you can't be considered for such an office because you are, after all, merely a teenager. *You* tell people that you're Ender Wiggin's older brother, that you and Valentine worked for years to try to hold the League together and to prepare for the League War so that your little brother's victory didn't lead to the self-destruction of humanity. But you are still too young to take an actual office of public trust. See how it works? Now your announcement won't be a confession or a scandal. It will be one more example of how nobly you place the interest of world peace and good order ahead of your own personal ambition."

"I'll still lose some of my contacts," said Peter.

"But not many. The news will be positive. It will have the right spin. All these years, Locke has been the brother of the genius Ender Wiggin. A prodigy."

"And there's no time to waste," said Bean. "You have to do it before Achilles can strike. Because you *will* be exposed within a few months."

"Weeks," said Sister Carlotta.

Peter was furious with himself. "Why didn't I see this? It's obvious."

"You've been doing this for years," said Bean. "You had a pattern that worked. But Achilles has changed everything. You've never had anybody gunning for you before. What matters to me is not that you failed to see it on your own. What matters is that when we pointed it out to you, you were willing to hear it."

"So I've passed your little test?" said Peter nastily.

"Just as I hope I'll pass yours," said Bean. "If we're going to work together, we have to be able to tell each other the truth. Now I know you'll listen to me. You just have to take my word for it that I'll listen to you. But I listen to *her,* don't I?"

Peter was churning with dread. They were right, the time had come, the old pattern was over. And it was frightening. Because now he had to put everything on the line, and he might fail.

But if he didn't act now, if he didn't risk everything, he would certainly fail. Achilles' presence in the equation made it inevitable.

"So how," said Peter, "will we get this groundswell started so I can decline the honor of being a candidate for the Hegemony?"

"Oh, that's easy," said Carlotta. "If you give the OK, then by tomorrow there can be news stories about how a highly placed source at the Vatican confirms that Locke's name is being floated as a possible successor when the current Hegemon's term expires."

"And then," said Bean, "a highly placed officer in the Hegemony—the Minister of Colonization, to be exact, though no one will say that—will be quoted as saying that Locke is not just a good candidate, he's the best candidate, and may be the only candidate, and with the support of the Vatican he thinks Locke is the frontrunner."

"You've planned this all out," said Peter.

"No," said Sister Carlotta. "It's just that the only two people we know are my highly placed friend in the Vatican and our good friend ex-Colonel Graff."

"We're committing all our assets," said Bean, "but they'll be enough. The moment those stories run—tomorrow—you be ready to reply for the next morning's nets. At the same time that everybody's giving their first reactions to your brand-new frontrunner status, the world will be reading your announcement that you refuse to be considered for such an office because your youth would make it too difficult for you to wield the authority that the office of Hegemon requires."

"And that," said Sister Carlotta, "is the very thing that gives you the moral authority to be accepted as Hegemon when the time comes."

"By declining the office," said Peter, "I make it more likely that I'll get it."

"Not in peacetime," said Carlotta. "Declining an office in peacetime takes you out of the running. But there's going to be war. And then the fellow who sacrificed his own ambition for the good of the world will look better and better. Especially when his last name is Wiggin."

Do they have to keep bringing up the fact that my relationship to Ender is more important than my years of work?

"You aren't against using that family connection, are you?" asked Bean.

"I'll do what it takes," said Peter, "and I'll use whatever works. But . . . tomorrow?"

"Achilles got to India yesterday, right?" said Bean. "Every day we delay this is a day that he has a chance to expose you. Do you think he'll wait? You exposed *him*—he'll crave the turnabout, and Chamrajnagar won't be shy about telling him, will he?"

"No," said Peter. "Chamrajnagar has already shown me how he feels about me. He'll do nothing to protect me."

"So here we are once again," said Bean. "We're giving you something, and you're going to use it. Are you going to help me? How can I get into a position where I have troops to train and command? Besides going back to Greece, I mean."

"No, not Greece," said Peter. "They're useless to you, and they'll end up doing only what Russia permits. No freedom of action."

"Where, then?" said Sister Carlotta. "Where do you have influence?"

"In all modesty," said Peter, "at this moment, I have influence everywhere. Day after tomorrow, I may have influence nowhere."

"So let's act now," said Bean. "Where?"

"Thailand," said Peter. "Burma has no hope of resisting an Indian attack, or of putting together an alliance that might have a chance. But Thailand is historically the leader of southeast Asia. The one nation that was never colonized. The natural leader of the

Tai-speaking peoples in the surrounding nations. And they have a strong military."

"But I don't speak the language," said Bean.

"Not a problem," said Peter. "The Thai have been multilingual for centuries, and they have a long history of allowing foreigners to take positions of power and influence in their government, as long as they're loyal to Thailand's interests. You have to throw in your lot with them. They have to trust you. But it seems plain enough that you know how to be loyal."

"Not at all," said Bean. "I'm completely selfish. I survive. That's all I do."

"But you survive," said Peter, "by being absolutely loyal to the few people you depend on. I read just as much about you as I did about Achilles."

"What was written about me reflects the fantasies of the newspeople," said Bean.

"I'm not talking about the news," said Peter. "I read Carlotta's memos to the I.F. about your childhood in Rotterdam."

They both stopped walking. Ah, have I surprised you? Peter couldn't help but take pleasure in knowing that he had shown that he, too, knew some things about *them*.

"Those memos were eyes only," said Carlotta. "There should have been no copies."

"Ah, but whose eyes?" said Peter. "There are no secrets to people with the right friends."

"*I* haven't read those memos," said Bean.

Carlotta looked searchingly at Peter. "Some information is worthless except to destroy," she said.

And now Peter wondered what secrets she had about Bean. Because when he spoke of "memos," he in fact was thinking of a report that had been in Achilles' file, which had drawn on a couple of those memos as a source about life on the streets of Rotterdam. The comments about Bean had been merely ancillary matters. He really hadn't read the actual memos. But now he wanted to, because there was clearly something that she didn't want Bean to know.

And Bean knew it, too.

"What's in those memos that you don't want Peter to tell me?" Bean demanded.

"I had to convince the Battle School people that I was being impartial about you," said Sister Carlotta. "So I had to make negative statements about you in order to get them to believe the positive ones."

"Do you think that would hurt my feelings?" said Bean.

"Yes, I do," said Carlotta. "Because even if you understand the reason why I said some of those things, you'll never forget that I said them."

"They can't be worse than what I imagine," said Bean.

"It's not a matter of being bad or worse. They can't be *too* bad or you wouldn't have got into Battle School, would you? You were too young and they didn't believe your test scores and they knew there wouldn't be time to train you unless you really were . . . what I said. I just don't want you to have my words in your memory. And if you have any sense, Bean, you'll never read them."

"Toguro," said Bean. "I've been gossiped about by the person I trust most, and it's so bad she begs me not to try to find out."

"Enough of this nonsense," said Peter. "We've all faced some nasty blows today. But we've got an alliance started here, haven't we? You're acting in my interest tonight, getting that groundswell started so I can reveal myself on the world's stage. And I've got to get you into Thailand, in a position of trust and influence, before I expose myself as a teenager. Which of us gets to sleep first, do you think?"

"Me," said Sister Carlotta. "Because I don't have any sins on my conscience."

"Kuso," said Bean. "You have all the sins of the world on your mind."

"You're confusing me with somebody else," said Sister Carlotta.

To Peter their banter sounded like family chatter—old jokes, repeated because they're comfortable.

Why didn't his own family have any of that? Peter had bantered with Valentine, but she had never really opened up to him and played that way. She always resented him, even feared him. And their parents were hopeless. There was no clever banter there, there were no shared jokes and memories.

Maybe I really was raised by robots, Peter thought.

"Tell your parents we really appreciated the dinner," said Bean.

"Home to bed," said Sister Carlotta.

"You won't be sleeping in your hotel tonight, will you?" said Peter. "You'll be leaving."

"We'll email you how to contact us," said Bean.

"You'll have to leave Greensboro yourself, you know," said Sister Carlotta. "Once you reveal your identity, Achilles will know where you are. And even though India has no reason to kill you, Achilles does. He kills anyone who has even *seen* him in a position of helplessness. You actually *put* him in that position. You're a dead man, as soon as he can reach you."

Peter thought of the attempt that had been made on Bean's life. "He was perfectly happy to kill your parents right along with you, wasn't he?" Peter asked.

"Maybe," said Bean, "you should tell your mom and dad who you are before they read about it on the nets. And then help them get out of town."

"At some point we have to stop hiding from Achilles and face him openly."

"Not until you have a government committed to keeping you alive," said Bean. "Until then, you stay in hiding. And your parents, too."

"I don't think they'll even believe me," said Peter. "My parents, I mean. When I tell them that I'm really Locke. What parents would? They'll probably try to commit me as delusional."

"Trust them," said Bean. "I think you think they're stupid. But I can assure you that they're not. Or at least your mother isn't. You got your brains from somebody. They'll deal with this."

So it was that when Peter got home at ten o'clock, he went to his parents' room and knocked on their door.

"What is it?" asked Father.

"Are you awake?" Peter asked.

"Come in," said Mother.

They chatted mindlessly for a few minutes about dinner and Sister Carlotta and that delightful little Julian Delphiki, so hard to believe that a child that young could possibly have done all that he had done in his short life. And on and on, until Peter interrupted them.

"I have something to tell you," said Peter. "Tomorrow, some friends of Bean's and Carlotta's will be starting a phony movement to get Locke nominated as Hegemon. You know who Locke is? The political commentator?"

They nodded.

"And the next morning," Peter went on, "Locke is going to come out with a statement that he has to decline such an honor because he's just a teenage boy living in Greensboro, North Carolina."

"Yes?" said Father.

Did they really not get it? "It's me, Dad," said Peter. "I'm Locke."

They looked at each other. Peter waited for them to say something stupid.

"Are you going to tell them that Valentine was Demosthenes, too?" asked Mother.

For a moment he thought she was saying that as a joke, that she thought that the only thing more absurd than Peter being Locke would be Valentine being Demosthenes.

Then he realized that there was no irony in her question at all. It was an important point, and one he needed to address—the contradiction between Locke and Demosthenes had to be resolved, or there *would* still be something for Chamrajnagar and Achilles to expose. And blaming Valentine for Demosthenes right from the start was an important thing to do.

But not as important to him as the fact that Mother knew it. "How long have you known?" he asked.

"We've been very proud of what you've accomplished," said Father.

"As proud as we've ever been of Ender," Mother added.

Peter almost staggered under the emotional blow. They had just told him the thing that he had wanted most to hear his entire life, without ever quite admitting it to himself. Tears sprang to his eyes.

"Thanks," he murmured. Then he closed the door and fled to his room. Somehow, fifteen minutes later, he got enough control of his emotions that he could write the letters he had to write to Thailand, and begin writing his self-exposure essay.

They knew. And far from thinking him a second-rater, a disappointment, they were as proud of him as they had ever been of Ender.

His whole world was about to change, his life would be transformed, he might lose everything, he might win everything. But all he could feel that night, as he finally went to bed and drifted off to sleep, was utter, foolish happiness.

Part Three

MANEUVERS

11

Bangkok

Posted on Military History Forum by HectorVictorious@firewall.net
Topic: Who Remembers Briseis?

When I read the Iliad, I see the same things everyone else does—the poetry, of course, and the information about heroic bronze-age warfare. But I see something else, too. It might have been Helen whose face launched a thousand ships, but it was Briseis who almost wrecked them. She was a powerless captive, a slave, and yet Achilles almost tore the Greek alliance apart because he wanted her.

The mystery that intrigues me is: Was she extraordinarily beautiful? Or was it her mind that Achilles coveted? No, seriously: Would she have been happy for long as Achilles' captive? Would she, perhaps, have gone to him willingly? Or remained a surly, resistant slave?

Not that it would have mattered to Achilles—he would have used his captive the same way, regardless of her feelings. But one imagines Briseis taking note of the tale about Achilles' heel and slipping that information to someone within the walls of Troy . . .

Briseis, if only I could have heard from you!

—Hector Victorious

Bean amused himself by leaving messages for Petra scattered all over the forums that she might visit—if she was alive, if Achilles allowed her to browse the nets, if she realized that a topic heading like "Who Remembers Briseis?" was a reference to her, and if she was free to reply as his message covertly begged her to do. He wooed her under other names of women loved by military leaders: Guinevere, Josephine, Roxane—even Barsine, the Persian wife of Alexander that Roxane murdered soon after his death. And he signed himself with the name of a nemesis or chief rival or successor: Mordred, Hector, Wellington, Cassander.

He took the dangerous step of allowing these identities to continue to exist, each consisting only of a forwarding order to another anonymous net identity that held all mail it received as encrypted postings on an open board with no-tracks protocols. He could visit and read the postings without leaving a trace. But firewalls could be pierced, protocols broken.

He could afford to be a little more careless now about his online identities, if only because his real-world location was now known to people whose trustworthiness he could not assess. Do you worry about the fifth lock on the back door, when the front door is open?

They had welcomed him generously in Bangkok. General Naresuan promised him that no one would know his real identity, that he would be given soldiers to train and intelligence to analyze and his advice would be sought constantly as the Thai military prepared for all kinds of future contingencies. "We are taking seriously Locke's assessment that India will soon pose a threat to Thai security, and we will of course want your help in preparing contingency plans." All so warm and courteous. Bean and Carlotta were installed in a general-officer-level apartment on a military base, given unlimited privileges concerning meals and purchases, and then . . . ignored.

No one called. No one consulted. The promised intelligence did not flow. The promised soldiers were never assigned.

Bean knew better than to even inquire. The promises were not forgotten. If he asked about them, Naresuan would be embarrassed, would feel challenged. That would never do. Something had happened. Bean could only imagine what.

At first, of course, he feared that Achilles had gotten to the Thai government somehow, that his agents now knew exactly where Bean was, that his death was imminent.

That was when he sent Carlotta away.

It was not a pleasant scene. "You should come with me," she said. "They won't stop you. Walk away."

"I'm not leaving," said Bean. "Whatever has gone wrong is probably local politics. Somebody here doesn't like having me around—maybe Naresuan himself, maybe someone else."

"If you feel safe enough to stay," said Sister Carlotta, "then there's no reason for me to go."

"You can't pass yourself off as my grandmother here," said Bean. "The fact that I have a guardian weakens me."

"Spare me the scene you're trying to play," said Carlotta. "I know there are reasons why you'd be better off without me, and I know there are ways that I could help you greatly."

"If Achilles knows where I am already, then his penetration of Bangkok is deep enough that I'll never get away," said Bean. "You might. The information that an older woman is with me might not have reached him yet. But it will soon, and he wants you dead as much as he wants to kill me. I don't want to have to worry about you here."

"I'll go," said Carlotta. "But how do I write to you, since you never keep the same address?"

He gave her the name of his folder on the no-tracks board he was using, and the encryption key. She memorized it.

"One more thing," said Bean. "In Greensboro, Peter said something about reading your memos."

"I think he was lying," said Carlotta.

"I think the way you reacted proved that whether he read them or not, there *were* memos, and you don't want me to read them."

"There were, and I don't," said Carlotta.

"And that's the other reason I want you to leave," said Bean.

The expression on her face turned fierce. "You can't trust me when I tell you that there is nothing in those memos that you need to know right now?"

"I need to know everything about myself. My strengths, my weaknesses. You know things about me that you told Graff and you didn't tell me. You're still not telling me. You think of yourself as my master, able to decide things for me. That means we're not partners after all."

"Very well," said Carlotta. "I am acting in your best interest, but I understand that you don't see it that way." Her manner was cold, but Bean knew her well enough to recognize that it was not anger she was controlling, but grief and frustration. It was a cold thing to do, but for her own sake he had to send her away and keep her from being in close contact with him until he understood what was going on here in Bangkok. The contretemps about the memos made her willing to go. And he really was annoyed.

She was out the door in fifteen minutes and on her way to the airport. Nine hours later he found a posting from her on his encrypted board: She was in Manila, where she could disappear within the Catholic establishment there. Not a word about their quarrel, if that's what it had been. Only a brief reference to "Locke's confession," as the newspeople were calling it. "Poor Peter," wrote Carlotta. "He's been hiding for so long, it's going to be hard for him to get used to having to face the consequences of his words."

To her secure address at the Vatican, Bean replied, "I just hope Peter has the brains to get out of Greensboro. What he needs right now is a small country to run, so he can get some administrative and political experience. Or at least a city water department."

And what I need, thought Bean, is soldiers to command. That's why I came here.

For weeks after Carlotta left, the silence continued. It became obvious, soon enough, that whatever was going on had nothing to do with Achilles, or Bean would be dead by now. Nor could it have had anything to do with Locke being revealed as Peter Wiggin—the freeze-out had already begun before Peter published his declaration.

Bean busied himself with whatever tasks seemed meaningful. Though he had no access to military-level maps, he could still access the publicly available satellite maps of the terrain between India and the heart of Thailand—the rough mountain country of northern and eastern Burma, the Indian Ocean coastal approaches. India had a substantial fleet, by Indian Ocean standards—might they attempt to run the Strait of Malacca and strike at the heart of Thailand from the gulf? All possibilities had to be prepared for.

Some basic intelligence about the makeup of the Indian and Thai military was available on the nets. Thailand had a powerful air force—there was a chance of achieving air dominance, if they could protect their bases. Therefore it would be essential to have the capability of laying down emergency airstrips in a thousand different places, an engineering feat well within the reach of the Thai military—if they trained for it now and dispersed crews and fuel and spare parts throughout the country. That, along with mines, would be the best protection against a coastal landing.

The other Indian vulnerability would be supply lines and lanes of advance. Since India's military strategy would inevitably depend on throwing vast, irresistible armies against the enemy, the defense was to keep those vast armies hungry and harry them constantly from the air and from raiding parties. And if, as was likely, the Indian Army reached the fertile plain of the Chao Phraya or the Aoray Plateau, they had to find the land utterly stripped, the food supplies dispersed and hidden—those that weren't destroyed.

It was a brutal strategy, because the Thai people would suffer along with the Indian Army—indeed, they would suffer more. So the destruction had to be set up so it would only take place at the last minute. And, as much as possible, they had to be able to evacuate women and children to remote areas or even to camps in Laos and Cambodia. Not that borders would stop the Indian army, but terrain might. Having many isolated targets for the Indians would force them to divide their forces. Then—and only then—would it make sense for the Thai military to take on smaller portions of the Indian army in hit-and-run engagements or, where possible, in pitched battles where the Thai side would have temporary numerical parity and superior air support.

Of course, for all Bean knew this was already the longstanding Thai military doctrine and if he made these suggestions he would only annoy them—or make them feel that he had contempt for them.

So he worded his memo very carefully. Lots of phrases like, "No doubt you already have this in place," and "as I'm sure you have long expected." Of course, even those phrases could backfire, if they *hadn't* thought of these things—it would sound patronizing. But he had to do something to break this stalemate of silence.

He read the memo over and over, revising each time.

He waited days to send it, so he could see it in new perspectives. Finally, certain that it was as rhetorically inoffensive as he could make it, he put it into an email and sent it to the Office of the Chakri—the supreme military commander. It was the most public and potentially embarrassing way he could deliver the memo, since mail to that address was inevitably sorted and read by aides. Even printing it out and carrying it by hand would have been more subtle. But the idea was to stir things up; if Naresuan wanted him to be subtle, he would have given him a private email address to write to.

Fifteen minutes after he sent the memo, his door unceremoniously opened and four military police came in. "Come with us, sir," said the sergeant in charge.

Bean knew better than to delay or to ask questions. These men knew nothing but the instructions they had been given, and Bean would find out what those were by waiting to see what they did.

They did not take him to the office of the Chakri. Instead he was taken to one of the temporary buildings that had been set up on the old parade grounds—the Thai military had only recently given up marching as part of the training of soldiers and the display of military might. Only three hundred years after the American Civil War had proven that the days of marching in formation into battle were over. For military organizations, that was about the normal time lag. Sometimes Bean half-expected to find some army somewhere that was still training its soldiers to fight with sabers from horseback.

There was no label, not even a number, on the door they led him to. And when he came inside, none of the soldier-clerks even looked up at him. His arrival was both expected and unimportant, their attitude said. Which meant, of course, that it was *very* important, or they would not be so studiously perfect about not noticing him.

He was led to an office door, which the sergeant opened for him. He went in; the military police did not. The door closed behind him.

Seated at the desk was a major. This was an awfully high rank to have manning a reception desk, but today, at least, that seemed to be the man's duty. He depressed the button on an intercom. "The package is here," he said.

"Send it in." The voice that came back sounded young. So young that Bean understood the situation at once.

Of course. Thailand had contributed its share of military geniuses to Battle School. And even though none of Ender's jeesh had been of Thai parentage, Thailand, like many east and south Asian countries, was overrepresented in the population of Battle School as a whole.

There had even been three Thai soldiers who served with Bean in Dragon Army. Bean remembered every kid in that army very well, along with his complete dossier, since he was the one who had drawn up the list of soldiers who should make up Ender's army. Since most countries seemed to value their returning Battle School graduates in proportion to their closeness to Ender Wiggin, it was most likely one of those three who had been given a position of such influence here that he would be able to intercept a memo to the Chakri so quickly. And of the three, the one Bean would expect to see in the most prominent position, taking the most aggressive role, was . . .

Surrey. Suriyawong. "Surly," as they called him behind his back, since he always seemed to be pissed off about something.

And there he was, standing behind a table covered with maps.

Bean saw, to his surprise, that he was actually almost as tall as Suriyawong. Surrey had not been very big, but everyone towered over Bean in Battle School. Bean was catching up. He might not spend his whole life hopelessly undersized. It was a promising thought.

There was nothing promising about Surrey's attitude, though. "So the colonial powers have decided to use India and Thailand to fight their surrogate wars," he said.

Bean knew at once what had gotten under Suriyawong's skin. Achilles was a Belgian Walloon by birth, and Bean, of course, was Greek. "Yes, of course," said Bean. "Belgium and Greece are bound to fight out their ancient differences on bloody battlefields in Burma."

"Just because you were in Ender's jeesh," said Suriyawong, "does not mean that you have any understanding of the military situation of Thailand."

"My memo was designed to show how limited my knowledge was, because Chakri Naresuan has not provided me with the access to intelligence that he indicated I would receive when I arrived."

"If we ever need your advice, we'll provide you with intelligence."

"If you only provide me with the intelligence you think I need," said Bean, "then my advice will only consist of telling you what you already know, and I might as well go home now."

"Yes," said Suriyawong. "That would be best."

"Suriyawong," said Bean, "you don't really know me."

"I know you were always an emossin' little showoff who always had to be smarter than everybody else."

"I *was* smarter than everybody else," said Bean. "I've got the test scores to prove it. So what? That didn't mean they made me commander of Dragon Army. It didn't mean Ender made me a toon leader. I know just how worthless being smart is, compared with being good at command. I also know just how ignorant I am here in Thailand. I didn't come here because I thought Thailand would be prostrate without my brilliant mind to lead you into battle. I came here because the most dangerous human on this planet is running the show in India and by my best calculations, Thailand is going to be his primary target. I came here because if Achilles is going to be stopped from setting up his tyranny over the world, this is where it has to be done. And I thought, like George Washington in the American revolution, you might actually welcome a Lafayette or a Steuben to help in the cause."

"If your foolish memo was an example of your 'help,' you can leave now."

"So you already have the capability of making temporary airstrips within the amount of time that a fighter is in the air? So they can land at an airstrip that didn't exist when they took off?"

"That *is* an interesting idea and we're having the engineers look at it and evaluate the feasibility."

Bean nodded. "Good. That tells me all I needed to know. I'll stay."

"No, you will not!"

"I'll stay because, despite the fact that you're pissed off that I'm here, you still recognized a good idea when you heard it and put it into play. You're not an idiot, and therefore you're worth working with."

Suriyawong slapped the table and leaned over it, furious. "You condescending little oomay, I'm not your moose."

Bean answered him calmly. "Suriyawong, I don't want your job. I don't want to run things here. I just want to be useful. Why not use me the way Ender did? Give me a few soldiers to train. Let me think of weird things to do and figure out how to do them. Let me be ready so that when the war comes, and there's some impossible thing you need done, you can call me in and say, Bean, I need you to do something to slow down this army for a day, and I've got no troops anywhere near there. And I'll say, Are they drawing water from a river? Good, then let's give their whole army dysentery for a week. That should slow them down. And I'll get in there, get a bioagent into the water, bypass their water purification system, and get out. Or do you already have a water-drugging diarrhea team?"

Suriyawong held his expression of cold anger for a few moments, and then it broke. He laughed. "Come on, Bean, did you make that up on the spot, or have you really planned an operation like that?"

"Made it up just now," said Bean. "But it's kind of a fun idea, don't you think? Dysentery has changed the course of history more than once."

"Everybody immunizes their soldiers against the known bioagents. And there's no way of stopping downstream collateral damage."

"But Thailand is bound to have some pretty hot and heavy bioresearch, right?"

"Purely defensive," said Suriyawong. Then he smiled and sat down. "Sit, sit. You really are content to take a background position?"

"Not only content, but eager," said Bean. "If Achilles knew I was here, he'd find a way to kill me. The last thing I need is to be prominent—until we actually get into combat, at which time it might be a nice psychological blow to give Achilles the idea that I'm running things. It won't be true, but it might make him even crazier to think it's me he's facing. I've outmaneuvered him before. He's afraid of me."

"It's not my own position I was trying to protect," said Suriyawong. Bean understood this to mean that of course it *was* his position he was protecting. "But Thailand kept its independence when every other country in this area was ruled by Europeans. We're very proud of keeping foreigners out."

"And yet," said Bean, "Thailand also has a history of letting foreigners in—and using them effectively."

"As long as they know their place," said Suriyawong.

"Give me a place, and I'll remember to stay in it," said Bean.

"What kind of contingent do you want to work with?"

What Bean asked for wasn't a large number of men, but he wanted to draw them from every branch of service. Only two fighter-bombers, two patrol boats, a handful of engineers, a couple of light armored vehicles to go along with a couple of hundred soldiers and enough choppers to carry everything but the boats and planes. "And the power to requisition odd things that we think of. Rowboats, for instance. High explosives so we can train in making cliffs fall and bridges collapse. Whatever I think of."

"But you don't actually commit to combat without permission."

"Permission," said Bean, "from whom?"

"Me," said Suriyawong.

"But you're not Chakri," said Bean.

"The Chakri," said Suriyawong, "exists to provide me with everything I ask for. The planning is entirely in my hands."

"Glad to know who's aboon here." Bean stood up. "For what it's worth, I was most help to Ender when I had access to everything he knew."

"In your dreams," said Suriyawong.

Bean grinned. "I'm dreaming of good maps," said Bean. "And an accurate assessment of the current situation of the Thai military."

Suriyawong thought about that for a long moment.

"How many of your soldiers are you sending into battle blindfolded?" asked Bean. "I hope I'm the only one."

"Until I'm sure you really are my soldier," said Suriyawong, "the blindfold stays on. But . . . you can have the maps."

"Thank you," said Bean.

He knew what Suriyawong feared: that Bean would use any information he got to come up with alternate strategies and persuade the Chakri that he would do a better job as chief strategist than Suriyawong. For it was patently untrue that Suriyawong was the aboon here. Chakri Naresuan might trust him and had obviously delegated great responsibility to him. But the authority remained in Naresuan's hands, and Suriyawong served at his pleasure. That's why Suriyawong feared Bean—he could be replaced.

He'd find out soon enough that Bean was not interested in palace politics. If he remembered correctly, Suriyawong was of the royal family—though the last few polygynist kings of Siam had had so many children that it was hard to imagine that there were many Thais who were not royal to one degree or another. Chulalongkorn had established the principle, centuries ago, that princes had a duty to serve, but not a right to high office. Suriyawong's life belonged to Thailand as a matter of honor, but he would hold his position in the military only as long as his superiors considered him the best for the job.

Now that Bean knew who it was who had been keeping him down, it would be easy enough to destroy Surrey and take his place. After all, Suriyawong had been given the responsibility to carry out Naresuan's promises to Bean. He had deliberately disobeyed the Chakri's orders. All Bean really needed to do was use a back door—some connection of Peter's, probably—to get word to Naresuan that Suriyawong had blocked Bean from getting what he needed, and there would be an inquiry and the first seeds of doubt about Suriyawong would be planted.

But Bean did not want Suriyawong's job.

He wanted a fighting force that he could train to work together so smoothly, so resourcefully, so brilliantly that when he made contact with Petra and found out where she was, he could go in and get her out alive. With or without Surly's permission. He'd help the Thai military as best he could, but Bean had his own objectives, and they had nothing to do with building a career in Bangkok.

"One last thing," said Bean. "I have to have a name here, something that won't alert anyone outside Thailand that I'm a child and a foreigner—that might be enough to tip off Achilles about who I am."

"What name do you have in mind? How about Süa—it means tiger."

"I have a better name," said Bean. "Borommakot."

Suriyawong looked puzzled for a moment, till he remembered the name from the history of Ayudhya, the ancient Tai city-state of which Siam was the successor. "That was the nickname of the uparat who stole the throne from Aphai, the rightful successor."

"I was just thinking of what the name means," said Bean. " 'In the urn. Awaiting cremation.' " He grinned. "As far as Achilles is concerned, I'm just a walking dead man."

Suriyawong relaxed. "Whatever. I thought as a foreigner you might appreciate having a shorter name."

"Why? I don't have to say it."

"You have to sign it."

"I'm not issuing written orders, and the only person I'll be reporting to is you. Besides, Borommakot is fun to say."

"You know your Thai history," said Suriyawong.

"Back in Battle School," said Bean. "I got fascinated with Thailand. A nation of survivors. The ancient Tai people managed to take over vast reaches of the Cambodian Empire and spread throughout southeast Asia, all without anybody noticing. They were conquered by Burma and emerged stronger than ever. When other countries were falling under European domination, Thailand managed to expand its borders for a surprisingly long time, and even when it lost Cambodia and Laos, it held its core. I think Achilles is going to find what everybody else has found—the Thai are not easily conquered, and, once conquered, not easily ruled."

"Then you have some idea of the soul of the Thai," said Suriyawong. "But no matter how long you study us, you will never be one of us."

"You're mistaken," said Bean. "I already am one of you. A survivor, a free man, no matter what."

Suriyawong took this seriously. "Then as one free

man to another, welcome to the service of Thailand."

They parted amicably, and by the end of the day, Bean saw that Suriyawong intended to keep his word. He was provided with a list of soldiers—four preexisting fifty-man companies with fair records, so they weren't giving him the dregs. And he would have his helicopters, his jets, his patrol boats to train with.

He should have been nervous, preparing to face soldiers who were bound to be skeptical about having him as their commander. But he had been in that situation before, in Battle School. He would win over these soldiers by the simplest expedient of all. Not flattery, not favors, not folksy friendliness. He would win their loyalty by showing them that he knew what to do with an army, so they would have the confidence that when they went into battle, their lives would not be wasted in some doomed enterprise. He would tell them, from the start, "I will never lead you into an action unless I know we can win it. Your job is to become such a brilliant fighting force that there is no action I can't lead you into. We're not in this for glory. We're in this to destroy the enemies of Thailand any way we can."

They'd get used to being led by a little Greek boy soon enough.

12

Islamabad

To: GuillaumeLeBon%Egalite@Haiti.gov
From: Locke%erasmus@polnet.gov
Re: Terms for Consultation

M. LeBon, I appreciate how difficult it was for you to approach me. I believe that I could offer you worthwhile views and suggestions, and, more to the point, I believe you are committed to acting courageously on behalf of the people you govern and therefore any suggestions I made would have an excellent chance of being put into effect.

But the terms you suggest are unacceptable to me. I will not come to Haiti by dark of night or masked as a tourist or student, lest anyone find out that you are consulting a teenage boy from America. I am still the author of every word written by Locke, and it is as that widely known figure, whose name is on the proposals that ended the League War, that I will come openly to consult with you. If my previous reputation were not reason enough for you to be able to invite me openly, then the fact that I am the brother of Ender Wiggin, on whose shoulders the fate of all humanity so recently was placed, should set a precedent you can follow without embarrassment. Not to mention the presence of children from Battle School in almost every military headquarters on Earth. The sum you offered is a princely one. But it will never be paid, for under the terms you suggested, I will not come, and if you invite me openly, I will certainly come but will accept no payment—not even for my expenses while I am in your country. As a foreigner, I could not possibly match your deep and abiding love for the people of Haiti, but I care very much that every nation and people on Earth share in the prosperity and freedom that are their birthright, and I will accept no fee for helping in that cause.

By bringing me openly, you decrease your personal risk, for if my suggestions are unpopular, you can lay the blame on me. And the personal risk I take by coming openly is far greater, for if the world judges my proposals to be unsound or if, in implementing them, you discover them to be unworkable, I will publicly bear the discredit. I speak candidly, because these are realities we both must face: Such is my confidence that my suggestions will be excellent and that you will be able to implement them effectively. When we have finished our work, you can play Cincinnatus and retire to your farm, while I will play Solon and leave the shores of Haiti, both of us confident that we have given your people a fair chance to take their proper place in the world.

Sincerely,
Peter Wiggin

Petra never forgot for an instant that she was a captive and a slave. But, like most captives, like most slaves, as she lived from day to day she became accustomed to her captivity and found ways to be herself within the tight boundaries around her.

She was guarded every moment, and her desk was crippled so she could send no outgoing messages. There would be no repetition of her message to Bean. And even when she saw that someone—could it be Bean, not killed after all?—was trying to speak to her, leaving messages on every military, historical, and geographic forum that spoke about women held in bondage to some warrior or other, she did not let it fret her. She could not answer, so she would waste no time trying.

Eventually the work that was forced on her became a challenge that she found interesting for its own sake. How to mount a campaign against Burma and Thailand and, eventually, Vietnam that would sweep all resistance before it, yet never provoke China to intervene. She saw at once that the vast size of the Indian Army was its greatest weakness, for the supply lines would be impossible to defend. So, unlike the other strategists Achilles was using—mostly Indian Battle School graduates—Petra did not bother with the logistics of a sledgehammer campaign. Eventually the Indian forces would have to divide anyway, unless the Burmese and Thai armies simply lined up to be slaughtered. So she planned an unpredictable campaign—dazzling thrusts by small, mobile forces that could live off the land. The few pieces of mobile armor would race forward, supplied with petrol by air tankers.

She knew her plan was the only one that made sense, and not just because of the intrinsic problems it solved. Any plan that involved putting ten million soldiers so near to the border with China would provoke Chinese intervention. Her plan would never put enough soldiers near China to constitute a threat. Nor would her plan lead to a war of attrition that would leave both sides exhausted and weak. Most of India's strength would remain in reserve, ready to strike wherever the enemy showed weakness.

Achilles gave copies of her plan to the others, of course—he called it "cooperation," but it functioned as an exercise in one-upmanship. All the others had quickly climbed into Achilles' pocket, and now were eager to please him. They sensed, of course, that Achilles wanted Petra humiliated, and duly gave him what he wanted. They mocked her plan as if any fool could see it was hopeless, even though their criticisms were specious and her main points were never even addressed. She bore it, because she was a slave, and because she knew that eventually, some of them were bound to catch on to the way Achilles manipulated them and used them. But she knew that she had done a brilliant job, and it would be a delicious irony if the Indian Army—no, be honest, if Achilles—did not use her plan, and marched head-on to destruction.

It did not bother her conscience to have come up with an effective strategy for Indian expansion in southeast Asia. She knew it would never be used. Even her strategy of small, quick strike forces did not change the fact that India could not afford a two-front war. Pakistan would not let the opportunity pass if India committed itself to an eastern war.

Achilles had simply chosen the wrong country to try to lead into war. Tikal Chapekar, the Indian prime minister, was an ambitious man with delusions of the nobility of his cause. He might very well believe in Achilles' persuasions and long to begin an attempt to "unify" southeast Asia. A war might even begin. But it would founder quickly as Pakistan prepared to attack in the west. Indian adventurism would evaporate as it always had.

She even said as much to Achilles when he visited her one morning after her plans had been so resoundingly rejected by her fellow strategists. "Follow whatever plan you like, nothing will ever work as you think it will."

Achilles simply changed the subject—when he visited her, he preferred to reminisce with her as if they were a couple of old people remembering their childhoods together. Remember this about Battle School? Remember that? She wanted to scream in his face that he had only been there for a few days before Bean had him chained up in an air shaft, confessing to his crimes. He had no right to be nostalgic for Battle School. All he was accomplishing was to poison her own memories of the place, for now when Battle School came up, she just wanted to change the subject, to forget it completely.

Who would have imagined that she would ever think of Battle School as her era of freedom and happiness? It certainly hadn't seemed that way at the time.

To be fair, her captivity was not painful. As long as Achilles was in Hyderabad, she had the run of the base, though she was never unobserved. She could go to the library and do research—though one of her guards had to thumb the ID pad, verifying that she had logged on as herself, with all the restrictions that implied, before she could access the nets. She could run through the dusty countryside that was used for military maneuvers—and sometimes could almost forget the other footfalls keeping syncopated rhythm with her own. She could eat what she wanted, sleep when she wanted. There were times when she almost forgot she wasn't free. There were far more times when, knowing she was not free, she almost decided to stop hoping that her captivity would ever end.

It was Bean's messages that kept her hope alive. She could not answer him, and therefore stopped thinking of his messages as actual communications. Instead they were something deeper than mere attempts at making contact. They were proof that she had not been forgotten. They were proof that Petra Arkanian, Battle

School brat, still had a friend who respected her and cared for her enough to refuse to give up. Each message was a cool kiss to her fevered brow.

And then one day Achilles came to her and told her he was going on a trip.

She assumed at once that this meant she would be confined to her room, locked down and under guard, until Achilles returned.

"No locks this time," said Achilles. "You're coming with me."

"So it's someplace inside India?"

"In one sense yes," said Achilles. "In another, no."

"I'm not interested in your games," she said, yawning. "I'm not going."

"Oh, you won't want to miss this," said Achilles. "And even if you did, it wouldn't matter, because I need you, so you'll be there."

"What can you possibly need me for?"

"Oh, well, when you put it that way, I suppose I should be more precise. I need you to see what takes place at the meeting."

"Why? Unless there's a successful assassination attempt, there's nothing I want to see you do."

"The meeting," said Achilles, "is in Islamabad."

Petra had no smart reply to that. The capital of Pakistan. It was unthinkable. What possible business could Achilles have there? And why would he bring her?

They flew—which of course reminded her of the eventful flight that had brought her to India as Achilles' prisoner. The open door—should I have pulled him out with me and brought him brutally down to earth?

During the flight Achilles showed her the letter he had sent to Ghaffar Wahabi, the "prime minister" of Pakistan—actually, of course, the military dictator . . .

or Sword of Islam, if you preferred it that way. The letter was a marvel of deft manipulation. It would never have attracted any attention in Islamabad, however, if it had not come from Hyderabad, the headquarters of the Indian Army. Even though Achilles' letter never actually said so, it would be assumed in Pakistan that Achilles came as an unofficial envoy of the Indian government.

How many times had an Indian military plane landed at this military airbase near Islamabad? How many times had Indian soldiers in uniform been allowed to set foot on Pakistani soil—bearing their sidearms, no less? And all to carry a Belgian boy and an Armenian girl to talk to whatever lower-level official the Pakistanis decided to fob off on them.

A bevy of stone-faced Pakistani officials led them to a building a short distance from where their plane was being refueled. Inside, on the second floor, the leading official said, "Your escort must remain outside."

"Of course," said Achilles. "But my assistant comes in with me. I must have a witness to remind me in case my memory flags."

The Indian soldiers stood near the wall at full attention. Achilles and Petra walked through the open door.

There were only two people in the room, and she recognized one of them immediately from his pictures. With a gesture, he indicated where they should sit.

Petra walked to her chair in silence, never taking her eyes off Ghaffar Wahabi, the prime minister of Pakistan. She sat beside and slightly behind Achilles, as a lone Pakistani aide sat just at Wahabi's right hand. This was no lower-level official. Somehow, Achilles' letter had opened all the doors, right to the very top.

They needed no interpreter, for Common was, though not their birth language, a childhood acquisition for both of them, and they spoke without accent. Wahabi seemed skeptical and distant, but at least he did not play any humiliation games—he did not keep them waiting, he ushered them into the room himself, and he did not challenge Achilles in any way.

"I have invited you because I wish to hear what you have to say," said Wahabi. "So please begin."

Petra wanted so badly for Achilles to do something horribly wrong—to simper and beam, or to try to strut and show off his intelligence.

"Sir, I'm afraid that it may sound at first as if I am trying to teach Indian history to you, a scholar in that field. It is from your book that I learned everything I'm about to say."

"It is easy to read my book," said Wahabi. "What did you learn from it that I do not already know?"

"The next step," said Achilles. "The step so obvious that I was stunned when you did not take it."

"So this is a book review?" asked Wahabi. But with those words he smiled faintly, to take away the edge of hostility.

"Over and over again, you show the great achievements of the Indian people, and how they are overshadowed, swallowed up, ignored, despised. The civilization of the Indus is treated as a poor also-ran to Mesopotamia and Egypt and even that latecomer China. The Aryan invaders brought their language and religion and imposed it on the people of India. The Moguls, the British, each with their overlay of beliefs and institutions. I must tell you that your book is regarded with great respect in the highest circles of the Indian government, because of the impartial way you treated the religions brought to India by invaders."

Petra knew that this was not idle flattery. For a Pakistani scholar, especially one with political ambitions, to write a history of the subcontinent without praising the Muslim influence and condemning the Hindu religion as primitive and destructive was brave indeed.

Wahabi raised a hand. "I wrote then as a scholar. Now I am the voice of the people. I hope my book has not led you into a quixotic quest for reunification of India. Pakistan is determined to remain pure."

"Please do not leap to conclusions," said Achilles. "I agree with you that reunification is impossible. Indeed, it is a meaningless term. Hindu and Muslim were never united except under an oppressor, so how could they be reunited?"

Wahabi nodded, and waited for Achilles to go on.

"What I saw throughout your account," said Achilles, "was a profound sense of the greatness inherent in the Indian people. Great religions have been born here. Great thinkers have arisen who have changed the world. And yet for two hundred years, when people think of the great powers, India and Pakistan are never on the list. And they never have been. And this makes you angry, and it makes you sad."

"More sad than angry," said Wahabi, "but then, I'm an old man, and my temper has abated."

"China rattles its swords, and the world shivers, but India is barely glanced at. The Islamic world trembles when Iraq or Turkey or Iran or Egypt swings one way or another, and yet Pakistan, stalwart for its entire history, is never treated as a leader. Why?"

"If I knew the answer," said Wahabi, "I would have written a different book."

"There are many reasons in the distant past," said Achilles, "but they all come down to one thing. The Indian people could never act together."

"Again, the language of unity," said Wahabi.

"Not at all," said Achilles. "Pakistan cannot take his rightful place of leadership in the Muslim world, because whenever he looks to the west, Pakistan hears the heavy steps of India behind him. And India cannot take her rightful place as the leader of the east, because the threat of Pakistan looms behind her."

Petra admired the deft way Achilles made his choice of pronouns seem casual, uncalculated—India the woman, Pakistan the man.

"The spirit of God is more at home in India and Pakistan than any other place. It is no accident that great religions have been born here, or have found their purest form. But Pakistan keeps India from being great in the east, and India keeps Pakistan from being great in the west."

"True, but insoluble," said Wahabi.

"Not so," said Achilles. "Let me remind you of another bit of history, from only a few years before Pakistan's creation as a state. In Europe, two great nations faced each other—Stalin's Russia and Hitler's Germany. These two leaders were great monsters. But they saw that their enmity had chained them to each other. Neither could accomplish anything as long as the other threatened to take advantage of the slightest opening."

"You compare India and Pakistan to Hitler and Stalin?"

"Not at all," said Achilles, "because so far, India and Pakistan have shown less sense and less self-control than either of those monsters."

Wahabi turned to his aide. "As usual, India has found a new way to insult us." The aide arose to help him to his feet.

"Sir, I thought you were a wise man," said Achilles.

"There is no one here to see you posture. No one to quote what I have said. You have nothing to lose by hearing me out, and everything to lose by leaving."

Petra was stunned to hear Achilles speak so sharply. Wasn't this taking his non-flatterer approach a little far? Any normal person would have apologized for the unfortunate comparison with Hitler and Stalin. But not Achilles. Well, this time he had surely gone too far. If this meeting failed, his whole strategy would come to nothing, and the tension he was under had led to this misstep.

Wahabi did not sit back down. "Say what you have to say, and be quick," he said.

"Hitler and Stalin sent their foreign ministers, Ribbentrop and Molotov, and despite the hideous denunciations that each had made against the other, they signed a nonaggression pact and divided Poland between them. It's true that a couple of years later, Hitler abrogated this pact, which led to millions of deaths and Hitler's eventual downfall, but that is irrelevant to your situation, because unlike Hitler and Stalin, you and Chapekar are men of honor—you are of India, and you both serve God faithfully."

"To say that Chapekar and I both serve God is blasphemy to one or the other of us, or both," said Wahabi.

"God loves this land and has given the Indian people greatness," said Achilles—so passionately that if Petra had not known better, she might have believed he had some kind of faith. "Do you really believe it is the will of God that both Pakistan and India remain in obscurity and weakness, solely because the people of India have not yet awakened to the will of Allah?"

"I do not care what atheists and madmen say about the will of Allah."

Good for you, thought Petra.

"Nor do I," said Achilles. "But I can tell you this. If you and Chapekar signed an agreement, not of unity, but of nonaggression, you could divide Asia between you. And if the decades pass and there is peace between these two great Indian nations, then will the Hindu not be proud of the Muslim, and the Muslim proud of the Hindu? Will it not be possible then for Hindus to hear the teachings of the Quran, not as the book of their deadly enemy, but rather as the book of their fellow Indians, who share with India the leadership of Asia? If you don't like the example of Hitler and Stalin, then look at Portugal and Spain, ambitious colonizers who shared the Iberian Peninsula. Portugal, to the west, was smaller and weaker—but it was also the bold explorer that opened up the seas. Spain sent one explorer, and he was Italian—but he discovered a new world."

Petra again saw the subtle flattery at work. Without saying so directly, Achilles had linked Portugal—the weaker but braver nation—to Pakistan, and the nation that prevailed through dumb luck to India.

"They might have gone to war and destroyed each other, or weakened each other hopelessly. Instead they listened to the Pope, who drew a line on the earth and gave everything east of it to Portugal and everything west of it to Spain. Draw your line across the Earth, Ghaffar Wahabi. Declare that you will not make war against the great Indian people who have not yet heard the word of Allah, but will instead show to all the world the shining example of the purity of Pakistan. While in the meantime, Tikal Chapekar will unite eastern Asia under Indian leadership, which they have long hungered for. Then, in the happy day when the Hindu people heed the Book, Islam will spread in one breath from New Delhi to Hanoi."

Wahabi slowly sat back down.

Achilles said nothing.

Petra knew then that his boldness had succeeded.

"Hanoi," said Wahabi. "Why not Beijing?"

"On the day that the Indian Muslims of Pakistan are made guardians of the sacred city, on that day the Hindus may imagine entering the forbidden city."

Wahabi laughed. "You are outrageous."

"I am," said Achilles. "But I'm right. About everything. About the fact that this is what your book was pointing to. That this is the obvious conclusion, if only India and Pakistan are blessed to have, at the same time, leaders with such vision and courage."

"And why does this matter to you?" said Wahabi.

"I dream of peace on Earth," said Achilles.

"And so you encourage Pakistan and India to go to war?"

"I encourage you to agree *not* to go to war with each other."

"Do you think Iran will peacefully accept Pakistan's leadership? Do you think the Turks will embrace us? It will have to be by conquest that we create this unity."

"But you *will* create it," said Achilles. "And when Islam is united under Indian leadership, it will no longer be humiliated by other nations. One great Muslim nation, one great Hindu nation, at peace with each other and too powerful for any other nation to dare to attack. That is how peace comes to Earth. God willing."

"Inshallah," echoed Wahabi. "But now it is time for me to know by what authority you say these things. You hold no office in India. How do I know you have not been sent to lull me while Indian armies amass for yet another unprovoked assault?"

Petra wondered if Achilles had planned to get Wahabi to say something so precisely calculated to give him the perfect dramatic moment, or if it was just chance. For Achilles' only answer to Wahabi was to draw from his portfolio a single sheet of paper, bearing a small signature at the bottom in blue ink.

"What is that?" said Wahabi.

"My authority," said Achilles. He handed the paper to Petra. She arose and carried it to the middle of the room, where Wahabi's aide took it from her hand.

Wahabi perused it, shaking his head. "And this is what he signed?"

"He more than signed it," said Achilles. "Ask your satellite team to tell you what the Indian Army is doing even as we speak."

"They are withdrawing from the border?"

"Someone has to be the first to offer trust. It's the opportunity you've been waiting for, you and all your predecessors. The Indian Army is withdrawing. You could send your troops forward. You could turn this gesture of peace into a bloodbath. Or you could give the orders to move your troops west and north. Iran is waiting for you to show them the purity of Islam. The Caliphate of Istanbul is waiting for you to unshackle it from the chains of the secular government of Turkey. Behind you, you will have only your brother Indians, wishing you well as you show the greatness of this land that God has chosen, and that finally is ready to rise."

"Save the speech," said Wahabi. "You understand that I have to verify that this signature is genuine, and that the Indian troops are moving in the direction that you say."

"You will do what you have to do," said Achilles. "I will return to India now."

"Without waiting for my answer?"

"I haven't asked you a question," said Achilles.

"Tikal Chapekar has asked that question, and it is to him you must give your answer. I am only the messenger."

With that, Achilles rose to his feet. Petra did, too. Achilles strode boldly to Wahabi and offered his hand. "I hope you will forgive me, but I could not bear to return to India without being able to say that the hand of Ghaffar Wahabi touched mine."

Wahabi reached out and took Achilles' hand. "Foreign meddler," said Wahabi, but his eyes twinkled, and Achilles smiled in reply.

Could this possibly have *worked*? Petra wondered. Molotov and Ribbentrop had to negotiate for weeks, didn't they? Achilles did this in a single meeting.

What were the magic words?

But as they walked out of the room, escorted again by the four Indian soldiers who had come with them—her guards—Petra realized there had been no magic words. Achilles had simply studied both men and recognized their ambitions, their yearning for greatness. He had told them what they most wanted to hear. He gave them the peace that they had secretly longed for.

She had not been there for the meeting with Chapekar that led to Achilles' getting that signed nonaggression pact and the promise to withdraw, but she could imagine it. "You must make the first gesture," Achilles must have said. "It's true that the Muslims might take advantage of it, might attack. But you have the largest army in the world, and govern the greatest people. Let them attack, and you will absorb the blow and then return to roll over them like water bursting from a dam. And no one will criticize you for taking a chance on peace."

And now it finally struck home. The plans she had

been drawing up for the invasion of Burma and Thailand were not mere foolery. They would be used. Hers or someone else's. The blood would begin to flow. Achilles would get his war.

I didn't sabotage my plans, she realized. I was so sure they could not be used that I didn't bother to build weaknesses into them. They might actually work.

What have I done?

And now she understood why Achilles had brought her along. He wanted to strut in front of her, of course—for some reason, he felt the need to have someone witness his triumphs. But it was more than that. He also wanted to rub her face in the fact that he was actually going to do what she had so often said could not be done.

Worst of all, she found herself hoping that her plan would be used, not because she wanted Achilles to win his war, but because she wanted to stick it to the other Battle School brats who had mocked her plan so mercilessly.

I have to get word to Bean somehow. I have to warn him, so he can get word to the governments of Burma and Thailand. I have to do something to subvert my own plan of attack, or their destruction will be on my shoulders.

She looked at Achilles, who was dozing in his seat, oblivious to the miles racing by beneath him, returning him to the place where his wars of conquest would begin. If she could only remove his murders from the equation, on balance he would be quite a remarkable boy. He was a Battle School discard with the label "psychopath" attached to him, and yet somehow he had gotten not one but three major world governments to do his bidding.

I was a witness to this most recent triumph, and I'm still not sure how he brought it off.

She remembered the story from her childhood, about Adam and Eve in the garden, and the talking snake. Even as a little girl she had said—to the consternation of her family—What kind of idiot was Eve, to believe a snake? But now she understood, for she had heard the voice of the snake and had watched as a wise and powerful man had fallen under its spell.

Eat the fruit and you can have the desires of your heart. It's not evil, it's noble and good. You'll be praised for it.

And it's delicious.

13

Warnings

To: Carlotta%agape@vatican.net/orders/sisters/ind
From: Graff%bonpassage@colmin.gov
Re: Found?

I think we've found Petra. A good friend in Islamabad who is aware of my interest in finding her tells me that a strange envoy from New Delhi came for a brief meeting with Wahabi yesterday—a teenage boy who could only be Achilles; and a teenage girl of the right description who said nothing. Petra? I think it likely.

Bean needs to know what I've learned. First, my friend tells me that this meeting was almost immediately followed by orders to the Pakistani military to move back from the border with India. Couple that with the already-noted Indian removal from that frontier, and I think we're witnessing the impossible—after two centuries of intermittent but chronic warfare, a real attempt at peace. And it seems to have been done by or with the help of Achilles. (Since so many of our colonists are Indian, there are those in my ministry who fear that an outbreak of peace on the subcontinent might jeopardize our work!)

Second, for Achilles to bring Petra along on this sensitive mission implies that she is not an unwilling participant in his projects. Given that in Russia Vlad also was seduced into working with Achilles, however briefly, it is not unthinkable that even as confirmed a skeptic as Petra might have become a true believer while in captivity. Bean must be made aware of this possibility, for he may be hoping to rescue someone who does not wish to be rescued.

Third, tell Bean that I can make contacts in Hyderabad, among former Battle School students working in the Indian high command. I will not ask them to compromise their loyalty to their country, but I will ask about Petra and find out what, if anything, they have seen or heard. I think old school loyalty may trump patriotic secrecy on this point.

Bean's little strike force was all that he could have hoped for. These were not elite soldiers the way Battle School students had been—they were not selected for the ability to command. But in some ways this made them easier to train. They weren't constantly analyzing and second-guessing. In Battle School, too, many soldiers kept trying to show off to everyone, so they could enhance their reputation in the school—commanders constantly had to struggle to keep their soldiers focused on the overall goal of the army.

Bean knew from his studies that in real-world armies, the opposite was more usually the problem—that soldiers tried *not* to do brilliantly at anything, or learn too quickly, for fear of being thought a suckup or show-off by their fellow soldiers. But the cure for both problems was the same. Bean worked hard to earn a reputation for tough, fair judgment.

He played no favorites, made no friends, but always noticed excellence and commented on it. His praise, however, was not effusive. Usually he would simply make a note about it in front of others. "Sergeant, your team made no mistakes." Only when an accomplishment was exceptional did he praise it explicitly, and then only with a terse "Good."

As he expected, the rarity of his praise as well as its fairness soon made it the most valued coin in his strike force. Soldiers who did good work did not have special privileges and were given no special authority, so they were not resented by the others. The praise was not effusive, so it never embarrassed them. Instead, they were admired by the others, and emulated. And the focus of the soldiers became the earning of Bean's recognition.

That was true power. Frederick the Great's dictum that soldiers had to fear their officers more than they feared the enemy was stupid. Soldiers needed to believe they had the respect of their officers, and to value that respect more than they valued life itself. Moreover, they had to know that their officers' respect was justified—that they really were the good soldiers their officers believed them to be.

In Battle School, Bean had used his brief time in command of an army to teach himself—he led his men to defeat every time, because he was more interested in learning what he could learn than in racking up points. This was demoralizing to his soldiers, but he didn't care—he knew that he would not be with them long, and that the time of the Battle School was nearly over. Here in Thailand, though, he knew that the battles coming up were real, the stakes high, and his soldiers' lives would be on the line. Victory, not information, was the goal.

And, behind that obvious motive, there lay an even deeper one. Sometime in the coming war—or even before, if he was lucky—he would be using a portion of this strike force to make a daring rescue attempt, probably deep inside India. There would be zero tolerance for error. He *would* bring Petra out. He *would* succeed.

He drove himself as hard as he drove any of his men. He made it a point to train alongside them—a child going through all the exercises the men went through. He ran with them, and if his pack was lighter it was only because he needed to carry fewer calories in order to survive. He had to carry smaller, lighter weapons, but no one begrudged him that—besides, they saw that his bullets went to the mark as often as theirs. There was nothing he asked them to do that he did not do himself. And when he was not as good as his men, he had no qualms about going to one of the best of them and asking him for criticism and advice—which he then followed.

This was unheard of, for a commander to risk allowing himself to appear unskilled or weak in front of his men. And Bean would not have done it, either, because the benefits did not usually outweigh the risks. However, he was planning to go along with them on difficult maneuvers, and his training had been theoretical and game-centered. He had to become a soldier, so he could be there to deal with problems and emergencies during operations, so he could keep up with them, and so that, in a pinch, he could join effectively in a fight.

At first, because of his youth and small stature, some of the soldiers had tried to make things easier for him. His refusal had been quiet but firm. "I have to learn this too," he would say, and that was the end of the discussion. Naturally, the soldiers watched him all the more intensely, to see how he measured up to the high standard he set for them. They saw him tax his body to the utmost. They saw that he shrank from nothing, that he came out of mudwork slimier than anyone, that he went over obstacles just as high as anyone's, that he ate no better food and slept on no better a patch of ground on maneuvers.

They did not see how much he modeled this strike force on the Battle School armies. With two hundred men, he divided them into five companies of forty. Each company, like Ender's Battle School army, was divided into five toons of eight men each. Every toon was expected to be able to carry out operations entirely on its own; every company was expected to be able to deal with complete independence. At the same time, he made sure that they became skilled observers, and trained them to see the kinds of things he needed them to see.

"You are my eyes," he said. "You need to see what I would look for *and* what you would see. I will always tell you what I am planning and why, so you will know if you see a problem I didn't anticipate, which might change my plan. Then you will make sure I know. My best chance of keeping you all alive is to know everything that is in your heads during battle, just as your best chance of staying alive is to know everything that is in my head."

Of course, he knew that he could not tell them everything. No doubt they understood this as well. But he spent an inordinate amount of time, by standard military doctrine, telling his men the reasoning behind his orders, and he expected his company and toon commanders to do the same with their men. "That way, when we give you an order without any reasons, you will know that it's because there's no time for explanation, that you must act now—but that there *is* a good reason, which we *would* tell you if we could."

Once when Suriyawong came to observe his training of his troops, he asked Bean if this was how he recommended training soldiers throughout the whole army.

"Not a chance," said Bean.

"If it works for you, why wouldn't it work everywhere?"

"Usually you don't need it and can't afford the time," said Bean.

"But you can?"

"These soldiers are going to be called on to do the impossible. They aren't going to be sent to hold a position or advance against an enemy posting. They're going to be sent to do difficult, complicated things right under the eyes of the enemy, under circumstances where they can't go back for new instructions but have to adapt and succeed. That is impossible if they don't understand the purpose behind all their orders. And they have to know exactly how their commanders think so that trust is perfect—and so they can compensate for their commanders' inevitable weaknesses."

"*Your* weaknesses?" asked Suriyawong.

"Hard to believe, Suriyawong, but yes, I have weaknesses."

That earned a faint smile from Surly—a rare prize. "Growing pains?" asked Suriyawong.

Bean looked down at his ankles. He had already had new uniforms made twice, and it was time for a third go. He was almost as tall now as Suriyawong had been when Bean first arrived in Bangkok half a year before. Growing caused him no pain. But it worried him, since it seemed unconnected with any other sign of puberty. Why, after all these years of being undersized, was his body now so determined to catch up?

He experienced none of the problems of adolescence—not the clumsiness that comes from having limbs that swing farther than they used to, not the rush of hormones that clouded judgment and distracted attention. So if he grew enough to carry better weapons, that could only be a plus.

"Someday I hope to be as fine a man as you," said Bean.

Suriyawong grunted. He knew that Surly would

take it as a joke. He also knew that, somewhere deeper than consciousness, Suriyawong would also take it at face value, for people always did. And it was important for Suriyawong to have the constant reassurance that Bean respected his position and would do nothing to undermine him.

That had been months ago, and Bean was able to report to Suriyawong a long list of possible missions that his men had been trained for and could perform at any time. It was his declaration of readiness.

Then came the letter from Graff. Carlotta forwarded it to him as soon as she got it. Petra was alive. She was probably with Achilles in Hyderabad.

Bean immediately notified Suriyawong that an intelligence source of a friend of his verified an apparent nonaggression pact between India and Pakistan, and a movement of troops away from the shared border—along with his opinion that this guaranteed an invasion of Burma within three weeks.

As to the other matters in the letter, Graff's assertion that Petra might have gone over to Achilles' cause was, of course, absurd—if Graff believed that, he didn't know Petra. What alarmed Bean was that she had been so thoroughly neutralized that she could *seem* to be on Achilles' side. This was the girl who always spoke her mind no matter how much abuse it caused to come down on her head. If she had fallen silent, it meant she was in despair.

Isn't she getting my messages? Has Achilles cut her off from information so thoroughly that she doesn't even roam the nets? That would explain her failure to answer. But still, Petra was used to standing alone. That wouldn't explain her silence.

It had to be her own strategy for mastery. Silence, so

that Achilles would forget how much she hated him. Though surely she knew him well enough by now to know that he never forgot anything. Silence, so that she could avoid even deeper isolation—that was possible. Even Petra could keep her mouth shut if every time she spoke up it cut her off from more and more information and opportunities.

Finally, though, Bean had to entertain the possibility that Graff was right. Petra was human. She feared death like anyone else. And if she had, in fact, witnessed the death of her two guardians in Russia, and if Achilles had committed the killings with his own hands—which Bean believed likely—then Petra was facing something she had never faced before. She could speak up to idiotic commanders and teachers in Battle School because the worst that could happen was reprimands. With Achilles, what she had to fear was death.

And the fear of death changed the way a person saw the world, Bean knew that. He had lived his first years of life under the constant pressure of that fear. Moreover, he had spent a considerable time specifically under Achilles' power. Even though he never forgot the danger Achilles posed, even Bean had come to think Achilles wasn't such a bad guy, that in fact he was a good leader, doing brave and bold things for his "family" of street urchins. Bean had admired him and learned from him—right up to the moment when Achilles murdered Poke.

Petra, fearing Achilles, submitting to his power, had to watch him closely just to stay alive. And, watching him, she would come to admire him. It's a common trait of primates to become submissive and even worshipful toward one who has the power to kill them.

Even if she fought off those feelings, they would still be there.

But she'll awaken from it, when she's out from under that power. I did. She will. So even if Graff is right, and Petra has become something of a disciple to Achilles, she will turn heretic once I get her out.

Still, the fact remained—he had to be prepared to bring her out even if she resisted rescue or tried to betray them.

He added dartguns and will-bending drugs to his army's arsenal and training.

Naturally, he would need more hard data than he had if he was to mount an operation to rescue her. He wrote to Peter, asking him to use some of his old Demosthenes contacts in the U.S. to get what intelligence data they had on Hyderabad. Beyond that, Bean really had no resources to tap without giving away his location. Because it was a sure thing that he couldn't ask Suriyawong for information about Hyderabad. Even if Suriyawong was feeling favorably disposed—and he *had* been sharing more information with Bean lately—there was no way to explain why he could possibly need information about the Indian high command base at Hyderabad.

Only after days of waiting for Peter, while training his men and himself in the use of darts and drugs, did Bean realize another important implication of discovering that Petra might actually be cooperating with Achilles. Because none of their strategy was geared to the kind of campaign Petra might design.

He requested a meeting with both Suriyawong and the Chakri. After all these months of never seeing the Chakri's face, he was surprised that the meeting was granted—and without delay. He sent his request when he got up at five in the morning. At seven, he was in the Chakri's office, with Suriyawong beside him.

Suriyawong only had time to mouth, with annoyance, the words "What is this?" before the Chakri started the meeting.

"What is this?" said the Chakri. He smiled at Suriyawong; he knew he was echoing Suriyawong's question. But Bean also knew that it was a smile of mockery. You couldn't control this Greek boy after all.

"I just found out information that you both need to know," said Bean. Of course, this implied that Suriyawong might not have recognized the importance of the information, so that Bean had to bring it to Chakri Naresuan directly. "I meant no lack of respect. Only that you must be aware of this immediately."

"What possible information can you have," said Chakri Naresuan, "that we don't already know?"

"Something that I learned from a well-connected friend," said Bean. "All our assumptions were based on the idea of the Indian Army using the obvious strategy—to overwhelm Burmese and Thai defenses with huge armies. But I just learned that Petra Arkanian, one of Ender Wiggin's jeesh, may be working with the Indian Army. I never thought she would collaborate with Achilles, but the possibility exists. And if she's directing the campaign, it won't be a flood of soldiers at all."

"Interesting," said the Chakri. "What strategy would she use?"

"She would still overwhelm you with numbers, but not with massed armies. Instead there would be probing raids, incursions by smaller forces, each one designed to strike, draw your attention, and then fade. They don't even have to retreat. They just live off the land until they can re-form later. Each one is easily beaten, except that there's nothing to beat. By the time we get there, they're gone. No supply lines. No vulnerabilities, just probe after probe until we can't respond to them all. Then the probes start getting bigger. When we get there, with our thinly stretched forces, the enemy is waiting. One of our groups destroyed, then another."

The Chakri looked at Suriyawong. "What Borommakot says is possible," said Suriyawong. "They can keep up such a strategy forever. We never damage them, because they have an infinite supply of troops, and they risk little on each attack. But every loss we suffer is irreplaceable, and every retreat gives them ground."

"So why wouldn't this Achilles think of such a strategy on his own?" asked the Chakri. "He's a very bright boy, they say."

"It's a cautious strategy," said Bean. "One that is very frugal with the lives of the soldiers. And it's slow."

"And Achilles is never careful with the lives of his soldiers?"

Bean thought back to his days in Achilles' "family" on the streets of Rotterdam. Achilles was, in fact, careful of the lives of the other children. He took great pains to make sure they were not exposed to risk. But that was because his power base absolutely depended on losing none of them. If any of the children had been hurt, the others would have melted away. That would not be the case with the Indian Army. Achilles would spend them like autumn leaves.

Except that Achilles' goal was not to rule India. It was to rule the world. So it did matter that he earn a reputation as a beneficent leader. That he seem to value the lives of his people.

"Sometimes he is, when it suits him," said Bean. "That's why he would follow such a plan if Petra outlined it for him."

"So what would it mean," said the Chakri, "if I told you that the attack on Burma has just been launched, and it is a massive frontal assault by huge Indian forces, just as you originally outlined in your first memo to us?"

Bean was stunned. Already? The apparent nonaggression pact between India and Pakistan was only a few days old. They could not possibly have amassed troops that quickly.

Bean was surprised to see that Suriyawong also had been unaware that war had begun.

"It was an extremely well-planned campaign," said the Chakri. "The Burmese only had a day's warning. The Indian troops moved like smoke. Whether it is your evil friend Achilles or your brilliant friend Petra or the mere simpletons of the Indian high command, they managed it superbly."

"What it means," said Bean, "is that Petra is not being listened to. Or that she is deliberately sabotaging the Indian Army's strategy. I'm relieved to know this, and I apologize for raising a warning that was not needed. May I ask, sir, if Thailand is coming into the war now?"

"Burma has not asked for help," said the Chakri.

"By the time Burma asks Thailand for help," said Bean, "the Indian Army will be at our borders."

"At that point," said the Chakri, "we will not wait for them to ask."

"What about China?" asked Bean.

The Chakri blinked twice before answering. "What about China?"

"Have they warned India? Have they responded in any way?"

"Matters with China are handled by a different branch of government," said the Chakri.

"India may have twice the population of China," said Bean, "but the Chinese Army is better equipped. India would think twice before provoking Chinese intervention."

"Better equipped," said the Chakri. "But is it deployed in a usable way? Their troops are kept along the Russian border. It would take weeks to bring them down here. If India plans a lightning strike, they have nothing to fear from China."

"As long as the I.F. keeps missiles from flying," said Suriyawong. "And with Chamrajnagar as Polemarch, you can be sure no missiles will attack India."

"Oh, that's another new development," said the Chakri. "Chamrajnagar submitted his resignation from the I.F. ten minutes after the attack on Burma was launched. He will return to Earth—to India—to accept his new appointment as leader of a coalition government that will guide the newly enlarged Indian empire. For of course, by the time a ship can bring him back to Earth, the war will be over, one way or another."

"Who is the new Polemarch?" asked Bean.

"That is the dilemma," said the Chakri. "There are those who wonder whom the Hegemon can nominate, considering that no one can quite trust anyone now. Some are wondering why the Hegemon should name a Polemarch at all. We've done without a Strategos since the League War. Why do we need the I.F. at all?"

"To keep the missiles from flying," said Suriyawong.

"That is the only serious argument in favor of keeping the I.F.," said the Chakri. "But many governments believe that the I.F. should be reduced to the role of policing above the atmosphere. There is no reason for any but a tiny fraction of the I.F.'s strength to be retained. And as for the colonization program, many are saying it is a waste of money, when war is erupting here on Earth. Well, enough of this little school class. There is grown-up work to be done. You will be consulted if we find that you are needed."

The Chakri's dismissive air was surprising. It revealed a high level of hostility to both of these Battle School graduates, not just the foreign one.

It was Suriyawong who challenged the Chakri on this. "Under what circumstances would we be called upon?" he asked. "Either the plans I drew up will work or they won't. If they work, you won't call on me. If they don't, you'll regard that as proof that I didn't know what I was doing, and you still won't call on me."

The Chakri pondered this for a few moments. "Why, I'd never thought of it that way. I believe you're right."

"No, you're wrong," said Suriyawong. "Nothing ever goes as planned during a war. We have to be able to adapt. I and the other Battle School graduates are trained for that. We should be kept informed of every development. Instead, you have cut me off from the intelligence that is flowing in. I should have seen this information the moment I woke up and looked at my desk. Why are you cutting me off?"

For the same reason you cut *me* off, Bean thought. So that when victory comes, all the credit can flow to the Chakri. "The Battle School children advised in the planning stages, but of course during the actual war, we did not leave it up to the children." And if things went badly, "We faithfully executed the plans drawn up by the Battle School children, but apparently schoolwork did not prepare them for the real world." The Chakri was covering his ass.

Suriyawong seemed to understand this also, for he gave no more argument. He arose. "Permission to leave, sir," he said.

"Granted. To you, too, Borommakot. Oh, and we'll probably be taking back the soldiers Suriyawong gave you to play with. Restoring them to their original units. Please prepare them to leave at once."

Bean also rose to his feet. "So Thailand is entering the war?"

"You will be informed of anything you need to know, when you need to know it."

As soon as they were outside the Chakri's office, Suriyawong sped up his pace. Bean had to run to catch up.

"I don't want to talk to you," said Suriyawong.

"Don't be a big baby about it," said Bean scornfully. "He's only doing to you what you already did to me. Did I run off and pout?"

Suriyawong stopped and whirled on Bean. "You and your stupid meeting!"

"He already cut you off," said Bean. "Already. Before I even asked to meet."

Suriyawong knew that Bean was right. "So I'm stripped of influence."

"And I never had any," said Bean. "What are we going to do about it?"

"Do?" said Suriyawong. "If the Chakri forbids it, no one will obey my orders. Without authority, I'm just a boy, still too young to enlist in the army."

"What we'll do first," said Bean, "is figure out what this all means."

"It means the Chakri is an oomay careerist," said Suriyawong.

"Come, let's walk out of the building."

"They can draw our words out of the open air, too, if they want," said Suriyawong.

"They have to *try* to do that. Here, anything we say is automatically recorded."

So Suriyawong walked with Bean out of the building that housed the highest of the Thai high command, and together they wandered toward the married officers' housing, to a park with playground equipment for the children of junior officers. When they sat on the swings, Bean realized that he was actually getting a little too big for them.

"Your strike force," said Suriyawong. "Just when it might have been most needed, it'll be dispersed."

"No it won't," said Bean.

"And why not?"

"Because you drew it from the garrison protecting the capital. Those troops won't be sent away. So they'll remain in Bangkok. The important thing is to keep all our matériel together and within easy reach. Do you think you still have authority for that?"

"As long as I call it routine cycling into storage," said Suriyawong, "I suppose so."

"And you'll know where these men are assigned, so when we need to, we can call them back to us."

"If I try that, I'll be cut off from the net," said Suriyawong.

"If we try that," said Bean, "it will be because the net doesn't matter."

"Because the war is lost."

"Think about it," said Bean. "Only a stupid careerist would openly disdain you like this. He *wanted* to shame and discourage you. Have you given him some offense?"

"I always give offense," said Suriyawong. "That's

why everyone called me Surly behind my back in Battle School. The only person I know who *is* more arrogant than I *seem* is you."

"Is Naresuan a fool?" asked Bean.

"I had not thought so," said Suriyawong.

"So this is a day for people who are not fools to act like fools."

"Are you saying I am also a fool?"

"I was saying that Achilles is apparently a fool."

"Because he is attacking with massed forces? You told us that was what we should expect. Apparently Petra did not give him the better plan."

"Or he's not using it."

"But he'd have to be a fool not to use it," said Suriyawong.

"So *if* Petra gave him the better plan, and he declined to use it, then he *and* the Chakri are both fools today. As when the Chakri pretended that he has no influence over foreign policy."

"About China, you mean?" Suriyawong thought about this for a moment. "You're right, of course he has influence. But perhaps he simply didn't want us to know what the Chinese were doing. Perhaps that was why he was so sure he didn't need us, that he didn't need to enter Burma. Because he *knows* the Chinese are coming in."

"So," said Bean. "While we sit here, watching the war, we will learn much from the plain events as they unfold. If China intervenes to stop the Indians before Achilles ever gets to Thailand, then we know Chakri Naresuan is a smart careerist, not a stupid one. But if China does not intervene, then we have to wonder why Naresuan, who is not a foolish man, has chosen to act like one."

"What do you suspect him of?" asked Suriyawong.

"As for Achilles," said Bean, "no matter how we construe these events, he has been a fool."

"No, he's only a fool if Petra actually gave him the better plan and he's ignoring it."

"On the contrary," said Bean. "He's a fool no matter what. To enter into this war with even the possibility that China will intervene, that is foolish in the extreme."

"So perhaps he knows that China will not intervene, and then the Chakri would be the only fool," said Suriyawong.

"Let's watch and see."

"I'll watch and grind my teeth," said Suriyawong.

"Watch with me," said Bean. "Let's drop this stupid competition between us. You care about Thailand. I care about figuring out what Achilles is doing and stopping him. At this moment, those two concerns coincide almost perfectly. Let's share everything we know."

"But you know nothing."

"I know nothing that *you* know," said Bean. "And you know nothing that I know."

"What can you possibly know?" said Suriyawong. "I'm the eemo who cut you off from the intelligence net."

"I knew about the deal between India and Pakistan."

"So did we."

"But you didn't tell me," said Bean. "And yet I knew."

Suriyawong nodded. "Even if the sharing is mostly one way, from me to you, it's long overdue, don't you think?"

"I'm not interested in what's early or late," said Bean. "Only what happens next."

They went to the officers' mess and had lunch, then walked back to Suriyawong's building, dismissed his staff for the rest of the day, and, with the building to themselves, sat in Suriyawong's office and watched the progress of the war on Worldnet. Burmese resistance was brave but futile.

"Poland in 1939," said Bean.

"And here in Thailand," said Suriyawong, "we're being as timid as France and England."

"At least China isn't invading Burma from the north, the way Russia invaded Poland from the east," said Bean.

"Small mercies," said Suriyawong.

But Bean wondered. Why *doesn't* China step in? Beijing wasn't saying anything to the press. No comment, about a war on their doorstep? What does China have up its sleeve?

"Maybe Pakistan wasn't the only country to sign a nonaggression pact with India," said Bean.

"Why? What would China gain?" asked Suriyawong.

"Vietnam?" said Bean.

"Worthless, compared to the menace of having India poised with a vast army at the underbelly of China."

Soon, to distract themselves from the news—and from their loss of any kind of influence—they stopped paying attention to the vids and reminisced about Battle School. Neither of them brought up the really bad experiences, only the funny things, the ridiculous things, and they laughed their way into the evening, until it was dark outside.

This afternoon with Suriyawong, now that they were friends, reminded Bean of home—in Crete, with his parents, with Nikolai. He tried to keep from thinking about them most of the time, but now, laughing with Suriyawong, he was filled with a bittersweet longing. He had that one year of something like a normal life, and now it was over. Blown to bits like the house they had been vacationing in. Like the government-protected apartment Graff and Sister Carlotta had taken them away from in the nick of time.

Suddenly a thrill of fear ran through Bean. He knew something, though he could not say how. His mind had made some connection and he didn't understand how, but he had no doubt that he was right.

"Is there any way out of this building that can't be seen from the outside?" asked Bean, in a whisper so faint he could hardly hear himself.

Suriyawong, who had been in the middle of a story about Major Anderson's penchant for nose-picking when he thought nobody was watching, looked at him like he was crazy. "What, you want to play hide-and-seek?"

Bean continued to whisper. "A way out."

Suriyawong took the hint and whispered back. "I don't know. I always use the doors. Like most doors, they're visible from both sides."

"A sewer line? A heating duct?"

"This is Bangkok. We don't have heating ducts."

"*Any* way out."

Suriyawong's whisper changed back to voice. "I'll look at the blueprints. But tomorrow, man, tomorrow. It's getting late and we talked right through dinner."

Bean grabbed his shoulder, forced him to look into his eyes. "Suriyawong," he whispered, even more softly, "I'm not joking. Right now, out of this building unobserved."

Finally Suriyawong got it: Bean was genuinely

afraid. His whisper was quiet again. "Why, what's happening?"

"Just tell me how."

Suriyawong closed his eyes. "Flood drainage," he whispered. "Old ditches. They just laid these temporary buildings down on top of the old parade ground. There's a shallow ditch that runs right under thc building. You can hardly tell it's there, but there's a gap."

"Where can we get under the building from inside?"

Suriyawang rolled his eyes. "These temporary buildings are made of lint." To prove his point, he pulled away the corner of the large rug in the middle of the room, rolled it back, and then, quite easily, pried up a floor section.

Underneath it was sod that had died from lack of sunlight. There were no gaps between floor and sod.

"Where's the ditch?" asked Bean.

Suriyawong thought again. "I think it crosses the hall. But the carpet is tacked down there."

Bean turned up the volume of the vid and went out the door of Suriyawong's office and through the anteroom to the hall. He pried up a corner of the carpet and ripped. Carpet fluff flew, and Bean kept pulling until Suriyawong stopped him. "I think about here," he said.

They pulled up another floor section. This time there was a depression in the yellowed sod.

"Can you get through that?" asked Bean.

"Hey, you're the one with the big head," said Suriyawong.

Bean threw himself down. The ground was damp—this *was* Bangkok—and he was clammy and filthy in moments as he wriggled along. Every floor joist was a challenge, and a couple of times he had to dig with his army-issue knife to make way for his head. But he made good progress anyway, and wriggled out into the darkness only a few minutes later. He stayed down, though, and saw that Suriyawong, despite not knowing what was going on, did not raise his head when he emerged from under the building, but continued to creep along just as Bean was doing.

They kept going until they reached the next point where the old eroded ditch went under another temporary building.

"Please tell me we're not going under another building."

Bean looked at the pattern of lights from the moon, from nearby porches and area lights. He had to count on his enemies being at least a little careless. If they were using infrared, this escape was meaningless. But if they were just eyeballing the place, watching the doors, he and Surly were already where slow, easy movement wouldn't be seen.

Bean started to roll himself up the incline.

Suriyawong grabbed him by the boot. Bean looked at him. Suriyawong pantomimed rubbing his cheeks, his forehead, his ears.

Bean had forgotten. His Greek skin was lighter than Suriyawong's. He would catch more light.

He rubbed his face, his ears, his hands with damp soil from under the grass. Suriyawong nodded.

They rolled—at a deliberate pace—up out of the ditch and wriggled slowly along the base of the building until they were around the corner. Here there were bushes to offer some shelter. They stood in the shadows for a moment, then walked, casually, away from the building as if they had just emerged from the door. Bean hoped not to be visible to anyone watching Suriyawong's building, but even if they could be seen, they shouldn't attract any attention, as long as no one noticed that they seemed to be just a little undersized.

Not until they were a quarter mile away did Suriyawong finally speak. "Do you mind telling me the name of this game?"

"Staying alive," said Bean.

"I never knew paranoid schizophrenia could strike so fast."

"They've tried twice," said Bean. "And they had no qualms about killing my family along with me."

"But we were just talking," said Suriyawong. "What did you see?"

"Nothing."

"Or hear?"

"Nothing," said Bean. "I had a feeling."

"Please don't tell me that you're a psychic."

"No, I'm not. But something about the events of the past few hours must have made some unconscious connection. I listen to my fears. I act on them."

"And this works?"

"I'm still alive," said Bean. "I need a public computer. Can we get off the base?"

"It depends on how all-pervasive this plot against you is," said Suriyawong. "You need a bath, by the way."

"What about some place with ordinary public computer access?"

"Sure, there are visitor facilities near the tram station entrance. But would it be ironic if your assassins were using it?"

"My assassins aren't visitors," said Bean.

This bothered Suriyawong. "You don't even know if anybody's really out to kill you, but you're sure it's somebody in the Thai Army?"

"It's Achilles," said Bean. "And Achilles isn't in Russia. India doesn't have any intelligence service that could carry out an operation like this inside the high command. So it has to be somebody that Achilles has corrupted."

"Nobody here is in the pay of India," said Suriyawong.

"Probably not," said Bean. "But India isn't the only place Achilles has friends by now. He was in Russia for a while. He has to have made other connections."

"It's so hard to take this seriously, Bean," said Suriyawong. "If you suddenly start laughing and say Gotcha that time, I *will* kill you."

"I might be wrong," said Bean, "but I'm not joking."

They got to the visitor facility and found no one using any of the computers. Bean logged on using one of his many false identities and wrote a message to Graff and Sister Carlotta.

> You know who this is. I believe an attempt is about to be made on my life. Would you send immediate messages to contacts within the Thai government, warning them that such an attempt is coming and tell them that it involves conspirators inside the Chakri's inner circle. No one else could have the access. And I believe the Chakri had prior knowledge. Any Indians supposedly involved are fall guys.

"You can't write that," said Suriyawong. "You have no evidence to accuse Naresuan. I'm annoyed with him, but he's a loyal Thai."

"He's a loyal Thai," said Bean, "but you can be loyal and still want me dead."

"But not *me,*" said Suriyawong.

"If you want it to look like the evil action of outsiders," said Bean, "then a brave Thai has to die along with me. What if they make our deaths look as if an Indian strike force did it? That would be provocation for a declaration of war, wouldn't it?"

"The Chakri doesn't need a provocation."

"He does if he wants the Burmese to believe that Thailand isn't just grabbing for a piece of Burma." Bean went back to his note.

> Please tell them that Suriyawong and I are alive. We will come out of hiding when we see Sister Carlotta with at least one high government official who Suriyawong would recognize on sight. Please act immediately. If I am wrong, you will be embarrassed. If I am right, you will have saved my life.

"I'm sick to my stomach thinking of how humiliated I'm going to be. Who are these people you're writing to?"

"People I trust. Like you."

Then, before sending the message, he added Peter's "Locke" address to the destination box.

"You know Ender Wiggin's brother?" asked Suriyawong.

"We've met."

Bean logged off.

"What now?" asked Suriyawong.

"We hide somewhere, I guess," said Bean.

Then they heard an explosion. Windows rattled. The floor trembled. The power flickered. The computers began to reboot.

"Got that done just in time," said Bean.

"Was that it?" asked Suriyawong.

"É," said Bean. "I think we're dead."

"Where do we hide?"

"If they did the deed, it's because they think we were still in there. So they won't be watching for us now. We can go to my barracks. My men will hide me."

"You're willing to bet my life on that?" asked Suriyawong.

"Yes," said Bean. "My track record of keeping you alive is pretty good so far."

As they walked out of the building, they saw military vehicles rushing toward where gray smoke was billowing up into the moonlit night. Others were heading for the entrances to the base. No one would be getting in or out.

By the time they reached the barracks where Bean's strike force was quartered, they could hear bursts of gunfire. "Now they're killing all the fake Indian spies this will be blamed on," said Bean. "The Chakri will regretfully inform the government that they all resisted capture and none were taken alive."

"Again you accuse him," said Suriyawong. "Why? How did you know this would happen?"

"I think I knew because there were too many smart people acting stupidly," said Bean. "Achilles *and* the Chakri. And he treated us angrily. Why? Because killing us bothered him. So he had to convince himself that we were disloyal children who had been corrupted by the I.F. We were a danger to Thailand. Once he hated us and feared us, killing us was justified."

"That's a long stretch from there to knowing they were about to kill us."

"They were probably set to do it at my quarters. But I stayed with you. It was quite possible they were planning for another opportunity—the Chakri would summon us to meet him somewhere, and we'd be killed instead. But when we stayed for hours and hours in your quarters, they realized *this* was the perfect opportunity. They had to check with the Chakri and get his consent to do it ahead of schedule. They probably had to rush to get the Indian stooges into place—they might even be genuine captured spies. Or they might be drugged Thai criminals who will have incriminating documents found on them."

"I don't care who they are," said Suriyawong. "I still don't understand how you knew."

"Neither do I," said Bean. "Most of the time, I analyze things very quickly and understand exactly why I know what I know. But sometimes my unconscious mind runs ahead of my conscious mind. It happened that way in the last battle, with Ender. We were doomed to defeat. I couldn't see a solution. And yet I said something, an ironic statement, a bitter joke—and it contained within it exactly the solution Ender needed. From then on, I've been trying to heed those unconscious processes that give me answers. I've thought back over my life and seen other times when I said things that were not really justified by my conscious analysis. Like the time when we stood over Achilles as he lay on the ground, and I told Poke to kill him. She wouldn't do it, and I couldn't persuade her, because I truly didn't understand why. Yet I understood what he was. I knew he had to die, or he would kill her."

"You know what I think?" said Suriyawong. "I think you heard something outside. Or noticed something subliminally on the way in. Somebody watching. And that's what triggered you."

Bean could only shrug. "You may well be right. As I said, I don't know."

It was after hours, but Bean could still palm his way through the locks to get in without setting off alarms. They hadn't bothered to deauthorize him. His entry into the building would show up on a computer somewhere, but it was a drone program and by the time any human looked at it, Bean's friends should have things well in motion.

Bean was glad to see that even though his men were in their home barracks on the grounds of the Thai high command base, they had not slacked in their discipline. No sooner were they inside the door than both Bean and Suriyawong were seized and pressed against the wall while they were checked for weapons.

"Good work," said Bean.

"Sir!" said the surprised soldier.

"And Suriyawong," said Bean.

"Sir!" said both the sentries.

A few others had been wakened by the scuffle.

"No lights," Bean said quickly. "And no loud talking. Weapons loaded. Prepare to move out on a moment's notice."

"Move out?" said Suriyawong.

"If they realize we're in here and decide to finish the job," said Bean, "this place is indefensible."

While some soldiers quietly woke the sleepers and all were busy dressing and loading their weapons, Bean had one of the sentries lead them to a computer. "You sign on," he said to the soldier.

As soon as he had logged on, Bean took his place and wrote, using the soldier's identity, to Graff, Carlotta, and Peter.

```
Both packages safe and awaiting pickup.
Please come right away before packages
are returned to sender.
```

Bean sent out one toon, divided into four pairs, to reconnoiter. When each pair returned another pair from another toon replaced them. Bean wanted to have enough warning to get these men out of the barracks before any kind of assault could be mounted.

In the meanwhile, they turned on a vid and watched the news. Sure enough, here came the first report. Indian agents had apparently penetrated the Thai command base and blown up a temporary building, killing Suriyawong, Thailand's most distinguished Battle School graduate, who had headed military doctrine and strategic planning for the past year and a half, since returning from space. It was a great national tragedy. There was no confirmation yet, but preliminary reports indicated that some of the Indian agents had been killed by the heroic soldiers defending Suriyawong. A visiting Battle School graduate had also been killed.

Some of Bean's soldiers chuckled, but soon enough they were all grim-faced. The fact that the reporters had been told Bean and Suriyawong were dead meant that whoever made the report believed they were both inside the offices at an hour when the only way anyone could know that was if the bodies had been found, or the building had been under observation. Since the bodies had obviously not been found, whoever was writing the official reports from the Chakri's office must have been part of the plot.

"I can understand someone wanting to kill Borommakot," said Suriyawong. "But why would anyone want to kill *me*?"

The soldiers laughed. Bean smiled.

Patrols returned and went out, again, again. No movement toward the barracks. The news carried the initial response from various commentators. India apparently wanted to cripple the Thai military by eliminating the nation's finest military mind. This was intolerable. The government would have no choice now but to declare war and join Burma in the struggle against Indian aggression.

Then new information came. The Prime Minister had declared that he would take personal control of this disaster. Someone in the military had obviously slipped badly to allow a foreign penetration of the high command's own base. Therefore, to protect the Chakri's reputation and make sure there was no hint of a cover-up of military errors, Bangkok city police would be supervising the investigation, and Bangkok city fire officials would investigate the wreckage of the exploded building.

"Good job," said Suriyawong. "The Prime Minister's cover story is strong and the Chakri won't resist letting police onto the base."

"If the fire investigators arrive soon enough," said Bean, "they might even prevent the Chakri's men from entering the building as soon as it cools enough from the fire. So they won't even know we weren't there."

Sirens moving through the base announced the arrival of the police and fire department. Bean kept waiting for the sound of gunfire. But it never came.

Instead, two of the patrols came rushing back.

"Someone is coming, but not soldiers. Bangkok police, sixteen of them, with a civilian."

"Just one?" asked Bean. "Is one of them a woman?"

"Not a woman, and just one. I believe, sir, that it is the Prime Minister himself."

Bean sent out more patrols to see if any military forces were within range.

"How did they know we were here?" asked Suriyawong.

"Once they took control of the Chakri's office," said Bean, "they could use the military personnel files to find out that the soldier who sent that last email was in this barracks when he sent it."

"So it's safe to come out?"

"Not yet," said Bean.

A patrol returned. "The Prime Minister wishes to enter this barracks alone, sir."

"Please," said Bean. "Invite him in."

"So you're sure he's not wired up with explosives to kill us all?" asked Suriyawong. "I mean, your paranoia has kept us alive so far."

As if in answer, the vid showed Chakri driving away from the main entrance to the base, under police escort. The reporter was explaining that Naresuan had resigned as Chakri, but the Prime Minister insisted that he merely take a leave of absence. In the meantime, the Minister of Defense was taking direct personal control of the Chakri's office, and generals from the field were being brought in to staff other positions of trust. Until then, the police had control of the command system. "Until we know how these Indian agents penetrated our most sensitive base," the Minister of Defense said, "we cannot be sure of our security."

The Prime Minister entered the barracks.

"Suriyawong," he said. He bowed deeply.

"Mr. Prime Minister," said Suriyawong, bowing noticeably less deeply. Ah, the vanity of a Battle School graduate, thought Bean.

"A certain nun is flying here as quickly as she can," said the Prime Minister, "but we hoped that you might trust me enough to come out without waiting for her arrival. She was on the opposite side of the world, you see."

Bean strode forward and spoke in his not-bad Thai. "Sir," he said, "I believe Suriyawong and I are safer here with these loyal troops than we would be anywhere else in Bangkok."

The Prime Minister looked at the soldiers standing, fully armed, at attention. "So someone has a private army right in the middle of this base," he said.

"I did not make my meaning clear," said Bean. "These soldiers are absolutely loyal to *you.* They are yours to command, because you are Thailand at this moment, sir."

The Prime Minister bowed, very slightly, and turned to the soldiers. "Then I order you to arrest this foreigner."

Immediately Bean's arms were gripped by the soldiers nearest to him, as another soldier patted him down for weapons.

Suriyawong's eyes widened, but he gave no other sign of surprise.

The Prime Minister smiled. "You may release him now," he said. "The Chakri warned me, before he took his voluntary leave of absence, that these soldiers had been corrupted and were no longer loyal to Thailand. I see now that he was misinformed. And since that is the case, I believe you are right. You are safer here, under their protection, until we explore the limits of the conspiracy. In fact, I would appreciate it if I could deputize a hundred of your men to serve with my police force as it takes control of this base."

"I urge you to take all but eight of them," said Bean.

"Which eight?" asked the Prime Minister.

"Any of these toons of eight, sir, could stand for a day against the Indian Army."

This was, of course, absurd, but it had a fine ring to it, and the men loved hearing him say it.

"Then, Suriyawong," said the Prime Minister, "I would appreciate your taking command of all but eight of these men and leading them in taking control of this base in my name. I will assign one policeman to each group, so that they can clearly be identified as acting under my authority. And one group of eight will, of course, remain with you for your protection at all times."

"Yes sir," said Suriyawong.

"I remember saying in my last campaign," said the Prime Minister, "that the children of Thailand held the keys to our national survival. I had no idea at the time how literally and how quickly that would be fulfilled."

"When Sister Carlotta arrives," said Bean, "you can tell her that she is no longer needed, but I would be glad to see her if she has the time."

"I'll tell her that," said the Prime Minister. "Now let's get to work. We have a long night ahead of us."

Everyone was quite solemn as Suriyawong called out the toon leaders. Bean was impressed that he knew who they were by name and face. Suriyawong might not have sought out Bean's company very much, but he had done an excellent job of keeping track of what Bean was doing. Only when everyone had moved out on their assignments, each toon with its own cop like a battle flag, did Suriyawong and the Prime Minister allow themselves to smile. "Good work," said the Prime Minister.

"Thank you for believing our message," said Bean.

"I wasn't sure I could believe Locke," said the Prime Minister, "and the Hegemon's Minister of Colonization is, after all, just a politician now. But when the Pope telephoned me personally, I had no choice but to believe. Now I must go out and tell the people the absolute truth about what happened here."

"That Indian agents did indeed attempt to kill me and an unnamed foreign visitor," asked Suriyawong, "but we survived because of quick action by heroic soldiers of the Thai Army? Or did the unnamed foreign visitor die?"

"I fear that he died," Bean suggested. "Blown to bits in the explosion."

"In any event," said Suriyawong, "you will assure the people, the enemies of Thailand have learned tonight that the Thai military may be challenged, but we cannot be defeated."

"I'm glad you were trained for the military, Suriyawong," said the Prime Minister. "I would not want to face you as an opponent in a political campaign."

"It is unthinkable that we would be opponents," said Suriyawong, "since we could not possibly disagree on any subject."

Everyone got the irony, but no one laughed. Suriyawong left with the Prime Minister and eight soldiers. Bean remained in the barracks with the last toon, and together they watched as the lies unfolded on the vid.

And as the news droned on, Bean thought of Achilles. Somehow he had found out Bean was alive—but that would be the Chakri, of course. But if the Chakri had turned to Achilles' side, why was he spinning the story of Suriyawong's death as a pretext for war with India? It made no sense. Having Thailand in the war from the beginning could only work against India. Add that to India's use of the clunky, obvious, life-wasting strategy of mass attack, and it began to look as though Achilles were some kind of idiot.

He was not an idiot. Therefore he was playing some sort of deeper game, and despite the much-vaunted cleverness of his unconscious mind, Bean did not yet know what it was. And Achilles would know soon enough, if he did not know already, that Bean was not dead.

He's in a killing mood, thought Bean.

Petra, thought Bean. Help me find a way to save you.

14

Hyderabad

Posted on the International Politics Forum by EnsiRaknor@TurkMilNet.gov
Topic: Where is Locke when we need him?

Am I the only one who wishes we had Locke's take on the recent developments in India? With India across the Burmese border and Pakistani troops massing in Baluchistan, threatening Iran and the gulf, we need a new way of looking at south Asia. The old models clearly don't work.

What I want to know is, did IntPolFor drop Locke's column when Peter Wiggin came forward as the author, or did Wiggin resign? Because if it was IPF's decision, it was, to put it bluntly, a stupid one. We never knew who Locke was—we listened to him because he made sense, and time after time he was the only one who made sense out of problematical situations, or at least was the first to see clearly what was going on. What does it matter if he's a teenager, an embryo, or a talking pig?

For that matter, as the Hegemon's term is near expiration, I am more and more uneasy with the current Hegemon-designate. Whoever suggested Locke almost a year ago had the right idea. Only now let's put him in office under his own name. What Ender Wiggin did in the Formic War, Peter Wiggin might be able to do in the conflagration that looms—put an end to it.

Reply 14, by Talleyrandophile@polnet.gov

I don't mean to be suspicious, but how do we know you're not Peter Wiggin, trying to put his name into play again?

Reply 14.1, by EnsiRaknor@TurkMilNet.gov

I don't mean to get personal, but Turkish Military Network IDs aren't given out to American teenagers doing consultation work in Haiti. I realize that international politics can make paranoids seem sane, but if Peter Wiggin could write under this ID, he must al-

```
ready run the world. But perhaps who I
am does make a difference. I'm in my
twenties now, but I'm a Battle School
grad. So maybe that's why the idea of
putting a kid in charge of things
doesn't sound so crazy to me.
```

Virlomi knew who Petra was the moment she first showed up in Hyderabad—they had met before. Even though she was considerably older, so her time in Battle School overlapped Petra's by only a year, in those days Virlomi took notice of every girl in the place. An easy task, since Petra's arrival brought the total number of girls to nine—five of whom graduated at the same time as Virlomi. It seemed as though having girls in the school were regarded as an experiment that had failed.

Back in Battle School, Petra had been a tough launchy with a smart mouth, who proudly refused all offers of advice. She seemed determined to make it as a girl among boys, meeting the same standards, taking their guff without help. Virlomi understood. She had had the same attitude herself, at first. She just hoped that Petra would not have to have such painful experiences as those Virlomi had had before finally realizing that the hostility of boys was, in most cases, insuperable, and a girl needed all the friends she could get.

Petra was memorable enough that of course Virlomi recognized her name when the stories of Ender's jeesh came out after the war. The one girl among them, the Armenian Joan of Arc. Virlomi read the articles and smiled. So Petra had been as tough as she thought she'd be. Good for her.

Then Ender's jeesh was kidnapped or killed, and when the kidnapped ones were returned from Russia,

Virlomi was heartsick to see that the only one whose fate remained unknown was Petra Arkanian.

Only she didn't have long to grieve. For suddenly the team of Indian Battle School graduates had a new commander, whom they immediately recognized as the same Achilles that Locke had accused of being a psychopathic killer. And soon they found that he was frequently shadowed by a silent, tired-looking girl whose name was never spoken.

But Virlomi knew her. Petra Arkanian.

Whatever Achilles' motive in keeping her name to himself, Virlomi didn't like it and so she made sure that everyone on the strategy team knew that this was the missing member of Ender's jeesh. They said nothing about Petra to Achilles, of course—merely responded to his instructions and reported to him as required. And soon enough Petra's silent presence was treated as if it were ordinary. The others hadn't known her.

But Virlomi knew that if Petra was silent, it meant something quite dreadful. It meant Achilles had some hold over her. A hostage—some kidnapped family member? Threats? Or something else? Had Achilles somehow overmastered Petra's will, which had once seemed so indomitable?

Virlomi took great pains to make sure that Achilles did not notice her paying special attention to Petra. But she watched the younger girl, learning all she could. Petra used her desk as the others did, and took part in reading intelligence reports and everything else that was sent to all of them. But something was wrong, and it took a while for Virlomi to realize what it was—Petra never typed anything at all while she was logged on to the system. There were a lot of netsites that required passwords or at least registration to sign on. But after typing her password to simply log on in the morning, Petra never typed again.

She's been blocked, Virlomi realized. That's why she never emails any of us. She's a prisoner here. She can't pass messages outside. And she doesn't talk to any of us because she's been forbidden to.

When she wasn't logged on, though, she must have been working furiously, because now and then Achilles would send a message to all of them, detailing new directions their planning should go. The language in these messages was not Achilles'—it was easy to spot the shift in style. He was getting these strategic insights—and they were good ones—from Petra, who was one of the nine who were chosen to save humanity from the Formics. One of the finest minds on Earth. And she was enslaved by this psychopathic Belgian.

So, while the others admired the brilliant strategies they were developing for aggressive war against Burma and Thailand, as Achilles' memos whipped up their enthusiasm for "India finally rising to take her rightful place among the nations," Virlomi grew more and more skeptical. Achilles cared nothing for India, no matter how good his rhetoric sounded. And when she found herself tempted to believe in him, she had only to look at Petra to remember what he was.

Because the others all seemed to buy into Achilles' version of India's future, Virlomi kept her opinions to herself. And she watched and waited for Petra to look at her, so she could give her a wink or a smile.

The day came. Petra looked. Virlomi smiled.

Petra looked away as casually as if Virlomi had been a chair and not a person trying to make contact.

Virlomi was not discouraged. She kept trying for eye contact until finally one day Petra passed near her on the way to a water fountain and slipped and caught herself on Virlomi's chair. In the midst of the noise of Petra's scuffling feet, Virlomi clearly heard her words: "Stop it. He's watching."

And that was it. Confirmation of what Virlomi had suspected about Achilles, proof that Petra had noticed her, and a warning that her help was not needed.

Well, that was nothing new. Petra never needed help, did she?

Then came the day, only a month ago, when Achilles sent a memo around ordering that they needed to update the old plans—the original strategy of mass assault, throwing huge armies with their huge supply lines against the Burmese. They were all stunned. Achilles gave no explanation, but he seemed unusually taciturn, and they all got the message. The brilliant strategy had been set aside by the adults. Some of the finest military minds in the world had come up with the strategy, and the adults were going to ignore them.

Everyone was outraged, but they soon settled back into the routine of work, trying to get the old plans into shape for the coming war. Troops had moved, supplies had been replenished in one area or fallen short in another. But they worked out the logistics. And when they received Achilles'—or, as Virlomi assumed, Petra's—plan for moving the bulk of the army from the Pakistani border to face the Burmese, they admired the brilliance of it, fitting the needs of the army into the existing rail and air traffic so that from satellites, no unusual movements would be visible until suddenly the armies were on the border, forming up. At most the enemy would have two days' notice; if they were careless, only a single day before it became obvious.

Achilles left on one of his frequent trips, only this

time Petra disappeared too. Virlomi feared for her. Had she served her purpose, and now that he was done with her, would he kill her?

But no. She came back the same night, when Achilles did.

And the next morning, word camc to begin the movement of troops. Following Petra's deft plan to get them to the Burmese border. And then, ignoring Petra's equally deft plan, they would launch their clumsy mass attack.

It makes no sense, thought Virlomi.

Then she got the email from the Hegemony Minister of Colonization—Colonel Graff, that old sabeek.

I'm sure you're aware that one of our Battle School graduates, Petra Arkanian, was not returned with the others who took part with Ender Wiggin in the final battle. I am very interested in locating her, and believe she may have been transported against her will to a place within the borders of India. If you know anything about her whereabouts and present condition, could you let someone know? I'm sure you'd want someone to do the same for you.

Almost immediately there came an e-mail from Achilles.

I'm sure you understand that because this is wartime, any attempt to convey information to someone outside the Indian military will be regarded as espi-

```
onage and treason, and you will be
killed forthwith.
```

So Achilles was definitely keeping Petra incommunicado, and cared very much that she remain hidden to outsiders.

Virlomi did not even have to think about what she would do. This had nothing to do with Indian military security. So, while she took his death threat seriously, she did not believe there was anything morally wrong with attempting to circumvent it.

She could not write directly to Colonel Graff. Nor could she send any kind of message containing any reference, however oblique, to Petra. Any email going out from Hyderabad was going to be scrutinized. And, now that Virlomi thought about it, she and the other Battle School graduates ensconced here in the Planning and Doctrine Division were only slightly more free than Petra. She could not leave the grounds. She could not have contact with anyone who was not military with a high-level security clearance.

Spies have radio equipment or dead drops, thought Virlomi. But how do you go about becoming a spy when you have no way to reach outside but writing letters, yet there's no one you can write a letter to and no way to say what you need to say without getting caught?

She might have thought of a solution on her own. But Petra simplified the process for her by coming up behind her at the drinking fountain. As Virlomi straightened up from drinking and Petra slipped in to take her place, Petra said, "I am Briseis."

And that was all.

The reference was obvious—everyone in Battle

School knew the Iliad. And with Achilles being their overseer at the moment, the Briseis reference was obvious. And yet it was not. Briseis had been held by someone else, and Achilles—the original one—had been furious because he felt slighted that he didn't have her. So what could she mean by saying she was Briseis?

It had to do with the letter from Graff and Achilles' warning. So it must be a key, a way to get word out about Petra. And to get word out required the net. So *Briseis* must mean something to someone out on the net. Perhaps there was some kind of coded electronic dead drop, keyed on the name Briseis. Perhaps Petra had already found someone to contact, but could not do it because she was cut off from the nets.

Virlomi didn't bother doing a general search. If someone out there was looking for Petra, the message would have to be at a site that Petra would be able to find without deviating from legitimate military research. Which meant that Virlomi probably already knew the site where the message was waiting.

The problem she was officially working on at the moment was to determine the most efficient way to minimize risk to supply helicopters while not consuming too much fuel. The problem was so technical that there was no way she could explain doing historical or theoretical research.

But Sayagi, a Battle School graduate five years her senior, was working on problems of pacifying and winning the allegiance of local populations in occupied countries. So Virlomi went to him. "I've gone greeyaz on my algorithms."

"You want my help?" he asked.

"No, no, I just need to set it aside for a couple of

hours so I can come back to it fresh. Anything I can help you look for?"

Of course Sayagi had received the same messages as Virlomi, and he was sharp enough not to take Virlomi's offer at face value.

"I don't know, what kind of thing could you do?"

"Any historical research? Or theoretical? On the nets?" She was tipping him to what she needed. And he understood.

"Toguro. I hate that stuff. I need data on failed approaches to pacification and conciliation. Besides killing or deporting everybody and moving in a new population."

"What do you already have?"

"You're wide open, I've been avoiding it."

"Thanks. You want a report or just links?"

"Paste-ups are enough. No links, though. That's too much like doing the work myself."

A perfectly innocent exchange. Virlomi had her cover now.

She went back to her desk and began browsing the historical and theoretical sites. She never actually ran a search on the name "Briseis"—that would be too obvious, the monitoring software would pick that right up and Achilles, if he saw it, would make the connection. Instead, Virlomi browsed through the sites, looking at subject headings.

Briseis showed up on the second site she tried.

It was a posting from someone calling himself HectorVictorious. Hector was not exactly an auspicious name—he was a hero, and the only person who was any kind of match for Achilles, but in the end Hector was killed and Achilles dragged his corpse around the walls of Troy.

Still, the message was clear, if you knew to think of Briseis as a codename for Petra.

Virlomi worked her way through several other postings, pretending to read them while actually composing her reply to HectorVictorious. When she was ready, she went back and typed it in, knowing as she did it that it might well be the cause of her own immediate execution.

> I vote for her remaining a resistant slave. Even if she was forced into silence, she would find a way to hold on to her soul. As for slipping a message to someone inside Troy, how do you know she didn't? And what good would it have done? It wasn't that long afterward that everyone in Troy was dead. Or didn't you ever hear of the Trojan horse? I know—Briseis should have warned the Trojans to beware of Greeks bearing gifts. Or found a friendly native to do it for her.

She signed it with her own name and email address. After all, this was supposed to be a perfectly innocent posting. Indeed, she worried that it might be *too* innocent. What if the person who was looking for Petra didn't realize that her references to Briseis resisting and being forced into silence were actually eyewitness reports? Or that the "friendly native" reference was to Virlomi herself?

But her address inside the Indian military network should alert whoever this was to pay special attention.

Now, of course, with the message posted, Virlomi

had to continue going through the motions of doing the useless research that Sayagi had "asked" her to do. It would be a couple of tedious hours—wasted time, if no one got the message.

—

Petra tried not to be obvious about watching what Virlomi was doing. After all, if Virlomi was as smart as she needed to be in order to bring this off, she wouldn't do anything that was worth watching. But Petra saw when Virlomi went over to Sayagi and talked for a while. And Petra noticed that Virlomi seemed to be browsing when she got back to her desk, mousing through online pages instead of writing or calculating. Was she going to spot those HectorVictorious postings?

Either she would or she wouldn't. Petra couldn't allow herself to think about it anymore. Because in a way it would be better for everyone if Virlomi simply didn't get it. Who knew how subtle Achilles was? For all Petra knew, those postings might be traps designed to catch her getting someone else to help her. That could be fatal all the way around.

But Achilles couldn't be everywhere. He was bright, he was suspicious, he played a deep game. But he was only one person and he couldn't think of everything. Besides, how important was Petra to him, really? He hadn't even used her campaign strategy. Surely he kept her around as a vanity, nothing more.

The reports coming back from the front were just what one might expect—Burmese resistance was only token, since they were massing their main forces in places where the terrain favored them. Canyons. River crossings.

All futile, of course. No matter where the Burmese made their stand, the Indian Army would simply flow around them. There weren't enough Burmese soldiers to make serious efforts at more than a handful of places, while there were so many Indians that they could press forward at every point, leaving only enough men at the Burmese strong points to keep them pinned down while the bulk of the Indian Army completed the takeover of Burma and moved on toward the mountain passes into Thailand.

That's where the challenge would begin, of course. For Indian supply lines would stretch all the way across Burma by then, and the Thai Air Force was formidable, especially since they had been observed testing a new temporary airfield system that could be built in many cases during the time a bomber was airborne. Not really worth it, bombing airfields when they could be replaced in two or three hours.

So even though the intelligence reports from inside Thailand were very good—detailed, accurate, and recent—on the most important points they didn't matter. There were few meaningful targets, given the strategy the Thai were using.

Petra knew Suriyawong, the Battle School grad who was running strategy and doctrine in Bangkok. He was good. But to Petra it looked a little suspicious that the new Thai strategy began, abruptly, only a few weeks after Petra and Achilles arrived in India from Russia. Suriyawong had already been in place in Bangkok for a year. Why the sudden change? It might be that someone had tipped them off about Achilles' presence in Hyderabad and what that might mean. Or it might be that someone else had joined Suriyawong and influenced his thinking.

Bean.

Petra refused to believe that he was dead. Those messages had to be from him. And even though Suriyawong was perfectly capable of thinking of the new Thai strategy himself, it was such a comprehensive set of changes, without any sign of gradual development, that it cried out for the obvious explanation—it came from a fresh set of eyes. Who else but Bean?

The trouble was, if it *was* Bean, Achilles' intelligence sources inside Thailand were so good that it was quite possible Bean would be spotted. And if Achilles' earlier attempt to kill Bean had failed, there was no chance that Achilles would refrain from trying again.

She couldn't think about that. If he had saved himself once, he could do it again. After all, maybe someone had excellent intelligence sources inside India, too.

And it might not be Bean leaving those Briseis messages. It might be Dink Meeker, for instance. Only that really wasn't Dink's style. Bean had always been something of a sneak. Dink was confrontational. He would go on the nets proclaiming that he knew Petra was in Hyderabad and demanding that she be released at once. Bean was the one who had figured out that the Battle School kept track of where students were by monitoring transmitters in their clothing. Take off all your clothes and go around buck naked, and the Battle School administrators wouldn't have a clue where you were. Not only had Bean thought of it, he had done it, climbing around in airshafts in the middle of the night. When he told her about it, as they waited around on Eros for the League War to settle down so they could go home, Petra hadn't really believed him at first. Not until he looked her coldly in the eye and said, "I don't joke, and if I did, this isn't particularly funny."

"I didn't think you were joking," said Petra. "I thought you were bragging."

"I was," said Bean. "But I wouldn't waste my time bragging about things I hadn't actually done."

That was Bean—admitting his faults right along with his virtues. No false modesty, and no vanity, either. If he bothered to talk to you at all, he never shaped his words to make himself look better or worse than he was.

She hadn't really known him in Battle School. How could she? She was older, and even though she noticed him and spoke to him a few times—she always made a point of speaking to new kids who were getting the pariah treatment, since she knew they needed friends, even if it was only a girl—she simply hadn't had much reason to talk to him.

And then there was the disastrous time when Petra had been suckered into trying to give Ender a warning—which turned out to be bogus, and in fact Ender's enemies were using Petra's attempt to warn Ender as the opportunity to jump him and beat him up. Bean was the one who saw through it and broke it up. And, quite naturally, he leapt to the conclusion that Petra was part of the conspiracy against Ender. He had continued to suspect her for quite a while. Petra wasn't really sure when he finally believed in her innocence. But it had been a barrier between them for a long time on Eros. So it wasn't until after the war ended that they even had a chance to get to know each other.

That was when Petra realized what Bean really was. It was hard to see past his small size and think of him as anything other than a preschooler or launchy or something. Even though everyone knew that he was the one that would have been chosen to take Ender's place, if Ender had broken under the strain of battle. A lot of them resented the fact. But Petra didn't. She knew Bean was the best of Ender's jeesh. It didn't bother her.

What was Bean, really? A dwarf. That's what she had to realize. With adult dwarfs, you could see in their faces that they were older than their size would indicate. But because Bean was still a child, and had none of the short-limbed deformations of dwarfism, he looked like the age his size implied. If you talked to him like a child, though, he tuned you out. Petra never had done that, so except when he thought she was a traitor to Ender, Bean always treated her with respect.

The funny thing was, it was all based on a misunderstanding. Bean thought Petra talked to him like a regular human being because she was so mature and wise that she didn't treat him like a little kid. But the truth was, she *did* treat him exactly the way she treated little kids. It's just that she always treated little kids like adults. So she got credit for being understanding, when in fact she was just lucky.

By the time the war was over, though, it didn't matter. They knew they were going home—all of them, it turned out, but Ender—and once they got back to Earth, they expected they wouldn't see each other again. So there was a kind of freedom, caution tossed to the wind. You could say what you wanted. You didn't have to take offense at anything because it wouldn't matter in a few months. It was the first time they could actually have fun.

And the person Petra enjoyed the most was Bean.

Dink, who had been close to Petra for a while in Battle School, was a little miffed by the way Petra was always with Bean. He even accused her—obliquely, because he didn't want to get frozen out completely—of having something romantic going on with Bean.

Well, of course he thought that way—puberty had already struck Dink Meeker, and like all boys that age, he thought everybody's mental processes were infused with testosterone.

It was something else, though, between Petra and Bean. Not brother and sister, either. Not mother-son or any other weird psychofake analogy she could think of. She just . . . liked him. She had spent so long having to prove to prickly, envious, and frightened boys that she was, in fact, smarter and better at everything than they were, that it took her quite by surprise to be with someone so arrogant, so absolutely sure of his own brilliance, that he didn't feel at all threatened by her. If she knew something that he didn't know, he listened, he watched, he learned. The only other person she'd known who was like that with her was Ender.

Ender. She missed him terribly sometimes. She had tutored him—and taken a lot of heat from Bonzo Madrid, their commander at the time, for doing it. And as it became clear what Ender was, and she joined gladly with those who followed him, obeyed him, gave themselves to him, she nevertheless had a secret place in her memory where she kept the knowledge that she had been Ender's friend at a time when no one else had the courage. She had made a difference in his life, and even when others thought she had betrayed him, Ender never thought that.

She loved Ender with a helpless mixture of worship and longing that led to foolish dreams of impossible futures, tying her life with his until they died. She fantasized about raising children together, the most brilliant children in the world. About being able to stand beside the greatest human being in the world—for so she thought he was—and having everybody recognize that he had chosen her to stand with him forever.

Dreams. After the war, Ender was beaten down. Broken. Finding out that he had actually caused the extermination of the Formics was more than he could bear. And because she, too, had broken during the war, her shame kept her away from him until it was too late, until they had divided Ender from the rest of them.

Which is why she knew that her feelings toward Bean were completely different. No such dreams and fantasies. Just a sense of complete acceptance. She belonged with Bean, not the way a wife belonged with a husband or, God forbid, a girlfriend with a boyfriend, but rather the way a left hand belonged with the right. They simply fit. Nothing exciting about it, nothing to write home about. But it could be counted on. She imagined that, of all the Battle School kids, of all the members of Ender's jeesh, it would be Bean that she would remain close to.

Then they got off the shuttle and were dispersed throughout the world. And even though Armenia and Greece were relatively close together—compared to, say, Shen in Japan or Hot Soup in China—they never saw each other, they never even wrote. She knew that Bean was going home to meet a family that he had never known, and she was busy trying to get involved with her own family again. She didn't exactly pine for him, or he for her. And besides, they didn't need to hang out together or chat all the time for her to know that, left hand with right hand, they were still friends, still belonged together. That when she needed someone, the first person she should call on was Bean.

In a world that didn't have Ender Wiggin in it, that

meant he was the person she loved most. That she would miss most if anything happened to him.

Which is why she could pretend that she wasn't going to worry about Bean getting folded by Achilles, but it wasn't true. She worried all the time. Of course, she worried about herself, too—and maybe a little more about herself than about him. But she'd already lost one love in her life, and even though she told herself that these childhood friendships wouldn't matter in twenty years, she didn't want to lose the other.

Her desk beeped at her.

There was a message in the display.

```
When did I designate this as naptime?
Come see me.
```

Only Achilles wrote with such peremptory rudeness. She hadn't been napping. She had been thinking. But it wasn't worth arguing with him about it.

She logged off and got up from her desk.

It was evening, getting dark outside. Her mind really had wandered. Most of the others on the day shift in Planning and Doctrine had already left, and the night response team was coming in. A couple of the day shift were still at their desks, though.

She caught a glance from Virlomi, one of the late ones. The girl looked worried. That meant she probably *had* done something in response to the Briseis posting, and now feared repercussions. Well, she was right to worry. Who knew how Achilles would speak or write or act if he was planning to kill somebody? Petra's personal opinion was that he was always planning to kill someone, so there was no difference in his behavior to warn you if you were next. Go home and try to get some sleep, Virlomi. Even if Achilles has caught you trying to help me and has decided to have you killed, you won't be able to do anything about it, so you might as well sleep the sleep of a child.

Petra left the big barn of a room they all worked in and moved through the corridors as if in a trance. Had she been asleep when Achilles wrote to her? Who cared.

As far as Petra knew, she was the only one in Planning and Doctrine who even knew where Achilles' office was. She had been in it often, but was not impressed by the privilege. She had the freedom of a slave or a captive. Achilles let her intrude on his privacy because he didn't think of her as a person.

One wall of his office was a 2D computer display, now showing a detailed map of the India-Burma border region. As reports came in from troops in the field and from satellites, it was updated by clerks, so Achilles could glance at it any time and see the best available intelligence on placement. Apart from that, the room was spartan. Two chairs—not comfortable ones—a table, a bookcase, and a cot. Petra suspected that somewhere on the base there was a comfortable suite of rooms with a soft bed that was never used. Whatever else Achilles was, he wasn't a hedonist. He never cared much about personal comfort, not that she had seen, anyway.

He didn't take his eyes off the map when she came in—but she was used to that. When he made a point of ignoring her, she took it as his perverse way of paying attention to her. It was when he looked right at her without seeing her that she felt truly invisible.

"The campaign's going very well," said Achilles.

"It's a stupid plan, and the Thai are going to cut it to shreds."

"They had a sort of coup a few minutes ago," said

Achilles. "The commander of the Thai military blew up young Suriyawong. Terrible case of professional jealousy, apparently."

Petra tried to keep from showing her sadness at Suriyawong's death and her disgust at Achilles. "You're not seriously expecting me to believe you had nothing to do with it?"

"Well, *they're* blaming it on Indian spies, of course. But there were no Indian spies involved."

"Not even the Chakri?"

"Definitely not spying for India," said Achilles.

"For whom, then?"

Achilles laughed. "You're so untrusting. My Briseis."

She had to work at staying relaxed, at not betraying anything when he called her that.

"Ah, Pet, you *are* my Briseis, don't you realize?"

"Not really," said Petra. "Briseis was in somebody else's tent."

"Oh, I have your *body* with me, and I get the product of your brain, but your heart still belongs to someone else."

"It belongs to me," said Petra.

"It belongs to Hector," said Achilles. "But . . . how can I bear to tell you this? Suriyawong was not alone in his office when the building was blown to bits. Another person contributed scraps of flesh and bone and a fine aerosol of blood to the general gore. Unfortunately, this means I can't drag his body around the walls of Troy."

Petra was sick inside. Had he heard her tell Virlomi, "I am Briseis"? And whom was he talking about, saying those things about Hector?

"Just tell me what you're talking about or don't," said Petra.

"Oh, don't tell me you haven't seen those little

messages all over the forums," said Achilles. "About Briseis, and Guinevere, and every other tragic romantic heroine who got trapped with some overbearing bunduck."

"What about them?"

"You know who wrote them," said Achilles.

"Do I?"

"I forgot. You refuse to play guessing games. All right, it was Bean, and you knew that."

Petra felt unwanted emotions welling up—she suppressed them. If those messages were posted by Bean, then he *had* lived through the previous assassination attempt. But that would mean Bean was "HectorVictorious," and Achilles' little allegory meant that Bean was indeed in Bangkok, and Achilles had spotted him and tried again to kill him. He had died along with Suriyawong.

"I'm glad to have you to tell me what I know. It saves my having to actually use my own memory."

"I know it's tearing you up, my poor Pet. The funny thing is, dear Briseis, Bean was just a bonus. It was Suriyawong that we targeted from the start."

"Fine. Congratulations. You're a genius. Whatever it is you want me to say so you'll shut up and let me get some dinner."

Talking rudely to Achilles was the only illusion of freedom Petra was able to retain. She figured it amused him. And she wasn't dumb enough to talk to him that way in front of anyone else.

"You had your heart set on Bean saving you, didn't you?" said Achilles. "That's why when old Graff sent that stupid request for information, you tipped that Virlomi kid to try responding to Bean."

Petra tasted despair. Achilles really did monitor everything.

"Come on, the water fountain's the most obvious place to bug," said Achilles.

"I thought you had important things to do."

"Nothing's more important in my life than you, Pet," said Achilles. "If I could just get you to come into my tent."

"You've kidnapped me twice. You watch me wherever I go. I don't know how I could be farther in your tent than I am."

"In . . . my . . . tent," said Achilles. "You're still my enemy."

"Oh, I forgot, I'm supposed to be so eager to please my captor that I surrender my volition to you."

"If I wanted that, I'd have you tortured, Pet," said Achilles. "But I don't want you that way."

"How kind of you."

"No, if I can't have you freely with me, as my friend and ally, then I'll just kill you. I'm not into torture."

"After you've used my work."

"But I'm not using your work," said Achilles.

"Oh, that's right. Because Suriyawong is dead, so you don't need to worry now about having any real opposition."

Achilles laughed. "Sure. That's it."

Which meant, of course, that she hadn't understood at all.

"It's easy to fool a person you keep living in a box. I only know what you tell me."

"But I tell you everything," said Achilles, "if only you were bright enough to get it."

Petra closed her eyes. She kept thinking of poor Suriyawong. So serious all the time. He had done his best for his country, and then it was his own commander-in-chief who killed him. Did he know? I hope not.

If she kept thinking of poor Suriyawong, she wouldn't have to think of Bean at all.

"You're not listening," said Achilles.

"Oh, thanks for telling me that," said Petra. "I thought I was."

Achilles was about to say something else, but then he cocked his head. The hearing aid he wore was a radio receiver tied to his desk. Somebody had just started talking to him.

Achilles turned from her to his desk. He typed a few things, read a few things. His face showed no emotion—but that was a real change, since he had been smiling and pleasant until the voice came. Something had gone wrong. Indeed, Petra knew him well enough now that she thought she recognized the signs of anger. Or maybe—she wondered, she hoped—fear.

"They aren't dead," Petra said.

"I'm busy," he said.

She laughed. "That's the message, isn't it? Once again, your assassins have piffed it. If you want a job done right, Achilles, you've got to do it yourself."

He turned away from the desk display and looked her in the eye. "He sent out a message from the barracks of his strike force there in Thailand. Of course the Chakri saw it."

"Not dead," said Petra. "He just keeps beating you."

"Narrowly escaping with his life while my plans are never interfered with at all . . ."

"Come on, you know he got you booted out of Russia."

Achilles raised his eyebrows. "So you admit you sent a coded message."

"Bean doesn't need coded messages to beat you," she said.

Achilles rose from his chair and walked over to her. She braced herself for a slap. But he planted a hand in her chest and shoved the chair over backward.

Her head hit the floor. It left her dazed, lights flashing through her peripheral vision. And then a wave of pain and nausea.

"He sent for dear old Sister Carlotta," said Achilles. His voice betrayed no emotion. "She's flying around the world to help him. Isn't that nice of her?"

Petra could barely comprehend what he was saying. The only thought she could hold on to was: Don't let there be any permanent brain damage. That was her whole self. She'd rather die than lose the brilliance that made her who she was.

"But that gives me time to set up a little surprise," said Achilles. "I think I'll make Bean very sorry that he's alive."

Petra wanted to say something to that, but she couldn't remember what. Then she couldn't remember what he had said. "What?"

"Oh, is your poor little head swimming, my Pet? You should be more careful with the way you lean back on that chair."

Now she remembered what he had said. A surprise. For Sister Carlotta. To make Bean sorry he's alive.

"Sister Carlotta is the one who got you off the streets of Rotterdam," said Petra. "You owe her everything. Your leg operation. Going to Battle School."

"I owe her nothing," said Achilles. "You see, she chose Bean. She sent him. Me, she passed over. I'm the one who brought civilization to the streets. I'm the one who kept her precious little Bean alive. But him she sends up into space, and me she leaves in the dirt."

"Poor baby," said Petra.

He kicked her, hard, in the ribs. She gasped.

"And as for Virlomi," he said, "I think I can use her to teach you a lesson about disloyalty to me."

"That's the way to bring me into your tent," said Petra.

Again he kicked her. She tried not to groan, but it came out anyway. This passive resistance strategy was not working.

He acted as if he hadn't done it. "Come on, why are you lying there? Get up."

"Just kill me and have done with it," she said. "Virlomi was just trying to be a decent human being."

"Virlomi was warned what would happen."

"Virlomi is nothing to you but a way to hurt me."

"You're not that important. And if I want to hurt you, I know how." He made as if to kick her again. She stiffened, curled away from the blow. But it didn't come.

Instead he reached down a hand to her. "Get up, my Pet. The floor is no place to nap."

She reached up and took his hand. She let him bear most of her weight as she rose up, so he was pulling hard.

Fool, she thought. I was trained for personal combat. You weren't in Battle School long enough to get that training.

As soon as her legs were under her, she shoved upward. Since that was the direction he had been pulling, he lost his balance and went over backward, falling over the legs of her chair.

He did not hit his head. He immediately tried to scramble to his feet. But she knew how to respond to his movements, kicking sharply at him with her heavy army-issue shoes, shifting her weight so that her kicks never came at the place he was protecting. Every kick hurt him. He tried to scramble backward, but she pressed on, relentless, and because he was using his arms to help him scuttle across the floor, she was able to kick him in the head, a solid blow that rocked him back and laid him out.

Not unconscious, but a little dizzy. Well, see how you like it.

He tried to do some kind of street-fighting move, kicking out with his legs while his eyes were looking elsewhere, but it was pathetic. She easily jumped over his legs and landed a scuffing kick right up between his legs.

He cried out in pain.

"Come on, get up," she said. "You're going to kill Virlomi, so kill me first. Do it. You're the killer. Get your gun. Come on."

And then, without her quite seeing how he did it, there was indeed a gun in his hand.

"Kick me again," he said through gritted teeth. "Kick me faster than this bullet."

She didn't move.

"I thought you wanted to die," he said.

She could see it now. He wouldn't shoot her. Not till he had shot Virlomi in front of her.

She had missed her chance. While he was down, before he got the gun—from the back of his waistband? from under the furniture?—she should have snapped his neck. This wasn't a wrestling match, this was her chance to put an end to him. But her instinct had taken over, and her instinct was not to kill, only to disable her opponent, because that's what she had practiced in Battle School.

Of all the things I could have learned from Ender,

the killer instinct, going for the final blow from the start, why was that the one I overlooked?

Something Bean had explained about Achilles. Something Graff had told him, after Bean had gotten him shipped back to Earth. That Achilles had to kill anyone who had ever seen him helpless. Even the doctor who had repaired his gimp leg, because she'd seen him laid out under anaesthetic and taken a knife to him.

Petra had just destroyed whatever feeling it was that had made him keep her alive. Whatever he had wanted from her, he wouldn't want it now. He wouldn't be able to bear having her around. She was dead.

Yet, no matter what else was going on, she was still a tactician. Thick headed as she was, her mind could still do this dance. The enemy saw things this way; so change it so he sees them another way.

Petra laughed. "I never thought you'd let me do that," she said.

He slowly, painfully, was getting to his feet, the gun trained on her.

She went on. "You always had to be el supremo, like the bunducks in Battle School. I never thought you had the guts to be like Ender or Bean, till now."

Still he said nothing. But he was standing there. He was listening.

"Crazy, isn't it? But Bean and Ender, they were so little. And they didn't care. Everybody looking down at them, *me* towering over them, they were the only guys in Battle School who weren't terrified of having somebody see a girl be better than them, bigger than them." Keep it going, keep spinning it. "They put Ender in Bonzo's army too early, he hadn't been trained. Didn't know how to do anything. And Bonzo gave orders, nobody was to work with him. So here I had this little kid, helpless, didn't know anything. That's what I like, Achilles. Smarter than me, but smaller. So I taught him. Chisel Bonzo, I didn't care. He was like *you've* always been, constantly showing me who's boss. But Ender knew how to let me run it. I taught him everything. I would have died for him."

"You're sick," said Achilles.

"Oh, you're going to tell me you didn't know that? You had the gun the whole time, why did you let me do that, if it wasn't—if you weren't trying to . . ."

"Trying to what?" he said. He was keeping his voice steady, but the craziness was plainly visible, and his voice trembled just a little. She had pushed him past the borders of sanity, deep into his madness. It was Caligula she was seeing now. But he was listening. If she found the right story to put on what just happened, maybe he would settle for . . . something else. Making his horse consul. Making Petra . . .

"Weren't you trying to seduce me?" she said.

"You don't even have your tits yet," he said.

"I don't think it's tits you're looking for," she said. "Or you would never have dragged me around with you in the first place. What was all that talk about wanting me in your tent? Loyal? You wanted me to belong to you. And all the time you did that sabeek stuff, pushing me around—that just made me feel contempt for you. I was looking down on you the whole time. You were nothing, just another sack of testosterone, another chimp hooting and beating his chest. But then you let me—you *did* let me, didn't you? You don't expect me to believe I really could have done that?"

A faint smile touched the corners of his lips.

"Doesn't that spoil it, if you think I did it on purpose?" he said.

She strode to him, right to the barrel of the gun, and, letting it press into her abdomen, she reached up, grabbed him by the neck, and pulled his head down to where she could kiss him.

She had no idea how to do it, except what she'd seen in movies. But she was apparently doing it well enough. The gun stayed in her belly, but his other arm wrapped around her, pulled her closer.

In the back of her mind, she remembered what Bean told her—that the last thing he had seen Achilles do before killing Bean's friend Poke was kiss her. Bean had had nightmares about it. Achilles kissing her, and then in the middle of the kiss, strangling her. Not that Bean actually saw that part. Maybe it didn't happen that way at all.

But no matter how you cut it, Achilles was a dangerous boy to kiss. And there was that gun in her belly. Maybe this was the moment he longed for. Maybe his dreams were about this—kissing a girl, and blowing a hole in her body while he did.

Well, blow away, she thought. Before I watch you kill Virlomi for the crime of having compassion for me and courage enough to act, I'd rather be dead myself. I'd rather kiss you than watch you kill her, and there's nothing in the world that could disgust me more than having to pretend that you're the . . . thing . . . I love.

The kiss ended. But she did not let go of him. She would not step back, she would not break this embrace. He had to believe that she wanted him. That she was in his emossin' tent.

He was breathing lightly, quickly. His heartbeat was rapid. Prelude to a kill? Or just the aftermath of a kiss.

"I said I'd kill anyone who tried to answer Graff," he said. "I have to."

"She didn't answer Graff, did she?" said Petra. "I know you have to keep control of things, but you don't have to be a strutting yelda about it. She doesn't know you know what she did."

"She'll think she got away with it."

"But *I'll* know," said Petra, "that you weren't afraid to give me what I want."

"What, you think you've found some way to make me do what you want?" he said.

Now she could back away from him. "I thought I'd found a man who didn't have to prove he was big by pushing people around. I guess I was wrong. Do what you want. Men like you disgust me." She put as much contempt into her voice, onto her face, as she could. "Here, prove you're a man. Shoot me. Shoot everybody. I've known *real* men. I thought you were one of them."

He lowered the gun. She did not show her relief. Just kept her eyes looking into his.

"Don't ever think you've got me figured out," he said.

"I don't care whether I figure you out or not," she said. "All I care about is, you're the first man since Ender and Bean who had guts enough to let me stand over him."

"Is that what you're going to say?" he asked.

"Say? Who to? I don't have any friends out there. The only person worth talking to in this whole place is you."

He stood there, breathing heavily again, a bit of the craziness back in his eyes.

What am I saying wrong?

"You're going to bring this off," she said. "I don't know how you're going to do it, but I can taste it. You're going to run the whole show. They're all going to be under you, Achilles. Governments, universities, corporations, all eager to please you. But when we're alone, where nobody else can see, we'll both know that you're strong enough to keep a strong woman with you."

"You?" said Achilles. "A woman?"

"If I'm not a woman, what were you doing with me in here?"

"Take off your clothes," he said.

The craziness was still there. He was testing her somehow. Waiting for her to show . . .

To show that she was faking. That she was really afraid of him, after all. That her story was all a lie, designed to trick him.

"No," she said. "You take off yours."

And the craziness faded.

He smiled.

He tucked the gun into the back of his pants.

"Get out of here," he said. "I've got a war to run."

"It's night," she said. "Nobody's moving."

"There's a lot more to this war than the armies," said Achilles.

"When do I get to stay in your tent?" she asked. "What do I have to do?" She could hardly believe she was saying this, when all she wanted was to get out.

"You have to be the thing I need," he said. "And right now, you're not."

He walked to his desk, sat down.

"And pick up your chair on the way out."

He started typing. Orders? For what? To kill whom?

She didn't ask. She picked up the chair. She walked out.

And kept walking, through the corridors to the room where she slept alone. Knowing, with every step, that she was monitored. There would be vids. He would check them, to see how she acted. To see if she meant what she'd said. So she couldn't stop and press her face against the wall and cry. She had to be . . . what? How would this play in a movie or a vid if she were a woman who was frustrated because she wanted to be with her man?

I don't know! she screamed inside. I'm not an actress!

And then, a much quieter voice in her head answered. Yes you are. And a pretty good one. Because for another few minutes, maybe another hour, maybe another night, you're alive.

No triumph, either. She couldn't seem to gloat, couldn't show relief. Frustration, annoyance—and some pain where he kicked her, where her head hit the floor—that's all she could show.

Even alone in her bed, the lights off, she lay there, pretending, lying. Hoping that whatever she did in her sleep would not provoke him. Would not bring that crazy frightened searching look into his eyes.

Not that it would be any guarantee, of course. There was no sign of craziness when he shot those men in the bread van back in Russia. Don't ever think you've got me figured out, he said.

You win, Achilles. I don't think I've got you figured out. But I've learned how to play one lousy string. That's something.

I also knocked you onto the floor, beat the goffno out of you, kicked you in your little kintamas, and made you think you liked it. Kill me tomorrow or whenever you want—my shoe going into your face, you can't take that away from me.

—

In the morning, Petra was pleased to find that she was still alive, considering what she had done the night before. Her head ached, her ribs were sore, but nothing was broken.

And she was starving. She had missed dinner the night before, and perhaps there was something about beating up her jailer that made her especially hungry. She didn't usually eat breakfast, so she had no accustomed place to sit. At other meals, she sat by herself, and others, respecting her solitude or fearing Achilles' displeasure, did not sit with her.

But today, on impulse, she took her tray to a table that had only a couple of empty spots. The conversation grew quiet when she first sat down, and a few people greeted her. She smiled back at them, but then concentrated on her food. Their conversation resumed.

"There's no way she got off the base."

"So she's still here."

"Unless someone *took* her."

"Maybe it's a special assignment or something."

"Sayagi says he thinks she's dead."

A chill ran through Petra's body.

"Who?" she asked.

The others glanced at her, but then glanced away. Finally one of them said, "Virlomi."

Virlomi was gone. And no one knew where she was.

He killed her. He said he would, and he did. The only thing I gained by what I did last night was that he didn't do it in front of me.

I can't stand this. I'm done. My life is not worth living. To be his captive, to have him kill anyone who tries to help me in any way . . .

No one was looking at her. Nor were they talking.

They know Virlomi tried to answer Graff, because she must have said something to Sayagi when she walked over to him yesterday. And now she's gone.

Petra knew she had to eat, no matter how sick at

heart she felt, no matter how much she wanted to cry, to run screaming from the room, to fall on the floor and beg their forgiveness for . . . for what? For being alive when Virlomi was dead.

She finished all she could bear to eat, and left the mess hall.

But as she walked through the corridors to the room where they all worked, she realized: Achilles would not have killed her like this. There was no point in killing her if the others didn't get to see her arrested and taken away. It wouldn't do what he needed it to do, if she just disappeared in the night.

At the same time, if she had escaped, he couldn't announce it. That would be even worse. So he would simply remain silent, and leave the impression with everyone that she was probably dead.

Petra imagined Virlomi walking boldly out of the building, her sheer bravado carrying the day. Or perhaps, dressed as one of the women who cleaned floors and windows, she had slipped out unnoticed. Or had she climbed a wall, or run a minefield? Petra didn't even know what the perimeter looked like, or how closely guarded it might be. She had never been given a tour.

Wishful thinking, that's all this is, she told herself as she sat down to the day's work. Virlomi is dead, and Achilles is simply waiting to announce it, to make us all suffer from not knowing.

But as the day wore on, and Achilles did not appear, Petra began to believe that perhaps she had gotten away. Maybe Achilles was staying away because he didn't want anyone speculating about any visible bruises he might have. Or maybe he's having some scrotal problems and he's having some doctor check him out—though heaven help him if Achilles decided that having a doctor handle his injured testes was worthy of the death penalty.

Maybe he was staying away because Virlomi was gone and Achilles did not want them to see him frustrated and helpless. When he caught her and could drag her into the room and shoot her dead in front of them, *then* he could face them.

And as long as that didn't happen, there was a chance Virlomi was alive.

Stay that way, my friend. Run far and don't pause for anything. Cross some border, find some refuge, swim to Sri Lanka, fly to the moon. Find some miracle, Virlomi, and live.

15

Murder

```
To:Graff%pilgrimage@colmin.gov
From:Carlotta%agape@vatican.net/or-
ders/sisters/ind
Re: Please forward

The attached file is encrypted. Please
wait twelve hours after the time of
sending and if you don't hear from me,
forward it to Bean. He'll know the key.
```

It took less than four hours to secure and inspect the entire high command base in Bangkok. Computer experts would be probing to try to find out whom it was that Naresuan had been communicating with outside, and whether he was in fact involved with a foreign power or this gambit was a private venture. When Suriyawong's work with the Prime Minister was finished, he came alone to the barracks where Bean was waiting.

Most of Bean's soldiers had already returned, and Bean had sent most of them to bed. He still watched the news in a desultory fashion—nothing new was being said, so he was interested only in seeing how the talking heads were spinning it. In Thailand, everything was charged with patriotic fervor. Abroad, of course, it was a different story. All the Common broadcasts were taking a more skeptical view that Indian operatives had really made the assassination attempt.

"Why would India want to provoke Thai entry into the war?"

"They know Thailand will come in eventually whether Burma asks them or not. So they felt they had to deprive Thailand of its best Battle School graduate."

"Is one child so dangerous?"

"Maybe you should ask the Formics. If you can find any."

And on and on, everyone trying to appear smart—or at least smarter than the Indian and Thai governments, which was the game the media always played. What mattered to Bean was how this would affect Peter. Was there any mention of the possibility that Achilles was running the show in India? Not a breath. Anything yet about Pakistani troop movements near Iran? The "Bangkok bombing" had driven that slow-moving story off the air. Nobody was giving this any global implications. As long as the I.F. was there to keep the nukes from flying, it was still just politics as usual in south Asia.

Except it wasn't. Everybody was so busy trying to look wise and unsurprised that nobody was standing up and screaming that this whole set of events was completely different from anything that had gone before. The most populous nation in the world has dared to turn its back on a two-hundred-year-old enemy and invade the small, weak country to its east. Now India was attacking Thailand. What did that mean? What was India's goal? What possible benefit could there be?

Why weren't they talking about these things?

"Well," said Suriyawong, "I don't think I'm going to go to sleep very soon."

"Everything all cleaned up?"

"More like everybody who worked closely with the Chakri has been sent home and put under house arrest while the investigation continues."

"That means the entire high command."

"Not really," said Suriyawong. "The best field commanders are out in the field. Commanding. One of them will be brought in as acting Chakri."

"They should give it to you."

"They should, but they won't. Aren't you just a little hungry?"

"It's late."

"This is Bangkok."

"Well, not really," said Bean. "This is a military base."

"When is your friend's flight due in?"

"Morning. Just after dawn."

"Ouch. She's going to be out of sorts. You going to meet her at the airport?"

"I didn't think about it."

"Let's go get dinner," said Suriyawong. "Officers do it all the time. We can take a couple of strike force soldiers with us to make sure we don't get hassled for being children."

"Achilles isn't going to give up on killing me."

"Us. He aimed at *us* this time."

"He might have a backup."

"Bean, I'm hungry. Are you hungry?" Suriyawong turned to the members of the toon that had been with him. "Any of you hungry?"

"Not really," said one of them. "We ate at the regular time."

"Sleepy," said another.

"Anybody awake enough to go into the city with us?"

Immediately all of them stepped forward.

"Don't ask perfect soldiers whether they want to protect their CO," said Bean.

"Designate a couple to go with us and let the others sleep," said Suriyawong.

"Yes sir," said Bean. He turned to the men. "Honest assessment. Which of you will be least impaired by failing to get enough sleep tonight?"

"Will we be allowed sleep tomorrow?" asked one.

"Yes," said Bean. "So it's a matter of how much it affects you to get off your rhythm."

"I'll be fine." Four others felt the same way. So Bean chose the two nearest. "Two of you keep watch for two more hours, then go back to the normal watch rotation."

Outside the building, with their two bodyguards walking five meters behind them, Bean and Suriyawong finally had a chance to talk candidly. First, though, Suriyawong had to know. "You really keep a regular watch rotation even here at the base?"

"Was I wrong?" asked Bean.

"Obviously not, but . . . you really are paranoid."

"I know I have an enemy who wants me dead. An

enemy who happens to be hopping from one powerful position to another."

"More powerful each time," said Suriyawong. "In Russia, he didn't have the power to start a war."

"He might not in India, either," said Bean.

"There's a war," said Suriyawong. "You're saying it isn't his?"

"It's his," said Bean. "But he's probably still having to persuade adults to go along with him."

"Win a few, and they hand you your own army," said Suriyawong.

"Win a few more, and they hand you the country," said Bean. "As Napoleon and Washington showed."

"How many do you have to win to get the world?"

Bean let the question hang.

"Why did he go after us?" asked Suriyawong. "I think you're right, that this operation at least was entirely Achilles'. It's not the kind of thing the Indian government goes for. India is a democracy. Folding children doesn't play well. No way he got approval."

"It might not even be India," said Bean. "We don't really know anything."

"Except that it's Achilles," said Suriyawong. "Think about the stuff that doesn't make sense. A second-rate, obvious campaign strategy that we're probably going to be able to take apart. A nasty bit of business like this that can only soil India's reputation in the rest of the world."

"Obviously he's not acting in India's best interest," said Bean. "But they think he is, if he's really the one who brought off this deal with Pakistan. He's acting for himself. And I can see what he gains by kidnapping Ender's jeesh and by trying to kill you."

"Fewer rivals?"

"No," said Bean. "He makes Battle School grads look like the most important weapons in the war."

"But he's not a Battle School grad."

"He was *in* Battle School, and he's that age. He doesn't want to have to wait till he grows up to be king of the world. He wants everyone to believe that a child should lead them. If you're worth killing, if Ender's jeesh is worth stealing . . ." It also helps Peter Wiggin, Bean realized. He didn't go to Battle School, but if children are plausible world leaders, his own track record as Locke raises him above any other contenders. Military ability is one thing. Ending the League War was a much stronger qualification. It trumped "psychopathic Battle School expulsee" hands down.

"Do you think that's all?" asked Suriyawong.

"What's all?" asked Bean. He had lost the thread. "Oh, you mean is that enough to explain why Achilles would want you dead?" Bean thought about it. "I don't know. Maybe. But it doesn't tell us why he's setting up India for a much bloodier war than it has to fight."

"What about this," said Suriyawong. "Make everybody fear what war will bring, so they want to strengthen the Hegemony to keep the war from spreading."

"That's fine, except nobody's going to nominate Achilles as Hegemon."

"Good point. Are we ruling out the possibility that Achilles is just stupid?"

"Yes, that's not a possibility."

"What about Petra, could she have fooled him into sticking with this obvious but somewhat dumb and wasteful strategy?"

"That *is* possible, except that Achilles is very sharp

at reading people. I don't know if Petra could lie to him. I never saw her lie to anybody. I don't know if she can."

"Never saw her lie to *anybody*?" asked Suriyawong.

Bean shrugged. "We became very good friends, at the end of the war. She speaks her mind. She may hold something back sometimes, but she tells you she's doing it. No smoke, no mirrors. The door's either open or it's shut."

"Lying takes practice," observed Suriyawong.

"Like the Chakri?"

"You don't get to that position by pure military ability. You have to make yourself look very good to a lot of people. And hide a lot of things you're doing."

"You're not suggesting Thailand's government is corrupt," said Bean.

"I'm suggesting Thailand's government is political. I hope this doesn't surprise you. Because I'd heard that you were bright."

They got a car to take them into town—Suriyawong had always had the authority to requisition a car and a driver, he just never used it till now.

"So where do we eat?" asked Bean. "It's not like I have a restaurant guide with me."

"I grew up in families with better chefs than any restaurant," said Suriyawong.

"So we go to your house?"

"My family lives near Chiang Mai."

"That's going to be a battle zone."

"Which is why I think they're actually in Vientiane, though security rules would keep them from telling me. My father is running a network of dispersed munitions factories." Suriyawong grinned. "I had to make sure I siphoned off some of these defense jobs for my family."

"In other words, he was best man for the task."

"My mother was best for the task, but this *is* Thailand. Our love affair with Western culture ended a century ago."

They ended up having to ask the soldiers, and they only knew the kind of place they could afford to eat. So they found themselves eating at a tiny all-night diner in a part of town that wasn't the worst, but wasn't the nicest, either. And the whole thing was so cheap it felt practically free.

Suriyawong and the soldiers went down on the food as if it were the best meal they'd ever had. "Isn't this *great*?" asked Suriyawong. "When my parents had company, and they were eating all the fancy stuff in the dining room with visitors, we kids would eat in the kitchen, the stuff the servants ate. *This* stuff. *Real* food."

No doubt that's why the Americans at Yum-Yum in Greensboro loved what they got there, too. Childhood memories. Food that tasted like safety and love and getting rewarded for good behavior. A treat—we're going out. Bean didn't have any such memories, of course. He had no nostalgia for picking up food wrappers and licking the sugar off the plastic and then trying to get at any of it that rubbed off on his nose.

What was he nostalgic for? Life in Achilles' "family"? Battle School? Not likely. And his time with his family in Greece had come too late to be part of his early childhood memories. He liked being in Crete, he loved his family, but no, the only good memories of his childhood were in Sister Carlotta's apartment when she took him off the street and fed him and kept him safe and helped him prepare to take the Battle School tests—his ticket off Earth, to where he'd be safe from Achilles.

It was the only time in his childhood when he felt safe. And even though he didn't believe it or understand it at the time, he felt loved, too. If he could sit down in some restaurant and eat a meal like the ones Sister Carlotta prepared there in Rotterdam, he'd probably feel the way those Americans felt about Yum-Yum, or these Thais felt about this place.

"Our friend Borommakot doesn't really like the food," said Suriyawong. He spoke in Thai, because Bean had picked up the language quite readily, and the soldiers weren't as comfortable in Common.

"He may not like it," said one soldier, "but it's making him grow."

"Soon he'll be as tall as you," said the other.

"How tall do Greeks get?" asked the first.

Bean froze.

So did Suriyawong.

The two soldiers looked at them with some alarm. "What, did you see something?"

"How did you know he was Greek?" asked Suriyawong.

The soldiers glanced at each other and then suppressed their smiles.

"I guess they're not stupid," said Bean.

"We saw all the vids on the Bugger War, we saw your face, you think you're not famous? Don't you know?"

"But you never said anything," said Bean.

"That would have been rude."

Bean wondered how many people made him in Araraquara and Greensboro, but were too polite to say anything.

It was three in the morning when they got to the airport. The plane was due in about six. Bean was too keyed up to sleep. He assigned himself to keep watch, and let the soldiers and Suriyawong doze.

So it was Bean who noticed when a flurry of activity began around the podium about forty-five minutes before the flight was supposed to arrive. He got up and went to ask what was going on.

"Please wait, we'll make an announcement," said the ticket agent. "Where are your parents? Are they here?"

Bean sighed. So much for fame. Suriyawong, at least, should have been recognized. Then again, everyone here had been on duty all night and probably hadn't heard any of the news about the assassination attempt, so they wouldn't have seen Suriyawong's face flashed in the vids again and again. He went back to waken one of the soldiers so he could find out, adult to adult, what was going on.

His uniform probably got him information that a civilian wouldn't have been told. He came back looking grim. "The plane went down," he said.

Bean felt his heart plummet. Achilles? Had he found a way to get to Sister Carlotta?

It couldn't be. How could he know? He couldn't be monitoring every airplane flight in the world.

The message Bean had sent via the computer in the barracks. The Chakri might have seen it. If he hadn't been arrested by then. He might have had time to relay the information to Achilles, or whatever intermediary they used. How else could Achilles have known that Carlotta would be coming?

"It's not him this time," said Suriyawong, when Bean told him what he was thinking. "There are plenty of reasons a plane can drop out of radar."

"She didn't say it disappeared," said the soldier. "She said it went down."

Suriyawong looked genuinely stricken. "Borommakot, I'm sorry." Then Suriyawong went to a telephone and contacted the Prime Minister's office. Being Thailand's pride and joy, who had just survived an assassination attempt, had its benefits. In a very few minutes they were escorted into the meeting room at the airport where officials from the government and the military were conferring, linked to aviation authorities and investigating agencies worldwide.

The plane had gone down over southern China. It was an Air Shanghai flight, and China was treating it as an internal matter, refusing to allow outside investigators to come to the crash site. But air traffic satellites had the story—there was an explosion, a big one, and the plane was in small fragments before any part of it reached the ground. No chance of survivors.

Only one faint hope remained. Maybe she hadn't made a connection somewhere. Maybe she wasn't on board.

But she was.

I could have stopped her, thought Bean. When I agreed to trust the Prime Minister without waiting for Carlotta to arrive, I could have sent word at once to have her go home. But instead he waited around and watched the vids and then went out for a night on the town. Because he wanted to see her. Because he had been frightened and he needed to have her with him.

Because he was too selfish even to think of the danger he was exposing her to. She flew under her own name—she had never done that when they were together. Was that his fault?

Yes. Because he had summoned her with such urgency that she didn't have time to do things covertly.

She just had the Vatican arrange her flights, and that was it. The end of her life.

The end of her ministry, that's how she'd think about it. The jobs left undone. The work that someone else would have to do.

All he'd done, ever since she met him, was steal time from her, keep her from the things that really mattered in her life. Having to do her work on the run, in hiding, for his sake. Whenever he needed her, she dropped everything. What had he ever done to deserve it? What had he ever given her in return? And now he had interrupted her work permanently. She would be so annoyed. But even now, if he could talk to her, he knew what she'd say.

It was always my choice, she'd say. You're part of the work God gave me. Life ends, and I'm not afraid to return to God. I'm only afraid for you, because you keep yourself such a stranger to him.

If only he could believe that she was still alive somehow. That she was there with Poke, maybe, taking her in now the way she took Bean in so many years ago. And the two of them laughing and reminiscing about clumsy old Bean, who just had a way of getting people killed.

Someone touched his arm. "Bean," whispered Suriyawong. "Bean, let's get you out of here."

Bean focused and realized that there were tears running down his cheeks. "I'm staying," he said.

"No," said Suriyawong. "Nothing's going to happen here. I mean let's go to the official residence. That's where the diplomatic greeyaz is flying."

Bean wiped his eyes on his sleeves, feeling like a little kid as he did it. What a thing to be seen doing in front of his men. But that was just too bad—it would be a far worse sign of weakness to try to conceal it or pathetically ask them not to tell. He did what he did, they saw what they saw, so be it. If Sister Carlotta wasn't worth some tears from someone who owed her as much as Bean did, then what were tears for, and when should they be shed?

There was a police escort waiting for them. Suriyawong thanked their bodyguards and ordered them back to the barracks. "No need to get up till you feel like it," he said.

They saluted Suriyawong. Then they turned to Bean and saluted him. Sharply. In best military fashion. No pity. Just honor. He returned their salute the same way—no gratitude, just respect.

—

The morning in the official residence was infuriating and boring by turns. China was being intransigent. Even though most of the passengers were Thai businessmen and tourists, it was a Chinese plane over Chinese airspace, and because there were indications that it might have been a ground-to-air missile attack rather than a planted bomb, it was being kept under tight military security.

Definitely Achilles, Bean and Suriyawong agreed. But they had talked enough about Achilles that Bean agreed to let Suriyawong brief the Thai military and state department leaders who needed to have all the information that might make sense of this.

Why would India want to blow up a passenger plane flying over China? Could it really have been solely to kill a nun who was coming to visit a Greek boy in Bangkok? That was simply too far-fetched to believe. Yet, bit by bit, and with the help of the Minister of Colonization, who could take them through details about Achilles' psychopathology that hadn't even been in Locke's reporting on him, they began to understand that yes, indeed, this might well have been a kind of defiant message from Achilles to Bean, telling him that he might have gotten away this time, but Achilles could still kill whomever he wanted.

While Suriyawong was briefing them, however, Bean was taken upstairs to the private residence, where the Prime Minister's wife very kindly led him to a guest bedroom and asked him if he had a friend or family member she should send for, or if he wanted a minister or priest of some religion or other. He thanked her and said that all he really needed was some time alone.

She closed the door behind her, and Bean cried silently until he was exhausted, and then, curled up on a mat on the floor, he went to sleep.

When he awoke it was still bright daylight beyond the louvered shutters. His eyes were still sore from crying. He was still exhausted. He must have woken up because his bladder was full. And he was thirsty. That was life. Pump it in, pump it out. Sleep and wake, sleep and wake. Oh, and a little reproduction here and there. But he was too young, and Sister Carlotta had opted out of that side of life. So for them the cycle had been pretty much the same. Find some meaning in life. But what? Bean was famous. His name would live in history books forever. Probably just as part of a list in the chapter on Ender Wiggin, but that was fine, that was more than most people got. When he was dead he wouldn't care.

Carlotta wouldn't be in any history books. Not even a footnote. Well, no, that wasn't true. Achilles was going to be famous, and she was the one who found him.

More than a footnote after all. Her name would be remembered, but always because it was linked with the koncho who killed her because she had seen how helpless he was and saved him from the life of the street.

Achilles killed her, but of course, he had my help.

Bean forced himself to think of something else. He could already feel that burning in his eyelids that meant tears were about to flow. That was done. He needed to keep his wits about him. Very important to keep thinking.

There was a courtesy computer in the room, with standard netlinks and some of Thailand's leading connection software. Soon Bean was signed on in one of his less-used identities. Graff would know things that the Thai government wasn't getting. So would Peter. And they would write to him.

Sure enough, there were messages from both of them encrypted on one of his dropsites. He pulled them both off.

They were the same. An email forwarded from Sister Carlotta herself.

Both of them said the same thing. The message had arrived at nine in the morning, Thailand time. They were supposed to wait twelve hours in case Sister Carlotta herself contacted them to retract the message. But when they learned with independent confirmation that there was no chance she was alive, they decided not to wait. Whatever the message was, Sister Carlotta had set it up so that if she didn't take an active step to block it, every day, it would automatically go to Graff and to Peter to send on to him.

Which meant that every day of her life, she had

thought of him, had done something to keep him from seeing this, and yet had also made sure that he would see whatever it was that this message contained.

Her farewell. He didn't want to read it. He had cried himself out. There was nothing left.

And yet she wanted him to read it. And after all she had done for him, he could surely do this for her.

The file was double-encrypted. Once he had opened it with his own decoding, it remained encoded by her. He had no idea what the password would be, and therefore it had to be something that she would expect him to think of.

And because he would only be trying to find the key after she was dead, the choice was obvious. He entered the name *Poke* and the decryption proceeded at once.

It was, as he expected, a letter to him.

Dear Julian, Dear Bean, Dear Friend,

Maybe Achilles killed me, maybe he didn't. You know how I feel about vengeance. Punishment belongs to God, and besides, anger makes people stupid, even people as bright as you. Achilles must be stopped because of what he is, not because of anything he did to me. My manner of death is meaningless to me. Only my manner of life mattered, and that is for my Redeemer to judge.

But you already know these things, and that is not why I wrote this letter.

There is information about you that you have a right to know. It's not pleasant information, and I was going to wait to tell you until you already had some inkling. I was not about to let my death keep you in ignorance, however. That would be giving either Achilles or the random chances of life—whichever caused my sudden death—too much power over you.

You know that you were born as part of an illegal scientific experiment using embryos stolen from your parents. You have preternatural memories of your own astonishing escape from the slaughter of your siblings when the experiment was terminated. What you did at that age tells anyone who knows the story that you are extraordinarily intelligent. What you have not known, until now, is why you are so intelligent, and what it implies about your future.

The person who stole your frozen embryo was a scientist, of sorts. He was working on the genetic enhancement of human intelligence. He based his experiment on the theoretical work of a Russian scientist named Anton. Though Anton was under an order of intervention and could not tell me directly, he courageously found a way to circumvent the programming and tell me of the genetic change that was made in you. (Though Anton was under the impression that the change could only be made in an unfertilized egg, this was really only a technical problem, not a theoretical one.)

There is a double key in the human genome. One of the keys deals with human intelligence. If turned one way, it places a block on the ability of the brain to function at peak capacity. In you, Anton's key has been turned. Your brain was not frozen in its growth. It did not stop making new neurons at an early age. Your brain continues to grow and make new connections. Instead of having a limited capacity, with patterns formed during early development, your brain adds new capacities and new patterns as they are needed. You are mentally like a one-year-old, but with experience. The mental feats that infants routinely perform, which are far greater than anything that adults manage, will always remain within your reach. For your entire life, for instance, you will be able to master new languages like a native speaker. You will be able to make and maintain connections with your own memory that are unlike those of anyone else. You are, in other words, uncharted—or perhaps self-charted—territory.

But there is a price for that unfettering of your brain. You have probably already guessed it. If your brain keeps growing, what happens to your head? How does all that brain matter stay inside?

Your head continues to grow, of course. Your skull has never fully closed. I have had your skull measurements tracked, naturally. The growth is slow, and much of the growth of your brain has involved the creation of more but smaller neurons. Also, there has been some thinning of your skull, so you may or may not have noticed the growth in the circumferences of your head—but it is real.

You see, the other side of Anton's key involves human growth. If we did not stop growing, we would die very young. Yet to live long requires that we give up more and more of our intelligence, because our brains must lock down and stop growing earlier in our life cycle. Most human beings fluctuate within a fairly narrow range. You are not even on the charts.

Bean, Julian, my child, you will die very young. Your body will continue to grow, not the way puberty would do it, with one growth spurt and then an adult height. As one scientist put it, you will never reach adult height, because there is no adult height. There is only height at time of death. You will steadily grow taller and larger until your heart gives out or your spine collapses. I tell you this bluntly, because there is no way to soften this blow.

No one knows what course your growth will take. At first I took great encouragement from the fact that you seemed to be growing more slowly than originally estimated. I was told that by the age of puberty, you would have caught up with other children your age—but you did not. You remained far behind them. So I hoped that perhaps he was wrong, that you might live to age forty or fifty, or even thirty. But in the year you were with your family, and in the time we have been together, you have been measured and your growth rate is accelerating. All indications are that it will continue to accelerate. If you live to be twenty, you will have defied all rational expectations. If you die before the age of fifteen, it will be only a mild surprise. I shed tears as I write these words, because if ever there was a child who could serve humanity by having a long adult life, it is you. No, I will be honest, my tears are because I think of you as being, in so many ways, my own son, and the only thing that makes me glad about the fact that you are learning of your future through this letter is that it means I have died before you. The worst fear of every loving parent, you see, is that they will have to bury a child. We nuns and priests are spared that grief. Except when we take it upon ourselves, as I so foolishly and gladly have done with you.

I have full documentation of all the findings of the team that has been studying you. They will continue to study you, if you allow them. The netlink is at the end of this letter. They can be trusted, because they are decent people, and because they also know that if the existence of their project becomes known, they will be in grave danger, for research into the genetic enhancement of human intelligence remains against the law. It is entirely your choice whether you cooperate. They already have valuable data. You may live your life without reference to them, or you may continue to provide them with information. I am not terribly interested in the science of it. I worked with them because I needed to know what would happen to you.

Forgive me for keeping this information from you. I know that you think you would have preferred to know it all along. I can only say, in my defense, that it is good for human beings to have a period of innocence and hope in their lives. I was afraid that if you knew this too soon, it would rob you of that hope. And yet to deprive you of this knowledge robbed you of the freedom to decide how to spend the years you have. I was going to tell you soon.

There are those who have said that because of this small genetic difference, you are not human. That because Anton's key requires two changes in the genome, not one, it could never have happened randomly, and therefore you represent a new species, created in the laboratory. But I tell you, you and Nikolai are twins, not separate species, and I, who have known you as well as any other person, have never seen anything from you but the best and purest of humanity. I know you will not accept my religious terminology, but you know what it means to me. You have a soul, my child. The Savior died for you as for every other human being ever born. Your life is of infinite worth to a loving God. And to me, my son.

You will find your own purpose for the time you have left to live. Do not be reckless with your life, just because it will not be long. But do not guard it overzealously, either. Death is not a tragedy to the one who dies. To have wasted the life before that death, that is the tragedy. Already you have used your years better than most. You will yet find many new purposes, and you will accomplish them. And if anyone in heaven heeds the voice of this old nun, you will be well watched over by angels and prayed for by many saints.

With love, Carlotta

Bean erased the letter. He could pull it from his dropsite and decode it again, if he needed to refer back to it. But it was burned into his memory. And not just as text on a desk display. He had heard it in Carlotta's voice, even as his eyes moved across the words that the desk put up before him.

He turned off the desk. He walked to the window and opened it. He looked out over the garden of the official residence. In the distance he could see airplanes making their approach to the airport, as others, having just taken off, rose up into the sky. He tried to picture Sister Carlotta's soul rising up like one of those airplanes. But the picture kept changing to an Air Shanghai flight coming in to land, and Sister Carlotta walking off the plane and looking him up and down and saying, "You need to buy new pants."

He went back inside and lay down on his mat, but

not to sleep. He did not close his eyes. He stared at the ceiling and thought about death and life and love and loss. And as he did, he thought he could feel his bones grow.

Part Four

DECISIONS

16

Treachery

To: Demosthenes%Tecumseh@freeamerica
.org
From: Unready%cincinnatus@anon.set
Re: Air Shanghai

The pinheads running this show have decided not to share satellite info on Air Shanghai with anyone outside the military, claiming that it involves vital interests of the United States. The only other countries with satellites capable of seeing what ours can see are China, Japan, and Brazil, and of these only China has a satellite in position to see it. So the Chinese know. And when I'm done with this letter, you'll know, and you'll know how to use the information. I don't like seeing big countries beat up on little ones, except when the big country is mine. So sue me.

The Air Shanghai flight was brought down by a ground-to-air missile, which was fired from INSIDE THAILAND. However, computer time-lapse tracking of movements in that area of Thailand show that the only serious candidate for how the ground-to-air missile got to its launch site is a utility truck whose movements originated in, get this, China.

Details: The truck (little white Vietnamese-made "Ho"-type vehicle) originated at a warehouse in Gejiu (which has already been tagged as a munitions clearinghouse) and crossed the Vietnamese border between Jinping, China, and Sinh Ho, Vietnam. It then crossed the Laotian border via the Ded Tay Chang pass. It traversed the widest part of Laos and entered Thailand near Tha Li, but at this point moved off the main roads. It passed near enough to the point from which the missile was launched for it to have been offloaded and transported manually to the site. And get this: All this movement happened MORE THAN A MONTH AGO.

I don't know about you, but to me and everybody else here, that looks like China wants a "provocation" to go to war against Thailand. Bangkok-bound Air Shanghai jet, carrying mostly Thai passengers, is shot down, over China, by a g-to-a launched from Thailand. China can make it look as though the Thai Army was trying to create a fake provocation against them, when in fact the reverse is the case. Very complicated, but the Chinese know they can show satellite proof that the missile was launched from inside Thailand. They can also prove that it had to have radar assistance from sophisticated military tracking systems—which will imply, in the Chinese version, that the Thai military was behind it, though WE know it means the Chinese military was in control. And when the Chinese ask for independent corroboration, you can count on it: Our beloved government, since it loves business better than honor, will back up the Chinese story, never mentioning the movements of that little truck. Thus America will stay in the good graces of its trading partner. And Thailand gets chiseled.

Do your thing, Demosthenes. Get this out into the public domain before our government can play toady. Just try to find a way to do it that doesn't point `at me. This isn't just job-losing territory. I could go to jail.`

When Suriyawong came to see if Bean wanted any dinner—a nine o'clock repast for the officers on duty, not an official meal with the P.M.—Bean almost followed him right down. He needed to eat, and now was as good a time as any. But he realized that he had not read any of his email after getting Sister Carlotta's last letter, so he told Suriyawong to start without him but save him a place.

He checked the dropsite that Peter had used to forward Carlotta's message, and found a more recent letter from Peter. This one included the text of a letter from one of Demosthenes' contacts inside the U.S. satellite intelligence service, and combined with Peter's own analysis of the situation, it made everything clear to Bean. He fired off a quick response, taking Peter's suspicions a step further, and then headed down to dinner.

Suriyawong and the adult officers—several of them field generals who had been summoned to Bangkok because of the crisis in the high command—were laughing. They fell silent when Bean entered the room. Ordinarily, he might have tried to put them at ease. Just because he was grieving did not change the fact that in the midst of crises, humor was needed to break the tension. But at this moment their silence was useful, and he used it.

"I just received information from one of my best sources of intelligence," Bean said. "You in this room are those who most need to hear it. But if the Prime Minister could also join us, it would save time."

One of the generals started to protest that a foreign child did not summon the Prime Minister of Thailand, but Suriyawong stood and bowed deeply to him. The man stopped talking. "Forgive me, sir," said Suriyawong, "but this foreign boy is Julian Delphiki, whose analysis of the final battle with the Formics led directly to Ender's victory."

Of course the general knew that already, but Suriyawong, by allowing him to pretend that he had not known, gave him a way to backpedal without losing face.

"I see," said the general. "Then perhaps the Prime Minister will not be offended at this summons."

Bean helped Suriyawong smooth things over as best he could. "Forgive me for having spoken with such rudeness. You were right to rebuke me. I can only hope you will excuse me for being forgetful of proper manners. The woman who raised me was on the Air Shanghai flight."

Again, the general certainly knew this; again, it allowed him to bow and murmur his commiseration. Proper respect had been shown to everyone. Now things could proceed.

The Prime Minister left his dinner with various high officials of the Chinese government, and stood against the wall, listening, as Bean relayed what he had learned from Peter about the source of the missile that brought down the jet.

"I have been in consultation off and on all day with the foreign minister of China," said the Prime Minister. "He has said nothing about the missile being launched from inside Thailand."

"When the Chinese government is ready to act on this provocation," said Bean, "they will pretend to have just discovered it."

The Prime Minister looked pained. "Could it not have been Indian operatives trying to make it seem that it was a Chinese venture?"

"It could have been anyone," said Bean. "But it was Chinese."

The prickly general spoke up. "How do you know this, if the satellite does not confirm it?"

"It would make little sense for it to be Indian," said Bean. "The only countries that could possibly detect the truck would be China and the U.S., which is well known to be in China's pocket. But China would know that they had not fired the missile, and they would know that Thailand had not fired it, so what would be the point?"

"It makes no sense for China to do it, either," said the Prime Minister.

"Sir," said Bean, "nothing makes sense in any of the things that have happened in the last few days. India has made a nonaggression pact with Pakistan and both nations have moved their troops away from their shared border. Pakistan is moving against Iran. India has invaded Burma, not because Burma is a prize, but because it stands between India and Thailand, which *is.* But India's attack makes no sense—right, Suriyawong?"

Suriyawong instantly understood that Bean was asking him to share in this, so that it would not all come from a European. "As Bean and I told the Chakri yesterday, the Indian attack on Burma is not just stupidly designed, it was *deliberately* stupidly designed. India has commanders wise enough and well-enough trained to know that sending masses of soldiers across the border, with the huge supply problem they represent, creates an easy target for our strategy of harassment. It also leaves them fully committed. And yet they have launched precisely such an attack."

"So much the better for us," said the prickly general.

"Sir," said Suriyawong, "it is important for you to

understand that they have the services of Petra Arkanian, and both Bean and I know that Petra would never sign off on the strategy they're using. So that is obviously *not* their strategy."

"What does this have to do with the Air Shanghai flight?" asked the Prime Minister.

"Everything," said Bean. "And with the attempt on Suriyawong's and my life last night. The Chakri's little game was meant to provoke Thailand into an immediate entry into the war with India. And even though the ploy did not work, and the Chakri was exposed, we are still maintaining the fiction that it was an Indian provocation. Your meetings with the Chinese foreign minister are part of your effort to involve the Chinese in the war against India—no, don't tell me that you can't confirm or deny it, it's obvious that's what such meetings would have to be about. And I'll bet the Chinese are telling you that they are massing troops on the Burmese border in order to attack the Indians suddenly, when they are most exposed."

The Prime Minister, who had indeed been opening his mouth to speak, held his silence.

"Yes, of course they are telling you this. But the Indians also know that the Chinese are massing on the Burmese border, and yet they proceed with their attack on Burma, and their forces are almost fully committed, making no provision for defense against a Chinese attack from the north. Why? Are we going to pretend that the Indians are *that* stupid?"

It was Suriyawong who answered as it dawned on him. "The Indians also have a nonaggression pact with China. They think the Chinese troops are massing at the border in order to attack *us*. They and the Indians have divided up southeast Asia."

"So this missile that the Chinese launched from

Thailand to shoot down their own airliner over their own territory," said the Prime Minister, "that will be their excuse to break off negotiations and attack us by surprise?"

"No one is surprised by Chinese treachery," said one of the generals.

"But that's not the whole picture," said Bean. "Because we have not yet accounted for Achilles."

"He's in India," said Suriyawong. "He planned the attempt to kill us last night."

"And we know he planned that attempt," said Bean, "because I was there. He wanted you dead as a provocation, but he gave approval for it to happen last night because we would both be killed in the same explosion. And we know that he is behind the downing of the Air Shanghai jet, because even though the missile was in place for a month, ready to be fired, this was not yet the right moment to create the provocation. The Chinese foreign minister is still in Bangkok. Thailand has not yet had several days to commit its troops to battle, depleting our supplies and sending most of our forces on missions far to the northwest. Chinese troops have not yet fully deployed to the north of us. That missile should not have been fired for several days, at least. But it was fired this morning because Achilles knew Sister Carlotta was on that airplane, and he could not pass up the opportunity to kill her."

"But you said the missile was a Chinese operation," said the Prime Minister. "Achilles is in India."

"Achilles is in India, but is Achilles working for India?"

"Are you saying he's working for China?" asked the Prime Minister.

"Achilles is working for Achilles," said Suriyawong. "But yes, now the picture is clear."

"Not to me," said the prickly general.

Suriyawong eagerly explained. "Achilles has been setting India up from the beginning. While Achilles was still in Russia, he doubtless used the Russian intelligence service to make contacts inside China. He promised he could hand them all of south and southeast Asia in a single blow. Then he goes to India and sets up a war in which India's army is fully committed in Burma. Until now, China has never been able to move against India, because the Indian Army was concentrated in the west and northwest, so that as Chinese troops came over the passes of the Himalayas, they were easily fought off by Indian troops. Now, though, the entire Indian Army is exposed, far from the heartland of India. If the Chinese can achieve a surprise attack and destroy that army, India will be defenseless. They will have no choice but to surrender. We're just a sideshow to them. They will attack us in order to lull the Indians into complacency."

"So they don't intend to invade Thailand?" asked the Prime Minister.

"Of course they do," said Bean. "They intend to rule from the Indus to the Mekong. But the Indian army is the main objective. Once that is destroyed, there is nothing in their way."

"And all this," said the prickly general, "we deduce from the fact that a certain Catholic nun was on the airplane?"

"We deduce this," said Bean, "from the fact that Achilles is controlling events in China, Thailand, and India. Achilles knew Sister Carlotta was on that plane because the Chakri intercepted my message to the Prime Minister. Achilles is running this show. He's betraying everybody to everybody else. And in the end, he stands at the top of a new empire that contains more than half the population of the world. China, India, Burma, Thailand, Vietnam. Everyone will have to accommodate this new superpower."

"But Achilles does not run China," said the Prime Minister. "As far as we know, he has never been *in* China."

"The Chinese no doubt think they're using him," said Bean. "But I know Achilles, and my guess is that within a year, the Chinese leaders will find themselves either dead or taking their orders from him."

"Perhaps," said the Prime Minister, "I should go warn the Chinese foreign minister of the great danger he is in."

The prickly general stood up. "This is what comes of allowing children to play at world affairs. They think that real life is like a computer game, a few mouse clicks and nations rise and fall."

"This is precisely how nations rise and fall," said Bean. "France in 1940. Napoleon remaking the map of Europe in the early 1800s, creating kingdoms so his brothers would have someplace to rule. The victors in World War I, cutting up kingdoms and drawing insane lines on the map that would lead to war again and again. The Japanese conquest of most of the western Pacific in December of 1941. The collapse of the Soviet Empire in 1989. Events can be sudden indeed."

"But those were great forces at work," said the general.

"Napoleon's whims were not a great force. Nor was Alexander, toppling empires wherever he went. There was nothing inevitable about Greeks reaching the Indus."

"I don't need history lessons from you."

Bean was about to retort that yes, apparently he

did—but Suriyawong shook his head. Bean got the message.

Suriyawong was right. The Prime Minister was not convinced, and the only generals who were speaking up were the ones who were downright hostile to Bean's and Suriyawong's ideas. If Bean continued to push, he would merely find himself marginalized in the coming war. And he needed to be in the thick of things, if he was to be able to use the strike force he had so laboriously created.

"Sir," said Bean to the general, "I did not mean to teach you anything. You have nothing to learn from me. I have merely offered you the information I received, and the conclusions I drew from it. If these conclusions are incorrect, I apologize for wasting your time. And if we proceed with the war against India, I ask only for the chance to serve Thailand honorably, in order to repay your kindness to me."

Before the general could say anything—and it was plain he was going to make a haughty reply—the Prime Minister intervened. "Thank you for giving us your best—Thailand survives in this difficult place because our people and our friends offer everything they have in the service of our small but beautiful land. Of course we will want to use you in the coming war. I believe you have a small strike force of highly trained and versatile Thai soldiers. I will see to it that your force is assigned to a commander who will find good use for that force, and for you."

It was a deft announcement to the generals at that table that Bean and Suriyawong were under his protection. Any general who attempted to quash their participation would simply find that they were assigned to another command. Bean could not have hoped for more.

"And now," said the Prime Minister, "while I am happy to have spent this quarter hour in your company, gentlemen, I have the foreign minister of China no doubt wondering why I am so rude as to stay away for all this time."

The Prime Minister bowed and left.

At once the prickly general and the others who were most skeptical returned to the joking conversation that Bean's arrival had interrupted, as if nothing had happened.

But General Phet Noi, who was field commander of all Thai forces in the Malay Peninsula, beckoned to Suriyawong and Bean. Suriyawong picked up his plate and moved to a place beside Phet Noi, while Bean paused only to fill his own plate from the pots on the serving table before joining them.

"So you have a strike force," said Phet Noi.

"Air, sea, and land," said Bean.

"The main Indian offensive," said Phet Noi, "is in the north. My army will be watching for Indian landings on the coast, but our role will be vigilance, not combat. Still, I think that if your strike force launched its missions from the south, you would be less likely to become tangled up in raids originating in the much more important northern commands."

Phet Noi obviously knew that his own command was the one least important to the conduct of the war—but he was as determined to get involved as Bean and Suriyawong were. They could help each other. For the rest of the meal, Bean and Suriyawong conversed earnestly with Phet Noi, discussing where in the Malay panhandle of Thailand the strike force might best be stationed. Finally, they were the last three at table.

"Sir," said Bean, "now that we're alone, the three of us, there is something I must tell you."

"Yes?"

"I will serve you loyally, and I will obey your orders. But if the opportunity comes, I will use my strike force to accomplish an objective that is not, strictly speaking, important to Thailand."

"And that is?"

"My friend Petra Arkanian is the hostage—no, I believe she is the virtual slave—of Achilles. Every day she lives in constant danger. When I have the information necessary to make success likely, I will use my strike force to bring her out of Hyderabad."

Phet Noi thought about this, his face showing nothing. "You know that Achilles may be holding on to her precisely because she is the bait that will lure you into a trap."

"That is possible," said Bean, "but I don't believe that it's what Achilles is doing. He believes he is able to kill anyone, anywhere. He doesn't need to set traps for me. To lie in wait is a sign of weakness. I believe he's holding on to Petra for his own reasons."

"You know him," said Phet Noi, "and I do not." He reflected for a moment. "As I listened to what you said about Achilles and his plans and treacheries, I believed that events might unfold exactly as you said. What I could not see was how Thailand could possibly turn this into victory. Even with advance warning, we can't prevail against China in the field of battle. China's supply lines into Thailand would be short. Almost a quarter of the population of Thailand is Chinese in origin, and while most of them are loyal Thai citizens, a large fraction of them still regard China as their homeland. China would not lack for saboteurs and collaborators within our country, while India has no such connection. How can we prevail?"

"There is only one way," said Bean. "Surrender at once."

"What?" said Suriyawong.

"Prime Minister Paribatra should go to the Chinese foreign minister, declare that Thailand wishes to be an ally of China. We will put most of our military temporarily under Chinese command to be used against the Indian aggressors as needed, and will supply not only our own armies, but the Chinese armies as well, to the limit of our abilities. Chinese merchants will have unrestricted access to Thai markets and manufacturing."

"But that would be shameful," said Suriyawong.

"It was shameful," said Bean, "when Thailand allied itself with Japan during World War II, but Thailand survived and Japanese troops did not occupy Thailand. It was shameful when Thailand bowed to the Europeans and surrendered Laos and Cambodia to France, but the heart of Thailand remained free. If Thailand doesn't preemptively ally itself to China and give China a free hand, then China will rule here anyway, but Thailand itself will utterly lose its freedom and its national existence, for many years at least, and perhaps forever."

"Am I listening to an oracle?" asked Phet Noi.

"You are listening to the fears of your own heart," said Bean. "Sometimes you have to feed the tiger so it won't devour you."

"Thailand will never do this," said Phet Noi.

"Then I suggest you make arrangements for your escape and life in exile," said Bean, "because when the Chinese take over, the ruling class is destroyed."

They all knew Bean was talking about the conquest

of Taiwan. All government officials and their families, all professors, all journalists, all writers, all politicians and their families were taken from Taiwan to reeducation camps in the western desert, where they were set to work performing manual labor, they and their children, for the rest of their lives. None of them ever returned to Taiwan. None of their children ever received approval for education beyond the age of fourteen. The method had been so effective in pacifying Taiwan that there was no chance they would not use the same method in their conquests now.

"Would I be a traitor, to plan for defeat by creating my own escape route?" Phet Noi wondered aloud.

"Or would you be a patriot, keeping at least one Thai general and his family out of the hands of the conquering enemy?" asked Bean.

"Is our defeat certain, then?" asked Suriyawong.

"You can read a map," said Bean. "But miracles happen."

Bean left them to their silent thoughts and returned to his room, to report to Peter on the likely Thai response.

17

On a Bridge

To: Chamrajnagar%sacredriver@ifcom.gov
From: Wiggin%resistance@haiti.gov
Re: For the sake of India, please do not set foot on Earth

Esteemed Polemarch Chamrajnagar,

For reasons that will be made clear by the attached essay, which I will soon publish, I fully expect that you will return to Earth just in time to be caught up in India's complete subjugation by China.

If your return to India had any chance of preserving her independence, you would bear any risk and return, regardless of any advice. And if your establishing a government in exile could accomplish anything for your native land, who would try to persuade you to do otherwise?

But India's strategic position is so exposed, and China's relentlessness in conquest is so well known, that you must know both courses of action are futile.

Your resignation as Polemarch does not take effect until you reach Earth. If you do not board the shuttle, but instead return to IFCom, you remain Polemarch. You are the only possible Polemarch who could secure the International Fleet. A new commander could not distinguish between Chinese who are loyal to the Fleet and those whose first allegiance is to their now-dominant homeland. The I.F. must not fall under the sway of Achilles. You, as Polemarch, could reassign suspect Chinese to innocuous postings, preventing any Chinese grab for control. If you return to Earth, and Achilles has influence over your successor as Polemarch, the I.F. will become a tool of conquest.

If you remain as Polemarch, you will be accused, as an Indian, of planning to pursue vengeance against China. Therefore, to prove your impartiality and avoid suspicion, you will have to remain utterly aloof from all Earthside wars and struggles. You can trust me and my allies to maintain the resistance to Achilles regardless of the apparent odds, if for no other reason than this: His ultimate triumph means our immediate death.

Stay in space and, by doing so, allow the possibility of humanity escaping the domination of a madman. In return, I vow to do all in my power to free India from Chinese rule and return it to self-rule.

Sincerely, Peter Wiggin

The soldiers around her knew perfectly well who Virlomi was. They also knew the reward that had been offered for her capture—or her dead body. The charge was treason and espionage. But from the start, as she passed through the checkpoint at the entrance of the base at Hyderabad, the common soldiers had believed in her and befriended her.

"You will hear me accused of spying or worse," she said, "but it isn't true. A treacherous foreign monster rules in Hyderabad, and he wants me dead for personal reasons. Help me."

Without a word, the soldiers walked her away from where the cameras might spot her, and waited. When an empty supply truck came up, they stopped it and while some of them talked to the driver, the others helped her get in. The truck drove through, and she was out.

Ever since, she had turned to the footsoldiers for help. Officers might or might not let compassion or righteousness interfere with obedience or ambition—the common soldiers had no such qualms. She was transported in the midst of a crush of soldiers on a crowded train, offered so much food smuggled out of mess halls that she could not eat it all, and given bunk space while weary men slept on the floor. No one laid a hand on her except to help her, and none betrayed her.

She moved across India to the east, toward the war zone, for she knew that her only hope, and the only hope for Petra Arkanian, was for her to find, or be found by, Bean.

Virlomi knew where Bean would be: making trouble for Achilles wherever and however he could. Since the Indian Army had chosen the dangerous and foolish strategy of committing all its manpower to battle, she knew that the effective counterstrategy would be harassment and disruption of supply lines. And Bean would come to whatever point on the supply line was most crucial and yet most difficult to disrupt.

So, as she neared the front, Virlomi went over in her mind the map she had memorized. To move large amounts of supplies and munitions quickly from India to the troops sweeping through the great plain where the Irrawaddy flowed, there were two general routes. The northern route was easier, but far more exposed to raids. The southern route was harder, but more protected. Bean would be working on disrupting the southern route.

Where? There were two roads over the mountains from Imphal in India to Kalemyo in Burma. They both passed through narrow canyons and crossed deep gorges. Where would it be hardest to rebuild a blown bridge or a collapsed highway? On both routes, there were candidate locations. But the hardest to rebuild was on the western route, a long stretch of road carved out of rock along the edge of a steep defile, leading to a bridge over a deep gorge. Bean would not just blow up this bridge, Virlomi thought, because it would not be that hard to span. He would also collapse the road in several places, so the engineers wouldn't be able to get to the place where the bridge must be anchored without first blasting and shaping a new road.

So that is where Virlomi went, and waited.

Water she found flowing cleanly through the side ravines. She was given food by passing soldiers, and soon learned that they were looking for her. Word had spread that the Woman-in-hiding needed food. And still no officer knew to look for her, and still no assassin from Achilles came to kill her. Poor as the soldiers were, apparently the reward did not tempt them. She was proud of her people even as she mourned for them, to have such a man as Achilles rule over them.

She heard of daring raids at easier spots on the eastern road, and traffic on the western road grew heavier, the roads trembling day and night as India burned up her fuel reserves supplying an army far larger than the war required. She asked the soldiers if they had heard of Thai raiders led by a child, and they laughed bitterly. "Two children," they said. "One white, one brown. They come in their helicopters, they destroy, they leave. Whomever they touch, they kill. Whatever they see, they destroy."

Now she began to worry. What if the one that came to take this bridge was not Bean, but the other one? No doubt another Battle School grad—Suriyawong came to mind—but would Bean have told him about her letter? Would he have any idea that she held within her head the plan of the base at Hyderabad? That she knew where Petra was?

Yet she had no choice. She would have to show herself, and hope.

So the days passed, waiting for the sound of the helicopters coming, bringing the strike force that would destroy this road.

—

Suriyawong had never been a commander in Battle School. They closed down the program before he rose to that position. But he had dreamed of command, studied it, planned it, and now, working with Bean in command of this or that configuration of their strike force, he finally understood the terror and exhilaration of having men listen to you, obey you, throw themselves into action and risk death because they trust you. Each time, because these men were so well-trained and resourceful and their tactics so effective, he brought back his whole complement. Injuries, but no deaths. Aborted missions, sometimes—but no deaths.

"It's the aborted missions," said Bean, "that earn you their trust. When you see that it's more dangerous than we anticipated, that it requires attrition to get the objective, then show the men you value their lives more than the objective of the moment. Later, when you have no choice but to commit them to grave risk, they'll know it's because this time it's worth dying. They know you won't spend them like a child, on candy and trash."

Bean was right, which hardly surprised Suriyawong. Bean was not just the smartest, he had also watched

Ender close at hand, had been Ender's secret weapon in Dragon Army, had been his backup commander on Eros. Of course he knew what leadership was.

What surprised Suriyawong was Bean's generosity. Bean had created this strike force, and trained these men, had earned their trust. Throughout that time, Suriyawong had been of little help, and had shown outright hostility at times. Yet Bean included Suriyawong, entrusted him with command, encouraged the men to help Suriyawong learn what they could do. Through it all, Bean had never treated Suriyawong as a subordinate or inferior, but rather had deferred to him as his superior officer.

In return, Suriyawong never commanded Bean to do anything. Rather, they reached a consensus on most things, and when they could not agree, Suriyawong deferred to Bean's decision and supported him in it.

Bean has no ambition, Suriyawong realized. He has no wish to be better than anyone else, or to rule over anyone, or to have more honor.

Then, on the missions where they worked together, Suriyawong saw something else: Bean had no fear of death.

Bullets could be flying, explosives could be near detonation, and Bean would move without fear and with only token concealment. It was as if he dared the enemy to shoot him, dared their own explosives to defy him and go off before he was ready.

Was this courage? Or did he wish for death? Had Sister Carlotta's death taken away some of his will to live? To hear him talk, Suriyawong would not have supposed it. Bean was too grimly determined to rescue Petra for Suriyawong to believe that he wanted to die. He had something urgent to live for. And yet he showed no fear of battle.

It was as if he knew the day that he would die, and this was not that day.

He certainly hadn't stopped caring about anything. Indeed, the quiet, icy, controlled, arrogant Bean that Suriyawong had known before had become, since the day Carlotta died, impatient and agitated. The calm he showed in battle, in front of the men, was certainly not there when he was alone with Suriyawong and Phet Noi. And the favorite object of his curses was not Achilles—he almost never spoke of Achilles—but Peter Wiggin.

"He's had everything for a month! And he does these little things—persuading Chamrajnagar not to return to Earth yet, persuading Ghaffar Wahabi not to invade Iran—and he tells me about them, but the big thing, publishing Achilles' whole treacherous strategy, he won't do that—and he tells *me* not to do it myself! Why not? If the Indian government could be forced to see how Achilles plans to betray them, they might be able to pull enough of their army out of Burma to make a stand against the Chinese. Russia might be able to intervene. The Japanese fleet might threaten Chinese trade. At the very least, the Chinese themselves might see Achilles for what he is, and jettison him even as they follow his plan! And all he says is, It's not the right moment, it's too soon, not yet, you have to trust me, I'm with you on this, right to the end."

He was scarcely kinder in his execrations of the Thai generals running the war—or ruining it, as he said. Suriyawong had to agree with him—the whole plan depended on keeping Thai forces dispersed, but now that the Thai Air Force had control of the air over Burma, they had concentrated their armies and airbases in forward positions. "I told them what the danger was," said Bean, "and they still gather their forces into one convenient place."

Phet Noi listened patiently; Suriyawong, too, gave up trying to argue with him. Bean was right. People were behaving foolishly, and not out of ignorance. Though of course they would say, later, "But we didn't *know* Bean was right."

To which Bean already had his answer: "You didn't know I was wrong! So you should have been prudent!"

The only thing different in Bean's diatribes was that he went hoarse for a week, and when his voice came back, it was lower. For a kid who had always been so tiny, even for his age, puberty—if that's what this was—certainly had struck him young. Or maybe he had just stretched out his vocal cords with all his ranting.

But now, on a mission, Bean was silent, the calm of battle already on him. Suriyawong and Bean boarded their choppers last, making sure all their men were aboard; one last salute to each other, and then they ducked inside and the door closed and the choppers rose into the air. They jetted along near the surface of the Indian Ocean, the chopper blades folded and enclosed until they got near Cheduba Island, today's staging area. Then the choppers dispersed, rose into the air, cut the jets, and opened their blades for vertical landing.

Now they would leave behind their reserves—the men and choppers that could bring out anyone stranded by a mechanical problem or unforeseen complication. Bean and Suriyawong never rode together—one chopper failure should not behead the mission. And each of them had redundant equipment, so that either could complete the whole mission. More than once, the redundancy had saved lives and missions—

Phet Noi made sure they were always equipped because, as he said, "You give the matériel to the commanders who know how to use it."

Bean and Suriyawong were too busy to chat in the staging area, but they did come together for a few moments, as they watched the reserve team camouflage their choppers and scrim their solar collectors. "You know what I wish?" said Bean.

"You mean besides wanting to be an astronaut when you grow up?" said Suriyawong.

"That we could scrub this mission and take off for Hyderabad."

"And get ourselves killed without ever seeing a sign of Petra, who has probably already been moved to someplace in the Himalayas."

"That's the genius of my plan," said Bean. "I take a herd of cattle hostage and threaten to shoot a cow a day till they bring her back."

"Too risky. The cows always make a break for it." But Suriyawong knew that to Bean, the inability to do anything for Petra was a constant ache. "We'll do it. Peter's looking for someone who'll give him current information about Hyderabad."

"Like he's working on publishing Achilles' plans." The favorite diatribe. Only because they were on a mission, Bean remained calm, ironic rather than furious.

"All done," said Suriyawong.

"See you in the mountains."

It was a dangerous mission. The enemy couldn't watch every kilometer of highway, but they had learned to converge quickly when the Thai choppers were spotted, and their strike force was having to finish their missions with less and less time to spare. And this spot was likely to be defended. That was why Bean's contingent—four of the five companies—

would be deployed to clear away any defenders and protect Suriyawong's group while they laid the charges and blew up the road and the bridge.

All was going according to plan—indeed, better than expected, because the enemy seemed not to know they were there—when one of the men pointed out, "There's a woman on the bridge."

"A civilian?"

"You need to see," said the soldier.

Suriyawong left the spot where the explosives were being placed and climbed back up to the bridge. Sure enough, a young Indian woman was standing there, her arms stretched out toward either side of the ravine.

"Has anyone mentioned to her that the bridge is going to explode, and we don't actually care if anyone's on it?"

"Sir," said the soldier, "she's asking for Bean."

"By name?"

He nodded.

Suriyawong looked at the woman again. A very young woman. Her clothing was filthy, tattered. Had it once been a military uniform? It certainly wasn't the way local women dressed.

She looked at him. "Suriyawong," she called.

Behind him, he could hear several soldiers exhale or gasp in surprise or wonder. How did this Indian woman know? It worried Suriyawong a little. The soldiers were reliable in almost everything, but if they once got god-stuff into their heads, it could complicate everything.

"I'm Suriyawong," he said.

"You were in Dragon Army," she said. "And you work with Bean."

"What do you want?" he demanded.

"I want to talk with you privately, here on the bridge."

"Sir, don't go," said the soldier. "Nobody's shooting, but we've spotted a half-dozen Indian soldiers. You're dead if you go out there."

What would Bean do?

Suriyawong stepped out onto the bridge, boldly but not in any hurry. He waited for the gunshot, wondering if he would feel the pain of impact before he heard the sound. Would the nerves of his ears report to his brain faster than the nerves of whatever body part the bullet tore into? Or would the sniper hit him in the head, mooting the point?

No bullet. He came near her, and stopped when she said, "This is as close as you should come, or they'll worry and shoot you."

"You control those soldiers?" asked Suriyawong.

"Don't you know me yet?" she said. "I'm Virlomi. I was ahead of you in Battle School."

He knew the name. He would never have recognized her face. "You left before I got there."

"Not many girls in Battle School. I thought the legend would live on."

"I heard of you."

"I'm a legend here, too. My people aren't firing because they think I know what I'm doing out here. And I thought you recognized me, because your soldiers on both sides of this ravine have refrained from shooting any of the Indian soldiers, even though I know they've spotted them."

"Maybe Bean recognized you," said Sirayawong. "In fact, I've heard your name more recently. You're the one who wrote back to him, aren't you? You were in Hyderabad."

"I know where Petra is."

"Unless they've moved her."

"Do you have any better sources? I tried to think of any way I could to get a message to Bean without getting caught. Finally I realized there was no computer solution. I had to bring the message in my head."

"So come with us."

"Not that simple," she said. "If they think I'm a captive, you'll never get out of here. Handheld g-to-a."

"Ouch," said Suriyawong. "Ambush. They knew we were coming?"

"No," said Virlomi. "They knew I was here. I didn't say anything, but they all knew that the Woman-in-hiding was at this bridge, so they figured that the gods were protecting this place."

"And the gods needed g-to-a missiles?"

"No, *I'm* the one they're protecting. The gods have the bridge, the men have me. So here's the deal. You pull your explosives off the bridge. Abort the mission. They see that I have the power to make the enemy go away without harming anything. And then they watch me call one of your departing choppers down to me, and I get on of my own free will. That's the only way you're getting out of here. Not really anything I designed, but I don't see any other way out."

"I always hate aborting missions," said Suriyawong. But before she could argue, he laughed and said, "No, don't worry, it's fine. It's a good plan. If Bean were down here on this bridge, he'd agree in a heartbeat."

Suriyawong walked back to his men. "No, it's not a god or a holy woman. She's Virlomi, a Battle School grad, and she has intelligence that's more valuable than this bridge. We're aborting the mission."

The soldier took this in, and Suriyawong could see

him trying to factor the magical element in with the orders.

"Soldier," said Suriyawong, "I have not been bewitched. This woman knows the groundplan of the Indian Army high command base in Hyderabad."

"Why would an Indian give that to us?" the soldier asked.

"Because the bunduck who's running the Indian side of the war has a prisoner there who's vital to the war."

Now it was making sense to the soldier. The magic element receded. He pulled his satrad off his belt and punched in the abort code. All the other satrads immediately vibrated in the preset pattern.

At once the explosives teams began dismantling. If they were to evacuate without dismantling, a second code, for urgency, would be sent. Suriyawong did not want any part of their matériel to fall into Indian hands. And he thought a more leisurely pace might be better.

"Soldier, I need to *seem* to be hypnotized by this woman," he said. "I am *not* hypnotized, but I'm faking it so the Indian soldiers all around us will think she's controlling me. Got that?"

"Yes sir."

"So while I walk back toward her, you call Bean and tell him that I need all the choppers but mine to evacuate, so the Indians can see they're gone. Then say 'Petra.' Got that? Tell him *nothing* else, no matter what he asks. We may be monitored, if not here, then in Hyderabad." Or Beijing, but he didn't want to complicate things by saying that.

"Yes sir."

Suriyawong turned his back on the soldier, walked three paces closer to Virlomi, and then prostrated himself before her.

Behind him, he could hear the soldier saying exactly what he had been told to say.

And after a very little while, choppers began to rise into the air from both sides of the ravine. Bean's troops were on the way out.

Suriyawong got up and returned to his men. His company had come in two choppers. "All of you get in the chopper with the explosives," he said. "Only the pilot and co-pilot stay in the other chopper."

The men obeyed immediately, and within three minutes Suriyawong was alone at his end of the bridge. He turned and bowed once again to Virlomi, then walked calmly to his chopper and climbed aboard.

"Rise slowly," he told the pilot, "and then pass slowly near the woman in the middle of the bridge, doorside toward her. At no point is any weapon to be trained on her. Nothing remotely threatening."

Suriyawong watched through the window. Virlomi was not signaling.

"Rise higher, as if we were leaving," said Suriyawong.

The pilot obeyed.

Finally, Virlomi began waving her arms, beckoning with both of them, slowly, as if she were reeling them back in with each movement of her arms.

"Slow down and then begin to descend toward her. I want no chance of error. The last thing we need is some downdraft to get her caught in the blades."

The pilot laughed grimly and brought the chopper like a dancer down onto the bridge, far enough away that Virlomi wasn't actually under the blades, but close enough that it would be only a few steps for her to come aboard.

Suriyawong ran to the door and opened it.

Virlomi did not just walk to the chopper. She danced to it, making ritual-like circling movements with each step.

On impulse, he got out of the chopper and prostrated himself again. When she got near enough, he said—loud enough to be heard over the chopper blades—"Walk on me!"

She did, planting her bare feet on his shoulders and walking down his back. Suriyawong didn't know how they could have communicated more clearly to the Indian soldiers that not only had Virlomi saved their bridge, she had also taken control of this chopper.

She was inside.

He got up, turned slowly, and sauntered onto the chopper.

The sauntering ended the moment he was inside. He rammed the door lever up into place and shouted, "I want jets as fast as you can!"

The chopper rose dizzily. "Strap down," Suriyawong ordered Virlomi. Then, seeing she wasn't familiar with the inside of this craft, he pushed her into place and put the ends of her harness into her hands. She got it at once and finished the job while he hurled himself into his place and got his straps in place just as the chopper cut the blades and plummeted for a moment before the jets kicked in. Then they rocketed down the ravine and out of range of the handheld g-to-a missiles.

"You just made my day," said Suriyawong.

"Took you long enough," said Virlomi. "I thought this bridge was one of the first places you'd hit."

"We figured that's what people would think, so we kept not coming here."

"Greeyaz," she said. "I should have remembered to

think completely ass-backward in order to predict what Battle School brats would do."

—

Bean had known the moment he saw her on the bridge that she had to be Virlomi, the Indian Battle Schooler who had answered his Briseis posting. He could only trust that Suriyawong would realize what was happening before he found the need to shoot somebody. And Surly had not let him down.

When they got back to the staging area, Bean barely greeted Virlomi before he started giving orders. "I want the whole staging area dismantled. Everybody's coming with us." While the company commanders saw to that, Bean ordered one of the chopper communications team to set up a net connection for him.

"That's satellite," the soldier said. "We'll be located right away."

"We'll be gone before anyone can react," said Bean.

Only then did he start explaining to Suriyawong and Virlomi. "We're fully equipped, right?"

"But not fully fueled."

"I'll take care of that," he said. "We're going to Hyderabad right now."

"But I haven't even drawn up the plans."

"Time for that in the air," he said. "This time we ride together, Suriyawong. Can't be helped—we both have to know the whole plan."

"We've waited this long," said Suriyawong. "What's the hurry now?"

"Two things," said Bean. "How long do you think it'll be before word reaches Achilles that our strike force picked up an Indian woman who was waiting for us on a bridge? Second thing—I'm going to force Peter Wiggin's hand. All hell is going to break loose, and we're riding the wave."

"What's the objective?" asked Virlomi. "To save Petra? To kill Achilles?"

"To bring out every Battle School kid who'll come with us."

"They'll never leave India," she said. "I may decide to stay myself."

"Wrong on both counts," said Bean. "I give India less than a week before Chinese troops have control of New Delhi and Hyderabad and any other city they want."

"Chinese?" asked Virlomi. "But there's some kind of—"

"Nonaggression pact?" said Bean. "Arranged by Achilles?"

"He's been working for China all along," said Suriyawong. "The Indian Army is exposed, undersupplied, exhausted, demoralized."

"But . . . if China comes in on the side of the Thai, isn't that what you want?"

Suriyawong gave a sharp, bitter laugh. "China comes in on the side of China. We tried to warn our own people, but they're sure *they* have a deal with Beijing."

Virlomi understood at once. Battle School–trained, she knew how to think the way Bean and Suriyawong did. "So that's why Achilles didn't use Petra's plan."

Bean and Suriyawong laughed and gave short little bows to each other.

"You knew about Petra's plan?"

"We assumed there'd be a better plan than the one India's using."

"So you have a plan to stop China?" said Virlomi.

"Not a chance," said Bean. "China might have been stopped a month ago, but nobody listened." He thought of Peter and barely stanched the fury. "Achilles himself may still be stopped, or at least weakened. But our goal is to keep the Indian Battle School team from falling into Chinese hands. Our Thai friends already have escape routes planned. So when we get to Hyderabad, we not only need to find Petra, we need to offer escape to anyone who'll come. Will they listen to you?"

"We'll see, won't we?" said Virlomi.

"The connection's ready," said a soldier. "I didn't actually link yet, because that's when the clock starts ticking."

"Do it," said Bean. "I've got some things to say to Peter Wiggin."

I'm coming, Petra. I'm getting you out.

As for Achilles, if he happens to come within my reach, there'll be no mercy this time, no relying on someone else to keep him out of circulation. I'll kill him without discussion. And my men will have orders to do the same.

18

Satyagraha

encrypt key ********
decrypt key *****
To: Locke%erasmus@polnet.gov
From: Borommakot@chakri.thai.gov/scom
Re: Now, or I will

I'm in a battlefield situation and I need two things from you, now.

First, I need permission from the Sri Lankan government to land at the base at Kilinochchi to refuel, ETA less than an hour. This is a nonmilitary rescue mission to retrieve Battle School graduates in imminent danger of capture, torture, enslavement, or at the very least imprisonment.

Second, to justify this and all other actions I'm about to take; to persuade those Battle Schoolers to come with me; and to create confusion in Hyderabad, I need you to publish now. Repeat, NOW. Or I will publish my own article, here attached, which specifically names you as a coconspirator with the Chinese, as proven by your failure to publish what you know in a timely manner. Even though I don't have Locke's worldwide reach, I have a nice little email list of my own, and my article will get attention. Yours, however, would have far faster results, and I would prefer it to come from you.

Pardon my threat. I can't afford to play any more of your "wait for the right time" games. I'm getting Petra out.

encrypt key *****
decrypt key ********
To: Borommakot@chakri.thai.gov/scom
From: Locke%erasmus@polnet.gov
Re: Done

Confirmed: Sri Lanka grants landing permission/refueling privileges at Kilinochchi for aircraft on humanitarian mission. Thai markings?

Confirmed: my essay released as of now, worldwide push distribution. This includes urgent fyi push into the systems at Hyderabad and Bangkok.

Your threat was sweetly loyal to your friend, but not necessary. This was the time I was waiting for. Apparently you didn't realize that the moment I published, Achilles would have to move his operations, and would probably take Petra with him. How would you have found her, if I had published a month ago?

encrypt key ********
decrypt key *****
To: Locke%erasmus@polnet.gov
From: Borommakot@chakri.thai.gov/scom
Re: Done

Confirm: Thai markings

As to your excuse: Kuso. If that had been your reason for delay, you would have told me a month ago. I know the real reason, even if you don't, and it makes me sick.

For two weeks after Virlomi disappeared, Achilles had not once come into the planning room—which no one minded, especially after the reward was issued for Virlomi's return. No one dared speak of it openly, but all were glad she had escaped Achilles' vengeance. They were all aware, of course, of the heightened security around them—for their "protection." But it didn't change their lives much. It wasn't as if any of them had ever had time to go frolicking in downtown Hyderabad, or fraternizing with officers twice or three times their age on the base.

Petra was skeptical of the reward offer, though. She knew Achilles well enough to know that he was perfectly capable of offering a reward for the capture of someone he had already killed. What safer cover could he have? Still, if that were the case it would imply that he did not have carte blanche from Tikal Chapekar—if he had to hide things from the Indian government, it meant Achilles was not yet running everything.

When he did return, there was no sign of a bruise on his face. Either Petra's kick had not left a mark, or it took two weeks for it to heal completely. Her own bruises were not yet gone, but no one could see them, since they were under her shirt. She wondered if he had any testicular pain. She wondered if he had had to see a urologist. She did not allow any trace of her gloating to appear on her face.

Achilles was full of talk about how well the war was going and what a good job they were doing in Planning. The army was well supplied and despite the harassment of the cowardly Thai military, the campaign was moving forward on schedule. The revised schedule, of course.

Which was such greeyaz. He was talking to the *planners*. They knew perfectly well that the army was bogged down, that they were still fighting the Burmese in the Irrawaddy plain because the Thai Army's harassment tactics made it impossible to mount the crushing offensive that would have driven the Burmese into the mountains and allowed the Indian Army to proceed into Thailand. Schedule? There was no schedule now.

What Achilles was telling them was: This is the party line. Make sure no memo or email from this room gives anyone even the slightest hint that events are not going according to plan.

It did not change the fact that everyone in Planning could smell defeat. Supplying a huge army on the move was taxing enough to India's limited resources. Supplying it when half the supplies were likely to disappear due to enemy action was chewing through India's resources faster than they could hope to replenish them.

At current rates of manufacture and consumption, the army would run out of munitions in seven weeks. But that would hardly matter—unless some miracle happened, they would run out of nonrenewable fuel in four.

Everyone knew that if Petra's plan had been followed, India would have been able to continue such an offensive indefinitely, and attrition would already have destroyed Burmese resistance. The war would already be on Thai soil, and the Indian Army would not bc limping along with a relentless deadline looming up behind them.

They did not talk in the planning room, but at meals they carefully, obliquely discussed things. Was it too late to revert to the other strategy? Not really—but it would require a strategic withdrawal of the bulk of India's army, which would be impossible to conceal from the people and the media. Politically, it would be a disaster. But then, running out of bullets or fuel would be even more disastrous.

"We have to draw up plans for withdrawal anyway," said Sayagi. "Unless some miracle happens in the field—some brilliance in a field commander that has hitherto been invisible, some political collapse in Burma or Thailand—we're going to need a plan to extricate our people."

"I don't think we'll get permission to spend time on that," someone answered.

Petra rarely said anything at meals, despite her new custom of sitting at table with one or another group from Planning. This time, though, she spoke up. "Do it in your heads," she said.

They paused for a moment, and then Sayagi nodded. "Good plan. No confrontation."

From then on, part of mealtime consisted of cryptic reports from each member of the team on the status of every portion of the withdrawal plan.

Another time that Petra spoke had nothing to do with military planning, per se. Someone had jokingly said that this would be a good time for Bose to return. Petra knew the story of Subhas Chandra Bose, the Netaji of the Japanese-backed anti-British-rule Indian National Army during World War II. When he died in a plane crash on the way to Japan at the end of the war, the legend among the Indian people was that he was not really dead, but lived on, planning to return someday to lead the people to freedom. In the centuries since then, invoking the return of Bose was both a joke and a serious comment—that the current leadership was as illegitimate as the British Raj had been.

From the mention of Bose, the conversation turned to a discussion of Gandhi. Someone started talking about "peaceful resistance"—never implying that anyone in Planning might contemplate such a thing, of course—and someone else said, "No, that's *passive* resistance."

That was when Petra spoke up. "This is India, and you know the word. It's satyagraha, and it doesn't mean peaceful or passive resistance at all."

"Not everyone here speaks Hindi," said a Tamil planner.

"But everyone here should know Gandhi," said Petra.

Sayagi agreed with her. "Satyagraha is something else. The willingness to endure great personal suffering in order to do what's right."

"What's the difference, really?"

"Sometimes," said Petra, "what's right is not peaceful or passive. What matters is that you do not hide from the consequences. You bear what must be borne."

"That sounds more like courage than anything else," said the Tamil.

"Courage to do right," said Sayagi. "Courage even when you can't win."

"What happened to 'discretion is the better part of valor'?"

"A quotation from a cowardly character in Shakespeare," someone else pointed out.

"Not contradictory anyway," said Sayagi. "Completely different circumstances. If there's a chance of victory later through withdrawal now, you keep your forces intact. But personally, as an individual, if you know that the price of doing right is terrible loss or suffering or even death, satyagraha means that you are all the more determined to do right, for fear that fear might make you unrighteous."

"Oh, paradoxes within paradoxes."

But Petra turned it from superficial philosophy to something else entirely. "I am trying," she said, "to achieve satyagraha."

And in the silence that followed, she knew that some, at least, understood. She was alive right now because she had *not* achieved satyagraha, because she had *not* always done the right thing, but had done only what was necessary to survive. And she was preparing to change that. To do the right thing regardless of whether she lived through it or not. And for whatever reason—respect for her, uncomfortableness with the intensity of it, or serious contemplation—they remained silent until the meal ended and they spoke again of quotidian things.

Now the war had been going for a month, and Achilles was giving them daily pep talks about how victory was imminent even as they wrestled privately with the growing problems of extricating the army. There *had* been some victories, and at two points the Indian Army was now in Thai territory—but that only lengthened the supply lines and put the army into mountainous country again, where their large numbers could not be brought to bear against the enemy, yet still had to be supplied. And these offensives had chewed through fuel and munitions. In a few days, they would have to choose between fueling tanks and fueling supply trucks. They were about to become a very hungry all-infantry army.

As soon as Achilles left, Sayagi stood up. "It is time to write down our plan for withdrawal and submit it. We must declare victory and withdraw."

There was no dissent. Even though the vids and the nets were full of stories of the great Indian victories, the advance into Thailand, these plans had to be written down, the orders drawn up, while there was still time and fuel enough to carry them out.

So they spent that morning writing each component of the plan. Sayagi, as their de facto leader, assembled them into a single, fairly coherent set of documents. In the meantime, Petra browsed the net and worked on the project she had been assigned by Achilles, taking no part in what they were doing. They didn't need her for this, and it was her desk that was most closely monitored by Achilles. As long as she was being obedient, Achilles might not notice that the others were not.

When they were almost done, she spoke up, even though she knew that Achilles would be notified quickly of what she said—that he might even be listening through that hearing aid in his ear. "Before you email it," she said, "post it."

At first they probably thought she meant the internal posting, where they could all read it. But then they saw that, using her fingernail on a piece of rough tan toilet paper, she had scratched a net address and was now holding it out.

It was Peter Wiggin's "Locke" forum.

They looked at her like she was crazy. To post military plans in a public place?

But then Sayagi began to nod. "They intercept all our emails," he said. "This is the only way it will get to Chapekar himself."

"To make military secrets public," someone said. He did not need to finish. They knew the penalty.

"Satyagraha," said Sayagi. He took the toilet paper with the address and sat down to go to that netsite. "I am the one doing this, and no one else," he said. "The rest of you warned me not to. There is no reason for more than one person to risk the consequences." Moments later, the data was flowing to Peter Wiggin's forum.

Only then did he send it as email to the general command—which would be routed through Achilles' computer.

"Sayagi," someone said. "Did you see what else is posted here? On this netsite?"

Petra also moved to the Locke forum and discovered that the lead essay on Locke's site was headed,

"Chinese treachery and the fall of India." The subhead said, "Will China, too, fall victim to a psychopath's twisted plans?"

Even as they were reading Locke's essay detailing how China had made promises to both Thailand and India, and would attack now that both armies were fully exposed and, in India's case, overextended, they received emails that contained the same essay, pushed into the system on an urgent basis. That meant it had already been cleared at the top—Chapekar knew what Locke was alleging.

Therefore, their emailed plans for immediate withdrawal of Indian troops from Burma had reached Chapekar at exactly the time when he knew they would be necessary.

"Toguro," breathed Sayagi. "We look like geniuses."

"We *are* geniuses," someone grumbled, and everyone laughed.

"Does anyone think," asked the Tamil, "we'll hear another pep talk from our Belgian friend about how well the war is going?"

Almost as an answer, they heard gunfire outside.

Petra felt a thrill of hope run through her: Achilles tried to make a run for it, and he was shot.

But then a more practical idea replaced her hope: Achilles foresaw this possibility, and has his own forces already in place to cover his escape.

And finally, despair: When he comes for me, will it be to kill me, or take me with him?

More gunfire.

"Maybe," said Sayagi, "we ought to disperse."

He was walking toward the door when it opened and Achilles came in, followed by six Sikhs carrying automatic weapons. "Have a seat, Sayagi," said Achilles. "I'm afraid we have a hostage situation here. Someone made some libelous assertions about me on the nets, and when I declined to be detained during the inquiry, shooting began. Fortunately, I have some friends, and while we're waiting for them to provide me with transportation to a neutral location, you are my guarantors of safety."

Immediately, the two Battle School grads who were Sikhs stood up and said, to Achilles' soldiers, "Are we under threat of death from you?"

"As long as you serve the oppressor," one of them answered.

"*He* is the oppressor!" one of the Sikh Battle Schoolers said, pointing to Achilles.

"Do you think the Chinese will be any kinder to our people than New Delhi has?" said the other.

"Remember how the Chinese treated Tibet and Taiwan! That is our future, because of *him*!"

The Sikh soldiers were obviously wavering.

Achilles drew a pistol from his back and shot the soldiers dead, one after another. The last two had time to try to rush at him, but every shot he fired struck home.

The pistol shots still rang in the room when Sayagi said, "Why didn't they shoot you?"

"I had them unload their weapons before entering the room," Achilles said. "I told them we didn't want any accidents. But don't think you can overpower me because I'm alone with a half-empty clip. This room has long been wired with explosives, and they go off when my heart stops beating or when I activate the controller implanted under the skin of my chest."

A pocket phone beeped and, without lowering his gun, Achilles answered it. "No, I'm afraid one of my soldiers went out of control, and in order to keep the children safe, I had to shoot some of my own men.

The situation is unchanged. I am monitoring the perimeter. Keep back, and these children will be safe."

Petra wanted to laugh. Most of the Battle Schoolers here were older than Achilles himself.

Achilles clicked off the phone and pocketed it. "I'm afraid I told them that I had you as my hostages before it was actually true."

"Caught you with your pants down, né?" said Sayagi. "You had no way of knowing you'd need hostages, or that we'd all be here. There are no explosives in this room."

Achilles turned to him and calmly shot him in the head. Sayagi crumpled and fell. Several of the others cried out. Achilles calmly changed clips.

No one charged him while he was reloading.

Not even, thought Petra, me.

There's nothing like casual murder to turn the onlookers into vegetables.

"Satyagraha," said Petra.

Achilles whirled on her. "What was that? What language?"

"Hindi," she said. "It means, 'One bears what one must.' "

"No more Hindi," said Achilles. "From anyone. Or any other language but Common. And if you talk, it had better be to me, and it had better not be something stupid and defiant like the words that got Sayagi killed. If all goes well, my relief should be here in only a few hours. And then Petra and I will go away and leave you to your new government. A Chinese government."

Many of them looked at Petra then. She smiled at Achilles. "So your tent door is still open?"

He smiled back. Warmly. Lovingly. Like a kiss.

But she knew that he was taking her away solely in order to relish the time in which she would have false hopes, before he pushed her from a helicopter or strangled her on the tarmac or, if he grew too impatient, simply shot her as she prepared to follow him out of this room. His time with her was over. His triumph was near—the architect of China's conquest of India, returning to China as a hero. Already plotting how he would take control of the Chinese government and then set out to conquer the other half of the world's population.

For now, though, she was alive, and so were the other Battle Schoolers, except Sayagi. The reason Sayagi died, of course, was not what he said to Achilles. He died because he was the one who posted the withdrawal plans on Locke's forum. Being plans for a retreat under unpredictable fire, they were still usable even with Chinese troops pouring down into Burma, even with Chinese planes bombing the retreating soldiers. The Indian commanders would be able to make a stand. The Chinese would have to fight hard before they won.

But they would win. The Indian defense could last no more than a few days, no matter how bravely they fought. That was when the trucks would stop rolling and food and munitions would run out. The war was already lost. There was only a little time for the Indian elite to attempt to flee before the Chinese swept in, unresisted, with their behead-the-society method of controlling an occupied country.

While these events unfolded, the Battle School graduates who would have kept India out of this dangerous situation in the first place, and whose planning was the only thing keeping the Chinese temporarily at bay, sat in a large room with seven corpses, one gun, and the young man who had betrayed them all.

More than three hours later, gunfire began again, in the distance. The booming sound of anti-aircraft guns.

Achilles was on the phone in an instant. "Don't fire at the incoming aircraft," he said, "or these geniuses start dying."

He clicked off before they could say anything in reply.

The shooting stopped.

They heard the rotors—choppers landing on the roof.

What a stupid place for them to land, thought Petra. Just because the roof is marked as a heliport doesn't mean they have to obey the signs. Up there, the Indian soldiers surrounding this place will have an easy target, and they'll see everything that happens. They'll know when Achilles is on the roof. They'll know which chopper to shoot down first, because he's in it. If this is the best plan the Chinese can come up with, Achilles is going to have a harder time using China as a base to take over the world than he thinks.

More choppers. Now that the roof was full, a few of them were landing on the grounds.

The door burst open, and a dozen Chinese soldiers fanned out through the room. A Chinese officer followed them in and saluted Achilles. "We came at once, sir."

"Good work," said Achilles. "Let's get them all up on the roof."

"You said you'd let us go!" said one of the Battle Schoolers.

"One way or another," said Achilles, "you're all going to end up in China anyway. Now get up and form into a line against that wall."

More choppers. And then the whoosh, whump of an explosion.

"Those stupid eemos," said the Tamil, "they're going to get us all killed."

"Such a shame," said Achilles, pointing his pistol at the Tamil's head.

The Chinese officer was already talking into his satrad. "Wait," he said. "It's not the Indians. They've got Thai markings."

Bean, thought Petra. You've come at last. Either that or death. Because if Bean wasn't running this Thai raid, the Thai could have no other objective than to kill everything that moved in Hyderabad.

Another whoosh-whump. Another. "They've taken out everything on the roof," the Chinese officer said. "The building's on fire, we've got to get out."

"Whose stupid idea was it to land up there anyway?" asked Achilles.

"It was the closest point to evacuate them from!" answered the officer angrily. "There aren't enough choppers left to take all these."

"They're coming," said Achilles, "even if we have to leave soldiers behind."

"We'll get them in a few days anyway. I don't leave my men behind!"

Not a bad commander, even if he's a little dim about tactics, thought Petra.

"They won't let us take off unless we've got their Indian geniuses with us."

"The Thai won't let us take off at all!"

"Of course they will," said Achilles. "They're here to kill me and rescue *her*." He pointed at Petra.

So Achilles knew it was Bean that was coming.

Petra showed nothing on her face.

If Achilles decided to leave without the hostages, there was a good chance he would kill them all. Deprive the enemy of a resource. And, more important, take away their hope.

"Achilles," she said, walking toward him. "Let's leave these others and get out. We'll be taking off from the ground. They won't know who's in what chopper. As long as we go *now*."

As she approached him, he swung his pistol to point at her chest. She did not even pause, merely walked toward him, past him, to the door. She opened it. "Now, Achilles. You don't have to die in flames today, but that's where you're headed, the longer you wait."

"She's right," said the Chinese officer.

Achilles grinned and looked from Petra to the officer and back again. We've shamed you in front of the others, thought Petra. We've shown that we knew what to do, and you didn't. Now you have to kill us both. This officer doesn't know he's dead, but I do. Then again, I was dead anyway. So now let's get out of here without killing anybody else.

"Nothing in this room matters but you," said Petra. She grinned back at him. "Soak a noky, boy."

Achilles turned back to point the gun, first at one Battle Schooler, then another. They recoiled or flinched, but he did not fire. He dropped his gun hand to his side and walked from the room, grabbing Petra by the arm as he passed her. "Come on, Pet," he said. "The future is calling."

Bean is coming, thought Petra, and Achilles is not going to let me get even a meter away from him. He knows Bean is here for me, so I'm the one person he'll make sure Bean never rescues.

Maybe we'll all kill each other today.

She thought back to the airplane ride that brought her and Achilles to India. The two of them standing at the open door. Maybe there would be another chance today—to die, taking Achilles with her. She wondered if Bean would understand that it was more important for Achilles to die than for her to live. More important, would he know that *she* understood that? It was the right thing to do, and now that she really knew Achilles, the kind of man he was, she would gladly pay that price and call it cheap.

19

Rescue

To:Wahabi%inshallah@Pakistan.gov
From:Chapekar%hope@India.gov
Re:For the Indian people

My Dear Friend Ghaffar,
I honor you because when I came to you with an offer of peace between our two families within the Indian people, you accepted and kept your word in every particular.

I honor you because you have lived a life that places the good of your people above your own ambition.

I honor you because in you rests the hope for my people's future.

I make this letter public even as I send it to you, not knowing what your response will be, for my people must know now, while I can still speak to them all, what I am asking of you and giving to you.

As the treacherous Chinese violate their promises and threaten to destroy our army, which has been weakened by the treachery of the one called Achilles, whom we treated as a guest and a friend, it is clear to me that without a miracle, the vast expanse of the nation of India will be defenseless against the invaders pouring into our country from the north. Soon the ruthless conqueror will work his will from Bengal to Punjab. Of all the Indian people, only those in Pakistan, led by you, will be free.

I ask you now to take upon yourself all the hopes of the Indian people. Our struggle over the next few days will give you time, I hope, to bring your armies back to our border, where you will be prepared to stand against the Chinese enemy.

I now give you permission to cross that border at any point where it is necessary, so you can establish stronger defensive positions. I order all Indian soldiers remaining at the Pakistani border to offer no resistance whatsoever to Pakistani forces entering our country, and to cooperate by providing full maps of all our defenses, and all codes and codebooks. All our matériel at the border is to be turned over to Pakistan as well.

I ask you that any citizens of India who come under the rule of the Pakistani government be treated as generously as you would wish us, were our situations reversed, to treat your people. Whatever past offenses have been committed between our families, let us forgive each other and commit no new offenses, but treat each other as brothers and sisters who have been faithful to different faces of the same God, and who must now stand shoulder to shoulder to defend India against the invader whose only god is power and whose worship is cruelty.

Many members of the Indian government, military, and educational system will flee to Pakistan. I beg you to open your borders to them, for if they remain in India, only death or captivity will be in their future. All other Indians have no reason to fear individual persecution from the Chinese, and I beg you not to flee to Pakistan, but rather to remain inside India, where, God willing, you will soon be liberated.

I myself will remain in India, to bear whatever burden is placed upon my people by the conqueror. I would rather be Mandela than de Gaulle. There is to be no government-in-exile. Pakistan is the government of the Indian people now. I say this with the full authority of Congress.

May God bless all honorable people, and keep them free.

Your brother and friend,
Tikal Chapekar

Jetting over the dry southern reaches of India felt to Bean like a strange dream, where the landscape never changed. Or no, it was a vidgame, with a computer making up scenery on the fly, recycling the same algorithms to create the same type of scenery in general, but never quite the same in detail.

Like human beings. DNA that differed by only the tiniest amounts from person to person, and yet those differences giving rise to saints and monsters, fools and geniuses, builders and wreckers, lovers and takers. More people live in this one country, India, than lived in the whole world only three or four centuries ago. More people live here today than lived in the entire history of the world up to the time of Christ. All the history of the Bible and the Iliad and Herodotus and Gilgamesh and everything that had been pieced together by archaeologists and anthropologists, all of those human relationships, all those achievements, could all have been played out by the people we're flying over right now, with people left over to live through new stories that no one would ever hear.

In these few days, China would conquer enough people to make five thousand years of human history, and they would treat them like grass, to be mown till all were the same level, with anything that rose above that level discarded to be mere compost.

And what am I doing? Riding along on a machine that would have given that old prophet Ezekiel a heart attack before he could even write about seeing a shark in the sky. Sister Carlotta used to joke that Battle School was the wheel in the sky that Ezekiel saw in his vision. So here I am, like a figure out of some ancient vision, and what am I doing? That's right, out of the billions of people I might have saved, I'm choosing the one I happen to know and like the best, and risking the lives of a couple of hundred good soldiers in order to do it. And if we get out of this alive, what will I do then? Spend the few years of life remaining to me, helping Peter Wiggin defeat Achilles so he can do exactly what Achilles is already so close to doing—unite humanity under the rule of one sick, ambitious marubo?

Sister Carlotta liked to quote from another biblical git—vanity, vanity, all is vanity. There is nothing new under the sun. A time to scatter rocks and a time to gather rocks together.

Well, as long as God didn't tell anybody what the rocks were for, I might as well leave the rocks and go get my friend, if I can.

As they approached Hyderabad, they picked up a lot of radio chatter. Tactical stuff from satrads, not just the net traffic you'd expect because of the Chinese surprise attack in Burma that had been triggered by Peter's essay. As they got closer, the onboard computers were able to distinguish the radio signatures of Chinese troops as well as Indian.

"Looks like Achilles' retrieval crew got here ahead of us," said Suriyawong.

"But no shooting," said Bean. "Which means they've already got to the planning room and they're holding the Battle Schoolers as hostages."

"You got it," said Suriyawong. "Three choppers on the roof."

"There'll be more on the ground, but let's complicate their lives and take out those three."

Virlomi had misgivings. "What if they think it's the Indian Army attacking and they kill the hostages?"

"Achilles is not so stupid he won't make sure who's doing the shooting before he starts using up his ticket home."

It was like target practice, and three missiles took out three choppers, just like that.

"Now get us onto blades and show the Thai markings," said Suriyawong.

It was, as usual, a sickening climb and drop before the blades took over. But Bean was used to the sense of clawing nausea and was able to notice, out the windows, that the Indian troops were cheering and waving.

"Oh, suddenly now we're the good guys," said Bean.

"I think we're just the not-quite-so-evil guys," said Suriyawong.

"I think you're taking irresponsible risks with the lives of my friends," said Virlomi.

Bean sobered at once. "Virlomi, I know Achilles, and the only way to keep him from killing your friends, just for spite, is to keep him worried and off balance. To give him no time to display his malice."

"I meant that if one of those missiles had gone astray," she said, "it could have hit the room they're in and killed them all."

"Oh, is that all you're worried about?" Bean said. "Virlomi, I *trained* these men. There are situations in which they might miss, but this was not one of them."

Virlomi nodded. "I understand. The confidence of the field commander. It's been a long time since I had a toon of my own."

A few choppers stayed aloft, watching the perimeter; most set down in front of the building where the planning room was located. Suriyawong had already briefed the company commanders he was taking into the building by satrad as they flew. Now he jumped from the chopper as soon as the door opened and, with Virlomi running behind him, he got his group moving, executing the plan.

At once, Bean's chopper lifted back up and, with another chopper, hopped the building to come down on the other side. This was where they found the two remaining Chinese helicopters, blades spinning. Bean had his pilot set down so the chopper's weapons were pointed at the sides of the two Chinese machines. Then he and the thirty men with him went out both doors as Chinese troops across the open space between them did the same.

Bean's other chopper remained airborne, waiting to see whether its missiles or the troops inside would be needed first.

The Chinese had Bean's troops outnumbered, but that wasn't really the issue. Nobody was shooting, because the Chinese wanted to get away alive, and there was no hope of that if shooting broke out, because the airborne chopper would simply destroy both the remaining Chinese machines and then it wouldn't matter what happened on the ground, they'd never get home and their mission would be a failure.

So the two little armies formed up just like regiments in the Napoleonic wars, neat little lines. Bean wanted to shout something like "fix bayonets" or "load"—but nobody was using muskets and besides, what interested him would be coming out the door of the building. . . .

And there he was, rushing straight for the nearest chopper, gripping Petra by the arm and half-dragging her along. Achilles held a pistol down at his side. Bean wanted to have one of his sharpshooters take him out, but he knew that then the Chinese would open fire and Petra would certainly be killed. So he called out to Achilles.

Achilles ignored him. Bean knew what he was thinking—get inside the chopper while everybody's holding their fire, and then Bean would be helpless, unable to do anything to Achilles without also harming Petra.

So Bean spoke into his satrad and the hovering chopper did what the gunner was trained to do—fired a missile that blew up just beyond the nearer Chinese chopper. The machine itself blocked the blast so Petra and Achilles weren't hurt—but the chopper was rocked over onto its side and then, as the blades chewed to bits against the ground, it flipped over and over and smashed up against a barracks. A few soldiers slithered out, trying to drag out others with broken limbs or other injuries before the machine went up in flames.

Achilles and Petra now stood in the middle of the open space. The only remaining Chinese chopper was too far for him to run to. He did the only thing he could do, under the circumstances. He held Petra in front of him with a gun pointed to her head. It wasn't a move they taught you in Battle School. It was straight from the vids.

In the meantime, the Chinese officer in charge—a colonel, if Bean remembered correctly how to translate the rank insignia, which was a very high rank for a small-scale operation like this one—strode out with his men. Bean did not have to instruct him to stay far away from Achilles and Petra. The colonel would know that any move to get between Achilles and Bean's men would lead to shooting, since there was only a stalemate as long as Bean had the ability to kill Achilles the moment he harmed Petra.

Without looking at the soldiers near him, Bean said, "Who has a trank pistol?"

One was slapped into his open hand. Someone murmured, "Keep your hand on a real gun, too."

And someone else said, "I hope the Indian Army doesn't realize that Achilles doesn't have *any* Indian kids with him. They couldn't care less about an Armenian." Bean appreciated it when his men thought through the whole situation. No time for praise now, though.

He stepped away from his men and walked toward Achilles and Petra. As he did, he saw Suriyawong and Virlomi come out the door through which the Chinese colonel had just come. Suriyawong called out, "All secure. Loading. Achilles murdered only one of ours."

"One of 'ours'?" said Achilles. "When did Sayagi become one of *yours*? You mean that I can kill anybody else and you don't care, but touch a Battle School brat and I'm a murderer?"

"You're never taking off in that chopper with Petra," said Bean.

"I know I'm never taking off *without* her," said

Achilles. "If I don't have her with me, you'll blow that chopper into bits so small they'd have to use a comb to gather them up."

"Then I guess I'll just have one of my sharpshooters kill you."

Petra smiled.

She was telling him yes, do it.

"Colonel Yuan-xi will then regard his mission as a failure, and he will kill as many of you as he can. Petra first."

Bean saw that the colonel had gotten his men on board the chopper—those who had come with him from the building and those who had deployed from the choppers when Bean first landed. Only he, Achilles, and Petra remained outside.

"Colonel," said Bean, "the only way this doesn't end in blood is if we can trust each other's word. I promise you that as long as Petra is alive, uninjured, and with me, you can take off safely with no interference from me or my strike force. Whether you have Achilles with you is of no importance to me."

Petra's smile vanished, replaced with a face that was an obvious mask of anger. She did not want Achilles to get away.

But she still hoped to live—that was why she was saying nothing, so Achilles wouldn't know that she was demanding his death, even at the cost of her own.

What she was ignoring was the fact that the Chinese commander had to meet the minimum conditions for mission success—he had to have Achilles with him when he left. If he didn't, a lot of people here would die, and for what? Achilles' worst deeds were already done. From here on, no one would ever trust his word on anything. Whatever power he got now would be by force and fear, not by deception. Which meant that he would be making enemies every day, driving people into the arms of his opponents.

He might still win more battles and more wars and he might even seem to triumph completely, but, like Caligula, he would make assassins out of the people closest to him. And when he died, men just as evil but perhaps not as crazy would take his place. Killing him now would not make that much difference to the world.

Keeping Petra alive, however, would make all the difference in the world to Bean. He had made the mistakes that killed Poke and Sister Carlotta. But he was going to make no mistakes today. Petra would live because Bean couldn't bear any other outcome. She didn't even get a vote on the matter.

The colonel was weighing the situation.

Achilles was not. "I'm moving to the chopper now. My fingers are pretty tight on this trigger. Don't make me flinch, Bean."

Bean knew what Achilles was thinking: Can I kill Bean at the last moment and still get away, or should I leave that pleasure for another time?

And that was an advantage for Bean, because his thinking was not clouded by thoughts of personal vengeance.

Except, he realized, that it was. Because he, too, was trying to think of some way to save Petra and still kill Achilles.

The colonel walked up closer behind Achilles before calling out his answer to Bean. "Achilles is the architect of a great Chinese victory, and he must come to

Beijing to be received in honor. My orders say nothing about the Armenian."

"They'll never let us take off without her, you fool," said Achilles.

"Sir, I give you my word, my parole. Even though Achilles has already murdered a woman and a girl who did nothing but good for him, and deserves to die for his crimes, I will let him go and let you go."

"Then our missions do not conflict," said the colonel. "I agree to your terms, provided you also agree to care for any of my men who remain behind according to the rules of war."

"I agree," said Bean.

"I'm in charge of our mission," said Achilles, "and I don't agree."

"You are not in charge of our mission, sir," said the colonel.

Bean knew exactly what Achilles would do. He would take the gun away from Petra's head long enough to shoot the colonel. Achilles would expect this move to surprise people, but Bean was not surprised at all. His hand with the trank gun was already rising before Achilles even started to turn to the colonel.

But Bean was not the only one who knew what to expect from Achilles. The colonel had deliberately moved close enough to Achilles that as he swung the gun around, the colonel slapped the weapon out of Achilles' hand. At the same moment, with his other hand the colonel slapped Achilles' arm close to the elbow, and even though there seemed to be almost no force behind the blow, Achilles' arm bent sickeningly backward. Achilles cried out in pain and dropped to his knees, letting go of Petra. She immediately launched herself to the side, out of the way, and at that moment Bean fired the trank gun. He was able to adjust the aim at the last split second, and the tiny pellet struck Achilles' shirt with such force that even though the casing collapsed against the cloth, the tranquilizer blew right through the fabric and penetrated Achilles' skin. He collapsed immediately.

"It's only a tranquilizer," said Bean. "He'll be awake in six hours or so, with a headache."

The colonel stood there, not bending yet to even notice Achilles, his eyes still fixed on Bean. "Now there is no hostage. Your enemy is on the ground. How good is your word, sir, when the circumstance in which it was given goes away?"

"Men of honor," said Bean, "are brothers no matter what uniform they wear. You may put him aboard, and take off. I recommend that you fly in formation with us until we are south of the defenses around Hyderabad. Then you may fly your own course, and we'll fly ours."

"That is a wise plan," said the colonel.

He knelt and started to pick up Achilles' limp body. It was tricky work, and so Bean, small as he was, stepped forward to help by taking Achilles' legs.

Petra was on her feet by then, and when Bean glanced at her he could see that she was eyeing Achilles' pistol, which lay on the ground near her. Bean could almost read her mind. To kill Achilles with his own gun had to be tempting—and Petra had not given her word.

But before she could even move toward the pistol, Bean had his trank gun pointed at her. "You could also wake up in six hours with a headache," he said.

"No need," she said. "I know that I'm also bound by your word." And, without stooping for the gun, she came and helped Bean carry his end of Achilles' body.

They rolled Achilles through the wide door of the chopper. Soldiers inside the machine took him and carried him back, presumably to a place where he could be secured during flight maneuvers. The chopper was grossly overcrowded, but only with men—there were no supplies or heavy munitions, so it would fly as well as normal. It would simply be uncomfortable for the passengers.

"You don't want to ride home on that chopper," said Bean. "I invite you to ride with us."

"But you're not going where I'm going," said the colonel.

"I know this boy you have just taken aboard," said Bean. "Even if he doesn't remember what you did when he wakes up, someone will tell him someday, and once he knows, you'll be marked. He never forgets. He will certainly kill you."

"Then I will have died obeying my orders and fulfilling my mission," said the colonel.

"Full asylum," said Bean, "and a life spent helping liberate China and all other nations from the kind of evil he represents."

"I know that you mean to be kind," said the colonel, "but it hurts my soul to be offered such rewards for betraying my country."

"Your country is led by men without honor," said Bean. "And yet they are sustained in power by the honor of men like you. Who, then, betrays his country? No, we have no time for arguments. I only plant the idea so it will fester in your soul." Bean smiled.

The colonel smiled back. "Then you are a devil, sir, as we Chinese always knew you Europeans to be."

Bean saluted him. He returned the salute and got on board.

The chopper door closed.

Bean and Petra ran out of the downdraft as the Chinese machine rose up into the air. There it hovered as Bean ordered everyone into the one chopper that remained on the ground. Less than two minutes later, his chopper, too, rose up, and the Thai and Chinese machines flew together over the building, where they were joined by the other helijets of Bean's strike force as they rose up from the ground or converged from their watching points at the perimeter.

They flew together toward the south, slowly, on blades. No Indian weapon was fired at them. For the Indian officers no doubt knew that their best young military minds were being taken to far more safety than they could possibly have in Hyderabad, or anywhere in India, once the Chinese came in force.

Then Bean gave the order, and all his choppers rose up, cut the blades, and dropped as the jets came on and the blades folded back for the quick ride back to Sri Lanka.

Inside the chopper, Petra sat glumly in her straps. Virlomi was beside her, but they did not speak to each other.

"Petra," said Bean.

She did not look up.

"Virlomi found us, we did not find her. Because of her, we were able to come for you."

Petra still did not look up, but she reached out a hand and laid it on Virlomi's hands, which were clasped in her lap. "You were brave and good," said Petra. "Thank you for having compassion for me."

Then she looked up to meet Bean's gaze. "But I don't thank *you,* Bean. I was ready to kill him. I would have done it. I would have found a way."

"He's going to kill himself in the end," said Bean. "He's going to overreach himself, like Robespierre, like Stalin. Others will see his pattern and when they realize he's finally about to put them to the guillotine, they'll decide they've had enough and he will, most certainly, die."

"But how many will he kill along the way? And now your hands are stained with all their blood, because you loaded him onto that chopper alive. Mine, too."

"You're wrong," said Bean. "He is the only one responsible for his killings. And you're wrong about what would have happened if we had let him take you along. You would not have lived through that ride."

"You don't know that."

"I know Achilles. When that chopper rose to about twenty stories up, you would have been pushed out the door. And do you know why?"

"So you could watch," she said.

"No, he would have waited till I was gone," said Bean. "He's not stupid. He regards his own survival as far more important than your death."

"Then why would he kill me now? Why are you so sure?"

"Because he had his arm around you like a lover," said Bean. "Standing there with the gun to your head, he held you with affection. I think he meant to kiss you before he took you on board. He'd want me to see that."

"She would never let him kiss her," said Virlomi with disgust.

But Petra met Bean's gaze, and the tears in her eyes were a truer answer than Virlomi's brave words. She had already let Achilles kiss her. Just like Poke.

"He marked you," said Bean. "He loved you. You had power over him. After he didn't need you anymore as the hostage to keep me from killing him, you could not go on living."

Suriyawong shuddered. "What made him that way?"

"Nothing *made* him that way," said Bean. "No matter what terrible things happened in his life, no matter what dreadful hungers rose up from his soul, he chose to act on those desires, he chose to do the things he did. *He's* responsible for his own actions, and no one else. Not even those who saved his life."

"Like you and me today," said Petra.

"Sister Carlotta saved his life today," said Bean. "The last thing she asked me was to leave vengeance up to God."

"Do you believe in God?" asked Suriyawong, surprised.

"More and more," said Bean. "And less and less."

Virlomi took Petra's hands between hers and said, "Enough of blame and enough of Achilles. You're free of him. You can have whole minutes and hours and days in which you don't have to think of what he'll do to you if he hears what you say, and how you have to act when he might be watching. The only way he can hurt you now is if you keep watching *him* in your own heart."

"Listen to her, Petra," said Suriyawong. "She's a goddess, you know."

Virlomi laughed. "I save bridges and summon choppers."

"And you blessed me," said Suriyawong.

"I never did," said Virlomi.

"When you walked on my back," said Suriyawong. "My whole body is now the path of a goddess."

"Only the back part," said Virlomi. "You'll have to find someone else to bless the front."

While they bantered, half-drunk with success and liberty and the overwhelming tragedy they were leaving behind them, Bean watched Petra, saw the tears drop from her eyes onto her lap, longed to be able to reach out and touch them away from her eyes. But what good would that do? Those tears had risen up from deep wells of pain, and his mere touch would do nothing to dry them at their source. It would take time to do that, and time was the one thing that he did not have. If Petra knew happiness in her life—happiness, that precious thing that Mrs. Wiggin talked about—it would come when she shared her life with someone else. Bean had saved her, had freed her, not so he could have her or be part of her life, but so that he did not have to bear the guilt of her death as he bore the deaths of Poke and Carlotta. It was a selfish thing he did, in a way. But in another way, there would be nothing for himself at all from this day's work.

Except that when his death came, sooner rather than later, he might well look back on this day's work with more pride than anything else in his life. Because today he won. In the midst of all this terrible defeat, he had found a victory. He had cheated Achilles out of one of his favorite murders. He had saved the life of his dearest friend, even though she wasn't quite grateful yet. His army had done what he needed it to do, and not one life had been lost out of the two hundred men he had first been given. Always before he had been part of someone else's victory. But today, today *he* won.

20

Hegemon

To: Chamrajnagar%Jawaharlal@ifcom.gov
From:PeterWiggin%freeworld@hegemon.gov
Re: Confirmation

Dear Polemarch Chamrajnagar,
Thank you for allowing me to reconfirm your appointment as Polemarch as my first official act. We both know that I was giving you only what you already had, while you, by accepting that reconfirmation as if it actually meant something, restored to the office of Hegemon some of the luster that has been torn from it by the events of recent months. There are many who feel that it is an empty gesture to appoint a Hegemon who leads only about a third

of the human race and has no particular influence over the third that officially supports him. Many nations are racing to find some accommodation with the Chinese and their allies, and I live under the constant threat of having my office abolished as one of the first gestures they can make to win the favor of the new superpower. I am, in short, a Hegemon without hegemony.

And it is all the more remarkable that you would make this generous gesture toward the very individual that you once regarded as the worst of all possible Hegemons. The weaknesses in my character that you saw then have not magically vanished. It is only by comparison with Achilles, and only in a world where your homeland groans under the Chinese lash, that I begin to look like an attractive alternative or a source of hope instead of despair. But regardless of my weaknesses, I also have strengths, and I make you a promise:

Even though you are bound by your oath of office never to use the International Fleet to influence the course of events on Earth, except to intercept nuclear weapons or punish those who use them, I know that you are still a man of Earth, a man of India, and you care deeply what happens to all people, and particularly to your people. Therefore I promise you that I will devote the rest of my life to reshaping this world into one that you would be glad of, for your people, and for all people. And I hope that I succeed well enough, before one or the other of us dies, that you will be glad of the support you gave to me today.

Sincerely,
Peter Wiggin, Hegemon

Over a million Indians made it out of India before the Chinese sealed the borders. Out of a population of a billion and a half, that was far too few. At least ten times that million were transported over the next year, from India to the cold lands of Manchuria and the high deserts of Sinkiang. Among the transported ones was Tikal Chapekar. The Chinese gave no report to outsiders about the fate of him or any of the other "former oppressors of the Indian people." The same, on a far smaller scale, happened to the governing elites of Burma, Thailand, Vietnam, Cambodia, and Laos.

As if this vast redrawing of the world's map were not enough, Russia announced that it had joined China as its ally, and that it considered the nations of eastern Europe that were not loyal members of the New Warsaw Pact to be provinces in rebellion. Without firing a shot, Russia was able, simply by promising not to be as dreadful an overlord as China, to rewrite the Warsaw Pact until it was more or less the constitution of an empire that included all of Europe east of Germany,

Austria, and Italy in the south, and east of Sweden and Norway in the north.

The weary nations of western Europe were quick to "welcome" the "discipline" that Russia would bring to Europe, and Russia was immediately given full membership in the European Community. Because Russia now controlled the votes of more than half the members of that community, it would require a constant tug of war to keep some semblance of independence, and rather than play that game, Great Britain, Ireland, Iceland, and Portugal left the European Community. But even they took great pains to assure the Russian bear that this was purely over economic issues and they really welcomed this renewed Russian interest in the West.

America, which had long since become the tail to China's dog in matters of trade, made a few grumpy noises about human rights and then went back to business as usual, using satellite cartography to redraw the map of the world to fit the new reality and then sell the atlases that resulted. In sub-Saharan Africa, where India had once been their greatest single trading partner and cultural influence, the loss of India was much more devastating, and they loyally denounced the Chinese conquest even as they scrambled to find new markets for their goods. Latin America was even louder in their condemnation of all the aggressors, but lacking serious military forces, their bluster could do no harm. In the Pacific, Japan, with its dominant fleet, could afford to stand firm; the other island nations that faced China across various not-so-wide bodies of water had no such luxury.

Indeed, the only force that stood firm against China and Russia while facing them across heavily defended borders were the Muslim nations. Iran generously forgot how threateningly Pakistani troops had loomed along their borders in the month before India's fall, and Arabs joined with Turks in Muslim solidarity against any Russian encroachment across the Caucasus or into the vast steppes of central Asia. No one seriously thought that Muslim military might could stand for long against a serious attack from China, and Russia was only scarcely less dangerous, but the Muslims laid aside their grievances, trusted in Allah, and kept their borders bristling with the warning that this nettle would be hard to grasp.

This was the world as it was the day that Peter "Locke" Wiggin was named as the new Hegemon. China let it be known that choosing any Hegemon at all was an affront, but Russia was a bit more tolerant, especially because many governments that cast their vote for Wiggin did so with the public declaration that the office was more ceremonial than practical, a gesture toward world unity and peace, and not at all an attempt to roll back the conquests that had brought "peace" to an unstable world.

But privately, many leaders of the very same governments assured Peter that they expected him to do all he could to bring about diplomatic "transformations" in the occupied countries. Peter listened to them politely and said reassuring things, but he felt nothing but scorn for them—for without military might, he had no way of negotiating with anyone about anything.

His first official act was to reconfirm the appointment of Polemarch Chamrajnagar—an action which China officially protested as illegal because the office of Hegemon no longer existed, and while they would do nothing to interfere with Chamrajnagar's continued leadership of the Fleet, they would no longer contribute financially either to the Hegemony or the Fleet.

Peter then confirmed Graff as Hegemony Minister of Colonization—and, again, because his work was off-world, China could do nothing more than cut off its contribution of funds.

But the lack of money forced Peter's next decision. He moved the Hegemony capital out of the former Netherlands and returned the Low Countries to self-government, which immediately put a stop to unrestricted immigration into those nations. He closed down most Hegemony services worldwide except for medical and agricultural research and assistance programs. He moved the main Hegemony offices to Brazil, which had several important assets:

First, it was a large enough and powerful enough country that the enemies of the Hegemony would not be quick to provoke it by assassinating the Hegemon within its borders.

Second, it was in the southern hemisphere, with strong economic ties to Africa, the Americas, and the Pacific, so that being there kept Peter within the mainstream of international commerce and politics.

And third, Brazil invited Peter Wiggin to come there. No one else did.

—

Peter had no delusions about what the office of Hegemon had become. He did not expect anyone to come to him. He went to them.

Which is why he left Haiti and crossed the Pacific to Manila, where Bean and his Thai army and the Indians they rescued had found temporary refuge. Peter knew that Bean was still angry at him, so he was relieved that Bean not only agreed to see him, but treated him with open respect when he arrived. His two hundred soldiers were crisply turned out to greet him, and when

Bean introduced him to Petra, Suriyawong, and Virlomi and the other Indian Battle Schoolers, he phrased everything as if he were presenting his friends to a man of higher rank.

In front of all of them, Bean then made a little speech. "To His Excellency the Hegemon, I offer the service of this band of soldiers—veterans of war, former opponents, and now, because of treachery, exiles from their homeland and brothers- and sisters-at-arms. This was not my decision, nor the decision of the majority. Each individual here was given the choice, and chose to make this offer of our service. We are few, but nations have found our service valuable before. We hope that we now can serve a cause that is higher than any nation, and whose end will be the establishment of a new and honorable order in the world."

Peter was surprised only by the formality of the offer, and the fact that it was made without any sort of negotiation beforehand. He also noticed that Bean had arranged to have cameras present. This would be news. So Peter made a brief, soundbite-oriented reply accepting their offer, praising their achievements, and expressing regret at the suffering of their people. It would play well—twenty seconds on the vids, and in full on the nets.

When the ceremonies were done, there was an inspection of their inventory—all the equipment they had been able to rescue from Thailand. Even their fighter-bomber pilots and patrol boat crews had managed to make their way from southern Thailand to the Philippines, so the Hegemon had an air force and a fleet. Peter nodded and commented gravely as he saw each item in the inventory—the cameras were still running.

Later, though, when they were alone, Peter finally

allowed himself a rueful, self-mocking laugh. "If it weren't for you I'd have nothing at all," he said. "But to compare this to the vast fleets and air forces and armies that the Hegemon once commanded . . ."

Bean looked at him coldly. "The office had to be greatly diminished," he said, "before they'd have given it to you."

The honeymoon, apparently, was over. "Yes," Peter said, "that's true, of course."

"And the world had to be in a desperate condition, with the existence of the office of Hegemon in doubt."

"That, too, is true," said Peter. "And for some reason you seem to be angry about this."

"That's because, apart from the not-trivial matter of Achilles' penchant for killing people now and then, I fail to see much difference between you and him. You're both content to let any number of people suffer needlessly in order to advance your personal ambitions."

Peter sighed. "If that's all the difference that you see, I don't understand how you could offer your service to me."

"I see other differences, of course," said Bean. "But they're matters of degree, not of kind. Achilles makes treaties he never intends to keep. You merely write essays that might have saved nations, but you delay publishing them so that those nations will fall, putting the world in a position desperate enough that they would make you Hegemon."

"Your statement is true," said Peter, "*only* if you believe that earlier publication would have saved India and Thailand."

"Early in the war," said Bean, "India still had the supplies and equipment to resist Chinese attack. Thailand's forces were still fully dispersed and hard to find."

"But if I had published early in the war," said Peter, "India and Thailand would not have seen their peril, and they wouldn't have believed me. After all, the Thai government didn't believe *you,* and you warned them of everything."

"You're Locke," said Bean.

"Ah yes. Because I had so much credibility and prestige, nations would tremble and believe my words. Aren't you forgetting something? At your insistence, I had declared myself to be a teenage college student. I was still recovering from that, trying to prove in Haiti that I could actually govern. I might have had the prestige left to be taken seriously in India and Thailand—but I might not. And if I published too soon, before China was ready to act, China would simply have denied everything to both sides, the war would have proceeded, and then there would have been no shock value at all to my publication. I wouldn't have been able to trigger the invasion at exactly the moment you needed me to."

"Don't pretend that this was your plan all along."

"It was my plan," said Peter, "to withhold publication until it could be an act of power instead of an act of futility. Yes, I was thinking of my prestige, because right now the only power I have is that prestige and the influence it gives me with the governments of the world. It's a coin that is minted very slowly, and if spent ineffectively, disappears. So yes, I protect that power very carefully, and use it sparingly, so that later, when I need to have it, it will still exist."

Bean was silent.

"You hate what happened in the war," said Peter. "So

do I. It's possible—not likely, but possible—that if I had published earlier, India might have been able to mount a real resistance. They might still have been fighting now. Millions of soldiers might have been dying even as we speak. Instead, there was a clean, almost bloodless victory for China. And now the Chinese have to govern a population almost twice the size of their own, with a culture every bit as old and all-absorbing as their own. The snake has swallowed a crocodile, and the question is going to arise again and again—who is digesting whom? Thailand and Vietnam will be just as hard to govern, and even the Burmese have never managed to govern Burma. What I did saved lives. It left the world with a clear moral picture of who did the stabbing in the back, and who was stabbed. And it leaves China victorious and Russia triumphant—but with captive, angry populations to govern who will not stand with them when the final struggle comes. Why do you think China made a quick peace with Pakistan? Because they knew they could not fight a war against the Muslim world with Indian revolt and sabotage a constant threat. And that alliance between China and Russia—what a joke! Within a year they'll be quarreling, and they'll be back to weakening each other across that long Siberian border. To people who think superficially, China and Russia look triumphant. But I never thought you were a superficial thinker."

"I see all that," said Bean.

"But you don't care. You're still angry at me."

Bean said nothing.

"It's hard," said Peter, "to see how all of this seems to work to my advantage, and not blame me for profiteering from the suffering of others. But the real issue is, What am I going to be able to do, and what will I actually do, now that I'm nominally the leader of the world, and actually the administrator of a small tax base, a few international service agencies, and this military force you gave to me today? I did the few things that were in my power to shape events so that when I got this office, it would still be worth having."

"But above all, to get that office."

"Yes, Bean. I'm arrogant. I think I'm the only person who understands what to do and has what it takes to do it. I think the world needs me. In fact, I'm even more arrogant than you. Is that what this comes down to? I should have been humbler? Only you are allowed to assess your own abilities candidly and decide that you're the best man for a particular job?"

"I don't want the job."

"I don't want *this* job, either," said Peter. "What I want is the job where the Hegemon speaks, and wars stop, where the Hegemon can redraw borders and strike down bad laws and break up international cartels and bring all of humanity a chance for a decent life in peace and whatever freedom their culture will allow. And I'm going to get that job, by creating it step by step. Not only that, I'm going to do it with your help, because you want somebody to do that job, and you know, just as surely as I do, that I'm the only one who can do it."

Bean nodded, saying nothing.

"You know all that, and you're still angry with me."

"I'm angry with Achilles," said Bean. "I'm angry with the stupidity of those who refused to listen to me. But you're here, and they're not."

"It's more than that," said Peter. "If that's all it was, you would have talked yourself out of your wrath long before we had this conversation."

"I know," said Bean. "But you don't want to hear it."

"Because it will hurt my feelings? Let me make a stab at it, then. You're angry because every word from my mouth, every gesture, every expression on my face reminds you of Ender Wiggin. Only I'm not Ender, I'll never be Ender, you think Ender should be doing what I'm doing, and you hate me for being the one who made sure Ender got sent away."

"It's irrational," said Bean. "I know that. I know that by sending him away you saved his life. The people who helped Achilles try to kill me would have worked day and night to kill Ender without any prompting from Achilles at all. They would have feared him far more than they feared you or me. I know that. But you look and talk so much like him. And I keep thinking, if Ender had been here, he wouldn't have botched things the way I did."

"The way I read it, it's the other way around. If *you* hadn't been there with Ender, *he* would have botched it at the end. No, don't argue, it doesn't matter. What *does* matter is, the world's the way it is right now, and we're in a position where, if we move carefully, if we think through and plan everything just right, we can fix this. We can make it better. No regrets. No wishing we could undo the past. We just look to the future and work our zhupas off."

"I'll look to the future," said Bean, "and I'll help you all I can. But I'll regret whatever I want to regret."

"Fair enough," said Peter. "Now that we've agreed on that, I think you should know. I've decided to revive the office of Strategos."

Bean gave one hoot of derision. "You're putting *that* title on the commander of a force of two hundred soldiers, a couple of planes, a couple of boats, and an overheated company of strategic planners?"

"Hey, if I can be called Hegemon, you can take on a title like that."

"I notice you didn't want any vids of me getting that title."

"No, I didn't," said Peter. "I don't want people to hear the news while looking at vids of a kid. I want them to learn of your appointment as Strategos while seeing stock footage of the victory over the Formics and hearing voice-overs about your rescue of the Indian Battle Schoolers."

"Well, fine," said Bean. "I accept. Do I get a fancy uniform?"

"No," said Peter. "At the rate you're growing lately, we'd have to pay for new ones too often, and you'd bankrupt us."

A thoughtful expression passed across Bean's face.

"What," said Peter, "did I offend again?"

"No," said Bean. "I was just wondering what your parents said, when you declared yourself to be Locke."

Peter laughed. "Oh, they pretended that they'd known it all along. Parents."

—

At Bean's suggestion, Peter located the headquarters of the Hegemony in a compound just outside the city of Ribeirão Preto in the state of São Paulo. There they would have excellent air connections anywhere in the world, while being surrounded by small towns and agricultural land. They'd be far from any government body. It was a pleasant place to live as they planned and trained to achieve the modest goal of freeing the captive nations while holding the line against any new aggressions.

The Delphiki family came out of hiding and joined

Bean in the safety of the Hegemony compound. Greece was part of the Warsaw Pact now, and there was no going home for them. Peter's parents also came, because they understood that they would become targets for anyone wanting to get to Peter. He gave them both jobs in the Hegemony, and if they minded the disruption of their lives, they never gave a sign of it.

The Arkanians left their homeland, too, and came gladly to live in a place where their children would not be stolen from them. Suriyawong's parents had made it out of Thailand, and they moved the family fortune and the family business to Ribeirão Preto. Other Thai and Indian families with ties to Bean's army or the Battle School graduates came as well, and soon there were thriving neighborhoods where Portuguese was rarely heard.

As for Achilles, month after month they heard nothing about him. Presumably he got back to Beijing. Presumably, he was worming his way into power one way or another. But they allowed themselves, as the silence about him continued, to hope that perhaps the Chinese, having made use of him, now knew him well enough to keep him away from the reins of power.

—

On a cloudy winter afternoon in June, Petra walked through the cemetery in the town of Araraquara, only twenty minutes by train from Ribeirão Preto. She took care to make sure she approached Bean from a direction where he could see her coming. Soon she stood beside him, looking at a marker.

"Who is buried here?" she asked.

"No one," said Bean, who showed no surprise at seeing her. "It's a cenotaph."

Petra read the names that were on it.

Poke.

Carlotta.

There was nothing else.

"There's a marker for Sister Carlotta somewhere in Vatican City," said Bean. "But there was no body recovered that could actually be buried anywhere. And Poke was cremated by people who didn't even know who she was. I got the idea for this from Virlomi."

Virlomi had set up a cenotaph for Sayagi in the small Hindu cemetery that already existed in Ribeirão Preto. It was a bit more elaborate—it included the dates of his birth and death, and called him "a man of satyagraha."

"Bean," said Petra, "it's quite insane of you to come here. No bodyguard. This marker standing here so that assassins can set their sights before you show up."

"I know," said Bean.

"At least you could have invited me along."

He turned to her, tears in his eyes. "This is my place of shame," he said. "I worked very hard to make sure your name would not be here."

"Is that what you tell yourself? There's no shame here, Bean. There's only love. And that's why I belong here—with the other lonely girls who gave their hearts to you."

Bean turned to her, put his arms around her, and wept into her shoulder. He had grown, to stand tall enough for that. "They saved my life," he said. "They *gave* me life."

"That's what good people do," said Petra. "And then they die, every one of them. It's a damned shame."

He gave one short laugh—whether at her small levity or at himself, for weeping, she did not know. "Nothing lasts long, does it," said Bean.

"They're still alive in you."

"Who am I alive in?" said Bean. "And don't say you."

"I will if I want. You saved *my* life."

"They never had children, either one of them," said Bean. "No one ever held either Poke or Carlotta the way a man does with a woman, or had a baby with them. They never got to see their children grow up and have children of their own."

"By Sister Carlotta's choice," said Petra.

"Not Poke's."

"They both had you."

"That's the futility of it," said Bean. "The only child they had was me."

"So . . . you owe it to them to carry on, to marry, to have more children who'll remember them both for your sake."

Bean stared off into space. "I have a better idea. Let me tell *you* about them. And you tell *your* children. Will you do that? If you could promise me that, then I think that I could bear all this, because they wouldn't just disappear from memory when I die."

"Of course I'll do that, Bean, but you're talking as if your life were already over, and it's just beginning. Look at you, you're getting along, you'll have a man's height before long, you'll—"

He touched her lips, gently, to silence her. "I'll have no wife, Petra. No babies."

"Why not? If you tell me you've decided to become a priest I'll kidnap you myself and get you out of this Catholic country."

"I'm not human, Petra," Bean replied. "And my species dies with me."

She laughed at his joke.

But as she looked into his eyes, she saw that it

wasn't a joke at all. Whatever he meant by that, he really thought that it was true. Not human. But how could he think that? Of all the people Petra knew, who was more human than Bean?

"Let's go back home," Bean finally said, "before somebody comes along and shoots us just for loitering."

"Home," said Petra.

Bean only halfway understood. "Sorry it's not Armenia."

"No, I don't think Armenia is home either," she said. "And Battle School sure wasn't, nor Eros. This *is* home, though. I mean, Ribeirão Preto. But here, too. Because . . . my family's here, of course, but . . ."

And then she realized what she was trying to say.

"It's because *you're* here. Because you're the one who went through it all with me. You're the one who knows what I'm talking about. What I'm remembering. Ender. That terrible day with Bonzo. And the day I fell asleep in the middle of a battle on Eros. You think *you* have shame." She laughed. "But it's OK to remember even *that* with you. Because you knew about that, and you still came to get me out."

"Took me long enough," said Bean.

They walked out of the cemetery toward the train station, holding hands because neither of them wanted to feel separate right now.

"I have an idea," said Petra.

"What?"

"If you ever change your mind—you know, about marrying and having babies—hang on to my address. Look me up."

Bean was silent for a long moment. "Ah," he finally said, "I get it. I rescued the princess, so now I can marry her if I want."

"That's the deal."

"Yeah, well, I notice you didn't mention it until after you heard my vow of celibacy."

"I suppose that was perverse of me."

"Besides, it's a cheat. Aren't I supposed to get half the kingdom, too?"

"I've got a better idea," she answered. "You can have it all."

Afterword

Just as *Speaker for the Dead* was a different kind of novel from *Ender's Game,* so also is *Shadow of the Hegemon* a different kind of book from *Ender's Shadow*. No longer are we in the close confines of Battle School or the asteroid Eros, fighting a war against insectoid aliens. Now, with *Hegemon,* we are on Earth, playing what amounts to a huge game of *Risk*—only you have to play politics and diplomacy as well in order to get power, hold onto it, and give yourself a place to land if you lose it.

Indeed, the game that this novel most resembles is the computer classic *Romance of the Three Kingdoms,* which is itself based on a Chinese historical novel, thus affirming the ties between history, fiction, and gaming. While history responds to irresistible forces and conditions (*pace* the extraordinarily illuminating book *Guns, Germs, and Steel,* which should be required reading by everyone who writes history or historical fiction, just so they understand the ground rules), in the specifics, history happens as it happens for highly personal reasons. The reasons European civilization prevailed over indigenous civilizations of the Americas consist of the implacable laws of history; but the reason why it was Cortez and Pizarro who prevailed over the Aztec and Inca empires by winning particular battles on particular days, instead of being cut down and destroyed as they might have been, had everything to do with their own character and the character and recent history of the emperors opposing them. And it happens that it is the novelist, not the historian, who has the freer hand at imagining what causes individual human beings to do the things they do.

Which is hardly a surprise. Human motivation cannot be documented, at least not with any kind of finality. After all, we rarely understand our own motivations, and so, even when we write down what we honestly believe to be our reasons for making the choices we make, our explanation is likely to be wrong or partly wrong or at least incomplete. So even when a historian or biographer has a wealth of information at hand, in the end he still has to make that uncomfortable leap into the abyss of ignorance before he can declare why a person did the things he did. The French Revolution inexorably led to anarchy and then tyranny for comprehensible reasons, following predictable paths. But nothing could have predicted Napoleon himself, or even that a single dictator of such gifts would emerge.

Novelists who write about Great Leaders, however, too often fall into the opposite trap. Able to imagine personal motivations, the people who write novels rarely have the grounding in historical fact or the grasp of historical forces to set their plausible characters into an equally plausible society. Most such attempts are laughably wrong, even when written by people who have actually been involved in the society of movers and shakers, for even those caught up in the maelstrom of politics are rarely able to see through the trees well enough to comprehend the forest. (Besides, most political or military novels by political or military leaders tend to be self-serving and self-justifying, which makes them almost as unreliable as books written by the ignorant.) How likely is it that someone who took part in the Clinton administration's immoral decision to launch unprovoked attacks on Afghanistan and the Sudan in the late summer of 1998 would be able to write a novel in which the political exigencies that led to these criminal acts are accurately recounted? Anyone in a position to know or guess the real interplay of human desires among the major players will also be so culpable that it will be impossible for him to tell the truth, even if he is honest enough to attempt it, simply because the people involved were so busy lying to themselves and to each other throughout the process that everyone involved is bound to be snow-blind.

In *Shadow of the Hegemon,* I have the advantage of writing a history that hasn't happened, because it is in the future. Not thirty million years in the future, as with my Homecoming books, or even three thousand years in the future, as with the trilogy of *Speaker for the Dead, Xenocide,* and *Children of the Mind,* but rather only a couple of centuries in the future, after nearly a century of international stasis caused by the Formic War. In the future history posited by *Hegemon,* nations and peoples of today are still recognizable, though the relative balance among them has changed. And I have both the perilous freedom and the solemn obligation to attempt to tell my characters' highly personal stories as they move (or are moved) amid the highest circles of power in the governing and military classes of the world.

If there is anything that can be called my "life study," it is precisely this subject area: great leaders and great forces shaping the interplay of nations and peoples throughout history. As a child, I would put myself to sleep at night imagining a map of the world as it existed in the late fifties, just as the great colonial empires were beginning to grant independence, one by one, to the colonies that had once made up those great swathes of British pink and French blue across Africa and southern Asia. I imagined all those colonies as free countries, and, choosing one of them or some other relatively small nation, I would imagine alliance, unifications, invasions, conquests, until all the world was united under one magnanimous, democratic government. Cincinnatus and George Washington, not Caesar or Napoleon, were my models. I read Machiavelli's *The Prince* and Shirer's *Rise and Fall of the Third Reich,* but I also read Mormon scripture (most notably the Book of Mormon stories of the generals Gideon, Moroni, Helaman, and Gidgiddoni, and Doctrine and Covenants section 121) and the Old and New Testaments, all the while trying to imagine how one might govern well when law gives way to exigency, and the circumstances under which war becomes righteous.

I don't pretend that the imaginings and studies of my life have brought me to great answers, and you will find no such answers in *Shadow of the Hegemon.* But I do believe I understand something of the workings of the world of government, politics, and war, both at their best and at their worst. I have sought the borderline between strength and ruthlessness, between ruthlessness and cruelty, and at the other extreme, between goodness and weakness, between weakness and betrayal. I have pondered how it is that some societies are able to get young men to kill and die with fervor trumping fear, and yet others seem to lose their will to survive or at least their will to do the things that make survival possible. And *Shadow of the Hegemon* and the two remaining books in this long tale of Bean, Petra, and Peter are my best attempt to use what I have learned in a tale in which great forces, large populations, and individuals of heroic if not always virtuous character combine to give shape to an imaginary, but I hope believable, history.

I am crippled in this effort by the factor that real life is rarely plausible—we believe that people would or could do these things only because we have documentation. Fiction, lacking that documentation, dares not be half so implausible. On the other hand, we can do what history never can—we can assign motive to human behavior, which cannot be refuted by any witness or evidence. So, despite doing my utmost to be truthful about how history happens, in the end I must depend on the novelist's tools. Do you care about this person, or that one? Do you believe such a person would do the things I say they do, for the reasons I assign?

History, when told as epic, often has the thrilling grandeur of Dvorak or Smetana, Borodin or Mussorgsky, but historical fiction must also find the intimacies and dissonances of the delicate little piano pieces of Satie and Debussy. For it is in the millions of small melodies that the truth of history is always found, for history only matters because of the effects we see or imagine in the lives of the ordinary people who are caught up in, or give shape to, the great events. Tchaikowsky can carry me away, but I tire quickly of the large effect, which feels so hollow and false on the second hearing. Of Satie I never tire, for his music is endlessly surprising and yet perfectly satisfying. If I can bring off this novel in Tchaikowsky's terms, that is well and good; but if I can also give you moments of Satie, I am far happier, for that is the harder and, ultimately, more rewarding task.

Besides my lifelong study of history in general, two books particularly influenced me during the writing of *Shadow of the Hegemon.* When I saw *Anna and the King,* I became impatient with my own ignorance of real Thai history, and so found David K. Wyatt's *Thailand: A Short History* (Yale, 1982, 1984). Wyatt writes clearly and convincingly, making the history of the Thai people both intelligible and fascinating. It is hard to imagine a nation that has been more lucky in the quality of its leaders as Thailand and its predecessor kingdoms, which managed to survive invasions from every direction and European and Japanese ambitions in Southeast Asia, all the while maintaining its own national character and remaining, more than many kingdoms and oligarchies, responsive to the needs of the Thai people. (I followed Wyatt's lead in calling the pre-Siamese language and the people who spoke it, in lands from Laos to upper Burma and southern China, "Tai," reserving "Thai" for the modern language and kingdom that bear that name.)

My own country once had leaders comparable to Siam's Mongkut and Chulalongkorn, and public servants as gifted and selfless as many of Chulalongkorn's brothers and nephews, but unlike Thailand, America is now a nation in decline, and my people have little will to be well led. America's past and its resources make it a major player for the nonce, but nations of small resources but strong will can change the course of world history, as the Huns, the Mongols, and the Arabs have shown, sometimes to devastating effect, and as the people of the Ganges have shown far more pacifically.

Which brings me to the second book, Lawrence James's *Raj: The Making and Unmaking of British India* (Little, Brown, 1997). Modern Indian history reads like one long tragedy of good, or at least bold, intentions leading to disaster, and in *Shadow of the Hegemon* I consciously echoed some of the themes I found in James's book.

As always, I relied on others to help me with this book by reading the first draft of each chapter to give me some idea whether I had wrought what I intended. My wife, Kristine; my son Geoffrey; and Kathy H. Kidd and Erin and Phillip Absher were my most immediate readers, and I thank them for helping prevent many a moment of inclarity or ineffectiveness.

The person most influential in giving this book the shape it has, however, is the aforementioned Phillip Absher, for when he read the first version of a chapter in which Petra was rescued from Russian captivity and united with Bean, he commented that I had built up her kidnapping so much that it was rather disappointing how easily the problem turned out to be resolved. I had not realized how high I had raised expectations, but I could see that he was right—that her easy release was not only a breaking of an implied promise with the reader, but also implausible under the circumstances. So instead of her kidnapping being an early event in a very involved story, I realized that it could and should provide the overarching structure of the entire novel, thus splitting what was to be one novel into two. As the story of Han Qing-jao took over *Xenocide* and caused it to become two books, so also the story of Petra took over this, Bean's second book, and caused there to be a third, *Shadow of Death* (which I may extend to the longer phrase from the Twenty-third Psalm, *The Valley of the Shadow of Death*; it would never do to become tied to a title too early). The book originally planned to be third will now be the fourth, *Shadow of the Giant.* All because Phillip felt a bit disappointed and, just as importantly, said so, causing me to think again about the structure I had unconsciously created in subversion of my conscious plans.

At the last minute, Ami Chopine of philoticweb.net found a real howler of an inconsistency between this book and *Ender's Game*. Ami, I owe you big time! (And thanks to Terry Jude, Matthew Schwartz, and Joshua Smith, too.)

I rarely write two novels at once, but I did this time, going back and forth between *Shadow of the Hegemon* and *Sarah,* my historical novel about the wife of Abraham (Shadow Mountain, 2000). The novels sustained each other in odd ways, each of them dealing with history during times of chaos and transformation—like the one the world is embarking upon at the time of this writing. In both stories, personal loyalties, ambitions, and passions sometimes shape the course of the history and sometimes surf upon history's wave, trying merely to stay just ahead of the breaking crest. May all who read these books find their own ways to do the same. It is in the turmoil of chaos that we discover what, if anything, we are.

As always, I have relied upon Kathleen Bellamy and Scott Allen to help keep communications open between me and my readers, and many who visited and took part in my online communities at *http://www.hatrack.com, http://www.frescopix.com,* and *http://www.-nauvoo.com*) helped me, often in ways they did not realize.

Many writers produce their art from a maelstrom of domestic chaos and tragedy. I am fortunate enough to write from within an island of peace and love, created by my wife, Kristine, my children, Geoffrey, Emily, Charlie Ben, and Zina, and good and dear friends and family who surround us and enrich our lives with their good will, kind help, and happy company. Perhaps I would write better were my life more miserable, but I have no interest in performing the experiment.

In particular, though, I write this book for my second son, Charlie Ben, who wordlessly has given great gifts to all who know him. Within the small community of his family, of school friends at Gateway Education Center, and of church friends in the Greensboro Summit Ward, Charlie Ben has given and received much friendship and love without uttering a word, as he patiently endures his pain and limitations, gladly receives the kindness of others, and generously shares his love and joy with all who care to receive it. Twisted by cerebral palsy, his body movements may look strange and disturbing to strangers, but to those willing to look more closely, a young man of beauty, humor, kindness, and joy can be found. May we all learn to see past such outward signs, and show our true selves through all barriers, however opaque they seem. And Charlie, who will never hold this book in his own hands or read it with his own eyes, will nevertheless hear it read to him by loving friends and family members. So to you, Charlie, I say: I am proud of all you do with your life, and glad to be your father; though you deserved a better one, you have been generous enough to love the one you have.

The next morning, Bean, Nikolai, and three other kids in their launch group had their assignments to Dragon Army. Months before they should have been promoted to soldiers. The unchosen kids were envious, furious by turn. Especially when they realized Bean was one of the chosen. "Do they *make* uniform flash suits that size?"

It was a good question. And the answer was no, they didn't. The colors of Dragon Army were grey, orange, grey. Because soldiers were usually a lot older than Bean when they came in, they had to cut a flash suit down for Bean, and they didn't do it all that well. Flash suits weren't manufactured in space, and nobody had the tools to do a first-rate job of alteration.

When they finally got it to fit him, Bean wore his flash suit to the Dragon Army barracks. Because it had taken him so long to be fitted, he was the last to arrive. Wiggin arrived at the door just as Bean was entering. "Go ahead," said Wiggin.

It was the first time Wiggin had ever spoken to him—for all Bean knew, the first time Wiggin had even noticed him. So thoroughly had Bean concealed his fascination with Wiggin that he had made himself effectively invisible.

Wiggin followed him into the room. Bean started down the corridor between the bunks, heading for the back of the room where the younger soldiers always had to sleep. He glanced at the other kids, who were all looking at him as he passed with a mixture of horror and amusement. They were in an army so lame that *this* little kid was part of it?

Behind him, Wiggin was starting his first speech. Voice confident, loud enough but not shouting, not nervous. "I'm Ender Wiggin. I'm your commander."

Tor Books by Orson Scott Card

Empire
The Folk of the Fringe
Future on Fire (editor)
Future on Ice (editor)
Hart's Hope
Hidden Empire
Invasive Procedures
(with Aaron Johnston)
Keeper of Dreams
The Lost Gate
Lovelock
(with Kathryn Kidd)
Pastwatch: The Redemption of Christopher Columbus
Saints
Songmaster
Treason
The Worthing Saga
Wyrms

Ender

Ender's Game
Speaker for the Dead
Xenocide
Children of the Mind
Ender's Shadow
Shadow of the Hegemon
Shadow Puppets
Shadow of the Giant
First Meetings: In the Enderverse
A War of Gifts
Ender in Exile

The Tales of Alvin Maker

Seventh Son
Red Prophet
Prentice Alvin
Alvin Journeyman
Heartfire
The Crystal City

Homecoming

The Memory of Earth
The Call of Earth
The Ships of Earth
Earthfall
Earthborn

Women of Genesis

Sarah
Rebekah
Rachel & Leah

Short Fiction

Maps in a Mirror: The Short Fiction of Orson Scott Card (hardcover)
Maps in a Mirror, Volume 1: The Changed Man (paperback)
Maps in a Mirror, Volume 2: Flux (paperback)
Maps in a Mirror, Volume 3: Cruel Miracles (paperback)
Maps in a Mirror, Volume 4: Monkey Sonatas (paperback)

ENDER'S SHADOW

ORSON SCOTT CARD

TOR®
A TOM DOHERTY ASSOCIATES BOOK
NEW YORK

ENDER'S SHADOW

Edited by Beth Meacham

A Tor Book
Published by Tom Doherty Associates, LLC
175 Fifth Avenue
New York, NY 10010

www.tor-forge.com

ISBN 978-0-8125-7571-2

First Edition: September 1999
First International Market Edition: August 2000
First U. S. Mass Market Edition: December 2000

Printed in the United States of America

19 18 17 16 15

TO DICK AND HAZIE BROWN

IN WHOSE HOME NO ONE IS HUNGRY

AND IN WHOSE HEARTS

NO ONE IS A STRANGER

CONTENTS

ENDER'S SHADOW

Foreword

This book is, strictly speaking, not a sequel, because it begins about where *Ender's Game* begins, and also ends, very nearly, at the same place. In fact, it is another telling of the same tale, with many of the same characters and settings, only from the perspective of another character. It's hard to know what to call it. A companion novel? A parallel novel? Perhaps a "parallax," if I can move that scientific term into literature.

Ideally, this novel should work as well for readers who have never read *Ender's Game* as for those who have read it several times. Because it is not a sequel, there is nothing you need to know from the novel *Ender's Game* that is not contained here. And yet, if I have achieved my literary goal, these two books complement and fulfill each other. Whichever one you read first, the other novel should still work on its own merits.

For many years, I have gratefully watched as *Ender's Game* has grown in popularity, especially among school-age readers. Though it was never intended as a young-adult novel, it has been embraced by many in that age group and by many teachers who find ways to use the book in their classrooms.

I have never found it surprising that the existing sequels—*Speaker for the Dead, Xenocide,* and *Children of the Mind*—never appealed as strongly to those younger readers. The obvious reason is that *Ender's Game* is centered around a child, while the sequels are about adults; perhaps more important, *Ender's Game* is, at least on the surface, a heroic, adventurous novel, while the sequels are a completely different kind of fiction, slower paced, more contemplative and idea-centered, and dealing with themes of less immediate import to younger readers.

Recently, however, I have come to realize that the 3,000-year gap between *Ender's Game* and its sequels leaves plenty of room for other sequels that are more closely tied to the original. In fact, in one sense *Ender's Game* has no sequels, for the other three books make one continuous story in themselves, while *Ender's Game* stands alone.

For a brief time I flirted seriously with the idea of opening up the *Ender's Game* universe to other writers, and went so far as to invite a writer whose work I greatly admire, Neal Shusterman, to consider working with me to create novels about Ender Wiggin's companions in Battle School. As we talked, it became clear that the most obvious character to begin with would be Bean, the child-soldier whom Ender treated as he had been treated by his adult teachers.

And then something else happened. The more we talked, the more jealous I became that Neal might be the one to write such a book, and not me. It finally dawned on me that, far from being finished with writing about "kids in space," as I cynically described the project, I actually had more to say, having actually learned something in the intervening dozen years since *Ender's Game* first appeared in 1985. And so, while still hoping that Neal and I can work together on something, I deftly swiped the project back.

I soon found that it's harder than it looks, to tell the same story twice, but differently. I was hindered by the fact that even though the viewpoint characters were different, the author was the same, with the same core beliefs about the world. I was helped by the fact that in the intervening years, I have learned a few things, and was able to bring different concerns and a deeper understanding to the project. Both books come from the same mind, but not the same; they draw on the same memories of childhood, but from a different perspective. For the reader, the parallax is created by Ender and Bean, standing a little ways apart as they move through the same events. For the writer, the parallax was created by a dozen years in which my older children grew up, and younger ones were born, and the world changed around me, and I learned a few things about human nature and about art that I had not known before.

Now you hold this book in your hands. Whether the literary experiment succeeds for you is entirely up to you to judge. For me it was worth dipping again into the same well, for the water was greatly changed this time, and if it has not been turned exactly into wine, at least it has a different flavor because of the different vessel that it was carried in, and I hope that you will enjoy it as much, or even more.

—Greensboro, North Carolina, January 1999

Part One

URCHIN

1

Poke

"You think you've found somebody, so suddenly my program gets the ax?"

"It's not about this kid that Graff found. It's about the low quality of what you've been finding."

"We knew it was long odds. But the kids I'm working with are actually fighting a war just to stay alive."

"Your kids are so malnourished that they suffer serious mental degradation before you even begin testing them. Most of them haven't formed any normal human bonds, they're so messed up they can't get through a day without finding something they can steal, break, or disrupt."

"They also represent possibility, as all children do."

"That's just the kind of sentimentality that discredits your whole project in the eyes of the I.F."

Poke kept her eyes open all the time. The younger children were supposed to be on watch, too, and sometimes they could be quite observant, but they just didn't notice all the things they needed to notice, and that meant that

Poke could only depend on herself to see danger.

There was plenty of danger to watch for. The cops, for instance. They didn't show up often, but when they did, they seemed especially bent on clearing the streets of children. They would flail about them with their magnetic whips, landing cruel stinging blows on even the smallest children, haranguing them as vermin, thieves, pestilence, a plague on the fair city of Rotterdam. It was Poke's job to notice when a disturbance in the distance suggested that the cops might be running a sweep. Then she would give the alarm whistle and the little ones would rush to their hiding places till the danger was past.

But the cops didn't come by that often. The real danger was much more immediate—big kids. Poke, at age nine, was the matriarch of her little crew (not that any of them knew for sure that she was a girl), but that cut no ice with the eleven- and twelve- and thirteen-year-old boys and girls who bullied their way around the streets. The adult-size beggars and thieves and whores of the street paid no attention to the little kids except to kick them out of the way. But the older children, who were among the kicked, turned around and preyed on the younger ones. Any time Poke's crew found something to eat—especially if they located a dependable source of garbage or an easy mark for a coin or a bit of food—they had to watch jealously and hide their winnings, for the bullies liked nothing better than to take away whatever scraps of food the little ones might have. Stealing from younger children was much safer than stealing from shops or passersby. And they enjoyed it, Poke could see that. They liked how the little kids cowered and obeyed and whimpered and gave them whatever they demanded.

So when the scrawny little two-year-old took up a perch on a garbage can across the street, Poke, being observant, saw him at once. The kid was on the edge of starvation. No, the kid was starving. Thin arms and legs, joints that looked ridiculously oversized, a distended belly. And if hunger didn't kill him soon, the onset of autumn would, because his clothing was thin and there wasn't much of it even at that.

Normally she wouldn't have paid him more than passing attention. But this one had eyes. He was still looking around with intelligence. None of that stupor of the walking dead, no longer searching for food or even caring to find a comfortable place to lie while breathing their last taste of the stinking air of Rotterdam. After all, death would not be such a change for them. Everyone knew that Rotterdam was, if not the capital, then the main seaport of Hell. The only difference between Rotterdam and death was that with Rotterdam, the damnation wasn't eternal.

This little boy—what was he doing? Not looking for food. He wasn't eyeing the pedestrians. Which was just as well—there was no chance that anyone would leave anything for a child that small. Anything he might get would be taken away by any other child, so why should he bother? If he wanted to survive, he should be following older scavengers and licking food wrappers behind them, getting the last sheen of sugar or dusting of flour clinging to the packaging, whatever the first comer hadn't licked off. There was nothing for this child out here on the street, not unless he got taken in by a crew, and Poke wouldn't have him. He'd be nothing but a drain, and her kids were already having a hard enough time without adding another useless mouth.

He's going to ask, she thought. He's going to whine and beg. But that only works on the rich people. I've got my crew to think of. He's not one of them, so I don't care about him. Even if he is small. He's nothing to me.

A couple of twelve-year-old hookers who didn't usually work this strip rounded a corner, heading toward Poke's base. She gave a low whistle. The kids immediately drifted apart, staying on the street but trying not to look like a crew.

It didn't help. The hookers knew already that Poke was a crew boss, and sure enough, they caught her by the arms and slammed her against a wall and demanded their "permission" fee. Poke knew better than to claim she had nothing to share—she always tried to keep a reserve in order to placate hungry bullies. These hookers, Poke could see why they were hungry. They didn't look like what the pedophiles wanted, when they came cruising through. They were too gaunt, too old-looking. So until they grew bodies and started attracting the slightly-less-perverted trade, they had to resort to scavenging. It made Poke's blood boil, to have them steal from her and her crew, but it was smarter to pay them off. If they beat her up, she couldn't look out for her crew now, could she? So she took them to one of her stashes and came up with a little bakery bag that still had half a pastry in it.

It was stale, since she'd been holding it for a couple of days for just such an occasion, but the two hookers grabbed it, tore open the bag, and one of them bit off more than half before offering the remainder to her friend. Or rather, her former friend, for of such predatory acts are feuds born. The two of them started fighting, screaming at each other, slapping, raking at each other with clawed hands. Poke watched closely, hoping that they'd drop the remaining fragment of pastry, but no such luck. It went into the mouth of the same girl who had already eaten the first bite—and it was that first girl who won the fight too, sending the other one running for refuge.

Poke turned around, and there was the little boy right behind her. She nearly tripped over him. Angry as she was at having had to give up food to those street-whores, she gave him a knee and knocked him to the ground. "Don't stand behind people if you don't want to land on your butt," she snarled.

He simply got up and looked at her, expectant, demanding.

"No, you little bastard, you're not getting nothing from me," said Poke. "I'm not taking one bean out of the mouths of my crew, you aren't *worth* a bean."

Her crew was starting to reassemble, now that the bullies had passed.

"Why you give your food to them?" said the boy. "You need that food."

"Oh, excuse me!" said Poke. She raised her voice, so her crew could hear her. "I guess you ought to be the crew boss here, is that it? You being so big, you got no trouble keeping the food."

"Not me," said the boy. "I'm not worth a bean, remember?"

"Yeah, I remember. Maybe *you* ought to remember and shut up."

Her crew laughed.

But the little boy didn't. "You got to get your own bully," he said.

"I don't *get* bullies, I get rid of them," Poke answered. She didn't like the way he kept talking, standing up to her. In a minute she was going to have to hurt him.

"You give food to bullies every day. Give that to *one* bully and get him to keep the others away from you."

"You think I never thought of that, stupid?" she said. "Only once he's bought, how I keep him? He won't fight for us."

"If he won't, then kill him," said the boy.

That made Poke mad, the stupid impossibility of it, the power of the idea that she knew she could never lay hands on. She gave him a knee again, and this time kicked him when he went down. "Maybe I start by killing you."

"I'm not worth a bean, remember?" said the boy. "You kill one bully, get another to fight for you, he want your food, he scared of you too."

She didn't know what to say to such a preposterous idea.

"They eating you up," said the boy. "Eating you up. So you got to kill one. Get him down, everybody as small as me. Stones crack any size head."

"You make me sick," she said.

"Cause you didn't think of it," he said.

He was flirting with death, talking to her that way. If

she injured him at all, he'd be finished, he must know that.

But then, he had death living with him inside his flimsy little shirt already. Hard to see how it would matter if death came any closer.

Poke looked around at her crew. She couldn't read their faces.

"I don't need no baby telling me to kill what we can't kill."

"Little kid come up behind him, you shove, he fall over," said the boy. "Already got you some big stones, bricks. Hit him in the head. When you see brains you done."

"He no good to me dead," she said. "I want my own bully, he keep us safe, I don't want no dead one."

The boy grinned. "So now you like my idea," he said.

"Can't trust no bully," she answered.

"He watch out for you at the charity kitchen," said the boy. "You get in at the kitchen." He kept looking her in the eye, but he was talking for the others to hear. "He get you *all* in at the kitchen."

"Little kid get into the kitchen, the big kids, they beat him," said Sergeant. He was eight, and mostly acted like he thought he was Poke's second-in-command, though truth was she didn't have a second.

"You get you a bully, he make them go away."

"How he stop two bullies? Three bullies?" asked Sergeant.

"Like I said," the boy answered. "You push him down, he not so big. You get your rocks. You be ready. Ben't you a soldier? Don't they call you Sergeant?"

"Stop talking to him, Sarge," said Poke. "I don't know why any of us is talking to some two-year-old."

"I'm four," said the boy.

"What your name?" asked Poke.

"Nobody ever said no name for me," he said.

"You mean you so stupid you can't remember your own name?"

"Nobody ever said no name," he said again. Still he looked her in the eye, lying there on the ground, the crew around him.

"Ain't worth a bean," she said.

"Am so," he said.

"Yeah," said Sergeant. "One damn bean."

"So now you got a name," said Poke. "You go back and sit on that garbage can, I think about what you said."

"I need something to eat," said Bean.

"If I get me a bully, if what you said works, then maybe I give you something."

"I need something now," said Bean.

She knew it was true.

She reached into her pocket and took out six peanuts she had been saving. He sat up and took just one from her hand, put it in his mouth and slowly chewed.

"Take them all," she said impatiently.

He held out his little hand. It was weak. He couldn't make a fist. "Can't hold them all," he said. "Don't hold so good."

Damn. She was wasting perfectly good peanuts on a kid who was going to die anyway.

But she was going to try his idea. It was audacious, but it was the first plan she'd ever heard that offered any hope of making things better, of changing something about their miserable life without her having to put on girl clothes and going into business. And since it was his idea, the crew had to see that she treated him fair. That's how you stay crew boss, they always see you be fair.

So she kept holding her hand out while he ate all six peanuts, one at a time.

After he swallowed the last one, he looked her in the eye for another long moment, and then said, "You better be ready to kill him."

"I want him alive."

"Be ready to kill him if he ain't the right one." With that, Bean toddled back across the street to his garbage can and laboriously climbed on top again to watch.

"You ain't no four years old!" Sergeant shouted over to him.

"I'm four but I'm just little," he shouted back.

Poke hushed Sergeant up and they went looking for stones and bricks and cinderblocks. If they were going to have a little war, they'd best be armed.

—

Bean didn't like his new name, but it was a name, and having a name meant that somebody else knew who he was and needed something to call him, and that was a good thing. So were the six peanuts. His mouth hardly knew what to do with them. Chewing hurt.

So did watching as Poke screwed up the plan he gave her. Bean didn't choose her because she was the smartest crew boss in Rotterdam. Quite the opposite. Her crew barely survived because her judgment wasn't that good. And she was too compassionate. Didn't have the brains to make sure she got enough food herself to look well fed, so while her own crew knew she was nice and liked her, to strangers she didn't look prosperous. Didn't look good at her job.

But if she really *was* good at her job, she would never have listened to him. He never would have got close. Or if she did listen, and did like his idea, she would have got rid of him. That's the way it worked on the street. Nice kids died. Poke was almost too nice to stay alive. That's what Bean was counting on. But that's what he now feared.

All this time he invested in watching people while his body ate itself up, it would be wasted if she couldn't bring it off. Not that Bean hadn't wasted a lot of time himself. At first when he watched the way kids did things on the street, the way they were stealing from each other, at each other's throats, in each other's pockets, selling every part of themselves that they could sell, he saw how things could be better if somebody had any brains, but he didn't trust his own insight. He was sure there must be something else that he just didn't get. He struggled to learn more—of everything. To learn to read so he'd know what the signs said on trucks and stores and wagons and bins. To learn enough Dutch and enough I.F. Common to understand everything that was said around him. It didn't help that hunger constantly distracted him. He probably could have found more to eat if he hadn't spent so much time studying the people. But finally he realized: He already understood it. He had understood it from the start. There was no secret that Bean just didn't get yet because he was only little. The reason all these kids handled everything so stupidly was because they were stupid.

They were stupid and he was smart. So why was he starving to death while these kids were still alive? That was when he decided to act. That was when he picked Poke as his crew boss. And now he sat on a garbage can watching her blow it.

She chose the wrong bully, that's the first thing she did. She needed a guy who made it on size alone, intimidating people. She needed somebody big and dumb, brutal but controllable. Instead, she thinks she needs somebody *small.* No, stupid! Stupid! Bean wanted to scream at her as she saw her target coming, a bully who called himself Achilles after the comics hero. He was little and mean and smart and quick, but he had a gimp leg. So she thought she could take him down more easily. Stupid! The idea isn't just to take him down—you can take *anybody* down the first time because they won't expect it. You need somebody who will *stay* down.

But he said nothing. Couldn't get her mad at him. See what happens. See what Achilles is like when he's beat. She'll see—it won't work and she'll have to kill him and hide the body and try again with another bully before word gets out that there's a crew of little kids taking down bullies.

So up comes Achilles, swaggering—or maybe that was just the rolling gait that his bent leg forced on him—and Poke makes an exaggerated show of cowering and trying to get away. Bad job, thought Bean. Achilles gets it already. Something's wrong. You were supposed to act like you normally do! Stupid! So Achilles looks around a lot more. Wary. She tells him she's got something stashed—that part's normal—and she leads him into the trap in the alley. But look, he's holding back. Being careful. It isn't going to work.

But it does work, because of the gimp leg. Achilles can see the trap being sprung but he can't get away, a couple of little kids pile into the backs of his legs while Poke and Sergeant push him from the front and down he goes. Then there's a couple of bricks hitting his body and his bad leg and they're thrown hard—the little kids get it, they do their job, even if Poke is stupid—and yeah, that's good, Achilles *is* scared, he thinks he's going to die.

Bean was off his perch by now. Down the alley, watching, closer. Hard to see past the crowd. He pushes his way in, and the little kids—who are all bigger than he is—recognize him, they know he earned a view of this, they let him in. He stands right at Achilles' head. Poke stands above him, holding a big cinderblock, and she's talking.

"You get us into the food line at the shelter."

"Sure, right, I will, I promise."

Don't believe him. Look at his eyes, checking for weakness.

"You get more food this way, too, Achilles. You get my crew. We get enough to eat, we have more strength, we bring more to you. You need a crew. The other bullies shove you out of the way—we've seen them!—but with us, you don't got to take no shit. See how we do it? An army, that's what we are."

OK, now he was getting it. It *was* a good idea, and he wasn't stupid, so it made sense to him.

"If this is so smart, Poke, how come you didn't do this before now?"

She had nothing to say to that. Instead, she glanced at Bean.

Just a momentary glance, but Achilles saw it. And Bean

knew what he was thinking. It was so obvious.

"Kill him," said Bean.

"Don't be stupid," said Poke. "He's in."

"That's right," said Achilles. "I'm in. It's a good idea."

"Kill him," said Bean. "If you don't kill him now, he's going to kill *you.*"

"You let this little walking turd get away with talking shit like this?" said Achilles.

"It's your life or his," said Bean. "Kill him and take the next guy."

"The next guy won't have my bad leg," said Achilles. "The next guy won't think he needs you. I know I do. I'm in. I'm the one you want. It makes sense."

Maybe Bean's warning made her more cautious. She didn't cave in quite yet. "You won't decide later that you're embarrassed to have a bunch of little kids in your crew?"

"It's *your* crew, not mine," said Achilles.

Liar, thought Bean. Don't you see that he's lying to you?

"What this is to me," said Achilles, "this is my family. These are my kid brothers and sisters. I got to look after my family, don't I?"

Bean saw at once that Achilles had won. Powerful bully, and he had called these kids his sisters, his brothers. Bean could see the hunger in their eyes. Not the regular hunger, for food, but the real hunger, the deep hunger, for family, for love, for belonging. They got a little of that by being in Poke's crew. But Achilles was promising more. He had just beaten Poke's best offer. Now it was too late to kill him.

Too late, but for a moment it looked as if Poke was so stupid she was going to go ahead and kill him after all. She raised the cinderblock higher, to crash it down.

"No," said Bean. "You can't. He's family now."

She lowered the cinderblock to her waist. Slowly she turned to look at Bean. "You get the hell out of here," she said. "You no part of my crew. You get *nothing* here."

"No," said Achilles. "You better go ahead and kill me, you plan to treat him that way."

Oh, that sounded brave. But Bean knew Achilles wasn't brave. Just smart. He had already won. It meant nothing that he was lying there on the ground and Poke still had the cinderblock. It was his crew now. Poke was finished. It would be a while before anybody but Bean and Achilles understood that, but the test of authority was here and now, and Achilles was going to win it.

"This little kid," said Achilles, "he may not be part of your crew, but he's part of my family. You don't go telling my brother to get lost."

Poke hesitated. A moment. A moment longer.

Long enough.

Achilles sat up. He rubbed his bruises, he checked out his contusions. He looked in joking admiration to the little kids who had bricked him. "Damn, you bad!" They laughed—nervously, at first. Would he hurt them because they hurt him? "Don't worry," he said. "You showed me what you can do. We have to do this to more than a couple of bullies, you'll see. I had to know you could do it right. Good job. What's your name?"

One by one he learned their names. Learned them and remembered them, or when he missed one he'd make a big deal about it, apologize, visibly work at remembering. Fifteen minutes later, they loved him.

If he could do this, thought Bean, if he's this good at making people love him, why didn't he do it before?

Because these fools always look up for power. People above you, they never want to share power with you. Why you look to them? They give you nothing. People below you, you give them hope, you give them respect, *they* give you power, cause they don't think they have any, so they don't mind giving it up.

Achilles got to his feet, a little shaky, his bad leg more sore than usual. Everybody stood back, gave him some space. He could leave now, if he wanted. Get away, never come back. Or go get some more bullies, come back and punish the crew. But he stood there, then smiled, reached into his pocket, took out the most incredible thing. A bunch of raisins. A whole handful of them. They looked at his hand as if it bore the mark of a nail in the palm.

"Little brothers and sisters first," he said. "Littlest first." He looked at Bean. "You."

"Not him!" said the next littlest. "We don't even know him."

"Bean was the one wanted us to *kill* you," said another.

"Bean," said Achilles. "Bean, you were just looking out for my family, weren't you?"

"Yes," said Bean.

"You want a raisin?"

Bean nodded.

"You first. You the one brought us all together, OK?"

Either Achilles would kill him or he wouldn't. At this moment, all that mattered was the raisin. Bean took it. Put it in his mouth. Did not even bite down on it. Just let his saliva soak it, bringing out the flavor of it.

"You know," said Achilles, "no matter how long you hold it in your mouth, it never turns back into a grape."

"What's a grape?"

Achilles laughed at him, still not chewing. Then he gave out raisins to the other kids. Poke had never shared out so many raisins, because she had never had so many to share. But the little kids wouldn't understand that. They'd think, Poke gave us garbage, and Achilles gave us raisins. That's because they were stupid.

2

Kitchen

"I know you've already looked through this area, and you're probably almost done with Rotterdam, but something's been happening lately, since you visited, that . . . oh, I don't know if it's really anything, I shouldn't have called."

"Tell me, I'm listening."

"There's always been fighting in the line. We try to stop them, but we only have a few volunteers, and they're needed to keep order inside the dining room, that and serve the food. So we know that a lot of kids who should get a turn can't even get in the line, because they're pushed out. And if we do manage to stop the bullies and let one of the little ones in, then they get beaten up afterward. We never see them again. It's ugly."

"Survival of the fittest."

"Of the cruelest. Civilization is supposed to be the opposite of that."

"*You're* civilized. They're not."

"Anyway, it's changed. All of a sudden. Just in the past few days. I don't know why. But I just—you said that anything unusual—and whoever's behind it—I mean, can civilization suddenly evolve all over again, in the middle of a jungle of children?"

"That's the only place it ever evolves. I'm through in Delft. There was nothing for us here. I already have enough blue plates."

Bean kept to the background during the weeks that followed. He had nothing to offer now—they already had his best idea. And he knew that gratitude wouldn't last long. He wasn't big and he didn't eat much, but if he was constantly underfoot, annoying people and chattering at them, it would soon become not only fun but popular to deny him food in hopes that he'd die or go away.

Even so, he often felt Achilles' eyes on him. He noticed this without fear. If Achilles killed him, so be it. He had been a few days from death anyway. It would just mean his plan didn't work so well after all, but since it was his only plan, it didn't matter if it turned out not to have been good. If Achilles remembered how Bean urged Poke to kill him—and of course he did remember—and if Achilles was planning how and when he would die, there was nothing Bean could do to prevent it.

Sucking up wouldn't help. That would just look like weakness, and Bean had seen for a long time how bullies—and Achilles was still a bully at heart—thrived on the terror of other children, how they treated people even worse when they showed their weakness. Nor would offering more clever ideas, first because Bean didn't have any, and second because Achilles would think it was an affront to his authority. And the other kids would resent it if Bean kept acting like he thought he was the only one with a brain. They already resented him for having thought of this plan that had changed their lives.

For the change was immediate. The very first morning, Achilles had Sergeant go stand in the line at Helga's Kitchen on Aert Van Nes Straat, because, he said, as long as we're going to get the crap beaten out of us anyway, we might as well try for the best free food in Rotterdam in case we get to eat before we die. He talked like that, but he had made them practice their moves till the last light of day the night before, so they worked together better and they didn't give themselves away so soon, the way they did when they were going after him. The practice gave them confidence. Achilles kept saying, "They'll expect this," and "They'll try that," and because he was a bully himself, they trusted him in a way they had never trusted Poke.

Poke, being stupid, kept trying to act as if she was in charge, as if she had only delegated their training to Achilles. Bean admired the way that Achilles did not argue with her, and did not change his plans or instructions in any way because of what she said. If she urged him to do what he was already doing, he'd keep doing it. There was no show of defiance. No struggle for power. Achilles acted as if he had already won, and because the other kids followed him, he had.

The line formed in front of Helga's early, and Achilles watched carefully as bullies who arrived later inserted themselves in line in a kind of hierarchy—the bullies knew which ones got pride of place. Bean tried to understand the principle Achilles used to pick which bully Sergeant should pick a fight with. It wasn't the weakest, but that was smart, since beating the weakest bully would only set them up for more fights every day. Nor was it the strongest. As Sergeant walked across the street, Bean tried to see what it was about the target bully that made Achilles pick him. And then Bean realized—this was the strongest bully who had no friends with him.

The target was big and he looked mean, so beating him would look like an important victory. But he talked to no one, greeted no one. He was out of his territory, and several of the other bullies were casting resentful glances at him, sizing him up. There might have been a fight here today even if Achilles hadn't picked this soup line, this stranger.

Sergeant was cool as you please, slipping into place directly in front of the target. For a moment, the target just stood there looking at him, as if he couldn't believe what he was seeing. Surely this little kid would realize his deadly mistake and run away. But Sergeant didn't even act as if he noticed the target was there.

"Hey!" said the target. He shoved Sergeant hard, and from the angle of the push, Sergeant should have been propelled away from the line. But, as Achilles had told him, he planted a foot right away and launched himself forward, hitting the bully in front of the target in line, even though that was not the direction in which the target had pushed him.

The bully in front turned around and snarled at Sergeant, who pleaded, "He pushed me."

"He hit you himself," said the target.

"Do I look that stupid?" said Sergeant.

The bully-in-front sized up the target. A stranger. Tough, but not unbeatable. "Watch yourself, skinny boy."

That was a dire insult among bullies, since it implied incompetence and weakness.

"Watch your own self."

During this exchange, Achilles led a picked group of younger kids toward Sergeant, who was risking life and limb by staying right up between the two bullies. Just before reaching them, two of the younger kids darted through the line to the other side, taking up posts against the wall just beyond the target's range of vision. Then Achilles started screaming.

"What the hell do you think you're doing, you turd-stained piece of toilet paper! I send my boy to hold my place in line and you *shove* him? You *shove* him into my *friend* here?"

Of course they weren't friends at all—Achilles was the lowest-status bully in this part of Rotterdam and he always took his place as the last of the bullies in line. But the target didn't know that, and he wouldn't have time to find out. For by the time the target was turned to face

Achilles, the boys behind him were already leaping against his calves. There was no waiting for the usual exchange of shoves and brags before the fight began. Achilles began it and ended it with brutal swiftness. He pushed hard just as the younger boys hit, and the target hit the cobbled street hard. He lay there dazed, blinking. But already two other little kids were handing big loose cobblestones to Achilles, who smashed them down, one, two, on the target's chest. Bean could hear the ribs as they popped like twigs.

Achilles pulled him by his shirt and flopped him right back down on the street. He groaned, struggled to move, groaned again, lay still.

The others in line had backed away from the fight. This was a violation of protocol. When bullies fought each other, they took it into the alleys, and they didn't try for serious injury, they fought until supremacy was clear and it was over. This was a new thing, using cobblestones, breaking bones. It scared them, not because Achilles was so fearsome to look at, but because he had done the forbidden thing, and he had done it right out in the open.

At once Achilles signaled Poke to bring the rest of the crew and fill in the gap in the line. Meanwhile, Achilles strutted up and down the line, ranting at the top of his voice. "You can disrespect me, I don't care, I'm just a cripple, I'm just a guy with a gimp leg! But don't you go shoving my family! Don't you go shoving one of my children out of line! You hear me? Because if you do that some truck's going to come down this street and knock you down and break your bones, just like happened to this little pinprick, and next time maybe your head's going to be what breaks till your brains fall out on the street. You got to watch out for speeding trucks like the one that knocked down this fart-for-brains right here in front of my soup kitchen!"

There it was, the challenge. *My* kitchen. And Achilles didn't hold back, didn't show a spark of timidity about it. He kept the rant going, limping up and down the line, staring each bully in the face, daring him to argue. Shadowing his movements on the other side of the line were the two younger boys who had helped take down the stranger, and Sergeant strutted at Achilles' side, looking happy and smug. They reeked of confidence, while the other bullies kept glancing over their shoulders to see what those leg-grabbers behind them were doing.

And it wasn't just talk and brag, either. When one of the bullies started looking belligerent, Achilles went right up into his face. However, as he had planned beforehand, he didn't actually go after the belligerent one—he was ready for trouble, asking for it. Instead, the boys launched themselves at the bully directly after him in line. Just as they leapt, Achilles turned and shoved the new target, screaming, "What do you think is so damn funny!" He had another cobblestone in his hands at once, standing over the fallen one, but he did not strike. "Go to the end of the line, you moron! You're lucky I'm letting you eat in my kitchen!"

It completely deflated the belligerent one, for the bully Achilles knocked down and obviously could have smashed was the one next *lower* in status. So the belligerent one hadn't been threatened or harmed, and yet Achilles had scored a victory right in his face and he hadn't been a part of it.

The door to the soup kitchen opened. At once Achilles was with the woman who opened it, smiling, greeting her like an old friend. "Thank you for feeding us today," he said. "I'm eating last today. Thank you for bringing in my friends. Thank you for feeding my family."

The woman at the door knew how the street worked. She knew Achilles, too, and that something very strange was going on here. Achilles always ate last of the bigger boys, and rather shamefacedly. But his new patronizing attitude hardly had time to get annoying before the first of Poke's crew came to the door. "My family," Achilles announced proudly, passing each of the little kids into the hall. "You take good care of my children."

Even Poke he called his child. If she noticed the humiliation of it, though, she didn't show it. All she cared about was the miracle of getting into the soup kitchen. The plan had worked.

And whether she thought of it as her plan or Bean's didn't matter to Bean in the least, at least not till he had the first soup in his mouth. He drank it as slowly as he could, but it was still gone so fast that he could hardly believe it. Was this all? And how had he managed to spill so much of the precious stuff on his shirt?

Quickly he stuffed his bread inside his clothing and headed for the door. Stashing the bread and leaving, that was Achilles' idea and it was a good one. Some of the bullies inside the kitchen were bound to plan retribution. The sight of little kids eating would be galling to them. They'd get used to it soon enough, Achilles promised, but this first day it was important that all the little kids get out while the bullies were still eating.

When Bean got to the door, the line was still coming in, and Achilles stood by the door, chatting with the woman about the tragic accident there in the line. Paramedics must have been summoned to carry the injured boy away—he was no longer groaning in the street. "It could have been one of the little kids," he said. "We need a policeman out here to watch the traffic. That driver would never have been so careless if there was a cop here."

The woman agreed. "It could have been awful. They said half his ribs were broken and his lung was punctured." She looked mournful, her hands fretting.

"This line forms up when it's still dark. It's dangerous. Can't we have a light out here? I've got my children to think about," said Achilles. "Don't you want my little kids to be safe? Or am I the only one who cares about them?"

The woman murmured something about money and how the soup kitchen didn't have much of a budget.

Poke was counting children at the door while Sergeant ushered them out into the street.

Bean, seeing that Achilles was trying to get the adults to protect them in line, decided the time was right for him to be useful. Because this woman was compassionate and Bean was by far the smallest child, he knew he had the most power over her. He came up to her, tugged on her woollen skirt. "Thank you for watching over us," he said. "It's the first time I ever got into a real kitchen. Papa Achilles told us that *you* would keep us safe so we little ones could eat here every day."

"Oh, you poor thing! Oh, look at you." Tears streamed down the woman's face. "Oh, oh, you poor darling." She embraced him.

Achilles looked on, beaming. "I got to watch out for them," he said quietly. "I got to keep them safe."

Then he led his family—it was no longer in any sense Poke's crew—away from Helga's kitchen, all marching in a line. Till they rounded the corner of a building and then they ran like hell, joining hands and putting as much distance between them and Helga's kitchen as they could. For the rest of the day they were going to have to lie low. In twos and threes the bullies would be looking for them.

But they *could* lie low, because they didn't need to forage for food today. The soup already gave them more calories than they normally got, and they had the bread.

Of course, the first tax on that bread belonged to Achilles, who had eaten no soup. Each child reverently offered his bread to their new papa, and he took a bite from each one and slowly chewed it and swallowed it before reaching for the next offered bread. It was quite a lengthy ritual. Achilles took a mouthful of every piece of bread except two: Poke's and Bean's.

"Thanks," said Poke.

She was so stupid, she thought it was a gesture of respect. Bean knew better. By not eating their bread, Achilles was putting them outside the family. We are dead, thought Bean.

That's why Bean hung back, why he held his tongue and remained unobtrusive during the next few weeks.

That was also why he endeavored never to be alone. Always he was within arm's reach of one of the other kids.

But he didn't linger near Poke. That was a picture he didn't want to get locked in anyone's memory, him tagging along with Poke.

From the second morning, Helga's soup kitchen had an adult outside watching, and a new light fixture on the third day. By the end of a week the adult guardian was a cop. Even so, Achilles never brought his group out of hiding until the adult was there, and then he would march the whole family right to the front of the line, and loudly thank the bully in first position for helping him look out for his children by saving them a place in line.

It was hard on all of them, though, seeing how the bullies looked at them. They had to be on their best behavior while the doorkeeper was watching, but murder was on their minds.

And it didn't get better; the bullies didn't "get used to it," despite Achilles' bland assurances that they would. So even though Bean was determined to be unobtrusive, he knew that something had to be done to turn the bullies away from their hatred, and Achilles, who thought the war was over and victory achieved, wasn't going to do it.

So as Bean took his place in line one morning, he deliberately hung back to be last of the family. Usually Poke brought up the rear—it was her way of trying to pretend that she was somehow involved in ushering the little ones in. But this time Bean deliberately got in place behind her, with the hate-filled stare of the bully who should have had first position burning on his head.

Right at the door, where the woman was standing with Achilles, both of them looking proud of his family, Bean turned to face the bully behind him and asked, in his loudest voice, "Where's *your* children? How come you don't bring *your* children to the kitchen?"

The bully would have snarled something vicious, but the woman at the door was watching with raised eyebrows. "You look after little children, too?" she asked. It was obvious she was delighted about the idea and wanted the answer to be yes. And stupid as this bully was, he knew that it was good to please adults who gave out food. So he said, "Of course I do."

"Well, you can bring them, you know. Just like Papa Achilles here. We're always glad to see the little children."

Again Bean piped up. "They let people with little children come inside *first!*"

"You know, that's such a good idea," said the woman. "I think we'll make that a rule. Now, let's move along, we're holding up the hungry children."

Bean did not even glance at Achilles as he went inside.

Later, after breakfast, as they were performing the ritual of giving bread to Achilles, Bean made it a point to offer his bread yet again, though there was danger in reminding everyone that Achilles never took a share from him. Today, though, he had to see how Achilles regarded him, for being so bold and intrusive.

"If they all bring little kids, they'll run out of soup faster," said Achilles coldly. His eyes said nothing at all—but that, too, was a message.

"If they all become papas," said Bean, "they won't be trying to kill us."

At that, Achilles' eyes came to life a little. He reached down and took the bread from Bean's hand. He bit down on the crust, tore away a huge piece of it. More than half. He jammed it into his mouth and chewed it slowly, then handed the remnant of the bread back to Bean.

It left Bean hungry that day, but it was worth it. It didn't mean that Achilles wasn't going to kill him someday, but at least he wasn't separating him from the rest of the family anymore. And that remnant of bread was far more food than he used to get in a day. Or a week, for that matter.

He was filling out. Muscles grew in his arms and legs again. He didn't get exhausted just crossing a street. He could keep up easily now, when the others jogged along.

They all had more energy. They were healthy, compared to street urchins who didn't have a papa. Everyone could see it. The other bullies would have no trouble recruiting families of their own.

—

Sister Carlotta was a recruiter for the International Fleet's training program for children. It had caused a lot of criticism in her order, and finally she won the right to do it by pointedly mentioning the Earth Defense Treaty, which was a veiled threat. If she reported the order for obstructing her work on behalf of the I.F., the order could lose its tax-exempt and draft-exempt status. She knew, however, that when the war ended and the treaty expired, she would no doubt be a nun in search of a home, for there would be no place for her among the Sisters of St. Nicholas.

But her mission in life, she knew, was to care for little children, and the way she saw it, if the Buggers won the next round of the war, all the little children of the Earth would die. Surely God did not mean that to happen—but in her judgment, at least, God did not want his servants to sit around waiting for God to work miracles to save them. He wanted his servants to labor as best they could to bring about righteousness. So it was her business, as a Sister of St. Nicholas, to use her training in child development in order to serve the war effort. As long as the I.F. thought it worthwhile to recruit extraordinarily gifted children to train them for command roles in the battles to come, then she would help them by finding the children that would otherwise be overlooked. They would never pay anyone to do something as fruitless as scouring the filthy streets of every overcrowded city in the world, searching among the malnourished savage children who begged and stole and starved there; for the chance of finding a child with the intelligence and ability and character to make a go of it in Battle School was remote.

To God, however, all things were possible. Did he not

say that the weak would be made strong, and the strong weak? Was Jesus not born to a humble carpenter and his bride in the country province of Galilee? The brilliance of children born to privilege and bounty, or even to bare sufficiency, would hardly show forth the miraculous power of God. And it was the miracle she was searching for. God had made humankind in his own image, male and female he created them. No Buggers from another planet were going to blow down what God had created.

Over the years, though, her enthusiasm, if not her faith, had flagged a little. Not one child had done better than a marginal success on the tests. Those children were indeed taken from the streets and trained, but it wasn't Battle School. They weren't on the course that might lead them to save the world. So she began to think that her real work was a different kind of miracle—giving the children hope, finding even a few to be lifted out of the morass, to be given special attention by the local authorities. She made it a point to indicate the most promising children, and then follow up on them with email to the authorities. Some of her early successes had already graduated from college; they said they owed their lives to Sister Carlotta, but she knew they owed their lives to God.

Then came the call from Helga Braun in Rotterdam, telling her of certain changes in the children who came to her charity kitchen. Civilization, she had called it. The children, all by themselves, were becoming civilized.

Sister Carlotta came at once, to see a thing that sounded like a miracle. And indeed, when she beheld it with her own eyes, she could hardly believe it. The line for breakfast was now flooded with little children. Instead of the bigger ones shoving them out of the way or intimidating them into not even bothering to try, they were shepherding them, protecting them, making sure each got his share. Helga had panicked at first, fearful that she would run out of food—but she found that when potential benefactors saw how these children were acting, donations increased.

There was always plenty now—not to mention an increase in volunteers helping.

"I was at the point of despair," she told Sister Carlotta. "On the day when they told me that a truck had hit one of the boys and broken his ribs. Of course that was a lie, but there he lay, right in the line. They didn't even try to conceal him from me. I was going to give up. I was going to leave the children to God and move in with my oldest boy in Frankfurt, where the government is not required by treaty to admit every refugee from any part of the globe."

"I'm glad you didn't," said Sister Carlotta. "You can't leave them to God, when God has left them to us."

"Well, that's the funny thing. Perhaps that fight in the line woke up these children to the horror of the life they were living, for that very day one of the big boys—but the weakest of them, with a bad leg, they call him Achilles—well, I suppose *I* gave him that name years ago, because Achilles had a weak heel, you know—Achilles, anyway—he showed up in the line with a group of little children. He as much as asked me for protection, warning me that what happened to that poor boy with the broken ribs—he was the one I call Ulysses, because he wanders from kitchen to kitchen—he's still in hospital, his ribs were completely smashed in, can you believe the brutality?—Achilles, anyway, he warned me that the same thing might happen to his little ones, so I made the special effort, I came early to watch over the line, and badgered the police to finally give me a man, off-duty volunteers at first, on part pay, but now regulars—you'd think I would have been watching over the line all along, but don't you see? It didn't make any difference because they didn't do their intimidation in the line, they did it where I couldn't see, so no matter how I watched over them, it was only the bigger, meaner boys who ended up in the line, and yes, I know they're God's children too and I fed them and tried to preach the gospel to them as they ate, but I was losing heart, they were so heartless themselves, so devoid of compassion, but Achilles, anyway, he had taken on a whole group of them, including the littlest child I ever saw on the streets, it just broke my heart, they call him Bean, so *small*, he looked to be two years old, though I've learned since that he thinks he's four, and he *talks* like he's ten at least, very precocious, I suppose that's why he lived long enough to get under Achilles' protection, but he was skin and bone, people say that when somebody's skinny, but in the case of this little Bean, it was true, I didn't know how he had muscles enough to walk, to *stand,* his arms and legs were as thin as an ant—oh, isn't that awful? To compare him to the Buggers? Or I should say, the Formics, since they're saying now that *Buggers* is a bad word in English, even though I.F. Common is *not* English, even though it began that way, don't you think?"

"So, Helga, you're telling me it began with this Achilles."

"Do call me Hazie. We're friends now, aren't we?" She gripped Sister Carlotta's hand. "You must meet this boy. Courage! Vision! Test him, Sister Carlotta. He is a leader of men! He is a civilizer!"

Sister Carlotta did not point out that civilizers often didn't make good soldiers. It was enough that the boy was interesting, and she had missed him the first time around. It was a reminder to her that she must be thorough.

In the dark of early morning, Sister Carlotta arrived at the door where the line had already formed. Helga beckoned to her, then pointed ostentatiously at a rather good-looking young man surrounded by smaller children. Only when she got closer and saw him take a couple of steps did she realize just how bad his right leg was. She tried to diagnose the condition. Was it an early case of rickets? A clubfoot, left uncorrected? A break that healed wrong?

It hardly mattered. Battle School would not take him with such an injury.

Then she saw the adoration in the eyes of the children,

the way they called him Papa and looked to him for approval. Few adult men were good fathers. This boy of—what, eleven? twelve?—had already learned to be an extraordinarily good father. Protector, provider, king, god to his little ones. Even as ye do it unto the least of these, ye have done it unto me. Christ had a special place deep in his heart for this boy Achilles. So she *would* test him, and maybe the leg could be corrected; or, failing that, she could surely find a place for him in some good school in one of the cities of the Netherlands—pardon, the International Territory—that was not completely overwhelmed by the desperate poverty of refugees.

He refused.

"I can't leave my children," he said.

"But surely one of the others can look after them."

A girl who dressed as a boy spoke up. "I can!"

But it was obvious she could not—she was too small herself. Achilles was right. His children depended on him, and to leave them would be irresponsible. The reason she was here was because he was civilized; civilized men do not leave their children.

"Then I will come to you," she said. "After you eat, take me where you spend your days, and let me teach you all in a little school. Only for a few days, but that would be good, wouldn't it?"

It *would* be good. It had been a long time since Sister Carlotta had actually taught a group of children. And never had she been given such a class as this. Just when her work had begun to seem futile even to her, God gave her such a chance. It might even be a miracle. Wasn't it the business of Christ to make the lame walk? If Achilles did well on the tests, then surely God would let the leg also be fixed, would let it be within the reach of medicine.

"School's good," said Achilles. "None of these little ones can read."

Sister Carlotta knew, of course, that if Achilles could read, he certainly couldn't do it well.

But for some reason, perhaps some almost unnoticeable

movement, when Achilles said that none of the little ones could read, the smallest of them all, the one called Bean, caught her eye. She looked at him, into eyes with sparks in them like distant campfires in the darkest night, and she knew that *he* knew how to read. She knew, without knowing how, that it was not Achilles at all, that it was this little one that God had brought her here to find.

She shook off the feeling. It was Achilles who was the civilizer, doing the work of Christ. It was the leader that the I.F. would want, not the weakest and smallest of the disciples.

—

Bean stayed as quiet as possible during the school sessions, never speaking up and never giving an answer even when Sister Carlotta tried to insist. He knew that it wouldn't be good for him to let anyone know that he could already read and do numbers, nor that he could understand every language spoken in the street, picking up new languages the way other children picked up stones. Whatever Sister Carlotta was doing, whatever gifts she had to bestow, if it ever seemed to the other children that Bean was trying to show them up, trying to get ahead of them, he knew that he would not be back for another day of school. And even though she mostly taught things he already knew how to do, in her conversation there were many hints of a wider world, of great knowledge and wisdom. No adult had ever taken the time to speak to them like this, and he luxuriated in the sound of high language well spoken. When she taught it was in I.F. Common, of course, that being the language of the street, but since many of the children had also learned Dutch and some were even native Dutch speakers, she would often explain hard points in that language. When she was frustrated though, and muttered under her breath, that was in Spanish, the language of the merchants of Jonker Frans Straat, and he tried to piece together the meanings of new words from her muttering. Her knowledge was a banquet, and if he remained quiet enough, he would be able to stay and feast.

School had only been going for a week, however, when he made a mistake. She passed out papers to them, and they had writing on them. Bean read his paper at once. It was a "Pre-Test" and the instructions said to circle the right answers to each question. So he began circling answers and was halfway down the page when he realized that the entire group had fallen silent.

They were all looking at him, because Sister Carlotta was looking at him.

"What are you doing, Bean?" she asked. "I haven't even told you what to do yet. Please give me your paper."

Stupid, inattentive, careless—if you die for this, Bean, you deserve it.

He handed her the paper.

She looked at it, then looked back at him very closely. "Finish it," she said.

He took the paper back from her hand. His pencil hovered over the page. He pretended to be struggling with the answer.

"You did the first fifteen in about a minute and a half," said Sister Carlotta. "Please don't expect me to believe that you're suddenly having a hard time with the next question." Her voice was dry and sarcastic.

"I can't do it," he said. "I was just playing anyway."

"Don't lie to me," said Carlotta. "Do the rest."

He gave up and did them all. It didn't take long. They were easy. He handed her the paper.

She glanced over it and said nothing. "I hope the rest of you will wait until I finish the instructions and read you the questions. If you try to guess at what the hard words are, you'll get all the answers wrong."

Then she proceeded to read each question and all the possible answers out loud. Only then could the other children set their marks on the papers.

Sister Carlotta didn't say another thing to call attention to Bean after that, but the damage was done. As soon as school was over, Sergeant came over to Bean. "So you can read," he said.

Bean shrugged.

"You been lying to us," said Sergeant.

"Never said I couldn't."

"Showed us all up. How come *you* didn't teach us?"

Because I was trying to survive, Bean said silently. Because I didn't want to remind Achilles that I was the smart one who thought up the original plan that got him this family. If he remembers that, he'll also remember who it was who told Poke to kill him.

The only answer he actually gave was a shrug.

"Don't like it when somebody holds out on us."

Sergeant nudged him with a foot.

Bean did not have to be given a map. He got up and jogged away from the group. School was out for him. Maybe breakfast, too. He'd have to wait till morning to find that out.

He spent the afternoon alone on the streets. He had to be careful. As the smallest and least important of Achilles' family, he might be overlooked. But it was more likely that those who hated Achilles would have taken special notice of Bean as one of the most memorable. They might take it into their heads that killing Bean or beating him to paste and leaving him would make a dandy warning to Achilles that he was still resented, even though life was better for everybody.

Bean knew there were plenty of bullies who felt that way. Especially the ones who weren't able to maintain a family, because they kept being too mean with the little children. The little ones learned quickly that when a papa got too nasty, they could punish him by leaving him alone at breakfast and attaching themselves to some other family. They would eat before him. They would have someone else's protection from him. He would eat last. If they ran out of food, he would get nothing, and Helga wouldn't even mind, because *he* wasn't a papa, *he* wasn't watching out for little ones. So those bullies, those marginal ones, they hated the way things worked these days, and they didn't forget that it was Achilles who had changed it all. Nor could they go to some other kitchen—the word had spread among the adults who gave out food, and now all the kitchens had a rule that groups with little children got to be first in line. If you couldn't hold on to a family, you could get pretty hungry. And nobody looked up to you.

Still, Bean couldn't resist trying to get close enough to some of the other families to hear their talk. Find out how the other groups worked.

The answer was easy to learn: They didn't work all that well. Achilles really was a good leader. That sharing of bread—none of the other groups did that. But there was a lot of punishing, the bully smacking kids who didn't do what he wanted. Taking their bread away from them because they didn't do something, or didn't do it quickly enough.

Poke had chosen right, after all. By dumb luck, or maybe she wasn't all that stupid. Because she had picked, not just the weakest bully, the easiest to beat, but also the smartest, the one who understood how to win and hold the loyalty of others. All Achilles had ever needed was the chance.

Except that Achilles still didn't share her bread, and now she was beginning to realize that this was a bad thing, not a good one. Bean could see it in her face when she watched the others do the ritual of sharing with Achilles. Because he got soup now—Helga brought it to him at the door—he took much smaller pieces, and instead of biting them off he tore them and ate them with a smile. Poke never got that smile from him. Achilles was never going to forgive her, and Bean could see that she was beginning to feel the pain of that. For she loved Achilles now, too, the way the other children did, and the way he kept her apart from the others was a kind of cruelty.

Maybe that's enough for him, thought Bean. Maybe that's his whole vengeance.

Bean happened to be curled up behind a newsstand

when several bullies began a conversation near him. "He's full of brag about how Achilles is going to pay for what he did."

"Oh, right, Ulysses is going to punish him, right."

"Well, maybe not directly."

"Achilles and his stupid family will just take him apart. And this time they won't aim for his chest. He said so, didn't he? Break open his head and put his brains on the street, that's what Achilles'll do."

"He's still just a cripple."

"Achilles gets away with everything. Give it up."

"I'm hoping Ulysses does it. Kills him, flat out. And then none of us take in any of his bastards. You got that? Nobody takes them in. Let them all die. Put them all in the river."

The talk went on that way until the boys drifted away from the newsstand.

Then Bean got up and went in search of Achilles.

3

Payback

"I think I have someone for you."

"You've thought that before."

"He's a born leader. But he does not meet your physical specifications."

"Then you'll pardon me if I don't waste time on him."

"If he passes your exacting intellectual and personality requirements, it is quite possible that for a minuscule portion of the brass button or toilet paper budget of the I.F., his physical limitations might be repaired."

"I never knew nuns could be sarcastic."

"I can't reach you with a ruler. Sarcasm is my last resort."

"Let me see the tests."

"I'll let you see the boy. And while we're at it, I'll let you see another."

"Also physically limited?"

"Small. Young. But so was the Wiggin boy, I hear. And this one—somehow on the streets he taught himself to read."

"Ah, Sister Carlotta, you help me fill the empty hours of my life."

"Keeping you out of mischief is how I serve God."

Bean went straight to Achilles with what he heard. It was too dangerous, to have Ulysses out of the hospital and word going around that he meant to get even for his humiliation.

"I thought that was all behind us," said Poke sadly. "The fighting I mean."

"Ulysses has been in bed for all this time," said Achilles. "Even if he knows about the changes, he hasn't had time to get how it works yet."

"So we stick together," said Sergeant. "Keep you safe."

"It might be safer for all," said Achilles, "if I disappear for a few days. To keep *you* safe."

"Then how will we get in to eat?" asked one of the younger ones. "They'll never let us in without you."

"Follow Poke," said Achilles. "Helga at the door will let you in just the same."

"What if Ulysses gets you?" asked one of the young ones. He rubbed the tears out of his eyes, lest he be shamed.

"Then I'll be dead," said Achilles. "I don't think he'll be content to put me in the hospital."

The child broke down crying, which set another to wailing, and soon it was a choir of boo-hoos, with Achilles shaking his head and laughing. "I'm not going to die. You'll be safe if I'm out of the way, and I'll come back after Ulysses has time to cool down and get used to the system."

Bean watched and listened in silence. He didn't think Achilles was handling it right, but he had given the warning and his responsibility was over. For Achilles to go into hiding was begging for trouble—it would be taken as a sign of weakness.

Achilles slipped away that night to go somewhere that he couldn't tell them so that nobody could accidentally let it slip. Bean toyed with the idea of following him to see what he really did, but realized he would be more useful with the main group. After all, Poke would be their leader now, and Poke was only an ordinary leader. In other words, stupid. She needed Bean, even if she didn't know it.

That night Bean tried to keep watch, for what he did not know. At last he did sleep, and dreamed of school, only it wasn't the sidewalk or alley school with Sister Carlotta, it was a real school, with tables and chairs. But in the dream Bean couldn't sit at a desk. Instead he hovered in the air over it, and when he wanted to he flew anywhere in the room. Up to the ceiling. Into a crevice in the wall, into a secret dark place, flying upward and upward as it got warmer and warmer and . . .

He woke in darkness. A cold breeze stirred. He needed to pee. He also wanted to fly. Having the dream end almost made him cry out with the pain of it. He couldn't remember ever dreaming of flying before. Why did he have to be little, with these stubby legs to carry him from place to place? When he was flying he could look down at everyone and see the tops of their silly heads. He could pee or poop on them like a bird. He wouldn't have to be afraid of them because if they got mad he could fly away and they could never catch him.

Of course, if I *could* fly, everyone else could fly too and I'd still be the smallest and slowest and they'd poop and pee on me anyway.

There was no going back to sleep. Bean could feel that in himself. He was too frightened, and he didn't know why. He got up and went into the alley to pee.

Poke was already there. She looked up and saw him.

"Leave me alone for a minute," she said.

"No," he said.

"Don't give me any crap, little boy," she said.

"I know you squat to pee," he said, "and I'm not looking anyway."

Glaring, she waited until he turned his back to urinate

against the wall. "I guess if you were going to tell about me you already would have," she said.

"They all know you're a girl, Poke. When you're not there, Papa Achilles talks about you as 'she' and 'her.' "

"He's not my papa."

"So I figured," said Bean. He waited, facing the wall.

"You can turn around now." She was up and fastening her pants again.

"I'm scared of something, Poke," said Bean.

"What?"

"I don't know."

"You don't know what you're scared of?

"That's why it's so scary."

She gave a soft, sharp laugh. "Bean, all that means is that you're four years old. Little kids see shapes in the night. Or they don't see shapes. Either way they're scared."

"Not me," said Bean. "When I'm scared, it's because something's wrong."

"Ulysses is looking to hurt Achilles, that's what."

"That wouldn't make you sad, would it?"

She glared at him. "We're eating better than ever. Everybody's happy. It was your plan. And I never cared about being the boss."

"But you hate him," said Bean.

She hesitated. "It feels like he's always laughing at me."

"How do *you* know what little kids are scared of?"

"Cause I used to be one," said Poke. "And I remember."

"Ulysses isn't going to hurt Achilles," said Bean.

"I know that," said Poke.

"Because you're planning to find Achilles and protect him."

"I'm planning to stay right here and watch out for the children."

"Or else maybe you're planning to find Ulysses first and kill him."

"How? He's bigger than me. By a lot."

"You didn't come out here to pee," said Bean. "Or else your bladder's the size of a gumball."

"You *listened?*"

Bean shrugged. "You wouldn't let me watch."

"You think too much, but you don't know enough to make sense of what's going on."

"I think Achilles was lying to us about what he's going to do," said Bean, "and I think you're lying to me right now."

"Get used to it," said Poke. "The world is full of liars."

"Ulysses doesn't care who he kills," said Bean. "He'd be just as happy to kill you as Achilles."

Poke shook her head impatiently. "Ulysses is nothing. He isn't going to hurt anybody. He's all brag."

"So why are you up?" asked Bean.

Poke shrugged.

"*You're* going to try to kill Achilles, aren't you," said Bean. "And make it look like Ulysses did it."

She rolled her eyes. "Did you drink a big glass of stupid juice tonight?"

"I'm smart enough to know you're lying!"

"Go back to sleep," she said. "Go back to the other children."

He regarded her for a while, and then obeyed.

Or rather, seemed to obey. He went back into the crawl space where they slept these days, but immediately crept out the back way and clambered up crates, drums, low walls, high walls, and finally got up onto a low-hanging roof. He walked to the edge in time to see Poke slip out of the alley into the street. She *was* going somewhere. To meet someone.

Bean slid down a pipe onto a rainbarrel, and scurried along Korte Hoog Straat after her. He tried to be quiet, but she wasn't trying, and there were other noises of the city, so she never heard his footfalls. He clung to the shadows of walls, but didn't dodge around too much. It was pretty straightforward, following her—she only turned twice. Headed for the river. Meeting someone.

Bean had two guesses. It was either Ulysses or Achilles. Who else did she know, that wasn't already asleep in the nest? But then, why meet either of them? To plead with Ulysses for Achilles' life? To heroically offer herself in his place? Or to try to persuade Achilles to come back and face down Ulysses instead of hiding? No, these were all things that Bean might have thought of doing—but Poke didn't think that far ahead.

Poke stopped in the middle of an open space on the dock at Scheepmakershaven and looked around. Then she saw what she was looking for. Bean strained to see. Someone waiting in a deep shadow. Bean climbed up on a big packing crate, trying to get a better view. He heard the two voices—both children—but he couldn't make out what they were saying. Whoever it was, he was taller than Poke. But that could be either Achilles or Ulysses.

The boy wrapped his arms around Poke and kissed her.

This was really weird. Bean had seen grownups do that plenty of times, but what would kids do it for? Poke was nine years old. Of course there were whores that age, but everybody knew that the johns who bought them were perverts.

Bean had to get closer, to hear what they were saying. He dropped down the back of the packing crate and slowly walked into the shadow of a kiosk. They, as if to oblige him, turned to face him; in the deep shadow he was invisible, at least if he kept still. He couldn't see them any better than they could see him, but he could hear snatches of their conversation now.

"You promised," Poke was saying. The guy mumbled in return.

A boat passing on the river scanned a spotlight across the riverside and showed the face of the boy Poke was with. It was Achilles.

Bean didn't want to see any more. To think he had once believed Achilles would someday kill Poke. This thing between girls and boys was something he just didn't get.

In the midst of hate, this happens. Just when Bean was beginning to make sense of the world.

He slipped away and ran up Posthoornstraat.

But he did not head back to their nest in the crawlspace, not yet. For even though he had all the answers, his heart was still jumping; something is wrong, it was saying to him, something is wrong.

And then he remembered that Poke wasn't the only one hiding something from him. Achilles had also been lying. Hiding something. Some plan. Was it just this meeting with Poke? Then why all this business about hiding from Ulysses? To take Poke as his girl, he didn't have to hide to do that. He could do that right out in the open. Some bullies did that, the older ones. They usually didn't take nine-year-olds, though. Was that what Achilles was hiding?

"You promised," Poke said to Achilles there on the dock.

What did Achilles promise? That was why Poke came to him—to pay him for his promise. But what could Achilles be promising her that he wasn't already giving her as part of his family? Achilles didn't have anything.

So he must have been promising *not* to do something. Not to kill her? Then that would be too stupid even for Poke, to go off alone with Achilles.

Not to kill *me,* thought Bean. That's the promise. Not to kill *me.*

Only I'm not the one in danger, or not the most danger. I might have said to kill him, but Poke was the one who knocked him down, who stood over him. That picture must still be in Achilles' mind, all the time he must remember it, must dream about it, him lying on the ground, a nine-year-old girl standing over him with a cinderblock, threatening to kill him. A cripple like him, somehow he had made it into the ranks of the bullies. So he was tough—but always mocked by the boys with two good legs, the lowest-status bully. And the lowest moment of his life had to be then, when a nine-year-old girl knocked him down and a bunch of little kids stood over him.

Poke, he blames you most. You're the one he has to smash in order to wipe out the agony of that memory.

Now it was clear. Everything Achilles had said today was a lie. He wasn't hiding from Ulysses. He would face Ulysses down—probably still would, tomorrow. But when he faced Ulysses, Achilles would have a much bigger grievance. You killed Poke! He would scream the accusation. Ulysses would look so stupid and weak, denying it after all the bragging he'd done about how he'd get even. He might even admit to killing her, just for the brag of it. And then Achilles would strike at Ulysses and nobody would blame him for killing the boy. It wouldn't be mere self-defense, it would be defense of his family.

Achilles was just too damn smart. And patient. Waiting to kill Poke until there was somebody else who could be blamed for it.

Bean ran back to warn her. As fast as his little legs would move, the longest strides he could take. He ran forever.

There was nobody there on the dock where Poke had met Achilles.

Bean looked around helplessly. He thought of calling out, but that would be stupid. Just because it was Poke that Achilles hated most didn't mean that he had forgiven Bean, even if he did let Bean give him bread.

Or maybe I've gone crazy over nothing. He was hugging her, wasn't he? She came willingly, didn't she? There are things between boys and girls that I just don't understand. Achilles is a provider, a protector, not a murderer. It's *my* mind that works that way, *my* mind that thinks of killing someone who is helpless, just because he might pose a danger later. Achilles is the good one. I'm the bad one, the criminal.

Achilles is the one who knows how to love. I'm the one who doesn't.

Bean walked to the edge of the dock and looked across the channel. The water was covered with a low-flowing mist. On the far bank, the lights of Boompjes Straat twinkled like Sinterklaas Day. The waves lapped like tiny kisses against the pilings.

He looked down into the river at his feet. Something was bobbing in the water, bumped up against the wharf.

Bean looked at it for a while, uncomprehending. But then he understood that he had known all along what it was, he just didn't want to believe it. It was Poke. She was dead. It was just as Bean had feared. Everybody on the street would believe that Ulysses was guilty of the murder, even if nothing could be proved. Bean had been right about everything. Whatever it was that passed between boys and girls, it didn't have the power to block hatred, vengeance for humiliation.

And as Bean stood there, looking down into the water, he realized: I either have to tell what happened, right now, this minute, to everybody, or I have to decide never to tell anybody, because if Achilles gets any hint that I saw what I saw tonight, he'll kill me and not give it a second thought. Achilles would simply say: Ulysses strikes again. Then he can pretend to be avenging two deaths, not one, when he kills Ulysses.

No, all Bean could do was keep silence. Pretend that he hadn't seen Poke's body floating in the river, her upturned face clearly recognizable in the moonlight.

She was stupid. Stupid not to see through Achilles' plans, stupid to trust him in any way, stupid not to listen to me. As stupid as I was, to walk away instead of calling out a warning, maybe saving her life by giving her a witness that Achilles could not hope to catch and therefore could not silence.

She was the reason Bean was alive. She was the one who gave him a name. She was the one who listened to his plan. And now she had died for it, and he could have saved her. Sure, he told her at the start to kill Achilles, but in the end she had been right to choose him—he was the only one of the bullies who could have figured it all out and brought it off with such style. But Bean had also been right. Achilles was a champion liar, and when he decided that Poke would die, he began building up the lies that would surround the murder—lies that would get Poke off by herself where he could kill her without witnesses; lies to alibi himself in the eyes of the younger kids.

I trusted him, thought Bean. I knew what he was from the start, and yet I trusted him.

Aw, Poke, you poor, stupid, kind, decent girl. You saved me and I let you down.

It's not *just* my fault. *She's* the one who went off alone with him.

Alone with him, trying to save my life? What a mistake, Poke, to think of anyone but yourself!

Am I going to die from her mistakes, too?

No. I'll die from my own damn mistakes.

Not tonight, though. Achilles had not set any plan in motion to get Bean off by himself. But from now on, when he lay awake at night, unable to drift off, he would think about how Achilles was just waiting. Biding his time. Till the day when Bean, too, would find himself in the river.

—

Sister Carlotta tried to be sensitive to the pain these children were suffering, so soon after one of their own was strangled and thrown in the river. But Poke's death was all the more reason to push forward on the testing. Achilles had not been found yet—with this Ulysses boy having already struck once, it was unlikely that Achilles would come out of hiding for some time. So Sister Carlotta had no choice but to proceed with Bean.

At first the boy was distracted, and did poorly. Sister Carlotta could not understand how he could fail even the elementary parts of the test, when he was so bright he had taught himself to read on the street. It had to be the death of Poke. So she interrupted the test and talked to him about death, about how Poke was caught up in spirit into the presence of God and the saints, who would care for her and make her happier than she had ever been in life. He did not seem interested. If anything, he did worse as they began the next phase of the test.

Well, if compassion didn't work, sternness might.

"Don't you understand what this test is for, Bean?" she asked.

"No," he said. The tone of his voice added the unmistakable idea "and I don't care."

"All you know about is the life of the street. But the streets of Rotterdam are only a part of a great city, and Rotterdam is only one city in a world of thousands of such cities. The whole human race, Bean, that's what this test is about. Because the Formics—"

"The Buggers," said Bean. Like most street urchins, he sneered at euphemism.

"They will be back, scouring the Earth, killing every living soul. This test is to see if you are one of the children who will be taken to Battle School and trained to be a commander of the forces that will try to stop them. This test is about saving the world, Bean."

For the first time since the test began, Bean turned his full attention to her. "Where is Battle School?"

"In an orbiting platform in space," she said. "If you do well enough on this test, you get to be a spaceman!"

There was no childlike eagerness in his face. Only hard calculation.

"I've been doing real bad so far, haven't I," he said.

"The test results so far show that you're too stupid to walk and breathe at the same time."

"Can I start over?"

"I have another version of the tests, yes," said Sister Carlotta.

"Do it."

As she brought out the alternate set, she smiled at him, tried to relax him again. "So you want to be a spaceman, is that it? Or is it the idea of being part of the International Fleet?"

He ignored her.

This time through the test, he finished everything, even though the tests were designed not to be finished in the allotted time. His scores were not perfect, but they were close. So close that nobody would believe the results.

So she gave him yet another battery of tests, this one designed for older children—the standard tests, in fact, that six-year-olds took when being considered for Battle School at the normal age. He did not do as well on these; there were too many experiences he had not had yet, to be able to understand the content of some of the questions. But he still did remarkably well. Better than any student she had ever tested.

And to think she had thought it was Achilles who had the real potential. This little one, this infant, really—he was astonishing. No one would believe she had found him on the streets, living at the starvation level.

A suspicion crept into her mind, and when the second test ended and she recorded the scores and set them aside, she leaned back in her chair and smiled at bleary-eyed little Bean and asked him, "Whose idea was it, this family thing that the street children have come up with?"

"Achilles' idea," said Bean.

Sister Carlotta waited.

"His idea to call it a family, anyway," said Bean.

She still waited. Pride would bring more to the surface, if she gave him time.

"But having a bully protect the little ones, that was my plan," said Bean. "I told it to Poke and she thought about it and decided to try it and she only made one mistake."

"What mistake was that?"

"She chose the wrong bully to protect us."

"You mean because he couldn't protect her from Ulysses?"

Bean laughed bitterly as tears slid down his cheeks.

"Ulysses is off somewhere bragging about what he's going to do."

Sister Carlotta knew but did not want to know. "Do you know who killed her, then?"

"I told her to kill him. I told her he was the wrong one. I saw it in his face, lying there on the ground, that he would never forgive her. But he's cold. He waited so long. But he never took bread from her. That should have told her. She shouldn't have gone off alone with him." He began crying in earnest now. "I think she was protecting *me*. Because I told her to kill him that first day. I think she was trying to get him not to kill me."

Sister Carlotta tried to keep emotion out of her voice. "Do you believe you might be in danger from Achilles?"

"I am now that I told you," he said. And then, after a moment's thought. "I was already. He doesn't forgive. He pays back, always."

"You realize that this isn't the way Achilles seems to me, or to Hazie. Helga, that is. To us, he seems—civilized."

Bean looked at her like she was crazy. "Isn't that what it *means* to be civilized? That you can *wait* to get what you want?"

"You want to get out of Rotterdam and go to Battle School so you can get away from Achilles."

Bean nodded.

"What about the other children. Do you think they're in danger from him?"

"No," said Bean. "He's their papa."

"But not yours. Even though he took bread from you."

"He hugged her and kissed her," said Bean. "I saw them on the dock, and she let him kiss her and then she said something about how he promised, and so I left, but then I realized and I ran back and it couldn't have been long, just running for maybe six blocks, and she was dead with her eye stabbed out, floating in the water, bumping up against the dock. He can kiss you and kill you, if he hates you enough."

Sister Carlotta drummed her fingers on the desk. "What a quandary."

"What's a quandary?"

"I was going to test Achilles, too. I think he could get into Battle School."

Bean's whole body tightened. "Then don't send me. Him or me."

"Do you really think . . ." Her voice trailed off. "You think he'd try to kill you there?"

"*Try?*" His voice was scornful. "Achilles doesn't just *try.*"

Sister Carlotta knew that the trait Bean was speaking of, that ruthless determination, was one of the things that they looked for in Battle School. It might make Achilles more attractive to them than Bean. And they could channel such murderous violence up there. Put it to good use.

But civilizing the bullies of the street had not been Achilles' idea. It had been Bean who thought of it. Incredible, for a child so young to conceive of it and bring it about. This child was the prize, not the one who lived for cold vengeance. But one thing was certain. It would be wrong of her to take them both. Though she could certainly take the other one and get him into a school here on Earth, get him off the street. Surely Achilles would become truly civilized then, where the desperation of the street no longer drove children to do such hideous things to each other.

Then she realized what nonsense she had been thinking. It wasn't the desperation of the street that drove Achilles to murder Poke. It was pride. It was Cain, who thought that being shamed was reason enough to take his brother's life. It was Judas, who did not shrink to kiss before killing. What was she thinking, to treat evil as if it were a mere mechanical product of deprivation? All the children of the street suffered fear and hunger, helplessness and desperation. But they didn't all become cold-blooded, calculating murderers.

If, that is, Bean was right.

But she had no doubt that Bean was telling her the truth. If Bean was lying, she would give up on herself as a judge of children's character. Now that she thought about it, Achilles was slick. A flatterer. Everything he said was calculated to impress. But Bean said little, and spoke plainly when he did speak. And he was young, and his fear and grief here in this room were real.

Of course, he also had urged that a child be killed.

But only because he posed a danger to others. It wasn't pride.

How can I judge? Isn't Christ supposed to be the judge of quick and dead? Why is this in my hands, when I am not fit to do it?

"Would you like to stay here, Bean, while I transmit your test results to the people who make the decisions about Battle School? You'll be safe here."

He looked down at his hands, nodded, then laid his head on his arms and sobbed.

—

Achilles came back to the nest that morning. "I couldn't stay away," he said. "Too much could go wrong." He took them to breakfast, just like always. But Poke and Bean weren't there.

Then Sergeant did his rounds, listening here and there, talking to other kids, talking to an adult here and there, finding out what was happening, anything that might be useful. It was along the Wijnhaven dock that he heard some of the longshoremen talking about the body found in the river that morning. A little girl. Sergeant found out where her body was being held till the authorities arrived. He didn't shy away, he walked right up to the body under a tarpaulin, and without asking permission from any of the others standing there, he pulled it back and looked at her.

"What are you doing, boy!"

"Her name is Poke," he said.

"You know her? Do you know who might have killed her?"

"A boy named Ulysses, that's who killed her," said

Sergeant. Then he dropped the tarp and his rounds were over. Achilles had to know that his fears had been justified, that Ulysses was taking out anybody he could from the family.

"We've got no choice but to kill him," said Sergeant.

"There's been enough bloodshed," said Achilles. "But I'm afraid you're right."

Some of the younger children were crying. One of them explained, "Poke fed me when I was going to die."

"Shut up," said Sergeant. "We're eating better now than we ever did when Poke was boss."

Achilles put a hand on Sergeant's arm, to still him. "Poke did the best a crew boss could do. And she's the one who got me into the family. So in a way, anything I get for you, she got for you."

Everyone nodded solemnly at that.

A kid asked, "You think Ulysses got Bean, too?"

"Big loss if he did," said Sergeant.

"Any loss to my family is a big loss," said Achilles. "But there'll be no more. Ulysses will either leave the city, now, or he's dead. Put the word out, Sergeant. Let it be known on the street that the challenge stands. Ulysses doesn't eat in any kitchen in town, until he faces me. That's what he decided for himself, when he chose to put a knife in Poke's eye."

Sergeant saluted him and took off at a run. The picture of businesslike obedience.

Except that as he ran, he, too, was crying. For he had not told anyone how Poke died, how her eye was a bloody wound. Maybe Achilles knew some other way, maybe he had already heard but didn't mention it till Sergeant came back with the news. Maybe maybe. Sergeant knew the truth. Ulysses didn't raise his hand against anybody. Achilles did it. Just as Bean warned in the beginning. Achilles would never forgive Poke for beating him. He killed her now because Ulysses would get blamed for it. And then sat there talking about how good she was and how they should all be grateful to her and everything

Achilles got for them, it was really Poke who got it.

So Bean was right all along. About everything. Achilles might be a good papa to the family, but he was also a killer, and he never forgives.

Poke knew that, though. Bean warned her, and she knew it, but she chose Achilles for their papa anyway. Chose him and then died for it. She was like Jesus that Helga preached about in her kitchen while they ate. She died for her people. And Achilles, he was like God. He made people pay for their sins no matter what they did.

The important thing is, stay on the good side of God. That's what Helga teaches, isn't it? Stay right with God.

I'll stay right with Achilles. I'll honor my papa, that's for sure, so I can stay alive until I'm old enough to go out on my own.

As for Bean, well, he was smart, but not smart enough to stay alive, and if you're not smart enough to stay alive, then you're better off dead.

By the time Sergeant got to his first corner to spread the word about Achilles' ban on Ulysses from any kitchen in town, he was through crying. Grief was done. This was about survival now. Even though Sergeant knew Ulysses hadn't killed anybody, he meant to, and it was still important for the family's safety that he die. Poke's death provided a good excuse to demand that the rest of the papas stand back and let Achilles deal with him. When it was all over, Achilles would be the leader among all the papas of Rotterdam. And Sergeant would stand beside him, knowing the secret of his vengeance and telling no one, because that's how Sergeant, that's how the family, that's how all the urchins of Rotterdam would survive.

4

Memories

"I was mistaken about the first one. He tests well, but his character is not well suited to Battle School."

"I don't see that on the tests you've shown me."

"He's very sharp. He gives the right answers, but they aren't true."

"And what test did you use to determine this?"

"He committed murder."

"Well, that is a drawback. And the other one? What am I supposed to do with so young a child? A fish this small I would generally throw back into the stream."

"Teach him. Feed him. He'll grow."

"He doesn't even have a name."

"Yes he does."

"Bean? That isn't a name, it's a joke."

"It won't be when he's done with it."

"Keep him until he's five. Make of him what you can and show me your results then."

"I have other children to find."

"No, Sister Carlotta, you don't. In all your years of

searching, this one is the best you've found. And there isn't time to find another. Bring this one up to snuff, and all your work will be worth it, as far as the I.F. is concerned."

"You frighten me, when you say there isn't time."

"I don't see why. Christians have been expecting the imminent end of the world for millennia."

"But it keeps not ending."

"So far, so good."

At first all Bean cared about was the food. There was enough of it. He ate everything they put before him. He ate until he was full—that most miraculous of words, which till now had had no meaning for him. He ate until he was stuffed. He ate until he was sick. He ate so often that he had bowel movements every day, sometimes twice a day. He laughed about it to Sister Carlotta. "All I do is eat and poop!" he said.

"Like any beast of the forest," said the nun. "It's time for you to begin to earn that food."

She was already teaching him, of course, daily lessons in reading and arithmetic, bringing him "up to level," though what level she had in mind, she never specified. She also gave him time to draw, and there were sessions where she had him sit there and try to remember every detail about his earliest memories. The clean place in particular fascinated her. But there were limits to memory. He was very small then, and had very little language. Everything was a mystery. He did remember climbing over the railing around his bed and falling to the floor. He didn't walk well at the time. Crawling was easier, but he liked walking because that's what the big people did. He clung to objects and leaned on walls and made good progress on two feet, only crawling when he had to cross an open space.

"You must have been eight or nine months old," Sister Carlotta said. "Most people don't remember that far back."

"I remember that everybody was upset. That's why I

climbed out of bed. All the children were in trouble."

"All the children?"

"The little ones like me. And the bigger ones. Some of the grownups came in and looked at us and cried."

"Why?"

"Bad things, that's all. I knew it was a bad thing coming and I knew it would happen to all of us who were in the beds. So I climbed out. I wasn't the first. I don't know what happened to the others. I heard the grownups yelling and getting all upset when they found the empty beds. I hid from them. They didn't find me. Maybe they found the others, maybe they didn't. All I know is when I came out all the beds were empty and the room was very dark except a lighted sign that said *exit*."

"You could read then?" She sounded skeptical.

"When I *could* read, I remembered that those were the letters on the sign," said Bean. "They were the only letters I saw back then. Of course I remembered them."

"So you were alone and the beds were empty and the room was dark."

"They came back. I heard them talking. I didn't understand most of the words. I hid again. And this time when I came out, even the beds were gone. Instead, there were desks and cabinets. An office. And no, I didn't know what an office was then, either, but now I do know what an office is and I remember that's what the rooms had all become. Offices. People came in during the day and worked there, only a few at first but my hiding place turned out not to be so good, when people were working there. And I was hungry."

"Where did you hide?"

"Come on, you know. Don't you?"

"If I knew, I wouldn't ask."

"You saw the way I acted when you showed me the toilet."

"You hid inside the toilet?"

"The tank on the back. It was hard to get the lid up. And it wasn't comfortable in there. I didn't know what it was for. But people started using it and the water rose and fell and the pieces moved and it scared me. And like I said, I was hungry. Plenty to drink, except that I peed in it myself. My diaper was so waterlogged it fell off my butt. I was naked."

"Bean, do you understand what you're telling me? That you were doing all this before you were a year old?"

"You're the one who said how old I was," said Bean. "I didn't know about ages then. You told me to remember. The more I tell you, the more comes back to me. But if you don't believe me . . ."

"I just . . . I do believe you. But who were the other children? What was the place where you lived, that clean place? Who were those grown-ups? Why did they take away the other children? Something illegal was going on, that's certain."

"Whatever," said Bean. "I was just glad to get out of the toilet."

"But you were naked, you said. And you left the place?"

"No, I got found. I came out of the toilet and a grownup found me."

"What happened?"

"He took me home. That's how I got clothing. I called them clothings then."

"You were talking."

"Some."

"And this grownup took you home and bought you clothing."

"I think he was a janitor. I know more about jobs now and I think that's what he was. It was night when he worked, and he didn't wear a uniform like a guard."

"What happened?"

"That's when I first found out about legal and illegal. It wasn't legal for him to have a child. I heard him yelling at this woman about me and most of it I didn't understand, but at the end I knew he had lost and she had won, and he started talking to me about how I had to go away, and so I went."

"He just turned you loose in the streets?"

"No, I left. I think now he was going to have to give me to somebody else, and it sounded scary, so I left before he could do it. But I wasn't naked or hungry anymore. He was nice. After I left I bet he didn't have any more trouble."

"And that's when you started living on the streets."

"Sort of. A couple of places I found, they fed me. But every time, other kids, big ones, would see that I was getting fed and they'd come shouting and begging and the people would stop feeding me or the bigger kids would shove me out of the way or take the food right out of my hands. I was scared. One time a big kid got so mad at me for eating that he put a stick down my throat and made me throw up what I just ate, right on the street. He even tried to eat it but he couldn't, it made him try to throw up, too. That was the scariest time. I hided all the time after that. Hid. All the time."

"And starved."

"And watched," said Bean. "I ate some. Now and then. I didn't die."

"No, you didn't."

"I saw plenty who did. Lots of dead children. Big ones and little ones. I kept wondering how many of them were from the clean place."

"Did you recognize any of them?"

"No. Nobody looked like they ever lived in the clean place. Everybody looked hungry."

"Bean, thank you for telling me all this."

"You asked."

"Do you realize that there is no way you could have survived for three years as an infant?"

"I guess that means I'm dead."

"I just . . . I'm saying that God must have been watching over you."

"Yeah. Well, sure. So why didn't he watch over all those dead kids?"

"He took them to his heart and loved them."

"So then he *didn't* love me?"

"No, he loved you too, he—"

" 'Cause if he was watching so careful, he could have given me something to eat now and then."

"He brought me to you. He has some great purpose in mind for you, Bean. You may not know what it is, but God didn't keep you alive so miraculously for no reason."

Bean was tired of talking about this. She looked so happy when she talked about God, but he hadn't figured it out yet, what God even was. It was like, she wanted to give God credit for every good thing, but when it was bad, then she either didn't mention God or had some reason why it was a good thing after all. As far as Bean could see, though, the dead kids would rather have been alive, just with more food. If God loved them so much, and he could do whatever he wanted, then why wasn't there more food for these kids? And if God just wanted them dead, why didn't he let them die sooner or not even be born at all, so they didn't have to go to so much trouble and get all excited about trying to be alive when he was just going to take them to his heart. None of it made any sense to Bean, and the more Sister Carlotta explained it, the less he understood it. Because if there was somebody in charge, then he ought to be fair, and if he wasn't fair, then why should Sister Carlotta be so happy that he was in charge?

But when he tried to say things like that to her, she got really upset and talked even more about God and used words he didn't know and it was better just to let her say what she wanted and not argue.

It was the reading that fascinated him. And the numbers. He loved that. Having paper and pencil so he could actually write things, that was really good.

And maps. She didn't teach him maps at first, but there were some on the walls and the shapes of them fascinated him. He would go up to them and read the little words written on them and one day he saw the name of the river and realized that the blue was rivers and even bigger blue areas were places with even more water than the river, and then he realized that some of the other words were the same names that had been written on the street signs and so he figured out that somehow this thing was a picture of Rotterdam, and then it all made sense. Rotterdam the way it would look to a bird, if the buildings were all invisible and the streets were all empty. He found where the nest was, and where Poke had died, and all kinds of other places.

When Sister Carlotta found out that he understood the map, she got very excited. She showed him maps where Rotterdam was just a little patch of lines, and one where it was just a dot, and one where it was too small even to be seen, but she knew where it *would* be. Bean had never realized the world was so big. Or that there were so many people.

But Sister Carlotta kept coming back to the Rotterdam map, trying to get him to remember where things from his earliest memories were. Nothing looked the same, though, on the map, so it wasn't easy, and it took a long time for him to figure out where some of the places were where people had fed him. He showed these to Sister Carlotta, and she made a mark right on the map, showing each place. And after a while he realized—all those places were grouped in one area, but kind of strung out, as if they marked a path from where he found Poke leading back through time to . . .

To the clean place.

Only that was too hard. He had been too scared, coming out of the clean place with the janitor. He didn't know where it was. And the truth was, as Sister Carlotta herself said, the janitor might have lived anywhere compared to the clean place. So all she was going to find by following Bean's path backward was maybe the janitor's flat, or at least where he lived three years ago. And even then, what would the janitor know?

He would know where the clean place was, that's what he'd know. And now Bean understood: It was very important to Sister Carlotta to find out where Bean came from.

To find out who he really was.

Only . . . he already knew who he really was. He tried to say this to her. "I'm right here. This is who I really am. I'm not pretending."

"I know that," she said, laughing, and she hugged him, which was all right. It felt good. Back when she first started doing it, he didn't know what to do with his hands. She had to show him how to hug her back. He had seen some little kids—the ones with mamas or papas—doing that but he always thought they were holding on tight so they wouldn't drop off onto the street and get lost. He didn't know that you did it just because it felt good. Sister Carlotta's body had hard places and squishy places and it was very strange to hug her. He thought of Poke and Achilles hugging and kissing, but he didn't want to kiss Sister Carlotta and after he got used to what hugging was, he didn't really want to do that either. He let her hug him. But he didn't ever think of hugging her himself. It just didn't come into his mind.

He knew that sometimes she hugged him instead of explaining things to him, and he didn't like that. She didn't want to tell him why it mattered that she find the clean place, so she hugged him and said, "Oh, you dear thing," or "Oh, you poor boy." But that only meant that it was even more important than she was saying, and she thought he was too stupid or ignorant to understand if she tried to explain.

He kept trying to remember more and more, if he could, only now he didn't tell her everything because she didn't tell *him* everything and fair was fair. He would find the clean room himself. Without her. And then tell her if he decided it would be good for him to have her know. Because what if she found the wrong answer? Would she put him back on the street? Would she keep him from going to school in the sky? Because that's what she promised at first, only after the tests she said he did very well only he would *not* go in the sky until he was five and maybe not even then because it was not entirely her decision and that's when he knew that she didn't have the power to keep her own promises. So if she found out the wrong thing about him, she might not be able to keep *any* of her promises. Not even the one about keeping him safe from Achilles. That's why he had to find out on his own.

He studied the map. He pictured things in his mind. He talked to himself as he was falling asleep, talked and thought and remembered, trying to get the janitor's face back into his mind, and the room he lived in, and the stairs outside where the mean lady stood to scream at him.

And one day, when he thought he had remembered enough, Bean went to the toilet—he liked the toilets, he liked to make them flush even though it scared him to see things disappear like that—and instead of coming back to Sister Carlotta's teaching place, he went the other way down the corridor and went right out the door onto the street and no one tried to stop him.

That's when he realized his mistake, though. He had been so busy trying to remember the janitor's place that it never occurred to him that he had no idea where *this* place was on the map. And it wasn't in a part of town that he knew. In fact, it hardly seemed like the same world. Instead of the street being full of people walking and pushing carts and riding bikes or skating to get from one place to another, the streets were almost empty, and there were cars parked everywhere. Not a single store, either. All houses and offices, or houses made into offices with little signs out front. The only building that was different was the very one he had just come out of. It was blocky and square and bigger than the others, but it had no sign out in front of it at all.

He knew where he was going, but he didn't know how

to get there from here. And Sister Carlotta would start looking for him soon.

His first thought was to hide, but then he remembered that she knew all about his story of hiding in the clean place, so she would also think of hiding and she would look for him in a hiding place close to the big building.

So he ran. It surprised him how strong he was now. It felt like he could run as fast as a bird flying, and he didn't get tired, he could run forever. All the way to the corner and around it onto another street.

Then down another street, and another, until he would have been lost except he started out lost and when you start out completely lost, it's hard to get loster. As he walked and trotted and jogged and ran up and down streets and alleys, he realized that all he had to do was find a canal or a stream and it would lead him to the river or to a place that he recognized. So the first bridge that went over water, he saw which way the water flowed and chose streets that would keep him close. It wasn't as if he knew where he was yet, but at least he was following a plan.

It worked. He came to the river and walked along it until he recognized, off in the distance and partly around a bend in the river, Maasboulevard, which led to the place where Poke was killed.

The bend in the river—he knew it from the map. He knew where all of Sister Carlotta's marks had been. He knew that he had to go through the place where he used to live on the streets in order to get past them and closer to the area where the janitor might have lived. And that wouldn't be easy, because he would be known there, and Sister Carlotta might even have the cops looking for him and *they* would look there because that's where all the street urchins were and they would expect him to become a street urchin again.

What they were forgetting was that Bean wasn't hungry anymore. And since he wasn't hungry, he wasn't in a hurry.

He walked the long way around. Far from the river, far from the busy part of town where the urchins were. Whenever the streets started looking crowded he would widen his circle and stay away from the busy places. He took the rest of that day and most of the next making such a wide circle that for a while he was not in Rotterdam anymore at all, and he saw some of the countryside, just like the pictures—farmland and the roads built up higher than the land around them. Sister Carlotta had explained to him once that most of the farmland was lower than the level of the sea, and great dikes were the only thing keeping the sea from rushing back onto the land and covering it. But Bean knew that he would never get close to any of the big dikes. Not by walking, anyway.

He drifted back into town now, into the Schiebroek district, and late in the afternoon of the second day he recognized the name of Rindijk Straat and soon found a cross street whose name he knew, Erasmus Singel, and then it was easy to get to the earliest place he could remember, the back door of a restaurant where he had been fed when he was still a baby and didn't talk right and grownups rushed to feed him and help him instead of kicking him out of the way.

He stood there in the dusk. Nothing had changed. He could almost picture the woman with the little bowl of food, holding it out to him and waving a spoon in her hand and saying something in a language he didn't understand. Now he could read the sign above the restaurant and realized that it was Armenian and that's probably what the woman had been speaking.

Which way had he walked to come here? He had smelled the food when he was walking along . . . here? He walked a little way up, a little way down the street, turning and turning to reorient himself.

"What are you doing here, fatso?"

It was two kids, maybe eight years old. Belligerent but not bullies. Probably part of a crew. No, part of a family, now that Achilles had changed everything. If the changes had spread to this part of town.

"I'm supposed to meet my papa here," said Bean.

"And who's your papa?"

Bean wasn't sure whether they took the word "papa" to mean his father or the papa of his "family." He took the chance, though, of saying "Achilles."

They scoffed at the idea. "He's way down by the river, why would he meet a fatso like you clear up here?"

But their derision was not important—what mattered was that Achilles' reputation had spread this far through the city.

"I don't have to explain his business to you," said Bean. "And all the kids in Achilles' family are fat like me. That's how well we eat."

"Are they all short like you?"

"I used to be taller, but I asked too many questions," said Bean, pushing past them and walking across Rozenlaan toward the area where the janitor's flat seemed likeliest to be.

They didn't follow him. Such was the magic of Achilles' name—or perhaps it was just Bean's utter confidence, paying them no notice as if he had nothing to fear from them.

Nothing looked familiar. He kept turning around and checking to see if he recognized things when looking in the direction he might have been going after leaving the janitor's flat. It didn't help. He wandered until it was dark, and kept wandering even then.

Until, quite by chance, he found himself standing at the foot of a street lamp, trying to read a sign, when a set of initials carved on the pole caught his attention. P♡DVM, it said. He had no idea what it meant; he had never thought of it during all his attempts to remember; but he knew that he had seen it before. And not just once. He had seen it several times. The janitor's flat was very close.

He turned slowly, scanning the area, and there it was:

A small apartment building with both an inside and an outside stairway.

The janitor lived on the top floor. Ground floor, first floor, second floor, third. Bean went to the mailboxes and tried to read the names, but they were set too high on the wall and the names were all faded, and some of the tags were missing entirely.

Not that he ever knew the janitor's name, truth to tell. There was no reason to think he would have recognized it even if he had been able to read it on the mailbox.

The outside stairway did not go all the way up to the top floor. It must have been built for a doctor's office on the first floor. And because it was dark, the door at the top of the stairs was locked.

There was nothing to do but wait. Either he would wait all night and get into the building through one entrance or another in the morning, or someone would come back in the night and Bean would slip through a door behind him.

He fell asleep and woke up, slept and woke again. He worried that a policeman would see him and shove him away, so when he woke the second time he abandoned all pretense of being on watch and crept under the stairs and curled up there for the night.

He was awakened by drunken laughter. It was still dark, and beginning to rain just a little—not enough to start dripping off the stairs, though, so Bean was dry. He stuck his head out to see who was laughing. It was a man and a woman, both merry with alcohol, the man furtively pawing and poking and pinching, the woman fending him off with halfhearted slaps. "Can't you wait?" she said.

"No," he said.

"You're just going to fall asleep without doing anything," she said.

"Not this time," he said. Then he threw up.

She looked disgusted and walked on without him. He staggered after her. "I feel better now," he said. "It'll be better."

"The price just went up," she said coldly. "And you brush your teeth first."

" 'Course I brush my teeth."

They were right at the front of the building now. Bean was waiting to slip in after them.

Then he realized that he didn't have to wait. The man *was* the janitor from all those years before.

Bean stepped out of the shadows. "Thanks for bringing him home," he said to the woman.

They both looked at him in surprise.

"Who are you?" asked the janitor.

Bean looked at the woman and rolled his eyes. "He's not *that* drunk, I hope," said Bean. To the janitor he said, "Mama will not be happy to see you come home like this again."

"Mama!" said the janitor. "Who the hell are you talking about?"

The woman gave the janitor a shove. He was so off balance that he lurched against the wall, then slid down it to land on his buttocks on the sidewalk. "I should have known," she said. "You bring me home to your *wife?*"

"I'm not married," said the janitor. "This kid isn't mine."

"I'm sure you're telling the truth on both points," said the woman. "But you better let him help you up the stairs anyway. Mama's waiting." She started to walk away.

"What about my forty gilders?" he asked plaintively, knowing the answer even as he asked.

She made an obscene gesture and walked on into the night.

"You little bastard," said the janitor.

"I had to talk to you alone," said Bean.

"Who the hell are you? Who's your mama?"

"That's what I'm here to find out," said Bean. "I'm the baby you found and brought home. Three years ago."

The man looked at him in stupefaction.

Suddenly a light went on, then another. Bean and the

janitor were bathed in overlapping flashlight beams. Four policemen converged on them.

"Don't bother running, kid," said a cop. "Nor you, Mr. Fun Time."

Bean recognized Sister Carlotta's voice. "They aren't criminals," she said. "I just need to talk to them. Up in his apartment."

"You followed me?" Bean asked her.

"I knew you were searching for him," she said. "I didn't want to interfere until you found him. Just in case you think you were really smart, young man, we intercepted four street thugs and two known sex offenders who were after you."

Bean rolled his eyes. "You think I've forgotten how to deal with them?"

Sister Carlotta shrugged. "I didn't want this to be the first time you ever made a mistake in your life." She did have a sarcastic streak.

"So as I told you, there was nothing to learn from this Pablo de Noches. He's an immigrant who lives to pay for prostitutes. Just another of the worthless people who have gravitated here ever since the Netherlands became international territory."

Sister Carlotta had sat patiently, waiting for the inspector to wind down his I-told-you-so speech. But when he spoke of a man's worthlessness, she could not let the remark go unchallenged. "He took in that baby," she said. "And fed the child and cared for him."

The inspector waved off the objection. "We needed one more street urchin? Because that's all that people like this ever produce."

"You didn't learn *nothing* from him," Sister Carlotta said. "You learned the location where the boy was found."

"And the people renting the building during that time are untraceable. A company name that never existed. Nothing to go on. No way to track them down."

"But that nothing *is* something," said Sister Carlotta. "I tell you that these people had many children in this place, which they closed down in a hurry, with all the children but one taken away. You tell me that the company was a false name and can't be traced. So now, in your experience, doesn't that tell you a great deal about what was going on in that building?"

The inspector shrugged. "Of course. It was obviously an organ farm."

Tears came to Sister Carlotta's eyes. "And that is the only possibility?"

"A lot of defective babies are born to rich families," said the inspector. "There is an illegal market in infant and toddler organs. We close down the organ farms whenever we find out where they are. Perhaps we were getting close to this organ farm and they got wind of it and closed up shop. But there is no paper in the department on any organ farm that we actually found at that time. So perhaps they closed down for another reason. Still, nothing."

Patiently, Sister Carlotta ignored his inability to realize how valuable this information was. "Where do the babies come from?"

The inspector looked at her blankly. As if he thought she was asking him to explain the facts of life.

"The organ farm," she said. "Where do they get the babies?"

The inspector shrugged. "Late-term abortions, usually. Some arrangement with the clinics, a kickback. That sort of thing."

"And that's the only source?"

"Well, I don't know. Kidnappings? I don't think that could be much of a factor, there aren't *that* many babies leaking through the security systems in the hospitals. People selling babies? It's been heard of, yes. Poor refugees arrive with eight children, and then a few years later they have only six, and they cry about the ones who died but who can prove anything? But nothing you can trace."

"The reason I'm asking," said Sister Carlotta, "is that this child is unusual. *Extremely* unusual."

"Three arms?" asked the inspector.

"Brilliant. Precocious. He escaped from this place before he was a year old. Before he could walk."

The inspector thought about that for a few moments. "He *crawled* away?"

"He hid in a toilet tank."

"He got the lid up before he was a year old?"

"He said it was hard to lift."

"No, it was probably cheap plastic, not porcelain. You know how these institutional plumbing fixtures are."

"You can see, though, why I want to know about the child's parentage. Some miraculous combination of parents."

The inspector shrugged. "Some children are born smart."

"But there is a hereditary component in this, inspector. A child like this must have . . . remarkable parents. Parents likely to be prominent because of the brilliance of their own minds."

"Maybe. Maybe not," said the inspector. "I mean, some of these refugees, they might be brilliant, but they're caught up in desperate times. To save the other children, maybe they sell a baby. That's even a *smart* thing to do. It doesn't rule out refugees as the parents of this brilliant boy you have."

"I suppose that's possible," said Sister Carlotta.

"It's the most information you'll ever have. Because this Pablo de Noches, he knows nothing. He barely could tell me the name of the town he came from in Spain."

"He was drunk when he was questioned," said Sister Carlotta.

"We'll question him again when he's sober," said the inspector. "We'll let you know if we learn anything more. In the meantime, though, you'll have to make do with what I've already told you, because there isn't anything more."

"I know all I need to know for now," said Sister Carlotta. "Enough to know that this child truly is a miracle, raised up by God for some great purpose."

"I'm not Catholic," said the inspector.

"God loves you all the same," said Sister Carlotta cheerfully.

Part Two

LAUNCHY

5

Ready or not

"Why are you giving me a five-year-old street urchin to tend?"

"You've seen the scores."

"Am I supposed to take those seriously?"

"Since the whole Battle School program is based on the reliability of our juvenile testing program, yes, I think you should take his scores seriously. I did a little research. No child has ever done better. Not even your star pupil."

"It's not the validity of the tests that I doubt. It's the tester."

"Sister Carlotta is a nun. You'll never find a more honest person."

"Honest people have been known to deceive themselves. To want so desperately, after all these years of searching, to find one—just one—child whose value will be worth all that work."

"And she's found him."

"Look at the *way* she found him. Her first report touts this Achilles child, and this—this Bean, this Legume—he's just an afterthought. Then Achilles is gone, not another mention of him—did he die? Wasn't she trying to get a leg operation for him?—and it's Haricot Vert who is now her candidate."

" 'Bean' is the name he calls himself. Rather as your Andrew Wiggin calls himself 'Ender.' "

"He's not *my* Andrew Wiggin."

"And Bean is not Sister Carlotta's child, either. If she were inclined to fudge the scores or administer tests unfairly, she would have pushed other students into the program long before now, and we'd already know how unreliable she was. She has never done that. She washes out her most hopeful children herself, then finds some place for them on Earth or in a non-command program. I think you're merely annoyed because you've already decided to focus all your attention and energy on the Wiggin boy, and you don't want any distraction."

"When did I lie down on your couch?"

"If my analysis is wrong, do forgive me."

"Of course I'll give this little one a chance. Even if I don't for one second believe these scores."

"Not just a chance. Advance him. Test him. Challenge him. Don't let him languish."

"You underestimate our program. We advance and test and challenge all our students."

"But some are more equal than others."

"Some take better advantage of the program than others."

"I'll look forward to telling Sister Carlotta about your enthusiasm."

Sister Carlotta shed tears when she told Bean that it was time for him to leave. Bean shed none.

"I understand that you're afraid, Bean, but don't be," she said. "You'll be safe there, and there's so much to learn. The way you drink down knowledge, you'll be very happy there in no time. So you won't really miss me at all."

Bean blinked. What sign had he given that made her think he was afraid? Or that he would miss her?

He felt none of those things. When he first met her, he might have been prepared to feel something for her. She was kind. She fed him. She was keeping him safe, giving him a life.

But then he found Pablo the janitor, and there was Sister Carlotta, stopping Bean from talking to the man who had saved him long before she did. Nor would she tell him anything that Pablo had said, or anything she had learned about the clean place.

From that moment, trust was gone. Bean knew that whatever Sister Carlotta was doing, it wasn't for him. She was using him. He didn't know what for. It might even be something he would have chosen to do himself. But she wasn't telling him the truth. She had secrets from him. The way Achilles kept secrets.

So during the months that she was his teacher, he had grown more and more distant from her. Everything she taught, he learned—and much that she didn't teach as well. He took every test she gave him, and did well; but he showed her nothing he had learned that she hadn't taught him.

Of course life with Sister Carlotta was better than life on the street—he had no intention of going back. But he did not trust her. He was on guard all the time. He was as careful as he had ever been back in Achilles' family. Those brief days at the beginning, when he wept in front of her, when he let go of himself and spoke freely—that had been a mistake that he would not repeat. Life was better, but he wasn't safe, and this wasn't home.

Her tears were real enough, he knew. She really did love him, and would really miss him when he left. After all, he had been a perfect child, compliant, quick, obedient. To her, that meant he was "good." To him, it was only a way of keeping his access to food and learning. He wasn't stupid.

Why did she assume he was afraid? Because she was

afraid *for* him. Therefore there might indeed be something to fear. He would be careful.

And why did she assume that he would miss her? Because she would miss him, and she could not imagine that what she was feeling, he might not feel as well. She had created an imaginary version of him. Like the games of Let's Pretend that she tried to play with him a couple of times. Harking back to her own childhood, no doubt, growing up in a house where there was always enough food. Bean didn't have to pretend things in order to exercise his imagination when he was on the street. Instead he had to imagine his plans for how to get food, for how to insinuate himself into a crew, for how to survive when he knew he seemed useless to everyone. He had to imagine how and when Achilles would decide to act against him for having advocated that Poke kill him. He had to imagine danger around every corner, a bully ready to seize every scrap of food. Oh, he had plenty of imagination. But he had no interest at all in playing Let's Pretend.

That was *her* game. She played it all the time. Let's pretend that Bean is a good little boy. Let's pretend that Bean is the son that this nun can never have for real. Let's pretend that when Bean leaves, he'll cry—that he's not crying now because he's too afraid of this new school, this journey into space, to let his emotions show. Let's pretend that Bean loves me.

And when he understood this, he made a decision: It will do no harm to me if she believes all this. And she wants very much to believe it. So why not give it to her? After all, Poke let me stay with the crew even though she didn't need me, because it would do no harm. It's the kind of thing Poke would do.

So Bean slid off his chair, walked around the table to Sister Carlotta, and put his arms as far around her as they would reach. She gathered him up onto her lap and held him tight, her tears flowing into his hair. He hoped her nose wasn't running. But he clung to her as long as she clung to him, letting go only when she let go of him. It was what she wanted from him, the only payment that she had ever asked of him. For all the meals, the lessons, the books, the language, for his future, he owed her no less than to join her in this game of Let's Pretend.

Then the moment passed. He slid off her lap. She dabbed at her eyes. Then she rose, took his hand, and led him out to the waiting soldiers, to the waiting car.

As he approached the car, the uniformed men loomed over him. It was not the grey uniform of the I.T. police, those kickers of children, those wielders of sticks. Rather it was the sky blue of the International Fleet that they wore, a cleaner look, and the people who gathered around to watch showed no fear, but rather admiration. This was the uniform of distant power, of safety for humanity, the uniform on which all hope depended. This was the service he was about to join.

But he was so small, and as they looked down at him he *was* afraid after all, and clung more tightly to Sister Carlotta's hand. Was he going to become one of them? Was he going to be a man in such a uniform, with such admiration directed at him? Then why was he afraid?

I'm afraid, Bean thought, because I don't see how I can ever be so tall.

One of the soldiers bent down to him, to lift him into the car. Bean glared up at him, defying him to dare such a thing. "I can do it," he said.

The soldier nodded slightly, and stood upright again. Bean hooked his leg up onto the running board of the car and hoisted himself in. It was high off the ground, and the seat he held to was slick and offered scant purchase to his hands. But he made it, and positioned himself in the middle of the back seat, the only position where he could see between the front seats and have some idea of where the car would be going.

One of the soldiers got into the driver's seat. Bean expected the other to get into the back seat beside Bean, and anticipated an argument about whether Bean could sit in the middle or not. Instead, he got into the front on the other side. Bean was alone in back.

He looked out the side window at Sister Carlotta. She was still dabbing at her eyes with a handkerchief. She gave him a little wave. He waved back. She sobbed a little. The car glided forward along the magnetic track in the road. Soon they were outside the city, gliding through the countryside at a hundred and fifty kilometers an hour. Ahead was the Amsterdam airport, one of only three in Europe that could launch one of the shuttles that could fly into orbit. Bean was through with Rotterdam. For the time being, at least, he was through with Earth.

Since Bean had never flown on an airplane, he did not understand how different the shuttle was, though that seemed to be all that the other boys could talk about at first. I thought it would be bigger. Doesn't it take off straight up? That was the old shuttle, stupid. There aren't any tray tables! That's cause in null-G you can't set anything down anyway, bonehead.

To Bean, the sky was the sky, and all he'd ever cared about was whether it was going to rain or snow or blow or burn. Going up into space did not seem any more strange to him than going up to the clouds.

What fascinated him were the other children. Boys, most of them, and all older than him. Definitely all larger. Some of them looked at him oddly, and behind him he heard one whisper, "Is he a kid or a doll?" But snide remarks about his size and his age were nothing new to him. In fact, what surprised him was that there was only the one remark, and it was whispered.

The kids themselves fascinated him. They were all so fat, so soft. Their bodies were like pillows, their cheeks full, their hair thick, their clothes well fitted. Bean knew, of course, that he had more fat on him now than at any time since he left the clean place, but he didn't see himself, he only saw them, and couldn't help comparing them to the kids on the street. Sergeant could take any of them apart. Achilles could . . . well, no use thinking about Achilles.

Bean tried to imagine them lining up outside a charity kitchen. Or scrounging for candy wrappers to lick. What a joke. They had never missed a meal in their lives. Bean wanted to punch them all so hard in the stomach that they would puke up everything they ate that day. Let them feel some pain there in their gut, that gnawing hunger. And then let them feel it again the next day, and the next hour, morning and night, waking and sleeping, the constant weakness fluttering just inside your throat, the faintness behind your eyes, the headache, the dizziness, the swelling of your joints, the distension of your belly, the thinning of your muscles until you barely have strength to stand. These children had never looked death in the face and then chosen to live anyway. They were confident. They were unwary.

These children are no match for me.

And, with just as much certainty: I will never catch up to them. They'll always be bigger, stronger, quicker, healthier. Happier. They talked to each other boastfully, spoke wistfully of home, mocked the children who had failed to qualify to come with them, pretended to have inside knowledge about how things really were in Battle School. Bean said nothing. Just listened, watched them maneuver, some of them determined to assert their place in the hierarchy, others quieter because they knew their place would be lower down; a handful relaxed, unworried, because they had never had to worry about the pecking order, having been always at the top of it. A part of Bean wanted to engage in the contest and win it, clawing his way to the top of the hill. Another part of him disdained the whole group of them. What would it mean, really, to be top dog in this mangy pack?

Then he glanced down at his small hands, and at the hands of the boy sitting next to him.

I really do look like a doll compared to the rest of them.

Some of the kids were complaining about how hungry they were. There was a strict rule against eating for twenty-four hours before the shuttle flight, and most of these kids had never gone so long without eating. For Bean, twenty-four hours without food was barely noticeable. In his crew, you didn't worry about hunger until the second week.

The shuttle took off, just like any airplane, though it had a long, long runway to get it up to speed, it was so heavy. Bean was surprised at the motion of the plane, the way it charged forward yet seemed to hold still, the way it rocked a little and sometimes bumped, as if it were rolling over irregularities in an invisible road.

When they got up to a high altitude, they rendezvoused with two fuel planes, in order to take on the rest of the rocket fuel needed to achieve escape velocity. The plane could never have lifted off the ground with that much fuel on board.

During the refueling, a man emerged from the control cabin and stood at the front of the rows of seats. His sky blue uniform was crisp and perfect, and his smile looked every bit as starched and pressed and unstainable as his clothes.

"My dear darling little children," he said. "Some of you apparently can't read yet. Your seat harnesses are to remain in place throughout the entire flight. Why are so many of them unfastened? Are you going somewhere?"

Lots of little clicks answered him like scattered applause.

"And let me also warn you that no matter how annoying or enticing some other child might be, keep your hands to yourself. You should keep in mind that the children around you scored every bit as high as you did on every test you took, and some of them scored higher."

Bean thought: That's impossible. Somebody here had to have the highest score.

A boy across the aisle apparently had the same thought. "Right," he said sarcastically.

"I was making a point, but I'm willing to digress," said the man. "Please, share with us the thought that so enthralled you that you could not contain it silently within you."

The boy knew he had made a mistake, but decided to tough it out. "Somebody here has the highest score."

The man continued looking at him, as if inviting him to continue.

Inviting him to dig himself a deeper grave, thought Bean.

"I mean, you said that everybody scored as high as everybody else, and some scored higher, and that's just obviously not true."

The man waited some more.

"That's all I had to say."

"Feel better?" said the man.

The boy sullenly kept his silence.

Without disturbing his perfect smile, the man's tone changed, and instead of bright sarcasm, there was now a sharp whiff of menace. "I asked you a question, boy."

"No, I don't feel better."

"What's your name?" asked the man.

"Nero."

A couple of children who knew a little bit about history laughed at the name. Bean knew about the emperor Nero. He did not laugh, however. He knew that a child named Bean was wise not to laugh at other kids' names. Besides, a name like that could be a real burden to bear. It said something about the boy's strength or at least his defiance that he didn't give some nickname.

Or maybe Nero *was* his nickname.

"Just . . . Nero?" asked the man.

"Nero Boulanger."

"French? Or just hungry?"

Bean did not get the joke. Was Boulanger a name that had something to do with food?

"Algerian."

"Nero, you are an example to all the children on this

shuttle. Because most of them are so foolish, they think it is better to keep their stupidest thoughts to themselves. You, however, understand the profound truth that you must reveal your stupidity openly. To hold your stupidity inside you is to embrace it, to cling to it, to protect it. But when you expose your stupidity, you give yourself the chance to have it caught, corrected, and replaced with wisdom. Be brave, all of you, like Nero Boulanger, and when you have a thought of such surpassing ignorance that you think it's actually smart, make sure to make some noise, to let your mental limitations squeak out some whimpering fart of a thought, so that you have a chance to learn."

Nero grumbled something.

"Listen—another flatulence, but this time even less articulate than before. Tell us, Nero. Speak up. You are teaching us all by the example of your courage, however half-assed it might be."

A couple of students laughed.

"And listen—your fart has drawn out other farts, from people equally stupid, for they think they are somehow superior to you, and that they could not just as easily have been chosen to be examples of superior intellect."

There would be no more laughter.

Bean felt a kind of dread, for he knew that somehow, this verbal sparring, or rather this one-sided verbal assault, this torture, this public exposure, was going to find some twisted path that led to him. He did not know how he sensed this, for the uniformed man had not so much as glanced at Bean, and Bean had made no sound, had done nothing to call attention to himself. Yet he knew that he, not Nero, would end up receiving the cruelest thrust from this man's dagger.

Then Bean realized why he was sure it would turn against him. This had turned into a nasty little argument about whether someone had higher test scores than anyone else on the shuttle. And Bean had assumed, for no reason whatsoever, that he was the child with the highest scores.

Now that he had seen his own belief, he knew it was

absurd. These children were all older and had grown up with far more advantages. He had had only Sister Carlotta as a teacher—Sister Carlotta and, of course, the street, though few of the things he learned *there* had shown up on the tests. There was no way that Bean had the highest score.

Yet he still knew, with absolute certainty, that this discussion was full of danger for him.

"I told you to speak up, Nero. I'm waiting."

"I still don't see how anything I said was stupid," said Nero.

"First, it was stupid because I have all the authority here, and you have none, so I have the power to make your life miserable, and you have no power to protect yourself. So how much intelligence does it take just to keep your mouth shut and avoid calling attention to yourself? What could be a more obvious decision to make when confronted with such a lopsided distribution of power?"

Nero withered in his seat.

"Second, you seemed to be listening to me, not to find out useful information, but to try to catch me in a logical fallacy. This tells us all that you are used to being smarter than your teachers, and that you listen to them in order to catch them making mistakes and prove how smart you are to the other students. This is such a pointless, stupid way of listening to teachers that it is clear you are going to waste months of our time before you finally catch on that the only transaction that matters is a transfer of useful information from adults who possess it to children who do not, and that catching mistakes is a criminal misuse of time."

Bean silently disagreed. The criminal misuse of time was *pointing out* the mistakes. Catching them—noticing them—that was essential. If you did not in your own mind distinguish between useful and erroneous information, then you were not *learning* at all, you were merely replacing ignorance with false belief, which was no improvement.

The part of the man's statement that was true, however, was about the uselessness of speaking up. If I know that the teacher is wrong, and say nothing, then I remain the only one who knows, and that gives me an advantage over those who believe the teacher.

"Third," said the man, "my statement only seems to be self-contradictory and impossible because you did not think beneath the surface of the situation. In fact it is not necessarily true that one person has the highest scores of everyone on this shuttle. That's because there were many tests, physical, mental, social, and psychological, and many ways to define 'highest' as well, since there are many ways to be physically or socially or psychologically fit for command. Children who tested highest on stamina may not have tested highest on strength; children who tested highest on memory may not have tested highest on anticipatory analysis. Children with remarkable social skills might be weaker in delay of gratification. Are you beginning to grasp the shallowness of your thinking that led you to your stupid and useless conclusion?"

Nero nodded.

"Let us hear the sound of your flatulence again, Nero. Be just as loud in acknowledging your errors as you were in making them."

"I was wrong."

There was not a boy on that shuttle who would not have avowed a preference for death to being in Nero's place at that moment. And yet Bean felt a kind of envy as well, though he did not understand why he would envy the victim of such torture.

"And yet," said the man, "you happen to be less wrong on this particular shuttle flight than you would have been in any other shuttle filled with launchies heading for Battle School. And do you know why?"

He did not choose to speak.

"Does anyone know why? Can anyone guess? I am inviting speculation."

No one accepted the invitation.

"Then let me choose a volunteer. There is a child here named—improbable as it might sound—'Bean.' Would that child please speak?"

Here it comes, thought Bean. He was filled with dread; but he was also filled with excitement, because this was what he wanted, though he did not know why. Look at me. Talk to me, you with the power, you with the authority.

"I'm here, sir," said Bean.

The man made a show of looking and looking, unable to see where Bean was. Of course it was a sham—he knew exactly where Bean was sitting before he ever spoke. "I can't see where your voice came from. Would you raise a hand?"

Bean immediately raised his hand. He realized, to his shame, that his hand did not even reach to the top of the high-backed seat.

"I still can't see you," said the man, though of course he could. "I give you permission to unstrap and stand on your seat."

Bean immediately complied, peeling off the harness and bounding to his feet. He was barely taller than the back of the seat in front of him.

"Ah, there you are," said the man. "Bean, would you be so kind as to speculate about why, in this shuttle, Nero comes closer to being correct than on any other?"

"Maybe somebody here scored highest on a lot of tests."

"Not just a lot of tests, Bean. All the tests of intellect. All the psychological tests. All the tests pertinent to command. Every one of them. Higher than anyone else on this shuttle."

"So I *was* right," said the newly defiant Nero.

"No you were not," said the man. "Because that remarkable child, the one who scored highest on all the tests related to command, happens to have scored the very lowest on the physical tests. And do you know why?"

No one answered.

"Bean, as long as you're standing, can you speculate about why this one child might have scored lowest on the physical tests?"

Bean knew how he had been set up. And he refused to try to hide from the obvious answer. He would say it, even though the question was designed to make the others detest him for answering it. After all, they would detest him anyway, no matter who said the answer.

"Maybe he scored lowest on the physical tests because he's very, very small."

Groans from many boys showed their disgust at his answer. At the arrogance and vanity that it suggested. But the man in uniform only nodded gravely.

"As should be expected from a boy of such remarkable ability, you are exactly correct. Only this boy's unusually small stature prevented Nero from being correct about there being one child with higher scores than everybody else." He turned to Nero. "So close to not being a complete fool," he said. "And yet . . . even if you had been right, it would only have been by accident. A broken clock is right two times a day. Sit down now, Bean, and put on your harness. The refueling is over and we're about to boost."

Bean sat down. He could feel the hostility of the other children. There was nothing he could do about that right now, and he wasn't sure that it was a disadvantage, anyway. What mattered was the much more puzzling question: Why did the man set him up like that? If the point was to get the kids competing with each other, they could have passed around a list with everyone's scores on all the tests, so they all could see where they stood. Instead, Bean had been singled out. He was already the smallest, and knew from experience that he was therefore a target for every mean-spirited impulse in a bully's heart. So why did they draw this big circle around him and all these arrows pointing at him, practically demanding that he be the main target of everyone's fear and hate?

Draw your targets, aim your darts. I'm going to do well enough in this school that someday I'll be the one with the authority, and then it won't matter who likes *me.* What will matter is who *I* like.

"As you may remember," said the man, "before the first fart from the mouthhole of Nero Bakerboy here, I was starting to make a point. I was telling you that even though some child here may seem like a prime target for your pathetic need to assert supremacy in a situation where you are unsure of being recognized for the hero that you want people to think you are, you must control yourself, and refrain from poking or pinching, jabbing or hitting, or even making snidely provocative remarks or sniggering like warthogs just because you think somebody is an easy target. And the reason why you should refrain from doing this is because you don't know who in this group is going to end up being *your* commander in the future, the admiral when you're a mere captain. And if you think for one moment that they will forget how you treated them now, today, then you really are a fool. If they're good commanders, they'll use you effectively in combat no matter how they despise you. But they don't have to be helpful to you in advancing your career. They don't have to nurture you and bring you along. They don't have to be kind and forgiving. Just think about that. The people you see around you will someday be giving you orders that will decide whether you live or die. I'd suggest you work on earning their respect, not trying to put them down so you can show off like some schoolyard punk."

The man turned his icy smile on Bean one more time.

"And I'll bet that Bean, here, is already planning to be the admiral who gives you all orders someday. He's even planning how he'll order *me* to stand solitary watch on some asteroid observatory till my bones melt from osteoporosis and I ooze around the station like an amoeba."

Bean hadn't given a moment's thought to some future

contest between him and this particular officer. He had no desire for vengeance. He wasn't Achilles. Achilles was stupid. And this officer was stupid for thinking that Bean would think that way. No doubt, however, the man thought Bean would be grateful because he had just warned the others not to pick on him. But Bean had been picked on by tougher bastards than these could possibly be; this officer's "protection" was not needed, and it made the gulf between Bean and the other children wider than before. If Bean could have lost a couple of tussles, he would have been humanized, accepted perhaps. But now there would be no tussles. No easy way to build bridges.

That was the reason for the annoyance that the man apparently saw on Bean's face. "I've got a word for you, Bean. I don't care what you do to me. Because there's only one enemy that matters. The Buggers. And if you can grow up to be the admiral who can give us victory over the Buggers and keep Earth safe for humanity, then make me eat my own guts, ass-first, and I'll still say, Thank you, sir. The Buggers are the enemy. Not Nero. Not Bean. Not even me. So keep your hands off each other."

He grinned again, mirthlessly.

"Besides, the last time somebody tried picking on another kid, he ended up flying through the shuttle in null-G and got his arm broken. It's one of the laws of strategy. Until you know that you're tougher than the enemy, you maneuver, you don't commit to battle. Consider that your first lesson in Battle School."

First lesson? No wonder they used this guy to tend children on the shuttle flights instead of having him teach. If you followed *that* little piece of wisdom, you'd be paralyzed against a vigorous enemy. Sometimes you *have* to commit to a fight even when you're weak. You don't *wait* till you *know* you're tougher. You *make* yourself tougher by whatever means you can, and then you strike by surprise, you sneak up, you backstab, you blindside, you cheat, you lie, you do whatever it takes to make sure that you come out on top.

This guy might be real tough as the only adult on a shuttle full of kids, but if he were a kid on the streets of Rotterdam, he'd "maneuver" himself into starvation in a month. If he wasn't killed before that just for talking like he thought his piss was perfume.

The man turned to head back to the control cabin.

Bean called out to him.

"What's your name?"

The man turned and fixed him with a withering stare. "Already drafting the orders to have my balls ground to powder, Bean?"

Bean didn't answer. Just looked him in the eye.

"I'm Captain Dimak. Anything else you want to know?"

Might as well find out now as later. "Do you teach at Battle School?"

"Yes," he said. "Coming down to pick up shuttle-loads of little boys and girls is how we get Earthside leave. Just as with you, my being on this shuttle means my vacation is over."

The refueling planes peeled away and rose above them. No, it was their own craft that was sinking. And the tail was sinking lower than the nose of the shuttle.

Metal covers came down over the windows. It felt like they were falling faster, faster . . . until, with a bone-shaking roar, the rockets fired and the shuttle began to rise again, higher, faster, faster, until Bean felt like he was going to be pushed right through the back of his chair. It seemed to go on forever, unchanging.

Then . . . silence.

Silence, and then a wave of panic. They were falling again, but this time there was no downward direction, just nausea and fear.

Bean closed his eyes. It didn't help. He opened them again, tried to reorient himself. No direction provided equilibrium. But he had schooled himself on the street not to succumb to nausea—a lot of the food he had to eat had already gone a little bad, and he couldn't afford to throw it up. So he went into his anti-nausea routine—deep breaths, distracting himself by concentrating on wiggling his toes. And, after a surprisingly short time, he was used to the null-G. As long as he didn't expect any direction to be down, he was fine.

The other kids didn't have his routine, or perhaps they were more susceptible to the sudden, relentless loss of balance. Now the reason for the prohibition against eating before the launch became clear. There was plenty of retching going on, but with nothing to throw up, there was no mess, no smell.

Dimak came back into the shuttle cabin, this time standing on the ceiling. Very cute, thought Bean. Another lecture began, this time about how to get rid of planetside assumptions about directions and gravity. Could these kids possibly be so stupid they needed to be told such obvious stuff?

Bean occupied the time of the lecture by seeing how much pressure it took to move himself around within his loosely-fitting harness. Everybody else was big enough that the harnesses fit snugly and prevented movement. Bean alone had room for a little maneuvering. He made the most of it. By the time they arrived at Battle School, he was determined to have at least a little skill at movement in null-G. He figured that in space, his survival might someday depend on knowing just how much force it would take to move his body, and then how much force it would take to stop. Knowing it in his mind wasn't half so important as knowing it with his body. Analyzing things was fine, but good reflexes could save your life.

6

Ender's shadow

"Normally your reports on a launch group are brief. A few troublemakers, an incident report, or—best of all—nothing."

"You're free to disregard any portion of my report, sir."

"Sir? My, but aren't we the prickly martinet today."

"What part of my report did you think was excessive?"

"I think this report is a love song."

"I realize that it might seem like sucking up, to use with every launch the technique you used with Ender Wiggin—"

"You use it with *every* launch?"

"As you noticed yourself, sir, it has interesting results. It causes an immediate sorting out."

"A sorting out into categories that might not otherwise exist. Nevertheless, I accept the compliment implied by your action. But seven pages about Bean—really, did you actually learn that much from a response that was primarily silent compliance?"

"That is just my point, sir. It was not compliance at all.

It was—I was performing the experiment, but it felt as though his were the big eye looking down the microscope, and I were the specimen on the slide."

"So he unnerved you."

"He would unnerve anyone. He's cold, sir. And yet—"

"And yet hot. Yes, I read your report. Every scintillating page of it."

"Yes sir."

"I think you know that it is considered good advice for us *not* to get crushes on our students."

"Sir?"

"In this case, however, I am delighted that you are so interested in Bean. Because, you see, I am not. I already have the boy I think gives us our best chance. Yet there is considerable pressure, because of Bean's damnable faked-up test scores, to give him special attention. Very well, he shall have it. And you shall give it to him."

"But sir . . ."

"Perhaps you are unable to distinguish an order from an invitation."

"I'm only concerned that . . . I think he already has a low opinion of me."

"Good. Then he'll underestimate you. Unless you think his low opinion might be correct."

"Compared to him, sir, we might all be a little dim."

"Close attention is your assignment. Try not to worship him."

All that Bean had on his mind was survival, that first day in Battle School. No one would help him—that had been made clear by Dimak's little charade in the shuttle. They were setting him up to be surrounded by . . . what? Rivals at best, enemies at worst. So it was the street again. Well, that was fine. Bean had survived on the street. And would have kept on surviving, even if Sister Carlotta hadn't found him. Even Pablo—Bean might have made it even without Pablo the janitor finding him in the toilet of the clean place.

So he watched. He listened. Everything the others learned, he had to learn just as well, maybe better. And on top of that, he had to learn what the others were oblivious to—the workings of the group, the systems of the Battle School. How teachers got on with each other. Where the power was. Who was afraid of whom. Every group had its bosses, its suckups, its rebels, its sheep. Every group had its strong bonds and its weak ones, friendships and hypocrisies. Lies within lies within lies. And Bean had to find them all, as quickly as possible, in order to learn the spaces in which he could survive.

They were taken to their barracks, given beds, lockers, little portable desks that were much more sophisticated than the one he had used when studying with Sister Carlotta. Some of the kids immediately began to play with them, trying to program them or exploring the games built into them, but Bean had no interest in that. The computer system of Battle School was not a person; mastering it might be helpful in the long run, but for today it was irrelevant. What Bean needed to find out was all outside the launchy barracks.

Which is where, soon enough, they went. They arrived in the "morning" according to space time—which, to the annoyance of many in Europe and Asia, meant Florida time, since the earliest stations had been controlled from there. For the kids, having launched from Europe, it was late afternoon, and that meant they would have a serious time-lag problem. Dimak explained that the cure for this was to get vigorous physical exercise and then take a short nap—no more than three hours—in the early afternoon, following which they would again have plenty of physical exercise so they could fall asleep that night at the regular bedtime for students.

They piled out to form a line in the corridor. "Green Brown Green," said Dimak, and showed them how those lines on the corridor walls would always lead them back to their barracks. Bean found himself jostled out of line several times, and ended up right at the back. He didn't care—mere jostling drew no blood and left no bruise, and last in line was the best place from which to observe.

Other kids passed them in the corridor, sometimes individuals, sometimes pairs or trios, most with brightly-colored uniforms in many different designs. Once they passed an entire group dressed alike and wearing helmets and carrying extravagant sidearms, jogging along with an intensity of purpose that Bean found intriguing. They're a crew, he thought. And they're heading off for a fight.

They weren't too intense to notice the new kids walking along the corridor, looking up at them in awe. Immediately there were catcalls. "Launchies!" "Fresh meat!" "Who make cocó in the hall and don't clean it up!" "They even smell stupid!" But it was all harmless banter, older kids asserting their supremacy. It meant nothing more than that. No real hostility. In fact it was almost affectionate. They remembered being launchies themselves.

Some of the launchies ahead of Bean in line were resentful and called back some vague, pathetic insults, which only caused more hooting and derision from the older kids. Bean had seen older, bigger kids who hated younger ones because they were competition for food, and drove them away, not caring if they caused the little ones to die. He had felt real blows, meant to hurt. He had seen cruelty, exploitation, molestation, murder. These other kids didn't know love when they saw it.

What Bean wanted to know was how that crew was organized, who led it, how he was chosen, what the crew was *for*. The fact that they had their own uniform meant that it had official status. So that meant that the adults were ultimately in control—the opposite of the way crews were organized in Rotterdam, where adults tried to break them up, where newspapers wrote about them as criminal conspiracies instead of pathetic little leagues for survival.

That, really, was the key. Everything the children did here was shaped by adults. In Rotterdam, the adults were either hostile, unconcerned, or, like Helga with her charity kitchen, ultimately powerless. So the children could shape their own society without interference. Everything was based on survival—on getting enough food without getting killed or injured or sick. Here, there were cooks and doctors, clothing and beds. Power wasn't about access to food—it was about getting the approval of adults.

That's what those uniforms meant. Adults chose them, and children wore them because adults somehow made it worth their while.

So the key to everything was understanding the teachers.

All this passed through Bean's mind, not so much verbally as with a clear and almost instantaneous understanding that within that crew there was no power at all, compared to the power of the teachers, before the uniformed catcallers reached him. When they saw Bean, so much smaller than any of the other kids, they broke out laughing, hooting, howling. "That one isn't big enough to be a turd!" "I can't believe he can *walk!*" "Did'ums wose um's mama?" "Is it even *human?*"

Bean tuned them out immediately. But he could feel the enjoyment of the kids ahead of him in line. They had been humiliated in the shuttle; now it was Bean's turn to be mocked. They loved it. And so did Bean—because it meant that he was seen as less of a rival. By diminishing him, the passing soldiers had made him just that much safer from . . .

From what? What was the *danger* here?

For there would be danger. That he knew. There was always danger. And since the teachers had all the power, the danger would come from them. But Dimak had started things out by turning the other kids against him. So the children themselves were the weapons of choice. Bean had to get to know the other kids, not because they themselves were going to be his problem, but because their weaknesses, their desires could be used against him by the teachers. And, to protect himself, Bean would have to work to undercut their hold on the other children. The only safety here was to subvert the teachers' influence.

And yet that was the greatest danger—if he was caught doing it.

They palmed in on a wall-mounted pad, then slid down a pole—the first time Bean had ever done it with a smooth shaft. In Rotterdam, all his sliding had been on rainspouts, signposts, and lightpoles. They ended up in a section of Battle School with higher gravity. Bean did not realize how light they must have been on the barracks level until he felt how heavy he was down in the gym.

"This is just a little heavier than Earth normal gravity," said Dimak. "You have to spend at least a half-hour a day here, or your bones start to dissolve. And you have to spend the time exercising, so you keep at peak endurance. And that's the key—endurance exercise, not bulking up. You're too small for your bodies to endure that kind of training, and it fights you here. Stamina, that's what we want."

The words meant almost nothing to the kids, but soon the trainer had made it clear. Lots of running on treadmills, riding on cycles, stair-stepping, pushups, situps, chinups, backups, but no weights. Some weight equipment was there, but it was all for the use of teachers. "Your heart rate is monitored from the moment you enter here," said the trainer. "If you don't have your heart rate elevated within five minutes of arrival and you don't keep it elevated for the next twenty-five minutes, it goes on your record *and* I see it on my control board here."

"I get a report on it too," said Dimak. "And you go on the pig list for everyone to see you've been lazy."

Pig list. So that's the tool they used—shaming them in front of the others. Stupid. As if Bean cared.

It was the monitoring board that Bean was interested in. How could they possibly monitor their heart rates and know what they were doing, automatically, from the moment they arrived? He almost asked the question, until he realized the only possible answer: The uniform. It was in the clothing. Some system of sensors. It probably told them a lot more than heart rate. For one thing, they could certainly track every kid wherever he was in the station, all the time. There must be hundreds and hundreds of kids here, and there would be computers reporting the whereabouts, the heart rates, and who could guess what other information about them. Was there a room somewhere with teachers watching every step they took?

Or maybe it wasn't the clothes. After all, they had to palm in before coming down here, presumably to identify themselves. So maybe there were special sensors in this room.

Time to find out. Bean raised his hand. "Sir," he said.

"Yes?" The trainer did a doubletake on seeing Bean's size, and a smile played around the corners of his mouth. He glanced at Dimak. Dimak did not crack a smile or show any understanding of what the trainer was thinking.

"Is the heart rate monitor in our clothing? If we take off any part of our clothes while we're exercising, does it—"

"You are not authorized to be out of uniform in the gym," said the trainer. "The room is kept cold on purpose so that you will not need to remove clothing. You will be monitored at all times."

Not really an answer, but it told him what he needed to know. The monitoring depended on the clothes. Maybe there was an identifier in the clothing and by palming in, they told the gym sensors which kid was wearing which set of clothing. That would make sense.

So clothing was probably anonymous from the time you put on a clean set until you palmed in somewhere. That was important—it meant that it might be possible to be untagged without being naked. Naked, Bean figured, would probably be conspicuous around here.

They all exercised and the trainer told them which of them were not up to the right heart rate and which of them were pushing too hard and would fatigue themselves too soon. Bean quickly got an idea of the level he had to work at, and then forgot about it. He'd remember by reflex, now that he knew.

It was mealtime, then. They were alone in the mess hall—as fresh arrivals, they were on a separate schedule that day. The food was good and there was a lot of it. Bean was stunned when some of the kids looked at their portion and complained about how little there was. It was a feast! Bean couldn't finish it. The whiners were informed by the cooks that the quantities were all adapted to their individual dietary needs—each kid's portion size came up on a computer display when he palmed in upon entering the mess hall.

So you don't eat without your palm on a pad. Important to know.

Bean soon found out that his size was going to get official attention. When he brought his half-finished tray to the disposal unit, an electronic chiming sound brought the on-duty nutritionist to speak to him. "It's your first day, so we aren't going to be rigid about it. But your portions are scientifically calibrated to meet your dietary needs, and in the future you will finish every bit of what you are served."

Bean looked at him without a word. He had already made his decision. If his exercise program made him hungrier, then he'd eat more. But if they were expecting him to gorge himself, they could forget it. It would be a simple enough matter to dump excess food onto the trays of the whiners. They'd be happy with it, and Bean would eat only as much as his body wanted. He remembered hunger very well, but he had lived with Sister Carlotta for many months, and he knew to trust his own appetite. For a while he had let her goad him into eating more than he actually was hungry for. The result had been a sense of loginess, a harder time sleeping and a harder time staying awake. He went back to eating only as much as his body wanted, letting his hunger be his guide, and it kept him sharp and quick. That was the only nutritionist he trusted. Let the whiners get sluggish.

Dimak stood after several of them had finished eating. "When you're through, go back to the barracks. If you think you can find it. If you have any doubt, wait for me and I'll bring the last group back myself."

The corridors were empty when Bean went out into the corridor. The other kids palmed the wall and their green-brown-green strip turned on. Bean watched them go. One of them turned back. "Aren't you coming?" Bean said nothing. There was nothing to say. He was obviously standing still. It was a stupid question. The kid turned around and jogged on down the corridor toward the barracks.

Bean went the other way. No stripes on the wall. He knew that there was no better time to explore than now. If he was caught out of the area he was supposed to be in, they'd believe him if he claimed to have got lost.

The corridor sloped up both behind him and in front of him. To his eyes it looked like he was always going uphill, and when he looked back, it was uphill to go back the way he had come. Strange. But Dimak had already explained that the station was a huge wheel, spinning in space so that centrifugal force would replace gravity. That meant the main corridor on each level was a big circle, so you'd always come back to where you started, and "down" was always toward the outside of the circle. Bean made the mental adjustment. It was dizzying at first, to picture himself on his side as he walked along, but then he mentally changed the orientation so that he imagined the station as a wheel on a cart, with him at the bottom of it no matter how much it turned. That put the people above him upside down, but he didn't care. Wherever he was was the bottom, and that way down stayed down and up stayed up.

The launchies were on the mess hall level, but the older kids must not be, because after the mess halls and the kitchens, there were only classrooms and unmarked doors with palmpads high enough that they were clearly not meant for children to enter. Other kids could probably reach those pads, but not even by jumping could Bean hope to palm one. It didn't matter. They wouldn't respond to any child's handprint, except to bring some adult to find out what the kid thought he was doing, trying to enter a room where he had no business.

By long habit—or was it instinct?—Bean regarded such barriers as only temporary blocks. He knew how to climb over walls in Rotterdam, how to get up on roofs. Short as he was, he still found ways to get wherever he needed to go. Those doors would not stop him if he decided he needed to get beyond them. He had no idea right now how he'd do it, but he had no doubt that he would find a way. So he wasn't annoyed. He simply tucked the information away, waiting until he thought of some way to use it.

Every few meters there was a pole for downward passage or a ladderway for going up. To get down the pole to the gym, he had had to palm a pad. But there seemed to be no pad on most of these. Which made sense. Most poles and ladderways would merely let you pass between floors—no, they called them decks; this was the International Fleet and so everything pretended to be a ship—while only one pole led down to the gym, to which they needed to control access so that it didn't get overcrowded with people coming when they weren't scheduled. As soon as he had made sense of it, Bean didn't have to think of it anymore. He scrambled up a ladder.

The next floor up had to be the barracks level for the older kids. Doors were more widely spaced, and each door had an insignia on it. Using the colors of some uniform—no doubt based on their stripe colors, though he doubted the older kids ever had to palm the wall to find their way around—there was also the silhouette of an animal. Some of them he didn't recognize, but he recognized a couple of birds, some cats, a dog, a lion. Whatever was in use symbolically on signs in Rotterdam. No pigeon. No fly. Only noble animals, or animals noted for courage. The dog silhouette looked like some kind of hunting animal, very thin around the hips. Not a mongrel.

So this is where the crews meet, and they have animal

symbols, which means they probably call themselves by animal names. Cat Crew. Or maybe Lion Crew. And probably not Crew. Bean would soon learn what they called themselves. He closed his eyes and tried to remember the colors and insignia on the crew that passed and mocked him in the corridor earlier. He could see the shape in his mind, but didn't see it on any of the doors he passed. It didn't matter—not worth traveling the whole corridor in search of it, when that would only increase his risk of getting caught.

Up again. More barracks, more classrooms. How many kids in a barracks? This place was bigger than he thought.

A soft chime sounded. Immediately, several doors opened and kids began to pour out into the corridor. A changeover time.

At first Bean felt more secure among the big kids, because he thought he could get lost in the crowd, the way he always did in Rotterdam. But that habit was useless here. This wasn't a random crowd of people on their own errands. These might be kids but they were military. They knew where everybody was supposed to be, and Bean, in his launchy uniform, was way out of place. Almost at once a couple of older kids stopped him.

"You don't belong on this deck," said one. At once several others stopped to look at Bean as if he were an object washed into the street by a storm.

"Look at the size of this one."

"Poor kid gots to sniff everybody's butt, neh?"

"Eh!"

"You're out of area, launchy."

Bean said nothing, just looked at each one as he spoke. Or she.

"What are your colors?" asked a girl.

Bean said nothing. Best excuse would be that he didn't remember, so he couldn't very well name them now.

"He's so small he could walk between my legs without touching my—"

"Oh, shut up, Dink, that's what you said when Ender—"

"Yeah, Ender, right."

"You don't think this is the kid they—"

"Was Ender *this* small when he arrived?"

"—been saying, he another Ender?"

"Right, like this one's going to shoot to the top of the standings."

"It wasn't Ender's fault that Bonzo wouldn't let him fire his weapon."

"But it's a fluke, that's all I'm saying—"

"This the one they talking about? One like Ender? Top scores?"

"Just get him down to the launchy level."

"Come with me," said the girl, taking him firmly by the hand.

Bean came along meekly.

"My name is Petra Arkanian," she said.

Bean said nothing.

"Come on, you may be little and you may be scared, but they don't let you in here if you're deaf or stupid."

Bean shrugged.

"Tell me your name before I break your stubby little fingers."

"Bean," he said.

"That's not a name, that's a lousy meal."

He said nothing.

"You don't fool me," she said. "This mute thing, it's just a cover. You came up here on purpose."

He kept his silence but it stabbed at him, that she had figured him out so easily.

"Kids for this school, they're chosen because they're smart and they've got initiative. So of course you wanted to explore. The thing is, they expect it. They probably know you're doing it. So there's no point in hiding it. What are they going to do, give you some big bad piggy points?"

So that's what the older kids thought about the pig list.

"This stubborn silence thing, it'll just piss people off. I'd forget about it if I were you. Maybe it worked with Mommy and Daddy, but it just makes you look stubborn and ridiculous because anything that matters, you're going to tell anyway, so why not just talk?"

"OK," said Bean.

Now that he was complying, she didn't crow about it. The lecture worked, so the lecture was over. "Colors?" she asked.

"Green brown green."

"Those launchy colors sound like something you'd find in a dirty toilet, don't you think?"

So she was just another one of the stupid kids who thought it was cute to make fun of launchies.

"It's like they designed everything to get the older kids to make fun of the younger ones."

Or maybe she wasn't. Maybe she was just talking. She was a talker. There weren't a lot of talkers on the streets. Not among the kids, anyway. Plenty of them among the drunks.

"The system around here is screwed. It's like they want us to act like little kids. Not that that's going to bother *you.* Hell, you're already doing some dumb lost-little-kid act."

"Not now," he said.

"Just remember this. No matter what you do, the teachers know about it and they already have some stupid theory about what this means about your personality or whatever. They *always* find a way to use it against you, if they want to, so you might as well not try. No doubt it's already in your report that you took this little jaunt when you were supposed to be having beddy-bye time and that probably tells them that you 'respond to insecurity by seeking to be alone while exploring the limits of your new environment.' " She used a fancy voice for the last part.

And maybe she had more voices to show off to him, but he wasn't going to stick around to find out. Apparently she was a take-charge person and didn't have anybody to take charge of until he came along. He wasn't interested in becoming her project. It was all right being Sister Carlotta's project because she could get him out of the street and into Battle School. But what did this Petra Arkanian have to offer him?

He slid down a pole, stopped in front of the first opening, pushed out into the corridor, ran to the next ladderway, and scooted up two decks before emerging into another corridor and running full out. She was probably right in what she said, but one thing was certain—he was not going to have her hold his hand all the way back to green-brown-green. The last thing he needed, if he was going to hold his own in this place, was to show up with some older kid holding his hand.

Bean was four decks above the mess level where he was supposed to be right now. There were kids moving through here, but nowhere near as many as the deck below. Most of the doors were unmarked, but a few stood open, including one wide arch that opened into a game room.

Bean had seen computer games in some of the bars in Rotterdam, but only from a distance, through the doors and between the legs of men and women going in and out in their endless search for oblivion. He had never seen a child playing a computer game, except on the vids in store windows. Here it was real, with only a few players catching quick games between classes so that each game's sounds stood out. A few kids playing solo games, and then four of them playing a four-sided space game with a holographic display. Bean stood back far enough not to intrude in their sightlines and watched them play. Each of them controlled a squadron of four tiny ships, with the goal of either wiping out all the other fleets or capturing—but not destroying—each player's slow-moving mothership. He learned the rules and the terminology by listening to the four boys chatter as they played.

The game ended by attrition, not by any cleverness—

the last boy simply happened to be the least stupid in his use of his ships. Bean watched as they reset the game. No one put in a coin. The games here were free.

Bean watched another game. It was just as quick as the first, as each boy committed his ships clumsily, forgetting about whichever one was not actively engaged. It was as if they thought of their force as one active ship and three reserves.

Maybe the controls didn't allow anything different. Bean moved closer. No, it was possible to set the course for one, flip to control another ship, and another, then return to the first ship to change its course at any time.

How did these boys get into Battle School if this was all they could think of? Bean had never played a computer game before, but he saw at once that any competent player could quickly win if this was the best competition available.

"Hey, dwarf, want to play?"

One of them had noticed him. Of course the others did, too.

"Yes," said Bean.

"Well Bugger that," said the one who invited him. "Who do you think you are, Ender Wiggin?"

They laughed and then all four of them walked away from the game, heading for their next class. The room was empty. Class time.

Ender Wiggin. The kids in the corridor talked about him, too. Something about Bean made these kids think of Ender Wiggin. Sometimes with admiration, sometimes with resentment. This Ender must have beaten some older kids at a computer game or something. And he was at the top of the standings, that's what somebody said. Standings in what?

The kids in the same uniform, running like one crew, heading for a fight—that was the central fact of life here. There was one core game that everyone played. They lived in barracks according to what team they were on. Every kid's standings were reported so everybody else knew them. And whatever the game was, the adults ran it.

So this was the shape of life here. And this Ender Wiggin, whoever he was, he was at the top of it all, he led the standings.

Bean reminded people of him.

That made him a little proud, yes, but it also annoyed him. It was safer not to be noticed. But because this other small kid had done brilliantly, everybody who saw Bean thought of Ender and that made Bean memorable. That would limit his freedom considerably. There was no way to disappear here, as he had been able to disappear in crowds in Rotterdam.

Well, who cared? He couldn't be hurt now, not really. No matter what happened, as long as he was here at Battle School he would never be hungry. He'd always have shelter. He had made it to heaven. All he had to do was the minimum required to not get sent home early. So who cared if people noticed him or not? It made no difference. Let them worry about their standings. Bean had already won the battle for survival, and after that, no other competition mattered.

But even as he had that thought, he knew it wasn't true. Because he did care. It wasn't enough just to survive. It never had been. Deeper than his need for food had been his hunger for order, for finding out how things worked, getting a grasp on the world around him. When he was starving, of course he used what he learned in order to get himself into Poke's crew and get her crew enough food that there would be enough to trickle some down to him at the bottom of the pecking order. But even when Achilles had turned them into his family and they had something to eat every day, Bean hadn't stopped being alert, trying to understand the changes, the dynamics in the group. Even with Sister Carlotta, he had spent a lot of effort trying to understand why and how she had the power to do for him what she was doing, and the basis on which she had chosen him. He had to know. He had to have the picture of everything in his mind.

Here, too. He could have gone back to the barracks and napped. Instead, he risked getting in trouble just to find out things that no doubt he would have learned in the ordinary course of events.

Why did I come up here? What was I looking for?

The key. The world was full of locked doors, and he had to get his hands on every key.

He stood still and listened. The room was nearly silent. But there was white noise, background rumble and hiss that made it so sounds didn't carry throughout the entire station.

With his eyes closed, he located the source of the faint rushing sound. Eyes open, he then walked to where the vent was. An out-flowing vent with slightly warmer air making a very slight breeze. The rushing sound was not the hiss of air here at the vent, but rather a much louder, more distant sound of the machinery that pumped air throughout the Battle School.

Sister Carlotta had told him that in space, there was no air, so wherever people lived, they had to keep their ships and stations closed tight, holding in every bit of air. And they also had to keep changing the air, because the oxygen, she said, got used up and had to be replenished. That's what this air system was about. It must go everywhere through the ship.

Bean sat before the vent screen, feeling around the edges. There were no visible screws or nails holding it on. He got his fingernails under the rim and carefully slid his fingers around it, prying it out a little, then a little more. His fingers now fit under the edges. He pulled straight forward. The vent came free, and Bean toppled over backward.

Only for a moment. He set aside the screen and tried to see into the vent. The vent duct was only about fifteen centimeters deep from front to back. The top was solid, but the bottom was open, leading down into the duct system.

Bean sized up the vent opening just the way he had, years before, stood on the seat of a toilet and studied the inside of the toilet tank, deciding whether he could fit in it. And the conclusion was the same—it would be cramped, it would be painful, but he could do it.

He reached an arm inside and down. He couldn't feel the bottom. But with arms as short as his, that didn't mean much. There was no way to tell by looking which way the duct went when it got down to the floor level. Bean could imagine a duct leading under the floor, but that felt wrong to him. Sister Carlotta had said that every scrap of material used to build the station had to be hauled up from Earth or the manufacturing plants on the moon. They wouldn't have big gaps between the decks and the ceilings below because that would be wasted space into which precious air would have to be pumped without anyone breathing it. No, the ductwork would be in the outside walls. It was probably no more than fifteen centimeters deep anywhere.

He closed his eyes and imagined an air system. Machinery making a warm wind blow through the narrow ducts, flowing into every room, carrying fresh breathable air everywhere.

No, that wouldn't work. There had to be a place where the air was getting sucked in and drawn back. And if the air blew in at the outside walls, then the intake would be . . . in the corridors.

Bean got up and ran to the door of the game room. Sure enough, the corridor's ceiling was at least twenty centimeters lower than the ceiling inside the room. But no vents. Just light fixtures.

He stepped back into the room and looked up. All along the top of the wall that bordered on the corridor there was a narrow vent that looked more decorative than practical. The opening was about three centimeters. Not even Bean could fit through the intake system.

He ran back to the open vent and took off his shoes.

No reason to get hung up because his feet were so much bigger than they needed to be.

He faced the vent and swung his feet down into the opening. Then he wriggled until his legs were entirely down the hole and his buttocks rested on the rim of the vent. His feet still hadn't found bottom. Not a good sign. What if the vent dropped straight down into the machinery?

He wriggled back out, then went in the other way. It was harder and more painful, but now his arms were more usable, giving him a good grip on the floor as he slid chest-deep into the hole.

His feet touched bottom.

Using his toes, he probed. Yes, the ductwork ran to the left and the right, along the outside wall of the room. And the opening was tall enough that he could slide down into it, then wriggle—always on his side—along from room to room.

That was all he needed to know at present. He gave a little jump so his arms reached farther out onto the floor, meaning to use friction to let him pull himself up. Instead, he just slid back down into the vent.

Oh, this was excellent. Someone would come looking for him, eventually, or he'd be found by the next batch of kids who came in to play games, but he did not want to be found like this. More to the point, the ductwork would only give him an alternate route through the station if he could climb out of the vents. He had a mental image of somebody opening a vent and seeing his skull looking out at them, his dead body completely dried up in the warm wind of the air ducts where he starved to death or died of thirst trying to get out of the vents.

As long as he was just standing there, though, he might as well find out if he could cover the vent opening from the inside.

He reached over and, with difficulty, got a finger on the screen and was able to pull it toward him. Once he got a hand solidly on it, it wasn't hard at all to get it over the opening. He could even pull it in, tightly enough that it probably wouldn't be noticeably different to casual observers on the other side. With the vent closed, though, he had to keep his head turned to one side. There wasn't room enough for him to turn it. So once he got in the duct system, his head would either stay turned to the left or to the right. Great.

He pushed the vent back out, but carefully, so that it didn't fall to the floor. Now it was time to climb out in earnest.

After a couple more failures, he finally realized that the screen was exactly the tool he needed. Laying it down on the floor in front of the vent, he hooked his fingers under the far end. Pulling back on the screen provided him with the leverage to lift his body far enough to get his chest over the rim of the vent opening. It hurt, to hang the weight of his body on such a sharp edge, but now he could get up on his elbows and then on his hands, lifting his whole body up through the opening and back into the room.

He thought carefully through the sequence of muscles he had used and then thought about the equipment in the gym. Yes, he could strengthen those muscles.

He put the vent screen back into place. Then he pulled up his shirt and looked at the red marks on his skin where the rim of the vent opening had scraped him mercilessly. There was some blood. Interesting. How would he explain it, if anyone asked? He'd have to see if he could reinjure the same spot by climbing around on the bunks later.

He jogged out of the game room and down the corridor to the nearest pole, then dropped to the mess hall level. All the way, he wondered why he had felt such urgency about getting into the ducts. Whenever he got like that in the past, doing some task without knowing why it even mattered, it had turned out that there was a danger that he had sensed but that hadn't yet risen to his conscious mind. What was the danger here?

Then he realized—in Rotterdam, out on the street, he

had always made sure he knew a back way out of everything, an alternate path to get from one place to another. If he was running from someone, he never dodged into a cul-de-sac to hide unless he knew another way out. In truth, he never really *hid* at all—he evaded pursuit by keeping on the move, always. No matter how awful the danger following him might be, he could not hold still. It felt terrible to be cornered. It hurt.

It hurt and was wet and cold and he was hungry and there wasn't enough air to breathe and people walked by and if they just lifted the lid they would find him and he had no way to run if they did that, he just had to sit there waiting for them to pass without noticing him. If they used the toilet and flushed it, the equipment wouldn't work right because the whole weight of his body was pressing down on the float. A lot of the water had spilled out of the tank when he climbed in. They'd notice something was wrong and they'd find him.

It was the worst experience of his life, and he couldn't stand the idea of ever hiding like that again. It wasn't the small space that bothered him, or that it was wet, or that he was hungry or alone. It was the fact that the only way out was into the arms of his pursuers.

Now that he understood that about himself, he could relax. He hadn't found the ductwork because he sensed some danger that hadn't yet risen to his conscious mind. He found the ductwork because he remembered how bad it felt to hide in the toilet tank as a toddler. So whatever danger there might be, he hadn't sensed it yet. It was just a childhood memory coming to the surface. Sister Carlotta had told him that a lot of human behavior was really acting out our responses to dangers long past. It hadn't sounded sensible to Bean at the time, but he didn't argue, and now he could see that she was right.

And how could he know there would never be a time when that narrow, dangerous highway through the ductwork might not be exactly the route he needed to save his life?

He never did palm the wall to light up green-brown-green. He knew exactly where his barracks was. How could he not? He had been there before, and knew every step between the barracks and every other place he had visited in the station.

And when he got there, Dimak had not yet returned with the slow eaters. His whole exploration hadn't taken more than twenty minutes, including his conversation with Petra and watching two quick computer games during the class break.

He awkwardly hoisted himself up from the lower bunk, dangling for a while from his chest on the rim of the second bunk. Long enough that it hurt in pretty much the same spot he had injured climbing out of the vent. "What are you doing?" asked one of the launchies near him.

Since the truth wouldn't be understood, he answered truthfully. "Injuring my chest," he said.

"I'm trying to sleep," said the other boy. "You're supposed to sleep, too."

"Naptime," said another boy. "I feel like I'm some stupid four-year-old."

Bean wondered vaguely what these boys' lives had been like, when taking a nap made them think of being four years old.

—

Sister Carlotta stood beside Pablo de Noches, looking at the toilet tank. "Old-fashioned kind," said Pablo. "Norteamericano. Very popular for a while back when the Netherlands first became international."

She lifted the lid on the toilet tank. Very light. Plastic.

As they came out of the lavatory, the office manager who had been showing them around looked at her curiously. "There's not any kind of danger from using the toilets, is there?" she asked.

"No," said Sister Carlotta. "I just had to see it, that's all. It's Fleet business. I'd appreciate it if you didn't talk about our visit here."

Of course, that almost guaranteed that she would talk about nothing else. But Sister Carlotta counted on it sounding like nothing more than strange gossip.

Whoever had run an organ farm in this building would not want to be discovered, and there was a lot of money in such evil businesses. That was how the devil rewarded his friends—lots of money, up to the moment he betrayed them and left them to face the agony of hell alone.

Outside the building, she spoke again to Pablo. "He really hid in there?"

"He was very tiny," said Pablo de Noches. "He was crawling when I found him, but he was soaking wet up to his shoulder on one side, and his chest. I thought he peed himself, but he said no. Then he showed me the toilet. And he was red here, here, where he pressed against the mechanism."

"He was talking," she said.

"Not a lot. A few words. So *tiny*. I could not believe a child so small could talk."

"How long was he in there?"

Pablo shrugged. "Shriveled up skin like old lady. All over. Cold. I was thinking, he will die. Not warm water like a swimming pool. Cold. He shivered all night."

"I can't understand why he *didn't* die," said Sister Carlotta.

Pablo smiled. "No hay nada que Dios no puede hacer."

"True," she answered. "But that doesn't mean we can't figure out *how* God works his miracles. Or why."

Pablo shrugged. "God does what he does. I do my work and live, the best man I can be."

She squeezed his arm. "You took in a lost child and saved him from people who meant to kill him. God saw you do that and he loves you."

Pablo said nothing, but Sister Carlotta could guess what he was thinking—how many sins, exactly, were washed away by that good act, and would it be enough to keep him out of hell?

"Good deeds do not wash away sins," said Sister Carlotta. "Solo el redentor puede limpiar su alma."

Pablo shrugged. Theology was not his skill.

"You don't do good deeds for yourself," said Sister Carlotta. "You do them because God is in you, and for those moments you are his hands and his feet, his eyes and his lips."

"I thought God was the baby. Jesus say, if you do it to this little one, you do it to me."

Sister Carlotta laughed. "God will sort out all the fine points in his own due time. It is enough that we try to serve him."

"He was so small," said Pablo. "But God was in him."

She bade him good-bye as he got out of the taxi in front of his apartment building.

Why did I have to see that toilet with my own eyes? My work with Bean is done. He left on the shuttle yesterday. Why can't I leave the matter alone?

Because he should have been dead, that's why. And after starving on the streets for all those years, even if he lived he was so malnourished he should have suffered serious mental damage. He should have been permanently retarded.

That was why she could not abandon the question of Bean's origin. Because maybe he *was* damaged. Maybe he *is* retarded. Maybe he started out so smart that he could lose half his intellect and still be the miraculous boy he is.

She thought of how St. Matthew kept saying that all the things that happened in Jesus' childhood, his mother treasured them in her heart. Bean is not Jesus, and I am not the Holy Mother. But he is a boy, and I have loved him as my son. What he did, no child of that age could do.

No child of less than a year, not yet walking by himself, could have such clear understanding of his danger that he would know to do the things that Bean did. Children that age often climbed out of their cribs, but they did not hide in a toilet tank for hours and then come out alive and ask for help. I can call it a miracle all I want, but I have to understand it. They use the dregs of the Earth in those organ farms. Bean has such extraordinary gifts that he could only have come from extraordinary parents.

And yet for all her research during the months that Bean lived with her, she had never found a single kidnapping that could possibly have been Bean. No abducted child. Not even an accident from which someone might have taken a surviving infant whose body was therefore never found. That wasn't proof—not every baby that disappeared left a trace of his life in the newspapers, and not every newspaper was archived and available for a search on the nets. But Bean had to be the child of parents so brilliant that the world took note of them—didn't he? Could a mind like his come from ordinary parents? Was that the miracle from which all other miracles flowed?

No matter how much Sister Carlotta tried to believe it, she could not. Bean was not what he seemed to be. He was in Battle School now, and there was a good chance he would end up someday as the commander of a great fleet. But what did anyone know about him? Was it possible that he was not a natural human being at all? That his extraordinary intelligence had been given him, not by God, but by someone or something else?

There was the question: If not God, then who could make such a child?

Sister Carlotta buried her face in her hands. Where did such thoughts come from? After all these years of searching, why did she have to keep doubting the one great success she had?

We have seen the beast of Revelation, she said silently. The Bugger, the Formic monster bringing destruction to the Earth, just as prophesied. We have seen the beast, and long ago Mazer Rackham and the human fleet, on the brink of defeat, slew that great dragon. But it will come again, and St. John the Revelator said that when it did, there would be a prophet who came with him.

No, no. Bean is good, a good-hearted boy. He is not

any kind of devil, not the servant of the beast, just a boy of great gifts that God may have raised up to bless this world in the hour of its greatest peril. I know him as a mother knows her child. I am not wrong.

Yet when she got back to her room, she set her computer to work, searching now for something new. For reports from or about scientists who had been working, at least five years ago, on projects involving alterations in human DNA.

And while the search program was querying all the great indexes on the nets and sorting their replies into useful categories, Sister Carlotta went to the neat little pile of folded clothing waiting to be washed. She would not wash it after all. She put it in a plastic bag along with Bean's sheets and pillowcase, and sealed the bag. Bean had worn this clothing, slept on this bedding. His skin was in it, small bits of it. A few hairs. Maybe enough DNA for a serious analysis.

He was a miracle, yes, but she would find out just what the dimensions of this miracle might be. For her ministry had not been to save the children of the cruel streets of the cities of the world. Her ministry had been to help save the one species made in the image of God. That was still her ministry. And if there was something wrong with the child she had taken into her heart as a beloved son, she would find out about it, and give warning.

7

Exploration

"So this launch group was slow getting back to their barracks."

"There is a twenty-one-minute discrepancy."

"Is that a lot? I didn't even know this sort of thing was tracked."

"For safety. And to have an idea, in the event of emergency, where everyone is. Tracking the uniforms that departed from the mess hall and the uniforms that entered the barracks, we come up with an aggregate of twenty-one minutes. That could be twenty-one children loitering for exactly one minute, or one child for twenty-one minutes."

"That's very helpful. Am I supposed to ask them?"

"No! They aren't supposed to know that we track them by their uniforms. It isn't good for them to know how much we know about them."

"And how little."

"Little?"

"If it was one student, it wouldn't be good for him to know that our tracking methods don't tell us who it was."

"Ah. Good point. And . . . actually, I came to you because I believe that it *was* one student only."

"Even though your data aren't clear?"

"Because of the arrival pattern. Spaced out in groups of two or three, a few solos. Just the way they left the mess hall. A little bit of clumping—three solos become a threesome, two twos arrive as four—but if there had been some kind of major distraction in the corridor, it would have caused major coalescing, a much larger group arriving at once after the disturbance ended."

"So. One student with twenty-one minutes unaccounted for."

"I thought you should at least be aware."

"What would he do with twenty-one minutes?"

"You know who it was?"

"I will, soon enough. Are the toilets tracked? Are we sure it wasn't somebody so nervous he went in to throw up his lunch?"

"Toilet entry and exit patterns were normal. In and out."

"Yes, I'll find out who it was. And keep watching the data for this launch group."

"So I was right to bring this to your attention?"

"Did you have any doubt of it?"

Bean slept lightly, listening, as he always did, waking twice that he remembered. He didn't get up, just lay there listening to the breathing of the others. Both times, there was a little whispering somewhere in the room. Always children's voices, no urgency about them, but the sound was enough to rouse Bean and kindle his attention, just for a moment till he was sure there was no danger.

Hc woke the third time when Dimak entered the room. Even before sitting up, Bean knew that's who it was, from the weight of his step, the sureness of his movement, the press of authority. Bean's eyes were open before Dimak spoke; he was on all fours, ready to move in any direction, before Dimak finished his first sentence.

"Naptime is over, boys and girls, time for work."

It was not about Bean. If Dimak knew what Bean had done after lunch and before their nap, he gave no sign. No immediate danger.

Bean sat on his bunk as Dimak instructed them in the use of their lockers and desks. Palm the wall beside the locker and it opens. Then turn on the desk and enter your name and a password.

Bean immediately palmed his own locker with his right hand, but did not palm the desk. Instead, he checked on Dimak—busy helping another student near the door—then scrambled to the unoccupied third bunk above his own and palmed *that* locker with his left hand. There was a desk inside that one, too. Quickly he turned on his own desk and typed in his name and a password. Bean. Achilles. Then he pulled out the other desk and turned it on. Name? Poke. Password? Carlotta.

He slipped the second desk back into the locker and closed the door, then tossed his first desk down onto his own bunk and slipped down after it. He did not look around to see if anyone noticed him. If they did, they'd say something soon enough; visibly checking around would merely call attention to him and make people suspect him who would not otherwise have noticed what he did.

Of course the adults would know what he had done. In fact, Dimak was certainly noticing already, when one child complained that his locker wouldn't open. So the station computer knew how many students there were and stopped opening lockers when the right total had been opened. But Dimak did not turn and demand to know who had opened two lockers. Instead, he pressed his own palm against the last student's locker. It popped open. He closed it again, and now it responded to the student's palm.

So they were going to let him have his second locker, his second desk, his second identity. No doubt they would watch him with special interest to see what he did with it. He would have to make a point of fiddling with it now and then, clumsily, so they'd think they knew what he wanted a second identity for. Maybe some kind of prank. Or to write down secret thoughts. That would be fun—Sister Carlotta was always prying after his secret thoughts, and no doubt these teachers would, too. Whatever he wrote, they'd eat it up.

Therefore they wouldn't be looking for his truly private work, which he would perform on his own desk. Or, if it was risky, on the desk of one of the boys across from him, both of whose passwords he had carefully noticed and memorized. Dimak was lecturing them about protecting their desks at all times, but it was inevitable that kids would be careless, and desks would be left lying around.

For now, though, Bean would do nothing riskier than what he had already done. The teachers had their own reasons for letting him do it. What mattered is that they not know his own.

After all, he didn't know himself. It was like the vent—if he thought of something that might get him some advantage later, he did it.

Dimak went on talking about how to submit homework, the directory of teachers' names, and the fantasy game that was on every desk. "You are not to spend study time playing the game," he said. "But when your studies are done, you are permitted a few minutes to explore."

Bean understood at once. The teachers *wanted* the students to play the game, and knew that the best way to encourage it was to put strict limits on it . . . and then not enforce them. A game—Sister Carlotta had used games to try to analyze Bean from time to time. So Bean always turned them into the same game: Try to figure out what Sister Carlotta is trying to learn from the way I play this game.

In this case, though, Bean figured that anything he did with the game would tell them things that he didn't want them to know about him. So he would not play at all, unless they compelled him. And maybe not even then. It was one thing to joust with Sister Carlotta; here, they no doubt had real experts, and Bean was not going to give them a chance to learn more about him than he knew himself.

Dimak took them on the tour, showing them most of what Bean had already seen. The other kids went ape over the game room. Bean did not so much as glance at the vent into which he had climbed, though he did make it a point to fiddle with the game he had watched the bigger boys play, figuring out how the controls worked and verifying that his tactics could, in fact, be carried out.

They did a workout in the gym, in which Bean immediately began working on the exercises that he thought he'd need—one-armed pushups and pullups being the most important, though they had to get a stool for him to stand on in order to reach the lowest chinning bar. No problem. Soon enough he'd be able to jump to reach it. With all the food they were giving him, he could build up strength quickly.

And they seemed grimly determined to pack food into him at an astonishing rate. After the gym they showered, and then it was suppertime. Bean wasn't even hungry yet, and they piled enough food onto his tray to feed his whole crew back in Rotterdam. Bean immediately headed for a couple of the kids who had whined about their small portions and, without even asking permission, scraped his excess onto their trays. When one of them tried to talk to him about it, Bean just put his finger to his lips. In answer, the boy grinned. Bean still ended up with more food than he wanted, but when he turned in his tray, it was scraped clean. The nutritionist would be happy. It remained to be seen if the janitors would report the food Bean left on the floor.

Free time. Bean headed back to the game room, hoping that tonight he'd actually see the famous Ender Wiggin. If he was there, he would no doubt be the center of a group of admirers. But at the center of the groups he saw were only the ordinary prestige-hungry clique-formers who thought they were leaders and so would follow their group anywhere in order to maintain that delusion. No way could any of them be Ender Wiggin. And Bean was not about to ask.

Instead, he tried his hand at several games. Each time, though, the moment he lost for the first time, other kids would push him out of the way. It was an interesting set of social rules. The students knew that even the shortest, greenest launchy was entitled to his turn—but the moment a turn ended, so did the protection of the rule. And they were rougher in shoving him than they needed to be, so the message was clear—you shouldn't have been using that game and making me wait. Just like the food lines at the charity kitchens in Rotterdam—except that absolutely nothing that mattered was at stake.

That was interesting, to find that it wasn't hunger that caused children to become bullies on the street. The bulliness was already in the child, and whatever the stakes were, they would find a way to act as they needed to act. If it was about food, then the children who lost would die; if it was about games, though, the bullies did not hesitate to be just as intrusive and send the same message. Do what I want, or pay for it.

Intelligence and education, which all these children had, apparently didn't make any important difference in human nature. Not that Bean had really thought they would.

Nor did the low stakes make any difference in Bean's response to the bullies. He simply complied without complaint and took note of who the bullies were. Not that he had any intention of punishing them or of avoiding them, either. He would simply remember who acted as a bully and take that into account when he was in a situation where that information might be important.

No point in getting emotional about anything. Being emotional didn't help with survival. What mattered was to learn everything, analyze the situation, choose a course of action, and then move boldly. Know, think, choose, do.

There was no place in that list for "feel." Not that Bean didn't have feelings. He simply refused to think about them or dwell on them or let them influence his decisions, when anything important was at stake.

"He's even smaller than Ender was."

Again, again. Bean was so tired of hearing that.

"Don't talk about that hijo de puta to me, bicho."

Bean perked up. Ender had an enemy. Bean was wondering when he'd spot one, for someone who was first in the standings *had* to have provoked something besides admiration. Who said it? Bean drifted nearer to the group the conversation had come from. The same voice came up again. Again. And then he knew: That one was the boy who had called Ender an hijo de puta.

He had the silhouette of some kind of lizard on his uniform. And a single triangle on his sleeve. None of the boys around him had the triangle. All were focused on him. Captain of the team?

Bean needed more information. He tugged on the sleeve of a boy standing near him.

"What," said the boy, annoyed.

"Who's that boy there?" asked Bean. "The team captain with the lizard."

"It's a salamander, pinhead. Salamander *army.* And he's the *commander.*"

Teams are called armies. Commander is the triangle rank. "What's his name?"

"Bonzo Madrid. And he's an even bigger asshole than you." The boy shrugged himself away from Bean.

So Bonzo Madrid was bold enough to declare his hatred for Ender Wiggin, but a kid who was not in Bonzo's army had contempt for *him* in turn and wasn't afraid to say so to a stranger. Good to know. The only enemy Ender had, so far, was contemptible.

But . . . contemptible as Bonzo might be, he *was* a commander. Which meant it was possible to become a commander without being the kind of boy that everybody respected. So what was their standard of judgment, in assigning command in this war game that shaped the life of Battle School?

More to the point, how do I get a command?

That was the first moment that Bean realized that he even had such a goal. Here in Battle School, he had arrived with the highest scores in his launch group—but he was the smallest and youngest and had been isolated even further by the deliberate actions of his teacher, making him a target of resentment. Somehow, in the midst of all this, Bean had made the decision that this would not be like Rotterdam. He was not going to live on the fringes, inserting himself only when it was absolutely essential for his own survival. As rapidly as possible, he was going to put himself in place to command an army.

Achilles had ruled because he was brutal, because he was willing to kill. That would always trump intelligence, when the intelligent one was physically smaller and had no strong allies. But here, the bullies only shoved and spoke rudely. The adults controlled things tightly and so brutality would not prevail, not in the assignment of command. Intelligence, then, had a chance to win out. Eventually, Bean might not have to live under the control of stupid people.

If this was what Bean wanted—and why not try for it, as long as some more important goal didn't come along first?—then he had to learn how the teachers made their decisions about command. Was it solely based on performance in classes? Bean doubted it. The International Fleet had to have smarter people than that running this school. The fact that they had that fantasy game on every desk suggested that they were looking at personality as well. Character. In the end, Bean suspected, character mattered more than intelligence. In Bean's litany of survival—know, think, choose, do—intelligence only mattered in the first three, and was the decisive factor only in the second one. The teachers knew that.

Maybe I *should* play the game, thought Bean.

Then: Not yet. Let's see what happens when I don't play.

At the same time he came to another conclusion he did not even know he had been concerned about. He would talk to Bonzo Madrid.

Bonzo was in the middle of a computer game, and he was obviously the kind of person who thought of anything unexpected as an affront to his dignity. That meant that for Bean to accomplish what he wanted, he could not approach Bonzo in a cringing way, like the suckups who surrounded him as he played, commending him even for his stupid mistakes in gameplay.

Instead, Bean pushed close enough to see when Bonzo's onscreen character died—again. "Señor Madrid, puedo hablar convozco?" The Spanish came to mind easily enough—he had listened to Pablo de Noches talk to fellow immigrants in Rotterdam who visited his apartment, and on the telephone to family members back in Valencia. And using Bonzo's native language had the desired effect. He didn't ignore Bean. He turned and glared at him.

"What do you want, bichinho?" Brazilian slang was common in Battle School, and Bonzo apparently felt no need to assert the purity of his Spanish.

Bean looked him in the eye, even though he was about twice Bean's height, and said, "People keep saying that I remind them of Ender Wiggin, and you're the only person around here who doesn't seem to worship him. I want to know the truth."

The way the other kids fell silent told Bean that he had judged aright—it was dangerous to ask Bonzo about Ender Wiggin. Dangerous, but that's why Bean had phrased his request so carefully.

"Damn right I don't worship the fart-eating insubordinate traitor, but why should I tell *you* about him?"

"Because you won't lie to me," said Bean, though he actually thought it was obvious Bonzo would probably lie outrageously in order to make himself look like the hero of what was obviously a story of his own humiliation at Ender's hands. "And if people are going to keep comparing me to the guy, I've got to know what he really is. I don't want to get iced because I do it all wrong here. You don't owe me nothing, but when you're small like me, you gots to have somebody who can tell you the stuff you gots to know to survive." Bean wasn't quite sure of the slang here yet, but what he knew, he used.

One of the other kids chimed in, as if Bean had written him a script and he was right on cue. "Get lost, launchy, Bonzo Madrid doesn't have time to change diapers."

Bean rounded on him and said fiercely, "I can't ask the teachers, they don't tell the truth. If Bonzo don't talk to me who I ask then? *You?* You don't know zits from zeroes."

It was pure Sergeant, that spiel, and it worked. Everybody laughed at the kid who had tried to brush him off, and Bonzo joined in, then put a hand on Bean's shoulder. "I'll tell you what I know, kid, it's about time somebody wanted to hear the truth about that walking rectum." To the kid that Bean had just fronted, Bonzo said, "Maybe you better finish my game, it's the only way you'll ever get to play at that level."

Bean could hardly believe a commander would say such a pointlessly offensive thing to one of his own subordinates. But the boy swallowed his anger and grinned and nodded and said, "That's right, Bonzo," and turned to the game, as instructed. A real suckup.

By chance Bonzo led him to stand right in front of the wall vent where Bean had been stuck only a few hours before. Bean gave it no more than a glance.

"Let me tell you about Ender. He's all about beating the other guy. Not just winning—he has to beat the other guy into the ground or he isn't happy. No rules for him. You give him a plain order, and he acts like he's going to obey it, but if he sees a way to make himself look good and all he has to do is disobey the order, well, all I can say is, I pity whoever has him in his army."

"He used to be Salamander?"

Bonzo's face reddened. "He wore a uniform with our colors, his name was on my roster, but he was *never* Salamander. The minute I saw him, I knew he was trouble. That cocky look on his face, like he thinks the whole Battle School was made just to give him a place to strut. I wasn't having it. I put in to transfer him the second he showed up and I refused to let him practice with us, I knew he'd learn our whole system and then take it to some other army and use what he learned from me to stick it to my army as fast as he could. I'm not stupid!"

In Bean's experience, that was a sentence never uttered except to prove its own inaccuracy.

"So he didn't follow orders."

"It's more than that. He goes crying like a baby to the teachers about how I don't let him practice, even though they *know* I've put in to transfer him out, but he whines and they let him go in to the battleroom during freetime and practice alone. Only he starts getting kids from his launch group and then kids from other armies, and they go in there as if he was their commander, doing what he tells them. That really pissed off a lot of us. And the teachers always give that little suckup whatever he wants, so when we commanders *demanded* that they bar our soldiers from practicing with him, they just said, 'Freetime is *free*,' but everything is part of the game, sabe? Everything, so they're letting him cheat, and every lousy soldier and sneaky little bastard goes to Ender for those freetime practices so every army's system is compromised, sabe? You plan your strategy for a game and you never know if your plans aren't being told to a soldier in the enemy army the second they come out of your mouth, sabe?"

Sabe sabe sabe. Bean wanted to shout back at him, Sí, yo *sé,* but you couldn't show impatience with Bonzo. Besides, this was all fascinating. Bean was getting a pretty good picture of how this army game shaped the life of Battle School. It gave the teachers a chance to see not only how the kids handled command, but also how they responded to incompetent commanders like Bonzo. Apparently, he had decided to make Ender the goat of his army, only Ender refused to take it. This Ender Wiggin was the kind of kid who got it that the teachers ran everything and used them by getting that practice room. He didn't ask them to get Bonzo to stop picking on him, he asked them for an alternate way to train himself. Smart. The teachers had to love that, and Bonzo couldn't do a thing about it.

Or could he?

"What did you do about it?"

"It's what we're going to do. I'm about fed up. If the teachers won't stop it, somebody else will have to, neh?" Bonzo grinned wickedly. "So I'd stay out of Ender Wiggin's freetime practice if I were you."

"Is he really number one in the standings?"

"Number one is piss," said Bonzo. "He's dead last in loyalty. There's not a commander who wants him in his army."

"Thanks," said Bean. "Only now it kind of pisses me off that people say I'm like him."

"Just because you're small. They made him a soldier when he was still way too young. Don't let them do that to you, and you'll be OK, sabe?"

"Ahora sé," said Bean. He gave Bonzo his biggest grin.

Bonzo smiled back and clapped him on his shoulder. "You'll do OK. When you get big enough, if I haven't graduated yet, maybe you'll be in Salamander."

If they leave you in command of an army for another day, it's just so that the other students can learn how to make the best of taking orders from a higher-ranking idiot. "I'm not going to be a soldier for a *long* time," said Bean.

"Work hard," said Bonzo. "It pays off." He clapped him on the shoulder yet again, then walked off with a big grin on his face. Proud of having helped a little kid. Glad to have convinced somebody of his own twisted version of dealing with Ender Wiggin, who was obviously smarter farting than Bonzo was talking.

And there was a threat of violence against the kids who practiced with Ender Wiggin in freetime. That was good to know. Bean would have to decide now what to do with that information. Get the warning to Ender? Warn the teachers? Say nothing? Be there to watch?

Freetime ended. The game room cleared out as everyone headed to their barracks for the time officially dedicated to independent study. Quiet time, in other words. For most of the kids in Bean's launch group, though, there was nothing to study—they hadn't had any classes yet. So for tonight, study meant playing the fantasy game on their desks and bantering with each other to assert position. Everybody's desk popped up with the suggestion that they could write letters home to their families. Some of the kids chose to do that. And, no doubt, they all assumed that's what Bean was doing.

But he was not. He signed on to his first desk as Poke and discovered that, as he suspected, it didn't matter which desk he used, it was the name and password that determined everything. He would never have to pull that second desk out of its locker. Using the Poke identity, he wrote a journal entry. This was not unexpected—"diary" was one of the options on the desk.

What should he be? A whiner? "Everybody pushed me out of the way in the game room just because I'm little, it isn't fair!" A baby? "I miss Sister Carlotta so so so much, I wish I could be in my own room back in Rotterdam." Ambitious? "I'll get the best scores on everything, they'll see."

In the end, he decided on something a little more subtle.

What would Achilles do if he were me? Of course he's not little, but with his bad leg it's almost the same thing. Achilles always knew how to wait and not show them anything. That's what I've got to do, too. Just wait and see what pops up. Nobody's going to want to be my friend at first. But after a while, they'll get used to me and we'll start sorting ourselves out in the classes. The first ones who'll let me get close will be the weaker ones, but that's not a problem. You build your crew based on loyalty first, that's what Achilles did, build loyalty and train them to obey. You work with what you have, and go from there.

Let them stew on *that*. Let them think he was trying to turn Battle School into the street life that he knew. They'd believe it. And in the meantime, he'd have time to learn as much as he could about how Battle School actually worked, and come up with a strategy that actually fit the situation.

Dimak came in one last time before lights out. "Your desks keep working after lights out," he said, "but if you use it when you're supposed to be sleeping, we'll know about it and we'll know what you're doing. So it better be important, or you go on the pig list."

Most of the kids put their desks away; a couple of them defiantly kept them out. Bean didn't care either way. He had other things to think about. Plenty of time for the desk tomorrow, or the next day.

He lay in the near-darkness—apparently the babies here had to have a little light so they could find their way to the toilet without tripping—and listened to the sounds around him, learning what they meant. A few whispers, a few shushes. The breathing of boys and girls as, one by one, they fell asleep. A few even had light child-snores. But under those human sounds, the windsound from the air system, and random clicking and distant voices, sounds of the flexing of a station rotating into and out of sunlight, the sound of adults working through the night.

This place was so expensive. Huge, to hold thousands of kids and teachers and staff and crew. As expensive as a ship of the fleet, surely. And all of it just to train little children. The adults may keep the kids wrapped up in a game, but it was serious business to *them*. This program of training children for war wasn't just some wacko educational theory gone mad, though Sister Carlotta was probably right when she said that a lot of people thought it was. The I.F. wouldn't maintain it at this level if it weren't expected to give serious results. So these kids snoring and soughing and whispering their way into the darkness, they really mattered.

They expect results from me. It's not just a party up here, where you come for the food and then do what you want. They really do want to make commanders out of us. And since Battle School has been going for a while, they probably have proof that it works—kids who already graduated and went on to compile a decent service record. That's what I've got to keep in mind. Whatever the system is here, it works.

A different sound. Not regular breathing. Jagged little breaths. An occasional gasp. And then . . . a sob.

Crying. Some boy was crying himself to sleep.

In the nest, Bean had heard some of the kids cry in their sleep, or as they neared sleep. Crying because they were hungry or injured or sick or cold. But what did these kids have to cry about here?

Another set of soft sobs joined the first.

They're homesick, Bean realized. They've never been away from mommy and daddy before, and it's getting to them.

Bean just didn't get it. He didn't feel that way about anybody. You just live in the place you're in, you don't worry about where you used to be or where you wish you were, *here* is where you are and here's where you've got to find a way to survive and lying in bed boo-hooing doesn't help much with *that.*

No problem, though. Their weakness just puts me farther ahead. One less rival on my road to becoming a commander.

Is that how Ender Wiggin thought about things? Bean recalled everything he had learned about Ender so far. The kid was resourceful. He didn't openly fight with Bonzo, but he didn't put up with his stupid decisions, either. It was fascinating to Bean, because on the street the one rule he knew for sure was, you don't stick your neck out unless your throat's about to be slit anyway. If you have a stupid crew boss, you don't tell him he's stupid, you don't show him he's stupid, you just go along and keep your head down. That's how kids survived.

When he had to, Bean had taken a bold risk. Got himself onto Poke's crew that way. But that was about food. That was about not dying. Why did Ender take such a risk when there was nothing at stake but his standing in the war game?

Maybe Ender knew something Bean didn't know. Maybe there was some reason why the game was more important than it seemed.

Or maybe Ender was one of those kids who just couldn't stand to lose, ever. The kind of kid who's for the team only as long as the team is taking him where he wants to go, and if it isn't, then it's every man for himself. That's what Bonzo thought. But Bonzo was stupid.

Once again, Bean was reminded that there were things he didn't understand. Ender wasn't doing every man for himself. He didn't practice alone. He opened his free time practice to other kids. Launchies, too, not just kids who could do things for him. Was it possible he did that just because it was a decent thing to do?

The way Poke had offered herself to Achilles in order to save Bean's life?

No, Bean didn't *know* that's what she did, he didn't *know* that's why she died.

But the possibility was there. And in his heart, he believed it. That was the thing he had always despised about her. She acted tough but she was soft at heart. And yet . . . that softness was what saved his life. And try as he might, he couldn't get himself to take the too-bad-for-her attitude that prevailed on the street. She listened to me when I talked to her, she did a hard thing that risked her own life on the chance that it would lead to a better life for all her crew. Then she offered me a place at her table and, in the end, she put herself between me and danger. Why?

What was this great secret? Did Ender know it? How did he learn it? Why couldn't Bean figure it out for himself? Try as he might, though, he couldn't understand Poke. He couldn't understand Sister Carlotta, either. Couldn't understand the arms she held him with, the tears she shed over him. Didn't they understand that no matter how much they loved him, he was still a separate person, and doing good for him didn't improve *their* lives in any way?

If Ender Wiggin has this weakness, then I will not be anything like him. I am not going to sacrifice myself for anybody. And the beginning of that is that I refuse to lie in my bed and cry for Poke floating there in the water with her throat slit, or boo-hoo because Sister Carlotta isn't asleep in the next room.

He wiped his eyes, rolled over, and willed his body to relax and go to sleep. Moments later, he was dozing in that light, easy-to-rouse sleep. Long before morning his pillow would be dry.

—

He dreamed, as human beings always dream—random firings of memory and imagination that the unconscious mind tries to put together into coherent stories. Bean rarely paid attention to his own dreams, rarely even remembered that he dreamed at all. But this morning he awoke with a clear image in his mind.

Ants, swarming from a crack in the sidewalk. Little black ants. And larger red ants, doing battle with them, destroying them. All of them scurrying. None of them looking up to see the human shoe coming down to stamp the life out of them.

When the shoe came back up, what was crushed under it was not ant bodies at all. They were the bodies of children, the urchins from the streets of Rotterdam. All of Achilles' family. Bean himself—he recognized his own face, rising above his flattened body, peering around for one last glimpse at the world before death.

Above him loomed the shoe that killed him. But now it was worn on the end of a bugger's leg, and the bugger laughed and laughed.

Bean remembered the laughing bugger when he awoke, and remembered the sight of all those children crushed flat, of his own body mashed like gum under a shoe. The meaning was obvious: While we children play at war, the buggers are coming to crush us. We must look above the level of our private struggles and keep in mind the greater enemy.

Except that Bean rejected that interpretation of his own dream the moment he thought of it. Dreams have no meaning at all, he reminded himself. And even if they do mean something, it's a meaning that reveals what I feel, what I fear, not some deep abiding truth. So the buggers are coming. So they might crush us all like ants under their feet. What's that to me? My business right now is to keep Bean alive, to advance myself to a position where I might be useful in the war against the buggers. There's nothing I can do to stop them right now.

Here's the lesson Bean took from his own dream: Don't be one of the scurrying, struggling ants.

Be the shoe.

—

Sister Carlotta had reached a dead end in her search of the nets. Plenty of information on human genetics studies, but nothing like what she was looking for.

So she sat there, doodling with a nuisance game on her desk while trying to think of what to do next and wondering why she was bothering to look into Bean's beginnings at all, when the secure message arrived from the I.F. Since the message would erase itself a minute after arrival, to be re-sent every minute until it was read by the recipient, she opened it at once and keyed in her first and second passwords.

FROM: Col.Graff@BattleSchool.IF
TO: Ss.Carlotta@SpecAsn.RemCon.IF
RE: Achilles

Please report all info on "Achilles" as known to subject.

As usual, a message so cryptic that it didn't actually have to be encrypted, though of course it had been. This was a secure message, wasn't it? So why not just use the kid's name. "Please report on 'Achilles' as known to *Bean.*"

Somehow Bean had given them the name Achilles, and under circumstances such that they didn't want to ask him directly to explain. So it had to be in something he had written. A letter to her? She felt a little thrill of hope and then scoffed at her own feelings. She knew perfectly well that mail from the kids in Battle School was almost never passed along, and besides, the chance of Bean actually writing to her was remote. But they had the name somehow, and wanted to know from her what it meant.

The trouble is, she didn't want to give him that information without knowing what it would mean for Bean.

So she prepared an equally cryptic reply:

Will reply by secure conference only.

Of course this would infuriate Graff, but that was just a perk. Graff was so used to having power far beyond his rank that it would be good for him to have a reminder that all obedience was voluntary and ultimately depended on the free choice of the person receiving the orders. And she *would* obey, in the end. She just wanted to make sure Bean was not going to suffer from the information. If they knew he had been so closely involved with both the perpetrator and the victim of a murder, they might drop him from the program. And even if she was sure it would be all right to talk about it, she might be able to get a quid pro quo.

It took another hour before the secure conference was set up, and when Graff's head appeared in the display above her computer, he was not happy. "What game are you playing today, Sister Carlotta?"

"You've been putting on weight, Colonel Graff. That's not healthy."

"Achilles," he said.

"Man with a bad heel," she said. "Killed Hector and dragged his body around the gates of Troy. Also had a thing for a captive girl named Briseis."

"You know that's not the context."

"I know more than that. I know you must have got the name from something Bean wrote, because the name is not pronounced uh-KILL-eez, it's pronounced ah-SHEEL. French."

"Someone local there."

"Dutch is the native language here, though Fleet Common has just about driven it out as anything but a curiosity."

"Sister Carlotta, I don't appreciate your wasting the expense of this conference."

"And I'm not going to talk about it until I know why you need to know."

Graff took a few deep breaths. She wondered if his mother taught him to count to ten, or if, perhaps, he had learned to bite his tongue from dealing with nuns in Catholic school.

"We are trying to make sense of something Bean wrote."

"Let me see it and I'll help you as I can."

"He's not your responsibility anymore, Sister Carlotta," said Graff.

"Then why are you asking me about him? He's your responsibility, yes? So I can get back to work, yes?"

Graff sighed and did something with his hands, out of sight in the display. Moments later the text of Bean's diary entry appeared on her display below and in front of Graff's face. She read it, smiling slightly.

"Well?" asked Graff.

"He's doing a number on you, Colonel."

"What do you mean?"

"He knows you're going to read it. He's misleading you."

"You *know* this?"

"Achilles might indeed be providing him with an example, but not a good one. Achilles once betrayed someone that Bean valued highly."

"Don't be vague, Sister Carlotta."

"I wasn't vague. I told you precisely what I wanted you to know. Just as Bean told you what he wanted you to hear. I can promise you that his diary entries will only make sense to you if you recognize that he is writing these things for you, with the intent to deceive."

"Why, because he didn't keep a diary down there?"

"Because his memory is perfect," said Sister Carlotta. "He would never, never commit his real thoughts to a readable form. He keeps his own counsel. Always. You will never find a document written by him that is not meant to be read."

"Would it make a difference if he was writing it under another identity? Which he thinks we don't know about?"

"But you *do* know about it, and so he *knows* you will know about it, so the other identity is there only to confuse you, and it's working."

"I forgot, you think this kid is smarter than God."

"I'm not worried that you don't accept my evaluation. The better you know him, the more you'll realize that I'm right. You'll even come to believe those test scores."

"What will it take to get you to help me with this?" asked Graff.

"Try telling me the truth about what this information will mean to Bean."

"He's got his primary teacher worried. He disappeared for twenty-one minutes on the way back from lunch—we have a witness who talked to him on a deck where he had no business, and that still doesn't account for that last seventeen minutes of his absence. He doesn't play with his desk—"

"You think setting up false identities and writing phony diary entries isn't playing?"

"There's a diagnostic/therapeutic game that all the children play—he hasn't even signed on yet."

"He'll know that the game is psychological, and he won't play it until he knows what it will cost him."

"Did you teach him that attitude of default hostility?"

"No, I learned it from him."

"Tell me straight. Based on this diary entry, it looks as though he plans to set up his own crew here, as if this were the street. We need to know about this Achilles so we'll know what he actually has in mind."

"He plans no such thing," said Sister Carlotta.

"You say it so forcefully, but without giving me a single reason to trust your conclusion."

"You called *me,* remember?"

"That's not enough, Sister Carlotta. Your opinions on this boy are suspect."

"He would never emulate Achilles. He would never write his true plans where you could find them. He does not build crews, he joins them and uses them and moves on without a backward glance."

"So investigating this Achilles won't give us a clue about Bean's future behavior?"

"Bean prides himself on not holding grudges. He thinks they're counterproductive. But at some level, I believe he wrote about Achilles specifically because you would read what he wrote and would want to know more about Achilles, and if you investigated him you would discover a very bad thing that Achilles did."

"To Bean?"

"To a friend of his."

"So he *is* capable of having friendships?"

"The girl who saved his life here on the street."

"And what's *her* name?"

"Poke. But don't bother looking for her. She's dead."

Graff thought about that a moment. "Is that the bad thing Achilles did?"

"Bean has reason to believe so, though I don't think it would be evidence enough to convict in court. And as I said, all these things may be unconscious. I don't think Bean would knowingly try to get even with Achilles, or anybody else, for that matter, but he might hope you'd do it for him."

"You're still holding back, but I have no choice but to trust your judgment, do I?"

"I promise you that Achilles is a dead end."

"And if you think of a reason why it might not be so dead after all?"

"I want your program to succeed, Colonel Graff, even more than I want Bean to succeed. My priorities are not skewed by the fact that I do care about the child. I really have told you everything now. But I hope you'll help me also."

"Information isn't traded in the I.F., Sister Carlotta. It flows from those who have it to those who need it."

"Let me tell you what I want, and you decide if I need it."

"Well?"

"I want to know of any illegal or top secret projects involving the alteration of the human genome in the past ten years."

Graff looked off into the distance. "It's too soon for you to be off on a new project, isn't it. So this is the same old project. This is about Bean."

"He came from somewhere."

"You mean his mind came from somewhere."

"I mean the whole package. I think you're going to end up relying on this boy, betting all our lives on him, and I think you need to know what's going on in his genes. It's a poor second to knowing what's happening in his mind, but that, I suspect, will always be out of reach for you."

"You sent him up here, and then you tell me something like this. Don't you realize that you have just guaranteed that I will never let him move to the top of our selection pool?"

"You say that now, when you've only had him for a day," said Sister Carlotta. "He'll grow on you."

"He damn well better not shrink or he'd get sucked away by the air system."

"Tut-tut, Colonel Graff."

"Sorry, Sister," he answered.

"Give me a high enough clearance and I'll do the search myself."

"No," he said. "But I'll get summaries sent to you."

She knew that they would give her only as much information as they thought she should have. But when he tried to fob her off with useless drivel, she'd deal with that problem, too. Just as she would try to get to Achilles before the I.F. found him. Get him away from the streets and into a school. Under another name. Because if the I.F. found him, in all likelihood they would test him—or find her scores on him. If they tested him, they would fix his foot and bring him up to Battle School. And she had promised Bean that he would never have to face Achilles again.

8

Good Student

"He doesn't play the fantasy game at *all?*"

"He has never so much as chosen a figure, let alone come through the portal."

"It's not possible that he hasn't discovered it."

"He reset the preferences on his desk so that the invitation no longer pops up."

"From which you conclude . . ."

"He knows it isn't a game. He doesn't want us analyzing the workings of his mind."

"And yet he wants us to advance him."

"I don't know that. He buries himself in his studies. For three months he's been getting perfect scores on every test. But he only reads the lesson material once. His study is on other subjects of his own choosing."

"Such as?"

"Vauban."

"Seventeenth-century fortifications? What is he *thinking?*"

"You see the problem?"

"How does he get along with the other children?"

"I think the classic description is 'loner.' He is polite. He volunteers nothing. He asks only what he's interested in. The kids in his launch group think he's strange. They know he scores better than them on everything, but they don't hate him. They treat him like a force of nature. No friends, but no enemies."

"That's important, that they don't hate him. They should, if he stays aloof like that."

"I think it's a skill he learned on the street—to turn away anger. He never gets angry himself. Maybe that's why the teasing about his size stopped."

"Nothing that you're telling me suggests that he has command potential."

"If you think he's trying to show command potential and failing at it, then you're right."

"So . . . what do you *think* he's doing?"

"Analyzing *us*."

"Gathering information without giving any. Do you really think he's that sophisticated?"

"He stayed alive on the street."

"I think it's time for you to probe a little."

"And let him know that his reticence bothers us?"

"If he's as clever as you think, he already knows."

Bean didn't mind being dirty. He had gone years without bathing, after all. A few days didn't bother him. And if other people minded, they kept their opinions to themselves. Let them add it to the gossip about him. Smaller and younger than Ender! Perfect scores on every test! Stinks like a pig!

That shower time was precious. That's when he could sign on to his desk as one of the boys bunking near him—while they were showering. They were naked, wearing only towels to the shower, so their uniforms weren't tracking them. During that time Bean could sign on and explore the system without letting the teachers know that he was learning the tricks of the system. It tipped his hand, just a little, when he altered the preferences so he didn't have to face that stupid invitation to play their mind game every time he changed tasks on his desk. But that wasn't a very difficult hack, and he decided they wouldn't be particularly alarmed that he'd figured it out.

So far, Bean had found only a few really useful things, but he felt as though he was on the verge of breaking through more important walls. He knew that there was a virtual system that the students were meant to hack through. He had heard the legends about how Ender (of course) had hacked the system on his first day and signed on as God, but he knew that while Ender might have been unusually quick about it, he wasn't doing anything that wasn't expected of bright, ambitious students.

Bean's first achievement was to find the way the teachers' system tracked student computer activity. By avoiding the actions that were automatically reported to the teachers, he was able to create a private file area that they wouldn't see unless they were deliberately looking for it. Then, whenever he found something interesting while signed on as someone else, he would remember the location, then go and download the information into his secure area and work on it at his leisure—while his desk reported that he was reading works from the library. He actually read those works, of course, but far more quickly than his desk reported.

With all that preparation, Bean expected to make real progress. But far too quickly he ran into the firewalls—information the system had to have but wouldn't yield. He found several workarounds. For instance, he couldn't find any maps of the whole station, only of the student-accessible areas, and those were always diagrammatic and cute, deliberately out of scale. But he did find a series of emergency maps in a program that would automatically display them on the walls of the corridors in the event of a pressure-loss emergency, showing the nearest safety locks. These maps *were* to scale, and by combining them into a single map in his secure area, he was able to create a schema of the whole station. Nothing was labeled except the locks, of course, but he learned of the existence of a parallel system of corridors on either side of the student area. The station must be not one but three parallel wheels, cross-linked at many points. That's where the teachers and staff lived, where the life support was located, the communications with the Fleet. The bad news was that they had separate air-circulation systems. The ductwork in one would not lead him to either of the others. Which meant that while he could probably spy on anything going on in the student wheel, the other wheels were out of reach.

Even within the student wheel, however, there were plenty of secret places to explore. The students had access to four decks, plus the gym below A-Deck and the battleroom above D-Deck. There were actually nine decks, however, two below A-Deck and three above D. Those spaces had to be used for something. And if they thought it was worth hiding it from the students, Bean figured it was worth exploring.

And he would have to start exploring soon. His exercise was making him stronger, and he was staying lean by not overeating—it was unbelievable how much food they tried to force on him, and they kept increasing his portions, probably because the previous servings hadn't caused him to gain as much weight as they wanted him to gain. But what he could not control was the increase in his height. The ducts would be impassable for him before too long—if they weren't already. Yet using the air system to get him access to the hidden decks was not something he could do during showers. It would mean losing sleep. So he kept putting it off—one day wouldn't make that much difference.

Until the morning when Dimak came into the barracks first thing in the morning and announced that everyone was to change his password immediately, with his back turned to the rest of the room, and was to tell no one what the new password was. "Never type it in where anyone can see," he said.

"Somebody's been using other people's passwords?" asked a kid, his tone suggesting that he thought this an appalling idea. Such dishonor! Bean wanted to laugh.

"It's required of all I.F. personnel, so you might as well develop the habit now," said Dimak. "Anyone found using the same password for more than a week will go on the pig list."

But Bean could only assume that they had caught on to what he was doing. That meant they had probably looked back into his probing for the past months and knew pretty much what he had found out. He signed on and purged his secure file area, on the chance that they hadn't actually found it yet. Everything he really needed there, he had already memorized. He would never rely on the desk again for anything his memory could hold.

Stripping and wrapping his towel around him, Bean headed for the showers with the others. But Dimak stopped him at the door.

"Let's talk," he said.

"What about my shower?" asked Bean.

"Suddenly you care about cleanliness?" asked Dimak.

So Bean expected to be chewed out for stealing passwords. Instead, Dimak sat beside him on a lower bunk near the door and asked him far more general questions. "How are you getting on here?"

"Fine."

"I know your test scores are good, but I'm concerned that you aren't making many friends among the other kids."

"I've got a lot of friends."

"You mean you know a lot of people's names and don't quarrel with anybody."

Bean shrugged. He didn't like this line of questioning any better than he would have liked an inquiry into his computer use.

"Bean, the system here was designed for a reason.

There are a lot of factors that go into our decisions concerning a student's ability to command. The classwork is an important part of that. But so is leadership."

"Everybody here is just full of leadership ability, right?"

Dimak laughed. "Well, that's true, you can't all be leaders at once."

"I'm about as big as a three-year-old," said Bean. "I don't think a lot of kids are eager to start saluting me."

"But you could be building networks of friendship. The other kids are. You don't."

"I guess I don't have what it takes to be a commander."

Dimak raised an eyebrow. "Are you suggesting you *want* to be iced?"

"Do my test scores look like I'm trying to fail?"

"What *do* you want?" asked Dimak. "You don't play the games the other kids play. Your exercise program is weird, even though you know the regular program is designed to strengthen you for the battleroom. Does that mean you don't intend to play that game, either? Because if that's your plan, you really *will* get iced. That's our primary means of assessing command ability. That's why the whole life of the school is centered around the armies."

"I'll do fine in the battleroom," said Bean.

"If you think you can do it without preparation, you're mistaken. A quick mind is no replacement for a strong, agile body. You have no idea how physically demanding the battleroom can be."

"I'll join the regular workouts, sir."

Dimak leaned back and closed his eyes with a small sigh. "My, but you're compliant, aren't you, Bean."

"I try to be, sir."

"That is such complete bullshit," said Dimak.

"Sir?" Here it comes, thought Bean.

"If you devoted the energy to making friends that you devote to hiding things from the teachers, you'd be the most beloved kid in the school."

"That would be Ender Wiggin, sir."

"And don't think we haven't picked up on the way you obsess about Wiggin."

"Obsess?" Bean hadn't asked about him after that first day. Never joined in discussions about the standings. Never visited the battleroom during Ender's practice sessions.

Oh. What an obvious mistake. Stupid.

"You're the only launchy who has completely avoided so much as seeing Ender Wiggin. You track his schedule so thoroughly that you are never in the same room with him. That takes real effort."

"I'm a launchy, sir. He's in an army."

"Don't play dumb, Bean. It's not convincing and it wastes my time."

Tell a useless and obvious truth, that was the rule. "Everyone compares me to Ender all the time 'cause I came here so young and small. I wanted to make my own way."

"I'll accept that for now because there's a limit to how deeply I want to wade into your bullshit," said Dimak.

But in saying what he'd said about Ender, Bean wondered if it might not be true. Why shouldn't I have such a normal emotion as jealousy? I'm not a machine. So he was a little offended that Dimak seemed to assume that something more subtle had to be going on. That Bean was lying no matter what he said.

"Tell me," said Dimak, "why you refuse to play the fantasy game."

"It looks boring and stupid," said Bean. That was certainly true.

"Not good enough," said Dimak. "For one thing, it *isn't* boring and stupid to any other kid in Battle School. In fact, the game adapts itself to your interests."

I have no doubt of *that,* thought Bean. "It's all pretending," said Bean. "None of it's real."

"Stop hiding for one second, can't you?" snapped Dimak. "You know perfectly well that we use the game to analyze personality, and that's why you refuse to play."

"Sounds like you've analyzed my personality anyway," said Bean.

"You just don't let up, do you?"

Bean said nothing. There was nothing to say.

"I've been looking at your reading list," said Dimak. "Vauban?"

"Yes?"

"Fortification engineering from the time of Louis the Fourteenth?"

Bean nodded. He thought back to Vauban and how his strategies had adapted to fit Louis's ever-more-straitened finances. Defense in depth had given way to a thin line of defenses; building new fortresses had largely been abandoned, while razing redundant or poorly placed ones continued. Poverty triumphing over strategy. He started to talk about this, but Dimak cut him off.

"Come on, Bean. Why are you studying a subject that has nothing to do with war in space?"

Bean didn't really have an answer. He had been working through the history of strategy from Xenophon and Alexander to Caesar and Machiavelli. Vauban came in sequence. There was no plan—mostly his readings were a cover for his clandestine computer work. But now that Dimak was asking him, what *did* seventeenth-century fortifications have to do with war in space?

"I'm not the one who put Vauban in the library."

"We have the full set of military writings that are found in every library in the fleet. Nothing more significant than that."

Bean shrugged.

"You spent two hours on Vauban."

"So what? I spent as long on Frederick the Great, and I don't think we're doing field drills, either, or bayoneting anyone who breaks ranks during a march into fire."

"You didn't actually read Vauban, did you," said Dimak. "So I want to know what you *were* doing."

"I *was* reading Vauban."

"You think we don't know how fast you read?"

"And *thinking* about Vauban?"

"All right then, what were you thinking?"

"Like you said. About how it applies to war in space." Buy some time here. What *does* Vauban have to do with war in space?

"I'm waiting," said Dimak. "Give me the insights that occupied you for two hours just yesterday."

"Well of course fortifications are impossible in space," said Bean. "In the traditional sense, that is. But there are things you can do. Like his mini-fortresses, where you leave a sallying force outside the main fortification. You can station squads of ships to intercept raiders. And there are barriers you can put up. Mines. Fields of flotsam to cause collisions with fast-moving ships, holing them. That sort of thing."

Dimak nodded, but said nothing.

Bean was beginning to warm to the discussion. "The real problem is that unlike Vauban, we have only one strong point worth defending—Earth. And the enemy is not limited to a primary direction of approach. He could come from anywhere. From anywhere all at once. So we run into the classic problem of defense, cubed. The farther out you deploy your defenses, the more of them you have to have, and if your resources are limited, you soon have more fortifications than you can man. What good are bases on moons Jupiter or Saturn or Neptune, when the enemy doesn't even have to come in on the plane of the ecliptic? He can bypass all our fortifications. The way Nimitz and MacArthur used two-dimensional island-hopping against the defense in depth of the Japanese in World War II. Only our enemy can work in three dimensions. Therefore we cannot possibly maintain defense in depth. Our only defense is early detection and a single massed force."

Dimak nodded slowly. His face showed no expression. "Go on."

Go on? That wasn't enough to explain two hours of reading? "Well, so I thought that even that was a recipe for disaster, because the enemy is free to divide his forces. So even if we intercept and defeat ninety-nine of a hundred attacking squadrons, he only has to get one squadron through to cause terrible devastation on Earth. We saw how much territory a single ship could scour when they first showed up and started burning over China. Get ten ships to Earth for a single day—and if they spread us out enough, they'd have a lot more than a day!—and they could wipe out most of our main population centers. All our eggs are in that one basket."

"And all this you got from Vauban," said Dimak.

Finally. That was apparently enough to satisfy him. "From thinking about Vauban, and how much harder our defensive problem is."

"So," said Dimak, "what's your solution?"

Solution? What did Dimak think Bean was? I'm thinking about how to get control of the situation here in Battle School, not how to save the world! "I don't think there is a solution," said Bean, buying time again. But then, having said it, he began to believe it. "There's no point in trying to defend Earth at all. In fact, unless they have some defensive device we don't know about, like some way of putting an invisible shield around a planet or something, the enemy is just as vulnerable. So the only strategy that makes any sense at all is an all-out attack. To send our fleet against *their* home world and destroy it."

"What if our fleets pass in the night?" asked Dimak. "We destroy each other's worlds and all we have left are ships?"

"No," said Bean, his mind racing. "Not if we sent out a fleet immediately after the Second Bugger War. After Mazer Rackham's strike force defeated them, it would take time for word of their defeat to come back to them. So we build a fleet as quickly as possible and launch it against their home world immediately. That way the news of their defeat reaches them at the same time as our devastating counterattack."

Dimak closed his eyes. "Now you tell us."

"No," said Bean, as it dawned on him that he was right about everything. "That fleet was already sent. Before anybody on this station was born, that fleet was launched."

"Interesting theory," said Dimak. "Of course you're wrong on every point."

"No I'm not," said Bean. He knew he wasn't wrong, because Dimak's air of calm was not holding. Sweat was standing out on his forehead. Bean had hit on something really important here, and Dimak knew it.

"I mean your theory is right, about the difficulty of defense in space. But hard as it is, we still have to do it, and that's why you're here. As to some fleet we supposedly launched—the Second Bugger War exhausted humanity's resources, Bean. It's taken us this long to get a reasonable-sized fleet again. And to get better weaponry for the next battle. If you learned anything from Vauban, you should have learned that you can't build more than your people have resources to support. Besides which, you're assuming we know where the enemy's home world is. But your analysis is good insofar as you've identified the magnitude of the problem we face."

Dimak got up from the bunk. "It's nice to know that your study time isn't completely wasted on breaking into the computer system," he said.

With that parting shot, he left the barracks.

Bean got up and walked back to his own bunk, where he got dressed. No time for a shower now, and it didn't matter anyway. Because he knew that he had struck a nerve in what he said to Dimak. The Second Bugger War hadn't exhausted humanity's resources, Bean was sure of that. The problems of defending a planet were so obvious that the I.F. couldn't possibly have missed them, especially not in the aftermath of a nearly-lost war. They knew they had to attack. They built the fleet. They launched it. It was gone. It was inconceivable that they had done anything else.

So what was all this nonsense with the Battle School for? Was Dimak right, that Battle School was simply about building up the defensive fleet around Earth to counter any enemy assault that might have passed our invasion fleet on the way?

If that were true, there would be no reason to conceal it. No reason to lie. In fact, all the propaganda on Earth was devoted to telling people how vital it was to prepare for the next Bugger invasion. So Dimak had done nothing more than repeat the story that the I.F. had been telling everybody on Earth for three generations. Yet Dimak was sweating like a fish. Which suggested that the story wasn't true.

The defensive fleet around Earth was already fully manned, that was the problem. The normal process of recruitment would have been enough. Defensive war didn't take brilliance, just alertness. Early detection, cautious interception, protection of an adequate reserve. Success depended not on the quality of command, but on the quantity of available ships and the quality of the weaponry. There was no reason for Battle School—Battle School only made sense in the context of an offensive war, a war where maneuver, strategy, and tactics would play an important role. But the offensive fleet was already gone. For all Bean knew, the battle had already been fought years ago and the I.F. was just waiting for news about whether we had won or lost. It all depended on how many lightyears away the Bugger home planet was.

For all we know, thought Bean, the war is already over, the I.F. knows that we won, and they simply haven't told anybody.

And the reason for that was obvious. The only thing that had ended war on Earth and bound together all of humanity was a common cause—defeating the Buggers. As soon as it was known that the Bugger threat was eliminated, all the pent-up hostilities would be released. Whether it was the Muslim world against the West, or long-restrained Russian imperialism and paranoia against the Atlantic alliance, or Indian adventurism, or . . . or all of them at once. Chaos. The resources of the International Fleet would be co-opted by mutinying commanders from one faction or another. Conceivably it could mean the destruction of Earth—without any help from the Formics at all.

That's what the I.F. was trying to prevent. The terrible cannibalistic war that would follow. Just as Rome tore itself apart in civil war after the final elimination of Carthage—only far worse, because the weapons were more terrible and the hatreds far deeper, national and religious hatreds rather than the mere personal rivalries among leading citizens of Rome.

The I.F. was determined to prevent it.

In that context, Battle School made perfect sense. For many years, almost every child on Earth had been tested, and those with any potential brilliance in military command were taken out of their homeland and put into space. The best of the Battle School graduates, or at least those most loyal to the I.F., might very well be used to command armies when the I.F. finally announced the end of the war and struck preemptively to eliminate national armies and unify the world, finally and permanently, under one government. But the main purpose of the Battle School was to get these kids off Earth so that they could not become commanders of the armies of any one nation or faction.

After all, the invasion of France by the major European powers after the French Revolution led to the desperate French government discovering and promoting Napoleon, even though in the end he seized the reins of power instead of just defending the nation. The I.F. was determined that there would be no Napoleons on Earth to lead the resistance. All the potential Napoleons were here, wearing silly uniforms and battling each other for supremacy in a stupid game. It was all pig lists. By taking us, they have tamed the world.

"If you don't get dressed, you'll be late for class," said

Nikolai, the boy who slept on the bottommost bunk directly across from Bean.

"Thanks," said Bean. He shed his dry towel and hurriedly pulled on his uniform.

"Sorry I had to tell them about your using my password," said Nikolai.

Bean was dumbfounded.

"I mean, I didn't *know* it was you, but they started asking me what I was looking for in the emergency map system, and since I didn't know what they were talking about, it wasn't hard to guess that somebody was signing on as me, and there you are, in the perfect place to see my desk whenever I sign on, and . . . I mean, you're really smart. But it's not like I set out to tell on you."

"That's fine," said Bean. "Not a problem."

"But, I mean, what *did* you find out? From the maps?"

Until this moment, Bean would have blown off the question—and the boy. Nothing much, I was just curious, that's what he would have said. But now his whole world had changed. Now it mattered that he have connections with the other boys, not so he could show his leadership ability to the teachers, but so that when war did break out on Earth, and when the I.F.'s little plan failed, as it was bound to do, he would know who his allies and enemies were among the commanders of the various national and factional armies.

For the I.F.'s plan *would* fail. It was a miracle it hadn't failed already. It depended too heavily on millions of soldiers and commanders being more loyal to the I.F. than to their homeland. It would not happen. The I.F. itself would break up into factions, inevitably.

But the plotters no doubt were aware of that danger. They would have kept the number of plotters as small as possible—perhaps only the triumvirate of Hegemon, Strategos, and Polemarch and maybe a few people here at Battle School. Because this station was the heart of the plan. Here was where every single gifted commander for two generations had been studied intimately. There were records on every one of them—who was most talented, most valuable. What their weaknesses were, both in character and in command. Who their friends were. What their loyalties were. Which of them, therefore, should be approached to command the I.F.'s forces in the intrahuman wars to come, and which should be stripped of command and held incommunicado until hostilities were over.

No wonder they were worried about Bean's lack of participation in their little mind game. It made him an unknown quantity. It made him dangerous.

Now it was even more dangerous for Bean to play than ever. Not playing might make them suspicious and fearful—but in whatever move they planned against him, at least they wouldn't know anything about him. While if he did play, then they might be less suspicious—but if they did move against him, they would do it knowing whatever information the game gave to them. And Bean was not at all confident of his ability to outplay the game. Even if he tried to give them misleading results, that strategy in itself might tell them more about him than he wanted them to know.

And there was another possibility, too. He might be completely wrong. There might be key information that he did not have. Maybe no fleet had been launched. Maybe they hadn't defeated the Buggers at their home world. Maybe there really was a desperate effort to build a defensive fleet. Maybe maybe maybe.

Bean had to get more information in order to have some hope that his analysis was correct and that his choices would be valid.

And Bean's isolation had to end.

"Nikolai," said Bean, "you wouldn't believe what I found out from those maps. Did you know there are nine decks, not just four?"

"Nine?"

"And that's just in this wheel. There are two other wheels they never tell us about."

"But the pictures of the station show only the one wheel."

"Those pictures were all taken when there *was* only one wheel. But in the plans, there are three. Parallel to each other, turning together."

Nikolai looked thoughtful. "But that's just the plans. Maybe they never built those other wheels."

"Then why would they still have maps for them in the emergency system?"

Nikolai laughed. "My father always said, bureaucrats never throw anything away."

Of course. Why hadn't he thought of that? The emergency map system was no doubt programmed before the first wheel was ever brought into service. So all those maps would already be in the system, even if the other wheels were never built, even if two-thirds of the maps would never have a corridor wall to be displayed on. No one would bother to go into the system and clean them out.

"I never thought of that," said Bean. He knew, given his reputation for brilliance, that he could pay Nikolai no higher compliment. As indeed the reaction of the other kids in nearby bunks showed. No one had ever had such a conversation with Bean before. No one had ever thought of something that Bean hadn't obviously thought of first. Nikolai was blushing with pride.

"But the nine decks, that makes sense," said Nikolai.

"Wish I knew what was on them," said Bean.

"Life support," said the girl named Corn Moon. "They got to be making oxygen somewhere here. That takes a lot of plants."

More kids joined in. "And staff. All we ever see are teachers and nutritionists."

"And maybe they *did* build the other wheels. We don't *know* they didn't."

The speculation ran rampant through the group. And at the center of it all: Bean.

Bean and his new friend, Nikolai.

"Come on," said Nikolai, "we'll be late for math."

Part Three

SCHOLAR

9

Garden of Sofia

"So he found out how many decks there are. What can he possibly do with that information?"

"Yes, that's the exact question. What was he planning, that he felt it necessary to find that out? Nobody else even looked for that, in the whole history of this school."

"You think he's plotting revolution?"

"All we know about this kid is that he survived on the streets of Rotterdam. It's a hellish place, from what I hear. The kids are vicious. They make *Lord of the Flies* look like *Pollyanna.*"

"When did you read *Pollyanna?*"

"It was a book?"

"How can he plot a revolution? He doesn't have any friends."

"I never said anything about revolution, that's *your* theory."

"I don't have a theory. I don't understand this kid. I never even wanted him up here. I think we should just send him home."

"No."

"No *sir,* I'm sure you meant to say."

"After three months in Battle School, he figured out that defensive war makes no sense and that we must have launched a fleet against the Bugger home worlds right after the end of the last war."

"He knows *that*? And you come telling me he knows how many *decks* there are?"

"He doesn't *know* it. He guessed. I told him he was wrong."

"I'm sure he believed you."

"I'm sure he's in doubt."

"This is all the more reason to send him back to Earth. Or out to some distant base somewhere. Do you realize the nightmare if there's a breach of security on this?"

"Everything depends on how he uses the information."

"Only we don't know anything about him, so we have no way of knowing how he'll use it."

"Sister Carlotta—"

"Do you *hate* me? That woman is even more inscrutable than your little dwarf."

"A mind like Bean's is not to be thrown away just because we fear there might be a security breach."

"Nor is security to be thrown away for the sake of one really smart kid."

"Aren't we smart enough to create new layers of deception for him? Let him find out something that he'll think is the truth. All we have to do is come up with a lie that we think he'll believe."

Sister Carlotta sat in the terrace garden, across the tiny table from the wizened old exile.

"I'm just an old Russian scientist living out the last years of his life on the shores of the Black Sea." Anton took a long drag on his cigarette and blew it out over the railing, adding it to the pollution flowing from Sofia out over the water.

"I'm not here with any law enforcement authority," said Sister Carlotta.

"You have something much more dangerous to me. You are from the Fleet."

"You're in no danger."

"That's true, but only because I'm not going to tell you anything."

"Thank you for your candor."

"You value candor, but I don't think you would appreciate it if I told you the thoughts your body arouses in the mind of this old Russian."

"Trying to shock nuns is not much sport. There is no trophy."

"So you take nunnitude seriously."

Sister Carlotta sighed. "You think I came here because I know something about you and you don't want me to find out more. But I came here because of what I can't find out about you."

"Which is?"

"Anything. Because I was researching a particular matter for the I.F., they gave me a summary of articles on the topic of research into altering the human genome."

"And my name came up?"

"On the contrary, your name was never mentioned."

"How quickly they forget."

"But when I read the few papers available from the people they did mention—always early work, before the I.F. security machine clamped down on them—I noticed a trend. Your name was always cited in their footnotes. Cited constantly. And yet not a word of yours could be found. Not even abstracts of papers. Apparently you have never published."

"And yet they quote me. Almost miraculous, isn't it? You people do collect miracles, don't you? To make saints?"

"No beatification until after you're dead, sorry."

"I have only one lung left as it is," said Anton. "So I don't have that long to wait, as long as I keep smoking."

"You could stop."

"With only one lung, it takes twice as many cigarettes to get the same nicotine. Therefore I have had to increase my smoking, not cut down. This should be obvious, but then, you do not think like a scientist, you think like a woman of faith. You think like an obedient person. When you find out something is bad, you don't do it."

"Your research was into genetic limitations on human intelligence."

"Was it?"

"Because it's in that area that you are always cited. Of course, these papers were never *about* that exact subject, or they too would have been classified. But the titles of the articles mentioned in the footnotes—the ones you never wrote, since you never published anything—are all tied to that area."

"It is so easy in a career to find oneself in a rut."

"So I want to ask you a hypothetical question."

"My favorite kind. Next to rhetorical ones. I can nap equally well through either kind."

"Suppose someone were to break the law and attempt to alter the human genome, specifically to enhance intelligence."

"Then someone would be in serious danger of being caught and punished."

"Suppose that, using the best available research, he found certain genes that he could alter in an embryo that would enhance the intelligence of the person when he was born."

"Embryo! Are you testing me? Such changes can only happen in the egg. A single cell."

"And suppose a child was born with these alterations in place. The child was born and he grew up enough for his great intelligence to be noticed."

"I assume you are not speaking of your own child."

"I'm speaking of no child at all. A hypothetical child. How would someone recognize that this child had been genetically altered? Without actually examining the genes."

Anton shrugged. "What does it matter if you examine the genes? They will be normal."

"Even though you altered them?"

"It is such a little change. Hypothetically speaking."

"Within the normal range of variation?"

"It is two switches, one that you turn on, one that you turn off. The gene is already there, you see."

"What gene?"

"Savants were the key, for me. Autistic, usually. Dysfunctional. They have extraordinary mental powers. Lightning-fast calculations. Phenomenal memories. But they are inept, even retarded in other areas. Square roots of twelve-digit numbers in seconds, but incapable of conducting a simple purchase in a store. How can they be so brilliant, and so stupid?"

"That gene?"

"No, it was another, but it showed me what was possible. The human brain could be far smarter than it is. But is there a, how you say, bargain?"

"Trade-off."

"A terrible bargain. To have this great intellect, you have to give up everything else. That's how the brains of autistic savants accomplish such feats. They do one thing, and the rest is a distraction, an annoyance, beyond the reach of any conceivable interest. Their attention truly is undivided."

"So all hyperintelligent people would be retarded in some other way."

"That is what we all assumed, because that is what we saw. The exceptions seemed to be only mild savants, who were thus able to spare some concentration on ordinary life. Then I thought . . . but I can't tell you what I thought, because I have been served with an order of inhibition."

He smiled helplessly. Sister Carlotta's heart fell. When someone was a proven security risk, they implanted in his brain a device that caused any kind of anxiety to launch a feedback loop, leading to a panic attack. Such people were then given periodic sensitization to make sure that they felt a great deal of anxiety when they contemplated talking about the forbidden subject. Viewed one way, it was a monstrous intrusion on a person's life; but if it was compared to the common practice of imprisoning or killing people who could not be trusted with a vital secret, an order of intervention could look downright humane.

That explained, of course, why Anton was amused by everything. He had to be. If he allowed himself to become agitated or angry—any strong negative emotion, really—then he would have a panic attack even without talking about forbidden subjects. Sister Carlotta had read an article once in which the wife of a man equipped with such a device said that their life together had never been happier, because now he took everything so calmly, with good humor. "The children love him now, instead of dreading his time at home." She said that, according to the article, only hours before he threw himself from a cliff. Life was better, apparently, for everyone but him.

And now she had met a man whose very memories had been rendered inaccessible.

"What a shame," said Sister Carlotta.

"But stay. My life here is a lonely one. You're a sister of mercy, aren't you? Have mercy on a lonely old man, and walk with me."

She wanted to say no, to leave at once. At that moment, however, he leaned back in his chair and began to breathe deeply, regularly, with his eyes closed, as he hummed a little tune to himself.

A ritual of calming. So . . . at the very moment of inviting her to walk with him, he had felt some kind of anxiety that triggered the device. That meant there was something important about his invitation.

"Of course I'll walk with you," she said. "Though technically my order is relatively unconcerned with mercy to individuals. We are far more pretentious than that. Our business is trying to save the world."

He chuckled. "One person at a time would be too slow, is that it?"

"We make our lives of service to the larger causes of humanity. The Savior already died for sin. We work on trying to clean up the consequences of sin on other people."

"An interesting religious quest," said Anton. "I wonder whether my old line of research would have been considered a service to humanity, or just another mess that someone like you would have to clean up."

"I wonder that myself," said Sister Carlotta.

"We will never know." They strolled out of the garden into the alley behind the house, and then to a street, and across it, and onto a path that led through an untended park.

"The trees here are very old," Sister Carlotta observed.

"How old are *you,* Carlotta?"

"Objectively or subjectively?"

"Stick to the Gregorian calendar, please, as most recently revised."

"That switch away from the Julian system still sticks in the Russian craw, does it?"

"It forced us for more than seven decades to commemorate an October Revolution that actually occurred in November."

"You are much too young to remember when there were Communists in Russia."

"On the contrary, I am old enough now to have all the memories of my people locked within my head. I remember things that happened long before I was born. I remember things that never happened at all. I live in memory."

"Is that a pleasant place to dwell?"

"Pleasant?" He shrugged. "I laugh at all of it because I must. Because it is so sweetly sad—all the tragedies, and yet nothing is learned."

"Because human nature never changes," she said.

"I have imagined," he said, "how God might have done

better, when he made man—in his own image, I believe."

"Male and female created he them. Making his image anatomically vague, one must suppose."

He laughed and clapped her rather too forcefully on the back. "I didn't know you could laugh about such things! I am pleasantly surprised!"

"I'm glad I could bring cheer into your bleak existence."

"And then you sink the barb into the flesh." They reached an overlook that had rather less of a view of the sea than Anton's own terrace. "It is not a bleak existence, Carlotta. For I can celebrate God's great compromise in making human beings as we are."

"Compromise?"

"Our bodies could live forever, you know. We don't have to wear out. Our cells are all alive; they can maintain and repair themselves, or be replaced by fresh ones. There are even mechanisms to keep replenishing our bones. Menopause need not stop a woman from bearing children. Our brains need not decay, shedding memories or failing to absorb new ones. But God made us with death inside."

"You are beginning to sound serious about God."

"God made us with death inside, and also with intelligence. We have our seventy years or so—perhaps ninety, with care—in the mountains of Georgia, a hundred and thirty is not unheard of, though I personally believe they are all liars. They would claim to be immortal if they thought they could get away with it. We could live forever, if we were willing to be stupid the whole time."

"Surely you're not saying that God had to choose between long life and intelligence for human beings!"

"It's there in your own Bible, Carlotta. Two trees—knowledge and life. You eat of the tree of knowledge, and you will surely die. You eat of the tree of life, and you remain a child in the garden forever, undying."

"You speak in theological terms, and yet I thought you were an unbeliever."

"Theology is a joke to me. Amusing! I laugh at it. I

can tell amusing stories about theology, to jest with believers. You see? It pleases me and keeps me calm."

At last she understood. How clearly did he have to spell it out? He was telling her the information she asked about, but doing it in code, in a way that fooled not only any eavesdroppers—and there might well be listeners to every word they said—but even his own mind. It was all a jest; therefore he could tell her the truth, as long as he did it in this form.

"Then I don't mind hearing your wild humorous forays into theology."

"Genesis tells of men who lived to be more than nine hundred years old. What it does not tell you is how very stupid these men all were."

Sister Carlotta laughed aloud.

"That's why God had to destroy humanity with his little flood," Anton went on. "Get rid of those stupid people and replace them with quicker ones. Quick quick quick, their minds moved, their metabolism. Rushing onward into the grave."

"From Methuselah at nearly a millennium of life to Moses with his hundred and twenty years, and now to us. But our lives are getting longer."

"I rest my case."

"Are we stupider now?"

"So stupid that we would rather have long life for our children than see them become too much like God, knowing . . . good and evil . . . knowing . . . everything." He clutched at his chest, gasping. "Ah, God! God in heaven!" He sank to his knees. His breath was shallow and rapid now. His eyes rolled back in his head. He fell over.

Apparently he hadn't been able to maintain his self-deception. His body finally caught on to how he had managed to tell his secret to this woman by speaking it in the language of religion.

She rolled him onto his back. Now that he had fainted, his panic attack was subsiding. Not that fainting was trivial in a man of Anton's age. But he would not need any heroism to bring him back, not this time. He would wake up calm.

Where were the people who were supposed to be monitoring him? Where were the spies who were listening in to their conversation?

Pounding feet on the grass, on the leaves.

"A bit slow, weren't you?" she said without looking up.

"Sorry, we didn't expect anything." The man was youngish, but not terribly bright-looking. The implant was supposed to keep him from spilling his tale; it was not necessary for his guards to be clever.

"I think he'll be all right."

"What were you talking about?"

"Religion," she said, knowing that her account would probably be checked against a recording. "He was criticizing God for mis-making human beings. He claimed to be joking, but I think that a man of his age is never really joking when he talks about God, do you?"

"Fear of death gets in them," said the young man sagely—or at least as sagely as he could manage.

"Do you think he accidentally triggered this panic attack by agitating his own anxiety about death?" If she asked it as a question, it wasn't actually a lie, was it?

"I don't know. He's coming around."

"Well, I certainly don't want to cause him any more anxiety about religious matters. When he wakes up, tell him how grateful I am for our conversation. Assure him that he has clarified for me one of the great questions about God's purpose."

"Yes, I'll tell him," said the young man earnestly.

Of course he would garble the message hopelessly.

Sister Carlotta bent over and kissed Anton's cold, sweaty forehead. Then she rose to her feet and walked away.

So that was the secret. The genome that allowed a human being to have extraordinary intelligence acted by speeding up many bodily processes. The mind worked faster. The child developed faster. Bean was indeed the product of an experiment in unlocking the savant gene. He had been given the fruit of the tree of knowledge. But there was a price. He would not be able to taste of the tree of life. Whatever he did with his life, he would have to do it young, because he would not live to be old.

Anton had not done the experiment. He had not played God, bringing forth human beings who would live in an explosion of intelligence, sudden fireworks instead of single, long-burning candles. But he had found a key God had hidden in the human genome. Someone else, some follower, some insatiably curious soul, some would-be visionary longing to take human beings to the next stage of evolution or some other such mad, arrogant cause—this someone had taken the bold step of turning that key, opening that door, putting the killing, brilliant fruit into the hand of Eve. And because of that act—that serpentine, slithering crime—it was Bean who had been expelled from the garden. Bean who would now, surely, die—but die like a god, knowing good and evil.

10

Sneaky

"I can't help you. You didn't give me the information I asked for."

"We gave you the damned summaries."

"You gave me nothing and you know it. And now you come to me asking me to evaluate Bean for you—but you do not tell me why, you give me no context. You expect an answer but you deprive me of the means of providing it."

"Frustrating, isn't it?"

"Not for me. I simply won't give you any answer."

"Then Bean is out of the program."

"If your mind is made up, no answer of mine will change you, especially because you have made certain my answer will be unreliable."

"You know more than you've told me, and I must have it."

"How marvelous. You have achieved perfect empathy with me, for that is the exact statement I have repeatedly made to you."

"An eye for an eye? How Christian of you."

"Unbelievers always want *other* people to act like Christians."

"Perhaps you haven't heard, but there's a war on."

"Again, I could have said the same thing to you. There's a war on, yet you fence me around with foolish secrecy. Since there is no evidence of the Formic enemy spying on us, this secrecy is not about the war. It's about the Triumvirate maintaining their power over humanity. And I am not remotely interested in that."

"You're wrong. That information is secret in order to prevent some terrible experiments from being performed."

"Only a fool closes the door when the wolf is already inside the barn."

"Do you have proof that Bean is the result of a genetic experiment?"

"How can I prove it, when you have cut me off from all evidence? Besides, what matters is not *whether* he has altered genes, but what those genetic changes, if he has them, might lead him to do. Your tests were all designed to allow you to predict the behavior of normal human beings. They may not apply to Bean."

"If he's that unpredictable, then we can't rely on him. He's out."

"What if he's the only one who can win the war? Do you drop him from the program then?"

Bean didn't want to have much food in his body, not tonight, so he gave away almost all his food and turned in a clean tray long before anyone else was done. Let the nutritionist be suspicious—he had to have time alone in the barracks.

The engineers had always located the intake at the top of the wall over the door into the corridor. Therefore the air must flow into the room from the opposite end, where the extra bunks were unoccupied. Since he had not been able to see a vent just glancing around that end of the room, it had to be located under one of the lower bunks. He couldn't search for it when others would see him, because no one could be allowed to know that he was interested in the vents. Now, alone, he dropped to the floor and in moments was jimmying at the vent cover. It came off readily. He tried putting it back on, listening carefully for the level of noise that operation caused. Too much. The vent screen would have to stay off. He laid it on the floor beside the opening, but out of the way so he wouldn't accidentally bump into it in the darkness. Then, to be sure, he took it completely out from under that bunk and slid it under the one directly across.

Done. He then resumed his normal activities.

Until night. Until the breathing of the others told him that most, if not all, were asleep.

Bean slept naked, as many of the boys did—his uniform would not give him away. They were told to wear their towels when going to and from the toilet in the night, so Bean assumed that it, too, could be tracked. So as Bean slid down from his bunk, he pulled his towel from its hook on the bunk frame and wrapped it around himself as he trotted to the door of the barracks.

Nothing unusual. Toilet trips were allowed, if not encouraged, after lights out, and Bean had made it a point to make several such runs during his time in Battle School. No pattern was being violated. And it was a good idea to make his first excursion with an empty bladder.

When he came back, if anyone was awake all they saw was a kid in a towel heading back to his bunk.

But he walked past his bunk and quietly sank down and slid under the last bunk, where the uncovered vent awaited him. His towel remained on the floor under the bunk, so that if anyone woke enough to notice that Bean's bunk was empty, they would see that his towel was missing and assume he had gone to the toilet.

It was no less painful this time, sliding into the vent, but once inside, Bean found that his exercise had paid off. He was able to slide down at an angle, always moving slowly enough to make no noise and to avoid snagging his skin on any protruding metal. He wanted no injuries he'd have to explain.

In the utter darkness of the air duct, he had to keep his mental map of the station constantly in mind. The faint nightlight of each barracks cast only enough light into the air ducts to allow him to make out the location of each vent. But what mattered was not the location of the other barracks on this level. Bean had to get either up or down to a deck where teachers lived and worked. Judging from the amount of time it took Dimak to get to their barracks the rare times that a quarrel demanded his attention, Bean assumed that his quarters were on another deck. And because Dimak always arrived breathing a little heavily, Bean also assumed it was a deck below their own level, not above—Dimak had to climb a ladder, not slide down a pole, to reach them.

Nevertheless, Bean had no intention of going down first. He had to see whether he could successfully climb to a higher deck before getting himself potentially trapped on a lower one.

So when he finally—after passing three barracks—came to a vertical shaft, he did not climb down. Instead, he probed the walls to see how much larger it was than the horizontals. It was much wider—Bean could not reach all the way across it. But it was only slightly deeper, front to back. That was good. As long as Bean didn't work too hard and sweat too much, friction between his skin and the front and back walls of the duct would allow him to inch his way upward. And in the vertical duct, he could face forward, giving his neck a much-needed respite from being perpetually turned to one side.

Downward was almost harder than upward, because once he started sliding it was harder to stop. He was also aware that the lower he went, the heavier he would become. And he had to keep checking the wall beside him, looking for another side duct.

But he didn't have to find it by probing, after all. He

could see the side duct, because there was light in both directions. The teachers didn't have the same lights-out rules as the students, and their quarters were smaller, so that vents came more frequently, spilling more light into the duct.

In the first room, a teacher was awake and working at his desk. The trouble was that Bean, peering out of a vent screen near the floor, could not see a thing he was typing.

It would be that way in all the rooms. The floor vents would not work for him. He had to get into the air-intake system.

Back to the vertical duct. The wind was coming from above, and so that was where he had to go if he was to cross over from one system to another. His only hope was that the duct system would have an access door before he reached the fans, and that he would be able to find it in the dark.

Heading always into the wind, and finding himself noticeably lighter after climbing past seven decks, he finally reached a wider area with a small light strip. The fans were much louder, but he still wasn't near enough to see them. It didn't matter. He would be out of this wind.

The access door was clearly marked. It also might be wired to sound an alarm if it was opened. But he doubted it. That was the kind of thing that was done in Rotterdam to guard against burglars. Burglary wasn't a serious problem on space stations. This door would only have been alarmed if all doors in the station were fitted with alarms. He'd find out soon enough.

He opened the door, slipped out into a faintly lighted space, closed the door behind him.

The structure of the station was visible here, the beams, the sections of metal plating. There were no solid surfaces. The room was also noticeably colder, and not just because he was out of the hot wind. Cold hard space was on the other side of those curved plates. The furnaces might be located here, but the insulation was very good, and they had not bothered to pump much of that hot air into this space, relying instead on seepage to heat it. Bean hadn't been this cold since Rotterdam . . . but compared to wearing thin clothing in the winter streets with the wind off the North Sea, this was still almost balmy. It annoyed Bean that he had become so pampered here that he even cared about such a slight chill. And yet he couldn't keep himself from shivering a couple of times. Even in Rotterdam, he hadn't been naked.

Following the ductwork, he climbed up the workmen's ladderways to the furnaces and then found the air-intake ducts and followed them back down. It was easy to find an access door and enter the main vertical duct.

Because the air in the intake system did not have to be under positive pressure, the ducts did not have to be so narrow. Also, this was the part of the system where dirt had to be caught and removed, so it was more important to maintain access; by the time air got past the furnaces, it was already as clean as it was ever going to get. So instead of shinnying up and down narrow shafts, Bean scrambled easily down a ladder, and in the low light still had no trouble reading the signs telling which deck each side opening led to.

The side passages weren't really ducts at all. Instead, they consisted of the entire space between the ceiling of one corridor and the floor of the one above. All the wiring was here, and the water pipes—hot, cold, sewer. And besides the strips of dim worklights, the space was frequently lighted by the vents on both sides of the space—those same narrow strips of vent openings that Bean had seen from the floor below on his first excursion.

Now he could see easily down into each teacher's quarters. He crept along, making as little noise as possible—a skill he had perfected prowling through Rotterdam. He quickly found what he was looking for—a teacher who was awake, but not working at his desk. The man was not well known to Bean, because he supervised an older group of launchies and did not teach any of the classes Bean was taking. He was heading for a shower. That meant he would come back to the room and, perhaps, would sign in again, allowing Bean to have a chance at getting both his log-in name and his password.

No doubt the teachers changed passwords often, so whatever he got wouldn't last long. Moreover, it was always possible that attempting to use a teacher's password on a student desk might set off some kind of alarm. But Bean doubted it. The whole security system was designed to shut students out, to monitor student behavior. The teachers would not be so closely watched. They frequently worked on their desks at odd hours, and they also frequently signed on to student desks during the day to call on their more powerful tools to help solve a student's problem or give a student more personalized computer resources. Bean was reasonably sure that the risk of discovery was outweighed by the benefits of snagging a teacher's identity.

While he waited, he heard voices a few rooms up. He wasn't quite close enough to make out the words. Did he dare risk missing the bather's return?

Moments later he was looking down into the quarters of . . . Dimak himself. Interesting. He was talking to a man whose holographic image appeared in the air over his desk. Colonel Graff, Bean realized. The commandant of Battle School.

"My strategy was simple enough," Graff was saying. "I gave in and got her access to the stuff she wanted. She was right, I can't get good answers from her unless I let her see the data she's asking for."

"So did she give you any answers?"

"No, too soon. But she gave me a very good question."

"Which is?"

"Whether the boy is actually human."

"Oh, come on. Does she think he's a Bugger larva in a human suit?"

"Nothing to do with the Buggers. Genetically enhanced. It would explain a lot."

"But still human, then."

"Isn't that debatable? The difference between humans and chimpanzees is genetically slight. Between humans and neanderthals it had to be minute. How much difference would it take for him to be a different species?"

"Philosophically interesting, but in practical terms—"

"In practical terms, we don't know what this kid will do. There's no data on his species. He's a primate, which suggests certain regularities, but we can't assume anything about his motivations that—"

"Sir, with all due respect, he's still a kid. He's a human being. He's not some alien—"

"That's precisely what we've got to find out before we determine how much we can rely on him. And that's why you are to watch him even more carefully. If you can't get him into the mind game, then find some other way to figure out what makes him tick. Because we can't use him until we know just how much we can rely on him."

Interesting that they openly call it the mind game among themselves, thought Bean.

Then he realized what they were saying. "Can't get him into the mind game." As far as Bean knew, he was the only kid who didn't play the fantasy game. They were talking about him. New species. Genetically altered. Bean felt his heart pounding in his chest. What am I? Not just smart, but . . . different.

"What about the breach of security?" Dimak asked.

"That's the other thing. You've got to figure out what he knows. Or at least how likely he is to spill it to any other kids. That's the greatest danger right now. Is the possibility of this kid being the commander we need great enough to balance the risk of breaching security and collapsing the program? I thought with Ender we had an all-or-nothing long-odds bet, but this one makes Ender look like a sure thing."

"I didn't think of you as a gambler, sir."

"I'm not. But sometimes you're forced into the game."

"I'm on it, sir."

"Encrypt everything you send me on him. No names.

No discussions with other teachers beyond the normal. Contain this."

"Of course."

"If the only way we can beat the Buggers is to replace ourselves with a new species, Dimak, then have we really saved humanity?"

"One kid is not replacement of a species," said Dimak.

"Foot in the door. Camel's nose in the tent. Give them an inch."

"*Them,* sir?"

"Yes, I'm paranoid and xenophobic. That's how I got this job. Cultivate those virtues and you, too, might rise to my lofty station."

Dimak laughed. Graff didn't. His head disappeared from the display.

Bean had the discipline to remember that he was waiting to get a password. He crept back to the bather's room.

Still not back.

What breach of security were they talking about? It must have been recent, for them to be discussing it with such urgency. That meant it had to be Bean's conversation with Dimak about what was really going on with the Battle School. And yet his guess that the battle had already happened could not be it, or Dimak and Graff would not be talking about how he might be the only way they could beat the Buggers. If the Buggers were still unbeaten, the breach of security had to be something else.

It could still be that his earlier guess was partly right, and Battle School existed as much to strip the Earth of good commanders as to beat the Buggers. Graff and Dimak's fear might be that Bean would let other kids in on the secret. For some of them, at least, it might rekindle their loyalty to the nation or ethnic group or ideology of their parents.

And since Bean had definitely been planning to probe the loyalties of other students over the next months and years, he now would have to be doubly cautious not to let his pattern of conversation attract the attention of the teachers. All he needed to know was which of the best and brightest kids had the strongest home loyalties. Of course, for that Bean would need to figure out just how loyalty worked, so he would have some idea of how to weaken it or strengthen it, how to exploit it or turn it.

But just because this first guess of Bean's could explain their words didn't mean it was right. And just because the final Bugger war had not yet been fought didn't mean his initial guess was completely wrong. They might, for instance, have launched a fleet against the Bugger home world years ago, but were still preparing commanders to fight off an invasion fleet now approaching Earth. In that case, the security breach Graff and Dimak feared was that Bean would frighten others by letting them know how urgent and dire the situation of humanity was.

The irony was that of all the children Bean had ever known, none could keep a secret as well as he did. Not even Achilles, for in refusing his share of Poke's bread, he had tipped his hand.

Bean could keep a secret, but he also knew that sometimes you had to give some hint of what you knew in order to get more information. That was what had prompted Bean's conversation with Dimak. It was dangerous, but in the long run, if he could keep them from removing him from the school entirely in order to silence him—not to mention keeping them from killing him—he had learned more important information than he had given them. In the end, the only things they could learn from him were about himself. And what he learned from them was about everything else—a much larger pool of knowledge.

Himself. That was their puzzle—who he was. Silly to be concerned about whether he was human. What else *could* he be? He had never seen any child show any desire or emotion that he himself had not felt. The only difference was that Bean was stronger, and did not let his fleeting needs and passions control his actions. Did that make him alien? He was human—only better.

The teacher came back into the room. He hung up his damp towel, but even before he dressed he sat back down and logged on. Bean watched his fingers move over the keys. It was so quick. A blur of keystrokes. He would have to replay the memory in his mind many times to make sure. But at least he had seen it; nothing obstructed his view.

Bean crawled back toward the vertical intake shaft. The evening's expedition had already taken as long as he dared—he needed his sleep, and every minute away increased the risk of chance discovery.

In fact, he had been very lucky on this first foray through the ducts. To happen to hear Dimak and Graff conversing about him, to happen to watch a teacher who conveniently gave him a clear view of his log-in. For a moment it crossed Bean's mind that they might know he was in the air system, might even have staged all this for him, to see what he'd do. It might be just one more experiment.

No. It wasn't just luck that this teacher showed him the log-in. Bean had chosen to watch him because he was going to shower, because his desk was sitting on the table in such a way that Bean had a reasonable chance of seeing the log-in. It was an intelligent choice on Bean's part. He had gone with the best odds, and it paid off.

As for Dimak and Graff, it might have been chance that he overheard them talking, but it was his own choice to move closer at once in order to hear. And, come to think of it, he had chosen to go exploring in the ducts because of precisely the same event that had prompted Graff and Dimak to be so concerned. Nor was it a surprise that their conversation happened after lights-out for the children—that's when things would have quieted down, and, with duties done, there would be time for a conversation without Graff calling Dimak in for a special meeting, which might arouse questions in the minds of the other teachers. Not luck, really—Bean had made his own luck. He saw the log-in and overheard the conversation because he had made that quick decision to get into the intake system and acted on it at once.

He had always made his own luck.

Maybe that was something that went along with whatever genetic alteration Graff had found out about.

She, they had said. *She* had raised the question of whether Bean was genetically human. Some woman who was searching for information, and Graff had given in, was letting her have access to facts that had been hidden from her. That meant that he would receive more answers from this woman as she began to use that new data. More answers about Bean's origins.

Could it be Sister Carlotta who had doubted Bean's humanity?

Sister Carlotta, who wept when he left her and went into space? Sister Carlotta, who loved him as a mother loves her child? How could *she* doubt him?

If they wanted to find some inhuman human, some alien in a human suit, they ought to take a good long look at a nun who embraces a child as her own, and then goes around casting doubt about whether he's a real boy. The opposite of Pinocchio's fairy. She touches a real boy and turns him into something awful and fearful.

It could not have been Sister Carlotta they were talking about. Just another woman. His guess that it might be her was simply wrong, just like his guess that the final battle with the Buggers had already happened. That's why Bean never fully trusted his own guesses. He acted on them, but always kept himself open to the possibility that his interpretations might be wrong.

Besides, *his* problem was not figuring out whether he really was human or not. Whatever he was, he was himself and must act in such a way as to not only stay alive but also get as much control over his own future as possible. The only danger to him was that *they* were concerned about the issue of his possible genetic alteration. Bean's task was therefore to appear so normal that their fears on that score would be dispelled.

But how could he pretend to be normal? He hadn't been brought here because he was normal, he was brought here because he was extraordinary. For that matter, so were all the other kids. And the school put so much strain on them that some became downright odd. Like Bonzo Madrid, with his loud vendetta against Ender Wiggin. So in fact, Bean shouldn't appear normal, he should appear weird in the expected ways.

Impossible to fake that. He didn't know yet what signs the teachers were looking for in the behavior of the children here. He could find ten things to do, and do them, never guessing that there were ninety things he hadn't noticed.

No, what he had to do was not to *act* in predictable ways, but to *become* what they hoped their perfect commander would be.

When he got back to his barracks, climbed back up to his bunk, and checked the time on his desk, he found that he had done it all in less than an hour. He put away his desk and lay there replaying in his mind the image in his memory of the teacher's fingers, logging in. When he was reasonably certain of what the log-in and password were, he allowed himself to drift toward sleep.

Only then, as he was beginning to doze, did he realize what his perfect camouflage would be, quelling their fears and bringing him both safety and advancement.

He had to become Ender Wiggin.

11

Daddy

"Sir. I asked for a private interview."

"Dimak is here because your breach of security affects his work."

"Breach of security! This is why you reassign me?"

"There is a child who used your log-in to the master teacher system. He found the log-in record files and rewrote them to give himself an identity."

"Sir, I have faithfully adhered to all regulations. I never sign on in front of the students."

"Everyone *says* they never sign on, but then it turns out they do."

"Excuse me, sir, but Uphanad does not. He's always on the others when he catches them doing it. Actually, he's kind of anal about it. Drives us all crazy."

"You can check my log-in records. I never sign on during teaching hours. In fact, I never sign on outside my quarters."

"Then how could this child possibly get in using your log-in?"

"My desk sits on my table, like so. If I may use your desk to demonstrate."

"Of course."

"I sit like so. I keep my back to the door so no one can even see in. I never sign on in any other position."

"Well it's not like there's a window he can peek through!"

"Yes there is, sir."

"Dimak?"

"There *is* a window, sir. Look. The vent."

"Are you seriously suggesting that he could—"

"He *is* the smallest child who ever—"

"It was that little *Bean* child who got my log-in?"

"Excellent, Dimak, you've managed to let his name slip out, haven't you."

"I'm sorry, sir."

"Ah. Another security breach. Will you send Dimak home with me?"

"I'm not sending anybody home."

"Sir, I must point out that Bean's intrusion into the master teacher system is an excellent opportunity."

"To have a student romping through the student data files?"

"To study Bean. We don't have him in the fantasy game, but now we have the game *he* chooses to play. We watch where he goes in the system, what he does with this power he has created for himself."

"But the damage he can do is—"

"He won't do any damage, sir. He won't do anything to give himself away. This kid is too street-smart. It's information he wants. He'll look, not touch."

"So you've got him analyzed already, is that it? You know what he's doing at all times?"

"I know that if there's a story we really want him to believe, he has to discover it himself. He has to *steal* it from us. So I think this little security breach is the perfect way to heal a much more important one."

"What I'm wondering is, if he's been crawling through the ducts, what *else* has he heard?"

"If we close off the duct system, he'll know he was caught, and then he won't trust what we set up for him to find."

"So I have to permit a child to crawl around through the ductwork and—"

"He can't do it much longer. He's growing, and the ducts are extremely shallow."

"That's not much comfort right now. And, unfortunately, we'll still have to kill Uphanad for knowing too much."

"Please assure me that you're joking."

"Yes, I'm joking. You'll have him as a student soon enough, Captain Uphanad. Watch him very carefully. Speak of him only with me. He's unpredictable and dangerous."

"Dangerous. Little Bean."

"He cleaned *your* clock, didn't he?"

"Yours too, sir, begging your pardon."

Bean worked his way through every student at Battle School, reading the records of a half dozen or so per day. Their original scores, he found, were the least interesting thing about them. Everyone here had such high scores on all the tests given back on Earth that the differences were almost trivial. Bean's own scores were the highest, and the gap between him and the next highest, Ender Wiggin, was wide—as wide as the gap between Ender and the next child after him. But it was all relative. The difference between Ender and Bean amounted to half of a percentage point; most of the children clustered between 97 and 98 percent.

Of course, Bean knew what they could not know, that for him getting the highest possible score on the tests had been easy. He could have done more, he could have done better, but he had reached the boundary of what the test could discover. The gap between him and Ender was much wider than they supposed.

And yet . . . in reading the records, Bean came to see that the scores were merely a guide to a child's potential. The teachers talked most about things like cleverness, insight, intuition; the ability to develop rapport, to outguess an opponent; the courage to act boldly, the caution to make certain before committing, the wisdom to know which course was the appropriate one. And in considering this, Bean realized that he was not necessarily any better at *these* things than the other students.

Ender Wiggin really did know things that Bean did not know. Bean might have thought to do as Wiggin did, arranging extra practices to make up for being with a commander who wouldn't train him. Bean even might have tried to bring in a few other students to train with him, since many things could not be done alone. But Wiggin had taken all comers, no matter how difficult it became to practice with so many in the battleroom, and according to the teachers' notes, he spent more time now training others than in working on his own technique. Of course, that was partly because he was no longer in Bonzo Madrid's army, so he got to take part in the regular practices. But he still kept working with the other kids, especially the eager launchies who wanted a head start before they were promoted into a regular army. Why?

Is he doing what I'm doing, studying the other students to prepare for a later war on Earth? Is he building some kind of network that reaches out into all the armies? Is he somehow mistraining them, so he can take advantage of their mistakes later?

From what Bean heard about Wiggin from the kids in his launch group who attended those practices, he came to realize that it was something else entirely. Wiggin seemed really to care about the other kids doing their best. Did he need so badly for them to like him? Because it was working, if that's what he was trying for. They worshiped him.

But there had to be more to it than some hunger for love. Bean couldn't get a handle on it.

He found that the teachers' observations, while helpful, didn't really help him get inside Wiggin's head. For one thing, they kept the psychological observations from the mind game somewhere else that Bean didn't have access to. For another, the teachers couldn't really get into Wiggin's mind because they simply didn't think at his level.

Bean did.

But Bean's project wasn't to analyze Wiggin out of scientific curiosity, or to compete with him, or even to understand him. It was to make himself into the kind of child that the teachers would trust, would rely on. Would regard as fully human. For that project, Wiggin was his teacher because Wiggin had already done what Bean needed to do.

And Wiggin had done it without being perfect. Without being, as far as Bean could tell, completely sane. Not that anyone was. But Wiggin's willingness to give up hours every day to training kids who could do nothing for him—the more Bean thought about it, the less sense it made. Wiggin was not building a network of supporters. Unlike Bean, he didn't have a perfect memory, so Bean was quite sure Wiggin was not compiling a mental dossier on every other kid in Battle School. The kids he worked with were not the best, and were often the most fearful and dependent of the launchies and of the losers in the regular armies. They came to him because they thought being in the same room with the soldier who was leading in the standings might bring some luck to them. But why did Wiggin keep giving his time to *them?*

Why did Poke die for me?

That was the same question. Bean knew it. He found several books about ethics in the library and called them up on his desk to read. He soon discovered that the only theories that explained altruism were bogus. The stupidest was the old sociobiological explanation of uncles dying for nephews—there were no blood ties in armies now, and people often died for strangers. Community theory was fine as far as it went—it explained why communities all honored sacrificial heroes in their stories and rituals, but it still didn't explain the heroes themselves.

For that was what Bean saw in Wiggin. This was the hero at his root.

Wiggin really does not care as much about himself as he does about these other kids who aren't worth five minutes of his time.

And yet this may be the very trait that makes everyone focus on him. Maybe this is why in all those stories Sister Carlotta told him, Jesus always had a crowd around him.

Maybe this is why I'm so afraid of Wiggin. Because *he's* the alien, not me. He's the unintelligible one, the unpredictable one. He's the one who doesn't do things for sensible, predictable reasons. I'm going to survive, and once you know that, there's nothing more to know about me. Him, though, he could do anything.

The more he studied Wiggin, the more mysteries Bean uncovered. The more he determined to act like Wiggin until, at some point, he came to see the world as Wiggin saw it.

But even as he tracked Wiggin—still from a distance—what Bean could not let himself do was what the younger kids did, what Wiggin's disciples did. He could not call him Ender. Calling him by his last name kept him at a distance. A microscope's distance, anyway.

What did Wiggin study when he read on his own? Not the books of military history and strategy that Bean had blown through in a rush and was now rereading methodically, applying everything to both space combat and modern warfare on Earth. Wiggin did his share of reading, too, but when he went into the library he was just as likely to look at combat vids, and the ones he watched most often were of Bugger ships. Those and the clips of Mazer Rackham's strike force in the heroic battle that broke the back of the Second Invasion.

Bean watched them too, though not over and over again—once he saw them, he remembered them perfectly and could replay them in his mind, with enough detail that he could notice things later that he hadn't realized at first. Was Wiggin seeing something new each time he went back to these vids? Or was he looking for something that he hadn't yet found?

Is he trying to understand the way the Buggers think? Why doesn't he realize that the library here simply doesn't have enough of the vids to make it useful? It's all propaganda stuff here. They withheld all the terrible scenes of dead guys, of fighting and killing hand to hand when ships were breached and boarded. They didn't have vids of defeats, where the Buggers blew the human ships out of the sky. All they had here was ships moving around in space, a few minutes of preparation for combat.

War in space? So exciting in the made-up stories, so boring in reality. Occasionally something would light up, mostly it was just dark.

And, of course, the obligatory moment of Mazer Rackham's victory.

What could Wiggin possibly hope to learn?

Bean learned more from the omissions than from what he actually saw. For instance, there was not one picture of Mazer Rackham anywhere in the library. That was odd. The Triumvirates' faces were everywhere, as were those of other commanders and political leaders. Why not Rackham? Had he died in the moment of victory? Or was he, perhaps, a fictitious figure, a deliberately-created legend, so that there could be a name to peg the victory to? But if that were the case, they'd have created a face for him—it was too easy to do that. Was he deformed?

Was he really, really small?

If I grow up to be the commander of the human fleet that defeats the Buggers, will they hide my picture, too, because someone so tiny can never be seen as a hero?

Who cares? I don't want to be a hero.

That's Wiggin's gig.

—

Nikolai, the boy across from him. Bright enough to make some guesses Bean hadn't made first. Confident enough not to get angry when he caught Bean intruding on him. Bean was so hopeful when he came at last to Nikolai's file.

The teacher evaluation was negative. "A place-holder." Cruel—but was it true?

Bean realized: I have been putting too much trust in the teachers' evaluations. Do I have any real evidence that they're right? Or do I believe in their evaluations because I am rated so highly? Have I let them flatter me into complacency?

What if all their evaluations were hopelessly wrong?

I had no teacher files on the streets of Rotterdam. I actually knew the children. Poke—I made my own judgment of her, and I was almost right, just a few surprises here and there. Sergeant—no surprises at all. Achilles—yes, I knew him.

So why have I stayed apart from the other students? Because they isolated me at first, and because I decided that the teachers had the power. But now I see that I was only partly right. The teachers have the power here and now, but someday I will not be in Battle School, and what does it matter then what the teachers think of me? I can learn all the military theory and history that I want, and it will do me no good if they never entrust me with command. And I will never be placed in charge of an army or a fleet unless they have reason to believe that other men would follow me.

Not men today, but boys, most of them, a few girls. Not men, but they *will* be men. How do they choose their leaders? How do I make them follow one who is so small, so resented?

What did Wiggin do?

Bean asked Nikolai which of the kids in their launch group practiced with Wiggin.

"Only a few. And they on the fringes, neh? Suckups and brags."

"But who are they?"

"You trying to get in with Wiggin?"

"Just want to find out about him."

"What you want to know?"

The questions bothered Bean. He didn't like talking so much about what he was doing. But he didn't sense any malice in Nikolai. He just wanted to know.

"History. He the best, neh? How he get that way?" Bean wondered if he sounded quite natural with the soldier slang. He hadn't used it that much. The music of it, he still wasn't quite there.

"You find out, you tell me." He rolled his eyes in self-derision.

"I'll tell you," said Bean.

"I got a chance to be best like Ender?" Nikolai laughed. "*You* got a chance, the way you learn."

"Wiggin's snot ain't honey," said Bean.

"What does that mean?"

"He human like anybody. I find out, I tell you, OK?"

Bean wondered why Nikolai already despaired about his own chances of being one of the best. Could it be that the teachers' negative evaluation was right after all? Or had they unconsciously let him see their disdain for him, and he believed them?

From the boys Nikolai had pointed out—the brags and suckups, which wasn't an inaccurate evaluation as far as it went—Bean learned what he wanted to know. The names of Wiggin's closest friends.

Shen. Alai. Petra—her again! But Shen the longest.

Bean found him in the library during study time. The only reason to go there was for the vids—all the books could be read from the desks. Shen wasn't watching vids, though. He had his desk with him, and he was playing the fantasy game.

Bean sat down beside him to watch. A lion-headed man in chain mail stood before a giant, who seemed to be offering him a choice of drinks—the sound was shaped so that Bean couldn't hear it from beside the desk, though

Shen seemed to be responding; he typed in a few words. His lion-man figure drank one of the substances and promptly died.

Shen muttered something and shoved the desk away.

"That the Giant's Drink?" said Bean. "I heard about that."

"You've never played it?" said Shen. "You can't win it. I *thought.*"

"I heard. Didn't sound fun."

"*Sound* fun? You haven't tried it? It's not like it's hard to find."

Bean shrugged, trying to fake the mannerisms he'd seen other boys use. Shen looked amused. Because Bean did the cool-guy shrug wrong? Or because it looked cute to have somebody so small do it?

"Come on, you don't play the fantasy game?"

"What you said," Bean prompted him. "You *thought* nobody ever won it."

"I saw a guy in a place I'd never seen. I asked him where it was, and he said, 'Other side of the Giant's Drink.' "

"He tell you how to get there?"

"I didn't ask."

"Why not?"

Shen grinned, looked away.

"It be Wiggin, neh?" asked Bean.

The grin faded. "I didn't say that."

"I know you're his friend, that's why I came here."

"What is this? You spying on him? You from Bonzo?"

This was not going well. Bean hadn't realized how protective Wiggin's friends might be. "I'm from me. Look, nothing bad, OK? I just—look, I just want to know about—you know him from the start, right? They say you been his friend from launchy days."

"So what?"

"Look, he got friends, right? Like you. Even though he always does better in class, always the best on everything, right? But they don't hate him."

"Plenty bichão hate him."

"I got to make some friends, man." Bean knew that he shouldn't try to sound pitiful. Instead, he should sound like a pitiful kid who was trying really hard *not* to sound pitiful. So he ended his maudlin little plea with a laugh. As if he was trying to make it sound like a joke.

"You're pretty short," said Shen.

"Not on the planet I'm from," said Bean.

For the first time, Shen let a genuine smile come to his face. "The planet of the pygmies."

"Them boys too big for me."

"Look, I know what you're saying," said Shen. "I had this funny walk. Some of the kids were ragging me. Ender stopped them."

"How?"

"Ragged them more."

"I never heard he got a mouth."

"No, he didn't say nada. Did it on the desk. Sent a message from God."

Oh, yeah. Bean had heard about that. "He did that for you?"

"They were making fun of my butt. I had a big butt. Before workouts, you know? Back then. So he make fun of them for looking at my butt. But he signs it God."

"So they didn't know it was him."

"Oh, they knew. Right away. But he didn't *say* anything. Out loud."

"That's how you got to be friends? He the protector of the little guys?" Like Achilles . . .

"*Little* guys?" said Shen. "He was the smallest in our launch group. Not like you, but way small. Younger, see."

"He was youngest, but he became your protector?"

"No. Not like that. No, he kept it from going on, that's all. He went to the group—it was Bernard, he was getting together the biggest guys, the tough guys—"

"The bullies."

"Yeah, I guess. Only Ender, he goes to Bernard's number one, his best friend. Alai. He gets Alai to be his friend, too."

"So he stole away Bernard's support?"

"No, man. No, it's not like that. He made friends with Alai, and then got Alai to help him make friends with Bernard."

"Bernard . . . he's the one, Ender broke his arm in the shuttle."

"That's right. And I think, really, Bernard never forgave him, but he saw how things were."

"How were things?"

"Ender's *good,* man. You just—he doesn't hate anybody. If you're a good person, you're going to like him. You want him to like you. If he likes you, then you're OK, see? But if you're scum, he just makes you mad. Just knowing he exists, see? So Ender, he tries to wake up the good part of you."

"How do you wake up 'good parts'?"

"I don't know, man. You think I know? It just . . . you know Ender long enough, he just makes you want him to be proud of you. That sounds so . . . sounds like I'm a baby, neh?"

Bean shook his head. What it sounded like to him was devotion. Bean hadn't really understood this. Friends were friends, he thought. Like Sergeant and Poke used to be, before Achilles. But it was never love. When Achilles came, they loved him, but it was more like worship, like . . . a god, he got them bread, they gave bread back to him. Like . . . well, like what he called himself. Papa. Was it the same thing? Was Ender Achilles all over again?

"You're smart, kid," said Shen. "I was there, neh? Only I never once thought, How did Ender *do* it? How can I do the same, be like him? It's like that was Ender, he's great, but it's nothing *I* could do. Maybe I should have tried. I just wanted to be . . . *with* him."

"Cause you're good, too," said Bean.

Shen rolled his eyes. "I guess that's what I was saying,

wasn't it? Implying, anyway. Guess that makes me a brag, neh?"

"Big old brag," said Bean, grinning.

"He's just . . . he makes you want to . . . I'd die for him. That sounds like hero talk, neh? But it's true. I'd die for him. I'd kill for him."

"You'd fight for him."

Shen got it at once. "That's right. He's a born commander."

"Alai fight for him too?"

"A lot of us."

"But some not, yes?"

"Like I said, the bad ones, they hate him, he makes them crazy."

"So the whole world divides up—good people love Wiggin, bad people hate Wiggin."

Shen's face went suspicious again. "I don't know why I told you all that merda. You too smart to believe any of it."

"I do believe it," said Bean. "Don't be mad at me." He'd learned that one a long time ago. Little kid says, Don't be mad at me, they feel a little silly.

"I'm not mad," said Shen. "I just thought you were making fun of me."

"I wanted to know how Wiggin makes friends."

"If I knew that, if I really understood that, I'd have more friends than I do, kid. But I got Ender as my friend, and all his friends are my friends too, and I'm their friend, so . . . it's like a family."

A family. Papa. Achilles again.

That old dread returned. That night after Poke died. Seeing her body in the water. Then Achilles in the morning. How he acted. Was that Wiggin? Papa until he got his chance?

Achilles was evil, and Ender was good. Yet they both created a family. Both had people who loved them, who would die for them. Protector, papa, provider, mama. Only parent to a crowd of orphans. We're all street kids up here in Battle School, too. We might not be hungry, but we're all still wishing for a family.

Except me. Last thing I need. Some papa smiling at me, waiting with a knife.

Better to *be* the papa than to have one.

How can I do that? Get somebody to love me the way Shen loves Wiggin?

No chance. I'm too little. Too cute. I got nothing they want. All I can do is protect myself, work the system. Ender's got plenty to teach those that have some hope of doing what he's done. But me, I have to learn my own way.

Even as he made the decision, though, he knew he wasn't done with Wiggin. Whatever Wiggin had, whatever Wiggin knew, Bean *would* learn it.

And so passed the weeks, the months. Bean did all his regular classwork. He attended the regular battleroom classes with Dimak teaching them how to move and shoot, the basic skills. On his own he completed all the enrichment courses you could take at your own desk, certifying in everything. He studied military history, philosophy, strategy. He read ethics, religion, biology. He kept track of every student in the school, from the newly arrived launchies to the students about to graduate. When he saw them in the halls, he knew more about them than they knew about themselves. He knew their nation of origin. He knew how much they missed their families and how important their native country or ethnic or religious group was to them. He knew how valuable they might be to a nationalist or idealist resistance movement.

And he kept reading everything Wiggin read, watching everything Wiggin watched. Hearing about Wiggin from the other kids. Watching Wiggin's standings on the boards. Meeting more of Wiggin's friends, hearing them talk about him. Bean listened to all the things Wiggin was quoted as saying and tried to fit them into some coherent philosophy, some worldview, some attitude, some plan.

And he found out something interesting. Despite Wiggin's altruism, despite his willingness to sacrifice, not one of his friends ever said that Wiggin came and talked over his problems. They all went to Wiggin, but who did Wiggin go to? He had no more *real* friends than Bean did. Wiggin kept his own counsel, just like Bean.

Soon Bean found himself being advanced out of classes whose work he had already mastered and being plunged into classwork with older and older groups, who looked at him with annoyance at first, but later simply with awe, as he raced past them and was promoted again before they were half done. Had Wiggin been pushed through his classwork at an accelerated rate? Yes, but not quite as fast. Was that because Bean was better? Or because the deadline was getting closer?

For the sense of urgency in teacher evaluations was getting greater. The ordinary students—as if any child here were ordinary—were getting briefer and briefer notations. They weren't being ignored, exactly. But the best were being identified and lifted out.

The *seeming* best. For Bean began to realize that the teachers' evaluations were often colored by which students they liked the best. The teachers pretended to be dispassionate, impartial, but in fact they got sucked in by the more charismatic children, just as the other students did. If a kid was likable, they gave him better comments on leadership, even if he was really just glib and athletic and needed to surround himself with a team. As often as not, they tagged the very students who would be the least effective commanders, while ignoring the ones who, to Bean, showed real promise. It was frustrating to watch them make such obvious mistakes. Here they had Wiggin right before their eyes—Wiggin, who was the real thing—and they still went on misreading everybody else. Getting all excited about some of these energetic, self-confident, ambitious kids even though they weren't actually producing excellent work.

Wasn't this whole school set up in order to find and train the best possible commanders? The Earthside testing did pretty well—there were no real dolts among the students. But the system had overlooked one crucial factor: How were the teachers chosen?

They were career military, all of them. Proven officers with real ability. But in the military you don't get trusted positions just because of your ability. You also have to attract the notice of superior officers. You have to be liked. You have to fit in with the system. You have to look like what the officers above you think that officers should look like. You have to think in ways that they are comfortable with.

The result was that you ended up with a command structure that was top-heavy with guys who looked good in uniform and talked right and did well enough not to embarrass themselves, while the really good ones quietly did all the serious work and bailed out their superiors and got blamed for errors they had advised against until they eventually got out.

That was the military. These teachers were all the kind of people who thrived in that environment. And they were selecting their favorite students based on precisely that same screwed-up sense of priorities.

No wonder a kid like Dink Meeker saw through it and refused to play. He was one of the few kids who was both likable *and* talented. His likability made them try to make him commander of his own army; his talent let him understand why they were doing it and turn them down because he couldn't believe in such a stupid system. And other kids, like Petra Arkanian, who had obnoxious personalities but could handle strategy and tactics in their sleep, who had the confidence to lead others into war, to trust their own decisions and act on them—they didn't care about trying to be one of the guys, and so they got overlooked, every flaw became magnified, every strength belittled.

So Bean began constructing his own anti-army. Kids who weren't getting picked out by the teachers, but were the real talents, the ones with heart and mind, not just face and chat. He began to imagine who among them should be officers, leading their own toons under the command of . . .

Of Ender Wiggin, of course. Bean could not imagine anyone else in that position. Wiggin would know how to use them.

And Bean knew just where he should be. Close to Wiggin. A toon leader, but the most trusted of them. Wiggin's righthand man. So when Wiggin was about to make a mistake, Bean could point out to him the error he was making. And so that Bean could be close enough to maybe understand why Wiggin was human and he himself was not.

—

Sister Carlotta used her new security clearance like a scalpel, most of the time, slicing her way into the information establishment, picking up answers here and new questions there, talking to people who never guessed what her project was, why she knew so much about their top-secret work, and quietly putting it all together in her own mind, in memos to Colonel Graff.

But sometimes she wielded her top security clearance like a meat-ax, using it to get past prison wardens and security officers, who saw her unbelievable level of need-to-know and then, when they checked to make sure her documents weren't a stupid forgery, were screamed at by officers so high-ranked that it made them want to treat Sister Carlotta like God.

That's how, at last, she came face to face with Bean's father. Or at least the closest thing to a father that he had.

"I want to talk to you about your installation in Rotterdam."

He looked at her sourly. "I already reported on everything. That's why I'm not dead, though I wonder if I made the right choice."

"They told me you were quite the whiner," said Sister

Carlotta, utterly devoid of compassion. "I didn't expect it to surface so quickly."

"Go to hell." He turned his back on her.

As if that meant anything. "Dr. Volescu, the records show that you had twenty-three babies in your organ farm in Rotterdam."

He said nothing.

"But of course that's a lie."

Silence.

"And, oddly enough, I know that the lie is not your idea. Because I know that your installation was not an organ farm indeed, and that the reason you aren't dead is because you agreed to plead guilty to running an organ farm in exchange for never discussing what you were *really* doing there."

He slowly turned around again. Enough that he could look up and see her with a sidelong glance. "Let me see that clearance you tried to show me before."

She showed it to him again. He studied it.

"What do you know?" he asked.

"I know your real crime was continuing a research project after it was closed down. Because you had these fertilized eggs that had been meticulously altered. You had turned Anton's key. You wanted them to be born. You wanted to see who they would become."

"If you know all that, why have you come to me? Everything I knew is in the documents you must have read."

"Not at all," said Sister Carlotta. "I don't care about confessions. I don't care about logistics. I want to know about the babies."

"They're all dead," he said. "We killed them when we knew we were about to be discovered." He looked at her with bitter defiance. "Yes, infanticide. Twenty-three murders. But since the government couldn't admit that such children had ever existed, I was never charged with the crimes. God judges me, though. God will press the charges. Is that why you're here? Is that who gave you your clearance?"

You make jokes about this? "All I want to know is what you learned about them."

"I learned nothing, there was no time, they were still babies."

"You had them for almost a year. They developed. All the work done since Anton found his key was theoretical. *You* watched the babies grow."

A slow smile crept across his face. "This is like those Nazi medical crimes all over again. You deplore what I did, but you still want to know the results of my research."

"You monitored their growth. Their health. Their intellectual development."

"We were about to start the tracking of intellectual development. The project wasn't funded, of course, so it's not as if we could provide much more than a clean warm room and basic bodily needs."

"Their bodies, then. Their motor skills."

"Small," he said. "They are born small, they grow slowly. Undersized and underweight, all of them."

"But very bright?"

"Crawling very young. Making pre-speech sounds far earlier than normal. That's all we knew. I didn't see them often myself. I couldn't afford the risk of detection."

"So what was your prognosis?"

"Prognosis?"

"How did you see their future?"

"Dead. That's everyone's future. What are you talking about?"

"If they hadn't been slaughtered, Dr. Volescu, what would have happened?"

"They would have kept on growing, of course."

"And later?"

"There *is* no later. They keep on growing."

She thought for a moment, trying to process the information.

"That's right, Sister. You're getting it. They grow

slowly, but they never stop. That's what Anton's key does. Unlocks the mind because the brain never stops growing. But neither does anything else. The cranium keeps expanding—it's never fully closed. The arms and legs, longer and longer."

"So when they reach adult height . . ."

"There is no adult height. There's just height at time of death. You can't keep growing like that forever. There's a reason why evolution builds a stop-clock into the growth control of long-lived bodies. You can't keep growing without some organ giving out, eventually. Usually the heart."

The implications filled Sister Carlotta with dread. "And the rate of this growth? In the children, I mean? How long until they are at normal height for their age?"

"My guess was that they'd catch up twice," said Volescu. "Once just before puberty, and then the normal kids would leap ahead for a while, but slow and steady wins the race, n'est-ce pas? By twenty, they would be giants. And then they'd die, almost certainly before age twenty-five. Do you have any idea how huge they would be? So my killing them, you see—it was a mercy."

"I doubt any of them would have chosen to miss out on even the mere twenty years you took from them."

"They never knew what happened to them. I'm not a monster. We drugged them all. They died in their sleep and then the bodies were incinerated."

"What about puberty? Would they ever mature sexually?"

"That's the part we'll never know, isn't it?"

Sister Carlotta got up to go.

"He lived, didn't he?" asked Volescu.

"Who?"

"The one we lost. The one whose body wasn't with the others. I counted only twenty-two going into the fire."

"When you worship Moloch, Dr. Volescu, you get no answers but the ones your chosen god provides."

"Tell me what he's like." His eyes were so hungry.

"You know it was a boy?"

"They were all boys," said Volescu.

"What, did you discard the girls?"

"How do you think I got the genes I worked with? I implanted my own altered DNA into denucleated eggs."

"God help us, they were all your own twins?"

"I'm not the monster you think I am," said Volescu. "I brought the frozen embryos to life because I had to know what they would become. Killing them was my greatest sorrow."

"And yet you did it—to save yourself."

"I was afraid. And the thought came to me: They're only copies. It isn't murder to discard the copies."

"Their souls and lives were their own."

"Do you think the government would have let them live? Do you really think they would have survived? Any of them?"

"You don't deserve to have a son," said Sister Carlotta.

"But I have one, don't I?" He laughed. "While you, Miss Carlotta, perpetual bride of the invisible God, how many do *you* have?"

"They may have been copies, Volescu, but even dead they're worth more than the original."

He continued laughing as she walked down the corridor away from him, but it sounded forced. She knew his laughter was a mask for grief. But it wasn't the grief of compassion, or even of remorse. It was the grief of a damned soul.

Bean. God be thanked, she thought, that you do not know your father, and never will. You're nothing like him. You're far more human.

In the back of her mind, though, she had one nagging doubt. Was she sure Bean had more compassion, more humanity? Or was Bean as cold of heart as this man? As incapable of empathy? Was he all mind?

Then she thought of him growing and growing, from this too-tiny child to a giant whose body could no longer sustain life. This was the legacy your father gave you.

This was Anton's key. She thought of David's cry, when he learned of the death of his son. Absalom! Oh Absalom! Would God I could die for thee, Absalom, my son!

But he was not dead yet, was he? Volescu might have been lying, might simply be wrong. There might be some way to prevent it. And even if there was not, there were still many years ahead of Bean. And how he lived those years still mattered.

God raises up the children that he needs, and makes men and women of them, and then takes them from this world at his good pleasure. To him all of life is but a moment. All that matters is what that moment was used for. And Bean *would* use it well. She was sure of that.

Or at least she hoped it with such fervor that it felt like certainty.

12

Roster

"If Wiggin's the one, then let's get him to Eros."

"He's not ready for Command School yet. It's premature."

"Then we have to go with one of the alternates."

"That's your decision."

"*Our* decision! What do we have to go on but what you tell us?"

"I've told you about those older boys, too. You have the same data I have."

"Do we have all of it?"

"Do you *want* all of it?"

"Do we have the data on all the children with scores and evaluations at such a high level?"

"No."

"Why not?"

"Some of them are disqualified for various reasons."

"Disqualified by whom?"

"By me."

"On what grounds?"

"One of them is borderline insane, for instance. We're trying to find some structure in which his abilities will be useful. But he could not possibly bear the weight of complete command."

"That's one."

"Another is undergoing surgery to correct a physical defect."

"Is it a defect that limits his ability to command?"

"It limits his ability to be trained to command."

"But it's being fixed."

"He's about to have his third operation. If it works, he might amount to something. But, as you say, there won't be time."

"How many more children have you concealed from us?"

"I have *concealed* none of them. If you mean how many have I simply not referred to you as potential commanders, the answer is *all* of them. Except the ones whose names you already have."

"Let me be blunt. We hear rumors about a very young one."

"They're all young."

"We hear rumors about a child who makes the Wiggin boy look slow."

"They all have their different strengths."

"There are those who want you relieved of your command."

"If I'm not to be allowed to select and train these kids properly, I'd prefer to be relieved, sir. Consider this a request."

"So it was a stupid threat. Advance them all as quickly as you can. Just keep in mind that they need a certain amount of time in Command School, too. It does us no good to give them all your training if they don't have time to get ours."

Dimak met Graff in the battleroom control center. Graff conducted all his secure meetings here, until they could be sure Bean had grown enough that he couldn't get through the ducts. The battlerooms had their own separate air systems.

Graff had an essay on his desk display. "Have you read this? 'Problems in Campaigning Between Solar Systems Separated by Lightyears.' "

"It's been circulating pretty widely among the faculty."

"But it isn't signed," said Graff. "You don't happen to know who wrote it, do you?"

"No, sir. Did you write it?"

"I'm no scholar, Dimak, you know that. In fact, this was written by a student."

"At Command School?"

"A student here."

At that moment Dimak understood why he had been called in. "Bean."

"Six years old. The paper reads like a work of scholarship!"

"I should have guessed. He picks up the voice of the strategists he's been reading. Or their translators. Though I don't know what will happen now that he's he's been reading Frederick and Bulow in the original—French and German. He inhales languages and breathes them back out."

"What did you think of this paper?"

"You already know it's killing me to keep key information from this boy. If he can write *this* with what he knows, what would happen if we told him everything? Colonel Graff, why can't we promote him right out of Battle School, set him loose as a theorist, and then watch what he spits out?"

"Our job isn't to find theorists here. It's too late for theory anyway."

"I just think . . . look, a kid so small, who'd follow him? He's being wasted here. But when he writes, nobody knows how little he is. Nobody knows how young he is."

"I see your point, but we're not going to breach security, period."

"Isn't he already a grave security risk?"

"The mouse who scutters through the ducts?"

"No. I think he's grown too big for that. He doesn't do those side-arm pushups anymore. I thought the security risk came from the fact that he guessed that an offensive fleet had been launched generations ago, so why were we still training children for command?"

"From analysis of his papers, from his activities when he signs on as a teacher, we think he's got a theory and it's wonderfully wrong. But he believes his false theory *only* because he doesn't know about the ansible. Do you understand? Because that's the main thing we'd have to tell him about, isn't it?"

"Of course."

"So you see, that's the one thing we can't tell him."

"What is his theory?"

"That we're assembling children here in preparation for a war between nations, or between nations and the I.F. A landside war, back on Earth."

"Why would we take the kids into space to prepare for a war on Earth?"

"Think just a minute and you'll get it."

"Because . . . because when we've licked the Formics, there probably *will* be a little landside conflict. And all the talented commanders—the I.F. would already have them."

"You see? We can't have this kid publishing, not even within the I.F. Not everybody has given up loyalty to groups on Earth."

"So why did you call me in?"

"Because I *do* want to use him. We aren't running the war here, but we *are* running a school. Did you read his paper about the ineffectiveness of using officers as teachers?"

"Yes. I felt slapped."

"This time he's mostly wrong, because he has no way of knowing how nontraditional our recruitment of faculty has always been. But he may also be a little bit right.

Because our system of testing for officer potential was designed to produce candidates with the traits identified in the most highly regarded officers in the Second Invasion."

"Hi-ho."

"You see? Some of the highly regarded were officers who performed well in battle, but the war was too short to weed out the deadwood. The officers they tested included just the kind of people he criticized in his paper. So . . ."

"So he had the wrong reason, but the right result."

"Absolutely. It gives us little pricks like Bonzo Madrid. You've known officers like him, haven't you? So why should we be surprised that our tests give him command of an army even though he has no idea what to do with it. All the vanity and all the stupidity of Custer or Hooker or—hell, pick your own vain incompetent, it's the most common kind of general officer."

"May I quote you?"

"I'll deny it. The thing is, Bean has been studying the dossiers of all the other students. We think he's evaluating them for loyalty to their native identity group, and also for their excellence as commanders."

"By *his* standards of excellence."

"We need to get Ender the command of an army. We're under a lot of pressure to get our leading candidates into Command School. But if we bust one of the current commanders in order to make a place for Ender, it'll cause too much resentment."

"So you have to give him a new army."

"Dragon."

"There are still kids here who remember the last Dragon Army."

"Right. I like that. The jinx."

"I see. You want to give Ender a running start."

"It gets worse."

"I thought it would."

"We also aren't going to give him any soldiers that

aren't already on their commanders' transfer list."

"The dregs? What are you *doing* to this kid?"

"If we choose them, by our ordinary standards, then yes, the dregs. But we aren't going to choose Ender's army."

"Bean?"

"Our tests are worthless on this, right? Some of those dregs are the very best students, according to Bean, right? And he's been studying the launchies. So give him an assignment. Tell him to solve a hypothetical problem. Construct an army only out of launchies. Maybe the soldiers on the transfer lists, too."

"I don't think there's any way to do that without telling him that we're on to his fake teacher log-in."

"So tell him."

"Then he won't believe anything he found while searching."

"He didn't find anything," said Graff. "We didn't have to plant anything fake for him to find, because he had his false theory. See? So whether he thinks we planted stuff or not, he'll stay deceived and we're still secure."

"You seem to be counting on your understanding of his psychology."

"Sister Carlotta assures me that he differs from ordinary human DNA in only one small area."

"So now he's human again?"

"I've got to make decisions based on *something,* Dimak!"

"So the jury's still out on the human thing?"

"Get me a roster of the hypothetical army Bean would pick, so we can give it to Ender."

"He'll put himself in it, you know."

"He damn well better, or he's not as smart as we've been thinking."

"What about Ender? Is he ready?"

"Anderson thinks he is." Graff sighed. "To Bean, it's still just a game, because none of the weight has fallen on him yet. But Ender . . . I think he knows, deep down, where this is going to lead. I think he feels it already."

"Sir, just because you're feeling the weight doesn't mean he is."

Graff laughed. "You cut straight to the heart of things, don't you!"

"Bean's hungry for it, sir. If Ender isn't, then why not put the burden where it's wanted?"

"If Bean's hungry for it, it proves he's still too young. Besides, the hungry ones always have something to prove. Look at Napoleon. Look at Hitler. Bold at first, yes, but then *still* bold later on, when they need to cautious, to pull back. Patton. Caesar. Alexander. Always overreaching, never quite putting the finish on it. No, it's Ender, not Bean. Ender doesn't want to do it, so he won't have anything to prove."

"Are you sure you're not just picking the kind of commander you'd want to serve under?"

"That's precisely what I'm doing," said Graff. "Can you think of a better standard?"

"The thing is, you can't pass the buck on this one, can you? Can't say how it was the tests, you just followed the tests. The scores. Whatever."

"Can't run this like a machine."

"That's why you don't want Bean, isn't it? Because he was *made,* like a machine."

"I don't analyze myself. I analyze *them.*"

"So if we win, who really won the war? The commander you picked? Or you, for picking him?"

"The Triumvirate, for trusting me. After their fashion. But if we lose . . ."

"Well *then* it's definitely you."

"We're *all* dead then. What will they do? Kill me first? Or leave me till last so I can contemplate the consequences of my error?"

"Ender, though. I mean if he's the one. *He* won't say it's you. He'll take it all on himself. Not the credit for victory—just the blame for failure."

"Win or lose, the kid I pick is going to have a brutal time of it."

—

Bean got his summons during lunch. He reported at once to Dimak's quarters.

He found his teacher sitting at his desk, reading something. The light was set so that Bean couldn't read it through the dazzle.

"Have a seat," said Dimak.

Bean jumped up and sat on Dimak's bed, his legs dangling.

"Let me read you something," said Dimak. " 'There are no fortifications, no magazines, no strong points. . . . In the enemy solar system, there can be no living off the land, since access to habitable planets will be possible only after complete victory. . . . Supply lines are not a problem, since there are none to protect, but the cost of that is that all supplies and ordnance must be carried with the invading fleet. . . . In effect, all interstellar invasion fleets are suicide attacks, because time dilation means that even if a fleet returns intact, almost no one they knew will still be alive. They can never return, and so must be sure that their force is sufficient to be decisive and therefore is worth the sacrifice. . . . Mixed-sex forces allow the possibility of the army becoming a permanent colony and/or occupying force on the captured enemy planet.' "

Bean listened complacently. He had left it in his desk for them to find it, and they had done so.

"You wrote this, Bean, but you never submitted it to anybody."

"There was never an assignment that it fit."

"You don't seem surprised that we found it."

"I assume that you routinely scan our desks."

"Just as you routinely scan ours?"

Bean felt his stomach twist with fear. They knew.

"Cute, naming your false log-in 'Graff' with a caret in front of it."

Bean said nothing.

"You've been scanning all the other students' records. Why?"

"I wanted to know them. I've only made friends with a few."

"Close friends with none."

"I'm little and I'm smarter than they are. Nobody's standing in line."

"So you use their records to tell you more about them. Why do you feel the need to understand them?"

"Someday I'll be in command of one of these armies."

"Plenty of time to get to know your soldiers then."

"No sir," said Bean. "No time at all."

"Why do you say that?"

"Because of the way I've been promoted. And Wiggin. We're the two best students in this school, and we're being raced through. I'm not going to have much time when I get an army."

"Bean, be realistic. It's going to be a long time before anybody's going to be willing to follow you into battle."

Bean said nothing. He knew that this was false, even if Dimak didn't.

"Let's see just how good your analysis is. Let me give you an assignment."

"For which class?"

"No class, Bean. I want you to create a hypothetical army. Working only with launchies, construct an entire roster, the full complement of forty-one soldiers."

"*No* veterans?"

Bean meant the question neutrally, just checking to make sure he understood the rules. But Dimak seemed to take it as criticism of the unfairness of it. "No, tell you what, you can include veterans who are posted for transfer at their commanders' request. That'll give you some experienced ones."

The ones the commander couldn't work with. Some really were losers, but some were the opposite. "Fine," said Bean.

"How long do you think it will take you?"

Bean already had a dozen picked out. "I can tell the list to you right now."

"I want you to think about it seriously."

"I already have. But you need to answer a couple of questions first. You said forty-one soldiers, but that would include the commander."

"All right, forty, and leave the commander blank."

"I have another question. Am I to command the army?"

"You can write it up that way, if you want."

But Dimak's very unconcern told Bean that the army was not for him. "This army's for Wiggin, isn't it?"

Dimak glowered. "It's hypothetical."

"Definitely Wiggin," said Bean. "You can't boot somebody else out of command to make room for him, so you're giving Wiggin a whole new army. I bet it's Dragon."

Dimak looked stricken, though he tried to cover it.

"Don't worry," said Bean. "I'll give him the best army you can form, following those rules."

"I *said* this was hypothetical!"

"You think I wouldn't figure it out when I found myself in Wiggin's army and everybody else in it was also on my roster?"

"Nobody's said we're actually going to follow your roster!"

"You will. Because I'll be right and you'll know it," said Bean. "And I can promise you, it'll be a hell of an army. With Wiggin to train us, we'll kick ass."

"Just do the hypothetical assignment, and talk to no one about it. Ever."

That was dismissal, but Bean didn't want to be dismissed yet. They came to *him*. They were having *him* do their work. He wanted to have his say while they were still listening. "The reason this army can be so good is that your system's been promoting a lot of the wrong kids. About half the best kids in this school are launchies or on the transfer lists, because they're the ones who haven't already been beaten into submission by the kiss-ass idiots you put in command of armies or toons. These misfits and little kids are the ones who can win. Wiggin will figure that out. He'll know how to use us."

"Bean, you're not as smart about everything as you think you are!"

"Yes I am, sir," said Bean. "Or you wouldn't have given this assignment to me. May I be dismissed? Or do you want me to tell you the roster now?"

"Dismissed," said Dimak.

I probably shouldn't have provoked him, thought Bean. Now it's possible that he'll fiddle with my roster just to prove he can. But that's not the kind of man he is. If I'm not right about that, then I'm not right about anybody else, either.

Besides, it felt good to speak the truth to someone in power.

After working with the list a little while, Bean was just as glad that Dimak hadn't taken him up on his foolish offer to make up the roster on the spot. Because it wasn't just a matter of naming the forty best soldiers among the launchies and the transfer lists.

Wiggin was way early for command, and that would make it harder for older kids to take it—getting put into a kid's army. So he struck off the list all who were older than Wiggin.

That left him with nearly sixty kids who were good enough to be in the army. Bean was ranking them in order of value when he realized that he was about to make another mistake. Quite a few of these kids were in the group of launchies and soldiers that practiced with Wiggin during free time. Wiggin would know these kids best, and naturally he'd look to them to be his toon leaders. The core of his army.

The trouble was, while a couple of them would do fine as toon leaders, relying on that group would mean passing over several who weren't part of that group. Including Bean.

So he doesn't choose me to lead a toon. He isn't going to choose me anyway, right? I'm too little. He won't look at me and see a leader.

Is this just about me, then? Am I corrupting this process just to get myself a chance to show what I can do?

And if I am, what's wrong with that? I know what I can do, and no one else really gets it. The teachers think I'm a scholar, they know I'm smart, they trust my judgment, but they aren't making this army for me, they're making it for him. I still have to prove to them what I can do. And if I really am one of the best, it would be to the benefit of the program to have it revealed as quickly as possible.

And then he thought: Is this how idiots rationalize their stupidity to themselves?

"Ho, Bean," said Nikolai.

"Ho," said Bean. He passed a hand across his desk, blanking the display. "Tell me."

"Nothing to tell. *You* looked grim."

"Just doing an assignment."

Nikolai laughed. "You never look that serious doing classwork. You just read for a while and then you type for a while. Like it was nothing. This is something."

"An extra assignment."

"A hard one, neh?"

"Not very."

"Sorry to break in. Just thought maybe something was wrong. Maybe a letter from home."

They both laughed at that. Letters weren't that common here. Every few months at the most. And the letters were pretty empty when they came. Some never got mail at all. Bean was one of them, and Nikolai knew why. It wasn't a secret, he was just the only one who noticed and the only one who asked about it. "No family at *all?*" he had said. "Some kids' families, maybe I'm the lucky one," Bean answered him, and Nikolai agreed. "But not mine.

I wish you had parents like mine." And then he went on about how he was an only child, but his parents really worked hard to get him. "They did it with surgery, fertilized five or six eggs, then twinned the healthiest ones a few more times, and finally they picked me. I grew up like I was going to be king or the Dalai Lama or something. And then one day the I.F. says, we need him. Hardest thing my parents ever did, saying yes. But I said, What if I'm the next Mazer Rackham? And they let me go."

That was months ago, but it was still between them, that conversation. Kids didn't talk much about home. Nikolai didn't discuss his family with anybody else, either. Just with Bean. And in return, Bean told him a little about life on the street. Not a lot of details, because it would sound like he was asking for pity or trying to look cool. But he mentioned how they were organized into a family. Talked about how it was Poke's crew, and then it became Achilles' family, and how they got into a charity kitchen. Then Bean waited to see how much of this story started circulating.

None of it did. Nikolai never said a word about it to anyone else. That was when Bean was sure that Nikolai was worth having as a friend. He could keep things to himself without even having to be asked to do it.

And now here Bean was, making up the roster for this great army, and here sat Nikolai, asking him what he was doing. Dimak had said to tell no one, but Nikolai could keep a secret. What harm could it do?

Then Bean recovered his senses. Knowing about this wouldn't help Nikolai in any way. Either he'd be in Dragon Army or he wouldn't. If he wasn't, he'd know Bean hadn't put him there. If he was, it would be worse, because he'd wonder if Bean had included him in the roster out of friendship instead of excellence.

Besides, Nikolai shouldn't be in Dragon Army. Bean liked him and trusted him, but Nikolai was not among the best of the launchies. He was smart, he was quick, he was good—but he was nothing special.

Except to me, thought Bean.

"It was a letter from *your* parents," said Bean. "They've stopped writing to you, they like me better."

"Yeah, and the Vatican is moving to Mecca."

"And I'm going to be made Polemarch."

"No jeito," said Nikolai. "You too tall, bicho." Nikolai picked up his desk. "I can't help you with your classwork tonight, Bean, so please don't beg me." He lay back on his bed, started into the fantasy game.

Bean lay back, too. He woke up his display and began wrestling with the names again. If he eliminated every one of the kids who'd been practicing with Wiggin, how many of the good ones would it leave? Fifteen veterans from the transfer lists. Twenty-two launchies, including Bean.

Why *hadn't* these launchies taken part in Wiggin's free-time practices? The veterans, they were already in trouble with their commanders, they weren't about to antagonize them any more, so it made sense for them not to have taken part. But these launchies, weren't they ambitious? Or were they bookish, trying to do it all through classwork instead of catching on that the battleroom was everything? Bean couldn't fault them for that—it had taken him a while to catch on, too. Were they so confident of their own abilities they didn't think they needed the extra prep? Or so arrogant they didn't want anybody to think they owed their success to Ender Wiggin? Or so shy they . . .

No. He couldn't possibly guess their motives. They were all too complex anyway. They were smart, with good evaluations—good by Bean's standards, not necessarily by the teachers'. That was all he needed to know. If he gave Wiggin an army without a single kid he'd worked with in practices, then all the army would start out equal in his eyes. Which meant Bean would have the same chance as any other kid to earn Wiggin's eye and maybe get command of a toon. If they couldn't compete with Bean for that position, then too damn bad for them.

But that left him with thirty-seven names on the roster. Three more slots to fill.

He went back and forth on a couple. Finally decided to include Crazy Tom, a veteran who held the unenviable record of being the most-transferred soldier in the history of the game who wasn't actually iced and sent home. So far. The thing was, Crazy Tom really was good. Sharp mind. But he couldn't stand it when somebody above him was stupid and unfair. And when he got pissed, he really went off. Ranting, throwing things, tearing bedding off every bed in his barracks once, another time writing a message about what an idiot his commander was and mailing it to every other student in the school. A few actually got it before the teachers intercepted it, and they said it was the hottest thing they ever read. Crazy Tom. Could be disruptive. But maybe he was just waiting for the right commander. He was in.

And a girl, Wu, which of course had become Woo and even Woo-*hoo.* Brilliant at her studies, absolutely a killer in the arcade games, but she refused to be a toon leader and as soon as her commanders asked her, she put in for a transfer and refused to fight until they gave it to her. Weird. Bean had no idea why she did that—the teachers were baffled, too. Nothing in her tests to show why. What the hell, thought Bean. She's in.

Last slot.

He typed in Nikolai's name.

Am I doing him a favor? He's not bad, he's just a little slower than these kids, just a little gentler. It'll be hard for him. And if he's left out of it, he won't mind. He'll just do his best with whatever army he gets sent to eventually.

And yet . . . Dragon Army is going to be a legend. Not just here in Battle School, either. These kids are going to go on to be leaders in the I.F. Or somewhere, anyway. And they'll tell stories about when they were in Dragon Army with the great Ender Wiggin. And if I include Nikolai, then even if he isn't the best of the soldiers, even if he's in fact the slowest, he'll still be *in,* he'll still be able to tell those stories someday. And he's not bad. He won't embarrass himself. He won't bring down the army. He'll do OK. So why not?

And I want him with me. He's the only one I've ever talked to. About personal things. The only one who knows the name of Poke. I want him. And there's a slot on the roster.

Bean went down the list one more time. Then he alphabetized it and mailed it to Dimak.

—

The next morning, Bean, Nikolai, and three other kids in their launch group had their assignment to Dragon Army. Months before they should have been promoted to soldiers. The unchosen kids were envious, hurt, furious by turn. Especially when they realized Bean was one of the chosen. "Do they *make* uniform flash suits that size?"

It was a good question. And the answer was no, they didn't. The colors of Dragon Army were grey, orange, grey. Because soldiers were usually a lot older than Bean when they came in, they had to cut a flash suit down for Bean, and they didn't do it all that well. Flash suits weren't manufactured in space, and nobody had the tools to do a first-rate job of alteration.

When they finally got it to fit him, Bean wore his flash suit to the Dragon Army barracks. Because it had taken him so long to be fitted, he was the last to arrive. Wiggin arrived at the door just as Bean was entering. "Go ahead," said Wiggin.

It was the first time Wiggin had ever spoken to him—for all Bean knew, the first time Wiggin had even noticed him. So thoroughly had Bean concealed his fascination with Wiggin that he had made himself effectively invisible.

Wiggin followed him into the room. Bean started down the corridor between the bunks, heading for the back of the room where the younger soldiers always had to sleep. He glanced at the other kids, who were all looking at him as he passed with a mixture of horror and amusement.

They were in an army so lame that *this* little tiny kid was part of it?

Behind him, Wiggin was starting his first speech. Voice confident, loud enough but not shouting, not nervous. "I'm Ender Wiggin. I'm your commander. Bunking will be arranged by seniority."

Some of the launchies groaned.

"Veterans to the back of the room, newest soldiers to the front."

The groaning stopped. That was the opposite of the way things were usually arranged. Wiggin was already shaking things up. Whenever he came into the barracks, the kids closest to him would be the new ones. Instead of getting lost in the shuffle, they'd always have his attention.

Bean turned around and headed back to the front of the room. He was still the youngest kid in Battle School, but five of the soldiers were from more recently arrived launch groups, so they got the positions nearest the door. Bean got an upper bunk directly across from Nikolai, who had the same seniority, being from the same launch group.

Bean clambered up onto his bed, hampered by his flash suit, and put his palm beside the locker. Nothing happened.

"Those of you who are in an army for the first time," said Wiggin, "just pull the locker open by hand. No locks. Nothing private here."

Laboriously Bean pulled off his flash suit to stow it in his locker.

Wiggin walked along between the bunks, making sure that seniority was respected. Then he jogged to the front of the room. "All right, everybody. Put on your flash suits and come to practice."

Bean looked at him in complete exasperation. Wiggin had been looking right at him when he started taking off his flash suit. Why didn't he suggest that Bean not take the damn thing off?

"We're on the morning schedule," Wiggin continued. "Straight to practice after breakfast. Officially you have a free hour between breakfast and practice. We'll see what happens after I find out how good you are."

Truth was, Bean felt like an idiot. Of course Wiggin would head for practice immediately. He shouldn't have needed a warning not to take the suit off. He should have *known.*

He tossed his suit pieces onto the floor and slid down the frame of the bunk. A lot of the other kids were talking, flipping clothes at each other, playing with their weapons. Bean tried to put on the cut-down suit, but couldn't figure out some of the jury-rigged fastenings. He had to take off several pieces and examine them to see how they fit, and finally gave up, took it all off, and started assembling it on the floor.

Wiggin, unconcerned, glanced at his watch. Apparently three minutes was his deadline. "All right, everybody out, now! On your way!"

"But I'm naked!" said one boy—Anwar, from Ecuador, child of Egyptian immigrants. His dossier ran through Bean's mind.

"Dress faster next time," said Wiggin.

Bean was naked, too. Furthermore, Wiggin was standing right there, watching him struggle with his suit. He could have helped. He could have waited. What am I getting myself in for?

"Three minutes from first call to running out the door—that's the rule this week," said Wiggin. "Next week the rule is two minutes. Move!"

Out in the corridor, kids who were in the midst of free time or were heading for class stopped to watch the parade of the unfamiliar uniforms of Dragon Army. And to mock the ones that were even more unusual.

One thing for sure. Bean was going to have to practice getting dressed in his cut-down suit if he was going to avoid running naked through the corridors. And if Wiggin didn't make any exceptions for him the first day, when he'd only just got his nonregulation flash suit, Bean certainly was *not* going to ask for special favors.

I chose to put myself in this army, Bean reminded himself as he jogged along, trying to keep pieces of his flash suit from spilling out of his arms.

Part Four

SOLDIER

13

Dragon Army

"I need access to Bean's genetic information," said Sister Carlotta.

"That's not for you," said Graff.

"And here I thought my clearance level would open *any* door."

"We invented a special new category of security, called 'Not for Sister Carlotta.' We don't want you sharing Bean's genetic information with anyone else. And you were already planning on putting it in other hands, weren't you?"

"Only to perform a test. So . . . you'll have to perform it for me. I want a comparison between Bean's DNA and Volescu's."

"I thought you told me Volescu was the source of the cloned DNA."

"I've been thinking about it since I told you that, Colonel Graff, and you know what? Bean doesn't look anything like Volescu. I couldn't see how he could possibly grow up to be like him, either."

"Maybe the difference in growth patterns makes him look different, too."

"Maybe. But it's also possible Volescu is lying. He's a vain man."

"Lying about everything?"

"Lying about anything. About paternity, quite possibly. And if he's lying about that—"

"Then maybe Bean's prognosis isn't so bleak? Don't you think we've already checked with our genetics people? Volescu wasn't lying about that, anyway. Anton's key will probably behave just the way he described."

"Please. Run the test and tell me the results."

"Because you don't want Bean to be Volescu's son."

"I don't want Bean to be Volescu's twin. And neither, I think, do you."

"Good point. Though I must tell you, the boy does have a vain streak."

"When you're as gifted as Bean, accurate self-assessment looks like vanity to other people."

"Yeah, but he doesn't have to rub it in, does he?"

"Uh-oh. Has someone's ego been hurt?"

"Not mine. Yet. But one of his teachers is feeling a little bruised."

"I notice you aren't telling me I faked his scores anymore."

"Yes, Sister Carlotta, you were right all along. He deserves to be here. And so does . . . Well, let's just say you hit the jackpot after all those years of searching."

"It's humanity's jackpot."

"I said he was worth bringing up here, not that he was the one who'll lead us to victory. The wheel's still spinning on that one. And my money's on another number."

Going up the ladderways while holding a flash suit wasn't practical, so Wiggin made the ones who were dressed run up and down the corridor, working up a sweat, while Bean and the other naked or partially-dressed kids got their suits on. Nikolai helped Bean get his suit fastened; it humiliated Bean to need help, but it would have been worse to be the last one finished—the pesky little teeny brat who slows everyone down. With Nikolai's help, he was not the last one done.

"Thanks."

"No ojjikay."

Moments later, they were streaming up the ladders to the battleroom level. Wiggin took them all the way to the upper door, the one that opened out into the middle of the battleroom wall. The one used for entering when it was an actual battle. There were handholds on the sides, the ceiling, and the floor, so students could swing out and hurl themselves into the null-G environment. The story was that gravity was lower in the battleroom because it was closer to the center of the station, but Bean had already realized that was bogus. There would still be some centrifugal force at the doors and a pronounced Coriolis effect. Instead, the battlerooms were completely null. To Bean, that meant that the I.F. had a device that would either block gravitation or, more likely, produce false gravity that was perfectly balanced to counter Coriolis and centrifugal forces in the battleroom, starting exactly at the door. It was a stunning technology—and it was never discussed inside the I.F., at least not in the literature available to students in Battle School, and completely unknown outside.

Wiggin assembled them in four files along the corridor and ordered them to jump up and use the ceiling handholds to fling their bodies into the room. "Assemble on the far wall, as if you were going for the enemy's gate." To the veterans that meant something. To the launchies, who had never been in a battle and had never, for that matter, entered through the upper door, it meant nothing at all. "Run up and go four at a time when I open the gate, one group per second." Wiggin walked to the back of the group and, using his hook, a controller strapped to the inside of his wrist and curved to conform to his left hand, he made the door, which had seemed quite solid, disappear.

"Go!" The first four kids started running for the gate. "Go!" The next group began to run before the first had even reached it. There would be no hesitation or somebody would crash into you from behind. "Go!" The first group grabbed and swung with varying degrees of clumsiness and heading out in various directions. "Go!" Later groups learned, or tried to, from the awkwardness of the earlier ones. "Go!"

Bean was at the end of the line, in the last group. Wiggin laid a hand on his shoulder. "You can use a side handhold if you want."

Right, thought Bean. *Now* you decide to baby me. Not because my meshugga flash suit didn't fit together right, but just because I'm short. "Go suck on it," said Bean.

"Go!"

Bean kept pace with the other three, though it meant pumping his legs half again as fast, and when he got near the gate he took a flying leap, tapped the ceiling handhold with his fingers as he passed, and sailed out into the room with no control at all, spinning in three nauseating directions at once.

But he didn't expect himself to do any better, and instead of fighting the spin, he calmed himself and did his anti-nausea routine, relaxing himself until he neared a wall and had to prepare for impact. He didn't land near one of the recessed handholds and wasn't facing the right way to grab anything even if he had. So he rebounded, but this time was a little more stable as he flew, and he ended up on the ceiling very near the back wall. It took him less time than some to make his way down to where the others were assembling, lined up along the floor under the middle gate on the back wall—the enemy gate.

Wiggin sailed calmly through the air. Because he had a hook, during practice he could maneuver in midair in ways that soldiers couldn't; during battle, though, the hook would be useless, so commanders had to make sure they didn't become dependent on the hook's added control. Bean noted approvingly that Wiggin seemed not to use the hook at all. He sailed in sideways, snagged a handhold on the floor about ten paces out from the back wall, and hung in the air. Upside down.

Fixing his gaze on one of them, Wiggin demanded, "Why are you upside down, soldier?"

Immediately some of the other soldiers started to turn themselves upside down like Wiggin.

"Attention!" Wiggin barked. All movement stopped. "I said why are you upside down!"

Bean was surprised that the soldier didn't answer. Had he forgotten what the teacher did in the shuttle on the way here? The deliberate disorientation? Or was that something that only Dimak did?

"I said why does every one of you have his feet in the air and his head toward the ground!"

Wiggin didn't look at Bean in particular, and this was one question Bean didn't want to answer. There was no assurance of which particular correct answer Wiggin was looking for, so why open his mouth just to get shut down?

It was a kid named Shame—short for Seamus—who finally spoke up. "Sir, this is the direction we were in coming out of the door." Good job, thought Bean. Better than some lame argument that there was no up or down in null-G.

"Well what difference is that supposed to make! What difference does it make what the gravity was back in the corridor! Are we going to fight in the corridor? Is there any gravity here?"

No sir, they all murmured.

"From now on, you forget about gravity before you go through that door. The old gravity is gone, erased. Understand me? Whatever your gravity is when you get to the door, remember—the enemy's gate is *down.* Your feet are toward the enemy gate. Up is toward your own gate. North is that way"—he pointed toward what had been the ceiling—"south is that way, east is that way, west is—what way?"

They pointed.

"That's what I expected," said Wiggin. "The only process you've mastered is the process of elimination, and the only reason you've mastered that is because you can do it in the toilet."

Bean watched, amused. So Wiggin subscribed to the you're-so-stupid-you-need-me-to-wipe-your-butts school of basic training. Well, maybe that was necessary. One of the rituals of training. Boring till it was over, but . . . commander's choice.

Wiggin glanced at Bean, but his eyes kept moving.

"What was the circus I saw out here! Did you call that forming up? Did you call that flying? Now everybody, launch and form up on the ceiling! Right now! Move!"

Bean knew what the trap was and launched for the wall they had just entered through before Wiggin had even finished talking. Most of the others also got what the test was, but a fair number of them launched the wrong way—toward the direction Wiggin had called *north* instead of the direction he had identified as *up*. This time Bean happened to arrive near a handhold, and he caught it with surprising ease. He had done it before in his launch group's battleroom practices, but he was small enough that, unlike the others, it was quite possible for him to land in a place that had no handhold within reach. Short arms were a definite drawback in the battleroom. On short bounds he could aim at a handhold and get there with some accuracy. On a cross-room jump there was little hope of that. So it felt good that this time, at least, he didn't look like an oaf. In fact, having launched first, he arrived first.

Bean turned around and watched as the ones who had blown it made the long, embarrassing second leap to join the rest of the army. He was a little surprised at who some of the bozos were. Inattention can make clowns of us all, he thought.

Wiggin was watching him again, and this time it was no passing glance.

"You!" Wiggin pointed at him. "Which way is down?"

Didn't we just cover this? "Toward the enemy door."

"Name, kid?"

Come on, Wiggin really didn't know who the short kid with the highest scores in the whole damn school was? Well, if we're playing mean sergeant and hapless recruit, I better follow the script. "This soldier's name is Bean, sir."

"Get that for size or for brains?"

Some of the other soldiers laughed. But not many of them. *They* knew Bean's reputation. To them it was no longer funny that he was so small—it was just embarrassing that a kid that small could make perfect scores on tests that had questions they didn't even understand.

"Well, Bean, you're right onto things." Wiggin now included the whole group as he launched into a lecture on how coming through the door feet first made you a much smaller target for the enemy to shoot at. Harder for him to hit you and freeze you. "Now, what happens when you're frozen?"

"Can't move," somebody said.

"That's what frozen *means,*" said Wiggin. "But what *happens* to you?"

Wiggin wasn't phrasing his question very clearly, in Bean's opinion, and there was no use in prolonging the agony while the others figured it out. So Bean spoke up. "You keep going in the direction you started in. At the speed you were going when you were flashed."

"That's true," said Wiggin. "You five, there on the end, move!" He pointed at five soldiers, who spent long enough looking at each other to make sure which five he meant that Wiggin had time to flash them all, freezing them in place. During practice, it took a few minutes for a freeze to wear off, unless the commander used his hook to unfreeze them earlier.

"The next five, move!"

Seven kids moved at once—no time to count. Wiggin flashed them as quickly as he flashed the others, but because they had already launched, they kept moving at a good clip toward the walls they had headed for.

The first five were hovering in the air near where they had been frozen.

"Look at these so-called soldiers. Their commander ordered them to move, and now look at them. Not only are they frozen, they're frozen right here, where they can get in the way. While the others, because they moved when they were ordered, are frozen down there, plugging up the enemy's lanes, blocking the enemy's vision. I imagine that about five of you have understood the point of this."

We all understand it, Wiggin. It's not like they bring stupid people up here to Battle School. It's not like I didn't pick you the best available army.

"And no doubt Bean is one of them. Right, Bean?"

Bean could hardly believe that Wiggin was singling him out *again.*

Just because I'm little, he's using me to embarrass the others. The little guy knows the answers, so why don't you big boys.

But then, Wiggin doesn't realize yet. He thinks he has an army of incompetent launchies and rejects. He hasn't had a chance to see that he actually has a select group. So he thinks of me as the most ludicrous of a sad lot. He's found out I'm not an idiot, but he still assumes the others are.

Wiggin was still looking at him. Oh, yeah, he had asked a question. "Right, sir," said Bean.

"Then what is the point?"

Spit back to him exactly what he just said to us. "When you are ordered to move, move fast, so if you get iced you'll bounce around instead of getting in the way of your own army's operations."

"Excellent. At least I have one soldier who can figure things out."

Bean was disgusted. This was the commander who was

supposed to turn Dragon into a legendary army? Wiggin was supposed to be the alpha and omega of the Battle School, and he's playing the game of singling me out to be the goat. Wiggin didn't even find out our scores, didn't discuss his soldiers with the teachers. If he did, he'd already know that I'm the smartest kid in the school. The others all know it. That's why they're looking at each other in embarrassment. Wiggin is revealing his own ignorance.

Bean saw how Wiggin seemed to be registering the distaste of his own soldiers. It was just an eyeblink, but maybe Wiggin finally got it that his make-fun-of-the-shrimp ploy was backfiring. Because he finally got on with the business of training. He taught them how to kneel in midair—even flashing their own legs to lock them in place—and then fire between their knees as they moved downward toward the enemy, so that their legs became a shield, absorbing fire and allowing them to shoot for longer periods of time out in the open. A good tactic, and Bean finally began to get some idea of why Wiggin might not be a disastrous commander after all. He could sense the others giving respect to their new commander at last.

When they'd got the point, Wiggin thawed himself and all the soldiers he had frozen in the demonstration. "Now," he said, "which way is the enemy's gate?"

"Down!" they all answered.

"And what is our attack position?"

Oh, right, thought Bean, like we can all give an explanation in unison. The only way to answer was to demonstrate—so Bean flipped himself away from the wall, heading for the other side, firing between his knees as he went. He didn't do it perfectly—there was a little rotation as he went—but all in all, he did OK for his first actual attempt at the maneuver.

Above him, he heard Wiggin shout at the others. "Is Bean the only one who knows how?"

By the time Bean had caught himself on the far wall, the whole rest of the army was coming after him, shouting as if they were on the attack. Only Wiggin remained at the ceiling. Bean noticed, with amusement, that Wiggin was standing there oriented the same way he had been in the corridor—his head "north," the old "up." He might have the theory down pat, but in practice, it's hard to shake off the old gravity-based thinking. Bean had made it a point to orient himself sideways, his head to the west. And the soldiers near him did the same, taking their orientation from him. If Wiggin noticed, he gave no sign.

"Now come back at me, all of you, attack *me!*"

Immediately his flash suit lit up with forty weapons firing at him as his entire army converged on him, firing all the way. "Ouch," said Wiggin when they arrived. "You got me."

Most of them laughed.

"Now, what are your legs good for, in combat?"

Nothing, said some boys.

"Bean doesn't think so," said Wiggin.

So he isn't going to let up on me even now. Well, what does he want to hear? Somebody else muttered "shields," but Wiggin didn't key in on that, so he must have something else in mind. "They're the best way to push off walls," Bean guessed.

"Right," said Wiggin.

"Come on, pushing off is movement, not combat," said Crazy Tom. A few others murmured their agreement.

Oh good, now it starts, thought Bean. Crazy Tom picks a meaningless quarrel with his commander, who gets pissed off at him and . . .

But Wiggin didn't take umbrage at Crazy Tom's correction. He just corrected him back, mildly. "There *is* no combat without movement. Now, with your legs frozen like this, can you push off walls?"

Bean had no idea. Neither did anyone else.

"Bean?" asked Wiggin. Of course.

"I've never tried it," said Bean, "but maybe if you faced the wall and doubled over at the waist—"

"Right but wrong. Watch me. My back's to the wall,

legs are frozen. Since I'm kneeling, my feet are against the wall. Usually, when you push off you have to push downward, so you string out your body behind you like a string *bean,* right?"

The group laughed. For the first time, Bean realized that maybe Wiggin wasn't being stupid to get the whole group laughing at the little guy. Maybe Wiggin knew perfectly well that Bean was the smartest kid, and had singled him out like this because he could tap into all the resentment the others felt for him. This whole session was guaranteeing that the other kids would all think it was OK to laugh at Bean, to despise him even though he was smart.

Great system, Wiggin. Destroy the effectiveness of your best soldier, make sure he gets no respect.

However, it was more important to learn what Wiggin was teaching than to feel sullen about the way he was teaching it. So Bean watched intently as Wiggin demonstrated a frozen-leg takeoff from the wall. He noticed that Wiggin gave himself a deliberate spin. It would make it harder for him to shoot as he flew, but it would also make it very hard for a distant enemy to focus enough light on any part of him for long enough to get a kill.

I may be pissed off, but that doesn't mean I can't learn.

It was a long and grueling practice, drilling over and over again on new skills. Bean saw that Wiggin wasn't willing to let them learn each technique separately. They had to do them all at once, integrating them into smooth, continuous movements. Like dancing, Bean thought. You don't learn to shoot and then learn to launch and then learn to do a controlled spin—you learn to launch-shoot-spin.

At the end, all of them dripping with sweat, exhausted, and flushed with the excitement of having learned stuff that they'd never heard of other soldiers doing, Wiggin assembled them at the lower door and announced that they'd have another practice during free time. "And don't tell me that free time is supposed to be free. I know that, and you're perfectly free to do what you want. I'm *invit-*

ing you to come to an extra, *voluntary* practice."

They laughed. This group consisted entirely of kids who had *not* chosen to do extra battleroom practice with Wiggin before, and he was making sure they understood that he expected them to change their priorities now. But they didn't mind. After this morning they knew that when Wiggin ran a practice, every second was effective. They couldn't afford to miss a practice or they'd fall significantly behind. Wiggin would get their free time. Even Crazy Tom wasn't arguing about it.

But Bean knew that he had to change his relationship with Wiggin right now, or there was no chance that he would get a chance for leadership. What Wiggin had done to him in today's practice, feeding on the resentment of the other kids for this little pipsqueak, would make it even less plausible for Bean to be made a leader within the army—if the other kids despised him, who would follow him?

So Bean waited for Wiggin in the corridor after the others had gone on ahead.

"Ho, Bean," said Wiggin.

"Ho, Ender," said Bean. Did Wiggin catch the sarcasm in the way Bean said his name? Was that why he paused a moment before answering?

"*Sir,*" said Wiggin softly.

Oh, cut out the merda, I've seen those vids, we all *laugh* at those vids. "I know what you're doing, *Ender,* sir, and I'm warning you."

"Warning me?"

"I can be the best man you've got, but don't play games with me."

"Or what?"

"Or I'll be the worst man you've got. One or the other." Not that Bean expected Wiggin to understand what he meant by that. How Bean could only be effective if he had Wiggin's trust and respect, how otherwise he'd just be the little kid, useful for nothing. Wiggin would probably take it to mean that Bean meant to cause trouble if

Wiggin didn't use him. And maybe he did mean that, a little.

"And what do you want?" asked Wiggin. "Love and kisses?"

Say it flat out, put it in his mind so plainly he can't pretend not to understand. "I want a toon."

Wiggin walked close to Bean, looked down at him. To Bean, though, it was a good sign that Wiggin hadn't just laughed. "Why should you get a toon?"

"Because I'd know what to do with it."

"Knowing what to do with a toon is easy. It's getting them to do it that's hard. Why should any soldier want to follow a little pinprick like you?"

Wiggin had got straight to the crux of the problem. But Bean didn't like the malicious way he said it. "They used to call *you* that, I hear. I hear Bonzo Madrid still does."

Wiggin wasn't taking the bait. "I asked you a question, soldier."

"I'll earn their respect, sir, if you don't stop me."

To his surprise, Wiggin grinned. "I'm helping you."

"Like hell."

"Nobody would notice you, except to feel sorry for the little kid. But I made sure they *all* noticed you today."

You should have done your research, Wiggin. You're the only one who didn't know already who I was.

"They'll be watching every move you make," said Wiggin. "All you have to do to earn their respect now is be perfect."

"So I don't even get a chance to learn before I'm being judged." That's not how you bring along talent.

"Poor kid. Nobody's treatin' him fair."

Wiggin's deliberate obtuseness infuriated Bean. You're smarter than this, Wiggin!

Seeing Bean's rage, Wiggin brought a hand forward and pushed him until his back rested firmly against the wall. "I'll tell you how to get a toon. Prove to me you know what you're doing as a soldier. Prove to me you know how to use other soldiers. And then prove to me that somebody's willing to follow you into battle. Then you'll get your toon. But not bloody well until."

Bean ignored the hand pressing against him. It would take a lot more than that to intimidate him physically. "That's fair," he said. "*If* you actually work that way, I'll be a toon leader in a month."

Now it was Wiggin's turn to be angry. He reached down, grabbed Bean by the front of his flash suit, and slid him up the wall so they stood there eye to eye. "When I say I work a certain way, Bean, then that's the way I work."

Bean just grinned at him. In this low gravity, so high in the station, picking up little kids wasn't any big test of strength. And Wiggin was no bully. There was no serious threat here.

Wiggin let go of him. Bean slid down the wall and landed gently on his feet, rebounded slightly, settled again. Wiggin walked to the pole and slid down. Bean had won this encounter by getting under Wiggin's skin. Besides, Wiggin knew he hadn't handled this situation very well. He wouldn't forget. In fact, it was Wiggin who had lost a little respect, and he knew it, and he'd be trying to earn it back.

Unlike you, Wiggin, I *do* give the other guy a chance to learn what he's doing before I insist on perfection. You screwed up with me today, but I'll give you a chance to do better tomorrow and the next day.

But when Bean got to the pole and reached out to take hold, he realized his hands were trembling and his grip was too weak. He had to pause a moment, leaning on the pole, till he had calmed enough.

That face-to-face encounter with Wiggin, he hadn't won that. It might even have been a stupid thing to do. Wiggin *had* hurt him with those snide comments, that ridicule. Bean had been studying Wiggin as the subject of his private theology, and today he had found out that all this time Wiggin didn't even know Bean existed. Everybody compared Bean to Wiggin—but apparently Wiggin hadn't heard or didn't care. He had treated Bean like nothing. And after having worked so hard this past year to earn respect, Bean didn't find it easy to be nothing again. It brought back feelings he thought he left behind in Rotterdam. The sick fear of imminent death. Even though he knew that no one here would raise a hand against him, he still remembered being on the edge of dying when he first went up to Poke and put his life in her hands.

Is that what I've done, once again? By putting myself on this roster, I gave my future into this boy's hands. I counted on him seeing in me what I see. But of course he couldn't. I have to give him time.

If there *was* time. For the teachers were moving quickly now, and Bean might not *have* a year in this army to prove himself to Wiggin.

14

Brothers

"You have results for me?"

"Interesting ones. Volescu *was* lying. Somewhat."

"I hope you're going to be more precise than that."

"Bean's genetic alteration was not based on a clone of Volescu. But they *are* related. Volescu is definitely not Bean's father. But he is almost certainly Volescu's half-uncle or a double cousin. I hope Volescu has a half-brother or double first cousin, because such a man is the only possible father of the fertilized egg that Volescu altered."

"You have a list of Volescu's relatives, I assume?"

"We didn't need any family at the trial. And Volescu's mother was not married. He uses her name."

"So Volescu's father had another child somewhere only you don't even know his name. I thought you knew everything."

"We know everything that we knew was worth knowing. That's a crucial distinction. We simply haven't looked for Volescu's father. He's not guilty of anything important. We can't investigate everybody."

"Another matter. Since you know everything that you know is worth knowing, perhaps you can tell me why a certain crippled boy has been removed from the school where I placed him?"

"Oh. Him. When you suddenly stopped touting him, we got suspicious. So we checked him out. Tested him. He's no Bean, but he definitely belongs here."

"And it never crossed your mind that I had good reason for keeping him out of Battle School?"

"We assumed that you thought that we might choose Achilles over Bean, who was, after all, far too young, so you offered only your favorite."

"You assumed. I've been dealing with you as if you were intelligent, and you've been dealing with me as if I were an idiot. Now I see it should have been the exact reverse."

"I didn't know Christians got so angry."

"Is Achilles already in Battle School?"

"He's still recovering from his fourth surgery. We had to fix the leg on Earth."

"Let me give you a word of advice. Do *not* put him in Battle School while Bean is still there."

"Bean is only six. He's still too young to *enter* Battle School, let alone graduate."

"If you put Achilles in, take Bean out. Period."

"Why?"

"If you're too stupid to believe me after all my other judgments turned out to be correct, why should I give you the ammunition to let you second-guess me? Let me just say that putting them in school together is a probable death sentence for one of them."

"Which one?"

"That rather depends on which one sees the other first."

"Achilles says he owes everything to Bean. He loves Bean."

"Then by all means, believe him and not me. But don't send the body of the loser back to me to deal with. You bury your own mistakes."

"That sounds pretty heartless."

"I'm not going to weep over the grave of either boy. I tried to save both their lives. You apparently seem determined to let them find out which is fittest in the best Darwinian fashion."

"Calm down, Sister Carlotta. We'll consider what you've told us. We won't be foolish."

"You've already been foolish. I have no high expectations for you now."

As days became weeks, the shape of Wiggin's army began to unfold, and Bean was filled with both hope and despair. Hope, because Wiggin was setting up an army that was almost infinitely adaptable. Despair, because he was doing it without any reliance on Bean.

After only a few practices, Wiggin had chosen his toon leaders—every one of them a veteran from the transfer lists. In fact, every veteran was either a toon leader or a second. Not only that, instead of the normal organization—four toons of ten soldiers each—he had created five toons of eight, and then made them practice a lot in half-toons of four men each, one commanded by the toon leader, the other by the second.

No one had ever fragmented an army like that before. And it wasn't just an illusion. Wiggin worked hard to make sure the toon leaders and seconds had plenty of leeway. He'd tell them their objective and let the leader decide how to achieve it. Or he'd group three toons together under the operational command of one of the toon leaders to handle one operation, while Wiggin himself commanded the smaller remaining force. It was an extraordinary amount of delegation.

Some of the soldiers were critical at first. As they were milling around near the entrance to the barracks, the veterans talked about how they'd practiced that day—in ten groups of four. "Everybody knows it's loser strategy to divide your army," said Fly Molo, who commanded A toon.

Bean was a little disgusted that the soldier with the highest rank after Wiggin would say something disparaging about his commander's strategy. Sure, Fly was learning, too. But there's such a thing as insubordination.

"He hasn't divided the army," said Bean. "He's just organized it. And there's no such thing as a rule of strategy that you can't break. The idea is to have your army concentrated at the decisive point. Not to keep it huddled together all the time."

Fly glared at Bean. "Just cause you little guys can hear us doesn't mean you understand what we're talking about."

"If you don't want to believe me, think what you want. My talking isn't going to make you stupider than you already are."

Fly came at him, grabbing him by the arm and dragging him to the edge of his bunk.

At once, Nikolai launched himself from the bunk opposite and landed on Fly's back, bumping his head into the front of Bean's bunk. In moments, the other toon leaders had pulled Fly and Nikolai apart—a ludicrous fight anyway, since Nikolai wasn't that much bigger than Bean.

"Forget it, Fly," said Hot Soup—Han Tzu, leader of D toon. "Nikolai thinks he's Bean's big brother."

"What's the kid doing mouthing off to a toon leader?" demanded Fly.

"You were being insubordinate toward our commander," said Bean. "And you were also completely wrong. By your view, Lee and Jackson were idiots at Chancellorsville."

"He keeps doing it!"

"Are you so stupid you can't recognize the truth just because the person telling it to you is short?" All of Bean's frustration at not being one of the officers was spilling out. He knew it, but he didn't feel like controlling it. They needed to hear the truth. And Wiggin needed to have the support when he was being taken down behind his back.

Nikolai was standing on the lower bunk, so he was as close to Bean as possible, affirming the bond between them. "Come on, Fly," said Nikolai. "This is *Bean,* remember?"

And, to Bean's surprise, that silenced Fly. Until this moment, Bean had not realized the power that his reputation had. He might be just a regular soldier in Dragon Army, but he was still the finest student of strategy and military history in the school, and apparently everybody—or at least everybody but Wiggin—knew it.

"I should have spoken with more respect," said Bean.

"Damn right," said Fly.

"But so should you."

Fly lunged against the grip of the boys holding him.

"Talking about Wiggin," said Bean. "You spoke without respect. 'Everybody knows it's loser strategy to divide your army.' " He got Fly's intonation almost exactly right. Several kids laughed. And, grudgingly, so did Fly.

"OK, right," said Fly. "I was out of line." He turned to Nikolai. "But I'm still an officer."

"Not when you're dragging a little kid off his bunk you're not," said Nikolai. "You're a bully when you do that."

Fly blinked. Wisely, no one else said a thing until Fly had decided how he was going to respond. "You're right, Nikolai. To defend your friend against a bully." He looked from Nikolai to Bean and back again. "Pusha, you guys even look like brothers." He walked past them, heading for his bunk. The other toon leaders followed him. Crisis over.

Nikolai looked at Bean then. "I was never as squished up and ugly as you," he said.

"And if I'm going to grow up to look like you, I'm going to kill myself now," said Bean.

"Do you have to talk to really *big* guys like that?"

"I didn't expect you to attack him like a one-man swarm of bees."

"I guess I wanted to jump on somebody," said Nikolai.

"You? Mr. Nice Guy?"

"I don't feel so nice lately." He climbed up on the bunk beside Bean, so they could talk more softly. "I'm out of my depth here, Bean. I don't belong in this army."

"What do you mean?"

"I wasn't ready to get promoted. I'm just average. Maybe not that good. And even though this army wasn't a bunch of heroes in the standings, these guys are good. Everybody learns faster than me. Everybody *gets* it and I'm still standing there thinking about it."

"So you work harder."

"I *am* working harder. You—you just get it, right away, everything, you see it all. And it's not that I'm stupid. I always get it, too. Just . . . a step behind."

"Sorry," said Bean.

"What are *you* sorry about? It's not *your* fault."

Yes it is, Nikolai. "Come on, you telling me you wish you weren't part of Ender Wiggin's army?"

Nikolai laughed a little. "He's really something, isn't he?"

"You'll do your part. You're a good soldier. You'll see. When we get into the battles, you'll do as well as anybody."

"Eh, probably. They can always freeze me and throw me around. A big lumpy projectile weapon."

"You're not so lumpy."

"Everybody's lumpy compared to you. I've watched you—you give away half your food."

"They feed me too much."

"I've got to study." Nikolai jumped across to his bunk.

Bean felt bad sometimes about having put Nikolai in this situation. But when they started winning, a lot of kids outside of Dragon Army would be wishing they could trade places with him. In fact, it was kind of surprising Nikolai realized he wasn't as qualified as the others. After all, the differences weren't that pronounced. Probably there were a lot of kids who felt just like Nikolai. But

Bean hadn't really reassured him. In fact, he had probably reaffirmed Nikolai's feelings of inferiority.

What a sensitive friend I am.

—

There was no point in interviewing Volescu again, not after getting such lies from him the first time. All that talk of copies, and him the original—there was no mitigation now. He was a murderer, a servant of the Father of Lies. He would do nothing to help Sister Carlotta. And the need to find out what might be expected of the one child who evaded Volescu's little holocaust was too great to rely again on the word of such a man.

Besides, Volescu had made contact with his half-brother or double cousin—how else could he have obtained a fertilized egg containing his DNA? So Sister Carlotta should be able either to follow Volescu's trail or duplicate his research.

She learned quickly that Volescu was the illegitimate child of a Romanian woman in Budapest, Hungary. A little checking—and the judicious use of her security clearance—got her the name of the father, a Greek-born official in the League who had recently been promoted to service on the Hegemon's staff. That might have been a roadblock, but Sister Carlotta did not need to speak to the grandfather. She only needed to know who he was in order to find out the names of his three legitimate children. The daughter was eliminated because the shared parent was a male. And in checking the two sons, she decided to go first to visit the married one.

They lived on the island of Crete, where Julian ran a software company whose only client was the International Defense League. Obviously this was not a coincidence, but nepotism was almost honorable compared to some of the outright graft and favor-trading that was endemic in the League. In the long run such corruption was basically harmless, since the International Fleet had seized control of its own budget early on and never let the League touch it again. Thus the Polemarch and the Strategos had far more money at their disposal than the Hegemon, which made him, though first in title, weakest in actual power and independence of movement.

And just because Julian Delphiki owed his career to his father's political connections did not necessarily mean that his company's product was not adequate and that he himself was not an honest man. By the standards of honesty that prevailed in the world of business, anyway.

Sister Carlotta found that she did not need her security clearance to get a meeting with Julian and his wife, Elena. She called and said she would like to see them on a matter concerning the I.F., and they immediately opened their calendar to her. She arrived in Knossos and was immediately driven to their home on a bluff overlooking the Aegean. They looked nervous—indeed, Elena was almost frantic, wringing a handkerchief.

"Please," she said, after accepting their offer of fruit and cheese. "Please tell me why you are so upset. There's nothing about my business that should alarm you."

The two of them glanced at each other, and Elena became flustered. "Then there's nothing wrong with our boy?"

For a moment, Sister Carlotta wondered if they already knew about Bean—but how could they?

"Your son?"

"Then he's all right!" Elena burst into tears of relief and when her husband knelt beside her, she clung to him and sobbed.

"You see, it was very hard for us to let him go into service," said Julian. "So when a religious person calls to tell us she needs to see us on business pertaining to the I.F., we thought—we leapt to the conclusion—"

"Oh, I'm so sorry. I didn't know you had a son in the military, or I would have been careful to assure you from the start that . . . but now I fear I am here under false pretenses. The matter I need to speak to you about is personal, so personal you may be reluctant to answer. Yet it *is* about a matter that is of some importance to the I.F. Truthful answers cannot possibly expose you to any personal risk, I promise."

Elena got control of herself. Julian seated himself again, and now they looked at Sister Carlotta almost with cheerfulness. "Oh, ask whatever you want," said Julian. "We're just happy that—whatever you want to ask."

"We'll answer if we can," said Elena.

"You say you have a son. This raises the possibility that—there is reason to wonder if you might not at some point have . . . was your son conceived under circumstances that would have allowed a clone of his fertilized egg to be made?"

"Oh yes," said Elena. "That is no secret. A defect in one fallopian tube and an ectopic pregnancy in the other made it impossible for me to conceive in utero. We wanted a child, so they drew out several of my eggs, fertilized them with my husband's sperm, and then cloned the ones we chose. There were four that we cloned, six copies of each. Two girls and two boys. So far, we have implanted only the one. He was such a—such a special boy, we did not want to dilute our attention. Now that his education is out of our hands, however, we have been thinking of bearing one of the girls. It's time." She reached over and took Julian's hand and smiled. He smiled back.

Such a contrast to Volescu. Hard to believe there was any genetic material in common.

"You said six copies of each of the four fertilized eggs," said Sister Carlotta.

"Six including the original," said Julian. "That way we have the best chance of implanting each of the four and carrying them through a full pregnancy."

"A total of twenty-four fertilized eggs. And only one of them was implanted?"

"Yes, we were very fortunate, the first one worked perfectly."

"Leaving twenty-three."

"Yes. Exactly."

"Mr. Delphiki, all twenty-three of those fertilized eggs remain in storage, waiting for implantation?"

"Of course."

Sister Carlotta thought for a moment. "How recently have you checked?"

"Just last week," said Julian. "As we began talking about having another child. The doctor assured us that nothing has happened to the eggs and they can be implanted with only a few hours' notice."

"But did the doctor actually check?"

"I don't know," said Julian.

Elena was starting to tense up a little. "What have you heard?" she asked.

"Nothing," said Sister Carlotta. "What I am looking for is the source of a particular child's genetic material. I simply need to make sure that your fertilized eggs were not the source."

"But of course they were not. Except for our son."

"Please don't be alarmed. But I would like to know the name of your doctor and the facility where the eggs are stored. And then I would be glad if you would call your doctor and have him go, in person, to the facility and insist upon seeing the eggs himself."

"They can't be seen without a microscope," said Julian.

"See that they have not been disturbed," said Sister Carlotta.

They had both become hyperalert again, especially since they had no idea what this was all about—nor could they be told. As soon as Julian gave her the name of doctor and hospital, Sister Carlotta stepped onto the porch and, as she gazed at the sail-specked Aegean, she used her global and got herself put through to the I.F. headquarters in Athens.

It would take several hours, perhaps, for either her call or Julian's to bring in the answer, so she and Julian and Elena made a heroic effort to appear unconcerned. They took her on a walking tour of their neighborhood, which offered views both ancient and modern, and of nature verdant, desert, and marine. The dry air was refreshing as long as the breeze from the sea did not lag, and Sister Carlotta enjoyed hearing Julian talk about his company and Elena talk about her work as a teacher. All thought of their having risen in the world through government corruption faded as she realized that however he got his contract, Julian was a serious, dedicated creator of software, while Elena was a fervent teacher who treated her profession as a crusade. "I knew as soon as I started teaching our son how remarkable he was," Elena told her. "But it wasn't until his pre-tests for school placement that we first learned that his gifts were particularly suited for the I.F."

Alarm bells went off. Sister Carlotta had assumed that their son was an adult. After all, they were not a young couple. "How old is your son?"

"Eight years old now," said Julian. "They sent us a picture. Quite a little man in his uniform. They don't let many letters come through."

Their son was in Battle School. They appeared to be in their forties, but they might not have started to have a family until late, and then tried in vain for a while, going through a tubal pregnancy before finding out that Elena could no longer conceive. Their son was only a couple of years older than Bean.

Which meant that Graff could compare Bean's genetic code with that of the Delphiki boy and find out if they were from the same cloned egg. There would be a control, to compare what Bean was like with Anton's key turned, as opposed to the other, whose genes were unaltered.

Now that she thought about it, of *course* any true sibling of Bean's would have exactly the abilities that would bring the attention of the I.F. Anton's key made a child into a savant in general; the particular mix of skills that the I.F. looked for were not affected. Bean would have had those skills no matter what; the alteration merely allowed him to bring a far sharper intelligence to bear on abilities he already had.

If Bean was in fact their child. Yet the coincidence of twenty-three fertilized eggs and the twenty-three children that Volescu had produced in the "clean room"—what other conclusion could she reach?

And soon the answer came, first to Sister Carlotta, but immediately thereafter to the Delphikis. The I.F. investigators had gone to the clinic with the doctor and together they had discovered that the eggs were missing.

It was hard news for the Delphikis to bear, and Sister Carlotta discreetly waited outside while Elena and Julian took some time alone together. But soon they invited her in. "How much can you tell us?" Julian asked. "You came here because you suspected our babies might have been taken. Tell me, were they born?"

Sister Carlotta wanted to hide behind the veil of military secrecy, but in truth there was no military secret involved—Volescu's crime was a matter of public record. And yet . . . weren't they better off not knowing?

"Julian, Elena, accidents happen in the laboratory. They might have died anyway. Nothing is certain. Isn't it better just to think of this as a terrible accident? Why add to the burden of the loss you already have?"

Elena looked at her fiercely. "You *will* tell me, Sister Carlotta, if you love the God of truth!"

"The eggs were stolen by a criminal who . . . illegally caused them to be brought through gestation. When his crime was about to be discovered, he gave them a painless death by sedative. They did not suffer."

"And this man will be put on trial?"

"He has already been tried and sentenced to life in prison," said Sister Carlotta.

"Already?" asked Julian. "How long ago were our babies stolen?"

"More than seven years ago."

"Oh!" cried Elena. "Then our babies . . . when they died . . ."

"They were infants. Not a year old yet."

"But why *our* babies? Why would he steal them? Was he going to sell them for adoption? Was he . . ."

"Does it matter? None of his plans came to fruition," said Sister Carlotta. The nature of Volescu's experiments *was* a secret.

"What was the murderer's name?" asked Julian. Seeing her hesitation, he insisted. "His name is a matter of public record, is it not?"

"In the criminal courts of Rotterdam," said Sister Carlotta. "Volescu."

Julian reacted as if slapped—but immediately controlled himself. Elena did not see it.

He knows about his father's mistress, thought Sister Carlotta. He understands now what part of the motive had to be. The legitimate son's children were kidnapped by the bastard, experimented on, and eventually killed—and the legitimate son didn't find out about it for seven years. Whatever privations Volescu fancied that his fatherlessness had caused him, he had taken his vengeance. And for Julian, it also meant that his father's lusts had come back to cause this loss, this pain to Julian and his wife. The sins of the fathers are visited upon the children unto the third and fourth generation. . . .

But didn't the scripture say the third and fourth generation of them that hate me? Julian and Elena did not hate God. Nor did their innocent babies.

It makes no more sense than Herod's slaughter of the babes of Bethlehem. The only comfort was the trust that a merciful God caught up the spirits of the slain infants into his bosom, and that he brought comfort, eventually, to the parents' hearts.

"Please," said Sister Carlotta. "I cannot say you should not grieve for the children that you will never hold. But you can still rejoice in the child that you have."

"A million miles away!" cried Elena.

"I don't suppose . . . you don't happen to know if the Battle School ever lets a child come home for a visit," said Julian. "His name is Nikolai Delphiki. Surely under the circumstances . . ."

"I'm so sorry," said Sister Carlotta. Reminding them of the child they had was not such a good idea after all, when they did not, in fact, have him. "I'm sorry that my coming led to such terrible news for you."

"But you learned what you came to learn," said Julian.

"Yes," said Sister Carlotta.

Then Julian realized something, though he said not a word in front of his wife. "Will you want to return to the airport now?"

"Yes, the car is still waiting. Soldiers are much more patient than cab drivers."

"I'll walk you to the car," said Julian.

"No, Julian," said Elena, "don't leave me."

"Just for a few moments, my love. Even now, we don't forget courtesy." He held his wife for a long moment, then led Sister Carlotta to the door and opened it for her.

As they walked to the car, Julian spoke of what he had come to understand. "Since my father's bastard is already in prison, you did not come here because of his crime."

"No," she said.

"One of our children is still alive," he said.

"What I tell you now I should not tell, because it is not within my authority," said Sister Carlotta. "But my first allegiance is to God, not the I.F. If the twenty-two children who died at Volescu's hand were yours, then a twenty-third may be alive. It remains for genetic testing to be done."

"But we will not be told," said Julian.

"Not yet," said Sister Carlotta. "And not soon. Perhaps not ever. But if it is within my power, then a day will come when you will meet your second son."

"Is he . . . do you know him?"

"If it is your son," she said, "then yes, I know him. His life has been hard, but his heart is good, and he is such a boy as to make any father or mother proud. Please don't ask me more. I've already said too much."

"Do I tell this to my wife?" asked Julian. "What will be harder for her, to know or not know?"

"Women are not so different from men. *You* preferred to know."

Julian nodded. "I know that you were only the bearer of news, not the cause of our loss. But your visit here will not be remembered with happiness. Yet I want you to know that I understand how kindly you have done this miserable job."

She nodded. "And you have been unfailingly gracious in a difficult hour."

Julian opened the door of her car. She stooped to the seat, swung her legs inside. But before he could close the door for her, she thought of one last question, a very important one.

"Julian, I know you were planning to have a daughter next. But if you had gone on to bring another son into the world, what would you have named him?"

"Our firstborn was named for my father, Nikolai," he said. "But Elena wanted to name a second son for me."

"Julian Delphiki," said Sister Carlotta. "If this truly is your son, I think he would be proud someday to bear his father's name."

"What name does he use now?" asked Julian.

"Of course I cannot say."

"But . . . not Volescu, surely."

"No. As far as I'm concerned, he'll never hear that name. God bless you, Julian Delphiki. I will pray for you and your wife."

"Pray for our children's souls, too, Sister."

"I already have, and do, and will."

—

Major Anderson looked at the boy sitting across the table from him. "Really, it's not that important a matter, Nikolai."

"I thought maybe I was in trouble."

"No, no. We just noticed that you seemed to be a particular friend of Bean. He doesn't have a lot of friends."

"It didn't help that Dimak painted a target on him in the shuttle. And now Ender's gone and done the same thing. I suppose Bean can take it, but smart as he is, he kind of pisses off a lot of the other kids."

"But not you?"

"Oh, he pisses me off, too."

"And yet you became his friend."

"Well, I didn't mean to. I just had the bunk across from him in launchy barracks."

"You traded for that bunk."

"Did I? Oh. Eh."

"And you did that before you knew how smart Bean was."

"Dimak told us in the shuttle that Bean had the highest scores of any of us."

"Was that why you wanted to be near him?"

Nikolai shrugged.

"It was an act of kindness," said Major Anderson. "Perhaps I'm just an old cynic, but when I see such an inexplicable act I become curious."

"He really does kind of look like my baby pictures. Isn't that dumb? I saw him and I thought, he looks just like cute little baby Nikolai. Which is what my mother always called me in my baby pictures. I never thought of them as *me*. I was big Nikolai. That was cute little baby Nikolai. I used to pretend that he was my little brother and we just happened to have the same name. Big Nikolai and Cute Little Baby Nikolai."

"I see that you're ashamed, but you shouldn't be. It's a natural thing for an only child to do."

"I wanted a brother."

"Many who have a brother wish they didn't."

"But the brother I made up for myself, he and I got along fine." Nikolai laughed at the absurdity of it.

"And you saw Bean and thought of him as the brother you once imagined."

"At first. Now I know who he really is, and it's better.

It's like . . . sometimes he's the little brother and I'm looking out for him, and sometimes he's the big brother and he's looking out for me."

"For instance?"

"What?"

"A boy that small—how does he look out for you?"

"He gives me advice. Helps me with classwork. We do some practice together. He's better at almost everything than I am. Only I'm bigger, and I think I like him more than he likes me."

"That may be true, Nikolai. But as far as we can tell, he likes you more than he likes anybody else. He just . . . so far, he may not have the same capacity for friendship that you have. I hope that my asking you these questions won't change your feelings and actions toward Bean. We don't assign people to be friends, but I hope you'll remain Bean's."

"I'm not his friend," said Nikolai.

"Oh?"

"I told you. I'm his brother." Nikolai grinned. "Once you get a brother, you don't give him up easy."

15

Courage

"Genetically, they're identical twins. The only difference is Anton's key."

"So the Delphikis have two sons."

"The Delphikis have one son, Nikolai, and he's with us for the duration. Bean was an orphan found on the streets of Rotterdam."

"Because he was kidnapped."

"The law is clear. Fertilized eggs are property. I know that this is a matter of religious sensitivity for you, but the I.F. is bound by law, not—"

"The I.F. uses law where possible to achieve its own ends. I know you're fighting a war. I know that some things are outside your power. But the war will not go on forever. All I ask is this: Make this information part of a record—part of many records. So that when the war ends, the proof of these things can and will survive. So the truth won't stay hidden."

"Of course."

"No, not of course. You know that the moment the

Formics are defeated, the I.F. will have no reason to exist. It will try to continue to exist in order to maintain international peace. But the League is not politically strong enough to survive in the nationalist winds that will blow. The I.F. will break into fragments, each following its own leader, and God help us if any part of the fleet ever should use its weapons against the surface of the Earth."

"You've been spending too much time reading the Apocalypse."

"I may not be one of the genius children in your school, but I see how the tides of opinion are flowing here on Earth. On the nets a demagogue named Demosthenes is inflaming the West about illegal and secret maneuvers by the Polemarch to give an advantage to the New Warsaw Pact, and the propaganda is even more virulent from Moscow, Baghdad, Buenos Aires, Beijing. There are a few rational voices, like Locke, but they're given lip service and then ignored. You and I can't do anything about the fact that world war will certainly come. But we *can* do our best to make sure these children don't become pawns in that game."

"The only way they won't be pawns is if they're players."

"You've been raising them. Surely you don't *fear* them. Give them their chance to play."

"Sister Carlotta, all my work is aimed at preparing for the showdown with the Formics. At turning these children into brilliant, reliable commanders. I can't look beyond that mark."

"Don't *look*. Just leave the door open for their families, their nations to claim them."

"I can't think about that right now."

"Right now is the only time you'll have the power to do it."

"You overestimate me."

"You underestimate yourself."

Dragon Army had only been practicing for a month when Wiggin came into the barracks only a few seconds after lights-on, brandishing a slip of paper. Battle orders. They would face Rabbit Army at 0700. And they'd do it without breakfast.

"I don't want anybody throwing up in the battleroom."

"Can we at least take a leak first?" asked Nikolai.

"No more than a decaliter," said Wiggin.

Everybody laughed, but they were also nervous. As a new army, with only a handful of veterans, they didn't actually expect to win, but they didn't want to be humiliated, either. They all had different ways of dealing with nerves—some became silent, others talkative. Some joked and bantered, others turned surly. Some just lay back down on their bunks and closed their eyes.

Bean watched them. He tried to remember if the kids in Poke's crew ever did these things. And then realized: They were *hungry,* not afraid of being shamed. You don't get this kind of fear until you have enough to eat. So it was the bullies who felt like these kids, afraid of humiliation but not of going hungry. And sure enough, the bullies standing around in line showed all these attitudes. They were always performing, always aware of others watching them. Fearful they would have to fight; eager for it, too.

What do I feel?

What's wrong with me that I have to think about it to know?

Oh . . . I'm just sitting here, watching. I'm one of *those.*

Bean pulled out his flash suit, but then realized he had to use the toilet before putting it on. He dropped down onto the deck and pulled his towel from its hook, wrapped it around himself. For a moment he flashed back to that night he had tossed his towel under a bunk and climbed into the ventilation system. He'd never fit now. Too thickly muscled, too tall. He was still the shortest kid in Battle School, and he doubted if anyone else would notice how he'd grown, but he was aware of how his arms and legs were longer. He could reach things more easily.

Didn't have to jump so often just to do normal things like palming his way into the gym.

I've changed, thought Bean. My body, of course. But also the way I think.

Nikolai was still lying in bed with his pillow over his head. Everybody had his own way of coping.

The other kids were all using the toilets and getting drinks of water, but Bean was the only one who thought it was a good idea to shower. They used to tease him by asking if the water was still warm when it got all the way down there, but the joke was old now. What Bean wanted was the steam. The blindness of the fog around him, of the fogged mirrors, everything hidden, so he could be anyone, anywhere, any size.

Someday they'll all see me as I see myself. Larger than any of them. Head and shoulders above the rest, seeing farther, reaching farther, carrying burdens they could only dream of. In Rotterdam all I cared about was staying alive. But here, well fed, I've found out who I am. What I might be. *They* might think I'm an alien or a robot or something, just because I'm not genetically ordinary. But when I've done the great deeds of my life, they'll be proud to claim me as a human, furious at anyone who questions whether I'm truly one of them.

Greater than Wiggin.

He put the thought out of his mind, or tried to. This wasn't a competition. There was room for two great men in the world at the same time. Lee and Grant were contemporaries, fought against each other. Bismarck and Disraeli. Napoleon and Wellington.

No, that's not the comparison. It's *Lincoln* and Grant. Two great men working together.

It was disconcerting, though, to realize how rare that was. Napoleon could never bear to let any of his lieutenants have real authority. All victories had to be his alone. Who was the great man beside Augustus? Alexander? They had friends, they had rivals, but they never had partners.

That's why Wiggin has kept me down, even though he knows by now from the reports they give to army commanders that I've got a mind better than anybody else in Dragon. Because I'm too obviously a rival. Because I made it clear that first day that I intended to rise, and he's letting me know that it won't happen while I'm with his army.

Someone came into the bathroom. Bean couldn't see who it was because of the fog. Nobody greeted him. Everybody else must have finished here and gone back to get ready.

The newcomer walked through the fog past the opening in Bean's shower stall. It was Wiggin.

Bean just stood there, covered with soap. He felt like an idiot. He was in such a daze he had forgotten to rinse, was just standing in the fog, lost in his thoughts. Hurriedly he moved under the water again.

"Bean?"

"Sir?" Bean turned to face him. Wiggin was standing in the shower entrance.

"I thought I ordered everybody to get down to the gym."

Bean thought back. The scene unfolded in his mind. Yes, Wiggin *had* ordered everybody to bring their flash suits to the gym.

"I'm sorry. I . . . was thinking of something else . . ."

"Everybody's nervous before their first battle."

Bean hated that. To have Wiggin see him doing something stupid. Not remembering an order—Bean remembered *everything.* It just hadn't registered. And now he was patronizing him. Everybody's nervous!

"*You* weren't," said Bean.

Wiggin had already stepped away. He came back. "Wasn't I?"

"Bonzo Madrid gave you orders not to take your weapon out. You were supposed to just stay there like a dummy. You weren't nervous about doing *that.*"

"No," said Wiggin. "I was pissed."

"Better than nervous."

Wiggin started to leave. Then returned again. "Are *you* pissed?"

"I did that before I showered," said Bean.

Wiggin laughed. Then his smile disappeared. "You're late, Bean, and you're still busy rinsing. I've already got your flash suit down in the gym. All we need now is your ass in it." Wiggin took Bean's towel off its hook. "I'll have this waiting for you down there, too. Now move."

Wiggin left.

Bean turned the water off, furious. That was completely unnecessary, and Wiggin knew it. Making him go through the corridor wet and naked during the time when other armies would be coming back from breakfast. That was low, and it was stupid.

Anything to put me down. Every chance he gets.

Bean, you idiot, you're still standing here. You could have run down to the gym and beaten him there. Instead, you're shooting your stupid self in the stupid foot. And why? None of this makes sense. None of this is going to help you. You want him to make you a toon leader, not think of you with contempt. So why are you doing things to make yourself look stupid and young and scared and unreliable?

And still you're standing here, frozen.

I'm a coward.

The thought ran through Bean's mind and filled him with terror. But it wouldn't go away.

I'm one of those guys who freezes up or does completely irrational things when he's afraid. Who loses control and goes slack-minded and stupid.

But I didn't do that in Rotterdam. If I had, I'd be dead.

Or maybe I *did* do it. Maybe that's why I didn't call out to Poke and Achilles when I saw them there alone on the dock. He wouldn't have killed her if I'd been there to witness what happened. Instead I ran off until I realized the danger she was in. But why didn't I realize it before? Because I *did* realize it, just as I heard Wiggin tell us to meet in the gym. Realized it, understood it completely, but was too cowardly to act. Too afraid that something would go wrong.

And maybe that's what happened when Achilles lay on the ground and I told Poke to kill him. I was wrong and she was right. Because *any* bully she caught that way would probably have held a grudge—and might easily have acted on it immediately, killing her as soon as they let him up. Achilles was the likeliest one, maybe the only one that would agree to the arrangement Bean had thought up. There was no choice. But I got scared. Kill him, I said, because I wanted it to go away.

And still I'm standing here. The water is off. I'm dripping wet and cold. But I can't move.

Nikolai was standing in the bathroom doorway. "Too bad about your diarrhea," he said.

"What?"

"I told Ender about how you were up with diarrhea in the night. That's why you had to go to the bathroom. You were sick, but you didn't want to tell him because you didn't want to miss the first battle."

"I'm so scared I couldn't take a dump if I wanted to," said Bean.

"He gave me your towel. He said it was stupid of him to take it." Nikolai walked in and gave it to him. "He said he needs you in the battle, so he's glad you're toughing it out."

"He doesn't need me. He doesn't even want me."

"Come on, Bean," said Nikolai. "You can do this."

Bean toweled off. It felt good to be moving. Doing something.

"I think you're dry enough," said Nikolai.

Again, Bean realized he was simply drying and drying himself, over and over.

"Nikolai, what's wrong with me?"

"You're afraid that you'll turn out to be just a little kid. Well, here's a clue: You *are* a little kid."

"So are you."

"So it's OK to be really bad. Isn't that what you keep telling me?" Nikolai laughed. "Come on, if I can do it, bad as I am, so can you."

"Nikolai," said Bean.

"What now?"

"I really *do* have to crap."

"I sure hope you don't expect me to wipe your butt."

"If I don't come out in three minutes, come in after me."

Cold and sweating—a combination he wouldn't have thought possible—Bean went into the toilet stall and closed the door. The pain in his abdomen was fierce. But he couldn't get his bowel to loosen up and let go.

What am I so *afraid* of?

Finally, his alimentary system triumphed over his nervous system. It felt like everything he'd ever eaten flooded out of him at once.

"Time's up," said Nikolai. "I'm coming in."

"At peril of your life," said Bean. "I'm done, I'm coming out."

Empty now, clean, and humiliated in front of his only real friend, Bean came out of the stall and wrapped his towel around him.

"Thanks for keeping me from being a liar," said Nikolai.

"What?"

"About your having diarrhea."

"For you I'd get dysentery."

"Now that's friendship."

By the time they got to the gym, everybody was already in their flash suits, ready to go. While Nikolai helped Bean get into his suit, Wiggin had the rest of them lie down on the mats and do relaxation exercises. Bean even had time to lie down for a couple of minutes before Wiggin had them get up. 0656. Four minutes to get to the battleroom. He was cutting it pretty fine.

As they ran along the corridor, Wiggin occasionally jumped up to touch the ceiling. Behind him, the rest of the army would jump up and touch the same spot when they reached it. Except the smaller ones. Bean, his heart still burning with humiliation and resentment and fear, did not try. You do that kind of thing when you belong with the group. And he didn't belong. After all his brilliance in class, the truth was out now. He was a coward. He didn't belong in the military at all. If he couldn't even risk playing a game, what would he be worth in combat? The real generals exposed themselves to enemy fire. Fearless, they had to be, an example of courage to their men.

Me, I freeze up, take long showers, and dump a week's rations into the head. Let's see them follow *that* example.

At the gate, Wiggin had time to line them up in toons, then remind them, "Which way is the enemy's gate?"

"Down!" they all answered.

Bean only mouthed the word. Down. Down down down.

What's the best way to get down off a goose?

What are you doing up on a goose in the first place, you fool!

The grey wall in front of them disappeared, and they could see into the battleroom. It was dim—not dark, but so faintly lighted that the only way they could see the enemy gate was the light of Rabbit Army's flash suits pouring out of it.

Wiggin was in no hurry to get out of the gate. He stood there surveying the room, which was arranged in an open grid, with eight "stars"—large cubes that served as obstacles, cover, and staging platforms—distributed fairly evenly if randomly through the space.

Wiggin's first assignment was to C toon. Crazy Tom's toon. The toon Bean belonged to. Word was whispered down the file. "Ender says slide the wall." And then, "Tom says flash your legs and go in on your knees. South wall."

Silently they swung into the room, using the handholds to propel themselves along the ceiling to the east wall. "They're setting up their battle formation. All we want to do is cut them up a little, make them nervous, confused, because they don't know what to do with us. We're raiders. So we shoot them up, then get behind that star. *Don't* get stuck out in the middle. And *aim.* Make every shot count."

Bean did everything mechanically. It was habit now to get in position, freeze his own legs, and then launch with his body oriented the right way. They'd done it hundreds of times. He did it exactly right; so did the other seven soldiers in the toon. Nobody was looking for anyone to fail. He was right where they expected him to be, doing his job.

They coasted along the wall, always within reach of a handhold. Their frozen legs were dark, blocking the lights of the rest of their flash suits until they were fairly close. Wiggin was doing something up near the gate to distract Rabbit Army's attention, so the surprise was pretty good.

As they got closer, Crazy Tom said, "Split and rebound to the star—me north, you south."

It was a maneuver that Crazy Tom had practiced with his toon. It was the right time for it, too. It would confuse the enemy more to have two groups to shoot at, heading different directions.

They pulled up on handholds. Their bodies, of course, swung against the wall, and suddenly the lights of their flash suits were quite visible. Somebody in Rabbit saw them and gave the alarm.

But C was already moving, half the toon diagonally south, the other half north, and all angling downward toward the floor. Bean began firing; the enemy was also firing at him. He heard the low whine that said somebody's beam was on his suit, but he was twisting slowly, and far enough from the enemy that none of the beams was in one place long enough to do damage. In the meantime, he found that his arm tracked perfectly, not trembling at all. He had practiced this a lot, and he was good at it. A clean kill, not just an arm or leg.

He had time for a second before he hit the wall and

had to rebound up to the rendezvous star. One more enemy hit before he got there, and then he snagged a handhold on the star and said, "Bean here."

"Lost three," said Crazy Tom. "But their formation's all gone to hell."

"What now?" said Dag.

They could tell from the shouting that the main battle was in progress.

Bean was thinking back over what he had seen as he approached the star.

"They sent a dozen guys to this star to wipe us out," said Bean. "They'll come around the east and west sides."

They all looked at him like he was insane. How could he know this?

"We've got about one more second," said Bean.

"All south," said Crazy Tom.

They swung up to the south side of the star. There were no Rabbits on that face, but Crazy Tom immediately led them in an attack around to the west face. Sure enough, there were Rabbits there, caught in the act of attacking what they clearly thought of as the "back" of the star—or, as Dragon Army was trained to think of it, the bottom. So to the Rabbits, the attack seemed to come from below, the direction they were least aware of. In moments, the six Rabbits on that face were frozen and drifting along below the star.

The other half of the attack force would see that and know what had happened.

"Top," said Crazy Tom.

To the enemy, that would be the front of the star—the position most exposed to fire from the main formation. The last place they'd expect Tom's toon to go.

And once they were there, instead of continuing to attempt to engage the strike force coming against them, Crazy Tom had them shoot at the main Rabbit formation, or what was left of it—mostly disorganized groups hiding behind stars and firing at Dragons coming down at them from several directions. The five of them in C toon had time to hit a couple of Rabbits each before the strike force found them again.

Without waiting for orders, Bean immediately launched away from the surface of the star so he could shoot downward at the strike force. This close, he was able to do four quick kills before the whining abruptly stopped and his suit went completely stiff and dark. The Rabbit who got him wasn't one of the strike force—it was somebody from the main force above him. And to his satisfaction, Bean could see that because of his firing, only one soldier from C toon was hit by the strike force sent against them. Then he rotated out of view.

It didn't matter now. He was out. But he had done well. Seven kills that he was sure of, maybe more. And it was more than his personal score. He had come up with the information Crazy Tom needed in order to make a good tactical decision, and then he had taken the bold action that kept the strike force from causing too many casualties. As a result, C toon remained in position to strike at the enemy from behind. Without any place to hide, Rabbit would be wiped out in moments. And Bean was part of it.

I didn't freeze once we got into action. I did what I was trained to do, and I stayed alert, and I thought of things. I can probably do better, move faster, see more. But for a first battle, I did fine. I can do this.

Because C toon was crucial to the victory, Wiggin used the other four toon leaders to press their helmets to the corners of the enemy gate, and gave Crazy Tom the honor of passing through the gate, which is what formally ended the game, bringing the lights on bright.

Major Anderson himself came in to congratulate the winning commander and supervise cleanup. Wiggin quickly unfroze the casualties. Bean was relieved when his suit could move again. Using his hook, Wiggin drew them all together and formed his soldiers into their five toons before he began unfreezing Rabbit Army. They stood at attention in the air, their feet pointed down, their heads up—and as Rabbit unfroze, they gradually oriented themselves in the same direction. They had no way of knowing it, but to Dragon, that was when victory became complete—for the enemy was now oriented as if their *own* gate was down.

—

Bean and Nikolai were already eating breakfast when Crazy Tom came to their table. "Ender says instead of fifteen minutes for breakfast, we have till 0745. And he'll let us out of practice in time to shower."

That was good news. They could slow down their eating.

Not that it mattered to Bean. His tray had little food on it, and he finished it immediately. Once he was in Dragon Army, Crazy Tom had caught him giving away food. Bean told him that he was always given too much, and Tom took the matter to Ender, and Ender got the nutritionists to stop overfeeding Bean. Today was the first time Bean ever wished for more. And that was only because he was so up from the battle.

"Smart," said Nikolai.

"What?"

"Ender tells us we've got fifteen minutes to eat, which feels rushed and we don't like it. Then right away he sends around the toon leaders, telling us we have till 0745. That's only ten minutes longer, but now it feels like forever. And a shower—we're supposed to be able to shower right after the game, but now we're grateful."

"*And* he gave the toon leaders the chance to bring good news," said Bean.

"Is that important?" asked Nikolai. "We know it was Ender's choice."

"Most commanders make sure all good news comes from them," said Bean, "and bad news from the toon leaders. But Wiggin's whole technique is building up his toon leaders. Crazy Tom went in there with nothing more than his training and his brains and a single objective—strike first from the wall and get behind them. All the rest was up to him."

"Yeah, but if his toon leaders screw up, it looks bad on Ender's record," said Nikolai.

Bean shook his head. "The point is that in his very first battle, Wiggin divided his force for tactical effect, and C toon was able to continue attacking even after we ran out of plans, because Crazy Tom was really, truly in charge of us. We didn't sit around wondering what Wiggin wanted us to do."

Nikolai got it, and nodded. "Bacana. That's right."

"Completely right," said Bean. By now everybody at the table was listening. "And that's because Wiggin isn't just thinking about Battle School and standings and merda like that. He keeps watching vids of the Second Invasion, did you know that? He's thinking about how to beat the *Buggers.* And he knows that the way you do that is to have as many commanders ready to fight them as you can get. Wiggin doesn't want to come out of this with Wiggin as the only commander ready to fight the Buggers. He wants to come out of this with him *and* the toon leaders *and* the seconds *and* if he can do it every single one of his soldiers ready to command a fleet against the Buggers if we have to."

Bean knew his enthusiasm was probably giving Wiggin credit for more than he had actually planned, but he was still full of the glow of victory. And besides, what he was saying was true—Wiggin was no Napoleon, holding on to the reins of control so tightly that none of his commanders was capable of brilliant independent command. Crazy Tom had performed well under pressure. He had made the right decisions—including the decision to listen to his smallest, most useless-looking soldier. And Crazy Tom had done that because Wiggin had set the example by listening to his toon leaders. You learn, you analyze, you choose, you act.

After breakfast, as they headed for practice, Nikolai asked him, "Why do you call him Wiggin?"

"Cause we're not friends," said Bean.

"Oh, so it's Mr. Wiggin and Mr. Bean, is that it?"

"No. *Bean* is my first name."

"Oh. So it's Mr. Wiggin and Who The Hell Are You."

"Got it."

—

Everybody expected to have at least a week to strut around and brag about their perfect won-lost record. Instead, the next morning at 0630, Wiggin appeared in the barracks, again brandishing battle orders. "Gentlemen, I hope you learned something yesterday, because today we're going to do it again."

All were surprised, and some were angry—it wasn't fair, they weren't ready. Wiggin just handed the orders to Fly Molo, who had just been heading out for breakfast. "Flash suits!" cried Fly, who clearly thought it was a cool thing to be the first army ever to fight two in a row like this.

But Hot Soup, the leader of D toon, had another attitude. "Why didn't you tell us earlier?"

"I thought you needed the shower," said Wiggin. "Yesterday Rabbit Army claimed we only won because the stink knocked them out."

Everybody within earshot laughed. But Bean was not amused. He knew that the paper hadn't been there first thing, when Wiggin woke up. The teachers planted it late. "Didn't find the paper till you got back from the showers, right?"

Wiggin gave him a blank look. "Of course. I'm not as close to the floor as you."

The contempt in his voice struck Bean like a blow. Only then did he realize that Wiggin had taken his question as a criticism—that Wiggin had been inattentive and hadn't *noticed* the orders. So now there was one more mark against Bean in Wiggin's mental dossier. But Bean couldn't let that upset him. It's not as if Wiggin didn't have him tagged as a coward. Maybe Crazy Tom told

Wiggin about how Bean contributed to the victory yesterday, and maybe not. It wouldn't change what Wiggin had seen with his own eyes—Bean malingering in the shower. And now Bean apparently taunting him for making them all have to rush for their second battle. Maybe I'll be made toon leader on my thirtieth birthday. And then only if everybody else is drowned in a boat accident.

Wiggin was still talking, of course, explaining how they should expect battles any time, the old rules were coming apart. "I can't pretend I like the way they're screwing around with us, but I do like one thing—that I've got an army that can handle it."

As he put on his flash suit, Bean thought through the implications of what the teachers were doing. They were pushing Wiggin faster and also making it harder for him. And this was only the beginning. Just the first few sprinkles of a snotstorm.

Why? Not because Wiggin was so good he needed the testing. On the contrary—Wiggin was training his army well, and the Battle School would only benefit from giving him plenty of time to do it. So it had to be something outside Battle School.

Only one possibility, really. The Bugger invaders were getting close. Only a few years away. They had to get Wiggin through training.

Wiggin. Not all of us, just Wiggin. Because if it were everybody, then everybody's schedule would be stepped up like this. Not just ours.

So it's already too late for me. Wiggin's the one they've chosen to rest their hopes on. Whether I'm toon leader or not will never matter. All that matters is: Will Wiggin be ready?

If Wiggin succeeds, there'll still be room for me to achieve greatness in the aftermath. The League will come apart. There'll be war among humans. Either I'll be used by the I.F. to help keep the peace, or maybe I can get into some army on Earth. I've got plenty of life ahead of me. Unless Wiggin commands our fleet against the invading

Buggers and loses. Then none of us has any life at all.

All I can do right now is my best to help Wiggin learn everything he can learn here. The trouble is, I'm not close enough to him for me to have any effect on him at all.

The battle was with Petra Arkanian, commander of Phoenix Army. Petra was sharper than Carn Carby had been; she also had the advantage of hearing how Wiggin worked entirely without formations and used little raiding parties to disrupt formations ahead of the main combat. Still, Dragon finished with only three soldiers flashed and nine partially disabled. A crushing defeat. Bean could see that Petra didn't like it, either. She probably felt like Wiggin had poured it on, deliberately setting her up for humiliation. But she'd get it, soon enough—Wiggin simply turned his toon leaders loose, and each of them pursued total victory, as he had trained them. Their system worked better, that's all, and the old way of doing battle was doomed.

Soon enough, all the other commanders would start adapting, learning from what Wiggin did. Soon enough, Dragon Army would be facing armies that were divided into five toons, not four, and that moved in a free-ranging style with a lot more discretion given to the toon leaders. The kids didn't get to Battle School because they were idiots. The only reason the techniques worked a second time was because there'd only been a day since the first battle, and nobody expected to have to face Wiggin again so soon. Now they'd know that changes would have to be made fast. Bean guessed that they'd probably never see another formation.

What then? Had Wiggin emptied his magazine, or would he have new tricks up his sleeve? The trouble was, innovation never resulted in victory over the long term. It was too easy for the enemy to imitate and improve on your innovations. The real test for Wiggin would be what he did when he was faced with slugfests between armies using similar tactics.

And the real test for me will be seeing if I can stand it

when Wiggin makes some stupid mistake and I have to sit here as an ordinary soldier and watch him do it.

The third day, another battle. The fourth day, another. Victory. Victory. But each time, the score was closer. Each time, Bean gained more confidence as a soldier—and became more frustrated that the most he could contribute, beyond his own good aim, was occasionally making a suggestion to Crazy Tom, or reminding him of something Bean had noticed and remembered.

Bean wrote to Dimak about it, explaining how he was being underused and suggesting that he would be getting better trained by working with a worse commander, where he'd have a better chance of getting his own toon.

The answer was short. "Who else would want you? Learn from Ender."

Brutal but true. No doubt even Wiggin didn't really want him. Either he was forbidden to transfer any of his soldiers, or he had tried to trade Bean away and no one would take him.

—

It was free time of the evening after their fourth battle. Most of the others were trying to keep up with their classwork—the battles were really taking it out of them, especially because they could all see that they needed to practice hard to stay ahead. Bean, though, coasted through classwork like always, and when Nikolai told him he didn't need any more damned help with his assignments, Bean decided that he should take a walk.

Passing Wiggin's quarters—a space even smaller than the cramped quarters the teachers had, just space for a bunk, one chair, and a tiny table—Bean was tempted to knock on the door and sit down and have it out with Wiggin once and for all. Then common sense prevailed over frustration and vanity, and Bean wandered until he came to the arcade.

It wasn't as full as it used to be. Bean figured that was because everyone was holding extra practices now, trying to implement whatever they thought it was Wiggin was doing before they actually had to face him in battle. Still, a few were still willing to fiddle with the controllers and make things move on screens or in holodisplays.

Bean found a flat-screen game that had, as its hero, a mouse. No one was using it, so Bean started maneuvering it through a maze. Quickly the maze gave way to the wallspaces and crawlspaces of an old house, with traps set here and there, easy stuff. Cats chased him—ho hum. He jumped up onto a table and found himself face to face with a giant.

A giant who offered him a drink.

This was the fantasy game. This was the psychological game that everybody else played on their desks all the time. No wonder no one was playing it here. They all recognized it and that wasn't the game they came here to play.

Bean was well aware that he was the only kid in the school who had never played the fantasy game. They had tricked him into playing this once, but he doubted that anything important could be learned from what he had done so far. So screw 'em. They could trick him into playing up to a point, but he didn't have to go further.

Except that the giant's face had changed. It was Achilles.

Bean stood there in shock for a moment. Frozen, frightened. How did they know? Why did they do it? To put him face-to-face with Achilles, by surprise like that. Those bastards.

He walked away from the game.

Moments later, he turned around and came back. The giant was no longer on the screen. The mouse was running around again, trying to get out of the maze.

No, I won't play. Achilles is far away and he does not have the power to hurt me. Or Poke either, not anymore. I don't have to think about him and I sure as hell don't have to drink anything he offers me.

Bean walked away again, and this time did not come back.

He found himself down by the mess. It had just closed, but Bean had nothing better to do, so he sat down in the corridor beside the mess hall door and rested his forehead on his knees and thought about Rotterdam and sitting on top of a garbage can watching Poke working with her crew and how she was the most decent crew boss he'd seen, the way she listened to the little kids and gave them a fair share and kept them alive even if it meant not eating so much herself and that's why he chose her, because she had mercy—mercy enough that she just might listen to a child.

Her mercy killed her.

I killed her when I chose her.

There better be a God. So he can damn Achilles to hell forever.

Someone kicked at his foot.

"Go away," said Bean, "I'm not bothering you."

Whoever it was kicked again, knocking Bean's feet out from under him. With his hands he caught himself from falling over. He looked up. Bonzo Madrid loomed over him.

"I understand you're the littlest dingleberry clinging to the butt hairs of Dragon Army," said Bonzo.

He had three other guys with him. Big guys. They all had bully faces.

"Hi, Bonzo."

"We need to talk, pinprick."

"What is this, espionage?" asked Bean. "You're not supposed to talk to soldiers in other armies."

"I don't need espionage to find out how to beat Dragon Army," said Bonzo.

"So you're just looking for the littlest Dragon soldiers wherever you can find them, and then you'll push them around a little till they cry?"

Bonzo's face showed his anger. Not that it didn't always show anger.

"Are you begging to eat out of your own asshole, pin-prick?"

Bean didn't like bullies right now. And since, at the moment, he felt guilty of murdering Poke, he didn't really care if Bonzo Madrid ended up being the one to administer the death penalty. It was time to speak his mind.

"You're at least three times my weight," said Bean, "except inside your skull. You're a second-rater who somehow got an army and never could figure out what to do with it. Wiggin is going to grind you into the ground and he isn't even going to have to try. So does it really matter what you do to me? I'm the smallest and weakest soldier in the whole school. Naturally *I'm* the one you choose to kick around."

"Yeah, the smallest and weakest," said one of the other kids.

Bonzo didn't say anything, though. Bean's words had stung. Bonzo had his pride, and he knew now that if he harmed Bean it would be a humiliation, not a pleasure.

"Ender Wiggin isn't going to beat me with that collection of launchies and rejects that he calls an army. He may have psyched out a bunch of dorks like Carn and . . . *Petra.*" He spat her name. "But whenever *we* find crap my army can pound it flat."

Bean affixed him with his most withering glare. "Don't you get it, Bonzo? The teachers have picked Wiggin. He's the best. The best ever. They didn't give him the worst army. They gave him the *best* army. Those veterans you call rejects—they were soldiers so good that the *stupid* commanders couldn't get along with them and tried to transfer them away. Wiggin knows how to use good soldiers, even if you don't. That's why Wiggin is winning. He's smarter than you. And his soldiers are all smarter than your soldiers. The deck is stacked against you, Bonzo. You might as well give up now. When your pathetic little Salamander Army faces us, you'll be so whipped you'll have to pee sitting down."

Bean might have said more—it's not like he had a plan,

and there was certainly a lot more he could have said—but he was interrupted. Two of Bonzo's friends scooped him up and held him high against the wall, higher than their own heads. Bonzo put one hand around his throat, just under his jaw, and pressed back. The others let go. Bean was hanging by his neck, and he couldn't breathe. Reflexively he kicked, struggling to get some purchase with his feet. But long-armed Bonzo was too far away for any of Bean's kicking to land on him.

"The game is one thing," Bonzo said quietly. "The teachers can rig that and give it to their little Wiggin catamite. But there'll come a time when it isn't a game. And when that time comes, it won't be a frozen flash suit that makes it so Wiggin can't move. Comprendes?"

What answer was he hoping for? It was a sure thing Bean couldn't nod or speak.

Bonzo just stood there, smiling maliciously, as Bean struggled.

Everything started turning black around the edges of Bean's vision before Bonzo finally let him drop to the floor. He lay there, coughing and gasping.

What have I done? I goaded Bonzo Madrid. A bully with none of Achilles' subtlety. When Wiggin beats him, Bonzo isn't going to take it. He won't stop with a demonstration, either. His hatred for Wiggin runs deep.

As soon as he could breathe again, Bean headed back to the barracks. Nikolai noticed the marks on his neck at once. "Who was choking you?"

"I don't know," said Bean.

"Don't give me that," said Nikolai. "He was facing you, look at the fingermarks."

"I don't remember."

"You remember the pattern of arteries on your own placenta."

"I'm not going to tell you," said Bean. To that, Nikolai had no answer, though he didn't like it.

Bean signed on as 'Graff and wrote a note to Dimak, even though he knew it would do no good.

"Bonzo is insane. He could kill somebody, and Wiggin's the one he hates the most."

The answer came back quickly, almost as if Dimak had been waiting for the message. "Clean up your own messes. Don't go crying to mama."

The words stung. It wasn't Bean's mess, it was Wiggin's. And, ultimately, the teachers', for having put Wiggin in Bonzo's army to begin with. And then to taunt him because he didn't have a mother—when did the teachers become the enemy here? They were supposed to protect us from crazy kids like Bonzo Madrid. How do they think I'm going to clean this mess up?

The only thing that will stop Bonzo Madrid is to kill him.

And then Bean remembered standing there looking down at Achilles, saying, "You got to kill him."

Why couldn't I have kept my mouth shut? Why did I have to goad Bonzo Madrid? Wiggin is going to end up like Poke. And it will be my fault again.

16

Companion

"So you see, Anton, the key you found has been turned, and it may be the salvation of the human race."

"But the poor boy. To live his life so small, and then die as a giant."

"Perhaps he'll be . . . amused at the irony."

"How strange to think that my little key might turn out to be the salvation of the human race. From the invading beasts, anyway. Who will save us when we become our own enemy again?"

"We are not enemies, you and I."

"Not many people are enemies to anyone. But the ones full of greed or hate, pride or fear—their passion is strong enough to lever all the world into war."

"If God can raise up a great soul to save us from one menace, might he not answer our prayers by raising up another when we need him?"

"But Sister Carlotta, you know the boy you speak of was not raised up by God. He was created by a kidnapper, a baby-killer, an outlaw scientist."

"Do you know why Satan is so angry all the time? Because whenever he works a particularly clever bit of mischief, God uses it to serve his own righteous purposes."

"So God uses wicked people as his tools."

"God gives us the freedom to do great evil, if we choose. Then he uses his own freedom to create goodness out of that evil, for that is what he chooses."

"So in the long run, God always wins."

"Yes."

"In the short run, though, it *can* be uncomfortable."

"And when, in the past, would you have preferred to die, instead of being alive here today?"

"There it is. We get used to everything. We find hope in anything."

"That's why I've never understood suicide. Even those suffering from great depression or guilt—don't they feel Christ the Comforter in their hearts, giving them hope?"

"You're asking me?"

"God not being convenient, I ask a fellow mortal."

"In my view, suicide is not really the wish for life to end."

"What is it, then?"

"It is the only way a powerless person can find to make everybody else look away from his shame. The wish is not to die, but to hide."

"As Adam and Eve hid from the Lord."

"Because they were naked."

"If only such sad people could remember: Everyone is naked. Everyone wants to hide. But life is still sweet. Let it go on."

"You don't believe that the Formics are the beast of the Apocalypse, then, Sister?"

"No, Anton. I believe they are also children of God."

"And yet you found this boy specifically so he could grow up to destroy them."

"*Defeat* them. Besides, if God does not want them to die, they will not die."

"And if God wants *us* to die, we will. Why do you work so hard, then?"

"Because these hands of mine, I gave them to God, and I serve him as best I can. If he had not wanted me to find Bean, I would not have found him."

"And if God wants the Formics to prevail?"

"He'll find some other hands to do it. For that job, he can't have mine."

Lately, while the toon leaders drilled the soldiers, Wiggin had taken to disappearing. Bean used his ^Graff logon to find what he was doing. He'd gone back to studying the vids of Mazer Rackham's victory, much more intensely and single-mindedly than ever before. And this time, because Wiggin's army was playing games daily and winning them all, the other commanders and many toon leaders and common soldiers as well began to go to the library and watch the same vids, trying to make sense of them, trying to see what Wiggin saw.

Stupid, thought Bean. Wiggin isn't looking for anything to use here in Battle School—he's created a powerful, versatile army and he'll figure out what to do with them on the spot. He's studying those vids in order to figure out how to beat the Buggers. Because he knows now: He will face them someday. The teachers would not be wrecking the whole system here in Battle School if they were not nearing the crisis, if they did not need Ender Wiggin to save us from the invading Buggers. So Wiggin studies the Buggers, desperate for some idea of what they want, how they fight, how they die.

Why don't the teachers see that Wiggin is done? He's not even thinking about Battle School anymore. They should take him out of here and move him into Tactical School, or whatever the next stage of his training will be. Instead, they're pushing him, making him tired.

Us too. We're tired.

Bean saw it especially in Nikolai, who was working harder than the others just to keep up. If we were an ordinary army, thought Bean, most of us would be like Nikolai. As it is, many of us are—Nikolai was not the first to show his weariness. Soldiers drop silverware or food trays at mealtimes. At least one has wet his bed. We argue more at practice. Our classwork is suffering. Everyone has limits. Even me, even genetically-altered Bean the thinking machine, I need time to relubricate and refuel, and I'm not getting it.

Bean even wrote to Colonel Graff about it, a snippy little note saying only, "It is one thing to train soldiers and quite another to wear them out." He got no reply.

Late afternoon, with a half hour before mess call. They had already won a game that morning and then practiced after class, though the toon leaders, at Wiggin's suggestion, had let their soldiers go early. Most of Dragon Army was now dressing after showers, though some had already gone on to kill time in the game room or the video room . . . or the library. Nobody was paying attention to classwork now, but a few still went through the motions.

Wiggin appeared in the doorway, brandishing the new orders.

A second battle on the *same day.*

"This one's hot and there's no time," said Wiggin. "They gave Bonzo notice about twenty minutes ago, and by the time we get to the door they'll have been inside for a good five minutes at least."

He sent the four soldiers nearest the door—all young, but not launchies anymore, they were veterans now—to bring back the ones who had left. Bean dressed quickly—he had learned how to do it by himself now, but not without hearing plenty of jokes about how he was the only soldier who had to practice getting dressed, and it was still slow.

As they dressed, there was plenty of complaining about how this was getting stupid, Dragon Army should have a break now and then. Fly Molo was the loudest, but even Crazy Tom, who usually laughed at everything, was pissed about it. When Tom said, "Same day nobody ever do two battles!" Wiggin answered, "Nobody ever beat Dragon Army, either. This be your big chance to lose?"

Of course not. Nobody intended to lose. They just wanted to complain about it.

It took a while, but finally they were gathered in the corridor to the battleroom. The gate was already open. A few of the last arrivals were still putting on their flash suits. Bean was right behind Crazy Tom, so he could see down into the room. Bright light. No stars, no grid, no hiding place of any kind. The enemy gate was open, and yet there was not a Salamander soldier to be seen.

"My heart," said Crazy Tom. "They haven't come out yet, either."

Bean rolled his eyes. Of course they were out. But in a room without cover, they had simply formed themselves up on the ceiling, gathered around Dragon Army's gate, ready to destroy everybody as they came out.

Wiggin caught Bean's facial expression and smiled as he covered his own mouth to signal them all to be silent. He pointed all around the gate, to let them know where Salamander was gathered, then motioned for them to move back.

The strategy was simple and obvious. Since Bonzo Madrid had kindly pinned his army against a wall, ready to be slaughtered, it only remained to find the right way to enter the battleroom and carry out the massacre.

Wiggin's solution—which Bean liked—was to transform the larger soldiers into armored vehicles by having them kneel upright and freeze their legs. Then a smaller soldier knelt on each big kid's calves, wrapped one arm around the bigger soldier's waist, and prepared to fire. The largest soldiers were used as launchers, throwing each pair into the battleroom.

For once being small had its advantages. Bean and Crazy Tom were the pair Wiggin used to demonstrate what he wanted them all to do. As a result, when the first two pairs were thrown into the room, Bean got to begin the slaughter. He had three kills almost at once—at such close range, the beam was tight and the kills came fast. And as they began to go out of range, Bean climbed around Crazy Tom and launched off of him, heading east and somewhat up while Tom went even faster toward the far side of the room. When other Dragons saw how Bean had managed to stay within firing range, while moving sideways and therefore remaining hard to hit, many of them did the same. Eventually Bean was disabled, but it hardly mattered—Salamander was wiped out to the last man, and without a single one of them getting off the wall. Even when it was obvious they were easy, stationary targets, Bonzo didn't catch on that he was doomed until he himself was already frozen, and nobody else had the initiative to countermand his original order and start moving so they wouldn't be so easy to hit. Just one more example of why a commander who ruled by fear and made all the decisions himself would always be beaten, sooner or later.

The whole battle had taken less than a full minute from the time Bean rode Crazy Tom through the door until the last Salamander was frozen.

What surprised Bean was that Wiggin, usually so calm, was pissed off and showing it. Major Anderson didn't even have a chance to give the official congratulations to the victor before Wiggin shouted at him, "I thought you were going to put us against an army that could match us in a fair fight."

Why would he think that? Wiggin must have had some kind of conversation with Anderson, must have been promised something that hadn't been delivered.

But Anderson explained nothing. "Congratulations on the victory, commander."

Wiggin wasn't going to have it. It wasn't going to be business as usual. He turned to his army and called out to Bean by name. "If you had commanded Salamander Army, what would you have done?"

Since another Dragon had used him to shove off in midair, Bean was now drifting down near the enemy gate, but he heard the question—Wiggin wasn't being subtle about this. Bean didn't want to answer, because he knew what a serious mistake this was, to speak slightingly of

Salamander and call on the smallest Dragon soldier to correct Bonzo's stupid tactics. Wiggin hadn't had Bonzo's hand around his throat the way Bean had. Still, Wiggin was commander, and Bonzo's tactics had been stupid, and it was fun to say so.

"Keep a shifting pattern of movement going in front of the door," Bean answered, loudly, so every soldier could hear him—even the Salamanders, still clinging to the ceiling. "You never hold still when the enemy knows exactly where you are."

Wiggin turned to Anderson again. "As long as you're cheating, why don't you train the other army to cheat intelligently!"

Anderson was still calm, ignoring Wiggin's outburst. "I suggest that you remobilize your army."

Wiggin wasn't wasting time with rituals today. He pressed the buttons to thaw both armies at once. And instead of forming up to receive formal surrender, he shouted at once, "Dragon Army dismissed!"

Bean was one of those nearest the gate, but he waited till nearly last, so that he and Wiggin left together. "Sir," said Bean. "You just humiliated Bonzo and he's—"

"I know," said Wiggin. He jogged away from Bean, not wanting to hear about it.

"He's dangerous!" Bean called after him. Wasted effort. Either Wiggin already knew he'd provoked the wrong bully, or he didn't care.

Did he do it deliberately? Wiggin was always in control of himself, always carrying out a plan. But Bean couldn't think of any plan that required yelling at Major Anderson and shaming Bonzo Madrid in front of his whole army.

Why would Wiggin do such a stupid thing?

—

It was almost impossible to think of geometry, even though there was a test tomorrow. Classwork was utterly unimportant now, and yet they went on taking the tests and turning in or failing to turn in their assignments. The last few days, Bean had begun to get less-than-perfect scores. Not that he didn't know the answers, or at least how to figure them out. It's that his mind kept wandering to things that mattered more—new tactics that might surprise an enemy; new tricks that the teachers might pull in the way they set things up; what might be, must be going on in the larger war, to cause the system to start breaking apart like this; what would happen on Earth and in the I.F. once the Buggers were defeated. If they were defeated. Hard to care about volumes, areas, faces, and dimensions of solids. On a test yesterday, working out problems of gravity near planetary and stellar masses, Bean finally gave up and wrote:

$$2 + 2 = \pi \sqrt{2 + n}$$

WHEN YOU KNOW THE VALUE OF N, I'LL FINISH THIS TEST.

He knew that the teachers all knew what was going on, and if they wanted to pretend that classwork still mattered, fine, let them, but *he* didn't have to play.

At the same time, he knew that the problems of gravity mattered to someone whose only likely future was in the International Fleet. He also needed a thorough grounding in geometry, since he had a pretty good idea of what math was yet to come. He wasn't going to be an engineer or artillerist or rocket scientist or even, in all likelihood, a pilot. But he had to know what they knew better than they knew it, or they'd never respect him enough to follow him.

Not tonight, that's all, thought Bean. Tonight I can rest. Tomorrow I'll learn what I need to learn. When I'm not so tired.

He closed his eyes.

He opened them again. He opened his locker and took out his desk.

Back on the streets of Rotterdam he had been tired,

worn out by hunger and malnutrition and despair. But he kept watching. Kept thinking. And therefore he was able to stay alive. In this army everyone was getting tired, which meant that there would be more and more stupid mistakes. Bean, of all of them, could least afford to become stupid. Not being stupid was the only asset he had.

He signed on. A message appeared in his display.

See me at once—Ender

It was only ten minutes before lights out. Maybe Wiggin sent the message three hours ago. But better late than never. He slid off his bunk, not bothering with shoes, and padded out into the corridor in his stocking feet. He knocked at the door marked

COMMANDER

DRAGON ARMY

"Come in," said Wiggin.

Bean opened the door and came inside. Wiggin looked tired in the way that Colonel Graff usually looked tired. Heavy skin around the eyes, face slack, hunched in the shoulders, but eyes still bright and fierce, watching, thinking. "Just saw your message," said Bean.

"Fine."

"It's near lights-out."

"I'll help you find your way in the dark."

The sarcasm surprised Bean. As usual, Wiggin had completely misunderstood the purpose of Bean's comment. "I just didn't know if you knew what time it was—"

"I always know what time it is."

Bean sighed inwardly. It never failed. Whenever he had any conversation with Wiggin, it turned into some kind of pissing contest, which Bean always lost even when it was Wiggin whose deliberate misunderstanding caused the whole thing. Bean hated it. He recognized Wiggin's genius and honored him for it. Why couldn't he see anything good in Bean?

But Bean said nothing. There was nothing he could say that would improve the situation. Wiggin had called him in. Let Wiggin move the meeting forward.

"Remember four weeks ago, Bean? When you told me to make you a toon leader?"

"Eh."

"I've made five toon leaders and five assistants since then. And none of them was you." Wiggin raised his eyebrows. "Was I right?"

"Yes, sir." But only because you didn't bother to give me a chance to prove myself before you made the assignments.

"So tell me how you've done in these eight battles."

Bean wanted to point out how time after time, his suggestions to Crazy Tom had made C toon the most effective in the army. How his tactical innovations and creative responses to flowing situations had been imitated by the other soldiers. But that would be brag and borderline insubordination. It wasn't what a soldier who wanted to be an officer would say. Either Crazy Tom had reported Bean's contribution or he hadn't. It wasn't Bean's place to report on anything about himself that wasn't public record. "Today was the first time they disabled me so early, but the computer listed me as getting eleven hits before I had to stop. I've never had less than five hits in a battle. I've also completed every assignment I've been given."

"Why did they make you a soldier so young, Bean?"

"No younger than you were." Technically not true, but close enough.

"But why?"

What was he getting at? It was the teachers' decision. Had he found out that Bean was the one who composed the roster? Did he know that Bean had chosen himself? "I don't know."

"Yes you do, and so do I."

No, Wiggin wasn't asking specifically about why *Bean* was made a soldier. He was asking why launchies were suddenly getting promoted so young. "I've tried to guess, but they're just guesses." Not that Bean's guesses were ever just guesses—but then, neither were Wiggin's. "You're—very good. They knew that, they pushed you ahead—"

"Tell me *why,* Bean."

And now Bean understood the question he was really asking. "Because they need us, that's why." He sat on the floor and looked, not into Wiggin's face, but at his feet. Bean knew things that he wasn't supposed to know. That the teachers didn't know he knew. And in all likelihood, there were teachers monitoring this conversation. Bean couldn't let his face give away how much he really understood. "Because they need somebody to beat the Buggers. That's the only thing they care about."

"It's important that you know that, Bean."

Bean wanted to demand, Why is it important that *I* know it? Or are you just saying that people in general should know it? Have you finally seen and understood who I am? That I'm *you,* only smarter and less likable, the better strategist but the weaker commander? That if you fail, if you break, if you get sick and die, then I'm the one? Is that why I need to know this?

"Because," Wiggin went on, "most of the boys in this school think the game is important *for itself,* but it isn't. It's only important because it helps them find kids who might grow up to be real commanders, in the real war. But as for the game, screw that. That's what they're doing. Screwing up the game."

"Funny," said Bean. "I thought they were just doing it to us." No, if Wiggin thought Bean needed to have this explained to him, he did *not* understand who Bean really was. Still, it was Bean in Wiggin's quarters, having this conversation with him. That was something.

"A game nine weeks earlier than it should have come. A game every day. And now two games in the same day.

Bean, I don't know what the teachers are doing, but my army is getting tired, and I'm getting tired, and they don't care at all about the rules of the game. I've pulled the old charts up from the computer. No one has ever destroyed so many enemies and kept so many of his own soldiers whole in the history of the game."

What was this, brag? Bean answered as brag was meant to be answered. "You're the best, Ender."

Wiggin shook his head. If he heard the irony in Bean's voice, he didn't respond to it. "Maybe. But it was no accident that I got the soldiers I got. Launchies, rejects from other armies, but put them together and my worst soldier could be a toon leader in another army. They've loaded things my way, but now they're loading it all against me. Bean, they want to break us down."

So Wiggin did understand how his army had been selected, even if he didn't know who had done the selecting. Or maybe he knew everything, and this was all that he cared to show Bean at this time. It was hard to guess how much of what Wiggin did was calculated and how much merely intuitive. "They can't break you."

"You'd be surprised." Wiggin breathed sharply, suddenly, as if there were a stab of pain, or he had to catch a sudden breath in a wind; Bean looked at him and realized that the impossible was happening. Far from baiting him, Ender Wiggin was actually confiding in him. Not much. But a little. Ender was letting Bean see that he was human. Bringing him into the inner circle. Making him . . . what? A counselor? A confidant?

"Maybe you'll be surprised," said Bean.

"There's a limit to how many clever new ideas I can come up with every day. Somebody's going to come up with something to throw at me that I haven't thought of before, and I won't be ready."

"What's the worst that could happen?" asked Bean. "You lose one game."

"Yes. That's the worst that could happen. I can't lose *any* games. Because if I lose *any* . . ."

He didn't complete the thought. Bean wondered what Ender imagined the consequences would be. Merely that the legend of Ender Wiggin, perfect soldier, would be lost? Or that his army would lose confidence in him, or in their own invincibility? Or was this about the larger war, and losing a game here in Battle School might shake the confidence of the teachers that Ender was the commander of the future, the one to lead the fleet, if he could be made ready before the Bugger invasion arrived?

Again, Bean did not know how much the teachers knew about what Bean had guessed about the progress of the wider war. Better to keep silence.

"I need you to be clever, Bean," said Ender. "I need you to think of solutions to problems we haven't seen yet. I want you to try things that no one has ever tried because they're absolutely stupid."

So what is this about, Ender? What have you decided about me, that brings me into your quarters tonight? "Why me?"

"Because even though there are some better soldiers than you in Dragon Army—not many, but some—there's nobody who can think better and faster than you."

He *had* seen. And after a month of frustration, Bean realized that it was better this way. Ender had seen his work in battle, had judged him by what he did, not by his reputation in classes or the rumors about his having the highest scores in the history of the school. Bean had earned this evaluation, and it had been given him by the only person in this school whose high opinion Bean longed for.

Ender held out his desk for Bean to see. On it were twelve names. Two or three soldiers from each toon. Bean immediately knew how Ender had chosen them. They were all good soldiers, confident and reliable. But not the flashy ones, the stunters, the show-offs. They were, in fact, the ones that Bean valued most highly among those who were not toon leaders. "Choose five of these," said Ender. "One from each toon. They're a special squad, and you'll train them. Only during the extra practice sessions. Talk to me about what you're training them to do. Don't spend too long on any one thing. Most of the time you and your squad will be part of the whole army, part of your regular toons. But when I need you. When there's something to be done that only you can do."

There was something else about these twelve. "These are all new. No veterans."

"After last week, Bean, all our soldiers are veterans. Don't you realize that on the individual soldier standings, all forty of our soldiers are in the top fifty? That you have to go down seventeen places to find a soldier who *isn't* a Dragon?"

"What if I can't think of anything?" asked Bean.

"Then I was wrong about you."

Bean grinned. "You weren't wrong."

The lights went out.

"Can you find your way back, Bean?"

"Probably not."

"Then stay here. If you listen very carefully, you can hear the good fairy come in the night and leave our assignment for tomorrow."

"They won't give us another battle tomorrow, will they?" Bean meant it as a joke, but Ender didn't answer.

Bean heard him climb into bed.

Ender was still small for a commander. His feet didn't come near the end of the bunk. There was plenty of room for Bean to curl up at the foot of the bed. So he climbed up and then lay still, so as not to disturb Ender's sleep. If he was sleeping. If he was not lying awake in the silence, trying to make sense of . . . what?

For Bean, the assignment was merely to think of the unthinkable—stupid ploys that might be used against them, and ways to counter them; equally stupid innovations they might introduce in order to sow confusion among the other armies and, Bean suspected, get them sidetracked into imitating completely nonessential strategies. Since few of the other commanders understood why

Dragon Army was winning, they kept imitating the nonce tactics used in a particular battle instead of seeing the underlying method Ender used in training and organizing his army. As Napoleon said, the only thing a commander ever truly controls is his own army—training, morale, trust, initiative, command and, to a lesser degree, supply, placement, movement, loyalty, and courage in battle. What the enemy will do and what chance will bring, those defy all planning. The commander must be able to change his plans abruptly when obstacles or opportunities appear. If his army isn't ready and willing to respond to his will, his cleverness comes to nothing.

The less effective commanders didn't understand this. Failing to recognize that Ender won because he and his army responded fluidly and instantly to change, they could only think to imitate the specific tactics they saw him use. Even if Bean's creative gambits were irrelevant to the outcome of the battle, they would lead other commanders to waste time imitating irrelevancies. Now and then something he came up with might actually be useful. But by and large, he was a sideshow.

That was fine with Bean. If Ender wanted a sideshow, what mattered was that he had chosen Bean to create that show, and Bean would do it as well as it could be done.

But if Ender was lying awake tonight, it was not because he was concerned about Dragon Army's battles tomorrow and the next day and the next. Ender was thinking about the Buggers and how he would fight them when he got through his training and was thrown into war, with the real lives of real men depending on his decisions, with the survival of humanity depending on the outcome.

In *that* scheme, what is my place? thought Bean. I'm glad enough that the burden is on Ender, not because I could not bear it—maybe I could—but because I have more confidence that Ender can bring it off than that I could. Whatever it is that makes men love the commander who decides when they will die, Ender has that, and if I have it no one has yet seen evidence of it. Besides, even without genetic alteration, Ender has abilities that the tests didn't measure for, that run deeper than mere intellect.

But he shouldn't have to bear all this alone. I can help him. I can forget geometry and astronomy and all the other nonsense and concentrate on the problems he faces most directly. I'll do research into the way other animals wage war, especially swarming hive insects, since the Formics resemble ants the way we resemble primates.

And I can watch his back.

Bean thought again of Bonzo Madrid. Of the deadly rage of bullies in Rotterdam.

Why have the teachers put Ender in this position? He's an obvious target for the hatred of the other boys. Kids in Battle School had war in their hearts. They hungered for triumph. They loathed defeat. If they lacked these attributes, they would never have been brought here. Yet from the start, Ender had been set apart from the others—younger but smarter, the leading soldier and now the commander who makes all other commanders look like babies. Some commanders responded to defeat by becoming submissive—Carn Carby, for instance, now praised Ender behind his back and studied his battles to try to learn how to win, never realizing that you had to study Ender's training, not his battles, to understand his victories. But most of the other commanders were resentful, frightened, ashamed, angry, jealous, and it was in their character to translate such feelings into violent action . . . if they were sure of victory.

Just like the streets of Rotterdam. Just like the bullies, struggling for supremacy, for rank, for respect. Ender has stripped Bonzo naked. It cannot be borne. He'll have his revenge, as surely as Achilles avenged his humiliation.

And the teachers understand this. They intend it. Ender has clearly mastered every test they set for him—whatever Battle School usually taught, he was done with. So why didn't they move him on to the next level? Because there was a lesson they were trying to teach, or a test they were trying to get him to pass, which was not within the usual curriculum. Only this particular test could end in death. Bean had felt Bonzo's fingers around his throat. This was a boy who, once he let himself go, would relish the absolute power that the murderer achieves at his victim's moment of death.

They're putting Ender into a street situation. They're testing him to see if he can survive.

They don't know what they're doing, the fools. The street is not a test. The street is a lottery.

I came out a winner—I was alive. But Ender's survival won't depend on his ability. Luck plays too large a role. Plus the skill and resolve and power of the opponent.

Bonzo may be unable to control the emotions that weaken him, but his presence in Battle School means that he is not without skill. He was made a commander because a certain type of soldier will follow him into death and horror. Ender is in mortal danger. And the teachers, who think of us as children, have no idea how quickly death can come. Look away for only a few minutes, step away far enough that you can't get back in time, and your precious Ender Wiggin, on whom all your hopes are pinned, will be quite, quite dead. I saw it on the streets of Rotterdam. It can happen just as easily in your nice clean rooms here in space.

So Bean set aside classwork for good that night, lying at Ender's feet. Instead, he had two new courses of study. He would help Ender prepare for the war he cared about, with the Buggers. But he would also help him in the street fight that was being set up for him.

It wasn't that Ender was oblivious, either. After some kind of fracas in the battleroom during one of Ender's early freetime practices, Ender had taken a course in self-defense, and knew something about fighting man to man. But Bonzo would not come at him man to man. He was too keenly aware of having been beaten. Bonzo's purpose would not be a rematch, it would not be vindication. It would be punishment. It would be elimination. He would bring a gang.

And the teachers would not realize the danger until it was too late. They still didn't think of anything the children did as "real."

So after Bean thought of clever, stupid things to do with his new squad, he also tried to think of ways to set Bonzo up so that, in the crunch, he would have to take on Ender Wiggin alone or not at all. Strip away Bonzo's support. Destroy the morale, the reputation of any bully who might go along with him.

This is one job Ender *can't* do. But it can be done.

Part Five

LEADER

17

Deadline

"I don't even know how to interpret this. The mind game had only one shot at Bean, and it puts up this one kid's face, and he goes off the charts with—what, fear? Rage? Isn't there anybody who knows how this so-called game works? It ran Ender through a wringer, brought in those pictures of his brother that it couldn't possibly have had, only it got them. And this one—was it some deeply insightful gambit that leads to powerful new conclusions about Bean's psyche? Or was it simply the only person Bean knew whose picture was already in the Battle School files?"

"Was that a rant, or is there any particular one of those questions you want answered?"

"What I want you to answer is this question: How the hell can you tell me that something was 'very significant' if you have no idea what it signifies!"

"If someone runs after your car, screaming and waving his arms, you know that something significant is intended, even if you can't hear a word he's saying."

"So that's what this was? Screaming?"

"That was an analogy. The image of Achilles was extraordinarily important to Bean."

"Important positive, or important negative?"

"That's too cut-and-dried. If it was negative, are his negative feelings because Achilles caused some terrible trauma in Bean? Or negative because having been torn away from Achilles was traumatic, and Bean longs to be restored to him?"

"So if we have an independent source of information that tells us to keep them apart . . ."

"Then either that independent source is really really right. . . ."

"Or really really wrong."

"I'd be more specific if I could. We only had a minute with him."

"That's disingenuous. You've had the mind game linked to all his work with his teacher-identity."

"And we've reported to you about that. It's partly his hunger to have control—that's how it began—but it has since become a way of taking responsibility. He has, in a way, *become* a teacher. He has also used his inside information to give himself the illusion of belonging to the community."

"He does belong."

"He has only one close friend, and that's more of a big brother, little brother thing."

"I have to decide whether I can put Achilles into Battle School while Bean is there, or give up one of them in order to keep the other. Now, from Bean's response to Achilles' face, what counsel can you give me."

"You won't like it."

"Try me."

"From that incident, we can tell you that putting them together will be either a really really bad thing, or—"

"I'm going to have to take a long, hard look at your budget."

"Sir, the whole purpose of the program, the way it

works, is that the computer makes connections we would never think of, and gets responses we weren't looking for. It's not actually under our control."

"Just because a program isn't out of control doesn't mean intelligence is present, either in the program or the programmer."

"We don't use the word 'intelligence' with software. We regard that as a naive idea. We say that it's 'complex.' Which means that we don't always understand what it's doing. We don't always get conclusive information."

"Have you *ever* gotten conclusive information about anything?"

"*I* chose the wrong word this time. 'Conclusive' isn't ever the goal when we are studying the human mind."

"Try 'useful.' Anything useful?"

"Sir, I've told you what we know. The decision was yours before we reported to you, and it's still your decision now. Use our information or not, but is it sensible to shoot the messenger?"

"When the messenger won't tell you what the hell the message *is*, my trigger finger gets twitchy. Dismissed."

Nikolai's name was on the list that Ender gave him, but Bean ran into problems immediately.

"I don't want to," said Nikolai.

It had not occurred to Bean that anyone would refuse.

"I'm having a hard enough time keeping up as it is."

"You're a good soldier."

"By the skin of my teeth. With a big helping of luck."

"That's how *all* good soldiers do it."

"Bean, if I lose one practice a day from my regular toon, then I'll fall behind. How can I make it up? And one practice a day with you won't be enough. I'm a smart kid, Bean, but I'm not Ender. I'm not you. That's the thing that I don't think you really get. How it feels *not* to be you. Things just aren't as easy and clear."

"It's not easy for me, either."

"Look, I know that, Bean. And there are some things I

can do for you. This isn't one of them. Please."

It was Bean's first experience with command, and it wasn't working. He found himself getting angry, wanting to say Screw you and go on to someone else. Only he couldn't be angry at the only true friend he had. And he also couldn't easily take no for an answer. "Nikolai, what we're doing won't be hard. Stunts and tricks."

Nikolai closed his eyes. "Bean, you're making me feel bad."

"I don't want you to feel bad, Sinterklaas, but this is the assignment I was given, because Ender thinks Dragon Army needs this. You were on the list, his choice not mine."

"But you don't have to choose me."

"So I ask the next kid, and he says, 'Nikolai's on this squad, right?' and I say, No, he didn't want to. That makes them all feel like they can say no. And they'll *want* to say no, because nobody wants to be taking orders from me."

"A month ago, sure, that would have been true. But they know you're a solid soldier. I've heard people talk about you. They respect you."

Again, it would have been so easy to do what Nikolai wanted and let him off the hook on this. And, as a friend, that would be the *right* thing to do. But Bean couldn't think as a friend. He had to deal with the fact that he had been given a command and he had to make it work.

Did he really need Nikolai?

"I'm just thinking out loud, Nikolai, because you're the only one I can say this to, but see, I'm scared. I wanted to lead a toon, but that's because I didn't know anything about what leaders do. I've had a week of battles to see how Crazy Tom holds the group of us together, the voice he uses for command. To see how Ender trains us and trusts us, and it's a dance, tiptoe, leap, spin, and I'm afraid that I'll fail, and there isn't *time* to fail, I have to make this work, and when you're with me, I know there's at least one person who isn't halfway hoping for this smart little kid to fail."

"Don't kid yourself," said Nikolai. "As long as we're being honest."

That stung. But a leader had to take that, didn't he? "No matter what you feel, Nikolai, you'll give me a chance," said Bean. "And because you're giving me a chance, the others will, too. I need . . . loyalty."

"So do I, Bean."

"You need my loyalty as a friend, in order to let you, personally, be happy," said Bean. "I need loyalty as a leader, in order to fulfil the assignment given to us by our commander."

"That's mean," said Nikolai.

"Eh," said Bean. "Also true."

"You're mean, Bean."

"Help me, Nikolai."

"Looks like our friendship goes only one way."

Bean had never felt like this before—this knife in his heart, just because of the words he was hearing, just because somebody *else* was angry with him. It wasn't just because he wanted Nikolai to think well of him. It was because he knew that Nikolai was at least partly right. Bean was using his friendship against him.

It wasn't because of that pain, however, that Bean decided to back off. It was because a soldier who was with him against his will would not serve him well. Even if he was a friend. "Look, if you won't, you won't. I'm sorry I made you mad. I'll do it without you. And you're right, I'll do fine. Still friends, Nikolai?"

Nikolai took his offered hand, held it. "Thank you," he whispered.

Bean went immediately to Shovel, the only one on Ender's list who was also from C toon. Shovel wasn't Bean's first choice—he had just the slightest tendency to delay, to do things halfheartedly. But because he was in C toon, Shovel had been there when Bean advised Crazy Tom. He had observed Bean in action.

Shovel set aside his desk when Bean asked if they could talk for a minute. As with Nikolai, Bean clambered up onto the bunk to sit beside the larger boy. Shovel was from Cagnes-sur-Mer, a little town on the French Riviera, and he still had that open-faced friendliness of Provence. Bean liked him. Everybody liked him.

Quickly Bean explained what Ender had asked him to do—though he didn't mention that it was just a sideshow. Nobody would give up a daily practice for a something that wouldn't be crucial to victory. "You were on the list Ender gave me, and I'd like you to—"

"Bean, what are you doing?"

Crazy Tom stood in front of Shovel's bunk.

At once Bean realized his mistake. "Sir," said Bean, "I should have talked to you first. I'm new at this and I just didn't think."

"New at what?"

Again Bean laid out what he had been asked to do by Ender.

"And Shovel's on the list?"

"Right."

"So I'm going to lose you *and* Shovel from my practices?"

"Just one practice per day."

"I'm the only toon leader who loses two."

"Ender said one from each toon. Five, plus me. Not my choice."

"Merda," said Crazy Tom. "You and Ender just didn't think of the fact that this is going to hit me harder than any of the other toon leaders. Whatever you're doing, why can't you do it with five instead of six? You and four others—one from each of the other toons?"

Bean wanted to argue, but realized that going head to head wasn't going to get him anywhere. "You're right, I didn't think of that, and you're right that Ender might very well change his mind when he realizes what he's doing to your practices. So when he comes in this morning, why don't you talk to him and let me know what the two of you decide? In the meantime, though, Shovel might tell me no, and then the question doesn't matter anymore, right?"

Crazy Tom thought about it. Bean could see the anger ticking away in him. But leadership had changed Crazy Tom. He no longer blew up the way he used to. He caught himself. He held it in. He waited it out.

"OK, I'll talk to Ender. If Shovel wants to do it."

They both looked at Shovel.

"I think it'd be OK," said Shovel. "To do something weird like this."

"I won't let up on either of you," said Crazy Tom. "And you don't talk about your wacko toon during my practices. You keep it outside."

They both agreed to that. Bean could see that Crazy Tom was wise to insist on that. This special assignment would set the two of them apart from the others in C toon. If they rubbed their noses in it, the others could feel shut out of an elite. That problem wouldn't show up as much in any of the other toons, because there'd only be one kid from each toon in Bean's squad. No chat. Therefore no nose-rubbing.

"Look, I don't have to talk to Ender about this," said Crazy Tom. "Unless it becomes a problem. OK?"

"Thanks," said Bean.

Crazy Tom went back to his own bunk.

I did that OK, thought Bean. I didn't screw up.

"Bean?" said Shovel.

"Eh?"

"One thing."

"Eh."

"Don't call me Shovel."

Bean thought back. Shovel's real name was Ducheval. "You prefer 'Two Horses'? Sounds kind of like a Sioux warrior."

Shovel grinned. "That's better than sounding like the tool you use to clean the stable."

"Ducheval," said Bean. "From now on."

"Thanks. When do we start?"

"Freetime practice today."

"Bacana."

Bean almost danced away from Ducheval's bunk. He had done it. He had handled it. Once, anyway.

And by the time breakfast was over, he had all five on his toon. With the other four, he checked with their toon leaders first. No one turned him down. And he got his squad to promise to call Ducheval by his right name from then on.

—

Graff had Dimak and Dap in his makeshift office in the battleroom bridge when Bean came. It was the usual argument between Dimak and Dap—that is, it was about nothing, some trivial question of one violating some minor protocol or other, which escalated quickly into a flurry of formal complaints. Just another skirmish in their rivalry, as Dap and Dimak tried to gain some advantage for their proteges, Ender and Bean, while at the same time trying to keep Graff from putting them in the physical danger that both saw looming. When the knock came at the door, voices had been raised for some time, and because the knock was not loud, it occurred to Graff to wonder what might have been overheard.

Had names been mentioned? Yes. Both Bean and Ender. And also Bonzo. Had Achilles' name come up? No. He had just been referred to as "another irresponsible decision endangering the future of the human race, all because of some insane theory about games being one thing and genuine life-and-death struggles being another, completely unproven and unprovable except in the blood of some child!" That was Dap, who had a tendency to wax eloquent.

Graff, of course, was already sick at heart, because he agreed with both teachers, not only in their arguments against each other, but also in their arguments against his own policy. Bean was demonstrably the better candidate on all tests; Ender was just as demonstrably the better candidate based on his performance in actual leadership situations. And Graff *was* being irresponsible to expose both boys to physical danger.

But in both cases, the child had serious doubts about his own courage. Ender had his long history of submission to his older brother, Peter, and the mind game had shown that in Ender's unconscious, Peter was linked to the Buggers. Graff knew that Ender had the courage to strike, without restraint, when the time came for it. That he could stand alone against an enemy, without anyone to help him, and destroy the one who would destroy him. But Ender didn't know it, and he had to know.

Bean, for his part, had shown physical symptoms of panic before his first battle, and while he ended up performing well, Graff didn't need any psychological tests to tell him that the doubt was there. The only difference was, in Bean's case Graff shared his doubt. There *was* no proof that Bean would strike.

Self-doubt was the one thing that neither candidate could afford to have. Against an enemy that did not hesitate—that *could* not hesitate—there could be no pause for reflection. The boys had to face their worst fears, knowing that no one would intervene to help. They had to know that when failure would be fatal, they would not fail. They had to pass the test and know that they had passed it. And both boys were so perceptive that the danger could not be faked. It had to *be* real.

Exposing them to that risk was utterly irresponsible of Graff. Yet he knew that it would be just as irresponsible not to. If Graff played it safe, no one would blame him if, in the actual war, Ender or Bean failed. That would be small consolation, though, given the consequences of failure. Whichever way he guessed, if he was wrong, everybody on Earth might pay the ultimate price. The only thing that made it possible was that if either of them was killed, or damaged physically or mentally, the other was still there to carry on as the sole remaining candidate.

If both failed, what then? There were many bright children, but none who were that much better than commanders already in place, who had graduated from Battle School many years ago.

Somebody has to roll the dice. Mine are the hands that hold those dice. I'm not a bureaucrat, placing my career above the larger purpose I was put here to serve. I will not put the dice in someone else's hands, or pretend that I don't have the choice I have.

For now, all Graff could do was listen to both Dap and Dimak, ignore their bureaucratic attacks and maneuvers against him, and try to keep them from each other's throats in their vicarious rivalry.

That small knock at the door—Graff knew before the door opened who it would be.

If he had heard the argument, Bean gave no sign. But then, that was Bean's specialty, giving no sign. Only Ender managed to be more secretive—and he, at least, had played the mind game long enough to give the teachers a map of his psyche.

"Sir," said Bean.

"Come in, Bean." Come in, Julian Delphiki, longed-for child of good and loving parents. Come in, kidnapped child, hostage of fate. Come and talk to the Fates, who are playing such clever little games with your life.

"I can wait," said Bean.

"Captain Dap and Captain Dimak can hear what you have to say, can't they?" asked Graff.

"If you say so, sir. It's not a secret. I would like to have access to station supplies."

"Denied."

"That's not acceptable, sir."

Graff saw how both Dap and Dimak glanced at him. Amused at the audacity of the boy? "Why do you think so?"

"Short notice, games every day, soldiers exhausted and yet still being pressured to perform in class—fine, Ender's dealing with it and so are we. But the only possible reason you could be doing this is to test our resourcefulness. So I want some resources."

"I don't remember your being commander of Dragon Army," said Graff. "I'll listen to a requisition for specific equipment from your commander."

"Not possible," said Bean. "He doesn't have time to waste on foolish bureaucratic procedures."

Foolish bureaucratic procedures. Graff had used that exact phrase in the argument just a few minutes ago. But Graff's voice had *not* been raised. How long *had* Bean been listening outside the door? Graff cursed himself silently. He had moved his office up here specifically because he knew Bean was a sneak and a spy, gathering intelligence however he could. And then he didn't even post a guard to stop the boy from simply walking up and listening at the door.

"And you do?" asked Graff.

"I'm the one he assigned to think of stupid things you might do to rig the game against us, and think of ways to deal with them."

"What do you think you're going to find?"

"I don't know," said Bean. "I just know that the only things *we* ever see are our uniforms and flash suits, our weapons and our desks. There are other supplies here. For instance, there's paper. We never get any except during written tests, when our desks are closed to us."

"What would you do with paper in the battleroom?"

"I don't know," said Bean. "Wad it up and throw it around. Shred it and make a cloud of dust out of it."

"And who would clean this up?"

"Not my problem," said Bean.

"Permission denied."

"That's not acceptable, sir," said Bean.

"I don't mean to hurt your feelings, Bean, but it matters less than a cockroach's fart whether you accept my decision or not."

"I don't mean to hurt *your* feelings, sir, but you clearly have no idea what you're doing. You're improvising.

Screwing with the system. The damage you're doing is going to take years to undo, and you don't care. That means that it doesn't matter what condition this school is in a year from now. That means that everybody who matters is going to be graduated soon. Training is being accelerated because the Buggers are getting too close for delays. So you're pushing. And you're especially pushing Ender Wiggin."

Graff felt sick. He knew that Bean's powers of analysis were extraordinary. So, also, were his powers of deception. Some of Bean's guesses weren't right—but was that because he didn't know the truth, or because he simply didn't want them to know how much he knew, or how much he guessed? I never wanted you here, Bean, because you're too dangerous.

Bean was still making his case. "When the day comes that Ender Wiggin is looking for ways to stop the Buggers from getting to Earth and scouring the whole planet the way they started to back in the First Invasion, are you going to give him some bullshit answer about what resources he can or cannot use?"

"As far as you're concerned, the ship's supplies don't exist."

"As far as I'm concerned," said Bean, "Ender is *this* close to telling you to fry up your game and eat it. He's sick of it—if you can't see that, you're not much of a teacher. He doesn't care about the standings. He doesn't care about beating other kids. All he cares about is preparing to fight the Buggers. So how hard do you think it will be for me to persuade him that your program here is crocked, and it's time to quit playing?"

"All right," said Graff. "Dimak, prepare the brig. Bean is to be confined until the shuttle is ready to take him back to Earth. This boy is out of Battle School."

Bean smiled slightly. "Go for it, Colonel Graff. I'm done here anyway. I've got everything *I* wanted here—a first-rate education. I'll never have to live on the street again. I'm home free. Let me out of your game, right now, I'm ready."

"You won't be free on Earth, either. Can't risk having you tell these wild stories about Battle School," said Graff.

"Right. Take the best student you ever had here and put him in jail because he asked for access to the supply closet and you didn't like it. Come on, Colonel Graff. Swallow hard and back down. You need my cooperation more than I need yours."

Dimak could barely conceal his smile.

If only confronting Graff like this were sufficient proof of Bean's courage. And for all that Graff had doubts about Bean, he didn't deny that he was good at maneuver. Graff would have given almost anything not to have Dimak and Dap in the room at this moment.

"It was your decision to have this conversation in front of witnesses," said Bean.

What, was the kid a mind reader?

No, Graff had glanced at the two teachers. Bean simply knew how to read his body language. The kid missed nothing. That's why he was so valuable to the program.

Isn't this why we pin our hopes on these kids? Because they're good at maneuver?

And if I know anything about command, don't I know this—that there are times when you cut your losses and leave the field?

"All right, Bean. One scan through supply inventory."

"With somebody to explain to me what it all is."

"I thought you already knew everything."

Bean was polite in victory; he did not respond to taunting. The sarcasm gave Graff a little compensation for having to back down. He knew that's all it was, but this job didn't have many perks.

"Captain Dimak and Captain Dap will accompany you," said Graff. "One scan, and either one of them can veto anything you request. They will be responsible for the consequences of any injuries resulting from your use of any item they let you have."

"Thank you, sir," said Bean. "In all likelihood I won't find anything useful. But I appreciate your fairmindedness in letting us search the station's resources to further the educational objectives of the Battle School."

The kid had the jargon down cold. All those months of access to the student data, with all the notations in the files, Bean had clearly learned more than just the factual contents of the dossiers. And now Bean was giving him the spin that he should use in writing up a report about his decision. As if Graff were not perfectly capable of creating his own spin.

The kid is patronizing me. Little bastard thinks that he's in control.

Well, I have some surprises for him, too.

"Dismissed," said Graff. "All of you."

They got up, saluted, left.

Now, thought Graff, I have to second-guess all my future decisions, wondering how much my choices are influenced by the fact that this kid really pisses me off.

—

As Bean scanned the inventory list, he was really searching primarily for something, anything, that might be made into a weapon that Ender or some of his army could carry to protect him from physical attack by Bonzo. But there was nothing that would be both concealable from the teachers and powerful enough to give smaller kids sufficient leverage over larger ones.

It was a disappointment, but he'd find other ways to neutralize the threat. And now, as long as he was scanning the inventory, *was* there anything that he might be able to use in the battleroom? Cleaning supplies weren't very promising. Nor would the hardware stocks make much sense in the battleroom. What, throw a handful of screws?

The safety equipment, though . . .

"What's a deadline?" asked Bean.

Dimak answered. "Very fine, strong cord that's used to secure maintenance and construction workers when they're working outside the station."

"How long?"

"With links, we can assemble several kilometers of secure deadline," said Dimak. "But each coil unspools to a hundred meters."

"I want to see it."

They took him into parts of the station that children never went to. The decor was far more utilitarian here. Screws and rivets were visible in the plates on the walls. The intake ducts were visible instead of being hidden inside the ceiling. There were no friendly lightstripes for a child to touch and get directions to his barracks. All the palm pads were too high for a child to comfortably use. And the staff they passed saw Bean and then looked at Dap and Dimak as if they were crazy.

The coil was amazingly small. Bean hefted it. Light, too. He unspooled a few decameters of it. It was almost invisible. "This will hold?"

"The weight of two adults," said Dimak.

"It's so fine. Will it cut?"

"Rounded so smoothly it can't cut anything. Wouldn't do us any good if it went slicing through things. Like spacesuits."

"Can I cut it into short lengths?"

"With a blowtorch," said Dimak.

"This is what I want."

"Just one?" asked Dap, rather sarcastically.

"And a blowtorch," said Bean.

"Denied," said Dimak.

"I was joking," said Bean. He walked out of the supply room and started jogging down the corridor, retracing the route they had just taken.

They jogged after him. "Slow down!" Dimak called out.

"Keep up!" Bean answered. "I've got a toon waiting for me to train them with this."

"Train them to do what!"

"I don't know!" He got to the pole and slid down. It passed him right through to the student levels. Going this direction, there was no security clearance at all.

His toon was waiting for him in the battleroom. They'd been working hard for him the past few days, trying all kinds of lame things. Formations that could explode in midair. Screens. Attacks without guns, disarming enemies with their feet. Getting into and out of spins, which made them almost impossible to hit but also kept them from shooting at anybody else.

The most encouraging thing was the fact that Ender spent almost the entire practice time watching Bean's squad whenever he wasn't actually responding to questions from leaders and soldiers in the other toons. Whatever they came up with, Ender would know about it and have his own ideas about when to use it. And, knowing that Ender's eyes were on them, Bean's soldiers worked all the harder. It gave Bean more stature in their eyes, that Ender really did care about what they did.

Ender's good at this, Bean realized again for the hundredth time. He knows how to form a group into the shape he wants it to have. He knows how to get people to work together. And he does it by the most minimal means possible.

If Graff were as good at this as Ender, I wouldn't have had to act like such a bully in there today.

The first thing Bean tried with the deadline was to stretch it across the battleroom. It reached, with barely enough slack to allow knots to be tied at both ends. But a few minutes of experimentation showed that it would be completely ineffective as a tripwire. Most enemies would simply miss it; those that did run into it might be disoriented or flipped around, but once it was known that it was there, it could be used like part of a grid, which meant it would work to the advantage of a creative enemy.

The deadline was designed to keep a man from drifting

off into space. What happens when you get to the end of the line?

Bean left one end fastened to a handhold in the wall, but coiled the other end around his waist several times. The line was now shorter than the width of the battleroom's cube. Bean tied a knot in the line, then launched himself toward the opposite wall.

As he sailed through the air, the deadline tautening behind him, he couldn't help thinking: I hope they were right about this wire not being capable of cutting. What a way to end—sliced in half in the battleroom. *That* would be an interesting mess for them to clean up.

When he was a meter from the wall, the line went taut. Bean's forward progress was immediately halted at his waist. His body jacknifed and he felt like he'd been kicked in the gut. But the most surprising thing was the way his inertia was translated from forward movement into a sideways arc that whipped him across the battleroom toward where D toon was practicing. He hit the wall so hard he had what was left of his breath knocked out of him.

"Did you see that!" Bean screamed, as soon as he could breathe. His stomach hurt—he might not have been sliced in half, but he would have a vicious bruise, he knew that at once, and if he hadn't had his flash suit on, he could well believe there would have been internal injuries. But he'd be OK, and the deadline had let him change directions abruptly in midair. "Did you see it! Did you see it!"

"Are you all right!" Ender shouted.

He realized that Ender thought he was injured. Slowing down his speech, Bean called out again, "Did you see how fast I went! Did you see how I changed direction!"

The whole army stopped practice to watch as Bean played more with the deadline. Tying two soldiers together got interesting results when one of them stopped, but it was hard to hold on. More effective was when Bean had Ender use his hook to pull a star out of the wall and put it into the middle of the battleroom. Bean tied himself and launched from the star; when the line went taut, the edge of the star acted as a fulcrum, shortening the length of the line as he changed direction. And as the line wrapped around the star, it shortened even more upon reaching each edge. At the end, Bean was moving so fast that he blacked out for a moment upon hitting the star. But the whole of Dragon Army was stunned at what they had seen. The deadline was completely invisible, so it looked as though this little kid had launched himself and then suddenly started changing direction and speeding up in midflight. It was seriously disturbing to see it.

"Let's do it again, and see if I can shoot while I'm doing it," said Bean.

—

Evening practice didn't end till 2140, leaving little time before bed. But having seen the stunts Bean's squad was preparing, the army was excited instead of weary, fairly scampering through the corridors. Most of them probably understood that what Bean had come up with were stunts, nothing that would be decisive in battle. It was fun anyway. It was new. And it was Dragon.

Bean started out leading the way, having been given that honor by Ender. A time of triumph, and even though he knew he was being manipulated by the system—behavior modification through public honors—it still felt good.

Not so good, though, that he let up his alertness. He hadn't gone far along the corridor until he realized that there were too many Salamander uniforms among the other boys wandering around in this section. By 2140, most armies were in their barracks, with only a few stragglers coming back from the library or the vids or the game room. Too many Salamanders, and the other soldiers were often big kids from armies whose commanders bore no special love toward Ender. It didn't take a genius to recognize a trap.

Bean jogged back and tagged Crazy Tom, Vlad, and

Hot Soup, who were walking together. "Too many Salamanders," Bean said. "Stay back with Ender." They got it at once—it was public knowledge that Bonzo was breathing out threats about what "somebody" ought to do to Ender Wiggin, just to put him in his place. Bean continued his shambling, easygoing run toward the back of the army, ignoring the smaller kids but tagging the other two toon leaders and all the seconds—the older kids, the ones who might have some chance of standing up to Bonzo's crew in a fight. Not *much* of a chance, but all that was needed was to keep them from getting at Ender until the teachers intervened. No way could the teachers stand aloof if an out-and-out riot erupted. Or could they?

Bean passed right by Ender, got behind him. He saw, coming up quickly, Petra Arkanian in her Phoenix Army uniform. She called out. "Ho, Ender!"

To Bean's disgust, Ender stopped and turned around. The boy was too trusting.

Behind Petra, a few Salamanders fell into step. Bean looked the other way, and saw a few more Salamanders and a couple of set-faced boys from other armies, drifting down the corridor past the last of the Dragons. Hot Soup and Crazy Tom were coming quickly, with more toon leaders and the rest of the larger Dragons coming behind them, but they weren't moving fast enough. Bean beckoned, and he saw Crazy Tom pick up his pace. The others followed suit.

"Ender, can I talk to you," said Petra.

Bean was bitterly disappointed. Petra was the Judas. Setting Ender up for Bonzo—who would have guessed? She *hated* Bonzo when she was in his army.

"Walk with me," said Ender.

"It's just for a moment," said Petra.

Either she was a perfect actress or she was oblivious, Bean realized. She only seemed aware of the other Dragon uniforms, never as much as glancing at anybody else. She isn't in on it after all, thought Bean. She's just an idiot.

At last, Ender seemed to be aware of his exposed position. Except for Bean, all the other Dragons were past him now, and that was apparently enough—at last—to make him uncomfortable. He turned his back on Petra and walked away, briskly, quickly closing the gap between him and the older Dragons.

Petra was angry for a moment, then jogged quickly to catch up with him. Bean stood his ground, looking at the oncoming Salamanders. They didn't even glance at him. They just picked up their pace, continuing to gain on Ender almost as fast as Petra was.

Bean took three steps and slapped the door of Rabbit Army barracks. Somebody opened it. Bean had only to say, "Salamander's making a move against Ender," and at once Rabbits started to pour out the door into the corridor. They emerged just as the Salamanders reached them, and started following along.

Witnesses, thought Bean. And helpers, too, if the fight seemed unfair.

Ahead of him, Ender and Petra were talking, and the larger Dragons fell in step around them. The Salamanders continued to follow closely, and the other thugs joined them as they passed. But the danger was dissipating. Rabbit Army and the older Dragons had done the job. Bean breathed a little easier. For the moment, at least, the danger was over.

Bean caught up with Ender in time to hear Petra angrily say, "How can you think I did? Don't you know who your friends are?" She ran off, ducked into a ladderway, scrambled upward.

Carn Carby of Rabbit caught up with Bean. "Everything OK?"

"I hope you don't mind my calling out your army."

"They came and got me. We seeing Ender safely to bed?"

"Eh."

Carn dropped back and walked along with the bulk of his soldiers. The Salamander thugs were now outnumbered about three to one. They backed off even more, and some of them peeled away and disappeared up ladderways or down poles.

When Bean caught up with Ender again, he was surrounded by his toon leaders. There was nothing subtle about it now—they were clearly his bodyguards, and some of the younger Dragons had realized what was happening and were filling out the formation. They got Ender to the door of his quarters and Crazy Tom pointedly entered before him, then allowed him to go in when he certified that no one was lying in wait. As if one of them could palm open a commander's door. But then, the teachers had been changing a lot of the rules lately. Anything could happen.

Bean lay awake for a while, trying to think what he could do. There was no way they could be with Ender every moment. There was classwork—armies were deliberately broken up then. Ender was the only one who could eat in the commanders' mess, so if Bonzo jumped him there . . . but he wouldn't, not with so many other commanders around him. Showers. Toilet stalls. And if Bonzo assembled the right group of thugs, they'd slap Ender's toon leaders aside like balloons.

What Bean had to do was try to peel away Bonzo's support. Before he slept, he had a half-assed little plan that might help a little, or might make things work, but at least it was something, and it would be public, so the teachers couldn't claim after the fact, in their typical bureaucrat cover-my-butt way that they hadn't known anything was going on.

He thought he could do something at breakfast, but of course there was a battle first thing in the morning. Pol Slattery, Badger Army. The teachers had found a new way to mess with the rules, too. When Badgers were flashed, instead of staying frozen till the end of the game they thawed after five minutes, the way it worked in practice. But Dragons, once hit, stayed rigid. Since the battleroom was packed with stars—plenty of hiding places—it took a while to realize that they were having to shoot the same soldiers more than once as they maneuvered through the stars, and Dragon Army came closer to losing than it ever had. It was all hand to hand, with a dozen of the remaining Dragons having to watch batches of frozen Badgers, reshooting them periodically and meanwhile frantically looking around for some other Badger sneaking up from behind.

The battle took so long that by the time they got out of the battleroom, breakfast was over. Dragon Army was pissed off—the ones who had been frozen early on, before they knew the trick, had spent more than an hour, some of them, floating in their rigid suits, growing more and more frustrated as the time wore on. The others, who had been forced to fight outnumbered and with little visibility against enemies who kept reviving, they were exhausted. Including Ender.

Ender gathered his army in the corridor and said, "Today you know everything. No practice. Get some rest. Have some fun. Pass a test."

They were all grateful for the reprieve, but still, they weren't getting any breakfast today and nobody felt like cheering. As they walked back to the barracks, some of them grumbled, "Bet they're serving breakfast to Badger Army right now."

"No, they got them up and served them breakfast before."

"No, they ate breakfast and then five minutes later they get to eat another."

Bean, however, was frustrated because he hadn't had a chance to carry out his plan at breakfast. It would have to wait till lunch.

The good thing was that because Dragon wasn't practicing, Bonzo's guys wouldn't know where to lie in wait for him. The bad thing was that if Ender went off by himself, there'd be nobody to protect him.

So Bean was relieved when he saw Ender go into his quarters. In consultation with the other toon leaders, Bean set up a watch on Ender's door. One Dragon sat outside the barracks for a half-hour shift, then knocked on the door and his replacement came out. No way was Ender going to go wandering off without Dragon Army knowing it.

But Ender never came out and finally it was lunchtime. All the toon leaders sent the soldiers on ahead and then detoured past Ender's door. Fly Molo knocked loudly—actually, he slapped the door hard five times. "Lunch, Ender."

"I'm not hungry." His voice was muffled by the door. "Go on and eat."

"We can wait," said Fly. "Don't want you walking to the commanders' mess alone."

"I'm not going to eat any lunch at all," said Ender. "Go on and I'll see you after."

"You heard him," said Fly to the others. "He'll be safe in here while we eat."

Bean had noticed that Ender did not promise to stay in his room throughout lunch. But at least Bonzo's people wouldn't know where he was. Unpredictability was helpful. And Bean wanted to get the chance to make his speech at lunch.

So he ran to the messroom and did not get in line, but instead bounded up onto a table and clapped his hands loudly to get attention. "Hey, everybody!"

He waited until the group went about as close to silent as it was going to get.

"There's some of you here who need a reminder of a couple of points of I.F. law. If a soldier is ordered to do something illegal or improper by his commanding officer, he has a responsibility to refuse the order and report it. A soldier who obeys an illegal or improper order is fully responsible for the consequences of his actions. Just in case any of you here are too dim to know what that means, the law says that if some commander orders you to commit a crime, that's no excuse. You are forbidden to obey."

Nobody from Salamander would meet Bean's gaze, but

a thug in Rat uniform answered in a surly tone. "You got something in mind, here, pinprick?"

"I've got *you* in mind, Lighter. Your scores are pretty much in the bottom ten percent in the school, so I thought you might need a little extra help."

"You can shut your facehole right now, that's the help I need!"

"Whatever Bonzo had you set to do last night, Lighter, you and about twenty others, what I'm telling you is *if* you'd actually tried something, every single one of you would have been out of Battle School on his ass. Iced. A complete failure, because you listened to Bonehead Madrid. Can I be any more clear than that?"

Lighter laughed—it sounded forced, but then, he wasn't the only one laughing. "You don't even know what's going on, pinprick," one of them said.

"I know Bonehead's trying to turn you into a street crew, you pathetic losers. He can't beat Ender in the battleroom, so he's going to get a dozen tough guys to beat up one little kid. You all hear that? You know what Ender is—the best damn commander ever to come through here. He might be the only one able to do what Mazer Rackham did and beat the Buggers when they come back, did you think of that? And these guys are so *smart* they want to beat his brains out. So when the Buggers come, and we've only got pus-brains like Bonzo Madrid to lead our fleets to defeat, then as the Buggers scour the Earth and kill every last man, woman, and child, the survivors will all know that *these* fools are the ones who got rid of the one guy who could have led us to victory!"

The whole place was dead silent now, and Bean could see, looking at the ones he recognized as having been with Bonzo's group last night, that he was getting through to them.

"Oh, you *forgot* the Buggers, is that it? You *forgot* that this Battle School wasn't put here so you could write home to Mommy about your high standings on the scoreboard. So you go ahead and help Bonzo out, and while you're at it, why not just slit your own throats, too, cause that's what you're doing if you hurt Ender Wiggin. But for the rest of us—well, how many here think that Ender Wiggin is the one commander we would all want to follow into battle? Come on, how many of you!"

Bean began to clap his hands slowly, rhythmically. Immediately, all the Dragons joined in. And very quickly, most of the rest of the soldiers were also clapping. The ones who weren't were conspicuous and could see how the others looked at them with scorn or hate.

Pretty soon, the whole room was clapping. Even the food servers.

Bean thrust both his hands straight up in the air. "The butt-faced Buggers are the only enemy! Humans are all on the same side! Anybody who raises a hand against Ender Wiggin is a Bugger-lover!"

They responded with cheers and applause, leaping to their feet.

It was Bean's first attempt at rabble-rousing. He was pleased to see that, as long as the cause was right, he was pretty damn good at it.

Only later, when he had his food and was sitting with C toon, eating it, did Lighter himself come up to Bean. He came up from behind, and the rest of C toon was on their feet, ready to take him on, before Bean even knew he was there. But Lighter motioned them to sit down, then leaned over and spoke right into Bean's ear. "Listen to this, Queen Stupid. The soldiers who are planning to take Wiggin apart aren't even *here.* So much for your stupid speech."

Then he was gone.

And, a moment later, so was Bean, with C toon gathering the rest of Dragon Army to follow behind him.

Ender wasn't in his quarters, or at least he didn't answer. Fly Molo, as A toon commander, took charge and divided them into groups to search the barracks, the game room, the vid room, the library, the gym.

But Bean called out for his squad to follow him. To

the bathroom. That's the one place that Bonzo and his boys could plan on Ender having to go, eventually.

By the time Bean got there, it was all over. Teachers and medical staff were clattering down the halls. Dink Meeker was walking with Ender, his arm across Ender's shoulder, away from the bathroom. Ender was wearing only his towel. He was wet, and there was blood all over the back of his head and dripping down his back. It took Bean only a moment to realize that it was not his blood. The others from Bean's squad watched as Dink led Ender back to his quarters and helped him inside. But Bean was already on his way to the bathroom.

The teachers ordered him out of the way, out of the corridor. But Bean saw enough. Bonzo lying on the floor, medical staff doing CPR. Bean knew that you don't do that to somebody whose heart is beating. And from the inattentive way the others were standing around, Bean knew it was only a formality. Nobody expected Bonzo's heart to start again. No surprise. His nose had been jammed up inside his head. His face was a mass of blood. Which explained the bloody back of Ender's head.

All our efforts didn't amount to squat. But Ender won anyway. He knew this was coming. He learned self-defense. He used it, and he didn't do a half-assed job of it, either.

If Ender had been Poke's friend, Poke wouldn't have died.

And if Ender had depended on Bean to save him, he'd be just as dead as Poke.

Rough hands dragged Bean off his feet, pushed him against a wall. "What did you see!" demanded Major Anderson.

"Nothing," said Bean. "Is that Bonzo in there? Is he hurt?"

"This is none of your business. Didn't you hear us order you away?"

Colonel Graff arrived then, and Bean could see that the teachers around him were furious at him—yet couldn't say anything, either because of military protocol or because one of the children was present.

"I think Bean has stuck his nose into things once too often," said Anderson.

"Are you going to send Bonzo home?" asked Bean. "Cause he's just going to try it again."

Graff gave him a withering glance. "I heard about your speech in the mess hall," said Graff. "I didn't know we brought you up here to be a politician."

"If you don't ice Bonzo and get him *out* of here, Ender's never going to be safe, and we won't stand for it!"

"Mind your own business, little boy," said Graff. "This is men's work here."

Bean let himself be dragged away by Dimak. Just in case they still wondered whether Bean saw that Bonzo was dead, he kept the act going just a little longer. "He's going to come after me, too," he said. "I don't want Bonzo coming after me."

"He's not coming after you," said Dimak. "He's going home. Count on it. But don't talk about this to anyone else. Let them find out when the official word is given out. Got it?"

"Yes, sir," said Bean.

"And where did you get all that nonsense about not obeying a commander who gives illegal orders?"

"From the Uniform Code of Military Conduct," said Bean.

"Well, here's a little fact for you—nobody has ever been prosecuted for obeying orders."

"That," said Bean, "is because nobody's done anything so outrageous that the general public got involved."

"The Uniform Code doesn't apply to students, at least not that part of it."

"But it applies to teachers," said Bean. "It applies to *you.* Just in case you obeyed any illegal or improper orders today. By . . . what, I don't know . . . standing by while a fight broke out in a bathroom? Just because your commanding officer told you to let a big kid beat up on a little kid."

If that information bothered Dimak, he gave no sign. He stood in the corridor and watched as Bean went into the Dragon Army barracks.

It was crazy inside. Dragon Army felt completely helpless and stupid, furious and ashamed. Bonzo Madrid had outsmarted them! Bonzo had gotten Ender alone! Where were Ender's soldiers when he needed them?

It took a long time for things to calm down. Through it all, Bean just sat on his bunk, thinking his own thoughts. Ender didn't just win his fight. Didn't just protect himself and walk away. Ender killed him. Struck a blow so devastating that his enemy will never, never come after him again.

Ender Wiggin, you're the one who was born to be commander of the fleet that defends Earth from the Third Invasion. Because that's what we need—someone who'll strike the most brutal blow possible, with perfect aim and with no regard for consequences. Total war.

Me, I'm no Ender Wiggin. I'm just a street kid whose only skill was staying alive. Somehow. The only time I was in real danger, I ran like a squirrel and took refuge with Sister Carlotta. Ender went alone into battle. I go alone into my hidey-hole. I'm the guy who makes big brave speeches standing on tables in the mess hall. Ender's the guy who meets the enemy naked and overpowers him against all odds.

Whatever genes they altered to make me, they weren't the ones that mattered.

Ender almost died because of me. Because I goaded Bonzo. Because I failed to keep watch at the crucial time. Because I didn't stop and think like Bonzo and figure out that he'd wait for Ender to be alone in the shower.

If Ender had died today, it would have been my fault all over again.

He wanted to kill somebody.

Couldn't be Bonzo. Bonzo was already dead.

Achilles. That's the one he needed to kill. And if Achilles had been there at that moment, Bean would have tried. Might have succeeded, too, if violent rage and desperate shame were enough to beat down any advantage of size and experience Achilles might have had. And if Achilles killed Bean anyway, it was no worse than Bean deserved, for having failed Ender Wiggin so completely.

He felt his bed bounce. Nikolai had jumped the gap between the upper bunks.

"It's OK," murmured Nikolai, touching Bean's shoulder.

Bean rolled onto his back, to face Nikolai.

"Oh," said Nikolai. "I thought you were crying."

"Ender won," said Bean. "What's to cry about?"

18

Friend

"This boy's death was not necessary."

"This boy's death was not foreseen."

"But it was foreseeable."

"You can always foresee things that already happened. These are children, after all. We did *not* anticipate this level of violence."

"I don't believe you. I believe that this is precisely the level of violence you anticipated. This is what you set up. You think that the experiment succeeded."

"I can't control your opinions. I can merely disagree with them."

"Ender Wiggin is ready to move on to Command School. That is my report."

"I have a separate report from Dap, the teacher assigned to watch him most closely. And that report—for which there are to be *no* sanctions against Captain Dap—tells me that Andrew Wiggin is 'psychologically unfit for duty.'"

"*If* he is, which I doubt, it is only temporary."

"How much time do you think we have? No, Colonel

Graff, for the time being we have to regard your course of action regarding Wiggin as a failure, and the boy as ruined not only for our purposes but quite possibly for any other as well. So, if it can be done without further killings, I want the other one pushed forward. I want him here in Command School as close to immediately as possible."

"Very well, sir. Though I must tell you that I regard Bean as unreliable."

"Why, because you haven't turned him into a killer yet?"

"Because he is not human, sir."

"The genetic difference is well within the range of ordinary variation."

"He was manufactured, and the manufacturer was a criminal, not to mention a certified loon."

"I could see some danger if his *father* were a criminal. Or his mother. But his *doctor?* The boy is exactly what we need, as quickly as we can get him."

"He is unpredictable."

"And the Wiggin boy is not?"

"Less unpredictable, sir."

"Very carefully answered, considering that you just insisted that the murder today was 'not foreseeable.' "

"*Not* murder, sir!"

"Killing, then."

"The mettle of the Wiggin boy is proved, sir, while Bean's is not."

"I have Dimak's report—for which, again, he is not to be—"

"Punished, I know, sir."

"Bean's behavior throughout this set of events has been exemplary."

"Then Captain Dimak's report was incomplete. Didn't he inform you that it was Bean who may have pushed Bonzo over the edge to violence by breaking security and informing him that Ender's army was composed of exceptional students?"

"That *was* an act with unforeseeable consequences."

"Bean was acting to save his own life, and in so doing he

shunted the danger onto Ender Wiggin's shoulders. That he later tried to ameliorate the danger does not change the fact that when Bean is under pressure, he turns traitor."

"Harsh language!"

"This from the man who just called an obvious act of self-defense 'murder'?"

"Enough of this! You are on leave of absence from your position as commander of Battle School for the duration of Ender Wiggin's so-called rest and recuperation. If Wiggin recovers enough to come to Command School, you may come with him and continue to have influence over the education of the children we bring here. If he does not, you may await your court-martial on Earth."

"I am relieved effective when?"

"When you get on the shuttle with Wiggin. Major Anderson will stand in as acting commander."

"Very well, sir. Wiggin *will* return to training, sir."

"*If* we still want him."

"When you are over the dismay we all feel at the unfortunate death of the Madrid boy, you will realize that I am right, and Ender is the only viable candidate, all the more now than before."

"I allow you that Parthian shot. And, if you are right, I wish you Godspeed on your work with the Wiggin boy. Dismissed."

Ender was still wearing only his towel when he stepped into the barracks. Bean saw him standing there, his face a rictus of death, and thought: He knows that Bonzo is dead, and it's killing him.

"Ho, Ender," said Hot Soup, who was standing near the door with the other toon leaders.

"There gonna be a practice tonight?" asked one of the younger soldiers.

Ender handed a slip of paper to Hot Soup.

"I guess that means not," said Nikolai softly.

Hot Soup read it. "Those sons of bitches! Two at once?"

Crazy Tom looked over his shoulder. "Two armies!"

"They'll just trip over each other," said Bean. What appalled him most about the teachers was not the stupidity of trying to combine armies, a ploy whose ineffectiveness had been proved time after time throughout history, but rather the get-back-on-the-horse mentality that led them to put *more* pressure on Ender at this of all times. Couldn't they see the damage they were doing to him? Was their goal to train him or break him? Because he was trained long since. He should have been promoted out of Battle School the week before. And now they give him one more battle, a completely meaningless one, when he's already over the edge of despair?

"I've got to clean up," said Ender. "Get them ready, get everybody together, I'll meet you there, at the gate." In his voice, Bean heard a complete lack of interest. No, something deeper than that. Ender doesn't *want* to win this battle.

Ender turned to leave. Everyone saw the blood on his head, his shoulders, down his back. He left.

They all ignored the blood. They had to. "Two fart-eating armies!" cried Crazy Tom. "We'll whip their butts!"

That seemed to be the general consensus as they got into their flash suits.

Bean tucked the coil of deadline into the waist of his flash suit. If Ender ever needed a stunt, it would be for this battle, when he was no longer interested in winning.

As promised, Ender joined them at the gate before it opened—just barely before. He walked down the corridor lined with his soldiers, who looked at him with love, with awe, with trust. Except Bean, who looked at him with anguish. Ender Wiggin was not larger than life, Bean knew. He was exactly life-sized, and so his larger-than-life burden was too much for him. And yet he was bearing it. So far.

The gate went transparent.

Four stars had been combined directly in front of the gate, completely blocking their view of the battleroom. Ender would have to deploy his forces blind. For all he knew, the enemy had already been let into the room fifteen minutes ago. For all he could possibly know, they were deployed just as Bonzo had deployed *his* army, only this time it would be completely effective, to have the gate ringed with enemy soldiers.

But Ender said nothing. Just stood there looking at the barrier.

Bean had halfway expected this. He was ready. What he did wasn't all that obvious—he only walked forward to stand directly beside Ender at the gate. But he knew that was all it would take. A reminder.

"Bean," said Ender. "Take your boys and tell me what's on the other side of this star."

"Yes *sir,*" said Bean. He pulled the coil of deadline from his waist, and with his five soldiers he made the short hop from the gate to the star. Immediately the gate he had just come through became the ceiling, the star their temporary floor. Bean tied the deadline around his waist while the other boys unspooled the line, arranging it in loose coils on the star. When it was about one-third played out, Bean declared it to be sufficient. He was guessing that the four stars were really eight—that they made a perfect cube. If he was wrong, then he had way too much deadline and he'd crash into the ceiling instead of making it back behind the star. Worse things could happen.

He slipped out beyond the edge of the star. He was right, it was a cube. It was too dim in the room to see well what the other armies were doing, but they seemed to be deploying. There had been no head start this time, apparently. He quickly reported this to Ducheval, who would repeat it to Ender while Bean did his stunt. Ender would no doubt start bringing out the rest of the army at once, before the time clicked down to zero.

Bean launched straight down from the ceiling. Above

him, his toon was holding the other end of the deadline secure, making sure it fed out properly and stopped abruptly.

Bean did not enjoy the wrenching of his gut when the deadline went taut, but there was kind of a thrill to the increase of speed as he suddenly moved south. He could see the distant flashing of the enemy firing up at him. Only soldiers from one half of the enemy's area were firing.

When the deadline reached the next edge of the cube, his speed increased again, and now he was headed upward in an arc that, for a moment, looked like it was going to scrape him against the ceiling. Then the last edge bit, and he scooted in behind the star and was caught deftly by his toon. Bean wiggled his arms and legs to show that he was none the worse for his ride. What the enemy was thinking about his magical maneuvers in midair he could only guess. What mattered was that Ender had *not* come through the gate. The timer must be nearly out.

Ender came alone through the gate. Bean made his report as quickly as possible. "It's really dim, but light enough you can't follow people easily by the lights on their suits. Worst possible for seeing. It's all open space from this star to the enemy side of the room. They've got eight stars making a square around their door. I didn't see anybody except the ones peeking around the boxes. They're just sitting there waiting for us."

In the distance, they heard the enemy begin catcalls. "Hey! We be hungry, come and feed us! Your ass is draggin'! Your ass is Dragon!"

Bean continued his report, but had no idea if Ender was even listening. "They fired at me from only one half their space. Which means that the two commanders are *not* agreeing and neither one has been put in supreme command."

"In a real war," said Ender, "any commander with brains at all would retreat and save this army."

"What the hell," said Bean. "It's only a game."

"It stopped being a game when they threw away the rules."

This wasn't good, thought Bean. How much time did they have to get their army through the gate? "So, you throw 'em away, too." He looked Ender in the eye, demanding that he wake up, pay attention, *act.*

The blank look left Ender's face. He grinned. It felt damn good to see that. "OK. Why not. Let's see how they react to a formation."

Ender began calling the rest of the army through the gate. It was going to get crowded on the top of that star, but there was no choice.

As it turned out, Ender's plan was to use another of Bean's stupid ideas, which he had watched Bean practice with his toon. A screen formation of frozen soldiers, controlled by Bean's toon, who remained unfrozen behind them. Having once told Bean what he wanted him to do, Ender joined the formation as a common soldier and left everything up to Bean to organize. "It's your show," he said.

Bean had never expected Ender to do any such thing, but it made a kind of sense. What Ender wanted was not to have this battle; allowing himself to be part of a screen of frozen soldiers, pushed through the battle by someone else, was as close to sleeping through it as he could get.

Bean set to work at once, constructing the screen in four parts consisting of one toon each. Each of toons A through C lined up four and three, arms interlocked with the men beside them, the upper row of three with toes hooked under the arms of the four soldiers below. When everybody was clamped down tight, Bean and his toon froze them. Then each of Bean's men took hold of one section of the screen and, careful to move very slowly so that inertia would not carry the screen out of their control, they maneuvered them out from above the star and slowly moved them down until they were just under it. Then they joined them back together into a single screen, with Bean's squad forming the interlock.

"When did you guys practice this?" asked Dumper, the leader of E toon.

"We've never done this before," Bean answered truthfully. "We've done bursting and linking with one-man screens, but seven men each? It's all new to us."

Dumper laughed. "And there's Ender, plugged into the screen like anybody. That's trust, Bean old boy."

That's despair, thought Bean. But he didn't feel the need to say *that* aloud.

When all was ready, E toon got into place behind the screen and, on Bean's command, pushed off as hard as they could.

The screen drifted down toward the enemy's gate at a pretty good clip. Enemy fire, though it was intense, hit only the already-frozen soldiers in front. E toon and Bean's squad kept moving, very slightly, but enough that no stray shot could freeze them. And they managed to do some return fire, taking out a few of the enemy soldiers and forcing them to stay behind cover.

When Bean figured they were as far as they could get before Griffin or Tiger launched an attack, he gave the word and his squad burst apart, causing the four sections of the screen also to separate and angle slightly so they were drifting now toward the corners of the stars where Griffin and Tiger were gathered. E toon went with the screens, firing like crazy, trying to make up for their tiny numbers.

After a count of three, the four members of Bean's squad who had gone with each screen pushed off again, this time angling to the middle and downward, so that they rejoined Bean and Ducheval, with momentum carrying them straight toward the enemy gate.

They held their bodies rigid, *not* firing a shot, and it worked. They were all small; they were clearly drifting, not moving with any particular purpose; the enemy took them for frozen soldiers if they were noticed at all. A few were partially disabled with stray shots, but even when under fire they never moved, and the enemy soon ignored them.

When they got to the enemy gate, Bean slowly, wordlessly, got four of them with their helmets in place at the corners of the gate. They pressed, just as in the end-of-game ritual, and Bean gave Ducheval a push, sending him through the gate as Bean drifted upward again.

The lights in the battleroom went on. The weapons all went dead. The battle was over.

It took a few moments before Griffin and Tiger realized what had happened. Dragon only had a few soldiers who weren't frozen or disabled, while Griffin and Tiger were mostly unscathed, having played conservative strategies. Bean knew that if either of them had been aggressive, Ender's strategy wouldn't have worked. But having seen Bean fly around the star, doing the impossible, and then watching this weird screen approach so slowly, they were intimidated into inaction. Ender's legend was such that they dared not commit their forces for fear of falling into a trap. Only . . . that *was* the trap.

Major Anderson came into the room through the teachergate. "Ender," he called.

Ender was frozen; he could only answer by grunting loudly through clenched jaws. That was a sound that victorious commanders rarely had to make.

Anderson, using the hook, drifted over to Ender and thawed him. Bean was half the battleroom away, but he heard Ender's words, so clear was his speech, so silent was the room. "I beat you again, sir."

Bean's squad members glanced at him, obviously wondering if he was resentful at Ender for claiming credit for a victory that was engineered and executed entirely by Bean. But Bean understood what Ender was saying. He wasn't talking about the victory over Griffin and Tiger armies. He was talking about a victory over the teachers. And *that* victory *was* the decision to turn the army over to Bean and sit it out himself. If they thought they were putting Ender to the ultimate test, making him fight two armies right after a personal fight for survival in the bathroom, he beat them—he sidestepped the test.

Anderson knew what Ender was saying, too. "Nonsense, Ender," said Anderson. He spoke softly, but the room was so silent that his words, too, could be heard. "Your battle was with Griffin and Tiger."

"How stupid do you think I am?" said Ender.

Damn right, said Bean silently.

Anderson spoke to the group at large. "After that little maneuver, the rules are being revised to require that all of the enemy's soldiers must be frozen or disabled before the gate can be reversed."

"Rules?" murmured Ducheval as he came back through the gate. Bean grinned at him.

"It could only work once anyway," said Ender.

Anderson handed the hook to Ender. Instead of thawing his soldiers one at a time, and only then thawing the enemy, Ender entered the command to thaw everyone at once, then handed the hook back to Anderson, who took it and drifted away toward the center, where the end-of-game rituals usually took place.

"Hey!" Ender shouted. "What is it next time? My army in a cage without guns, with the rest of the Battle School against them? How about a little equality?"

So many soldiers murmured their agreement that the sound of it was loud, and not all came from Dragon Army. But Anderson seemed to pay no attention.

It was William Bee of Griffin Army who said what almost everyone was thinking. "Ender, if you're on one side of the battle, it won't be equal no matter what the conditions are."

The armies vocally agreed, many of the soldiers laughing, and Talo Momoe, not to be outclassed by Bee, started clapping his hands rhythmically. "Ender Wiggin!" he shouted. Other boys took up the chant.

But Bean knew the truth—knew, in fact, what Ender knew. That no matter how good a commander was, no matter how resourceful, no matter how well-prepared his army, no matter how excellent his lieutenants, no matter how courageous and spirited the fight, victory almost always went to the side with the greater power to inflict damage. Sometimes David kills Goliath, and people never forget. But there were a lot of little guys Goliath had already mashed into the ground. Nobody sang songs about *those* fights, because they knew that was the likely outcome. No, that was the *inevitable* outcome, except for the miracles.

The Buggers wouldn't know or care how legendary a commander Ender might be to his own men. The human ships wouldn't have any magical tricks like Bean's deadline to dazzle the Buggers with, to put them off their stride. Ender knew that. Bean knew that. What if David hadn't had a sling, a handful of stones, and the time to throw? What good would the excellence of his aim have done him then?

So yes, it was good, it was right for the soldiers of all three armies to cheer Ender, to chant his name as he drifted toward the enemy gate, where Bean and his squad waited for him. But in the end it meant nothing, except that everyone would have too much hope in Ender's ability. It only made the burden on Ender heavier.

I would carry some of it if I could, Bean said silently. Like I did today, you can turn it over to me and I'll do it, if I can. You don't have to do this alone.

Only even as he thought this, Bean knew it wasn't true. If it could be done, Ender was the one who would have to do it. All those months when Bean refused to see Ender, hid from him, it was because he couldn't bear to face the fact that Ender was what Bean only wished to be—the kind of person on whom you could put all your hopes, who could carry all your fears, and he would not let you down, would not betray you.

I want to be the kind of boy you are, thought Bean. But I don't want to go through what you've been through to get there.

And then, as Ender passed through the gate and Bean

followed behind him, Bean remembered falling into line behind Poke or Sergeant or Achilles on the streets of Rotterdam, and he almost laughed as he thought, I don't want to have to go through what *I've* gone through to get here, either.

Out in the corridor, Ender walked away instead of waiting for his soldiers. But not fast, and soon they caught up with him, surrounded him, brought him to a stop through their sheer ebullience. Only his silence, his impassivity, kept them from giving full vent to their excitement.

"Practice tonight?" asked Crazy Tom.

Ender shook his head.

"Tomorrow morning then?"

"No."

"Well, when?"

"Never again, as far as I'm concerned."

Not everyone had heard, but those who did began to murmur to each other.

"Hey, that's not fair," said a soldier from B toon. "It's not our fault the teachers are screwing up the game. You can't just stop teaching us stuff because—"

Ender slammed his hand against the wall and shouted at the kid. "I don't care about the game anymore!" He looked at other soldiers, met their gaze, refused to let them pretend they didn't hear. "Do you understand that?" Then he whispered. "The game is over."

He walked away.

Some of the boys wanted to follow him, took a few steps. But Hot Soup grabbed a couple of them by the neck of their flash suits and said, "Let him be alone. Can't you see he wants to be alone?"

Of course he wants to be alone, thought Bean. He killed a kid today, and even if he doesn't know the outcome, he knows what was at stake. These teachers were willing to let him face death without help. Why should he play along with them anymore? Good for you, Ender.

Not so good for the rest of us, but it's not like you're our father or something. More like a brother, and the thing with brothers is, you're supposed to take turns being the keeper. Sometimes you get to sit down and be the brother who is kept.

Fly Molo led them back to the barracks. Bean followed along, wishing he could go with Ender, talk to him, assure him that he agreed completely, that he understood. But that was pathetic, Bean realized. Why should Ender care whether *I* understand him or not? I'm just a kid, just one of his army. He knows me, he knows how to use me, but what does he care whether I know him?

Bean climbed to his bunk and saw a slip of paper on it.

Transfer

Bean

Rabbit Army

Commander

That was Carn Carby's army. Carn was being removed from command? He was a good guy—not a great commander, but why couldn't they wait till he graduated?

Because they're through with this school, that's why. They're advancing everybody they think needs some experience with command, and they're graduating other students to make room for them. I might have Rabbit Army, but not for long, I bet.

He pulled out his desk, meaning to sign on as ^Graff and check the rosters. Find out what was happening to everybody. But the ^Graff log-in didn't work. Apparently they no longer considered it useful to permit Bean to keep his inside access.

From the back of the room, the older boys were raising a hubbub. Bean heard Crazy Tom's voice rising above the rest. "You mean I'm supposed to figure out how to beat Dragon Army?" Word soon filtered to the front. The toon leaders and seconds had all received transfer orders. Every single one of them was being given command of an army. Dragon had been stripped.

After about a minute of chaos, Fly Molo led the other toon leaders along between the bunks, heading toward the door. Of course—they had to go tell Ender what the teachers had done to him now.

But to Bean's surprise, Fly stopped at his bunk and looked up at him, then glanced at the other toon leaders behind him.

"Bean, somebody's got to tell Ender."

Bean nodded.

"We thought . . . since you're his friend . . ."

Bean let nothing show on his face, but he was stunned. Me? Ender's friend? No more than anyone else in this room.

And then he realized. In this army, Ender had everyone's love and admiration. And they all knew they had Ender's trust. But only Bean had been taken inside Ender's confidence, when Ender assigned him his special squad. And when Ender wanted to stop playing the game, it was Bean to whom he had turned over his army. Bean was the closest thing to a friend they had seen Ender have since he got command of Dragon.

Bean looked across at Nikolai, who was grinning his ass off. Nikolai saluted him and mouthed the word *commander.*

Bean saluted Nikolai back, but could not smile, knowing what this would do to Ender. He nodded to Fly Molo, then slid off the bunk and went out the door.

He didn't go straight to Ender's quarters, though. Instead, he went to Carn Carby's room. No one answered. So he went on to Rabbit barracks and knocked. "Where's Carn?" he asked.

"Graduated," said Itú, the leader of Rabbit's A toon. "He found out about half an hour ago."

"We were in a battle."

"I know—two armies at once. You won, right?"

Bean nodded. "I bet Carn wasn't the only one graduated early."

"A lot of commanders," said Itú. "More than half."

"Including Bonzo Madrid? I mean, he graduated?"

"That's what the official notice said." Itú shrugged. "Everybody knows that if anything, Bonzo was probably iced. I mean, they didn't even list his assignment. Just 'Cartagena.' His hometown. Is that iced or what? But let the teachers call it what they want."

"I'll bet the total who graduated was nine," said Bean. "Neh?"

"Eh," said Itú. "Nine. So you know something?"

"Bad news, I think," said Bean. He showed Itú his transfer orders.

"Santa merda," said Itú. Then he saluted. Not sarcastically, but not enthusiastically, either.

"Would you mind breaking it to the others? Give them a chance to get used to the idea before I show up for real? I've got to go talk to Ender. Maybe he already knows they've just taken his entire leadership and given them armies. But if he doesn't, I've got to tell him."

"*Every* Dragon toon leader?"

"And every second." He thought of saying, Sorry Rabbit got stuck with me. But Ender would never have said anything self-belittling like that. And if Bean was going to be a commander, he couldn't start out with an apology. "I think Carn Carby had a good organization," said Bean, "so I don't expect to change any of the toon leadership for the first week, anyway, till I see how things go in practice and decide what shape we're in for the kind of battles we're going to start having now that most of the commanders are kids trained in Dragon."

Itú understood immediately. "Man, that's going to be strange, isn't it? Ender trained all you guys, and now you've got to fight each other."

"One thing's for sure," said Bean. "I have no intention of trying to turn Rabbit into a copy of Ender's Dragon. We're not the same kids and we won't be fighting the same opponents. Rabbit's a good army. We don't have to copy anybody."

Itú grinned. "Even if that's just bullshit, sir, it's first-rate bullshit. I'll pass it on." He saluted.

Bean saluted back. Then he jogged to Ender's quarters.

Ender's mattress and blankets and pillow had been thrown out into the corridor. For a moment Bean wondered why. Then he saw that the sheets and mattress were still damp and bloody. Water from Ender's shower. Blood from Bonzo's face. Apparently Ender didn't want them in his room.

Bean knocked on the door.

"Go away," said Ender softly.

Bean knocked again. Then again.

"Come in," said Ender.

Bean palmed the door open.

"Go away, Bean," said Ender.

Bean nodded. He understood the sentiment. But he had to deliver his message. So he just looked at his shoes and waited for Ender to ask him his business. Or yell at him. Whatever Ender wanted to do. Because the other toon leaders were wrong. Bean didn't have any special relationship with Ender. Not outside the game.

Ender said nothing. And continued to say nothing.

Bean looked up from the ground and saw Ender gazing at him. Not angry. Just . . . watching. What does he see in me, Bean wondered. How well does he know me? What does he think of me? What do I amount to in his eyes?

That was something Bean would probably never know. And he had come here for another purpose. Time to carry it out.

He took a step closer to Ender. He turned his hand so the transfer slip was visible. He didn't offer it to Ender, but he knew Ender would see it.

"You're transferred?" asked Ender. His voice sounded dead. As if he'd been expecting it.

"To Rabbit Army," said Bean.

Ender nodded. "Carn Carby's a good man. I hope he recognizes what you're worth."

The words came to Bean like a longed-for blessing. He swallowed the emotion that welled up inside him. He still had more of his message to deliver.

"Carn Carby was graduated today," said Bean. "He got his notice while we were fighting our battle."

"Well," said Ender. "Who's commanding Rabbit then?" He didn't sound all that interested. The question was expected, so he asked it.

"Me," said Bean. He was embarrassed; a smile came inadvertently to his lips.

Ender looked at the ceiling and nodded. "Of course. After all, you're only four years younger than the regular age."

"It isn't funny," said Bean. "I don't know what's going on here." Except that the system seems to be running on sheer panic. "All the changes in the game. And now this. I wasn't the only one transferred, you know. They graduated half the commanders, and transferred a lot of our guys to command their armies."

"Which guys?" Now Ender did sound interested.

"It looks like—every toon leader and every assistant."

"Of course. If they decide to wreck my army, they'll cut it to the ground. Whatever they're doing, they're thorough."

"You'll still win, Ender. We all know that. Crazy Tom, he said, 'You mean I'm supposed to figure out how to beat Dragon Army?' Everybody knows you're the best." His words sounded empty even to himself. He wanted to be encouraging, but he knew that Ender knew better. Still he babbled on. "They can't break you down, no matter what they—"

"They already have."

They've broken trust, Bean wanted to say. That's not the same thing. *You* aren't broken. *They're* broken. But all that came out of his mouth were empty, limping words. "No, Ender, they can't—"

"I don't care about their game anymore, Bean," said Ender. "I'm not going to play it anymore. No more practices. No more battles. They can put their little slips of paper on the floor all they want, but I won't go. I decided that before I went through the door today. That's why I had you go for the gate. I didn't think it would work, but I didn't care. I just wanted to go out in style."

I know that, thought Bean. You think I didn't know that? But if it comes down to style, you certainly got *that.* "You should've seen William Bee's face. He just stood there trying to figure out how he had lost when you only had seven boys who could wiggle their toes and he only had three who couldn't."

"Why should I want to see William Bee's face?" said Ender. "Why should I want to beat anybody?"

Bean felt the heat of embarrassment in his face. He'd said the wrong thing. Only . . . he didn't know what the right thing was. Something to make Ender feel better. Something to make him understand how much he was loved and honored.

Only that love and honor were part of the burden Ender bore. There was nothing Bean could say that would not make it all the heavier on Ender. So he said nothing.

Ender pressed his palms against his eyes. "I hurt Bonzo really bad today, Bean. I really hurt him bad."

Of course. All this other stuff, that's nothing. What weighs on Ender is that terrible fight in the bathroom. The fight that your friends, your army, did nothing to prevent. And what hurts you is not the danger you were in, but the harm you did in protecting yourself.

"He had it coming," said Bean. He winced at his own words. Was that the best he could come up with? But what else could he say? No problem, Ender. Of course, he looked dead to *me,* and I'm probably the only kid in this school who actually knows what death looks like, but . . . no problem! Nothing to worry about! He had it coming!

"I knocked him out standing up," said Ender. "It was

like he was dead, standing there. And I kept hurting him."

So he did know. And yet . . . he didn't actually *know.* And Bean wasn't about to tell him. There were times for absolute honesty between friends, but this wasn't one of them.

"I just wanted to make sure he never hurt me again."

"He won't," said Bean. "They sent him home."

"Already?"

Bean told him what Itú had said. All the while, he felt like Ender could see that he was concealing something. Surely it was impossible to deceive Ender Wiggin.

"I'm glad they graduated him," said Ender.

Some graduation. They're going to bury him, or cremate him, or whatever they're doing with corpses in Spain this year.

Spain. Pablo de Noches, who saved his life, came from Spain. And now a body was going back there, a boy who turned killer in his heart, and died for it.

I must be losing it, thought Bean. What does it matter that Bonzo was Spanish and Pablo de Noches was Spanish? What does it matter that anybody is anything?

And while these thoughts ran through Bean's mind, he babbled, trying to talk like someone who didn't know anything, trying to reassure Ender but knowing that if Ender believed that he knew nothing, then his words were meaningless, and if Ender realized that Bean was only faking ignorance, then his words were all lies. "Was it true he had a whole bunch of guys gang up on you?" Bean wanted to run from the room, he sounded so lame, even to himself.

"No," said Ender. "It was just him and me. He fought with honor."

Bean was relieved. Ender was turned so deeply inward right now that he didn't even register what Bean was saying, how false it was.

"I didn't fight with honor," said Ender. "I fought to win."

Yes, that's right, thought Bean. Fought the only way

that's worth fighting, the only way that has any point. "And you did. Kicked him right out of orbit." It was as close as Bean could come to telling him the truth.

There was a knock on the door. Then it opened, immediately, without waiting for an answer. Before Bean could turn to see who it was, he knew it was a teacher—Ender looked up too high for it to be a kid.

Major Anderson and Colonel Graff.

"Ender Wiggin," said Graff.

Ender rose to his feet. "Yes sir." The deadness had returned to his voice.

"Your display of temper in the battleroom today was insubordinate and is not to be repeated."

Bean couldn't believe the stupidity of it. After what Ender had been through—what the teachers had *put* him through—and they have to keep playing this oppressive game with him? Making him feel utterly alone even *now?* These guys were relentless.

Ender's only answer was another lifeless "Yes sir." But Bean was fed up. "I think it was about time somebody told a teacher how we felt about what you've been doing."

Anderson and Graff didn't show a sign they'd even heard him. Instead, Anderson handed Ender a full sheet of paper. Not a transfer slip. A full-fledged set of orders. Ender was being transferred out of the school.

"Graduated?" Bean asked.

Ender nodded.

"What took them so long?" asked Bean. "You're only two or three years early. You've already learned how to walk and talk and dress yourself. What will they have left to teach you?" The whole thing was such a joke. Did they really think anybody was fooled? You reprimand Ender for insubordination, but then you graduate him because you've got a war coming and you don't have a lot of time to get him ready. He's your hope of victory, and you treat him like something you scrape off your shoe.

"All I know is, the game's over," said Ender. He folded the paper. "None too soon. Can I tell my army?"

"There isn't time," said Graff. "Your shuttle leaves in twenty minutes. Besides, it's better not to talk to them after you get your orders. It makes it easier."

"For them or for you?" Ender asked.

He turned to Bean, took his hand. To Bean, it was like the touch of the finger of God. It sent light all through him. Maybe I am his friend. Maybe he feels toward me some small part of the . . . feeling I have for him.

And then it was over. Ender let go of his hand. He turned toward the door.

"Wait," said Bean. "Where are you going? Tactical? Navigational? Support?"

"Command School," said Ender.

"*Pre*-command?"

"Command." Ender was out the door.

Straight to Command School. The elite school whose location was even a secret. Adults went to Command School. The battle must be coming very soon, to skip right past all the things they were supposed to learn in Tactical and Pre-Command.

He caught Graff by the sleeve. "Nobody goes to Command School until they're sixteen!" he said.

Graff shook off Bean's hand and left. If he caught Bean's sarcasm, he gave no sign of it.

The door closed. Bean was alone in Ender's quarters.

He looked around. Without Ender in it, the room was nothing. Being here meant nothing. Yet it was only a few days ago, not even a week, when Bean had stood here and Ender told him he was getting a toon after all.

For some reason what came into Bean's mind was the moment when Poke handed him six peanuts. It was life that she handed to him then.

Was it life that Ender gave to Bean? Was it the same thing?

No. Poke gave him life. Ender gave it meaning.

When Ender was here, this was the most important room in Battle School. Now it was no more than a broom closet.

Bean walked back down the corridor to the room that had been Carn Carby's until today. Until an hour ago. He palmed it—it opened. Already programmed in.

The room was empty. Nothing in it.

This room is mine, thought Bean.

Mine, and yet still empty.

He felt powerful emotions welling up inside him. He should be excited, proud to have his own command. But he didn't really care about it. As Ender said, the game was nothing. Bean would do a decent job, but the reason he'd have the respect of his soldiers was because he would carry some of Ender's reflected glory with him, a shrimpy little Napoleon flumping around wearing a man's shoes while he barked commands in a little tiny child's voice. Cute little Caligula, "Little Boot," the pride of Germanicus's army. But when he was wearing his father's boots, those boots were empty, and Caligula knew it, and nothing he ever did could change that. Was that his madness?

It won't drive *me* mad, thought Bean. Because I don't covet what Ender has or what he is. It's enough that *he* is Ender Wiggin. I don't have to be.

He understood what this feeling was, welling up in him, filling his throat, making tears stand out in his eyes, making his face burn, forcing a gasp, a silent sob. He bit on his lip, trying to let pain force the emotion away. It didn't help. Ender was gone.

Now that he knew what the feeling was, he could control it. He lay down on the bunk and went into the relaxing routine until the need to cry had passed. Ender had taken his hand to say good-bye. Ender had said, "I hope he recognizes what you're worth." Bean didn't really have anything left to prove. He'd do his best with Rabbit Army because maybe at some point in the future, when Ender was at the bridge of the flagship of the human fleet, Bean might have some role to play, some way to help. Some stunt that Ender might need him to pull to dazzle the Buggers. So he'd please the teachers, impress the hell out of them, so that they would keep opening doors for him, until one day a door would open and his friend Ender would be on the other side of it, and he could be in Ender's army once again.

19

Rebel

"Putting in Achilles was Graff's last act, and we know there were grave concerns. Why not play it safe and at least change Achilles to another army?"

"This is not necessarily a Bonzo Madrid situation for Bean."

"But we have no assurance that it's not, sir. Colonel Graff kept a lot of information to himself. A lot of conversations with Sister Carlotta, for instance, with no memo of what was said. Graff knows things about Bean and, I can promise you, about Achilles as well. I think he's laid a trap for us."

"Wrong, Captain Dimak. If Graff laid a trap, it was not for us."

"You're sure of that?"

"Graff doesn't play bureaucratic games. He doesn't give a damn about you and me. If he laid a trap, it's for Bean."

"Well, that's my point!"

"I understand your point. But Achilles stays."

"Why?"

"Achilles' tests show him to be of a remarkably even temperament. He is no Bonzo Madrid. Therefore Bean is in no physical danger. The stress seems to be psychological. A test of character. And that is precisely the area where we have the very least data about Bean, given his refusal to play the mind game and the ambiguity of the information we got from his playing with his teacher log-in. Therefore I think this forced relationship with his bugbear is worth pursuing."

"Bugbear or nemesis, sir?"

"We will monitor closely. I will *not* be keeping adults so far removed that we can't get there to intervene in time, the way Graff arranged it with Ender and Bonzo. Every precaution will be taken. I am not playing Russian roulette the way Graff was."

"Yes you are, sir. The only difference is that he knew he had only one empty chamber, and you don't know how many chambers are empty because he loaded the gun."

On his first morning as commander of Rabbit Army, Bean woke to see a paper lying on his floor. For a moment he was stunned at the thought that he would be given a battle before he even met his army, but to his relief the note was about something much more mundane.

Because of the number of new commanders, the tradition of not joining the commanders' mess until after the first victory is abolished. You are to dine in the commanders' mess starting immediately.

It made sense. Since they were going to accelerate the battle schedule for everyone, they wanted to have the commanders in a position to share information right from the start. And to be under social pressure from their peers, as well.

Holding the paper in his hand, Bean remembered how Ender had held his orders, each impossible new permutation of the game. Just because this order made sense did not make it a good thing. There was nothing sacred about the game itself that made Bean resent changes in the rules and customs, but the way the teachers were manipulating them *did* bother him.

Cutting off his access to student information, for instance. The question wasn't why they cut it off, or even why they let him have it for so long. The question was why the other commanders didn't have that much information all along. If they were supposed to be learning to lead, then they should have the tools of leadership.

And as long as they were changing the system, why not get rid of the really pernicious, destructive things they did? For instance, the scoreboards in the mess halls. Standings and scores! Instead of fighting the battle at hand, those scores made soldiers and commanders alike more cautious, less willing to experiment. That's why the ludicrous custom of fighting in formations had lasted so long—Ender can't have been the first commander to see a better way. But nobody wanted to rock the boat, to be the one who innovated and paid the price by dropping in the rankings. Far better to treat each battle as a completely separate problem, and to feel free to engage in battles as if they were *play* rather than work. Creativity and challenge would increase drastically. And commanders wouldn't have to worry when they gave an order to a toon or an individual whether they were causing a particular soldier to sacrifice his standing for the good of the army.

Most important, though, was the challenge inherent in Ender's decision to reject the game. The fact that he graduated before he could really go on strike didn't change the fact that if he had done so, Bean would have supported him in it.

Now that Ender was gone, a boycott of the game didn't make sense. Especially if Bean and the others were to advance to a point where they might be part of Ender's fleet when the real battles came. But they could take charge of the game, use it for their own purposes.

So, dressed in his new—and ill-fitting—Rabbit Army

uniform, Bean soon found himself once again standing on a table, this time in the much smaller officers' mess. Since Bean's speech the day before was already the stuff of legend, there was laughter and some catcalling when he got up.

"Do people where you come from eat with their feet, Bean?"

"Instead of getting up on tables, why don't you just *grow*, Bean?"

"Put some stilts on so we can keep the tables clean!"

But the other new commanders who had, until yesterday, been toon leaders in Dragon Army, made no catcalls and did not laugh. Their respectful attention to Bean soon prevailed, and silence fell over the room.

Bean flung up an arm to point to the scoreboard that showed the standings. "Where's Dragon Army?" he asked.

"They dissolved it," said Petra Arkanian. "The soldiers have been folded into the other armies. Except for you guys who used to be Dragon."

Bean listened, keeping his opinion of her to himself. All he could think of, though, was two nights before, when she was, wittingly or not, the Judas who was supposed to lure Ender into a trap.

"Without Dragon up there," said Bean, "that board means nothing. Whatever standing any of us gets would not be the same if Dragon were still there."

"There's not a hell of a lot we can do about it," said Dink Meeker.

"The problem isn't that Dragon is missing," said Bean. "The problem is that we shouldn't have that board at all. *We're* not each other's enemies. The *Buggers* are the only enemy. *We're* supposed to be allies. We should be learning from each other, sharing information and ideas. We should feel free to experiment, trying new things without being afraid of how it will affect our standings. That board up there, that's the *teachers'* game, getting us to turn against each other. Like Bonzo. Nobody here is as crazy with jealousy as he was, but come on, he was what those standings were bound to create. He was all set to beat in the brains of our best commander, our best hope against the next Bugger invasion, and why? Because Ender humiliated him in the *standings.* Think about that! The standings were more important to him than the war against the Formics!"

"Bonzo was crazy," said William Bee.

"So let's *not* be crazy," said Bean. "Let's get those standings out of the game. Let's take each battle one at a time, a clean slate. Try anything you can think of to win. And when the battle is over, both commanders sit down and explain what they were thinking, why they did what they did, so we can learn from each other. No secrets! Everybody try everything! And screw the standings!"

There were murmurs of assent, and not just from the former Dragons.

"That's easy for you to say," said Shen. "*Your* standing right now is tied for last."

"And there's the problem, right there," said Bean. "You're suspicious of my motives, and why? Because of the standings. But aren't we all supposed to be commanders in the same fleet someday? Working together? Trusting each other? How sick would the I.F. be, if all the ship captains and strike force commanders and fleet admirals spent all their time worrying about their standings instead of working together to try to beat the Formics! I want to learn from you, Shen. I don't want to *compete* with you for some empty rank that the teachers put up on that wall in order to manipulate us."

"I'm sure you guys from Dragon are all concerned about learning from us losers," said Petra.

There it was, out in the open.

"Yes! Yes, I *am* concerned. Precisely because I've been in Dragon Army. There are nine of us here who know pretty much only what we learned from Ender. Well, brilliant as he was, he's not the only one in the fleet or even in the school who knows anything. I need to learn how *you* think. I don't need you keeping secrets from me, and you don't need me keeping secrets from you. Maybe part of what made Ender so good was that he kept all his toon leaders talking to each other, free to try things but only as long as we shared what we were doing."

There was more assent this time. Even the doubters were nodding thoughtfully.

"So what I propose is this. A unanimous rejection of that board up there, not only the one in here but the one in the soldiers' mess, too. We all agree not to pay attention to it, period. We ask the teachers to disconnect the things or leave them blank. If they refuse, we bring in sheets to cover it, or we throw chairs until we break it. We don't have to play *their* game. We can take charge of our own education and get ready to fight the *real* enemy. We have to remember, always, who the real enemy is."

"Yeah, the teachers," said Dink Meeker.

Everybody laughed. But then Dink Meeker stood up on the table beside Bean. "I'm the senior commander here, now they've graduated all the oldest guys. I'm probably the oldest soldier left in Battle School. So I propose that we adopt Bean's proposal right now, and I'll go to the teachers to demand that the boards be shut off. Is there anyone opposed?"

Not a sound.

"That makes it unanimous. If the boards are still on at lunch, let's bring sheets to cover them up. If they're still on at dinner, then forget using chairs to vandalize, let's just refuse to take our armies to any battles until the boards are off."

Alai spoke up from where he stood in the serving line. "*That'll* shoot our standings all to . . ."

Then Alai realized what he was saying, and laughed at himself. "Damn, but they've got us brainwashed, haven't they!"

—

Bean was still flushed with victory when, after breakfast, he made his way to Rabbit barracks in order to meet his soldiers officially for the first time. Rabbit was on a midday practice schedule, so he only had about half an hour between breakfast and the first classes of the morning. Yesterday, when he talked to Itú, his mind had been on other things, with only the most cursory attention to what was going on inside Rabbit barracks. But now he realized that, unlike Dragon Army, the soldiers in Rabbit were all of the regular age. Not one was even close to Bean's height. He looked like somebody's doll, and worse, he felt like that too, walking down the corridor between the bunks, seeing all these huge boys—and a couple of girls—looking down at him.

Halfway down the bunks, he turned to face those he had already passed. Might as well address the problem immediately.

"The first problem I see," said Bean loudly, "is that you're all way too tall."

Nobody laughed. Bean died a little. But he had to go on.

"I'm growing as fast as I can. Beyond that, I don't know what I can do about it."

Only now did he get a chuckle or two. But that was a relief, that even a few were willing to meet him partway.

"Our first practice together is at 1030. As to our first battle together, I can't predict that, but I can promise you this—the teachers are *not* going to give me the traditional three months after my assignment to a new army. Same with all the other new commanders just appointed. They gave Ender Wiggin only a few weeks with Dragon before they went into battle—and Dragon was a new army, constructed out of nothing. Rabbit is a good army with a solid record. The only new person here is me. I expect the battles to begin in a matter of days, a week at most, and I expect battles to come frequently. So for the first couple of practices, you'll really be training me in your existing system. I need to see how you work with your toon leaders, how the toons work with each other, how you respond to orders, what commands you use. I'll have a couple of things to say that are more about attitude than tactics, but by and large, I want to see you doing things as you've always done them under Carn. It would help me, though, if you practiced with intensity, so I can see you at your sharpest. Are there any questions?"

None. Silence.

"One other thing. Day before yesterday, Bonzo and some of his friends were stalking Ender Wiggin in the halls. I saw the danger, but the soldiers in Dragon Army were mostly too small to stand up against the crew Bonzo had assembled. It wasn't an accident that when I needed help for my commander, I came to the door of Rabbit Army. This wasn't the closest barracks. I came to you because I knew that you had a fair-minded commander in Carn Carby, and I believed that his army would have the same attitude. Even if you didn't have any particular love for Ender Wiggin or Dragon Army, I knew that you would not stand by and let a bunch of thugs pound on a smaller kid that they couldn't beat fair and square in battle. And I was right about you. When you poured out of this barracks and stood as witnesses in the corridor, I was proud of what you stood for. I'm proud now to be one of you."

That did it. Flattery rarely fails, and never does if it's sincere. By letting them know they had already earned his respect, he dissipated much of the tension, for of course they were worried that as a former Dragon he would have contempt for the first army that Ender Wiggin beat. Now they knew better, and so he'd have a chance to win their respect as well.

Itú started clapping, and the other boys joined in. It wasn't a long ovation, but it was enough to let him know the door was open, at least a crack.

He raised his hands to silence the applause—just in time, since it was already dying down. "I'd like to speak to the toon leaders for a few minutes in my quarters. The rest of you are dismissed till practice."

Almost at once, Itú was beside him. "Good job," he said. "Only one mistake."

"What was that?"

"You aren't the only new person here."

"They assigned one of the Dragon soldiers to Rabbit?" For a moment, Bean allowed himself to hope that it would be Nikolai. He could use a reliable friend.

No such luck.

"No, a Dragon soldier would be a veteran! I mean this guy is *new.* He just got to Battle School yesterday afternoon and he was assigned here last night, after you came by."

"A launchy? Assigned straight to an army?"

"Oh, we asked him about that, and he's had a lot of the same classwork. He went through a bunch of surgeries down on Earth, and he studied through it all, but—"

"You mean he's recovering from surgery, too?"

"No, he walks fine, he's—look, why don't you just meet him? All I need to know is, do you want to assign him to a toon or what?"

"Eh, let's see him."

Itú led him to the back of the barracks. There he was, standing beside his bunk, several inches taller than Bean remembered, with legs of even length now, both of them straight. The boy he had last seen fondling Poke, minutes before her dead body went into the river.

"Ho, Achilles," said Bean.

"Ho, Bean," said Achilles. He grinned winningly. "Looks like you're the big guy here."

"So to speak," said Bean.

"You two know each other?" said Itú.

"We knew each other in Rotterdam," said Achilles.

They can't have assigned him to me by accident. I never told anybody but Sister Carlotta about what he did, but how can I guess what she told the I.F.? Maybe they put him here because they thought both of us being from the Rotterdam streets, from the same crew—the same family—I might be able to help him get into the mainstream of the school faster. Or maybe they knew that he was a murderer who was able to hold a grudge for a long, long time, and strike when least expected. Maybe they knew that he planned for my death as surely as he planned for Poke's. Maybe he's here to be my Bonzo Madrid.

Except that I haven't taken any personal defense classes. And I'm half his size—I couldn't jump high enough to hit him in the nose. Whatever they were trying to accomplish by putting Ender's life at risk, Ender always had a better chance of surviving than I will.

The only thing in my favor is that Achilles wants to survive and prosper more than he wants vengeance. Since he can hold a grudge forever, he's in no hurry to act on it. And, unlike Bonzo, he'll never allow himself to be goaded into striking under circumstances where he'd be identifiable as the killer. As long as he thinks he needs me and as long as I'm never alone, I'm probably safe.

Safe. He shuddered. Poke felt safe, too.

"Achilles was *my* commander there," said Bean. "He kept a group of us kids alive. Got us into the charity kitchens."

"Bean is too modest," said Achilles. "The whole thing was his idea. He basically taught us the whole idea of working together. I've studied a lot since then, Bean. I've had a year of nothing but books and classes—when they weren't cutting into my legs and pulverizing and regrowing my bones. And I finally know enough to understand just what a leap you helped us make. From barbarism into civilization. Bean here is like a replay of human evolution."

Bean was not so stupid as to fail to recognize when flattery was being used on him. At the same time, it was more than a little useful to have this new boy, straight from Earth, already know who Bean was and show respect for him.

"The evolution of the pygmies, anyway," said Bean.

"Bean was the toughest little bastard you ever saw on the street, I got to tell you."

No, this was not what Bean needed right now. Achilles had just crossed the line from flattery into possession. Stories about Bean as a "tough little bastard" would, of necessity, set Achilles up as Bean's superior, able to evaluate him. The stories might even be to Bean's credit—but they would serve more to validate Achilles, make him an insider far faster than he would otherwise have been. And Bean did not want Achilles to be inside yet.

Achilles was already going on, as more soldiers gathered closer to hear. "The way I got recruited into Bean's crew was—"

"It wasn't my crew," said Bean, cutting him off. "And here in Battle School, we don't tell stories about home and we don't listen to them either. So I'd appreciate it if you never spoke again of anything that happened Rotterdam, not while you're in my army."

He'd done the nice bit during his opening speech. But now was the time for authority.

Achilles didn't show any sign of embarrassment at the reprimand. "I get it. No problem."

"It's time for you to get ready to go to class," said Bean to the soldiers. "I need to confer with my toon leaders only." Bean pointed to Ambul, a Thai soldier who, according to what Bean read in the student reports, would have been a toon leader long ago, except for his tendency to disobey stupid orders. "You, Ambul. I assign you to get Achilles to and from his correct classes and acquaint him with how to wear a flash suit, how it works, and the basics of movement in the battleroom. Achilles, you are to obey Ambul like God until I assign you to a regular toon."

Achilles grinned. "But I don't obey God."

You think I don't know that? "The correct answer to an order from me is 'Yes sir.' "

Achilles' grin faded. "Yes sir."

"I'm glad to have you here," Bean lied.

"Glad to be here, sir," said Achilles. And Bean was reasonably sure that while Achilles was *not* lying, his reason for being glad was very complicated, and certainly included, by now, a renewed desire to see Bean die.

For the first time, Bean understood the reason Ender had almost always acted as if he was oblivious to the danger from Bonzo. It was a simple choice, really. Either he could act to save himself, or he could act to maintain control over his army. In order to hold real authority, Bean had to insist on complete obedience and respect from his soldiers, even if it meant putting Achilles down, even if it meant increasing his personal danger.

And yet another part of him thought: Achilles wouldn't be here if he didn't have the ability to be a leader. He performed extraordinarily well as our papa in Rotterdam. It's my responsibility now to get him up to speed as quickly as possible, for the sake of his potential usefulness to the I.F. I can't let my personal fear interfere with that, or my hatred of him for what he did to Poke. So even if Achilles is evil incarnate, my job is to turn him into a highly effective soldier with a good shot at becoming a commander.

And in the meantime, I'll watch my back.

20

Trial and Error

"You brought him up to Battle School, didn't you?"

"Sister Carlotta, I'm on a leave of absence right now. That means I've been sacked, in case you don't understand how the I.F. handles these things."

"Sacked! A miscarriage of justice. You ought to be shot."

"If the Sisters of St. Nicholas had convents, your abbess would make you do serious penance for that un-Christian thought."

"You took him out of the hospital in Cairo and directly into space. Even though I warned you."

"Didn't you notice that you telephoned me on a regular exchange? I'm on Earth. Someone else is running Battle School."

"He's a serial murderer now, you know. Not just the girl in Rotterdam. There was a boy there, too, the one Helga called Ulysses. They found his body a few weeks ago."

"Achilles has been in medical care for the past year."

"The coroner estimates that the killing took place at

least that long ago. The body was hidden behind some long-term storage near the fish market. It covered the smell, you see. And it goes on. A teacher at the school I put him in."

"Ah. That's right. *You* put him in a school long before I did."

"The teacher fell to his death from an upper story."

"No witnesses. No evidence."

"Exactly."

"You see a trend here?"

"But that's *my* point. Achilles does not kill carelessly. Nor does he choose his victims at random. Anyone who has seen him helpless, crippled, beaten—he can't bear the shame. He has to expunge it by getting absolute power over the person who dared to humiliate him."

"You're a psychologist now?"

"I laid the facts before an expert."

"The supposed facts."

"I'm not in court, Colonel. I'm talking to the man who put this killer in school with the child who came up with the original plan to humiliate him. Who called for his death. My expert assured me that the chance of Achilles *not* striking against Bean is zero."

"It's not as easy as you think, in space. No dock, you see."

"Do you know how I knew you had taken him into space?"

"I'm sure you have your sources, both mortal and heavenly."

"My dear friend, Dr. Vivian Delamar, was the surgeon who reconstructed Achilles' leg."

"As I recall, you recommended her."

"Before I knew what Achilles really was. When I found out, I called her. Warned her to be careful. Because my expert also said that *she* was in danger."

"The one who restored his leg? Why?"

"No one has seen him more helpless than the surgeon who cuts into him as he lies there drugged to the gills.

Rationally, I'm sure he knew it was wrong to harm this woman who did him so much good. But then, the same would apply to Poke, the first time he killed. *If* it was the first time."

"So . . . Dr. Vivian Delamar. You alerted her. What did she see? Did he murmur a confession under anaesthetic?"

"We'll never know. He killed her."

"You're joking."

"I'm in Cairo. Her funeral is tomorrow. They were calling it a heart attack until I urged them to look for a hypodermic insertion mark. Indeed they found one, and now it's on the books as a murder. Achilles *does* know how to read. He learned which drugs would do the job. How he got her to sit still for it, I don't know."

"How can I believe this, Sister Carlotta? The boy is generous, gracious, people are drawn to him, he's a born leader. People like that don't kill."

"Who are the dead? The teacher who mocked him for his ignorance when he first arrived in the school, showed him up in front of the class. The doctor who saw him laid out under anaesthetic. The street girl whose crew took him down. The street boy who vowed to kill him and made him go into hiding. Maybe the coincidence argument would sway a jury, but it shouldn't sway you."

"Yes, you've convinced me that the danger might well be real. But I already alerted the teachers at Battle School that there might be some danger. And now I really am not in charge of Battle School."

"You're still in *touch.* If you give them a more urgent warning, they'll take steps."

"I'll give the appropriate warning."

"You're lying to me."

"You can tell that over the phone?"

"You *want* Bean exposed to danger!"

"Sister . . . yes, I do. But not this much of it. Whatever I can do, I'll do."

"If you let Bean come to harm, God will have an accounting from you."

"He'll have to get in line, Sister Carlotta. The I.F. court-martial takes precedence."

Bean looked down into the air vent in his quarters and marveled that he had ever been small enough to fit in there. What was he then, the size of a rat?

Fortunately, with a room of his own now he wasn't limited to the outflow vents. He put his chair on top of his table and climbed up to the long, thin intake vents along the wall on the corridor side of his room. The vent trim pried out as several long sections. The paneling above it was separate from the riveted wall below. And it, too, came off fairly easily. Now there was room enough for almost any kid in Battle School to shinny in to the crawl space over the corridor ceiling.

Bean stripped off his clothes and once again crawled into the air system.

It was more cramped this time—it was surprising how much he'd grown. He made his way quickly to the maintenance area near the furnaces. He found how the lighting systems worked, and carefully went around removing lightbulbs and wall glow units in the areas he'd be needing. Soon there was a wide vertical shaft that was utterly dark when the door was closed, with deep shadows even when it was open. Carefully he laid his trap.

—

Achilles never ceased to be astonished at how the universe bent to his will. Whatever he wished seemed to come to him. Poke and her crew, raising him above the other bullies. Sister Carlotta, bringing him to the priests' school in Bruxelles. Dr. Delamar, straightening his leg so he could *run*, so he looked no different from any other boy his age. And now here he was in Battle School, and who should be his first commander but little Bean, ready to take him under his wing, help him rise within this school. As if the universe were created to serve him, with all the people in it tuned to resonate with his desires.

The battleroom was cool beyond belief. War in a box. Point the gun, the other kid's suit freezes. Of course, Ambul had made the mistake of demonstrating this by freezing Achilles and then laughing at his consternation at floating in the air, unable to move, unable to change the direction of his drift. People shouldn't do that. It was wrong, and it always gnawed at Achilles until he was able to set things right. There should be more kindness and respect in the world.

Like Bean. It looked so promising at first, but then Bean started putting him down. Making sure the others saw that Achilles *used* to be Bean's papa, but now he was just a soldier in Bean's army. There was no need for that. You don't go putting people down. Bean had changed. Back when Poke first put Achilles on his back, shaming him in front of all those little children, it was Bean who showed him respect. "Kill him," Bean had said. He knew, then, that tiny boy, he knew that even on his back, Achilles was dangerous. But he seemed to have forgotten that now. In fact, Achilles was pretty sure that Bean must have told Ambul to freeze his flash suit and humiliate him in the practice room, setting him up for the others to laugh at him.

I was your friend and protector, Bean, because you showed respect for me. But now I have to weigh that in the balance with your behavior here in Battle School. No respect for me at all.

The trouble was, the students in Battle School were given nothing that could be used as a weapon, and everything was made completely safe. No one was ever alone, either. Except the commanders. Alone in their quarters. That was promising. But Achilles suspected that the teachers had a way of tracking where every student was at any given time. He'd have to learn the system, learn how to evade it, before he could start setting things to rights.

But he knew this: He'd learn what he needed to learn. Opportunities would appear. And he, being Achilles, would see those opportunities and seize them. Nothing could interrupt his rise until he held all the power there was to hold within his hands. Then there would be perfect justice in the world, not this miserable system that left so many children starving and ignorant and crippled on the streets while others lived in privilege and safety and health. All those adults who had run things for thousands of years were fools or failures. But the universe obeyed Achilles. He and he alone could correct the abuses.

On his third day in Battle School, Rabbit Army had its first battle with Bean as commander. They lost. They would not have lost if Achilles had been commander. Bean was doing some stupid touchy-feely thing, leaving things up to the toon leaders. But it was obvious that the toon leaders had been badly chosen by Bean's predecessor. If Bean was to win, he needed to take tighter control. When he tried to suggest this to Bean, the child only smiled knowingly—a maddeningly superior smile—and told him that the key to victory was for each toon leader and, eventually, each soldier to see the whole situation and act independently to bring about victory. It made Achilles want to slap him, it was so stupid, so wrongheaded. The one who knew how to order things did not leave it up to others to create their little messes in the corners of the world. He took the reins and pulled, sharp and hard. He whipped his men into obedience. As Frederick the Great said: The soldier must fear his officers more than he fears the bullets of the enemy. You could not rule without the naked exercise of power. The followers must bow their heads to the leader. They must *surrender* their heads, using only the mind and will of the leader to rule them. No one but Achilles seemed to understand that this was the great strength of the Buggers. They had no individual minds, only the mind of the hive. They submitted perfectly to the queen. We cannot defeat the Buggers until we learn from them, become like them.

But there was no point in explaining this to Bean. He would not listen. Therefore he would never make Rabbit

Army into a hive. He was working to create chaos. It was unbearable.

Unbearable—yet, just when Achilles thought he couldn't bear the stupidity and waste any longer, Bean called him to his quarters.

Achilles was startled, when he entered, to find that Bean had removed the vent cover and part of the wall panel, giving him access to the air-duct system. This was not at all what Achilles had expected.

"Take your clothes off," said Bean.

Achilles smelled an attempt at humiliation.

Bean was taking off his own uniform. "They track us through the uniforms," said Bean. "If you aren't wearing one, they don't know where you are, except in the gym and the battleroom, where they have really expensive equipment to track each warm body. We aren't going to either of those places, so strip."

Bean was naked. As long as Bean went first, Achilles could not be shamed by doing the same.

"Ender and I used to do this," said Bean. "Everybody thought Ender was such a brilliant commander, but the truth is he knew all the plans of the other commanders because we'd go spying through the air ducts. And not just the commanders, either. We found out what the teachers were planning. We always knew it in advance. Not hard to win that way."

Achilles laughed. This was too cool. Bean might be a fool, but this Ender that Achilles had heard so much about, *he* knew what he was doing.

"It takes two people, is that it?"

"To get where I can spy on the teachers, there's a wide shaft, pitch black. I can't climb down. I need somebody to lower me down and haul me back up. I didn't know who in Rabbit Army I could trust, and then . . . there you were. A friend from the old days."

It was happening again. The universe, bending to his will. He and Bean would be alone. No one would be tracking where they were. No one would know what had happened.

"I'm in," said Achilles.

"Boost me up," said Bean. "You're tall enough to climb up alone."

Clearly, Bean had come this way many times before. He scampered through the crawl space, his feet and butt flashing in the spill from the corridor lights. Achilles noted where he put his hands and feet, and soon was as adept at Bean at picking his way through. Every time he used his leg, he marveled at the use of it. It went where he wanted it to go, and had the strength to hold him. Dr. Delamar might be a skilled surgeon, but even she said that she had never seen a body respond to the surgery as Achilles' did. His body knew how to be whole, expected to be strong. All the time before, those crippled years, had been the universe's way of teaching Achilles the unbearability of disorder. And now Achilles was perfect of body, ready to move ahead in setting things to rights.

Achilles very carefully noted the route they took. If the opportunity presented itself, he would be coming back alone. He could not afford to get lost, or give himself away. No one could know that he had ever been in the air system. As long as he gave them no reason, the teachers would never suspect him. All they knew was that he and Bean were friends. And when Achilles grieved for the child, his tears would be real. They always were, for there was a nobility to these tragic deaths. A grandeur as the great universe worked its will through Achilles' adept hands.

The furnaces roared as they came into a room where the framing of the station was visible. Fire was good. It left so little residue. People died when they accidentally fell into fire. It happened all the time. Bean, crawling around alone . . . it would be good if they went near the furnace.

Instead, Bean opened a door into a dark space. The light from the opening showed a black gap not far inside.

"Don't step over the edge of that," Bean said cheerfully. He picked up a loop of very fine cord from the ground. "It's a deadline. Safety equipment. Keeps workmen from drifting off into space when they're working on the outside of the station. Ender and I set it up—it goes over a beam up there and keeps me centered in the shaft. You can't grip it in your hands, it cuts too easily if it slides across your skin. So you loop it tight around your body—no sliding, see?—and brace yourself. The gravity's not that intense, so I just jump off. We measured it out, so I stop right at the level of the vents leading to the teachers' quarters."

"Doesn't it hurt when you stop?"

"Like a bitch," said Bean. "No pain no gain, right? I take off the deadline, I snag it on a flap of metal and it stays there till I get back. I'll tug on it three times when I get it back on. Then you pull me back up. But *not* with your hands. You go out the door and walk out there. When you get to place where we came in, go around the beam there and go till you touch the wall. Just wait there until I can get myself swinging and land back here on this ledge. Then I unloop myself and you come back in and we leave the deadline for next time. Simple, see?"

"Got it," said Achilles.

Instead of walking to the wall, it would be simple enough to just keep walking. Get Bean floating in the air where he couldn't get hold of anything. Plenty of time, then, to find a way to tie it off inside that dark room. With the roar of the furnaces and fans, nobody would hear Bean calling for help. Then Achilles would have time to explore. Figure out how to get into the furnaces. Swing Bean back, strangle him, carry the body to the fire. Drop the deadline down the shaft. Nobody would find it. Quite possibly no one would ever find Bean, or if they did, his soft tissues would be consumed. All evidence of strangulation would be gone. Very neat. There'd be some improvisation, but there always was. Achilles could handle little problems as they came up.

Achilles looped the deadline over his head, then drew it tight under his arms as Bean climbed into the loop at the other end.

"Set," said Achilles.

"Make sure it's tight, so it doesn't have any slack to cut you when I hit bottom."

"Yes, it's tight."

But Bean had to check. He got a finger under the line. "Tighter," said Bean.

Achilles tightened it more.

"Good," said Bean. "That's it. Do it."

Do it? Bean was the one who was supposed to do it.

Then the deadline went taut and Achilles was lifted off his feet. With a few more yanks, he hung in the air in the dark shaft. The deadline dug harshly into his skin.

When Bean said "do it" he was talking to someone else. Someone who was already here, lying in wait. The traitorous little bastard.

Achilles said nothing, however. He reached up to see if he could touch the beam above him, but it was out of reach. Nor could he climb the line, not with bare hands, not with the line drawn taut by his own body weight.

He wriggled on the line, starting himself swinging. But no matter how far he went in any direction, he touched nothing. No wall, no place where he might find purchase.

Time to talk.

"What's this about, Bean?"

"It's about Poke," said Bean.

"She's dead, Bean."

"You kissed her. You killed her. You put her in the river."

Achilles felt the blood run hot into his face. No one saw that. He was guessing. But then . . . how did he know that Achilles had kissed her first, unless he saw?

"You're wrong," said Achilles.

"How sad if I am. Then the wrong man will die for the crime."

"Die? Be serious, Bean. You aren't a killer."

"But the hot dry air of the shaft will do it for me. You'll dehydrate in a day. Your mouth's already a little dry, isn't it? And then you'll just keep hanging here, mummifying. This is the intake system, so the air gets filtered and purified. Even if your body stinks for a while, nobody will smell it. Nobody will see you—you're above where the light shines from the door. And nobody comes in here anyway. No, the disappearance of Achilles will be the mystery of Battle School. They'll tell ghost stories about you to frighten the launchies."

"Bean, I didn't do it."

"I saw you, Achilles, you poor fool. I don't care what you say, I *saw* you. I never thought I'd have the chance to make you pay for what you did to her. Poke did nothing but good to you. I told her to kill you, but she had mercy. She made you king of the streets. And for that you killed her?"

"I didn't kill her."

"Let me lay it out for you, Achilles, since you're clearly too stupid to see where you are. First thing is, you forgot where you were. Back on Earth, you were used to being a lot smarter than everybody around you. But here in Battle School, *everybody* is as smart as you, and most of us are smarter. You think Ambul didn't see the way you looked at him? You think he didn't know he was marked for death after he laughed at you? You think the other soldiers in Rabbit doubted me when I told them about you? They'd already seen that there was something wrong with you. The adults might have missed it, they might buy into the way you suck up to them, but *we* didn't. And since we just had a case of one kid trying to kill another, nobody was going to put up with it again. Nobody was going to wait for you to strike. Because here's the thing—we don't give a shit about fairness here. We're soldiers. Soldiers do not give the other guy a sporting chance. Soldiers shoot in the back, lay traps and ambushes, lie to the enemy and outnumber the other bastard every chance they get. Your kind of murder only works among civilians.

And you were too cocky, too stupid, too insane to realize that."

Achilles knew that Bean was right. He had miscalculated grossly. He had forgotten that when Bean said for Poke to kill him, he had not just been showing respect for Achilles. He had also been trying to get Achilles killed.

This just wasn't working out very well.

"So you have only two ways for this to end. One way, you just hang there, we take turns watching to make sure you don't figure some way out of this, until you're dead and then we leave you and go about our lives. The other way, you confess to everything—and I mean everything, not just what you think I already know—and you keep confessing. Confess to the teachers. Confess to the psychiatrists they send you to. Confess your way into a mental hospital back on Earth. We don't care which you choose. All that matters is that you never again walk freely through the corridors of Battle School. Or anywhere else. So . . . what will it be? Dry out on the line, or let the teachers know just how crazy you are?"

"Bring me a teacher, I'll confess."

"Didn't you hear me explain how stupid we're not? You confess now. Before witnesses. With a recorder. We don't bring some teacher up here to see you hanging there and feel all squishy sorry for you. Any teacher who comes here will know exactly what you are, and there'll be about six marines to keep you subdued and sedated because, Achilles, they don't play around here. They don't give people chances to escape. You've got no rights here. You don't get rights again until you're back on Earth. Here's your last chance. Confession time."

Achilles almost laughed out loud. But it was important for Bean to think that he had won. As, for the moment, he had. Achilles could see now that there was no way for him to remain in Battle School. But Bean wasn't smart enough just to kill him and have done. No, Bean was, completely unnecessarily, allowing him to live. And as long as Achilles was alive, then time would move things his way. The universe would bend until the door was opened and Achilles went free. And it would happen sooner rather than later.

You shouldn't have left a door open for me, Bean. Because I *will* kill you someday. You and everyone else who has seen me helpless here.

"All right," said Achilles. "I killed Poke. I strangled her and put her in the river."

"Go on."

"What more? You want to know how she wet herself and took a shit while she was dying? You want to know how her eyes bugged out?"

"One murder doesn't get you psychiatric confinement, Achilles. You know you've killed before."

"What makes you think so?"

"Because it didn't bother you."

It never bothered, not even the first time. You just don't understand power. If it *bothers* you, you aren't fit to *have* power. "I killed Ulysses, of course, but just because he was a nuisance."

"And?"

"I'm not a mass murderer, Bean."

"You live to kill, Achilles. Spill it all. And then convince me that it really *was* all."

But Achilles had just been playing. He had already decided to tell it all.

"The most recent was Dr. Vivian Delamar," he said. "I told her not to do the operations under total anaesthetic. I told her to leave me alert, I could take it even if there was pain. But she had to be in control. Well, if she really loved control so much, why did she turn her back on me? And why was she so stupid as to think I really had a gun? By pressing hard in her back, I made it so she didn't even feel the needle go in right next to where the tongue depressors were poking her. Died of a heart attack right there in her own office. Nobody even knew I'd been in there. You want more?"

"I want it all, Achilles."

It took twenty minutes, but Achilles gave them the whole chronicle, all seven times he had set things right. He liked it, actually, telling them like this. Nobody had ever had a chance to understand how powerful he was till now. He wanted to see their faces, that's the only thing that was missing. He wanted to see the disgust that would reveal their weakness, their inability to look power in the face. Machiavelli understood. If you intend to rule, you don't shrink from killing. Saddam Hussein knew it—you have to be willing to kill with your own hand. You can't stand back and let others do it for you all the time. And Stalin understood it, too—you can never be loyal to anybody, because that only weakens you. Lenin was good to Stalin, gave him his chance, raised him out of nothing to be the keeper of the gate to power. But that didn't stop Stalin from imprisoning Lenin and then killing him. That's what these fools would never understand. All those military writers were just armchair philosophers. All that military history—most of it was useless. War was just one of the tools that the great men used to get and keep their power. And the only way to stop a great man was the way Brutus did it.

Bean, you're no Brutus.

Turn on the light. Let me see the faces.

But the light did not go on. When he was finished, when they left, there was only the light through the door, silhouetting them as they left. Five of them. All naked, but carrying the recording equipment. They even tested it, to make sure it had picked up Achilles' confession. He heard his own voice, strong and unwavering. Proud of what he'd done. That would prove to the weaklings that he was "insane." They would keep him alive. Until the universe bent things to his will yet again, and set him free to reign with blood and horror on Earth. Since they hadn't let him see their faces, he'd have no choice. When all the power was in his hands, he'd have to kill everyone who was in Battle School at this time. That would be a good idea, anyway. Since all the brilliant military minds of the age had been assembled here at one time or another, it was obvious that in order to rule safely, Achilles would have to get rid of everyone whose name had ever been on a Battle School roster. Then there'd be no rivals. And he'd keep testing children as long as he lived, finding any with the slightest spark of military talent. Herod understood how you stay in power.

Part Six

VICTOR

21

Guesswork

"We're not waiting any longer for Colonel Graff to repair the damage done to Ender Wiggin. Wiggin doesn't need Tactical School for the job he'll be doing. And we need the others to move on at once. *They* have to get the feel of what the old ships can do before we bring them here and put them on the simulators, and that takes time."

"They've only had a few games."

"I shouldn't have allowed them as much time as I have. ISL is two months away from you, and by the time they're done with Tactical, the voyage from there to FleetCom will be four months. That gives them only three months in Tactical before we have to bring them to Command School. Three months in which to compress three years of training."

"I should tell you that Bean seems to have passed Colonel Graff's last test."

"Test? When I relieved Colonel Graff, I thought his sick little testing program ended as well."

"We didn't know how dangerous this Achilles was. We

had been warned of *some* danger, but . . . he seemed so likable . . . I'm not faulting Colonel Graff, you understand, *he* had no way of knowing."

"Knowing what?'

"That Achilles is a serial killer."

"That should make Graff happy. Ender's count is up to two."

"I'm not joking, sir. Achilles has seven murders on his tally."

"And he passed the screening?"

"He knew how to answer the psychological tests."

"Please tell me that none of the seven took place at Battle School."

"Number eight would have. But Bean got him to confess."

"Bean's a priest now?"

"Actually, sir, it was deft strategy. He outmaneuvered Achilles—led him into an ambush, and confession was the only escape."

"So Ender, the nice middle-class American boy, kills the kid who wants to beat him up in the bathroom. And Bean, the hoodlum street kid, turns a serial killer over to law enforcement."

"The more significant thing for our purposes is that Ender was good at building teams, but he beat Bonzo hand to hand, one on one. And then Bean, a loner who had almost no friends after a year in the school, he beats Achilles by assembling a team to be his defense and his witnesses. I have no idea if Graff predicted these outcomes, but the result was that his tests got each boy to act not only against our expectations, but also against his own predilections."

"Predilections. Major Anderson."

"It will all be in my report."

"Try to write the entire thing without using the word *predilection* once."

"Yes, sir."

"I've assigned the destroyer *Condor* to take the group."

"How many do you want, sir?"

"We have need of a maximum of eleven at any one time. We have Carby, Bee, and Momoe on their way to Tactical already, but Graff tells me that of those three, only Carby is likely to work well with Wiggin. We do need to hold a slot for Ender, but it wouldn't hurt to have a spare. So send ten."

"*Which* ten?"

"How the hell should I know? Well . . . Bean, him for sure. And the nine others that you think would work best with either Bean or Ender in command, whichever one it turns out to be."

"One list for both possible commanders?"

"With Ender as the first choice. We want them all to train together. Become a team."

The orders came at 1700. Bean was supposed to board the *Condor* at 1800. It's not as if he had anything to pack. An hour was more time than they gave Ender. So Bean went and told his army what was happening, where he was going.

"We've only had five games," said Itú.

"Got to catch the bus when it comes to the stop, neh?" said Bean.

"Eh," said Itú.

"Who else?" asked Ambul.

"They didn't tell me. Just . . . Tactical School."

"We don't even know where it is."

"Somewhere in space," said Itú.

"No, really?" It was lame, but they laughed. It wasn't all that hard a good-bye. He'd only been with Rabbit for eight days.

"Sorry we didn't win any for you," said Itú.

"We would have won, if I'd wanted to," said Bean.

They looked at him like he was crazy.

"I was the one who proposed that we get rid of the standings, stop caring who wins. How would it look if we do that and I win every time?"

"It would look like you really did care about the standings," said Itú.

"That's not what bothers me," said another toon leader. "Are you telling me you set us up to *lose?*"

"No, I'm telling you I had a different priority. What do we learn from beating each other? Nothing. We're never going to have to fight human children. We're going to have to fight Buggers. So what do we need to learn? How to coordinate our attacks. How to respond to each other. How to feel the course of the battle, and take responsibility for the whole thing even if you don't have command. *That's* what I was working on with you guys. And if we *won,* if we went in and mopped up the walls with them, using *my* strategy, what does that teach *you?* You already worked with a good commander. What you needed to do was work with each other. So I put you in tough situations and by the end you were finding ways to bail each other out. To make it work."

"We never made it work well enough to win."

"That's not how I measured it. You made it work. When the Buggers come again, they're going to make things go wrong. Besides the normal friction of war, they're going to be doing stuff we couldn't think of because they're not human, they don't think like us. So plans of attack, what good are they then? We try, we do what we can, but what really counts is what you do when command breaks down. When it's just you with your squadron, and you with your transport, and you with your beat-up strike force that's got only five weapons among eight ships. How do you help each other? How do you make do? That's what I was working on. And then I went back to the officers' mess and told them what I learned. What you guys showed me. I learned stuff from them, too. I told you all the stuff I learned from them, right?"

"Well, you *could* have told us what you were learning from *us,*" said Itú. They were all still a bit resentful.

"I didn't have to *tell* you. You learned it."

"At least you could have told us it was OK not to win."

"But you were supposed to *try* to win. I didn't tell you because it only works if you think it counts. Like when the Buggers come. It'll count then, for real. That's when you get really smart, when losing means that you and everybody you ever cared about, the whole human race, will die. Look, I didn't think we'd have long together. So I made the best use of the time, for you and for me. You guys are all ready to take command of armies."

"What about you, Bean?" asked Ambul. He was smiling, but there was an edge to it. "You ready to command a fleet?"

"I don't know. It depends on whether they want to win." Bean grinned.

"Here's the thing, Bean," said Ambul. "Soldiers don't like to lose."

"And *that,*" said Bean, "is why losing is a much more powerful teacher than winning."

They heard him. They thought about it. Some of them nodded.

"*If* you live," Bean added. And grinned at them.

They smiled back.

"I gave you the best thing I could think of to give you during this week," said Bean. "And learned from you as much as I was smart enough to learn. Thank you." He stood and saluted them.

They saluted back.

He left.

And went to Rat Army barracks.

"Nikolai just got his orders," a toon leader told him.

For a moment Bean wondered if Nikolai would be going to Tactical School with him. His first thought was, No way is he ready. His second thought was, I wish he could come. His third thought was, I'm not much of a friend, to think first how he doesn't deserve to be promoted.

"What orders?" Bean asked.

"He's got him an army. Hell, he wasn't even a toon leader here. Just *got* here last week."

"Which army?"

"Rabbit." The toon leader looked at Bean's uniform again. "Oh. I guess he's replacing *you.*"

Bean laughed and headed for the quarters he had just left.

Nikolai was sitting inside with the door open, looking lost.

"Can I come in?"

Nikolai looked up and grinned. "Tell me you're here to take your army back."

"I've got a hint for you. Try to win. They think that's important."

"I couldn't believe you lost all five."

"You know, for a school that doesn't list standings anymore, everybody sure keeps track."

"I keep track of *you.*"

"Nikolai, I wish you were coming with me."

"What's happening, Bean? Is this it? Are the Buggers here?"

"I don't know."

"Come on, you figure these things out."

"If the Buggers were really coming, would they leave all you guys here in the station? Or send you back to Earth? Or evacuate you to some obscure asteroid? I don't know. Some things point to the end being really close. Other things seem like nothing important's going to happen anywhere around here."

"So maybe they're about to launch this huge fleet against the Bugger world and you guys are supposed to grow up on the voyage."

"Maybe," said Bean. "But the time to launch *that* fleet was right after the Second Invasion."

"Well, what if they didn't find out where the Bugger home world *was* until now?"

That stopped Bean cold. "Never crossed my mind," said Bean. "I mean, they must have been sending signals home. All we had to do was track that direction. Follow the light, you know. That's what it says in the manuals."

"What if they don't communicate by light?"

"Light may take a year to go a lightyear, but it's still faster than anything else."

"Anything else that we know about," said Nikolai.

Bean just looked at him.

"Oh, I know, that's stupid. The laws of physics and all that. I just—you know, I keep thinking, that's all. I don't like to rule things out just because they're impossible."

Bean laughed. "Merda, Nikolai, I should have let you talk more and me talk less back when we slept across from each other."

"Bean, you know I'm not a genius."

"All geniuses here, Nikolai."

"I was scraping by."

"So maybe you're not a Napoleon, Nikolai. Maybe you're just an Eisenhower. Don't expect me to cry for you."

It was Nikolai's turn to laugh.

"I'll miss you, Bean."

"Thanks for coming with me to face Achilles, Nikolai."

"Guy gave me nightmares."

"Me too."

"And I'm glad you brought the others along too. Itú, Ambul, Crazy Tom, I felt like we could've used six more, and Achilles was hanging from a wire. Guys like him, you can understand why they invented hanging."

"Someday," said Bean, "you're going to need me the way I needed you. And I'll be there."

"I'm sorry I didn't join your squad, Bean."

"You were right," said Bean. "I asked you because you were my friend, and I thought I needed a friend, but I should have *been* a friend, too, and seen what *you* needed."

"I'll never let you down again."

Bean threw his arms around Nikolai. Nikolai hugged him back.

Bean remembered when he left Earth. Hugging Sister

Carlotta. Analyzing. This is what she needs. It costs me nothing. Therefore I'll give her the hug.

I'm not that kid anymore.

Maybe because I was able to come through for Poke after all. Too late to help her, but I still got her killer to admit it. I still got him to pay something, even if it can never be enough.

"Go meet your army, Nikolai," said Bean. "I've got a spaceship to catch."

He watched Nikolai go out the door and knew, with a sharp pang of regret, that he would never see his friend again.

—

Dimak stood in Major Anderson's quarters.

"Captain Dimak, I watched Colonel Graff indulge your constant complaints, your resistance to his orders, and I kept thinking, Dimak might be right, but I would never tolerate such lack of respect if *I* were in command. I'd throw him out on his ass and write 'insubordinate' in about forty places in his dossier. I thought I should tell you that before you make your complaint."

Dimak blinked.

"Go ahead, I'm waiting."

"It isn't so much a complaint as a question."

"Then ask your question."

"I thought you were supposed to choose a team that was equally compatible with Ender *and* with Bean."

"The word *equally* was never used, as far as I can recall. But even if it was, did it occur to you that it might be impossible? I could have chosen forty brilliant children who would all have been proud and eager to serve under Andrew Wiggin. How many would be *equally* proud and eager to serve under Bean?"

Dimak had no answer for that.

"The way I analyze it, the soldiers I chose to send on this destroyer are the students who are emotionally closest and most responsive to Ender Wiggin, while also being among the dozen or so best commanders in the school. These soldiers also have no particular animosity toward Bean. So if they find him placed over them, they'll probably do their best for him."

"They'll never forgive him for not being Ender."

"I guess that will be Bean's challenge. Who else should I have sent? Nikolai is Bean's friend, but he'd be out of his depth. Someday he'll be ready for Tactical School, and then Command, but not yet. And what other friends does Bean have?"

"He's won a lot of respect."

"And lost it again when he lost all five of his games."

"I've explained to you why he—"

"Humanity doesn't need explanations, Captain Dimak! It needs winners! Ender Wiggin had the fire to win. Bean is capable of losing five in a row as if they didn't even matter."

"They didn't matter. He learned what he needed to learn from them."

"Captain Dimak, I can see that I'm falling into the same trap that Colonel Graff fell into. You have crossed the line from teaching into advocacy. I would dismiss you as Bean's teacher, were it not for the fact that the question is already moot. I'm sending the soldiers I decided on already. If Bean is really so brilliant, he'll figure out a way to work with them."

"Yes sir," said Dimak.

"If it's any consolation, do remember that Crazy Tom was one of the ones Bean brought along to hear Achilles' confession. Crazy Tom *went*. That suggests that the better they know Bean, the more seriously they take him."

"Thank you, sir."

"Bean is no longer your responsibility, Captain Dimak. You did well with him. I salute you for it. Now . . . get back to work."

Dimak saluted.

Anderson saluted.

Dimak left.

—

On the destroyer *Condor,* the crew had no idea what to do with these children. They all knew about the Battle School, and both the captain and the pilot were Battle School graduates. But after perfunctory conversation—What army were you in? Oh, in my day Rat was the best, Dragon was a complete loser, how things change, how things stay the same—there was nothing more to say.

Without the shared concerns of being army commanders, the children drifted into their natural friendship groups. Dink and Petra had been friends almost from their first beginnings in Battle School, and they were so senior to the others that no one tried to penetrate that closed circle. Alai and Shen had been in Ender Wiggin's original launch group, and Vlad and Dumper, who had commanded B and E toons and were probably the most worshipful of Ender, hung around with them. Crazy Tom, Fly Molo, and Hot Soup had already been a trio back in Dragon Army. On a personal level, Bean did not expect to be included in any of these groups, and he wasn't particularly excluded, either; Crazy Tom, at least, showed real respect for Bean, and often included him in conversation. If Bean belonged to any of these groups, it was Crazy Tom's.

The only reason the division into cliques bothered him was that this group was clearly being assembled, not just randomly chosen. Trust needed to grow between them all, strongly if not equally. But they had been chosen for Ender—any idiot could see that—and it was not Bean's place to suggest that they play the onboard games together, learn together, do anything together. If Bean tried to assert any kind of leadership, it would only build more walls between him and the others than already existed.

There was only one of the group that Bean didn't think belonged there. And he couldn't do anything about that. Apparently the adults did not hold Petra responsible for her near-betrayal of Ender in the corridor the evening before Ender's life-or-death struggle with Bonzo. But Bean was not so sure. Petra was one of the best of the commanders, smart, able to see the big picture. How could she possibly have been fooled by Bonzo? Of course she couldn't have been hoping for Ender's destruction. But she had been careless, at best, and at worst might have been playing some kind of game that Bean did not yet understand. So he remained suspicious of her. Which wasn't good, to have such mistrust, but there it was.

Bean passed the four months of the voyage in the ship's library, mostly. Now that they were out of Battle School, he was reasonably sure that they weren't being spied on so intensely. The destroyer simply wasn't equipped for it. So he no longer had to choose his reading material with an eye to what the teachers would make of his selections.

He read no military history or theory whatsoever. He had already read all the major writers and many of the minor ones and knew the important campaigns backward and forward, from both sides. Those were in his memory to be called upon whenever he needed them. What was missing from his memory was the big picture. How the world worked. Political, social, economic history. What happened in nations when they weren't at war. How they got into and out of wars. How victory and defeat affected them. How alliances were formed and broken.

And, most important of all, but hardest to find: What was going on in the world today. The destroyer library had only the information that had been current when last it docked at Interstellar Launch—ISL—which is where the authorized list of documents was made available for download. Bean could make requests for more information, but that would require the library computer to make requisitions and use communications bandwidth that would have to be justified. It would be noticed, and then they'd wonder why this child was studying matters that could have no possible concern for him.

From what he could find on board, however, it was still possible to piece together the basic situation on Earth, and to reach some conclusions. During the years before the First Invasion, various power blocs had jockeyed for position, using some combination of terrorism, "surgical" strikes, limited military operations, and economic sanctions, boycotts, and embargos to gain the upper hand or give firm warnings or simply express national or ideological rage. When the Buggers showed up, China had just emerged as the dominant world power, economically and militarily, having finally reunited itself as a democracy. The North Americans and Europeans played at being China's "big brothers," but the economic balance had finally shifted.

What Bean saw as the driving force of history, however, was the resurgent Russian Empire. Where the Chinese simply took it for granted that they were and should be the center of the universe, the Russians, led by a series of ambitious demagogues and authoritarian generals, felt that history had cheated them out of their rightful place, century after century, and it was time for that to end. So it was Russia that forced the creation of the New Warsaw Pact, bringing its effective borders back to the peak of Soviet power—and beyond, for this time Greece was its ally, and an intimidated Turkey was neutralized. Europe was on the verge of being neutralized, the Russian dream of hegemony from the Pacific to the Atlantic at last within reach.

And then the Formics came and cut a swath of destruction through China that left a hundred million dead. Suddenly land-based armies seemed trivial, and questions of international competition were put on hold.

But that was only superficial. In fact, the Russians used their domination of the office of the Polemarch to build up a network of officers in key places throughout the fleet. Everything was in place for a vast power play the moment the Buggers were defeated—or before, if they thought it was to their advantage. Oddly, the Russians were rather open about their intentions—they always had been. They had no talent for subtlety, but they made up for it with amazing stubbornness. Negotiations for anything could take decades. And meanwhile, their penetration of the fleet was nearly total. Infantry forces loyal to the Strategos would be isolated, unable to get to the places where they were needed because there would be no ships to carry them.

When the war with the Buggers ended, the Russians clearly planned that within hours they would rule the fleet and therefore the world. It was their destiny. The North Americans were as complacent as ever, sure that destiny would work everything out in their favor. Only a few demagogues saw the danger. The Chinese and the Muslim world were alert to the danger, and even they were unable to make any kind of stand for fear of breaking up the alliance that made resistance to the Buggers possible.

The more he studied, the more Bean wished that he did not have to go to Tactical School. This war would belong to Ender and his friends. And while Bean loved Ender as much as any of them, and would gladly serve with them against the Buggers, the fact was that they didn't need him. It was the next war, the struggle for world domination, that fascinated him. The Russians *could* be stopped, if the right preparations were made.

But then he had to ask himself: *Should* they be stopped? A quick, bloody, but effective coup which would bring the world under a single government—it would mean the end of war among humans, wouldn't it? And in such a climate of peace, wouldn't all nations be better off?

So, even as Bean developed his plan for stopping the Russians, he tried to evaluate what a worldwide Russian Empire would be like.

And what he concluded was that it would not last. For along with their national vigor, the Russians had also nurtured their astonishing talent for misgovernment, that sense of personal entitlement that made corruption a way of life. The institutional tradition of competence that would be essential for a successful world government was nonexistent. It was in China that those institutions and values were most vigorous. But even China would be a poor substitute for a genuine world government that transcended any national interest. The wrong world government would eventually collapse under its own weight.

Bean longed to be able to talk these things over with someone—with Nikolai, or even with one of the teachers. It slowed him down to have his own thoughts move around in circles—without outside stimulation it was hard to break free of his own assumptions. One mind can think only of its own questions; it rarely surprises itself. But he made progress, slowly, during that voyage, and then during the months of Tactical School.

Tactical was a blur of short voyages and detailed tours of various ships. Bean was disgusted that they seemed to concentrate entirely on older designs, which seemed pointless to him—why train your commanders in ships they won't actually be using in battle? But the teachers treated his objection with contempt, pointing out that ships were ships, in the long run, and the newest vessels had to be put into service patrolling the perimeters of the solar system. There were none to spare for training children.

They were taught very little about the art of pilotry, for they were not being trained to fly the ships, only to command them in battle. They had to get a sense of how the weapons worked, how the ships moved, what could be expected of them, what their limitations were. Much of it was rote learning . . . but that was precisely the kind of learning Bean could do almost in his sleep, being able to recall anything that he had read or heard with any degree of attention.

So throughout Tactical School, while he performed as well as anyone, his real concentration was still on the problems of the current political situation on Earth. For Tactical School was at ISL, and so the library there was constantly being updated, and not just with the material authorized for inclusion in finite ships' libraries. For the first time, Bean began to read the writings of current political thinkers on Earth. He read what was coming out of Russia, and once again was astonished at how nakedly they pursued their ambitions. The Chinese writers saw the danger, but being Chinese, made no effort to rally support in other nations for any kind of resistance. To the Chinese, once something was known in China, it was known everywhere that mattered. And the Euro-American nations seemed dominated by a studied ignorance that to Bean appeared to be a death wish. Yet there were some who were awake, struggling to create coalitions.

Two popular commentators in particular came to Bean's attention. Demosthenes at first glance seemed to be a rabble-rouser, playing on prejudice and xenophobia. But he was also having considerable success in leading a popular movement. Bean didn't know if life under a government headed by Demosthenes would be any better than living under the Russians, but Demosthenes would at least make a contest out of it. The other commentator that Bean took note of was Locke, a lofty, high-minded fellow who nattered about world peace and forging alliances—yet amid his apparent complacency, Locke actually seemed to be working from the same set of facts as Demosthenes, taking it for granted that the Russians were vigorous enough to "lead" the world, but unprepared to do so in a "beneficial" way. In a way, it was as if Demosthenes and Locke were doing their research together, reading all the same sources, learning from all the same correspondents, but then appealing to completely different audiences.

For a while, Bean even toyed with the possibility that Locke and Demosthenes were the same person. But no, the writing styles were different, and more importantly, they thought and analyzed differently. Bean didn't think anyone was smart enough to fake that.

Whoever they were, these two commentators were the people who seemed to see the situation most accurately, and so Bean began to conceive of his essay on strategy in the post-Formic world as a letter to both Locke and Demosthenes. A private letter. An anonymous letter. Because his observations should be known, and these two seemed to be in the best position to bring Bean's ideas to fruition.

Resorting to old habits, Bean spent some time in the library watching several officers log on to the net, and soon had six log-ins that he could use. He then wrote his letter in six parts, using a different log-in for each part, and then sent the parts to Locke and Demosthenes within minutes of each other. He did it during an hour when the library was crowded, and made sure that he himself was logged on to the net on his own desk in his barracks, ostensibly playing a game. He doubted they'd be counting his keystrokes and realize that he wasn't actually doing anything with his desk during that time. And if they did trace the letter back to him, well, too bad. In all likelihood, Locke and Demosthenes would not try to trace him—in his letter he asked them not to. They would either believe him or not; they would agree with him or not; beyond that he could not go. He had spelled out for them exactly what the dangers were, what the Russian strategy obviously was, and what steps must be taken to ensure that the Russians did not succeed in their preemptive strike.

One of the most important points he made was that the children from Battle, Tactical, and Command School had to be brought back to Earth as quickly as possible, once the Buggers were defeated. If they remained in space, they would either be taken by the Russians or kept in ineffectual isolation by the I.F. But these children were the finest military minds that humanity had produced in this generation. If the power of one great nation was to be subdued, it would require brilliant commanders in opposition to them.

Within a day, Demosthenes had an essay on the nets calling for the Battle School to be dissolved at once and all those children brought home. "They have kidnapped our most promising children. Our Alexanders and Napoleons, our Rommels and Pattons, our Caesars and Fredericks and Washingtons and Saladins are being kept in a tower where we can't reach them, where they can't help their own people remain free from the threat of Russian domination. And who can doubt that the Russians intend to seize those children and use them? Or, if they can't, they will certainly try, with a single well-placed missile, to blast them all to bits, depriving us of our natural military leadership." Delicious demagoguery, designed to spark fear and outrage. Bean could imagine the consternation in the military as their precious school became a political issue. It was an emotional issue that Demosthenes would not let go of and other nationalists all over the world would fervently echo. And because it was about children, no politician could dare oppose the principle that all the children in Battle School would come home the *moment* the war ended. Not only that, but on this issue, Locke lent his prestigious, moderate voice to the cause, openly supporting the principle of the return of the children. "By all means, pay the piper, rid us of the invading rats—and then bring our children home."

I saw, I wrote, and the world changed a little. It was a heady feeling. It made all the work at Tactical School seem almost meaningless by comparison. He wanted to bound into the classroom and tell the others about his triumph. But they would look at him like he was crazy. They knew nothing about the world at large, and took no responsibility for it. They were closed into the military world.

Three days after Bean sent his letters to Locke and Demosthenes, the children came to class and found that they were to depart immediately for Command School, this time joined by Carn Carby, who had been a class ahead of them in Tactical School. They had spent only three months at ISL, and Bean couldn't help wondering if his letters had not had some influence over the timing. If there was some danger that the children might be sent home prematurely, the I.F. had to make sure their prize specimens were out of reach.

22

Reunion

"I suppose I should congratulate you for undoing the damage you did to Ender Wiggin."

"Sir, I respectfully disagree that I did any damage."

"Ah, good then, I *don't* have to congratulate you. You do realize that your status here will be as observer."

"I hope that I will also have opportunities to offer advice based on my years of experience with these children."

"Command School has worked with children for years."

"Respectfully, sir, Command School has worked with adolescents. Ambitious, testosterone-charged, competitive teenagers. And quite aside from that, we have a lot riding on these particular children, and I know things about them that must be taken into account."

"All those things should be in your reports."

"They are. But with all respect, is there anyone there who has memorized my reports so thoroughly that the appropriate details will come to mind the instant they're needed?"

"I'll listen to you, Colonel Graff. And please stop assuring me of how respectful you are whenever you're about to tell me I'm an idiot."

"I thought that my leave of absence was designed to chasten me. I'm trying to show that I've been chastened."

"Are there any of these details about the children that come to mind right now?"

"An important one, sir. Because so much depends on what Ender does or does not know, it is vital that you isolate him from the other children. During actual practices he can be there, but under no circumstances can you allow free conversation or sharing of information."

"And why is that?"

"Because if Bean ever comes to know about the ansible, he'll leap straight to the core situation. He may figure it out on his own as it is—you have no idea how difficult it is to conceal information from him. Ender is more trusting—but Ender can't do his job *unless* he knows about the ansible. You see? He and Bean cannot be allowed to have any free time together. Any conversation that is not on point."

"But if this is so, then Bean is not capable of being Ender's backup, because then he would *have* to be told about the ansible."

"It won't matter then."

"But you yourself were the author of the proposition that only a child—"

"Sir, none of that applies to Bean."

"Because?"

"Because he's not human."

"Colonel Graff, you make me tired."

The voyage to Command School was four long months, and this time they were being trained continuously, as thorough an education in the mathematics of targeting, explosives, and other weapons-related subjects as could be managed on board a fast-moving cruiser. Finally, too, they were being forged again into a team, and it quickly became clear to everyone that the leading student was

Bean. He mastered everything immediately, and was soon the one whom the others turned to for explanations of concepts they didn't grasp at once. From being the lowest in status on the first voyage, a complete outsider, Bean now became an outcast for the opposite reason—he was alone in the position of highest status.

He struggled with the situation, because he knew that he needed to be able to function as part of the team, not just as a mentor or expert. Now it became vital that he take part in their downtime, relaxing with them, joking, joining in with reminiscences about Battle School. And about even earlier times.

For now, at last, the Battle School tabu against talking about home was gone. They all spoke freely of mothers and fathers who by now were distant memories, but who still played a vital role in their lives.

The fact that Bean had no parents at first made the others a little shy with him, but he seized the opportunity and began to speak openly about his entire experience. Hiding in the toilet tank in the clean room. Going home with the Spanish custodian. Starving on the streets as he scouted for his opportunity. Telling Poke how to beat the bullies at their own game. Watching Achilles, admiring him, fearing him as he created their little street family, marginalized Poke, and finally killed her. When he told them of finding Poke's body, several of them wept. Petra in particular broke down and sobbed.

It was an opportunity, and Bean seized it. Naturally, she soon fled the company of others, taking her emotions into the privacy of her quarters. As soon afterward as he could, Bean followed her.

"Bean, I don't want to talk."

"I do," said Bean. "It's something we have to talk about. For the good of the team."

"Is that what we are?" she asked.

"Petra, you know the worst thing I've ever done. Achilles was dangerous, I knew it, and I still went away and left Poke alone with him. She died for it. That burns in me every day of my life. Every time I start to feel happy, I remember Poke, how I owe my life to her, how I could have saved her. Every time I love somebody, I have that fear that I'll betray them the same way I did her."

"Why are you telling me this, Bean?"

"Because you betrayed Ender and I think it's eating at you."

Her eyes flashed with rage. "I did not! And it's eating at *you,* not me!"

"Petra, whether you admit it to yourself or not, when you tried to slow Ender down in the corridor that day, there's no way you didn't know what you were doing. I've seen you in action, you're sharp, you see everything. In some ways you're the best tactical commander in the whole group. It's absolutely impossible that you didn't see how Bonzo's thugs were all there in the corridor, waiting to beat the crap out of Ender, and what did you do? You tried to slow him down, peel him off from the group."

"And you stopped me," said Petra. "So it's moot, isn't it?"

"I have to know why."

"You don't have to know squat."

"Petra, we have to fight shoulder to shoulder someday. We have to be able to trust each other. I don't trust you because I don't know why you did that. And now you won't trust me because you know I don't trust *you.*"

"Oh what a tangled web we weave."

"What the hell does that mean?"

"My father said it. Oh what a tangled web we weave when first we practice to deceive."

"Exactly. Untangle this for me."

"You're the one who's weaving a web for me, Bean. You know things you don't tell the rest of us. You think I don't see that? So you want me to restore your trust in me, but you don't tell me anything useful."

"I opened my soul to you," said Bean.

"You told me about your *feelings.*" She said it with utter contempt. "So good, it's a relief to know you have them, or at least to know that you think it's worth pretending to have them, nobody's quite sure about that. But what you don't ever tell us is what the hell is actually going on here. We think you know."

"All I have are guesses."

"The teachers told you things back in Battle School that none of the rest of us knew. You knew the name of every kid in the school, you knew things about us, all of us. You knew things you had no business knowing."

Bean was stunned to realize that his special access had been so noticeable to her. Had he been careless? Or was she even more observant than he had thought? "I broke into the student data," said Bean.

"And they didn't catch you?"

"I think they did. Right from the start. Certainly they knew about it later." And he told her about choosing the roster for Dragon Army.

She flopped down on her bunk and addressed the ceiling. "You chose them! All those rejects and those little launchy bastards, *you* chose them!"

"Somebody had to. The teachers weren't competent to do it."

"So Ender had the best. He didn't *make* them the best, they already *were* the best."

"The best that weren't already in armies. I'm the only one who was a launchy when Dragon was formed who's with this team now. You and Shen and Alai and Dink and Carn, you weren't in Dragon, and you're obviously among the best. Dragon won because they were good, yes, but also because Ender knew what to do with them."

"It still turns one little corner of my universe upside down."

"Petra, this was a trade."

"Was it?"

"Explain why you weren't a Judas back in Battle School."

"I was a Judas," said Petra. "How's that for an explanation?"

Bean was sickened. "You can say it like that? Without shame?"

"Are you stupid?" asked Petra. "I was doing the same thing you were doing, trying to save Ender's life. I knew Ender had trained for combat, and those thugs hadn't. I was also trained. Bonzo had been working these guys up into a frenzy, but the fact is, they didn't like Bonzo very much, he had just pissed them off at Ender. So if they got in a few licks against Ender, right there in the corridor where Dragon Army and other soldiers would get into it right away, where Ender would have me beside him in a limited space so only a few of them could come at us at once—I figured that Ender would get bruised, get a bloody nose, but he'd come out of it OK. And all those walking scabies would be satisfied. Bonzo's ranting would be old news. Bonzo would be alone again. Ender would be safe from anything worse."

"You were gambling a lot on your fighting ability."

"And Ender's. We were both damn good then, and in excellent shape. And you know what? I think Ender understood what I was doing, and the only reason he didn't go along with it was you."

"Me?"

"He saw you plunging right into the middle of everything. You'd get your head beaten in, that was obvious. So he had to avoid the violence then. Which means that because of you, he got set up the next day when it really *was* dangerous, when Ender was completely alone with no one for backup."

"So why didn't you explain this before?"

"Because you were the only one besides Ender who knew I was setting him up, and I didn't really care what you thought then, and I'm not that concerned about it now."

"It was a stupid plan," said Bean.

"It was better than yours," said Petra.

"Well, I guess when you look at how it all turned out,

we'll never know how stupid your plan was. But we sure know that mine was shot to hell."

Petra flashed him a brief, insincere grin. "Now, do you trust me again? Can we go back to the intimate friendship we've shared for so long?"

"You know something, Petra? All that hostility is wasted on me. In fact, it's bad aim on your part to even try it. Because I'm the best friend you've got here."

"Oh really?"

"Yes, really. Because I'm the only one of these boys who ever chose to have a girl as his commander."

She paused a moment, staring at him blankly before saying, "I got over the fact that I'm a girl a long time ago."

"But they didn't. And you know they didn't. You know that it bothers them all the time, that you're not really one of the guys. They're your friends, sure, at least Dink is, but they all like you. At the same time, there were what, a dozen girls in the whole school? And except for you, none of them were really topflight soldiers. They didn't take you seriously."

"Ender did," said Petra.

"And I do," said Bean. "The others all know what happened in the corridor, you know. It's not like it was a secret. But you know why they haven't had this conversation with you?"

"Why?"

"Because *they* all figured you were an idiot and didn't realize how close you came to getting Ender pounded into the deck. I'm the only one who had enough respect for you to realize that you would never make such a stupid mistake by accident."

"I'm supposed to be flattered?"

"You're supposed to stop treating me like the enemy. You're almost as much of an outsider in this group as I am. And when it comes down to actual combat, you need someone who'll take you as seriously as you take yourself."

"Do me no favors."

"I'm leaving now."

"About time."

"And when you think about this more and you realize I'm right, you don't have to apologize. You cried for Poke, and that makes us friends. You can trust me, and I can trust you, and that's all."

She was starting some retort as he left, but he didn't stick around long enough to hear what it was. Petra was just that way—she had to act tough. Bean didn't mind. He knew they'd said the things they needed to say.

—

Command School was at FleetCom, and the location of FleetCom was a closely guarded secret. The only way you ever found out where it was was to be assigned there, and very few people who had been there ever came back to Earth.

Just before arrival, the kids were briefed. FleetCom was in the wandering asteroid Eros. And as they approached, they realized that it really was *in* the asteroid. Almost nothing showed on the surface except the docking station. They boarded the shuttlebug, which reminded them of schoolbuses, and took the five-minute ride down to the surface. There the shuttlebug slid inside what looked like a cave. A snakelike tube reached out to the bug and enclosed it completely. They got out of the shuttlebug into near-zero gravity, and a strong air current sucked them like a vacuum cleaner up into the bowels of Eros.

Bean knew at once that this place was not shaped by human hands. The tunnels were all too low—and even then, the ceilings had obviously been raised after the initial construction, since the lower walls were smooth and only the top half-meter showed tool marks. The Buggers made this, probably when they were mounting the Second Invasion. What was once their forward base was now the center of the International Fleet. Bean tried to imagine the battle required to take this place. The Buggers scuttering along the tunnels, the infantry coming in with low-power explosives to burn them out. Flashes of light. And then cleanup, dragging the Formic bodies out of the tunnels and bit by bit converting it into a human space.

This is how we got our secret technologies, thought Bean. The Buggers had gravity-generating machines. We learned how they worked and built our own, installing them in the Battle School and wherever else they were needed. But the I.F. never announced the fact, because it would have frightened people to realize how advanced their technology was.

What else did we learn from them?

Bean noticed how even the children hunched a little to walk through the tunnels. The headroom was at least two meters, and not one of the kids was nearly that tall, but the proportions were all wrong for human comfort, so the roof of the tunnels seemed oppressively low, ready to collapse. It must have been even worse when we first arrived, before the roofs were raised.

Ender would thrive here. He'd hate it, of course, because he was human. But he'd also use the place to help him get inside the minds of the Buggers who built it. Not that you could ever really understand an alien mind. But this place gave you a decent chance to try.

The boys were bunked up in two rooms; Petra had a smaller room to herself. It was even more bare here than Battle School, and they could never escape the coldness of the stone around them. On Earth, stone had always seemed solid. But in space, it seemed downright porous. There were bubble holes all through the stone, and Bean couldn't help feeling that air was leaking out all the time. Air leaking out, and cold leaking in, and perhaps something else, the larvae of the Buggers chewing like earthworms through the solid stone, crawling out of the bubble holes at night when the room was dark, crawling over their foreheads and reading their minds and . . .

He woke up, breathing heavily, his hand clutching his

forehead. He hardly dared to move his hand. Had something been crawling on him?

His hand was empty.

He wanted to go back to sleep, but it was too close to reveille for him to hope for that. He lay there thinking. The nightmare was absurd—there could not possibly be any Buggers alive here. But something made him afraid. Something was bothering him, and he wasn't sure what.

He thought back to a conversation with one of the technicians who serviced the simulators. Bean's had malfunctioned during practice, so that suddenly the little points of light that represented his ships moving through three-dimensional space were no longer under his control. To his surprise, they didn't just drift on in the direction of the last orders he gave. Instead, they began to swarm, to gather, and then changed color as they shifted to be under someone else's control.

When the technician arrived to replace the chip that had blown, Bean asked him why the ships didn't just stop or keep drifting. "It's part of the simulation," the technician said. "What's being simulated here is not that you're the pilot or even the captain of these ships. You're the admiral, and so inside each ship there's a simulated captain and a simulated pilot, and so when your contact got cut off, they acted the way the real guys would act if they lost contact. See?"

"That seems like a lot of trouble to go to."

"Look, we've had a lot of time to work on these simulators," said the technician. "They're *exactly* like combat."

"Except," said Bean, "the time-lag."

The technician looked blank for a moment. "Oh, right. The time-lag. Well, that just wasn't worth programming in." And then he was gone.

It was that moment of blankness that was bothering Bean. These simulators were as perfect as they could make them, *exactly* like combat, and yet they didn't include the time-lag that came from lightspeed communications. The distances being simulated were large enough that most of the time there should be at least a slight delay between a command and its execution, and sometimes it should be several seconds. But no such delay was programmed in. All communications were being treated as instantaneous. And when Bean asked about it, his question was blown off by the teacher who first trained them on the simulators. "It's a simulation. Plenty of time to get used to the lightspeed delay when you train with the real thing."

That sounded like typically stupid military thinking even at the time, but now Bean realized it was simply a lie. If they programmed in the behavior of pilots and captains when communications were cut off, they could very easily have included the time-lag. The reason these ships were simulated with instantaneous response was because that *was* an accurate simulation of conditions they would meet in combat.

Lying awake in the darkness, Bean finally made the connection. It was so obvious, once he thought of it. It wasn't just gravity control they got from the Buggers. It was faster-than-light communication. It's a big secret from people on Earth, but our ships can talk to each other instantaneously.

And if the ships can, why not FleetCom here on Eros? What was the range of communication? Was it truly instantaneous regardless of distance, or was it merely faster than light, so that at truly great distances it began to have its own time-lag?

His mind raced through the possibilities, and the implications of those possibilities. Our patrol ships will be able to warn us of the approaching enemy fleet long before it reaches us. They've probably known for years that it was coming, and how fast. That's why we've been rushed through our training like this—they've known for years when the Third Invasion would begin.

And then another thought. If this instantaneous communication works regardless of distance, then we could even be talking to the invasion fleet we sent against the Formic home planet right after the Second Invasion. If our starships were going near lightspeed, the relative time differential would complicate communication, but as long as we're imagining miracles, that would be easy enough to solve. We'll know whether our invasion of their world succeeded or not, moments afterward. Why, if the communication is really powerful, with plenty of bandwidth, FleetCom could even watch the battle unfold, or at least watch a simulation of the battle, and . . .

A simulation of the battle. Each ship in the expeditionary force sending back its position at all times. The communications device receives that data and feeds it into a computer and what comes out is . . . the simulation we've been practicing with.

We are training to command ships in combat, not here in the solar system, but lightyears away. They sent the pilots and the captains, but the admirals who will command them are still back here. At FleetCom. They had generations to find the right commanders, and we're the ones.

It left him gasping, this realization. He hardly dared to believe it, and yet it made far better sense than any of the other more plausible scenarios. For one thing, it explained perfectly why the kids had been trained on older ships. The fleet they would be commanding had launched decades ago, when those older designs were the newest and the best.

They didn't rip us through Battle School and Tactical School because the Bugger fleet is about to reach our solar system. They're in a hurry because *our* fleet is about to reach the Buggers' world.

It was like Nikolai said. You can't rule out the impossible, because you never know which of your assumptions about what was possible might turn out, in the real universe, to be false. Bean hadn't been able to think of this simple, rational explanation because he had been locked in the box of thinking that lightspeed limited both travel *and* communication. But the technician let down just the tiniest part of the veil they had covering the truth, and because Bean finally found a way to open his mind to the possibility, he now knew the secret.

Sometime during their training, anytime at all, without the slightest warning, without ever even telling us they're doing it, they can switch over and we'll be commanding real ships in a real battle. We'll think it's a game, but we'll be fighting a war.

And they don't tell us because we're children. They think we can't handle it. Knowing that our decisions will cause death and destruction. That when we lose a ship, real men die. They're keeping it a secret to protect us from our own compassion.

Except me. Because now I know.

The weight of it suddenly came upon him and he could hardly breathe, except shallowly. Now I know. How will it change the way I play? I can't let it, that's all. I was already doing my best—knowing this won't make me work harder or play better. It might make me do worse. Might make me hesitate, might make me lose concentration. Through their training, they had all learned that winning depended on being able to forget everything but what you were doing at that moment. You could hold all your ships in your mind at once—but only if any ship that no longer matters could be blocked out completely. Thinking about dead men, about torn bodies having the air sucked out of their lungs by the cold vacuum of space, who could still play the game knowing that this was what it really meant?

The teachers were right to keep this secret from us. That technician should be court-martialed for letting me see behind the curtain.

I can't tell anyone. The other kids shouldn't know this. And if the teachers know that I know it, they'll take me out of the game.

So I have to fake it.

No. I have to disbelieve it. I have to forget that it's

true. It *isn't* true. The truth is what they've been telling us. The simulation is simply ignoring lightspeed. They trained us on old ships because the new ones are all deployed and can't be wasted. The fight we're preparing for is to repel invading Formics, not to invade their solar system. This was just a crazy dream, pure self-delusion. Nothing goes faster than light, and therefore information can't be transmitted faster than light.

Besides, if we really did send an invasion fleet that long ago, they don't need little kids to command them. Mazer Rackham must be with that fleet, no way would it have launched without him. Mazer Rackham is still alive, preserved by the relativistic changes of near-lightspeed travel. Maybe it's only been a few years to him. And he's ready. We aren't needed.

Bean calmed his breathing. His heartrate slowed. I can't let myself get carried away with fantasies like that. I would be so embarrassed if anyone knew the stupid theory I came up with in my sleep. I can't even tell this as a dream. The game is as it always was.

Reveille sounded over the intercom. Bean got out of bed—a bottom bunk, this time—and joined in as normally as possible with the banter of Crazy Tom and Hot Soup, while Fly Molo kept his morning surliness to himself and Alai did his prayers. Bean went to mess and ate as he normally ate. Everything was normal. It didn't mean a thing that he couldn't get his bowels to unclench at the normal time. That his belly gnawed at him all day, and at mealtime he was faintly nauseated. That was just lack of sleep.

Near the end of three months on Eros, their work on the simulators changed. There would be ships directly under their control, but they also had others under them to whom they had to give commands out loud, besides using the controls to enter them manually. "Like combat," said their supervisor.

"In combat," said Alai, "we'd know who the officers serving under us were."

"That would matter if you depended on them to give you information. But you do not. All the information you need is conveyed to your simulator and appears in the display. So you give your orders orally as well as manually. Just assume that you will be obeyed. Your teachers will be monitoring the orders you give to help you learn to be explicit and immediate. You will also have to master the technique of switching back and forth between cross-talk among yourselves and giving orders to individual ships. It's quite simple, you see. Turn your heads to the left or right to speak to each other, whichever is more comfortable for you. But when your face is pointing straight at the display, your voice will be carried to whatever ship or squadron you have selected with your controls. And to address all the ships under your control at once, head straight forward and duck your chin, like this."

"What happens if we raise our heads?" asked Shen.

Alai answered before the teacher could. "Then you're talking to God."

After the laughter died down, the teacher said, "Almost right, Alai. When you raise your chin to speak, you'll be talking to *your* commander."

Several spoke at once. "*Our* commander?"

"You did not think we were training all of you to be supreme commander at once, did you? No no. For the moment, we will assign one of you at random to be that commander, just for practice. Let's say . . . the little one. You. Bean."

"I'm supposed to be commander?"

"Just for the practices. Or is he not competent? You others will not obey him in battle?"

The others answered the teacher with scorn. Of course Bean was competent. Of course they'd follow him.

"But then, he never did win a battle when he commanded Rabbit Army," said Fly Molo.

"Excellent. That means that you will all have the challenge of making this little one a winner in spite of himself. If you do not think *that* is a realistic military situation, you have not been reading history carefully enough."

So it was that Bean found himself in command of the ten other kids from Battle School. It was exhilarating, of course, for neither he nor the others believed for one moment that the teacher's choice had been random. They knew that Bean was better at the simulator than anybody. Petra was the one who said it after practice one day. "Hell, Bean, I think you have this all in your head so clear you could close your eyes and still play." It was almost true. He did not have to keep checking to see where everyone was. It was all in his head at once.

It took a couple of days for them to handle it smoothly, taking orders from Bean and giving their own orders orally along with the physical controls. There were constant mistakes at first, heads in the wrong position so that comments and questions and orders went to the wrong destination. But soon enough it became instinctive.

Bean then insisted that others take turns being in the command position. "I need practice taking orders just like they do," he said. "And learning how to change my head position to speak up and sideways." The teacher agreed, and after another day, Bean had mastered the technique as well as any of the others.

Having other kids in the master seat had another good effect as well. Even though no one did so badly as to embarrass himself, it was clear that Bean was sharper and faster than anyone else, with a keener grasp of developing situations and a better ability to sort out what he was hearing and remember what everybody had said.

"You're not *human,*" said Petra. "*Nobody* can do what you do!"

"Am so human," said Bean mildly. "And I know somebody who can do it better than me."

"Who's that?" she demanded.

"Ender."

They all fell silent for a moment.

"Yeah, well, he ain't here," said Vlad.

"How do *you* know?" said Bean. "For all we know, he's been here all along."

"That's stupid," said Dink. "Why wouldn't they have him practice with us? Why would they keep it a secret?"

"Because they like secrets," said Bean. "And maybe because they're giving him different training. And maybe because it's like Sinterklaas. They're going to bring him to us as a present."

"And maybe you're full of merda," said Dumper.

Bean just laughed. Of course it would be Ender. This group was assembled for Ender. Ender was the one all their hopes were resting on. The reason they put Bean in that master position was because Bean was the substitute. If Ender got appendicitis in the middle of the war, it was Bean they'd switch the controls to. Bean who'd start giving commands, deciding which ships would be sacrificed, which men would die. But until then, it would be Ender's choice, and for Ender, it would only be a game. No deaths, no suffering, no fear, no guilt. Just . . . a game.

Definitely it's Ender. And the sooner the better.

The next day, their supervisor told them that Ender Wiggin was going to be their commander starting that afternoon. When they didn't act surprised, he asked why. "Because Bean already told us."

—

"They want me to find out how you've been getting your inside information, Bean." Graff looked across the table at the painfully small child who sat there looking at him without expression.

"I don't have any inside information," said Bean.

"You knew that Ender was going to be the commander."

"I *guessed,*" said Bean. "Not that it was hard. Look at who we are. Ender's closest friends. Ender's toon leaders. He's the common thread. There were plenty of other kids you could have brought here, probably about as good as us. But these are the ones who'd follow Ender straight into space without a suit, if he told us he needed us to do it."

"Nice speech, but you have a history of sneaking."

"Right. *When* would I be doing this sneaking? When are any of us alone? Our desks are just dumb terminals and we never get to see anybody else log on so it's not like I can capture another identity. I just do what I'm told all day every day. You guys keep assuming that we kids are stupid, even though you chose us because we're really, really smart. And now you sit there and accuse me of having to *steal* information that any idiot could guess."

"Not *any* idiot."

"That was just an expression."

"Bean," said Graff, "I think you're feeding me a line of complete bullshit."

"Colonel Graff, even if that were true, which it isn't, so what? So I found out Ender was coming. I'm secretly monitoring your dreams. So *what?* He'll still come, he'll be in command, he'll be brilliant, and then we'll all graduate and I'll sit in a booster seat in a ship somewhere and give commands to grownups in my little-boy voice until they get sick of hearing me and throw me out into space."

"I don't care about the fact that you knew about Ender. I don't care that it was a guess."

"I know you don't care about those things."

"I need to know what else you've figured out."

"Colonel," said Bean, sounding very tired, "doesn't it occur to you that the very fact that you're asking me this question *tells* me there's something else for me to figure out, and therefore greatly increases the chance that I *will* figure it out?"

Graff's smile grew even broader. "That's just what I told the . . . officer who assigned me to talk to you and ask these questions. I told him that we would end up telling you more, just by having the interview, than you would ever tell us, but he said, 'The kid is *six,* Colonel Graff.' "

"I think I'm seven."

"He was working from an old report and hadn't done the math."

"Just tell me what secret you want to make sure I don't know, and I'll tell you if I already knew it."

"Very helpful."

"Colonel Graff, am I doing a good job?"

"Absurd question. Of course you are."

"If I do know anything that you don't want us kids to know, have I talked about it? Have I told any of the other kids? Has it affected my performance in any way?"

"No."

"To me that sounds like a tree falling in the forest where no one can hear. If I *do* know something, because I figured it out, but I'm not telling anybody else, and it's not affecting my work, then why would you waste time finding out whether I know it? Because after this conversation, you may be sure that I'll be looking very hard for any secret that might be lying around where a seven-year-old might find it. Even if I do find such a secret, though, I *still* won't tell the other kids, so it *still* won't make a difference. So why don't we just drop it?"

Graff reached under the table and pressed something.

"All right," said Graff. "They've got the recording of our conversation and if that doesn't reassure them, nothing will."

"Reassure them of what? And who is 'them'?"

"Bean, this part is not being recorded."

"Yes it is," said Bean.

"I turned it off."

"Puh-leeze."

In fact, Graff was not altogether sure that the recording *was* off. Even if the machine he controlled was off, that didn't mean there wasn't another.

"Let's walk," said Graff.

"I hope not outside."

Graff got up from the table—laboriously, because he'd put on a lot of weight and they kept Eros at full gravity—and led the way out into the tunnels.

As they walked, Graff talked softly. "Let's at least make them work for it," he said.

"Fine," said Bean.

"I thought you'd want to know that the I.F. is going crazy because of an apparent security leak. It seems that someone with access to the most secret archives wrote letters to a couple of net pundits who then started agitating for the children of Battle School to be sent home to their native countries."

"What's a pundit?" asked Bean.

"My turn to say puh-leeze, I think. Look, I'm not accusing you. I just happen to have seen a text of the letters sent to Locke and Demosthenes—they're both being closely watched, as I'm sure you would expect—and when I read those letters—interesting the differences between them, by the way, very cleverly done—I realized that there was not really any top secret information in there, beyond what any child in Battle School knows. No, the thing that's really making them crazy is that the political analysis is dead on, even though it's based on insufficient information. From what is publicly known, in other words, the writer of those letters couldn't have figured out what he figured out. The Russians are claiming that somebody's been spying on them—and lying about what they found, of course. But I accessed the library on the destroyer *Condor* and found out what you were reading. And then I checked your library use on the ISL while you were in Tactical School. You've been a busy boy."

"I try to keep my mind occupied."

"You'll be happy to know that the first group of children has already been sent home."

"But the war's not over."

"You think that when you start a political snowball rolling, it will always go where you wanted it to go? You're smart but you're naive, Bean. Give the universe a push, and you don't know which dominoes will fall. There are always a few you never thought were connected. Someone will always push back a little harder than you expected.

But still, I'm happy that you remembered the other children and set the wheels in motion to free them."

"But not us."

"The I.F. has no obligation to remind the agitators on Earth that Tactical School and Command School are still full of children."

"I'm not going to remind them."

"I know you won't. No, Bean, I got a chance to talk to you because you panicked some of the higher-ups with your educated guess about who would command your team. But I was hoping for a chance to talk to you because there are a couple of things I wanted to tell you. Besides the fact that your letter had pretty much the desired effect."

"I'm listening, though I admit to no letter."

"First, you'll be fascinated to know the identity of Locke and Demosthenes."

"Identity? Just one?"

"One mind, two voices. You see, Bean, Ender Wiggin was born third in his family. A special waiver, not an illegal birth. His older brother and sister are just as gifted as he is, but for various reasons were deemed inappropriate for Battle School. But the brother, Peter Wiggin, is a very ambitious young man. With the military closed off to him, he's gone into politics. Twice."

"He's Locke *and* Demosthenes," said Bean.

"He plans the strategy for both of them, but he only writes Locke. His sister Valentine writes Demosthenes."

Bean laughed. "Now it makes sense."

"So both your letters went to the same people."

"If I wrote them."

"And it's driving poor Peter Wiggin crazy. He's really tapping into all his sources inside the fleet to find out who sent those letters. But nobody in the Fleet knows, either. The six officers whose log-ins you used have been ruled out. And as you can guess, *nobody* is checking to see if the only seven-year-old ever to go to Tactical School might have dabbled in political epistolary in his spare time."

"Except you."

"Because, by God, I'm the only person who understands exactly how brilliant you children actually are."

"How brilliant are we?" Bean grinned.

"Our walk won't last forever, and I won't waste time on flattery. The other thing I wanted to tell you is that Sister Carlotta, being unemployed after you left, devoted a lot of effort to tracking down your parentage. I can see two officers approaching us right now who will put an end to this unrecorded conversation, and so I'll be brief. You have a name, Bean. You are Julian Delphiki."

"That's Nikolai's last name."

"Julian is the name of Nikolai's father. And of your father. Your mother's name is Elena. You are identical twins. Your fertilized eggs were implanted at different times, and your genes were altered in one very small but significant way. So when you look at Nikolai, you see yourself as you would have been, had you not been genetically altered, and had you grown up with parents who loved you and cared for you."

"Julian Delphiki," said Bean.

"Nikolai is among those already heading for Earth. Sister Carlotta will see to it that, when he is repatriated to Greece, he is informed that you are indeed his brother. His parents already know that you exist—Sister Carlotta told them. Your home is a lovely place, a house on the hills of Crete overlooking the Aegean. Sister Carlotta tells me that they are good people, your parents. They wept with joy when they learned that you exist. And now our interview is coming to an end. We were discussing your low opinion of the quality of teaching here at Command School."

"How did you guess."

"You're not the only one who can do that."

The two officers—an admiral and a general, both wearing big false smiles—greeted them and asked how the interview had gone.

"You have the recording," said Graff. "Including the part where Bean insisted that it was still being recorded."

"And yet the interview continued."

"I was telling him," said Bean, "about the incompetence of the teachers here at Command School."

"Incompetence?"

"Our battles are always against exceptionally stupid computer opponents. And then the teachers insist on going through long, tedious analyses of these mock combats, even though no enemy could possibly behave as stupidly and predictably as these simulations do. I was suggesting that the only way for us to get decent competition here is if you divide us into two groups and have us fight each other."

The two officers looked at each other. "Interesting point," said the general.

"Moot," said the admiral. "Ender Wiggin is about to be introduced into your game. We thought you'd want to be there to greet him."

"Yes," said Bean. "I do."

"I'll take you," said the admiral.

"Let's talk," the general said to Graff.

On the way, the admiral said little, and Bean could answer his chat without thought. It was a good thing. For he was in turmoil over the things that Graff had told him. It was almost not a surprise that Locke and Demosthenes were Ender's siblings. If they were as intelligent as Ender, it was inevitable that they would rise into prominence, and the nets allowed them to conceal their identity enough to accomplish it while they were still young. But part of the reason Bean was drawn to them had to be the sheer familiarity of their voices. They must have sounded like Ender, in that subtle way in which people who have lived long together pick up nuances of speech from each other. Bean didn't realize it consciously, but unconsciously it would have made him more alert to those essays. He should have known, and at some level he did know.

But the other, that Nikolai was really his brother—how could he believe that? It was as if Graff had read his heart and found the lie that would penetrate most deeply into his soul and told it to him. I'm Greek? My brother happened to be in my launch group, the boy who became my dearest friend? Twins? Parents who love me?

Julian Delphiki?

No, I can't believe this. Graff has never dealt honestly with us. Graff was the one who did not lift a finger to protect Ender from Bonzo. Graff does nothing except to accomplish some manipulative purpose.

My name is Bean. Poke gave me that name, and I won't give it up in exchange for a lie.

—

They heard his voice, first, talking to a technician in another room. "How can I work with squadron leaders I never see?"

"And why would you need to see them?" asked the technician.

"To know who they are, how they think—"

"You'll learn who they are and how they think from the way they work with the simulator. But even so, I think you won't be concerned. They're listening to you right now. Put on the headset so you can hear them."

They all trembled with excitement, knowing that he would soon hear their voices as they now heard his.

"Somebody say something," said Petra.

"Wait till he gets the headset on," said Dink.

"How will we know?" asked Vlad.

"Me first," said Alai.

A pause. A new faint hiss in their earphones.

"Salaam," Alai whispered.

"Alai," said Ender.

"And me," said Bean. "The dwarf."

"Bean," said Ender.

Yes, thought Bean, as the others talked to him. That's who I am. That's the name that is spoken by the people who know me.

23

Ender's Game

"General, you are the Strategos. You have the authority to do this, and you have the obligation."

"I don't need disgraced former Battle School commandants to tell me my obligations."

"If you do not arrest the Polemarch and his conspirators—"

"Colonel Graff, if I *do* strike first, then I will bear the blame for the war that ensues."

"Yes, you would, sir. Now tell me, which would be the better outcome—everybody blames you, but we win the war, or nobody blames you, because you've been stood up against a wall and shot after the Polemarch's coup results in worldwide Russian hegemony?"

"I will not fire the first shot."

"A military commander not willing to strike preemptively when he has firm intelligence—"

"The politics of the thing—"

"If you let them win it's the end of politics!"

"The Russians stopped being the bad guys back in the twentieth century!"

"Whoever is doing the bad things, that's the bad guy. You're the sheriff, sir, whether people approve of you or not. Do your job."

With Ender there, Bean immediately stepped back into his place among the toon leaders. No one mentioned it to him. He had been the leading commander, he had trained them well, but Ender had always been the natural commander of this group, and now that he was here, Bean was small again.

And rightly so, Bean knew. He had led them well, but Ender made him look like a novice. It wasn't that Ender's strategies were better than Bean's—they weren't, really. Different sometimes, but more often Bean watched Ender do exactly what he would have done.

The important difference was in the way he led the others. He had their fierce devotion instead of the ever-so-slightly-resentful obedience Bean got from them, which helped from the start. But he also earned that devotion by noticing, not just what was going on in the battle, but what was going on in his commanders' minds. He was stern, sometimes even snappish, making it clear that he expected better than their best. And yet he had a way of giving an intonation to innocuous words, showing appreciation, admiration, closeness. They felt known by the one whose honor they needed. Bean simply did not know how to do that. His encouragement was always more obvious, a bit heavy-handed. It meant less to them because it felt more calculated. It *was* more calculated. Ender was just . . . himself. Authority came from him like breath.

They flipped a genetic switch in me and made me an intellectual athlete. I can get the ball into the goal from anywhere on the field. But knowing *when* to kick. Knowing how to forge a team out of a bunch of players. What switch was it that was flipped in Ender Wiggin's genes?

Or is that something deeper than the mechanical genius of the body? Is there a spirit, and is what Ender has a gift from God? We follow him like disciples. We look to him to draw water from the rock.

Can I learn to do what he does? Or am I to be like so many of the military writers I've studied, condemned to be second-raters in the field, remembered only because of their chronicles and explanations of other commanders' genius? Will I write a book after this, telling all about how Ender did it?

Let Ender write that book. Or Graff. I have work to do here, and when it's done, I'll choose my own work and do it as well as I can. If I'm remembered only because I was one of Ender's companions, so be it. Serving with Ender is its own reward.

But ah, how it stung to see how happy the others were, and how they paid no attention to him at all, except to tease him like a little brother, like a mascot. How they must have hated it when he was their leader.

And the worst thing was, that's how Ender treated him, too. Not that any of them were ever allowed to see Ender. But during their long separation, Ender had apparently forgotten how he once relied on Bean. It was Petra that he leaned on most, and Alai, and Dink, and Shen. The ones who had never been in an army with him. Bean and the other toon leaders from Dragon Army were still used, still trusted, but when there was something hard to do, something that required creative flair, Ender never thought of Bean.

Didn't matter. Couldn't think about that. Because Bean knew that along with his primary assignment as one of the squadron chiefs, he had another, deeper work to do. He had to watch the whole flow of each battle, ready to step in at any moment, should Ender falter. Ender seemed not to guess that Bean had that kind of trust from the teachers, but Bean knew it, and if sometimes it made him a little distracted in fulfilling his official assignments, if sometimes Ender grew impatient with him for being a little late, a little inattentive, that was to be expected. For what Ender did not know was that at any moment, if the supervisor signaled him, Bean could take over and continue Ender's plan, watching over all of the squadron leaders, saving the game.

At first, that assignment seemed empty—Ender was healthy, alert. But then came the change.

It was the day after Ender mentioned to them, casually, that he had a different teacher from theirs. He referred to him as "Mazer" once too often, and Crazy Tom said, "He must have gone through hell, growing up with that name."

"When he was growing up," said Ender, "the name wasn't famous."

"Anybody that old is dead," said Shen.

"Not if he was put on a lightspeed ship for a lot of years and then brought back."

That's when it dawned on them. "Your teacher is *the* Mazer Rackham?"

"You know how they say he's a brilliant hero?" said Ender.

Of course they knew.

"What they don't mention is, he's a complete hard-ass."

And then the new simulation began and they got back to work.

Next day, Ender told them that things were changing. "So far we've been playing against the computer or against each other. But starting now, every few days Mazer himself and a team of experienced pilots will control the opposing fleet. Anything goes."

A series of tests, with Mazer Rackham himself as the opponent. It smelled fishy to Bean.

These aren't tests, these are setups, preparations for the conditions that might come when they face the actual Bugger fleet near their home planet. The I.F. is getting preliminary information back from the expeditionary fleet, and they're preparing us for what the Buggers are actually going to throw at us when battle is joined.

The trouble was, no matter how bright Mazer Rackham

and the other officers might be, they were still human. When the real battle came, the Buggers were bound to show them things that humans simply couldn't think of.

Then came the first of these "tests"—and it was embarrassing how juvenile the strategy was. A big globe formation, surrounding a single ship.

In this battle it became clear that Ender knew things that he wasn't telling them. For one thing, he told them to ignore the ship in the center of the globe. It was a decoy. But how could Ender know that? Because he knew that the Buggers would *show* a single ship like that, and it was a lie. Which means that the Buggers expect us to go for that one ship.

Except, of course, that this was not really the Buggers, this was Mazer Rackham. So why would Rackham expect the Buggers to expect humans to strike for a single ship?

Bean thought back to those vids that Ender had watched over and over in Battle School—all the propaganda film of the Second Invasion.

They never showed the battle because there wasn't one. Nor did Mazer Rackham command a strike force with a brilliant strategy. Mazer Rackham hit a single ship and the war was over. That's why there's no video of hand-to-hand combat. Mazer Rackham killed the queen. And now he expects the Buggers to show a central ship as a decoy, because that's how we won last time.

Kill the queen, and all the Buggers are defenseless. Mindless. That's what the vids meant. Ender knows that, but he also knows that the Buggers know that we know it, so he doesn't fall for their sucker bait.

The second thing that Ender knew and they didn't was the use of a weapon that hadn't been in any of their simulations till this first test. Ender called it "Dr. Device" and then said nothing more about it—until he ordered Alai to use it where the enemy fleet was most concentrated. To their surprise, the thing set off a chain reaction that leapt from ship to ship, until all but the most outlying Formic ships were destroyed. And it was an easy matter to mop up those stragglers. The playing field was clear when they finished.

"Why was their strategy so stupid?" asked Bean.

"That's what I was wondering," said Ender. "But we didn't lose a ship, so that's OK."

Later, Ender told them what Mazer said—they were simulating a whole invasion sequence, and so he was taking the simulated enemy through a learning curve. "Next time they'll have learned. It won't be so easy."

Bean heard that and it filled him with alarm. An invasion sequence? Why a scenario like that? Why not warm-ups before a single battle?

Because the Buggers have more than one world, thought Bean. Of course they do. They found Earth and expected to turn it into yet another colony, just as they've done before.

We have more than one fleet. One for each Formic world.

And the reason they can learn from battle to battle is because they, too, have faster-than-light communication across interstellar space.

All of Bean's guesses were confirmed. He also knew the secret behind these tests. Mazer Rackham wasn't commanding a simulated Bugger fleet. It was a real battle, and Rackham's only function was to watch how it flowed and then coach Ender afterward on what the enemy strategies meant and how to counter them in future.

That was why they were giving most of their commands orally. They were being transmitted to real crews of real ships who followed their orders and fought real battles. Any ship we lose, thought Bean, means that grown men and women have died. Any carelessness on our part takes lives. Yet they don't tell us this precisely because we can't afford to be burdened with that knowledge. In wartime, commanders have always had to learn the concept of "acceptable losses." But those who keep their humanity never really accept the idea of acceptability, Bean understood that. It gnaws at them. So they protect us child-soldiers by keeping us convinced that it's only games and tests.

Therefore I can't let on to anyone that I do know. Therefore I must accept the losses without a word, without a visible qualm. I must try to block out of my mind the people who will die from our boldness, whose sacrifice is not of a mere counter in a game, but of their lives.

The "tests" came every few days, and each battle lasted longer. Alai joked that they ought to be fitted with diapers so they didn't have to be distracted when their bladder got full during a battle. Next day, they were fitted out with catheters. It was Crazy Tom who put a stop to that. "Come on, just get us a jar to pee in. We can't play this game with something hanging off our dicks." Jars it was, after that. Bean never heard of anyone using one, though. And though he wondered what they provided for Petra, no one ever had the courage to brave her wrath by asking.

Bean began to notice some of Ender's mistakes pretty early on. For one thing, Ender was relying too much on Petra. She always got command of the core force, watching a hundred different things at once, so that Ender could concentrate on the feints, the ploys, the tricks. Couldn't Ender see that Petra, a perfectionist, was getting eaten alive by guilt and shame over every mistake she made? He was so good with people, and yet he seemed to think she was really tough, instead of realizing that toughness was an act she put on to hide her intense anxiety. Every mistake weighed on her. She wasn't sleeping well, and it showed up as she got more and more fatigued during battles.

But then, maybe the reason Ender didn't realize what he was doing to her was that he, too, was tired. So were all of them. Fading a little under the pressure, and sometimes a lot. Getting more fatigued, more error-prone as the tests got harder, as the odds got longer.

Because the battles were harder with each new "test," Ender was forced to leave more and more decisions up to others. Instead of smoothly carrying out Ender's detailed commands, the squadron leaders had more and more of the battle to carry on their own shoulders. For long sequences, Ender was too busy in one part of the battle to give new orders in another. The squadron leaders who were affected began to use crosstalk to determine their tactics until Ender noticed them again. And Bean was grateful to find that, while Ender never gave him the interesting assignments, some of the others talked to him when Ender's attention was elsewhere. Crazy Tom and Hot Soup came up with their own plans, but they routinely ran them past Bean. And since, in each battle, he was spending half his attention observing and analyzing Ender's plan, Bean was able to tell them, with pretty good accuracy, what they should do to help make the overall plan work out. Now and then Ender praised Tom or Soup for decisions that came from Bean's advice. It was the closest thing to praise that Bean heard.

The other toon leaders and the older kids simply didn't turn to Bean at all. He understood why; they must have resented it greatly when the teachers placed Bean above them during the time before Ender was brought in. Now that they had their true commander, they were never again going to do anything that smacked of subservience to Bean. He understood—but that didn't keep it from stinging.

Whether or not they wanted him to oversee their work, whether or not his feelings were hurt, that was still his assignment and he was determined never to be caught unprepared. As the pressure became more and more intense, as they became wearier and wearier, more irritable with each other, less generous in their assessment of each other's work, Bean became all the more attentive because the chances of error were all the greater.

One day Petra fell asleep during battle. She had let her force drift too far into a vulnerable position, and the enemy took advantage, tearing her squadron to bits. Why didn't she give the order to fall back? Worse yet, Ender didn't notice soon enough, either. It was Bean who told him: Something's wrong with Petra.

Ender called out to her. She didn't answer. Ender flipped control of her two remaining ships to Crazy Tom and then tried to salvage the overall battle. Petra had, as usual, occupied the core position, and the loss of most of her large squadron was a devastating blow. Only because the enemy was overconfident during mop-up was Ender able to lay a couple of traps and regain the initiative. He won, but with heavy losses.

Petra apparently woke up near the end of the battle and found her controls cut off, with no voice until it was all over. Then her microphone came on again and they could hear her crying, "I'm sorry, I'm sorry. Tell Ender I'm sorry, he can't hear me, I'm so sorry . . ."

Bean got to her before she could return to her room. She was staggering along the tunnel, leaning against the wall and crying, using her hands to find her way because she couldn't see through her tears. Bean came up and touched her. She shrugged off his hand.

"Petra," said Bean. "Fatigue is fatigue. You can't stay awake when your brain shuts down."

"It was *my* brain that shut down! You don't know how that feels because you're always so smart you could do all our jobs and play chess while you're doing it!"

"Petra, he was relying on you too much, he never gave you a break—"

"He doesn't take breaks either, and I don't see him—"

"Yes you *do.* It was obvious there was something wrong with your squadron for several seconds before somebody called his attention to it. And even then, he tried to rouse you before assigning control to somebody else. If he'd acted faster you would have had six ships left, not just two."

"*You* pointed it out to him. You were watching me. Checking up on me."

"Petra, I watch everybody."

"You said you'd trust me, but you don't. And you shouldn't, nobody should trust me."

She broke into uncontrollable sobbing, leaning against the stone of the wall.

A couple of officers showed up then, led her away. Not to her room.

—

Graff called him in soon afterward. "You handled it just right," said Graff. "That's what you're there for."

"I wasn't quick either," said Bean.

"You were watching. You saw where the plan was breaking down, you called Ender's attention to it. You did your job. The other kids don't realize it and I know that has to gall you—"

"I don't care what they notice—"

"But you did the job. On that battle you get the save."

"Whatever the hell that means."

"It's baseball. Oh yeah. That wasn't big on the streets of Rotterdam."

"Can I please go sleep now?"

"In a minute. Bean, Ender's getting tired. He's making mistakes. It's all the more important that you watch everything. Be there for him. You saw how Petra was."

"We're all getting fatigued."

"Well, so is Ender. Worse than anyone. He cries in his sleep. He has strange dreams. He's talking about how Mazer seems to know what he's planning, spying on his dreams."

"You telling me he's going crazy?"

"I'm telling you that the only person he pushed harder than Petra is himself. Cover for him, Bean. Back him up."

"I already am."

"You're angry all the time, Bean."

Graff's words startled him. At first he thought, No I'm not! Then he thought, Am I?

"Ender isn't using you for anything important, and after having run the show that has to piss you off, Bean. But it's not Ender's fault. Mazer has been telling Ender that he has doubts about your ability to handle large numbers of ships. That's why you haven't been getting the complicated, interesting assignments. Not that Ender takes Mazer's word for it. But everything you do, Ender sees it through the lens of Mazer's lack of confidence."

"Mazer Rackham thinks I—"

"Mazer Rackham knows exactly what you are and what you can do. But we had to make sure Ender didn't assign you something so complicated you couldn't keep track of the overall flow of the game. And we had to do it without telling Ender you're his backup."

"So why are you telling me this?"

"When this test is over and you go on to real commands, we'll tell Ender the truth about what you were doing, and why Mazer said what he said. I know it means a lot to you to have Ender's confidence, and you don't feel like you have it, and so I wanted you to know why we did it."

"Why this sudden bout of honesty?"

"Because I think you'll do better knowing it."

"I'll do better *believing* it whether it's true or not. You could be lying. So do I really know anything at all from this conversation?"

"Believe what you want, Bean."

—

Petra didn't come to practice for a couple of days. When she came back, of course Ender didn't give her the heavy assignments anymore. She did well at the assignments she had, but her ebullience was gone. Her heart was broken.

But dammit, she had *slept* for a couple of days. They were all just the tiniest bit jealous of her for that, even though they'd never willingly trade places with her. Whether they had any particular god in mind, they all prayed: Let it not happen to me. Yet at the same time they also prayed the opposite prayer: Oh, let me sleep, let me have a day in which I don't have to think about this game.

The tests went on. How many worlds did these bastards colonize before they got to Earth? Bean wondered. And are we sure we have them all? And what good does it do to destroy their fleets when we don't have the forces there to occupy the defeated colonies? Or do we just leave our ships there, shooting down anything that tries to boost from the surface of the planet?

Petra wasn't the only one to blow out. Vlad went catatonic and couldn't be roused from his bunk. It took three days for the doctors to get him awake again, and unlike Petra, he was out for the duration. He just couldn't concentrate.

Bean kept waiting for Crazy Tom to follow suit, but despite his nickname, he actually seemed to get saner as he got wearier. Instead it was Fly Molo who started laughing when he lost control of his squadron. Ender cut him off immediately, and for once he put Bean in charge of Fly's ships. Fly was back the next day, no explanation, but everyone understood that he wouldn't be given crucial assignments now.

And Bean became more and more aware of Ender's decreasing alertness. His orders came after longer and longer pauses now, and a couple of times his orders weren't clearly stated. Bean immediately translated them into a more comprehensible form, and Ender never knew there had been confusion. But the others were finally becoming aware that Bean was following the whole battle, not just his part of it. Perhaps they even saw how Bean would ask a question during a battle, make some comment that alerted Ender to something that he needed to be aware of, but never in a way that sounded like Bean was criticizing anybody. After the battles one or two of the older kids would speak to Bean. Nothing major. Just a hand on his shoulder, on his back, and a couple of words. "Good game." "Good work." "Keep it up." "Thanks, Bean."

He hadn't realized how much he needed the honor of others until he finally got it.

—

"Bean, this next game, I think you should know something."

"What?"

Colonel Graff hesitated. "We couldn't get Ender awake this morning. He's been having nightmares. He doesn't eat unless we make him. He bites his hand in his sleep—bites it bloody. And today we couldn't get him to wake up. We were able to hold off on the . . . test . . . so he's going to be in command, as usual, but . . . not as usual."

"I'm ready. I always am."

"Yeah, but . . . look, advance word on this test is that it's . . . there's no . . ."

"It's hopeless."

"Anything you can do to help. Any suggestion."

"This Dr. Device thing, Ender hasn't let us use it in a long time."

"The enemy learned enough about how it works that they never let their ships get close enough together for a chain reaction to spread. It takes a certain amount of mass to be able to maintain the field. Basically, right now it's just ballast. Useless."

"It would have been nice if you'd told *me* how it works before now."

"There are people who don't want us to tell you anything, Bean. You have a way of using every scrap of information to guess ten times more than we want you to know. It makes them a little leery of giving you those scraps in the first place."

"Colonel Graff, you know that I know that these battles are real. Mazer Rackham isn't making them up. When we lose ships, real men die."

Graff looked away.

"And these are men that Mazer Rackham knows, neh?"

Graff nodded slightly.

"You don't think Ender can sense what Mazer is feeling? I don't know the guy, maybe he's like a rock, but *I* think that when he does his critiques with Ender, he's letting his . . . what, his anguish . . . Ender feels it. Because Ender is a lot more tired *after* a critique than before it. He may not know what's really going on, but he knows that something terrible is at stake. He knows that Mazer Rackham is really upset with every mistake Ender makes."

"Have you found some way to sneak into Ender's room?"

"I know how to listen to Ender. I'm not wrong about Mazer, am I?"

Graff shook his head.

"Colonel Graff, what you don't realize, what nobody seems to remember—that last game in Battle School, where Ender turned his army over to me. That wasn't a strategy. He was quitting. He was through. He was on strike. You didn't find that out because you graduated him. The thing with Bonzo finished him. I think Mazer Rackham's anguish is doing the same thing to him now. I think even when Ender doesn't *consciously* know that he's killed somebody, he knows it deep down, and it burns in his heart."

Graff looked at him sharply.

"I know Bonzo was dead. I saw him. I've seen death before, remember? You don't get your nose jammed into your brain and lose two gallons of blood and get up and walk away. You never told Ender that Bonzo was dead, but you're a fool if you think he doesn't know. And he knows, thanks to Mazer, that every ship we've lost means good men are dead. He can't stand it, Colonel Graff."

"You're more insightful than you get credit for, Bean," said Graff.

"I know, I'm the cold inhuman intellect, right?" Bean laughed bitterly. "Genetically altered, therefore I'm just as alien as the Buggers."

Graff blushed. "No one's ever said that."

"You mean you've never said it in front of me. Knowingly. What you don't seem to understand is, sometimes you have to just tell people the truth and ask them to do the thing you want, instead of trying to trick them into it."

"Are you saying we should tell Ender the game is real?"

"No! Are you insane? If he's this upset when the knowledge is unconscious, what do you think would happen if he *knew* that he knew? He'd freeze up."

"But you don't freeze up. Is that it? You should command this next battle?"

"You still don't get it, Colonel Graff. I don't freeze up because it isn't my battle. I'm helping. I'm watching. But I'm free. Because it's Ender's game."

Bean's simulator came to life.

"It's time," said Graff. "Good luck."

"Colonel Graff, Ender may go on strike again. He may walk out on it. He might give up. He might tell himself, It's only a game and I'm sick of it, I don't care what they do to me, I'm done. That's in him, to do that. When it seems completely unfair and utterly pointless."

"What if I promised him it was the last one?"

Bean put on his headset as he asked, "Would it be true?"

Graff nodded.

"Yeah, well, I don't think it would make much difference. Besides, he's Mazer's student now, isn't he?"

"I guess. Mazer was talking about telling him that it was the final exam."

"Mazer is Ender's teacher now," Bean mused. "And you're left with me. The kid you didn't want."

Graff blushed again. "That's right," he said. "Since you seem to know everything. I didn't want you."

Even though Bean already knew it, the words still hurt.

"But Bean," said Graff, "the thing is, I was wrong." He put a hand on Bean's shoulder and left the room.

Bean logged on. He was the last of the squadron leaders to do so.

"Are you there?" asked Ender over the headsets.

"All of us," said Bean. "Kind of late for practice this morning, aren't you?"

"Sorry," said Ender. "I overslept."

They laughed. Except Bean.

Ender took them through some maneuvers, warming up for the battle. And then it was time. The display cleared.

Bean waited, anxiety gnawing at his gut.

The enemy appeared in the display.

Their fleet was deployed around a planet that loomed in the center of the display. There had been battles near planets before, but every other time, the world was near the edge of the display—the enemy fleet always tried to lure them away from the planet.

This time there was no luring. Just the most incredible swarm of enemy ships imaginable. Always staying a certain distance away from each other, thousands and thousands of ships followed random, unpredictable, intertwining paths, together forming a cloud of death around the planet.

This is the home planet, thought Bean. He almost said it aloud, but caught himself in time. This is a *simulation* of the Bugger defense of their home planet.

They've had generations to prepare for us to come. All the previous battles were nothing. These Formics can lose any number of individual Buggers and they don't care. All that matters is the queen. Like the one Mazer Rackham killed in the Second Invasion. And they haven't put a queen at risk in any of these battles. Until now.

That's why they're swarming. There's a queen here.

Where?

On the planet surface, thought Bean. The idea is to keep us from getting to the planet surface.

So that's precisely where we need to go. Dr. Device needs mass. Planets have mass. Pretty simple.

Except that there was no way to get this small force of human ships through that swarm and near enough to the planet to deploy Dr. Device. For if there was anything that history taught, it was this: Sometimes the other side is irresistibly strong, and then the only sensible course of action is to retreat in order to save your force to fight another day.

In this war, however, there would be no other day. There was no hope of retreat. The decisions that lost this battle, and therefore this war, were made two generations ago when these ships were launched, an inadequate force from the start. The commanders who set this fleet in motion may not even have known, then, that this was the Buggers' home world. It was no one's fault. They simply didn't have enough of a force even to make a dent in the enemy's defenses. It didn't matter how brilliant Ender was. When you have only one guy with a shovel, you can't build a dike to hold back the sea.

No retreat, no possibility of victory, no room for delay or maneuver, no reason for the enemy to do anything but continue to do what they were doing.

There were only twenty starships in the human fleet, each with four fighters. And they were the oldest design, sluggish compared to some of the fighters they'd had in earlier battles. It made sense—the Bugger home world was probably the farthest away, so the fleet that got there now had left before any of the other fleets. Before the better ships came on line.

Eighty fighters. Against five thousand, maybe ten thousand enemy ships. It was impossible to determine the number. Bean saw how the display kept losing track of individual enemy ships, how the total count kept fluctuating. There were so many it was overloading the system. They kept winking in and out like fireflies.

A long time passed—many seconds, perhaps a minute. By now Ender usually had them all deployed, ready to move. But still there was nothing from him but silence.

A light blinked on Bean's console. He knew what it meant. All he had to do was press a button, and control of the battle would be his. They were offering it to him, because they thought that Ender had frozen up.

He hasn't frozen up, thought Bean. He hasn't panicked.

He has simply understood the situation, exactly as I understand it. There *is* no strategy. Only he doesn't see that this is simply the fortunes of war, a disaster that can't be helped. What he sees is a test set before him by his teachers, by Mazer Rackham, a test so absurdly unfair that the only reasonable course of action is to refuse to take it.

They were so clever, keeping the truth from him all this time. But now was it going to backfire on them. If Ender understood that it was not a game, that the real war had come down to this moment, then he might make some desperate effort, or with his genius he might even come up with an answer to a problem that, as far as Bean could see, had no solution. But Ender did not understand the reality, and so to him it was like that day in the battleroom, facing two armies, when Ender turned the whole thing over to Bean and, in effect, refused to play.

For a moment Bean was tempted to scream the truth. It's not a game, it's the real thing, this is the last battle, we've lost this war after all! But what would be gained by that, except to panic everyone?

Yet it was absurd to even contemplate pressing that button to take over control himself. Ender hadn't collapsed or failed. The battle was unwinnable; it should not even be fought. The lives of the men on those ships were not to be wasted on such a hopeless Charge of the Light Brigade. I'm not General Burnside at Fredericksburg. I don't send my men off to senseless, hopeless, meaningless death.

If I had a plan, I'd take control. I have no plan. So for good or ill, it's Ender's game, not mine.

And there was another reason for not taking over.

Bean remembered standing over the supine body of a bully who was too dangerous to ever be tamed, telling Poke, Kill him now, kill him.

I was right. And now, once again, the bully must be killed. Even though I don't know how to do it, we *can't* lose this war. I don't know how to win it, but I'm not God, I don't see everything. And maybe Ender doesn't *see* a solution either, but if anyone can find one, if anyone can make it happen, it's Ender.

Maybe it isn't hopeless. Maybe there's some way to get down to the planet's surface and wipe the Buggers out of the universe. Now is the time for miracles. For Ender, the others will do their best work. If I took over, they'd be so upset, so distracted that even if I came up with a plan that had some kind of chance, it would never work because their hearts wouldn't be in it.

Ender has to try. If he doesn't, we all die. Because even if they weren't going to send another fleet against us, after this they'll *have* to send one. Because we beat all their fleets in every battle till now. If we don't win this one, with finality, destroying their capability to make war against us, then they'll be back. And this time they'll have figured out how to make Dr. Device themselves.

We have only the one world. We have only the one hope.

Do it, Ender.

There flashed into Bean's mind the words Ender said in their first day of training as Dragon Army: Remember, the enemy's gate is down. In Dragon Army's last battle, when there was no hope, that was the strategy that Ender had used, sending Bean's squad to press their helmets against the floor around the gate and win. Too bad there was no such cheat available now.

Deploying Dr. Device against the planet's surface to blow the whole thing up, that might do the trick. You just couldn't get there from here.

It was time to give up. Time to get out of the game, to tell them not to send children to do grownups' work. It's hopeless. We're done.

"Remember," Bean said ironically, "the enemy's gate is down."

Fly Molo, Hot Soup, Vlad, Dumper, Crazy Tom—they grimly laughed. They had been in Dragon Army. They remembered how those words were used before.

But Ender didn't seem to get the joke.

Ender didn't seem to understand that there was no way to get Dr. Device to the planet's surface.

Instead, his voice came into their ears, giving them orders. He pulled them into a tight formation, cylinders within cylinders.

Bean wanted to shout, Don't do it! There are real men on those ships, and if you send them in, they'll die, a sacrifice with no hope of victory.

But he held his tongue, because, in the back of his mind, in the deepest corner of his heart, he still had hope that Ender might do what could not be done. And as long as there was such a hope, the lives of those men were, by their own choice when they set out on this expedition, expendable.

Ender set them in motion, having them dodge here and there through the ever-shifting formations of the enemy swarm.

Surely the enemy sees what we're doing, thought Bean. Surely they see how every third or fourth move takes us closer and closer to the planet.

At any moment the enemy could destroy them quickly by concentrating their forces. So why weren't they doing it?

One possibility occurred to Bean. The Buggers didn't dare concentrate their forces close to Ender's tight formation, because the moment they drew their ships that close together, Ender could use Dr. Device against them.

And then he thought of another explanation. Could it be that there were simply too many Bugger ships? Could it be that the queen or queens had to spend all their concentration, all their mental strength just keeping ten thousand ships swarming through space without getting too close to each other?

Unlike Ender, the Bugger queen couldn't turn control of her ships over to subordinates. She *had* no subordinates. The individual Buggers were like her hands and her feet. Now she had hundreds of hands and feet, or perhaps thousands of them, all wiggling at once.

That's why she wasn't responding intelligently. Her forces were too numerous. That's why she wasn't making the obvious moves, setting traps, blocking Ender from taking his cylinder ever closer to the planet with every swing and dodge and shift that he made.

In fact, the maneuvers the Buggers were making were ludicrously wrong. For as Ender penetrated deeper and deeper into the planet's gravity well, the Buggers were building up a thick wall of forces *behind* Ender's formation.

They're blocking our retreat!

At once Bean understood a third and most important reason for what was happening. The Buggers had learned the wrong lessons from the previous battles. Up to now, Ender's strategy had always been to ensure the survival of as many human ships as possible. He had always left himself a line of retreat. The Buggers, with their huge numerical advantage, were finally in a position to guarantee that the human forces would not get away.

There was no way, at the beginning of this battle, to predict that the Buggers would make such a mistake. Yet throughout history, great victories had come as much because of the losing army's errors as because of the winner's brilliance in battle. The Buggers have finally, finally learned that we humans value each and every individual human life. We don't throw our forces away because every soldier is the queen of a one-member hive. But they've learned this lesson just in time for it to be hopelessly wrong—for we humans *do,* when the cause is sufficient, spend our own lives. We throw ourselves onto the grenade to save our buddies in the foxhole. We rise out of the trenches and charge the entrenched enemy and die like maggots under a blowtorch. We strap bombs on our bodies and blow ourselves up in the midst of our enemies. We are, when the cause is sufficient, insane.

They don't believe we'll use Dr. Device because the only way to use it is to destroy our own ships in the process. From the moment Ender started giving orders, it was obvious to everyone that this was a suicide run. These ships were not made to enter an atmosphere. And yet to get close enough to the planet to set off Dr. Device, they had to do exactly that.

Get down into the gravity well and launch the weapon just before the ship burns up. And if it works, if the planet is torn apart by whatever force it is in that terrible weapon, the chain reaction will reach out into space and take out any ships that might happen to survive.

Win or lose, there'd be no human survivors from this battle.

They've never seen us make a move like that. They don't understand that, yes, humans will always act to preserve their own lives—except for the times when they don't. In the Buggers' experience, autonomous beings do not sacrifice themselves. Once they understood our autonomy, the seed of their defeat was sown.

In all of Ender's study of the Buggers, in all his obsession with them over the years of his training, did he somehow come to *know* that they would make such deadly mistakes?

I did not know it. I would not have pursued this strategy. I *had* no strategy. Ender was the only commander who could have known, or guessed, or unconsciously hoped that when he flung out his forces the enemy would falter, would trip, would fall, would fail.

Or *did* he know at all? Could it be that he reached the same conclusion as I did, that this battle was unwinnable? That he decided not to play it out, that he went on strike, that he quit? And then my bitter words, "the enemy's gate is down," triggered his futile, useless gesture of despair, sending his ships to certain doom because he did not know that there were real ships out there, with real men aboard, that he was sending to their deaths? Could it be that he was as surprised as I was by the mistakes of the enemy? Could our victory be an accident?

No. For even if my words provoked Ender into action, he was still the one who chose *this* formation, *these* feints and evasions, *this* meandering route. It was Ender whose previous victories taught the enemy to think of us as one kind of creature, when we are really something quite different. He pretended all this time that humans were rational beings, when we are really the most terrible monsters these poor aliens could ever have conceived of in their nightmares. They had no way of knowing the story of blind Samson, who pulled down the temple on his own head to slay his enemies.

On those ships, thought Bean, there are individual men who gave up homes and families, the world of their birth, in order to cross a great swatch of the galaxy and make war on a terrible enemy. Somewhere along the way they're bound to understand that Ender's strategy requires them all to die. Perhaps they already have. And yet they obey and will continue to obey the orders that come to them. As in the famous Charge of the Light Brigade, these soldiers give up their lives, trusting that their commanders are using them well. While we sit safely here in these simulator rooms, playing an elaborate computer game, they are obeying, dying so that all of humankind can live.

And yet we who command them, we children in these elaborate game machines, have no idea of their courage, their sacrifice. We cannot give them the honor they deserve, because we don't even know they exist.

Except for me.

There sprang into Bean's mind a favorite scripture of Sister Carlotta's. Maybe it meant so much to her because she had no children. She told Bean the story of Absalom's rebellion against his own father, King David. In the course of a battle, Absalom was killed. When they brought the news to David, it meant victory, it meant that no more of his soldiers would die. His throne was safe. His *life* was safe. But all he could think about was his son, his beloved son, his dead boy.

Bean ducked his head, so his voice would be heard only by the men under his command. And then, for just long enough to speak, he pressed the override that put his voice into the ears of all the men of that distant fleet. Bean had no idea how his voice would sound to them; would they hear his childish voice, or were the sounds distorted, so they would hear him as an adult, or perhaps as some metallic, machinelike voice? No matter. In some form the men of that distant fleet would hear his voice, transmitted faster than light, God knows how.

"O my son Absalom," Bean said softly, knowing for the first time the kind of anguish that could tear such words from a man's mouth. "My son, my son Absalom. Would God I could die for thee, O Absalom, my son. My sons!"

He had paraphrased it a little, but God would understand. Or if he didn't, Sister Carlotta would.

Now, thought Bean. Do it now, Ender. You're as close as you can get without giving away the game. They're beginning to understand their danger. They're concentrating their forces. They'll blow us out of the sky before our weapons can be launched—

"All right, everybody except Petra's squadron," said Ender. "Straight down, as fast as you can. Launch Dr. Device against the planet. Wait till the last possible second. Petra, cover as you can."

The squadron leaders, Bean among them, echoed Ender's commands to their own fleets. And then there was nothing to do but watch. Each ship was on its own.

The enemy understood now, and rushed to destroy the plummeting humans. Fighter after fighter was picked off by the inrushing ships of the Formic fleet. Only a few human fighters survived long enough to enter the atmosphere.

Hold on, thought Bean. Hold on as long as you can.

The ships that launched too early watched their Dr. Device burn up in the atmosphere before it could go off. A few other ships burned up themselves without launching.

Two ships were left. One was in Bean's squadron.

"Don't launch it," said Bean into his microphone, head down. "Set it off inside your ship. God be with you."

Bean had no way of knowing whether it was his ship or the other that did it. He only knew that both ships disappeared from the display without launching. And then the surface of the planet started to bubble. Suddenly a vast eruption licked outward toward the last of the human fighters, Petra's ships, on which there might or might not still be men alive to see death coming at them. To see their victory approach.

The simulator put on a spectacular show as the exploding planet chewed up all the enemy ships, engulfing them in the chain reaction. But long before the last ship was swallowed up, all the maneuvering had stopped. They drifted, dead. Like the dead Bugger ships in the vids of the Second Invasion. The queens of the hive had died on the planet's surface. The destruction of the remaining ships was a mere formality. The Buggers were already dead.

—

Bean emerged into the tunnel to find that the other kids were already there, congratulating each other and commenting on how cool the explosion effect was, and wondering if something like that could really happen.

"Yes," said Bean. "It could."

"As if you know," said Fly Molo, laughing.

"Of course I know it could happen," said Bean. "It *did* happen."

They looked at him uncomprehendingly. When did it happen? I never heard of anything like that. Where could they have tested that weapon against a planet? I know, they took out Neptune!

"It happened just now," said Bean. "It happened at the home world of the Buggers. We just blew it up. They're all dead."

They finally began to realize that he was serious. They fired objections at him. He explained about the faster-than-light communications device. They didn't believe him.

Then another voice entered the conversation. "It's called the ansible."

They looked up to see Colonel Graff standing a ways off, down the tunnel.

Is Bean telling the truth? Was that a real battle?

"They were all real," said Bean. "All the so-called tests. Real battles. Real victories. Right, Colonel Graff? We were fighting the real war all along."

"It's over now," said Graff. "The human race will continue. The Buggers won't."

They finally believed it, and became giddy with the realization. It's over. We won. We weren't practicing, we were actually commanders.

And then, at last, a silence fell.

"They're *all* dead?" asked Petra.

Bean nodded.

Again they looked at Graff. "We have reports. All life activity has ceased on all the other planets. They must have gathered their queens back on their home planet. When the queens die, the Buggers die. There is no enemy now."

Petra began to cry, leaning against the wall. Bean wanted to reach out to her, but Dink was there. Dink was the friend who held her, comforted her.

Some soberly, some exultantly, they went back to their barracks. Petra wasn't the only one who cried. But whether the tears were shed in anguish or in relief, no one could say for sure.

Only Bean did not return to his room, perhaps because Bean was the only one not surprised. He stayed out in the tunnel with Graff.

"How's Ender taking it?"

"Badly," said Graff. "We should have broken it to him more carefully, but there was no holding back. In the moment of victory."

"All your gambles paid off," said Bean.

"I know what happened, Bean," said Graff. "Why did

you leave control with him? How did you know he'd come up with a plan?"

"I didn't," said Bean. "I only knew that I had no plan at all."

"But what you said—'the enemy's gate is down.' That's the plan Ender used."

"It wasn't a plan," said Bean. "Maybe it made him think of a plan. But it was him. It was Ender. You put your money on the right kid."

Graff looked at Bean in silence, then reached out and put a hand on Bean's head, tousled his hair a little. "I think perhaps you pulled each other across the finish line."

"It doesn't matter, does it?" said Bean. "It's finished, anyway. And so is the temporary unity of the human race."

"Yes," said Graff. He pulled his hand away, ran it through his own hair. "I believed in your analysis. I tried to give warning. *If* the Strategos heeded my advice, the Polemarch's men are getting arrested here on Eros and all over the fleet."

"Will they go peacefully?" asked Bean.

"We'll see," said Graff.

The sound of gunfire echoed from some distant tunnel.

"Guess not," said Bean.

They heard the sound of men running in step. And soon they saw them, a contingent of a dozen armed marines.

Bean and Graff watched them approach. "Friend or foe?"

"They all wear the same uniform," said Graff. "You're the one who called it, Bean. Inside those doors"—he gestured toward the doors to the kids' quarters—"those children are the spoils of war. In command of armies back on Earth, they're the hope of victory. *You* are the hope."

The soldiers came to a stop in front of Graff. "We're here to protect the children, sir," said their leader.

"From what?"

"The Polemarch's men seem to be resisting arrest, sir,"

said the soldier. "The Strategos has ordered that these children be kept safe at all costs."

Graff was visibly relieved to know which side these troops were on. "The girl is in that room over there. I suggest you consolidate them all into those two barrack rooms for the duration."

"Is this the kid who did it?" asked the soldier, indicating Bean.

"He's one of them."

"It was Ender Wiggin who did it," said Bean. "Ender was our commander."

"Is he in one of those rooms?" asked the soldier.

"He's with Mazer Rackham," said Graff. "And this one stays with me."

The soldier saluted. He began positioning his men in more advanced positions down the tunnel, with only a single guard outside each door to prevent the kids from going out and getting lost somewhere in the fighting.

Bean trotted along beside Graff as he headed purposefully down the tunnel, beyond the farthest of the guards.

"If the Strategos did this right, the ansibles have already been secured. I don't know about you, but I want to be where the news is coming in. And going out."

"Is Russian a hard language to learn?" asked Bean.

"Is that what passes for humor with you?" asked Graff.

"It was a simple question."

"Bean, you're a great kid, but shut up, OK?"

Bean laughed. "OK."

"You don't mind if I still call you Bean?"

"It's my name."

"Your name should have been Julian Delphiki. If you'd had a birth certificate, that's the name that would have been on it."

"You mean that was true?"

"Would I lie about something like that?"

Then, realizing the absurdity of what he had just said, they laughed. Laughed long enough to still be smiling when they passed the detachment of marines protecting the entrance to the ansible complex.

"You think anybody will ask me for military advice?" asked Bean. "Because I'm going to get into this war, even if I have to lie about my age and enlist in the marines."

24

Homecoming

"I thought you'd want to know. Some bad news."

"There's no shortage of that, even in the midst of victory."

"When it became clear that the IDL had control of Battle School and was sending the kids home under I.F. protection, the New Warsaw Pact apparently did a little research and found that there was one student from Battle School who wasn't under our control. Achilles."

"But he was only there a couple of days."

"He passed our tests. He got in. He was the only one they could get."

"Did they? Get him?"

"All the security there was designed to keep inmates inside. Three guards dead, all the inmates released into the general population. They've all been recovered, except one."

"So he's loose."

"I wouldn't call it loose, exactly. They intend to use him."

"Do they know what he is?"

"No. His records were sealed. A juvenile, you see. They weren't coming for his dossier."

"They'll find out. They don't like serial killers in Moscow, either."

"He's hard to pin down. How many died before any of us suspected him?"

"The war is over for now."

"And the jockeying for advantage in the next war has begun."

"With any luck, Colonel Graff, I'll be dead by then."

"I'm not actually a colonel anymore, Sister Carlotta."

"They're really going to go ahead with that court-martial?"

"An investigation, that's all. An inquiry."

"I just don't understand why they have to find a scapegoat for victory."

"I'll be fine. The sun still shines on planet Earth."

"But never again on *their* tragic world."

"Is your God also their God, Sister Carlotta? Did he take them into heaven?"

"He's not *my* God, Mr. Graff. But I am his child, as are you. I don't know whether he looks at the Formics and sees them, too, as his children."

"Children. Sister Carlotta, the things I did to these children."

"You gave them a world to come home to."

"All but one of them."

It took days for the Polemarch's men to be subdued, but at last Fleetcom was entirely under the Strategos's command, and not one ship had been launched under rebel command. A triumph. The Hegemon resigned as part of the truce, but that only formalized what had already been the reality.

Bean stayed with Graff throughout the fighting, as they read every dispatch and listened to every report about what was happening elsewhere in the fleet and back on Earth. They talked through the unfolding situation, tried to read between the lines, interpreted what was happening as best they could. For Bean, the war with the Buggers was already behind him. All that mattered now was how things went on Earth. When a shaky truce was signed, temporarily ending the fighting, Bean knew that it would not last. He would be needed. Once he got to Earth, he could prepare himself to play his role. Ender's war is over, he thought. This next one will be mine.

While Bean was avidly following the news, the other kids were confined to their quarters under guard, and during the power failures in their part of Eros they did their cowering in darkness. Twice there were assaults on that section of the tunnels, but whether the Russians were trying to get at the kids or merely happened to probe in that area, looking for weaknesses, no one could guess.

Ender was under much heavier guard, but didn't know it. Utterly exhausted, and perhaps unwilling or unable to bear the enormity of what he had done, he remained unconscious for days.

Not till the fighting stopped did he come back to consciousness.

They let the kids get together then, their confinement over for now. Together they made the pilgrimage to the room where Ender had been under protection and medical care. They found him apparently cheerful, able to joke. But Bean could see a deep weariness, a sadness in Ender's eyes that it was impossible to ignore. The victory had cost him deeply, more than anybody.

More than me, thought Bean, even though I knew what I was doing, and he was innocent of any bad intent. He tortures himself, and I move on. Maybe because to me the death of Poke was more important than the death of an entire species that I never saw. I knew her—she has stayed with me in my heart. The Buggers I never knew. How can I grieve for them?

Ender can.

After they filled Ender in on the news about what happened while he slept, Petra touched his hair. "You OK?"

she asked. "You scared us. They said you were crazy, and we said *they* were crazy."

"I'm crazy," said Ender. "But I think I'm OK."

There was more banter, but then Ender's emotions overflowed and for the first time any of them could remember, they saw Ender cry. Bean happened to be standing near him, and when Ender reached out, it was Bean and Petra that he embraced. The touch of his hand, the embrace of his arm, they were more than Bean could bear. He also cried.

"I missed you," said Ender. "I wanted to see you so bad."

"You saw us pretty bad," said Petra. She was not crying. She kissed his cheek.

"I saw you magnificent," said Ender. "The ones I needed most, I used up soonest. Bad planning on my part."

"Everybody's OK now," said Dink. "Nothing was wrong with any of us that five days of cowering in blacked-out rooms in the middle of a war couldn't cure."

"I don't have to be your commander anymore, do I?" asked Ender. "I don't want to command anybody again."

Bean believed him. And believed also that Ender never *would* command in battle again. He might still have the talents that brought him to this place. But the most important ones didn't have to be used for violence. If the universe had any kindness in it, or even simple justice, Ender would never have to take another life. He had surely filled his quota.

"You don't have to command anybody," said Dink, "but you're always our commander."

Bean felt the truth of that. There was not one of them who would not carry Ender with them in their hearts, wherever they went, whatever they did.

What Bean didn't have the heart to tell them was that on Earth, both sides had insisted that they be given custody of the hero of the war, young Ender Wiggin, whose great victory had captured the popular imagination. Whoever had him would not only have the use of his fine military mind—they thought—but would also have the benefit of all the publicity and public adulation that surrounded him, that filled every mention of his name.

So as the political leaders worked out the truce, they reached a simple and obvious compromise. All the children from Battle School would be repatriated. Except Ender Wiggin.

Ender Wiggin would not be coming home. Neither party on Earth would be able to use him. That was the compromise.

And it had been proposed by Locke. By Ender's own brother.

When he learned that it made Bean seethe inside, the way he had when he thought Petra had betrayed Ender. It was wrong. It couldn't be borne.

Perhaps Peter Wiggin did it to keep Ender from becoming a pawn. To keep him free. Or perhaps he did it so that Ender could not use his celebrity to make his own play for political power. Was Peter Wiggin saving his brother, or eliminating a rival for power?

Someday I'll meet him and find out, thought Bean. And if he betrayed his brother, I'll destroy him.

When Bean shed his tears there in Ender's room, he was weeping for a cause the others did not yet know about. He was weeping because, as surely as the soldiers who died in those fighting ships, Ender would not be coming home from the war.

"So," said Alai, breaking the silence. "What do we do now? The Bugger War's over, and so's the war down there on Earth, and even the war here. What do we do now?"

"We're kids," said Petra. "They'll probably make us go to school. It's a law. You have to go to school till you're seventeen."

They all laughed until they cried again.

They saw each other off and on again over the next few days. Then they boarded several different cruisers and destroyers for the voyage back to Earth. Bean knew well why they traveled in separate ships. That way no one would ask why Ender wasn't on board. If Ender knew, before they left, that he was not going back to Earth, he said nothing about it.

—

Elena could hardly contain her joy when Sister Carlotta called, asking if she and her husband would both be at home in an hour. "I'm bringing you your son," she said.

Nikolai, Nikolai, Nikolai. Elena sang the name over and over again in her mind, with her lips. Her husband Julian, too, was almost dancing as he hurried about the house, making things ready. Nikolai had been so little when he left. Now he would be so much older. They would hardly know him. They would not understand what he had been through. But it didn't matter. They loved him. They would learn who he was all over again. They would not let the lost years get in the way of the years to come.

"I see the car!" cried Julian.

Elena hurriedly pulled the covers from the dishes, so that Nikolai could come into a kitchen filled with the freshest, purest food of his childhood memories. Whatever they ate in space, it couldn't be as good as this.

Then she ran to the door and stood beside her husband as they watched Sister Carlotta get out of the front seat.

Why didn't she ride in back with Nikolai?

No matter. The back door opened, and Nikolai emerged, unfolding his lanky young body. So tall he was growing! Yet still a boy. There was a little bit of childhood left for him.

Run to me, my son!

But he didn't run to her. He turned his back on his parents.

Ah. He was reaching into the back seat. A present, perhaps?

No. Another boy.

A smaller boy, but with the same face as Nikolai. Perhaps too careworn for a child so small, but with the same open goodness that Nikolai had always had. Nikolai was smiling so broadly he could not contain it. But the small one was not smiling. He looked uncertain. Hesitant.

"Julian," said her husband.

Why would he say his own name?

"Our second son," he said. "They didn't all die, Elena. One lived."

All hope of those little ones had been buried in her heart. It almost hurt to open that hidden place. She gasped at the intensity of it.

"Nikolai met him in Battle School," he went on. "I told Sister Carlotta that if we had another son, you meant to name him Julian."

"You knew," said Elena.

"Forgive me, my love. But Sister Carlotta wasn't sure then that he was ours. Or that he would ever be able to come home. I couldn't bear it, to tell you of the hope, only to break your heart later."

"I have two sons," she said.

"If you want him," said Julian. "His life has been hard. But he's a stranger here. He doesn't speak Greek. He's been told that he's coming just for a visit. That legally he is not our child, but rather a ward of the state. We don't have to take him in, if you don't want to, Elena."

"Hush, you foolish man," she said. Then, loudly, she called out to the approaching boys. "Here are my two sons, home from the wars! Come to your mother! I have missed you both so much, and for so many years!"

They ran to her then, and she held them in her arms, and her tears fell on them both, and her husband's hands rested upon both boys' heads.

Her husband spoke. Elena recognized his words at once, from the gospel of St. Luke. But because he had only memorized the passage in Greek, the little one did not understand him. No matter. Nikolai began to translate into Common, the language of the fleet, and almost at once the little one recognized the words, and spoke them correctly, from memory, as Sister Carlotta had once read it to him years before.

"Let us eat, and be merry: for this my son was dead, and is alive again; he was lost, and is found." Then the little one burst into tears and clung to his mother, and kissed his father's hand.

"Welcome home, little brother," said Nikolai. "I told you they were nice."

Acknowledgments

One book was particularly useful in preparing this novel: Peter Paret, ed., *Makers of Modern Strategy: From Machiavelli to the Nuclear Age* (Princeton University Press, 1986). The essays are not all of identical quality, but they gave me a good idea of the writings that might be in the library in Battle School.

I have nothing but fond memories of Rotterdam, a city of kind and generous people. The callousness toward the poor shown in this novel would be impossible today, but the business of science fiction is sometimes to show impossible nightmares.

I owe individual thanks to:

Erin and Phillip Absher, for, among other things, the lack of vomiting on the shuttle, the size of the toilet tank, and the weight of the lid;

Jane Brady, Laura Morefield, Oliver Withstandley, Matt Tolton, Kathryn H. Kidd, Kristine A. Card, and others who read the advance manuscript and made suggestions and corrections. Some annoying contradictions between *Ender's Game* and this book were thereby averted; any that remain are not errors at all, but merely subtle literary effects designed to show the difference in perception and memory between the two accounts of the same event. As my programmer friends would say, there are no bugs, only features;

Tom Doherty, my publisher; Beth Meacham, my editor; and Barbara Bova, my agent, for responding so positively to the idea of this book when I proposed it as a collaborative project and then realized I wanted to write it entirely myself. And if I still think *Urchin* was the better title for this book, it doesn't mean that I don't agree that my second title, *Ender's Shadow,* is the more marketable one;

My assistants, Scott Allen and Kathleen Bellamy, who at various times defy gravity and perform other useful miracles;

My son Geoff, who, though he is no longer the five-year-old he was when I wrote the novel *Ender's Game,* is still the model for Ender Wiggin;

My wife, Kristine, and the children who were home during the writing of this book: Emily, Charlie Ben, and Zina. Their patience with me when I was struggling to figure out the right approach to this novel was surpassed only by their patience when I finally found it and became possessed by the story. When I brought Bean home to a loving family I knew what it should look like, because I see it every day.

ROB HENDERSON, HENDERSON PHOTOGRAPHY, INC.

ORSON SCOTT CARD is the award-winning author of dozens of bestselling science fiction and fantasy novels, including the Ender quartet: *Ender's Game, Speaker for the Dead, Xenocide,* and *Children of the Mind.*

He lives in Greensboro, North Carolina.

A COMPANION VOLUME TO *ENDER'S GAME,* ONE THAT EXPANDS AND COMPLIMENTS THE FIRST, ENHANCING ITS POWER, ILLUMINATING ITS EVENTS AND ITS POWERFUL CONCLUSION.

Andrew "Ender" Wiggin was not the only child in the Battle School; he was just the best of the best. Here is the story of another of those precocious generals, the one they called Bean—the one who became Ender's right hand, his strategist, and his friend.

Bean's past was a battle just to survive on the streets of Rotterdam. He was a tiny child with a mind leagues beyond anyone else's. Bean's desperate struggle, and his remarkable success, brought him to the attention of the Battle School's recruiters, those people scouring the planet for leaders, tacticians, and generals to save Earth from the threat of alien invasion. Bean was sent into orbit, to the Battle School. And there he met Ender....

"Orson Scott Card made a strong case for being the best writer science fiction has to offer."
THE HOUSTON POST

"The publishing equivalent of a *Star Wars* blockbuster."
NEW YORK DAILY NEWS

"[*Ender's Shadow*] is entertaining, fast-paced science fiction. Don't be surprised if [it] wins the Hugo and Nebula like its acclaimed predecessor."
CNN.com

COVER ART BY LISA FALKENSTERN • TOM DOHERTY ASSOCIATES, LLC
WWW.TOR-FORGE.COM • PRINTED IN THE USA

“Card understands the human condition and has things of real value to say about it. He tells the truth well—ultimately the only criterion of greatness. *Ender’s Game* will still be finding new readers when 99 percent of the books published this year are completely forgotten.”

—Gene Wolfe

“A gripping tale of adventure in space and a scathing indictment of the military mind. Recommended.”

—*Library Journal*

“The games are fierce and consistently exciting. The cast . . . offers memorable characters. . . . And the aliens leave an intriguing heritage to mankind.”

—*Locus*

Tor Books by Orson Scott Card

Empire
The Folk of the Fringe
Future on Fire (editor)
Future on Ice (editor)
The Gate Thief
Hart's Hope
Hidden Empire
Invasive Procedures (with Aaron Johnston)
Keeper of Dreams
The Lost Gate
Lovelock (with Kathryn Kidd)
Pastwatch
Saints
Songmaster
Treason
The Worthing Saga
Wyrms

The First Formic War
Earth Unaware (with Aaron Johnston)
Earth Afire (with Aaron Johnston)

Ender
Ender's Game
Speaker for the Dead
Xenocide
Children of the Mind
Ender's Shadow
Shadow of the Hegemon
Shadow Puppets
Shadow of the Giant
First Meetings
A War of Gifts
Ender in Exile
Shadows in Flight

The Tales of Alvin Maker
Seventh Son
Red Prophet
Prentice Alvin
Alvin Journeyman
Heartfire
The Crystal City

Homecoming
The Memory of Earth
The Call of Earth
The Ships of Earth
Earthfall
Earthborn

Women of Genesis
Sarah
Rebekah
Rachel & Leah

Short Fiction
Maps in a Mirror: The Short Fiction of Orson Scott Card (hardcover)
Maps in a Mirror, Volume 1: The Changed Man (paperback)
Maps in a Mirror, Volume 2: Flux (paperback)
Maps in a Mirror, Volume 3: Cruel Miracles (paperback)
Maps in a Mirror, Volume 4: Monkey Sonatas (paperback)

ORSON SCOTT CARD

ENDER'S GAME

A TOM DOHERTY ASSOCIATES BOOK
NEW YORK

ENDER'S GAME

A Tor Book
Published by Tom Doherty Associates, LLC
175 Fifth Avenue
New York, NY 10010

www.tor-forge.com

Tor® is a registered trademark of Tom Doherty Associates, LLC.

ISBN 978-0-7653-7062-4

Revised Edition: August 1991

First Mass Market Movie Tie-In Edition: October 2013

Printed in the United States of America

10 9 8 7 6 5 4 3 2 1

For Geoffrey,
who makes me remember
how young and how old
children can be

CONTENTS

Acknowledgments

Portions of this book were recounted in my first published science fiction story, "Ender's Game," in the August 1977 *Analog*, edited by Ben Bova; his faith in me and this story are the foundation of my career.

Harriet McDougal of Tor is that rarest of editors—one who understands a story and can help the author make it exactly what he meant it to be. They don't pay her enough. Harriet's task was made more than a little easier, however, because of the excellent work of my resident editor, Kristine Card. I don't pay her enough, either.

I am grateful also to Barbara Bova, who has been my friend and agent through thin and, sometimes, thick; and to Tom Doherty, my publisher, who let me talk him into doing this book at the ABA in Dallas, which shows either his superb judgment or how weary one can get at a convention.

Introduction

It makes me a little uncomfortable, writing an introduction to *Ender's Game*. After all, the book has been in print for six years now, and in all that time, nobody has ever written to me to say, "You know, *Ender's Game* was a pretty good book, but you know what it really needs? An introduction!" And yet when a novel goes back to print for a new hardcover edition, there ought to be *something* new in it to mark the occasion (something besides the minor changes as I fix the errors and internal contradictions and stylistic excesses that have bothered me ever since the novel first appeared). So be assured—the novel stands on its own, and if you skip this intro and go straight to the story, I not only won't stand in your way, I'll even *agree* with you!

The novelet "Ender's Game" was my first published science fiction. It was based on an idea—the Battle Room—that came to me when I was sixteen years old. I had just read Isaac Asimov's *Foundation* trilogy, which was (more or less) an extrapolation of the ideas in Gibbon's *Decline and Fall of the Roman Empire,* applied to a galaxy-wide empire in some far future time.

The novel set me, not to dreaming, but to *thinking*, which is Asimov's most extraordinary ability as a fiction writer. What *would* the future be like? How would things change? What would remain the same? The premise of *Foundation* seemed to be that even though you might change the props and the actors, the play of human history is always the same. And yet that fundamentally pessimistic premise (you mean we'll *never* change?) was tempered by Asimov's idea of a group of human beings who, not through genetic change, but through learned skills, are able to understand and heal the minds of other people.

It was an idea that rang true with me, perhaps in part because of my Mormon upbringing and beliefs: Human beings may be miserable specimens, in the main, but we *can* learn, and, through learning, become decent people.

Those were some of the ideas that played through my mind as I read *Foundation*, curled on my bed—a thin mattress on a slab of plywood, a bed my father had made for me—in my basement bedroom in our little rambler on 650 East in Orem, Utah. And then, as so many science fiction readers have done over the years, I felt a strong desire to write stories that would do for others what Asimov's story had done for me.

In other genres, that desire is usually expressed by producing thinly veiled rewrites of the great work: Tolkien's disciples far too often simply rewrite Tolkien, for example. In science fiction, however, the whole point is that the ideas are fresh and startling and intriguing; you imitate the great ones, not by rewriting *their* stories, but rather by creating stories that are just as startling and new.

But new in what way? Asimov was a scientist, and approached every field of human knowledge in a scientific manner—assimilating data, combining it in new and startling ways, thinking through the implications of each new idea. I was no scientist, and unlikely ever to be one, at least not a *real* scientist—not a physicist, not a chemist, not a biologist, not even an engineer. I had no gift for mathematics and no great love for it, either. Though I relished the study of logic and languages, and virtually inhaled histories and biographies, it never occurred to me at the time that these were just as valid sources of science fiction stories as astronomy or quantum mechanics.

How, then, could I possibly come up with a science fiction idea? What did *I* actually know about anything?

At that time my older brother Bill was in the army, stationed at Fort Douglas in Salt Lake City; he was nursing a hip-to-heel cast from a bike-riding accident, however, and came home on weekends. It was then that he had met his future wife, Laura Dene Low, while attending a church meeting on the BYU campus; and it was Laura who gave me *Foundation* to read. Perhaps, then, it was natural for my thoughts to turn to things military.

To me, though, the military didn't mean the Vietnam War, which was then nearing its peak of American involvement. I had no experience of that, except for Bill's stories of the miserable life in basic training, the humiliation of officer's candidate school, and his lonely but in many ways successful life as a noncom in Korea. Far more deeply rooted in my mind was my experience, five or six years earlier, of reading Bruce Catton's three-volume *Army of the Potomac*. I remembered so well the stories of the commanders in that war—the struggle to find a Union general capable of using McClellan's magnificent army to defeat Lee and Jackson and Stuart, and then, finally, Grant, who brought death to far too many of his soldiers, but also made their deaths mean something, by grinding away at Lee, keeping him from dancing and maneuvering out of reach. It was because of Catton's history that I had stopped enjoying chess, and had to revise the rules of *Risk* in order to play it—I had come to understand something of war, and not just because of the conclusions Catton himself had reached. I found meanings of my own in that history.

I learned that history is shaped by the use of power, and that different people, leading the same army, with, therefore, approximately the same power, applied it so differently that the army seemed to change from a pack of noble fools at Fredericksburg to panicked cowards melting away at Chancellorsville, then to the grimly determined, stubborn soldiers who held the ridges at Gettysburg, and then, finally, to the disciplined, professional army that ground Lee to dust in Grant's long campaign. It wasn't the soliders who changed. It was the leader. And even though I could not then have articulated what I understood of military leadership, I knew that I *did* understand it. I understood, at levels deeper than speech, how a great military leader imposes his will on his enemy, and makes his own army a willing extension of himself.

So one morning, as my Dad drove me to Brigham Young High School along Carterville Road in the heavily wooded bottoms of the Provo River, I wondered: How would you train soldiers for combat in the future? I didn't bother thinking of new land-based weapons systems—what was on my mind, after *Foundation*, was space. Soldiers and commanders would have to think very differently in space, because the old ideas of up and down simply wouldn't apply anymore. I had read in Nordhoff's and Hall's history of World War I flying that it was very hard at first for new pilots to learn to look above and below them rather than merely to the right and left, to find the enemy approaching them in the air. How much worse, then, would it be to learn to think with no up and down at all?

The essence of training is to allow error without consequence. Three-dimensional warfare would need to be practiced in an enclosed space, so mistakes wouldn't send trainees flying off to Jupiter. It would need to offer a way to practice shooting without risk of injury; and yet trainees who were "hit" would need to be disabled, at least temporarily. The environment would need to be changeable, to simulate the different conditions of warfare—near a ship, in the midst of debris, near tiny asteroids. And it would need to have some of the confusion of real battle, so that the play-combat didn't evolve into something as rigid and formal as the meaningless marching and maneuvers that still waste an astonishing amount of a trainee's precious hours in basic training in our modern military.

The result of my speculations that morning was the Battle Room, exactly as you will see it (or have already seen it) in this book. It was a good idea, and something like it will certainly be used for training if ever there is a manned military in space. (Something very much like it has already been used in various amusement halls throughout America.)

But, having thought of the Battle Room, I hadn't the faintest idea of how to go about turning the idea into a story. It occurred to me then for the first time that the *idea* of the story is nothing compared to the importance of knowing how to find a character and a story to tell around that idea. Asimov, having had the idea of paralleling *The Decline and Fall*, still had no story; his genius—and the soul of the story—came when he personalized his history, making the psychohistorian Hari Seldon the god-figure, the planmaker, the apocalyptic prophet of the story. I had no such character, and no idea of how to make one.

Years passed. I graduated from high school as a junior (just in time—Brigham Young High School was discontinued with the class of 1968) and went on to Brigham Young University. I started there as an archaeology major, but quickly discovered that doing archaeology is unspeakably boring compared to reading the books by Thor Heyerdahl (*Aku-Aku, Kon-Tiki*), Yigael Yadin (*Masada*), and James Michener (*The Source*) that had set me dreaming. Potsherds! Better to be a *dentist* than to spend your life trying to put together fragments of old pottery in endless desert landscapes in the Middle East.

By the time I realized that not even the semi-science of archaeology was for someone as impatient as me, I was already immersed in my real career. At the time, of course, I misunderstood myself: I thought I was in theatre because I loved performing. And I *do* love performing, don't get me wrong. Give me an audience and I'll hold onto them as long as I can, on any subject. But I'm not a good actor, and theatre was not to be my career. At the time, though, all I cared about was doing plays. Directing them. Building sets and making costumes and putting on makeup for them.

And, above all, *rewriting* those *lousy* scripts. I kept thinking, Why couldn't the playwright hear how dull that speech was? This scene could so easily be punched up and made far more effective.

Then I tried my hand at writing adaptations of novels for a reader's theatre class, and my fate was sealed. I was a playwright.

People came to my plays and clapped at the end. I learned—from actors and from audiences—how to shape a scene, how to build tension, and—above all—the necessity of being harsh with your own material, excising or rewriting anything that doesn't work. I learned to separate the *story* from the *writing*, probably the most important thing that any storyteller has to learn—that there are a thousand right ways to tell a story, and ten million wrong ones, and you're a lot more likely to find one of the latter than the former your first time through the tale.

My love of theatre lasted through my mission for the LDS Church. Even while I was in São Paulo, Brazil, as a missionary, I wrote a play called *Stone Tables* about the relationship between Moses and Aaron in the book of Exodus, which had standing-room-only audiences at its premiere (which I didn't attend, since I was still in Brazil!).

At the same time, though, that original impetus to write science fiction persisted.

I had taken fiction writing courses at college, for which I don't think I ever wrote science fiction. But on the side, I had started a series of stories about people with psionic powers (I had no idea this was a sci-fi cliché at the time) that eventually grew into *The Worthing Saga*. I had even sent one of the stories off to *Analog* magazine before my mission, and on my mission I wrote several long stories in the same series (as well as a couple of stabs at mainstream stories).

In all that time, the Battle Room remained an idea in the back of my mind. It wasn't until 1975, though, that I dusted it off and tried to write it. By then I had started a theatre company that managed to do reasonably well during the first summer and then collapsed under the weight of bad luck and bad management (myself) during the fall and winter. I was deeply in debt on the pathetic salary of an editor at BYU Press. Writing was the only thing I knew how to do *besides* proofreading and editing. It was time to get serious about writing something that might actually earn some money—and, plainly, playwriting wasn't going to be it.

I first rewrote and sent out "Tinker," the first Worthing story I wrote and the one that was still most effective. I got a rejection letter from Ben Bova at *Analog*, pointing out that "Tinker" simply didn't feel like science fiction—it felt like fantasy. So the Worthing stories were out for the time being.

What was left? The old Battle Room idea. It happened one spring day that a friend of mine, Tammy Mikkelson, was taking her boss's children to the circus in Salt Lake City; would I like to come along? I would. And since there was no ticket for me (and I've always detested the circus anyway—the clowns drive me up a wall), I spent the hours of the performance out on the lawn of the Salt Palace with a notebook on my lap, writing "Ender's Game" as I had written all my plays, in longhand on narrow-ruled paper. "Remember," said Ender. "The enemy's gate is *down*."

Maybe it was because of the children in the car on the way up that I decided that the trainees in the Battle Room were so young. Maybe it was because I, barely an adolescent myself, understood only childhood well enough to write about it. Or maybe it was because of something that impressed me in Catton's *Army of the Potomac*: that the soldiers were all so young and innocent. That they shot and bayoneted the enemy, and then slipped across the neutral ground between armies to trade tobacco, jokes, liquor, and food. Even though it was a deadly game, and the suffering and fear were terrible and real, it was still a game played by children, not all that different from the wargames my brothers and I had played, firing water-filled squirt bottles at each other.

"Ender's Game" was written and sold. I knew it was a strong story because *I* cared about it and believed in it. I had no idea that it would have the effect it had on the science fiction audience. While most people ignored it, of course, and continue to live full and happy lives without reading it or anything else by me, there was still a surprisingly large group who responded to the story with some fervency.

Ignored on the Nebula ballot, "Ender's Game" got onto the Hugo ballot and came in second. More to the point, I was awarded the John W. Campbell Award for best new writer. Without doubt, "Ender's Game" wasn't just my first sale—it was the launching pad of my career.

The same story did it again in 1985, when I rewrote it at novel length—the book, now slightly revised, that you are holding in your hands. At that point I thought of *Ender's Game*, the novel, existing only to set up the much more powerful (I thought) story of *Speaker for the Dead*. But when I finished the novel, I knew that the story had new strength. I had learned a great deal, about life and about writing, in the decade since I wrote the novelet, and it came together for the first time in this book. Again the audience was kind to me: the Nebula and Hugo awards, foreign translations, and strong, steady sales that, for the first time in my career, actually earned out my advance and allowed me to receive royalties.

But it wasn't just a matter of having a quiet little cult novel that brought in a steady income. There was something more to the way that people responded to *Ender's Game*.

For one thing, the people that hated it *really* hated it. The attacks on the novel—and on me—were astonishing. Some of it I expected—I have a master's degree in literature, and in writing *Ender's Game* I deliberately avoided all the little literary games and gimmicks that make "fine" writing so impenetrable to the general audience. All the layers of meaning are there to be decoded, if you like to play the game of literary criticism—but if you don't care to play that game, that's fine with me. I designed *Ender's Game* to be as clear and accessible as any story of mine could possibly be. My goal was that the reader wouldn't have to be trained in literature or even in science fiction to receive the tale in its simplest, purest form. And, since a great many writers and critics have based their entire careers on the premise that anything that the general public can understand without mediation is worthless drivel, it is not surprising that they found my little novel to be despicable. If everybody came to agree that stories should be told this clearly, the professors of literature would be out of a job, and the writers of obscure, encoded fiction would be, not honored, but pitied for their impenetrability.

For some people, however, the loathing for *Ender's Game* transcended mere artistic argument. I recall a letter to the editor of *Isaac Asimov's Science Fiction Magazine*, in which a woman who worked as a guidance counselor for gifted children reported that she had only picked up *Ender's Game* to read it because her son had kept telling her it was a wonderful book. She read it and loathed it. Of course, I wondered what kind of guidance counselor would hold her son's tastes up to public ridicule, but the criticism that left me most flabbergasted was her assertion that my depiction of gifted children was hopelessly unrealistic. They just don't talk like that, she said. The don't *think* like that.

And it wasn't just her. There have been others with that criticism. Thus I began to realize that, as it is, *Ender's Game* disturbs some people because it challenges their assumptions about reality. In fact, the novel's very clarity may make it *more* challenging, simply because the story's vision of the world is so relentlessly plain. It was important to her, and to others, to believe that children don't actually think or speak the way the children in *Ender's Game* think and speak.

Yet I knew—I *knew*—that this was one of the truest things about *Ender's Game*. In fact, I realized in retrospect that this may indeed be part of the reason why it was so important to me, there on the lawn in front of the Salt

Palace, to write a story in which gifted children are trained to fight in adult wars. Because never in my entire childhood did I feel like a child. I felt like a person all along—the same person that I am today. I never felt that I spoke childishly. I never felt that my emotions and desires were somehow less real than adult emotions and desires. And in writing *Ender's Game*, I forced the audience to experience the lives of these children from that perspective—the perspective in which their feelings and decisions are just as real and important as any adult's.

The nasty side of myself wanted to answer that guidance counselor by saying, The only reason you don't think gifted children talk this way is because they know better than to talk this way in front of *you*. But the truer answer is that *Ender's Game* asserts the personhood of children, and those who are used to thinking of children in another way—especially those whose whole career is based on that—are going to find *Ender's Game* a very unpleasant place to live. Children are a perpetual, self-renewing underclass, helpless to escape from the decisions of adults until they become adults themselves. And *Ender's Game*, seen in that context, might even be a sort of revolutionary tract.

Because the book *does* ring true with the children who read it. The highest praise I ever received for a book of mine was when the school librarian at Farrer Junior High in Provo, Utah, told me, "You know, *Ender's Game* is our most-lost book."

And then there are the letters. This one, for instance, which I received in March of 1991:

> Dear Mr. Card,
>
> I am writing to you on behalf of myself and my twelve friends and fellow students who joined me at a two-week residential program for gifted and talented students at Purdue University this summer. We attended the class, "Philosophy and Science Fiction," instructed by Peter Robinson, and we range in age from thirteen through fifteen.

> We are all in about the same position; we are very intellectually oriented and have found few people at home who share this trait. Hence, most of us are lonely, and have been since kindergarten. When teachers continually compliment you, your chances of "fitting in" are about nil.
>
> All our lives we've unconsciously been living by the philosophy, "The only way to gain respect is doing so well you can't be ignored." And, for me and Mike, at least, "beating the system" at school is how we've chosen to do this. Both Mike and I plan to be in calculus our second year of high school, schedules permitting. (Both of us are interested in science/math related careers.) Not to get me wrong; we're all bright and at the top of our class. However, in choosing these paths, most of us have wound up satisfied in ourselves, but very lonely.
>
> This is why *Ender's Game* and *Speaker for the Dead* really hit home for us. These books were our "texts" for the class. We would read one hundred to two hundred pages per night and then discuss them (and other short stories and essays) during the day. At Purdue, it wasn't a "classroom" discussion, however. It was a group of friends talking about how their feelings and philosophies corresponded to or differed from the books'.
>
> You couldn't *imagine* the impact your books had on us; *we* are the Enders of today. Almost everything written in *Ender's Game* and *Speaker* applied to each one of us on a very, very personal level. No, the situation isn't as drastic today, but all the feelings are there. Both your books, along with the excellent work of Peter Robinson, unified us into a tight web of people.

Ingrid's letter goes on, talking of the *Phoenix Rising*, the magazine that these students publish together in order to maintain their sense of community. (In response I have given them this introduction to publish in their magazine before its appearance in book form.)

Of course, I'm always glad when people like a story of mine; but something much more important is gong on here. These readers found that *Ender's Game* was not merely a "mythic" story, dealing with general truths, but something much more personal: To them, *Ender's Game* was an epic tale, a story that expressed who they are as a community, a story that distinguished them from the other people around them. They didn't love Ender, or pity Ender (a frequent adult response); they *were* Ender, all of them. Ender's experience was not foreign or strange to them; in their minds, Ender's life echoed their own lives. The truth of the story was not truth in general, but *their* truth.

Stories can be read so differently—even clear stories, even stories that deliberately avoid surface ambiguities. For instance, here's another letter, likewise one that I received in mid-March of 1991. It was written on 16 February and postmarked the 18th. Those dates are important.

> Mr. Card,
>
> I'm an army aviator waiting out a sandstorm in Saudi Arabia. I've always wanted to write you and since my future is in doubt—I know when the ground war will begin—I decided today would be the day I'd write.
>
> I read *Ender's Game* during flight school four years ago. I'm a warrant officer, and our school, at least the first six weeks, is very different from the commissioned officers'. I was eighteen years old when I arrived at Ft. Rucker to start flight training, and the first six weeks almost beat me. Ender gave me courage then and many times after that. I've experienced the tiredness Ender felt, the kind that goes deep to your soul. It would be interesting to know what caused you to feel the same way. No one

could describe it unless they experienced it, but I understand how personal that can be. There is one other novel that describes that frame of soul and mind that I cherish as much as *Ender's Game*. It's called *Armour* and its author is John Steakley. Ender and Felix [the protagonist of *Armour*] are always close by in my mind. Sadly, there is no sequel to *Armour* as there is to *Ender's Game*.

We are the bastards of military aviation. Our helicopters may be the best in the world, but the equipment we wear and the systems in our helicopter, such as the navigation instruments, are at least twenty years behind the Navy and Air Force. I am very happy with the Air Force's ability to bomb with precision, but if they miss, the bombs still land on the enemy's territory. If we screw up, the guys we haul to the battle, the "grunts," die. We don't even have the armour plate for our chests—"chicken plate"—that the helicopter pilots did in Vietnam. Last year in El Salvador, army aviators flew a couple of civilian VIPs and twenty reporters over guerrilla-controlled territory and there were no flares in their launchers to counteract the heat-seeking missiles we knew the rebels had. One of our pilots and a crew member were killed last year on a training flight because they flew the sling load they were carrying into the trees at 70 miles an hour. It could have been prevented if our night vision goggles had a heads-up display like the Air Force has had for forty years. I'm sure you heard about Colonel Pickett being shot down in a Huey in El Salvador just a few months ago. That type of aircraft is at least thirty years old and there are no survivability measures installed. He was a good man, I knew him.

The reason I told you about these things is because I wanted to paint a picture for you. I love

> my job but we aren't like the "zoomies" that everyone makes movies about. We do our job with less technology, less political support, less recognition, and more risk than the rest, while the threat to us continues to modernize at an unbelievable rate. I'm not asking for sympathy but I was wondering if you and Mr. Steakley could write a novel about helicopters and the men that fly them for the Army twenty years in the future. There are many of us that read science fiction and after I read *Ender's Game* and *Armour* three times each I started letting my comrades read them. My wife cried when she read *Ender's Game*. There is a following here for a book like the one I requested. We have no speaker for us, the ones that will soon die, or the ones that survive. . .

As with those gifted young students who read this book as "their" story, this soldier—who, like most but not all of the Army aviators in the Gulf War, survived—did not read *Ender's Game* as a "work of literature." He read it as epic, as a story that helped define his community. It was not his only epic, of course—*Armour*, John Steakley's fine novel, was an equal candidate to be part of his self-story. What matters most, though, was his clear sense that, no matter how much these stories spoke to him, they were still not *exactly* his community's epic. He still felt the need for a "speaker for the dead" and for the living. He still felt a hunger, especially at a time when death might well be near, to have his own story, his friends' stories, told.

Why else do we read fiction, anyway? Not to be impressed by somebody's dazzling language—or at least I hope that's not our reason. I think that most of us, anyway, read these stories that we know are not "true" because we're hungry for another kind of truth: The mythic truth about human nature in general, the particular truth about those life-communities that define our own identity, and the most specific truth of all: our own self-story. Fiction, because it is not about somebody who actually lived in the real world, always has the possibility of being about ourself.

Ender's Game is a story about gifted children. It is also a story about soldiers. Captain John F. Schmitt, the author of the Marine Corp's *Warfighting,* the most brilliant concise book of military strategy ever written by an American (and a proponent of the kind of thinking that was at the heart of the allied victory in the Gulf War), found *Ender's Game* to be a useful enough story about the nature of leadership to use it in courses he taught at the Marine University at Quantico. Watauga College, the interdisciplinary studies program at Appalachian State University—as *un*military a community as you could ever hope to find!—uses *Ender's Game* for completely different purposes—to talk about problem-solving and the self-creation of the individual. A graduate student in Toronto explored the political ideas in *Ender's Game*. A writer and critic at Pepperdine has seen *Ender's Game* as, in some ways, religious fiction.

All these uses are valid; all these readings of the book are "correct." For all these readers have placed themselves inside this story, not as spectators, but as participants, and so have looked at the world of *Ender's Game,* not with my eyes only, but also with their own.

This is the essence of the transaction between storyteller and audience. The "true" story is not the one that exists in my mind; it is *certainly* not the written words on the bound paper that you hold in your hands. The story in my mind is nothing but a hope; the text of the story is the tool I created in order to try to make that hope a reality. The story itself, the true story, is the one that the audience members create in their minds, guided and shaped by my text, but then transformed, elucidated, expanded, edited, and clarified by their own experience, their own desires, their own hopes and fears.

The story of *Ender's Game* is not this book, though it has that title emblazoned on it. The story is one that you and I will construct together in your memory. If the story means anything to you at all, then when you remember it afterward, think of it, not as something I created, but rather as something that we made together.

Orson Scott Card
Greensboro, North Carolina
March 1991

1

Third

"I've watched through his eyes, I've listened through his ears, and I tell you he's the one. Or at least as close as we're going to get."

"That's what you said about the brother."

"The brother tested out impossible. For other reasons. Nothing to do with his ability."

"Same with the sister. And there are doubts about him. He's too malleable. Too willing to submerge himself in someone else's will."

"Not if the other person is his enemy."

"So what do we do? Surround him with enemies all the time?"

"If we have to."

"I thought you said you liked this kid."

"If the buggers get him, they'll make me look like his favorite uncle."

"All right. We're saving the world, after all. Take him."

—

The monitor lady smiled very nicely and tousled his hair and said, "Andrew, I suppose by now you're just absolutely sick of having that horrid monitor. Well, I have good news for you. That monitor is going to come out today. We're going to take it right out, and it won't hurt a bit."

Ender nodded. It was a lie, of course, that it wouldn't hurt a bit. But since adults always said it when it *was* going to hurt, he could count on that statement as an accurate prediction of the future. Sometimes lies were more dependable than the truth.

"So if you'll just come over here, Andrew, just sit right up here on the examining table. The doctor will be in to see you in a moment."

The monitor gone. Ender tried to imagine the little device missing from the back of his neck. I'll roll over on my back in bed and it won't be pressing there. I won't feel it tingling and taking up the heat when I shower.

And Peter won't hate me anymore. I'll come home and show him that the monitor's gone, and he'll see that I didn't make it, either. That I'll just be a normal kid now, like him. That won't be so bad then. He'll forgive me that I had my monitor a whole year longer than he had his. We'll be—

Not friends, probably. No, Peter was too dangerous. Peter got so angry. Brothers, though. Not enemies, not friends, but brothers—able to live in the same house. He won't hate me, he'll just leave me alone. And when he wants to play buggers and astronauts, maybe I won't have to play, maybe I can just go read a book.

But Ender knew, even as he thought it, that Peter wouldn't leave him alone. There was something in Peter's eyes, when he was in his mad mood, and whenever Ender saw that look, that glint, he knew that the one thing Peter would *not* do was leave him alone. I'm practicing piano, Ender. Come turn the pages for me. Oh, is the monitor boy too busy to help his brother? Is he too smart? Got to go kill some buggers, astronaut? No, no, I don't *want* your help. I can do it on my own, you little bastard, you little *Third*.

"This won't take long, Andrew," said the doctor.

Ender nodded.

"It's designed to be removed. Without infection, without damage. But there'll be some tickling, and some people say they have a feeling of something *missing*. You'll keep looking around for something, something you were looking for, but you can't find it, and you can't remember what it was. So I'll tell you. It's the monitor you're looking for, and it isn't there. In a few days that feeling will pass."

The doctor was twisting something at the back of Ender's head. Suddenly a pain stabbed through him like a needle from his neck to his groin. Ender felt his back spasm, and his body arched violently backward; his head struck the bed. He could feel his legs thrashing, and his hands were clenching each other, wringing each other so tightly that they arched.

"Deedee!" shouted the doctor. "I need you!" The nurse ran in, gasped. "Got to relax these muscles. Get it to me, now! What are you waiting for!"

Something changed hands; Ender could not see. He lurched to one side and fell off the examining table. "Catch him!" cried the nurse.

"Just hold him steady—"

"You hold him, doctor, he's too strong for me—"

"Not the whole thing! You'll stop his heart—"

Ender felt a needle enter his back just above the neck of his shirt. It burned, but wherever in him the fire spread, his muscles gradually unclenched. Now he could cry for the fear and pain of it.

"Are you all right, Andrew?" the nurse asked.

Andrew could not remember how to speak. They lifted him onto the table. They checked his pulse, did other things; he did not understand it all.

The doctor was trembling; his voice shook as he spoke. "They leave these things in the kids for three years, what do they expect? We could have switched him off, do you realize that? We could have unplugged his brain for all time.''

''When does the drug wear off?'' asked the nurse.

''Keep him here for at least an hour. Watch him. If he doesn't start talking in fifteen minutes, call me. Could have unplugged him forever. I don't have the brains of a bugger.''

—

He got back to Miss Pumphrey's class only fifteen minutes before the closing bell. He was still a little unsteady on his feet.

''Are you all right, Andrew?'' asked Miss Pumphrey.

He nodded.

''Were you ill?''

He shook his head.

''You don't look well.''

''I'm OK.''

''You'd better sit down, Andrew.''

He started toward his seat, but stopped. Now what was I looking for? I can't think what I was looking for.

''Your seat is over there,'' said Miss Pumphrey.

He sat down, but it was something else he needed, something he had lost. I'll find it later.

''Your monitor,'' whispered the girl behind him.

Andrew shrugged.

''His monitor,'' she whispered to the others.

Andrew reached up and felt his neck. There was a bandaid. It was gone. He was just like everybody else now.

''Washed out, Andy?'' asked a boy who sat across the aisle and behind him. Couldn't think of his name. Peter. No, that was someone else.

''Quiet, Mr. Stilson,'' said Miss Pumphrey. Stilson smirked.

Miss Pumphrey talked about multiplication. Ender doodled on his desk, drawing contour maps of mountainous islands and then telling his desk to display them in three dimensions from every angle. The teacher would know, of course, that he wasn't paying attention, but she wouldn't bother him. He always knew the answer, even when she thought he wasn't paying attention.

In the corner of his desk a word appeared and began marching around the perimeter of the desk. It was upside down and backward at first, but Ender knew what it said long before it reached the bottom of the desk and turned right side up.

THIRD

Ender smiled. He was the one who had figured out how to send messages and make them march—even as his secret enemy called him names, the method of delivery praised him. It was not *his* fault he was a Third. It was the government's idea, they were the ones who authorized it—how else could a Third like Ender have got into school? And now the monitor was gone. The experiment entitled Andrew Wiggin hadn't worked out after all. If they could, he was sure they would like to rescind the waivers that had allowed him to be born at all. Didn't work, so erase the experiment.

The bell rang. Everyone signed off their desks or hurriedly typed in reminders to themselves. Some were dumping lessons or data into their computers at home. A few gathered at the printers while something they wanted to show was printed out. Ender spread his hands over the child-size keyboard near the edge of the desk and wondered what it would feel like to have hands as large as a grown-up's. They must feel so big and awkward, thick stubby fingers and beefy palms. Of course, they had bigger keyboards—but how could their thick fingers draw a fine line, the way Ender could, a thin line so precise that he could make it spiral seventy-nine times from the center to the edge of the desk without the lines ever touching or overlapping. It gave him something to do while the teacher droned on about arithmetic. Arithmetic! Valentine had taught him arithmetic when he was three.

"Are you all right, Andrew?"

"Yes, ma'am."

"You'll miss the bus."

Ender nodded and got up. The other kids were gone. They would be waiting, though, the bad ones. His monitor wasn't perched on his neck, hearing what he heard and seeing what he saw. They could say what they liked. They might even hit him now—no one could see them anymore, and so no one would come to Ender's rescue. There were advantages to the monitor, and he would miss them.

It was Stilson, of course. He wasn't bigger than most other kids, but he was bigger than Ender. And he had some others with him. He always did.

"Hey Third."

Don't answer. Nothing to say.

"Hey, Third, we're talkin to you, Third, hey bugger-lover, we're talkin to you."

Can't think of anything to answer. Anything I say will make it worse. So will saying nothing.

"Hey, Third, hey, turd, you flunked out, huh? Thought you were better than us, but you lost your little birdie, Thirdie, got a bandaid on your neck."

"Are you going to let me through?" Ender asked.

"Are we going to let him through? Should we let him through?" They all laughed. "Sure we'll let you through. First we'll let your arm through, then your butt through, then maybe a piece of your knee."

The others chimed in now. "Lost your birdie, Thirdie. Lost your birdie, Thirdie."

Stilson began pushing him with one hand; someone behind him then pushed him toward Stilson.

"See-saw, marjorie daw," somebody said.

"Tennis!"

"Ping-pong!"

This would not have a happy ending. So Ender decided that he'd rather not be the unhappiest at the end. The next time Stilson's arm came out to push him, Ender grabbed at it. He missed.

"Oh, gonna fight me, huh? Gonna fight me, Thirdie?"

The people behind Ender grabbed at him, to hold him.

Ender did not feel like laughing, but he laughed. "You mean it takes this many of you to fight one Third?"

"We're *people*, not *Thirds*, turd face. You're about as strong as a fart!"

But they let go of him. And as soon as they did, Ender kicked out high and hard, catching Stilson square in the breastbone. He dropped. It took Ender by surprise—he hadn't thought to put Stilson on the ground with one kick. It didn't occur to him that Stilson didn't take a fight like this seriously, that he wasn't prepared for a truly desperate blow.

For a moment, the others backed away and Stilson lay motionless. They were all wondering if he was dead. Ender, however, was trying to figure out a way to forestall vengeance. To keep them from taking him in a pack tomorrow. I have to win this now, and for all time, or I'll fight it every day and it will get worse and worse.

Ender knew the unspoken rules of manly warfare, even though he was only six. It was forbidden to strike the opponent who lay helpless on the ground; only an animal would do that.

So Ender walked to Stilson's supine body and kicked him again, viciously, in the ribs. Stilson groaned and rolled away from him. Ender walked around him and kicked him again, in the crotch. Stilson could not make a sound; he only doubled up and tears streamed out of his eyes.

Then Ender looked at the others coldly. "You might be having some idea of ganging up on me. You could probably beat me up pretty bad. But just remember what I do to people who try to hurt me. From then on you'd be wondering when I'd get you, and how bad it would be." He kicked Stilson in the face. Blood from his nose spattered the ground nearby. "It wouldn't be this bad," Ender said. "It would be worse."

He turned and walked away. Nobody followed him. He turned a corner into the corridor leading to the bus stop. He could hear the boys behind him saying, "Geez. Look at him. He's wasted." Ender leaned his head against the wall of the corridor and cried until the bus came. I am just like Peter. Take my monitor away, and I am just like Peter.

2

Peter

"All right, it's off. How's he doing."

"You live inside somebody's body for a few years, you get used to it. I look at his face now. I can't tell what's going on. I'm not used to seeing his facial expressions. I'm used to feeling them."

"Come on, we're not talking about psychoanalysis here. We're soldiers, not witch doctors. You just saw him beat the guts out of the leader of a gang."

"He was thorough. He didn't just beat him, he beat him deep. Like Mazer Rackham at the—"

"Spare me. So in the judgment of the committee, he passes."

"Mostly. Let's see what he does with his brother, now that the monitor's off."

"His brother. Aren't you afraid of what his brother will do to *him*?"

"You were the one who told me that this wasn't a no-risk business."

"I went back through some of the tapes. I can't help it. I like the kid. I think we're going to screw him up."

"Of course we are. It's our job. We're the wicked witch. We promise gingerbread, but we eat the little bastards alive."

"I'm sorry, Ender," Valentine whispered. She was looking at the bandaid on his neck.

Ender touched the wall and the door closed behind him. "I don't care. I'm glad it's gone."

"What's gone?" Peter walked into the parlor, chewing on a mouthful of bread and peanut butter.

Ender did not see Peter as the beautiful ten-year-old boy that grown-ups saw, with dark, thick, tousled hair and a face that could have belonged to Alexander the Great. Ender looked at Peter only to detect anger or boredom, the dangerous moods that almost always led to pain. Now as Peter's eyes discovered the bandaid on his neck, the telltale flicker of anger appeared.

Valentine saw it too. "Now he's like us," she said, trying to soothe him before he had time to strike.

But Peter would not be soothed. "Like us? He keeps the little sucker till he's six years old. When did you lose yours? You were three. I lost mine before I was five. *He* almost made it, little bastard, little bugger."

This is all right, Ender thought. Talk and talk, Peter. Talk is fine.

"Well, now your guardian angels aren't watching over you," Peter said. "Now they aren't checking to see if you feel pain, listening to hear what I'm saying, seeing what I'm doing to you. How about that? How about it?"

Ender shrugged.

Suddenly Peter smiled and clapped his hands together in a mockery of good cheer. "Let's play buggers and astronauts," he said.

"Where's Mom?" asked Valentine.

"Out," said Peter. "I'm in charge."

"I think I'll call Daddy."

"Call away," said Peter. "You know he's never in."

"I'll play," Ender said.

"You be the bugger," said Peter.

"Let him be the astronaut for once," Valentine said.

"Keep your fat face out of it, fart mouth," said Peter. "Come on upstairs and choose your weapons."

It would not be a good game, Ender knew. It was not a question of winning. When kids played in the corridors, whole troops of them, the buggers never won, and sometimes the games got mean. But here in their flat, the game would start mean, and the bugger couldn't just go empty and quit the way buggers did in the real wars. The bugger was in it until the astronaut decided it was over.

Peter opened his bottom drawer and took out the bugger mask. Mother had got upset at him when Peter bought it, but Dad pointed out that the war wouldn't go away just because you hid bugger masks and wouldn't let your kids play with make-believe laser guns. Better to play the war games, and have a better chance of surviving when the buggers came again.

If I survive the games, thought Ender. He put on the mask. It closed him in like a hand pressed tight against his face. But this isn't how it feels to be a bugger, thought Ender. They don't wear this face like a mask, it *is* their face. On their home worlds, do the buggers put on human masks, and play? And what do they call us? Slimies, because we're so soft and oily compared to them?

"Watch out, Slimy," Ender said.

He could barely see Peter through the eyeholes. Peter smiled at him. "Slimy, huh? Well, bugger-wugger, let's see how to break that face of yours."

Ender couldn't see it coming, except a slight shift of Peter's weight; the mask cut out his peripheral vision. Suddenly there was the pain and pressure of a blow to the side of his head; he lost balance, fell that way.

"Don't see too well, do you, bugger?" said Peter.

Ender began to take off the mask. Peter put his toe against Ender's groin. "Don't take off the mask," Peter said.

Ender pulled the mask down into place, took his hands away.

Peter pressed with his foot. Pain shot through Ender; he doubled up.

"Lie flat, bugger. We're gonna vivisect you, bugger. At long last we've got one of you alive, and we're going to see how you work."

"Peter, stop it," Ender said.

"Peter, stop it. Very good. So you buggers can guess our names. You can make yourselves sound like pathetic, cute little children so we'll love you and be nice to you. But it doesn't work. I can see you for what you really are. They meant you to be human, little Third, but you're really a bugger, and now it shows."

He lifted his foot, took a step, and then knelt on Ender, his knee pressing into Ender's belly just below the breastbone. He put more and more of his weight on Ender. It became hard to breathe.

"I could kill you like this," Peter whispered. "Just press and press until you're dead. And I could say that I didn't know it would hurt you, that we were just playing, and they'd believe me, and everything would be fine. And you'd be dead. Everything would be fine."

Ender could not speak; the breath was being forced from his lungs. Peter might mean it. Probably didn't mean it, but then he might.

"I do mean it," Peter said. "Whatever you think, I mean it. They only authorized you because I was so promising. But I didn't pan out. You did better. They think you're better. But I don't want a better little brother, Ender. I don't want a Third."

"I'll tell," Valentine said from the doorway.

"No one would believe you."

"They'd believe me."

"Then you're dead, too, sweet little sister."

"Oh, yes," said Valentine. "They'll believe that. 'I didn't know it would kill Andrew. And when he was dead, I didn't know it would kill Valentine *too*.' "

The pressure let up a little.

"So. Not today. But someday you two won't be together. And there'll be an accident."

"You're all talk," Valentine said. "You don't mean any of it."

"I don't?"

"And do you know why you don't mean it?" Valentine asked. "Because you want to be in government someday. You want to be elected. And they won't elect you if your opponents can dig up the fact that your brother and sister both died in suspicious accidents when they were little. Especially because of the letter I've put in my secret file in the city library, which will be opened in the event of my death."

"Don't give me that kind of crap," Peter said.

"It says, I didn't die a natural death. Peter killed me, and if he hasn't already killed Andrew, he will soon. Not enough to convict you, but enough to keep you from ever getting elected."

"You're his monitor now," said Peter. "You better watch him, day and night. You better be there."

"Ender and I aren't stupid. We scored as well as you did on everything. Better on some things. We're all such wonderfully bright children. You're not the smartest, Peter, just the biggest."

"Oh, I know. But there'll come a day when you aren't there with him, when you forget. And suddenly you'll remember, and you'll rush to him, and there he'll be, perfectly all right. And the next time you won't worry so much, and you won't come so fast. And every time, he'll be all right. And you'll think that I forgot. Even though you'll remember that I said this, you'll think that I forgot. And years will pass. And then there'll be a terrible accident, and I'll find his body, and I'll cry and cry over him, and you'll remember this conversation, Vally, but you'll be ashamed of yourself for remembering, because you'll know that I changed, that it really was an accident, that it's cruel of you even to remember what I said in a childhood quarrel. Except that it'll be true. I'm gonna save this up, and he's gonna die, and you won't do a thing, not a thing. But you go on believing that I'm just the biggest."

"The biggest asshole," Valentine said.

Peter leaped to his feet and started for her. She shied away. Ender pried off his mask. Peter flopped back on his bed and started to laugh. Loud, but with real mirth, tears coming to his eyes. "Oh, you guys are just super, just the biggest suckers on the planet earth."

"Now he's going to tell us it was all a joke," Valentine said.

"Not a joke, a game. I can make you guys believe anything. I can make you dance around like puppets." In a phony monster voice he said, "I'm going to kill you and chop you into little pieces and put you into the garbage hole." He laughed again. "Biggest suckers in the solar system."

Ender stood there watching him laugh and thought of Stilson, thought of how it felt to crunch into his body. This is who needed it. This is who should have got it.

As if she could read his mind, Valentine whispered, "No, Ender."

Peter suddenly rolled to the side, flipped off the bed, and got in position for a fight. "Oh, yes, Ender," he said. "Any time, Ender."

Ender lifted his right leg and took off his shoe. He held it up. "See there, on the toe? That's blood, Peter. It's not mine."

"Ooh. Ooh, I'm gonna die, I'm gonna die. Ender squished a capper-tiller and now he's gonna squish me."

There was no getting to him. Peter was a murderer at heart, and nobody knew it but Valentine and Ender.

Mother came home and commiserated with Ender about

the monitor. Father came home and kept saying it was such a wonderful surprise, they had such fantastic children that the government told them to have three, and now the government didn't want to take any of them after all, so here they were with three, they still had a Third . . . until Ender wanted to scream at him, I know I'm a Third, I know it, if you want I'll go away so you don't have to be embarrassed in front of everybody, I'm sorry I lost the monitor and now you have three kids and no obvious explanation, so inconvenient for you, I'm sorry sorry sorry.

He lay in bed staring upward into the darkness. On the bunk above him, he could hear Peter turning and tossing restlessly. Then Peter slid off the bunk and walked out of the room. Ender heard the hushing sound of the toilet clearing; then Peter stood silhouetted in the doorway.

He thinks I'm asleep. He's going to kill me.

Peter walked to the bed, and sure enough, he did not lift himself up to his bed. Instead he came and stood by Ender's head.

But he did not reach for a pillow to smother Ender. He did not have a weapon.

He whispered, "Ender, I'm sorry, I'm sorry, I know how it feels, I'm sorry, I'm your brother, I love you."

A long time later, Peter's even breathing said that he was asleep. Ender peeled the bandaid from his neck. And for the second time that day he cried.

3

Graff

"The sister is our weak link. He really loves her."

"I know. She can undo it all, from the start. He won't want to leave her."

"So, what are you going to do?"

"Persuade him that he wants to come with us more than he wants to stay with her."

"How will you do that?"

"I'll lie to him."

"And if that doesn't work?"

"Then I'll tell the truth. We're allowed to do that in emergencies. We can't plan for everything, you know."

Ender wasn't very hungry during breakfast. He kept wondering what it would be like at school. Facing Stilson after yesterday's fight. What Stilson's friends would do. Probably nothing, but he couldn't be sure. He didn't want to go.

"You're not eating, Andrew," his mother said.

Peter came into the room. ''Morning, Ender. Thanks for leaving your slimy washcloth in the middle of the shower.''

''Just for you,'' Ender murmured.

''Andrew, you have to eat.''

Ender held out his wrists, a gesture that said, So feed it to me through a needle.

''Very funny,'' Mother said. ''I try to be concerned, but it makes no difference to my genius children.''

''It was all your genes that made us geniuses, Mom,'' said Peter. ''We sure didn't get any from Dad.''

''I heard that,'' Father said, not looking up from the news that was being displayed on the table while he ate.

''It would've been wasted if you hadn't.''

The table beeped. Someone was at the door.

''Who is it?'' Mother asked.

Father thumbed a key and a man appeared on his video. He was wearing the only military uniform that meant anything anymore, the I.F., the International Fleet.

''I thought it was over,'' said Father.

Peter said nothing, just poured milk over his cereal.

And Ender thought, Maybe I won't have to go to school today after all.

Father coded the door open and got up from the table. ''I'll see to it,'' he said. ''Stay and eat.''

They stayed, but they didn't eat. A few moments later, Father came back into the room and beckoned to Mother.

''You're in deep poo,'' said Peter. ''They found out what you did to that kid at school, and now they're gonna make you do time out in the Belt.''

''I'm only six, moron, I'm a juvenile.''

''You're a Third, turd. You've got no rights.''

Valentine came in, her hair in a sleepy halo around her face. ''Where's Mom and Dad? I'm too sick to go to school.''

''Another oral exam, huh?'' Peter said.

''Shut up, Peter,'' said Valentine.

"You should relax and enjoy it," said Peter. "It could be worse."

"I don't know how."

"It could be an anal exam."

"Hyuk hyuk," Valentine said. "Where are Mother and Father?"

"Talking to a guy from IF."

Instinctively she looked at Ender. After all, for years they had expected someone to come and tell them that Ender had passed, that Ender was needed.

"That's right, look at him," Peter said. "But it might be me, you know. They might have realized I was the best of the lot after all." Peter's feelings were hurt, and so he was being a snot, as usual.

The door opened. "Ender," said Father, "you better come in here."

"Sorry, Peter," Valentine taunted.

Father glowered. "Children, this is no laughing matter."

Ender followed Father into the parlor. The I.F. officer rose to his feet when they entered, but he did not extend a hand to Ender.

Mother was twisting her wedding band on her finger. "Andrew," she said, "I never thought you were the kind to get in a fight."

"The Stilson boy is in the hospital," Father said. "You really did a number on him. With your shoe, Ender. That wasn't exactly fair."

Ender shook his head. He had expected someone from the school to come about Stilson, not an officer of the fleet. This was more serious than he had thought. And yet he couldn't think what else he could have done.

"Do you have any explanation for your behavior, young man?" asked the officer.

Ender shook his head again. He didn't know what to say, and he was afraid to reveal himself to be any more monstrous than his actions had made him out to be. I'll take it, whatever the punishment is, he thought. Let's get it over with.

"We're willing to consider extenuating circumstances," the officer said. "But I must tell you it doesn't look good. Kicking him in the groin, kicking him repeatedly in the face and body when he was down—it sounds like you really enjoyed it."

"I didn't," Ender whispered.

"Then why did you do it?"

"He had his gang there," Ender said.

"So? This excuses anything?"

"No."

"Tell me why you kept on kicking him. You had already won."

"Knocking him down won the first fight. I wanted to win all the next ones, too. So they'd leave me alone." Ender couldn't help it, he was too afraid, too ashamed of his own acts; though he tried not to, he cried again. Ender did not like to cry and rarely did; now, in less than a day, he had done it three times. And each time was worse. To cry in front of his mother and father and this military man, that was shameful. "You took away the monitor," Ender said. "I had to take care of myself, didn't I?"

"Ender, you should have asked a grown-up for help," Father began.

But the officer stood up and stepped across the room to Ender. He held out his hand. "My name is Graff, Ender. Colonel Hyrum Graff. I'm director of primary training at Battle School in the Belt. I've come to invite you to enter the school."

After all. "But the monitor—"

"The final step in your testing was to see what would happen when the monitor came off. We don't always do it that way, but in your case—"

"And he passed?" Mother was incredulous. "Putting the Stilson boy in the hospital? What would you have done if Andrew had killed him, given him a medal?"

"It isn't *what* he did, Mrs. Wiggin. It's why." Colonel Graff handed her a folder full of papers. "Here are the requisitions. Your son has been cleared by the I.F. Selective Service. Of course we already have your consent, granted in writing at the time conception was confirmed, or he could not have been born. He has been ours from then, if he qualified.''

Father's voice was trembling as he spoke. ''It's not very kind of you, to let us think you didn't want him, and then to take him after all.''

''And this charade about the Stilson boy,'' Mother said.

''It wasn't a charade, Mrs. Wiggin. Until we knew what Ender's motivation was, we couldn't be sure he wasn't another—we had to know what the action meant. Or at least what Ender believed that it meant.''

''Must you call him that stupid nickname?'' Mother began to cry.

''That's the name he calls himself.''

''What are you going to do, Colonel Graff?'' Father asked. ''Walk out the door with him now?''

''That depends,'' said Graff.

''On what?''

''On whether Ender wants to come.''

Mother's weeping turned to bitter laughter. ''Oh, so it's voluntary after all, how sweet!''

''For the two of you, the choice was made when Ender was conceived. But for Ender, the choice has not been made at all. Conscripts make good cannon fodder, but for officers we need volunteers.''

''Officers?'' Ender asked. At the sound of his voice, the others fell silent.

''Yes,'' said Graff. ''Battle School is for training future starship captains and commodores of flotillas and admirals of the fleet.''

''Let's not have any deception here!'' Father said angrily. ''How many of the boys at the Battle School actually end up in command of ships!''

''Unfortunately, Mr. Wiggin, that is classified information. But I *can* say that none of our boys who makes it through the first year has ever failed to receive a commission as an officer. And none has retired from a position of lower rank than chief executive officer of an interplanetary vessel. Even in the domestic defense forces within our own solar system, there's honor to be had."

"How many make it through the first year?" asked Ender.

"All who want to," said Graff.

Ender almost said, I want to. But he held his tongue. This would keep him out of school, but that was stupid, that was just a problem for a few days. It would keep him away from Peter—that was more important, that might be a matter of life itself. But to leave Mother and Father, and above all, to leave Valentine. And become a soldier. Ender didn't like fighting. He didn't like Peter's kind, the strong against the weak, and he didn't like his own kind either, the smart against the stupid.

"I think," Graff said, "that Ender and I should have a private conversation."

"No," Father said.

"I won't take him without letting you speak to him again," Graff said. "And you really can't stop me."

Father glared at Graff a moment longer, then got up and left the room. Mother paused to squeeze Ender's hand. She closed the door behind her when she left.

"Ender," Graff said, "if you come with me, you won't be back here for a long time. There aren't any vacations from Battle School. No visitors, either. A full course of training lasts until you're sixteen years old—you get your first leave, under certain circumstances, when you're twelve. Believe me, Ender, people change in six years, in ten years. Your sister Valentine will be a woman when you see her again, if you come with me. You'll be strangers. You'll still love her, Ender, but you won't know her. You see I'm not pretending it's easy."

"Mom and Daddy?"

"I know you, Ender. I've been watching the monitor disks for some time. You won't miss your mother and father, not much, not for long. And they won't miss you long, either."

Tears came to Ender's eyes, in spite of himself. He turned his face away, but would not reach up to wipe them.

"They *do* love you, Ender. But you have to understand what your life has cost them. They were born religious, you know. Your father was baptized with the name John Paul Wieczorek. Catholic. The seventh of nine children."

Nine children. That was unthinkable. Criminal.

"Yes, well, people do strange things for religion. You know the sanctions, Ender—they were not as harsh then, but still not easy. Only the first two children had a free education. Taxes steadily rose with each new child. Your father turned sixteen and invoked the Noncomplying Families Act to separate himself from his family. He changed his name, renounced his religion, and vowed never to have more than the allotted two children. He meant it. All the shame and persecution he went through as a child—he vowed no child of his would go through it. Do you understand?"

"He didn't want me."

"Well, no one *wants* a Third anymore. You can't expect them to be glad. But your father and mother are a special case. They both renounced their religions—your mother was a Mormon—but in fact their feelings are still ambiguous. Do you know what ambiguous means?"

"They feel both ways."

"They're ashamed of having come from noncompliant families. They conceal it. To the degree that your mother refuses to admit to anyone that she was born in Utah, lest they suspect. Your father denies his Polish ancestry, since Poland is still a noncompliant nation, and under international sanction because of it. So, you see, having a Third, even under the government's direct instructions, undoes everything they've been trying to do."

"I know that."

"But it's more complicated than that. Your father still

named you with legitimate saints' names. In fact, he baptized all three of you himself as soon as he got you home after you were born. And your mother objected. They quarreled over it each time, not because she didn't want you baptized, but because she didn't want you baptized Catholic. They haven't really given up their religion. They look at you and see you as a badge of pride, because they were able to circumvent the law and have a Third. But you're also a badge of cowardice, because they dare not go further and practice the noncompliance they still feel is right. And you're a badge of public shame, because at every step you interfere with their efforts at assimilation into normal complying society."

"How can you know all this?"

"We monitored your brother and sister, Ender. You'd be amazed at how sensitive the instruments are. We were connected directly to your brain. We heard all that you heard, whether you were listening carefully or not. Whether you understood or not. *We* understand."

"So my parents love me and don't love me?"

"They love you. The question is whether they want you here. Your presence in this house is a constant disruption. A source of tension. Do you understand?"

"*I'm* not the one who causes tension."

"Not anything you *do*, Ender. Your life itself. Your brother hates you because you are living proof that he wasn't good enough. Your parents resent you because of all the past they are trying to evade."

"Valentine loves me."

"With all her heart. Completely, unstintingly, she's devoted to you, and you adore her. I told you it wouldn't be easy."

"What is it like, there?"

"Hard work. Studies, just like school here, except we put you into mathematics and computers much more heavily. Military history. Strategy and tactics. And above all, the Battle Room."

"What's that?"

"War games. All the boys are organized into armies. Day after day, in zero gravity, there are mock battles. Nobody gets hurt, but winning and losing matter. Everybody starts as a common soldier, taking orders. Older boys are your officers, and it's their duty to train you and command you in battle. More than that I can't tell you. It's like playing buggers and astronauts—except that you have weapons that work, and fellow soldiers fighting beside you, and your whole future and the future of the human race depends on how well you learn, how well you fight. It's a hard life, and you won't have a normal childhood. Of course, with your mind, and as a Third to boot, you wouldn't have a particularly normal childhood anyway."

"All boys?"

"A few girls. They don't often pass the tests to get in. Too many centuries of evolution are working against them. None of them will be like Valentine, anyway. But there'll be brothers there, Ender."

"Like Peter?"

"Peter wasn't accepted, Ender, for the very reasons that you hate him."

"I don't hate him. I'm just—"

"Afraid of him. Well, Peter isn't all bad, you know. He was the best we'd seen in a long time. We asked your parents to choose a daughter next—they would have anyway—hoping that Valentine would be Peter, but milder. She was too mild. And so we requisitioned you."

"To be half Peter and half Valentine."

"If things worked out right."

"Am I?"

"As far as we can tell. Our tests are very good, Ender. But they don't tell us everything. In fact, when it comes down to it, they hardly tell us anything. But they're better than nothing." Graff leaned over and took Ender's hands in his. "Ender Wiggin, if it were just a matter of choosing the best and happiest future for you, I'd tell you to stay home. Stay here, grow up, be happy. There are worse things than being a Third, worse things than a big brother who can't make up his mind whether to be a human being or a jackal. Battle School is one of those worse things. But we need you. The buggers may seem like a game to you now, Ender, but they damn near wiped us out last time. They had us cold, outnumbered and outweaponed. The only thing that saved us was that we had the most brilliant military commander we ever found. Call it fate, call it God, call it damnfool luck, we had Mazer Rackham.

"But we don't have him now, Ender. We've scraped together everything mankind could produce, a fleet that makes the one they sent against us last time seem like a bunch of kids playing in a swimming pool. We have some new weapons, too. But it might not be enough, even so. Because in the eighty years since the last war, they've had as much time to prepare as we have. We need the best we can get, and we need them fast. Maybe you're not going to work out for us, and maybe you are. Maybe you'll break down under the pressure, maybe it'll ruin your life, maybe you'll hate me for coming here to your house today. But if there's a chance that because you're with the fleet, mankind might survive and the buggers might leave us alone forever—then I'm going to ask you to do it. To come with me."

Ender had trouble focusing on Colonel Graff. The man looked far away and very small, as if Ender could pick him up with tweezers and drop him in a pocket. To leave everything here, and go to a place that was very hard, with no Valentine, no Mom and Dad.

And then he thought of the films of the buggers that everyone had to see at least once a year. The Scathing of China. The Battle of the Belt. Death and suffering and terror. And Mazer Rackham and his brilliant maneuvers, destroying an enemy fleet twice his size and twice his firepower, using the little human ships that seemed so frail and weak. Like children fighting with grown-ups. And we won.

"I'm afraid," said Ender quietly. "But I'll go with you."

"Tell me again," said Graff.

"It's what I was born for, isn't it? If I don't go, why am I alive?"

"Not good enough," said Graff.

"I don't want to go," said Ender, "but I will."

Graff nodded. "You can change your mind. Up until the time you get in my car with me, you can change your mind. After that, you stay at the pleasure of the International Fleet. Do you understand that?"

Ender nodded.

"All right. Let's tell them."

Mother cried. Father held Ender tight. Peter shook his hand and said, "You lucky little pinheaded fart-eater." Valentine kissed him and left her tears on his cheek.

There was nothing to pack. No belongings to take. "The school provides everything you need, from uniforms to school supplies. And as for toys—there's only one game."

"Good-bye," Ender said to his family. He reached up and took Colonel Graff's hand and walked out the door with him.

"Kill some buggers for me!" Peter shouted.

"I love you, Andrew!" Mother called.

"We'll write to you!" Father said.

And as he got into the car that waited silently in the corridor, he heard Valentine's anguished cry. "Come back to me! I love you forever!"

4

Launch

"With Ender, we have to strike a delicate balance. Isolate him enough that he remains creative—otherwise he'll adopt the system here and we'll lose him. At the same time, we need to make sure he keeps a strong ability to lead."

"If he earns rank, he'll lead."

"It isn't that simple. Mazer Rackham could handle his little fleet and win. By the time this war happens, there'll be too much, even for a genius. Too many little boats. He has to work smoothly with his subordinates."

"Oh, good. He has to be a genius and nice, too."

"Not *nice*. Nice will let the buggers have us all."

"So you're going to isolate him."

"I'll have him completely separated from the rest of the boys by the time we get to the School."

"I have no doubt of it. I'll be waiting for you to get here. I watched the vids of what he did to the Stilson boy. This is not a sweet little kid you're bringing up here."

"That's where you're mistaken. He's even sweeter than he looks. But don't worry. We'll purge *that* in a hurry."

"Sometimes I think you enjoy breaking these little geniuses."

"There *is* an art to it, and I'm very, very good at it. But enjoy? Well, maybe. When they put back the pieces afterward, and it makes them better."

"You're a monster."

"Thanks. Does this mean I get a raise?"

"Just a medal. The budget isn't inexhaustible."

They say that weightlessness can cause disorientation, especially in children, whose sense of direction isn't yet secure. But Ender was disoriented before he left Earth's gravity. Before the shuttle launch even began.

There were nineteen other boys in his launch. They filed out of the bus and into the elevator. They talked and joked and bragged and laughed. Ender kept his silence. He noticed how Graff and the other officers were watching them. Analyzing. Everything we do means something, Ender realized. Them laughing. Me not laughing.

He toyed with the idea of trying to be like the other boys. But he couldn't think of any jokes, and none of theirs seemed funny. Wherever their laughter came from, Ender couldn't find such a place in himself. He was afraid, and fear made him serious.

They had dressed him in a uniform, all in a single piece; it felt funny not to have a belt cinched around his waist. He felt baggy and naked, dressed like that. There were TV cameras going, perched like animals on the shoulders of crouching, prowling men. The men moved slowly, catlike, so the camera motion would be smooth. Ender caught himself moving smoothly, too.

He imagined himself being on TV, in an interview. The announcer asking him, How do you feel, Mr. Wiggin? Actually quite well, except hungry. Hungry? Oh, yes, they don't let you eat for twenty hours before the launch. How interesting, I never knew that. All of us are quite hungry, actually. And all the while, during the interview, Ender and the TV guy would slink along smoothly in front of the cameraman, taking long, lithe strides. The TV guy was letting him be the spokesman for all the boys, though Ender was barely competent to speak for himself. For the first time, Ender felt like laughing. He smiled. The other boys near him were laughing at the moment, too, for another reason. They think I'm smiling at their joke, thought Ender. But I'm smiling at something much funnier.

"Go up the ladder one at a time," said an officer. "When you come to an aisle with empty seats, take one. There aren't any window seats."

It was a joke. The other boys laughed.

Ender was near the last, but not the very last. The TV cameras did not give up, though. Will Valentine see me disappear into the shuttle? He thought of waving at her, of running to the cameraman and saying, "Can I tell Valentine good-bye?" He didn't know that it would be censored out of the tape if he did, for the boys soaring out to Battle School were all supposed to be heroes. They weren't supposed to miss anybody. Ender didn't know about the censorship, but he did know that running to the cameras would be wrong.

He walked the short bridge to the door in the shuttle. He noticed that the wall to his right was carpeted like a floor. That was where the disorientation began. The moment he thought of the wall as a floor, he began to feel like he was walking on a wall. He got to the ladder, and noticed that the vertical surface behind it was also carpeted. I am climbing up the floor. Hand over hand, step by step.

And then, for fun, he pretended that he was climbing *down* the wall. He did it almost instantly in his mind, convinced himself against the best evidence of gravity until he reached an empty seat. He found himself gripping the seat tightly, even though gravity pulled him firmly against it.

The other boys were bouncing on their seats a little, poking and pushing, shouting. Ender carefully found the straps, figured out how they fit together to hold him at crotch, waist, and shoulders. He imagined the ship dangling upside down on the undersurface of the Earth, the giant fingers of gravity holding them firmly in place. But we will slip away, he thought. We are going to fall off this planet.

He did not know its significance at the time. Later, though, he would remember that it was even before he left Earth that he first thought of it as a planet, like any other, not particularly his own.

"Oh, already figured it out," said Graff. He was standing on the ladder.

"Coming with us?" Ender asked.

"I don't usually come down for recruiting," Graff said. "I'm kind of in charge there. Administrator of the School. Like a principal. They told me I had to come back or I'd lose my job." He smiled.

Ender smiled back. He felt comfortable with Graff. Graff was good. And he was principal of the Battle School. Ender relaxed a little. He would have a friend there.

Adults helped the other boys belt themselves in place, those who hadn't done as Ender did. Then they waited for an hour while a TV at the front of the shuttle introduced them to shuttle flight, the history of space flight, and their possible future with the great starships of the I.F. Very boring stuff. Ender had seen such films before.

Except that he had not been belted into a seat inside the shuttle. Hanging upside down from the belly of Earth.

The launch wasn't bad. A little scary. Some jolting, a few moments of panic that this might be the first failed launch since the early days of the shuttle. The movies hadn't made it plain how much violence you could experience, lying on your back in a soft chair.

Then it was over, and he really was hanging by the straps, no gravity anywhere.

But because he had already reoriented himself, he was not surprised when Graff came up the ladder backward, as if he were climbing down to the front of the shuttle. Nor did it bother him when Graff hooked his feet under a rung and pushed off with his hands, so that suddenly he swung upright, as if this were an ordinary airplane.

The reorientations were too much for some. One boy gagged; Ender understood then why they had been forbidden to eat anything for twenty hours before the launch. Vomiting in null gravity wouldn't be fun.

But for Ender, Graff's gravity game was fun. And he carried it further, imagining that Graff was actually hanging upside down from the center aisle, and then picturing him sticking straight out from a side wall. Gravity could go any which way. However I want it to go. I can make Graff stand on his head and he doesn't even know it.

"What do you think is so funny, Wiggin?"

Graff's voice was sharp and angry. What did I do wrong, thought Ender. Did I laugh out loud?

"I asked you a question, soldier!" barked Graff.

Oh yes. This is the beginning of the training routine. Ender had seen some military shows on TV, and they always shouted a lot at the beginning of training before the soldiers and the officer became good friends.

"Yes sir," Ender said.

"Well answer it, then!"

"I thought of you hanging upside down by your feet. I thought it was funny."

It sounded stupid, now, with Graff looking at him coldly. "To you I suppose it *is* funny. Is it funny to anybody else here?"

Murmurs of no.

"Well why isn't it?" Graff looked at them all with contempt. "Scumbrains, that's what we've got in this launch. Pinheaded little morons. Only one of you had the brains to realize that in null gravity directions are whatever you conceive them to be. Do you understand that, Shafts?"

The boy nodded.

"No you didn't. Of course you didn't. Not only stupid, but a liar too. There's only one boy on this launch with any brains *at all*, and that's Ender Wiggin. Take a good look at him, little boys. He's going to be a commander when you're still in diapers up there. Because he knows how to think in null gravity, and you just want to throw up."

This wasn't the way the show was supposed to go. Graff was supposed to pick on him, not set him up as the best. They were supposed to be against each other at first, so they could become friends later.

"Most of you are going to ice out. Get used to that, little boys. Most of you are going to end up in Combat School, because you don't have the brains to handle deep-space piloting. Most of you aren't worth the price of bringing you up here to Battle School because you don't have what it takes. Some of you might make it. *Some* of you might be worth something to humanity. But don't bet on it. I'm betting on only one."

Suddenly Graff did a backflip and caught the ladder with his hands, then swung his feet away from the ladder. Doing a handstand, if the floor was down. Dangling by his hands, if the floor was up. Hand over hand he swung himself back along the aisle to his seat.

"Looks like *you've* got it made here," whispered the boy next to him.

Ender shook his head.

"Oh, won't even talk to me?" the boy said.

"I didn't ask him to say that stuff," Ender whispered.

He felt a sharp pain on the top of his head. Then again. Some giggles from behind him. The boy in the next seat back must have unfastened his straps. Again a blow to the head. Go away, Ender thought. I didn't do anything to you.

Again a blow to the head. Laughter from the boys. Didn't Graff see this? Wasn't he going to stop it? Another blow. Harder. It really hurt. Where was Graff?

Then it became clear. Graff had deliberately caused it. It was worse than the abuse in the shows. When the sergeant picked on you, the others liked you better. But when the officer prefers you, the others hate you.

"Hey, fart-eater," came the whisper from behind him. He was hit on the head again. "Do you like this? Hey, super-brain, is this fun?" Another blow, this one so hard that Ender cried out softly with the pain.

If Graff was setting him up, there'd be no help unless he helped himself. He waited until he thought another blow was about to come. Now, he thought. And yes, the blow was there. It hurt, but Ender was already trying to sense the coming of the next blow. Now. And yes, right on time. I've got you, Ender thought.

Just as the next blow was coming, Ender reached up with both hands, snatched the boy by the wrist, and then pulled down on the arm, hard.

In gravity, the boy would have been jammed against Ender's seat back, hurting his chest. In null gravity, however, he flipped over the seat completely, up toward the ceiling. Ender wasn't expecting it. He hadn't realized how null gravity magnified the effects of even a child's movements. The boy sailed through the air, bouncing against the ceiling, then down against another boy in his seat, then out into the aisle, his arms flailing until he screamed as his body slammed into the bulkhead at the front of the compartment, his left arm twisted under him.

It took only seconds. Graff was already there, snatching the boy out of the air. Deftly he propelled him down the aisle toward the other man. "Left arm. Broken, I think," he said. In moments the boy had been given a drug and lay quietly in the air as the officer ballooned a splint around his arm.

Ender felt sick. He had only meant to catch the boy's arm. No. No, he had meant to hurt him, and had pulled with all his strength. He hadn't meant it to be so public, but the boy was feeling exactly the pain Ender had meant him to feel. Null gravity had betrayed him, that was all. I am Peter. I'm just like him. And Ender hated himself.

Graff stayed at the front of the cabin. "What are you, slow learners? In your feeble little minds, haven't you picked up one little fact? You were brought here to be *soldiers*. In your old schools, in your old families, maybe you were the big shot, maybe you were tough, maybe you were smart. But we chose the best of the best, and that's the only kind of kid you're going to meet now. And when I tell you Ender Wiggin is the best in this launch, take the hint, my little dorklings. Don't mess with him. Little boys have died in Battle School before. Do I make myself clear?"

There was silence the rest of the launch. The boy sitting next to Ender was scrupulously careful not to touch him.

I am not a killer, Ender said to himself over and over. I am not Peter. No matter what Graff says, I'm not. I was defending myself. I bore it a long time. I was patient. I'm not what he said.

A voice over the speaker told them they were approaching the school; it took twenty minutes to decelerate and dock. Ender lagged behind the others. They were not unwilling to let him be the last to leave the shuttle, climbing upward in the direction that had been down when they embarked. Graff was waiting at the end of the narrow tube that led from the shuttle into the heart of the Battle School.

"Was it a good flight, Ender?" Graff asked cheerfully.

"I thought you were my friend." Despite himself, Ender's voice trembled.

Graff looked puzzled. "Whatever gave you that idea, Ender?"

"Because you—" Because you spoke nicely to me, and honestly. "You didn't lie."

"I won't lie now, either," said Graff. "My job isn't to be friends. My job is to produce the best soldiers in the world. In the whole history of the world. We need a Napoleon. An Alexander. Except that Napoleon lost in the end, and Alexander flamed out and died young. We need a Julius Caesar, except that he made himself dictator, and died for it. My job is to produce such a creature, and all the men and women he'll need to help him. Nowhere in that does it say I have to make friends with children."

"You made them hate me."

"So? What will you do about it? Crawl into a corner? Start kissing their little backsides so they'll love you again? There's only one thing that will make them stop hating you. And that's being so good at what you do that they can't ignore you. I told them you were the best. Now you damn well better be."

"What if I can't?"

"Then too bad. Look, Ender, I'm sorry if you're lonely and afraid. But the buggers are out there. Ten billion, a hundred billion, a million billion of them, for all we know. With as many ships, for all we know. With weapons we can't understand. And a willingness to use those weapons to wipe us out. It isn't the world at stake, Ender. Just us. Just humankind. As far as the rest of the biosphere is concerned, we could be wiped out and it would adjust, it would get on with the next step in evolution. But humanity doesn't want to die. As a species, we have evolved to survive. And the way we do it is by straining and straining and, at last, every few generations, giving birth to genius. The one who invents the wheel. And light. And flight. The one who builds a city, a nation, an empire. Do you understand any of this?"

Ender thought he did, but wasn't sure, and so said nothing.

"No. Of course not. So I'll put it bluntly. Human beings are free except when humanity needs them. Maybe humanity needs you. To do something. Maybe humanity needs *me*—to find out what you're good for. We might both do despicable things, Ender, but if humankind survives, then we were good tools."

"Is that all? Just tools?"

"Individual human beings are all tools, that the others use to help us all survive."

"That's a lie."

"No. It's just a half truth. You can worry about the other half after we win this war."

"It'll be over before I grow up," Ender said.

"I hope you're wrong," said Graff. "By the way, you aren't helping yourself at all, talking to me. The other boys are no doubt telling each other that old Ender Wiggin is back there licking up to Graff. If word once gets around that you're a teachers' boy, you're iced for sure."

In other words, go away and leave me alone. "Good-bye," Ender said. He pulled himself hand over hand along the tube where the other boys had gone.

Graff watched him go.

One of the teachers near him said, "Is that the one?"

"God knows," said Graff. "If Ender isn't him, then he'd better show up soon."

"Maybe it's nobody," said the teacher.

"Maybe. But if that's the case, Anderson, then in my opinion God is a bugger. You can quote me on that."

"I will."

They stood in silence a while longer.

"Anderson."

"Mmm."

"The kid's wrong. I *am* his friend."

"I know."

"He's clean. Right to the heart, he's good."

"I've read the reports."

"Anderson, think what we're going to do to him."

Anderson was defiant. "We're going to make him the best military commander in history."

"And then put the fate of the world on his shoulders. For his sake, I hope it isn't him. I do."

"Cheer up. The buggers may kill us all before he graduates."

Graff smiled. "You're right. I feel better already."

5

Games

"You have my admiration. Breaking an arm—that was a master stroke."

"That was an accident."

"Really? And I've already commended you in your official report."

"It's too strong. It makes that other little bastard into a hero. It could screw up training for a lot of kids. I thought Ender might call for help."

"Call for help? I thought that was what you valued most in him—that he settles his own problems. When he's out there surrounded by an enemy fleet, there ain't gonna be nobody to help him if he calls."

"Who would have guessed the little sucker'd be out of his seat? And that he'd land just wrong against the bulkhead?"

"Just one more example of the stupidity of the military. If you had any brains, you'd be in a real career, like selling life insurance."

"You, too, mastermind."

"We've just got to face the fact that we're second rate. With the fate of humanity in our hands. Gives you a delicious feeling of power, doesn't it? Especially because this time if we lose there won't be any criticism of us at all."

"I never thought of it that way. But let's not lose."

"See how Ender handles it. If we've already lost him, if he can't handle this, who next? Who else?"

"I'll make up a list."

"In the meantime, figure out how to unlose Ender."

"I told you. His isolation can't be broken. He can never come to believe that anybody will ever help him out, *ever*. If he once thinks there's an easy way out, he's wrecked."

"You're right. That would be terrible, if he believed he had a friend."

"He can have friends. It's parents he can't have."

The other boys had already chosen their bunks when Ender arrived. Ender stopped in the doorway of the dormitory, looking for the sole remaining bed. The ceiling was low—Ender could reach up and touch it. A child-sized room, with the bottom bunk resting on the floor. The other boys were watching him, cornerwise. Sure enough, the bottom bunk right by the door was the only empty bed. For a moment it occurred to Ender that by letting the others put him in the worst place, he was inviting later bullying. Yet he couldn't very well oust someone else.

So he smiled broadly. "Hey, thanks," he said. Not sarcastically at all. He said it as sincerely as if they had reserved for him the best position. "I thought I was going to have to *ask* for low bunk by the door."

He sat down and looked in the locker that stood open at the foot of the bunk. There was a paper taped to the inside of the door.

PLACE YOUR HAND ON THE SCANNER
AT THE HEAD OF YOUR BUNK
AND SPEAK YOUR NAME TWICE.

Ender found the scanner, a sheet of opaque plastic. He put his left hand on it and said, "Ender Wiggin. Ender Wiggin."

The scanner glowed green for a moment. Ender closed his locker and tried to reopen it. He couldn't. Then he put his hand on the scanner and said, "Ender Wiggin." The locker popped open. So did three other compartments.

One of them contained four jumpsuits like the one he was wearing, and one white one. Another compartment contained a small desk, just like the ones at school. So they weren't through with studies yet.

It was the largest compartment that contained the prize. It looked like a spacesuit at first glance, complete with helmet and gloves. But it wasn't. There was no airtight seal. Still, it would effectively cover the whole body. It was thickly padded. It was also a little stiff.

And there was a pistol within. A lasergun, it looked like, since the end was solid, clear glass. But surely they wouldn't let children have lethal weapons—

"Not laser," said a man. Ender looked up. It was one he hadn't seen before. A young and kind-looking man. "But it has a tight enough beam. Well-focused. You can aim it and make a three-inch circle of light on a wall a hundred meters off."

"What's it for?" Ender asked.

"One of the games we play during recreation. Does anyone else have his locker open?" The man looked around. "I mean, have you followed directions and coded in your voices and hands? You can't get into the lockers until you do. This room is your home for the first year or so here at the Battle School, so get the bunk you want and stay with it. Ordinarily, we let you elect your chief officer and install him in the lower bunk by the door, but apparently that position has been taken. Can't recode the lockers now. So think about whom you want to choose. Dinner in seven minutes. Follow the lighted dots on the floor. Your color code is red yellow yellow—whenever you're assigned a path to follow, it will be red yellow yellow, three dots side by side—go where those lights indicate. What's your color code, boys?''

''Red, yellow, yellow.''

''Very good. My name is Dap. I'm your mom for the next few months.''

The boys laughed.

''Laugh all you like, but keep it in mind. If you get lost in the school, which is quite possible, don't go opening doors. Some of them lead outside.'' More laughter. ''Instead just tell someone that your mom is Dap, and they'll call me. Or tell them your color, and they'll light up a path for you to get home. If you have a problem, come talk to me. Remember, I'm the only person here who's paid to be nice to you. But not too nice. Give me any lip and I'll break your face. OK?''

They laughed again. Dap had a room full of friends. Frightened children are so easy to win.

''Which way is down, anybody tell me?''

They told him.

''OK, that's true. But that direction is toward the *outside*. The ship is spinning, and that's what makes it feel like that is down. The floor actually curves around in *that* direction. Keep going long enough that way, and you come back to where you started. Except don't try it. Because up that way is teachers' quarters, and up that way is the bigger kids. And the bigger kids don't like Launchies butting in. You might get pushed around. In fact, you *will* get pushed around. And when you do, don't come crying to me. Got it? This is Battle School, not nursery school.''

''What are we supposed to do, then?'' asked a boy, a really small black kid who had a top bunk near Ender's.

''If you don't like getting pushed around, figure out for yourself what to do about it. But I warn you—murder is strictly against the rules. So is any deliberate injury. I understand there was one attempted murder on the way up here.

A broken arm. That kind of thing happens again, somebody ices out. You got it?"

"What's icing out?" asked the boy with his arm puffed up in a splint.

"Ice. Put out in the cold. Sent Earthside. Finished at Battle School."

Nobody looked at Ender.

"So, boys, if any of you are thinking of being troublemakers, at least be clever about it, OK?"

Dap left. They still didn't look at Ender.

Ender felt the fear growing in his belly. The kid whose arm he broke—Ender didn't feel sorry for him. He was a Stilson. And like Stilson, he was already gathering a gang. A little knot of kids, several of the bigger ones. They were laughing at the far end of the room, and every now and then one of them would turn to look at Ender.

With all his heart, Ender wanted to go home. What did any of this have to do with saving the world? There was no monitor now. It was Ender against the gang again, only they were right in his room. Peter again, but without Valentine.

The fear stayed, all through dinner as no one sat by him in the mess hall. The other boys were talking about things—the big scoreboard on one wall, the food, the bigger kids. Ender could only watch in isolation.

The scoreboards were team standings. Win-loss records, with the most recent scores. Some of the bigger boys apparently had bets on the most recent games. Two teams, Manticore and Asp, had no recent score—these boxes were flashing. Ender decided they must be playing right now.

He noticed that the older boys were divided into groups, according to the uniforms they wore. Some with different uniforms were talking together, but generally the groups each had their own area. Launchies—their own group, and the two or three next older groups—all had plain blue uniforms. But the big kids, the ones that were on teams, they were wearing much more flamboyant clothing. Ender tried to guess which ones went with which name. Scorpion and Spider were easy. So were Flame and Tide.

A bigger boy came to sit by him. Not just a little bigger—he looked to be twelve or thirteen. Getting his man's growth started.

"Hi," he said.

"Hi," Ender said.

"I'm Mick."

"Ender."

"That's a name?"

"Since I was little. It's what my sister called me."

"Not a bad name here. Ender. Finisher. Hey."

"Hope so."

"Ender, you the bugger in your launch?"

Ender shrugged.

"I noticed you eating all alone. Every launch has one like that. Kid that nobody takes to right away. Sometimes I think the teachers do it on purpose. The teachers aren't very nice. You'll notice that."

"Yeah."

"So you the bugger?"

"I guess so."

"Hey. Nothing to cry about, you know?" He gave Ender his roll, and took Ender's pudding. "Eat nutritious stuff. It'll keep you strong." Mick dug into the pudding.

"What about you?" asked Ender.

"Me? I'm nothing. I'm a fart in the air conditioning. I'm always there, but most of the time nobody knows it."

Ender smiled tentatively.

"Yeah, funny, but no joke. I got nowhere here. I'm getting big now. They're going to send me to my next school pretty soon. No way it'll be Tactical School for me. I've never been a leader, you see. Only the guys who get to be leaders have a shot at it."

"How do you get to be a leader?"

"Hey, if I knew, you think I'd be like this? How many guys my size you see in here?"

Not many. Ender didn't say it.

"A few. I'm not the only half-iced bugger-fodder. A few of us. The other guys—they're all commanders. All the guys from my launch have their own teams now. Not me."

Ender nodded.

"Listen, little guy. I'm doing you a favor. Make friends. Be a leader. Kiss butts if you've got to, but if the other guys despise you—you know what I mean?"

Ender nodded again.

"Naw, you don't know nothing. You Launchies are all alike. You don't know nothing. Minds like space. Nothing there. And if anything hits you, you fall apart. Look, when you end up like me, don't forget that somebody warned you. It's the last nice thing anybody's going to do for you."

"So why did you tell me?" asked Ender.

"What are you, a smartmouth? Shut up and eat."

Ender shut up and ate. He didn't like Mick. And he knew there was no chance he would end up like that. Maybe that was what the teachers were planning, but Ender didn't intend to fit in with their plans.

I will not be the bugger of my group, Ender thought. I didn't leave Valentine and Mother and Father to come here just to be iced.

As he lifted the fork to his mouth, he could feel his family around him, as they always had been. He knew just which way to turn his head to look up and see Mother, trying to get Valentine not to slurp. He knew just where Father would be, scanning the news on the table while pretending to be part of the dinner conversation. Peter, pretending to take a crushed pea out of his nose—even Peter could be funny.

It was a mistake to think of them. He felt a sob rise in his throat and swallowed it down; he could not see his plate.

He could not cry. There was no chance that he would be treated with compassion. Dap was not Mother. Any sign of weakness would tell the Stilsons and Peters that this boy could be broken. Ender did what he always did when Peter tormented him. He began to count doubles. One, two, four, eight, sixteen, thirty-two, sixty-four. And on, as high as he could hold the numbers in his head: 128, 256, 512, 1024, 2048, 4096, 8192, 16384, 32768, 65536, 131072, 262144. At 67108864 he began to be unsure—had he slipped out a digit? Should he be in the ten millions or the hundred millions or just the millions? He tried doubling again and lost it. 1342 something. 16? Or 17738? It was gone. Start over again. All the doubling he could hold. The pain was gone. The tears were gone. He would not cry.

Until that night, when the lights went dim, and in the distance he could hear several boys whimpering for their mothers or fathers or dogs. Then he could not help himself. His lips formed Valentine's name. He could hear her voice laughing in the distance, just down the hall. He could see Mother passing his door, looking in to be sure he was all right. He could hear Father laughing at the video. It was all so clear, and it would *never* be that way again. I'll be old when I ever see them again, twelve at the earliest. Why did I say yes? What was I such a fool for? Going to school would have been nothing. Facing Stilson every day. And Peter. He was a pissant, Ender wasn't afraid of him.

I want to go home, he whispered.

But his whisper was the whisper he used when he cried out in pain when Peter tormented him. The sound didn't travel farther than his own ears, and sometimes not that far.

And his tears could fall unwanted on his sheet, but his sobs were so gentle that they did not shake the bed, so quiet they could not be heard. But the ache was there, thick in his throat and the front of his face, hot in his chest and in his eyes. I want to go home.

Dap came to the door that night and moved quietly among the beds, touching a hand here, a forehead there. Where he went there was more crying, not less. The touch of kindness in this frightening place was enough to push some over the edge into tears. Not Ender, though. When Dap came, his crying was over, and his face was dry. It was the lying face he presented to Mother and Father, when Peter had been cruel to him and he dared not let it show. Thank you for this, Peter. For dry eyes and silent weeping. You taught me how to hide anything I felt. More than ever, I need that now.

—

This was school. Every day, hours of classes. Reading. Numbers. History. Videos of the bloody battles in space, the Marines spraying their guts all over the walls of the bugger ships. Holos of the clean wars of the fleet, ships turning into puffs of light as the spacecraft killed each other deftly in the deep night. Many things to learn. Ender worked as hard as anyone; all of them struggled for the first time in their lives, as for the first time in their lives they competed with classmates who were at least as bright as they.

But the games—that was what they lived for. That was what filled the hours between waking and sleeping.

Dap introduced them to the game room on their second day. It was up, way above the decks where the boys lived and worked. They climbed ladders to where the gravity weakened, and there in the cavern they saw the dazzling lights of the games.

Some of the games they knew; some they had even played at home. Simple ones and hard ones. Ender walked past the two-dimensional games on video and began to study the games the bigger boys played, the holographic games with objects hovering in the air. He was the only Launchy in that part of the room, and every now and then one of the bigger boys would shove him out of the way. What're you doing here? Get lost. Fly off. And of course he would fly, in the lower gravity here, leave his feet and soar until he ran into something or someone.

Every time, though, he extricated himself and went back, perhaps to a different spot, to get a different angle on the game. He was too small to see the controls, how the game was actually done. That didn't matter. He got the movement of it in the air. The way the player dug tunnels in the darkness, tunnels of light, which the enemy ships would search for and then follow mercilessly until they caught the player's ship. The player could make traps: mines, drifting bombs, loops in the air that forced the enemy ships to repeat endlessly. Some of the players were clever. Others lost quickly.

Ender liked it better, though, when two boys played against each other. Then they had to use each other's tunnels, and it quickly became clear which of them was worth anything at the strategy of it.

Within an hour or so, it began to pall. Ender understood the regularities by then. Understood the rules the computer was following, so that he knew he could always, once he mastered the controls, outmaneuver the enemy. Spirals when the enemy was like this; loops when the enemy was like that. Lie in wait at one trap. Lay seven traps and then lure them like this. There was no challenge to it, then, just a matter of playing until the computer got so fast that no human reflexes could overcome it. That wasn't fun. It was the other boys he wanted to play. The boys who had been so trained by the computer that even when they played against each other they each tried to emulate the computer. Think like a machine instead of a boy.

I could beat them this way. I could beat them that way.

"I'd like a turn against you," he said to the boy who had just won.

"Lawsy me, what is this?" asked the boy. "Is it a bug or a bugger?"

"A new flock of dwarfs just came aboard," said another boy.

"But it *talks*. Did you know they could talk?"

"I see," said Ender. "You're afraid to play me two out of three."

"Beating you," said the boy, "would be as easy as pissing in the shower."

"And not half as fun," said another.

"I'm Ender Wiggin."

"Listen up, scrunchface. You nobody. Got that? You *nobody*, got that? You not anybody till you gots you first kill. Got that?"

The slang of the older boys had its own rhythm. Ender picked it up quick enough. "If I'm nobody, then how come you scared to play me two out of three?"

Now the other guys were impatient. "Kill the squirt quick and let's get on with it."

So Ender took his place at the unfamiliar controls. His hands were small, but the controls were simple enough. It took only a little experimentation to find out which buttons used certain weapons. Movement control was a standard wireball. His reflexes were slow at first. The other boy, whose name he still didn't know, got ahead quickly. But Ender learned a lot and was doing much better by the time the game ended.

"Satisfied, Launchy?"

"Two out of three."

"We don't allow two out of three games."

"So you beat me the first time I ever touched the game," Ender said. "If you can't do it twice, you can't do it at all."

They played again, and this time Ender was deft enough to pull off a few maneuvers that the boy had obviously never seen before. His patterns couldn't cope with them. Ender didn't win easily, but he won.

The bigger boys stopped laughing and joking then. The third game went in total silence. Ender won it quickly and efficiently.

When the game ended, one of the older boys said, "Bout time they replaced this machine. Getting so any pinbrain can beat it now."

Not a word of congratulation. Just total silence as Ender walked away.

He didn't go far. Just stood off in the near distance and watched as the next players tried to use the things he had shown them. Any pinbrain? Ender smiled inwardly. They won't forget me.

He felt good. He had won something, and against older boys. Probably not the best of the older boys, but he no longer had the panicked feeling that he might be out of his depth, that Battle School might be too much for him. All he had to do was watch the game and understand how things worked, and then he could use the system, and even excel.

It was the waiting and watching that cost the most. For during that time he had to endure. The boy whose arm he had broken was out for vengeance. His name, Ender quickly learned, was Bernard. He spoke his own name with a French accent, since the French, with their arrogant Separatism, insisted that the teaching of Standard not begin until the age of four, when the French language patterns were already set. His accent made him exotic and interesting; his broken arm made him a martyr; his sadism made him a natural focus for all those who loved pain in others.

Ender became their enemy.

Little things. Kicking his bed every time they went in and out of the door. Jostling him with his meal tray. Tripping him on the ladders. Ender learned quickly not to leave anything of his outside his lockers; he also learned to be quick on his feet, to catch himself. ''Maladroit,'' Bernard called him once, and the name stuck.

There were times when Ender was very angry. With Bernard, of course, anger was inadequate. It was the kind of person he was—a tormentor. What enraged Ender was how willingly the others went along with him. Surely they knew there was no justice in Bernard's revenge. Surely they knew that he had struck first at Ender in the shuttle, that Ender had only been responding to violence. If they knew, they acted as if they didn't; even if they did not know, they should be able to tell from Bernard himself that he was a snake.

After all, Ender wasn't his only target. Bernard was setting up a kingdom, wasn't he?

Ender watched from the fringes of the group as Bernard

established the hierarchy. Some of the boys were useful to him, and he flattered them outrageously. Some of the boys were willing servants, doing whatever he wanted even though he treated them with contempt.

But a few chafed under Bernard's rule.

Ender, watching, knew who resented Bernard. Shen was small, ambitious, and easily needled. Bernard had discovered that quickly, and started calling him Worm. "Because he's so *small*," Bernard said, "and because he *wriggles*. Look how he shimmies his butt when he walks."

Shen stormed off, but they only laughed louder. "Look at his *butt*. See ya, Worm!"

Ender said nothing to Shen—it would be too obvious, then, that he was starting his own competing gang. He just sat with his desk on his lap, looking as studious as possible.

He was not studying. He was telling his desk to keep sending a message into the interrupt queue every thirty seconds. The message was to everyone, and it was short and to the point. What made it hard was figuring out how to disguise who it was from, the way the teachers could. Messages from one of the boys always had their name automatically inserted. Ender hadn't cracked the teachers' security system yet, so he couldn't pretend to be a teacher. But he *was* able to set up a file for a nonexistent student, whom he whimsically named *God*.

Only when the message was ready to go did he try to catch Shen's eye. Like all the other boys, he was watching Bernard and his cronies laugh and joke, making fun of the math teacher, who often stopped in midsentence and looked around as if he had been let off the bus at the wrong stop and didn't know where he was.

Eventually, though, Shen glanced around. Ender nodded to him, pointed to his desk, and smiled. Shen looked puzzled. Ender held up his desk a little and then pointed at it. Shen reached for his own desk. Ender sent the message then. Shen saw it almost at once. Shen read it, then laughed aloud. He looked at Ender as if to say, Did you do this? Ender shrugged, to say, I don't know who did it but it sure wasn't me.

Shen laughed again, and several of the other boys who were not close to Bernard's group got out their desks and looked. Every thirty seconds the message appeared on every desk, marched around the screen quickly, then disappeared. The boys laughed together.

"What's so funny?" Bernard asked. Ender made sure he was not smiling when Bernard looked around the room, imitating the fear that so many others felt. Shen, of course, smiled all the more defiantly. It took a moment; then Bernard told one of his boys to bring out a desk. Together they read the message.

COVER YOUR BUTT. BERNARD IS WATCHING.
—GOD

Bernard went red with anger. "Who did this!" he shouted.

"God," said Shen.

"It sure as hell wasn't *you*," Bernard said. "This takes too much *brains* for a *worm*."

Ender's message expired after five minutes. After a while, a message from Bernard appeared on his desk.

I KNOW IT WAS YOU.
—BERNARD.

Ender didn't look up. He acted, in fact, as if he hadn't seen the message. Bernard just wants to catch me looking guilty. He doesn't know.

Of course, it didn't matter if he knew. Bernard would punish him all the more, because he had to rebuild his position. The one thing he couldn't stand was having the other boys laughing at him. He had to make clear who was boss. So Ender got knocked down in the shower that morning. One of Bernard's boys pretended to trip over him, and managed to plant a knee in his belly. Ender took it in silence. He was still watching, as far as the open war was concerned. He would do nothing.

But in the other war, the war of desks, he already had his next attack in place. When he got back from the shower, Bernard was raging, kicking beds and yelling at boys. "I didn't write it! Shut up!"

Marching constantly around every boy's desk was this message:

I LOVE YOUR BUTT. LET ME KISS IT.
—BERNARD

"I didn't write that message!" Bernard shouted. After the shouting had been going on for some time, Dap appeared at the door.

"What's the fuss?" he asked.

"Somebody's been writing messages using my name." Bernard was sullen.

"What message?"

"It doesn't matter what message!"

"It does to me." Dap picked up the nearest desk, which happened to belong to the boy who bunked above Ender. Dap read it, smiled very slightly, gave back the desk.

"Interesting," he said.

"Aren't you going to find out who did it?" demanded Bernard.

"Oh, I know who did it," Dap said.

Yes, Ender thought. The system was too easily broken. They mean us to break it, or sections of it. They know it was me.

"Well, who, then?" Bernard shouted.

"Are you shouting at me, soldier?" asked Dap, very softly.

At once the mood in the room changed. From rage on the part of Bernard's closest friends and barely contained mirth among the rest, all became somber. Authority was about to speak.

"No, sir," said Bernard.

"Everybody knows that the system automatically puts on the name of the sender."

"I didn't write that!" Bernard said.

"Shouting?" asked Dap.

"Yesterday someone sent a message that was signed GOD," Bernard said.

"Really?" said Dap. "I didn't know he was signed onto the system." Dap turned and left, and the room filled with laughter.

Bernard's attempt to be ruler of the room was broken—only a few stayed with him now. But they were the most vicious. And Ender knew that until he was through watching, it would go hard on him. Still, the tampering with the system had done its work. Bernard was contained, and all the boys who had some quality were free of him. Best of all, Ender had done it without sending him to the hospital. Much better this way.

Then he settled down to the serious business of designing a security system for his own desk, since the safeguards built into the system were obviously inadequate. If a six-year-old could break them down, they were obviously put there as a plaything, not serious security. Just another game that the teachers set up for us. And this is one I'm good at.

"How did you do that?" Shen asked him at breakfast.

Ender noted quietly that this was the first time another Launchy from his own class had sat with him at a meal. "Do what?" he asked.

"Send a message with a fake name. And Bernard's name! That was great. They're calling him Buttwatcher now. Just Watcher in front of the teachers, but everybody knows what he's watching."

"Poor Bernard," Ender murmured. "And he's so sensitive."

"Come on, Ender. You broke into the system. How'd you do it?"

Ender shook his head and smiled. "Thanks for thinking I'm bright enough to do that. I just happened to see it first, that's all."

"OK, you don't have to tell me," said Shen. "Still, it was great." They ate in silence for a moment. "*Do* I wiggle my butt when I walk?"

"Naw," Ender said. "Just a little. Just don't take such big long steps, that's all."

Shen nodded.

"The only person who'd ever notice was Bernard."

"He's a pig," said Shen.

Ender shrugged. "On the whole, pigs aren't so bad."

Shen laughed. "You're right. I wasn't being fair to the pigs."

They laughed together, and two other Launchies joined them. Ender's isolation was over. The war was just beginning.

6

The Giant's Drink

"We've had our disappointments in the past, hanging on for years, hoping they'll pull through, and then they don't. Nice thing about Ender, he's determined to ice within the first six months."

"Oh?"

"Don't you see what's going on here? He's stuck at the Giant's Drink in the mind game. Is the boy suicidal? You never mentioned it."

"Everybody gets the Giant sometime."

"But Ender won't leave it alone. Like Pinual."

"Everybody looks like Pinual at one time or another. But he's the only one who killed himself. I don't think it had anything to do with the Giant's Drink."

"You're betting my life on that. And look what he's done with his launch group."

"Wasn't his fault, you know."

"I don't care. His fault or not, he's poisoning that group.

They're supposed to bond, and right where he stands there's a chasm a mile wide."

"I don't plan to leave him there very long, anyway."

"Then you'd better plan again. That launch is sick, and he's the source of the disease. He stays till it's cured."

"*I* was the source of the disease. I was isolating him, and it worked."

"Give him time with the group. To see what he does with it."

"We don't have time."

"We don't have time to rush too fast with a kid who has as much chance of being a monster as a military genius."

"Is this an order?"

"The recorder's on, it's always on, your ass is covered, go to hell."

"If it's an order, then I'll—"

"It's an order. Hold him where he is until we see how he handles things in his launch group. Graff, you give me ulcers."

"You wouldn't have ulcers if you'd leave the school to me and take care of the fleet yourself."

"The fleet is looking for a battle commander. There's nothing to take care of until you get me *that*."

They filed clumsily into the battleroom, like children in a swimming pool for the first time, clinging to the handholds along the side. Null gravity was frightening, disorienting; they soon found that things went better if they didn't use their feet at all.

Worse, the suits were confining. It was harder to make precise movements, since the suits bent just a bit slower, resisted a bit more than any clothing they had ever worn before.

Ender gripped the handhold and flexed his knees. He noticed that along with the sluggishness, the suit had an amplifying effect on movement. It was hard to get them started, but the suit's legs kept moving, and strongly, after his muscles had stopped. Give them a push *this* strong, and the suit pushes with twice the force. I'll be clumsy for a while. Better get started.

So, still grasping the handhold, he pushed off strongly with his feet.

Instantly he flipped around, his feet flying over his head, and landed flat on his back against the wall. The rebound was stronger, it seemed, and his hands tore loose from the handhold. He flew across the battleroom, tumbling over and over.

For a sickening moment he tried to retain his old up-and-down orientation, his body attempting to right itself, searching for the gravity that wasn't there. Then he forced himself to change his view. He was hurtling toward a wall. That was down. And at once he had control of himself. He wasn't flying, he was falling. This was a dive. He could choose how he would hit the surface.

I'm going too fast to catch ahold and stay, but I can soften the impact, I can fly off at an angle if I roll when I hit and use my feet—

It didn't work at all the way he had planned. He went off at an angle, but it was not the one he had predicted. Nor did he have time to consider. He hit another wall, this time too soon to have prepared for it. But quite accidently he discovered a way to use his feet to control the rebound angle. Now he was soaring across the room again, toward the other boys who still clung to the wall. This time he had slowed enough to be able to grip a rung. He was at a crazy angle in relation to the other boys, but once again his orientation had changed, and as far as he could tell, they were all lying on the floor, not hanging on a wall, and he was no more upside down than they were.

"What are you trying to do, kill yourself?" asked Shen.

"Try it," Ender said. "The suit keeps you from hurting yourself, and you can control your bouncing with your legs, like this." He approximated the movement he had made.

Shen shook his head—he wasn't trying any fool stunt like that. But one boy did take off, not as fast as Ender had, because he didn't begin with a flip, but fast enough. Ender didn't even have to see his face to know that it was Bernard. And right after him, Bernard's best friend, Alai.

Ender watched them cross the huge room, Bernard struggling to orient himself to the direction he thought of as the floor, Alai surrendering to the movement and preparing to rebound from the wall. No wonder Bernard broke his arm in the shuttle, Ender thought. He tightens up when he's flying. He panics. Ender stored the information away for future reference.

And another bit of information, too. Alai did not push off in the same direction as Bernard. He aimed for a corner of the room. Their paths diverged more and more as they flew, and where Bernard made a clumsy, crunching landing and bounce on his wall, Alai did a glancing triple bounce on three surfaces near the corner that left him most of his speed and sent him flying off at a surprising angle. Alai shouted and whooped, and so did the boys watching him. Some of them forgot they were weightless and let go of the wall to clap their hands. Now they drifted lazily in many directions, waving their arms, trying to swim.

Now, that's a problem, thought Ender. What if you catch yourself drifting? There's no way to push off.

He was tempted to set himself adrift and try to solve the problem by trial and error. But he could see the others, their useless efforts at control, and he couldn't think of what he would do that they weren't already doing.

Holding onto the floor with one hand, he fiddled idly with the toy gun that was attached to his suit in front, just below the shoulder. Then he remembered the hand rockets sometimes used by marines when they did a boarding assault on an enemy station. He pulled the gun from his suit and examined it. He had pushed all the buttons back in the room, but the gun did nothing there. Maybe here in the battleroom it would work. There were no instructions on it. No labels on the controls. The trigger was obvious—he had had toy guns, as all children had, almost since infancy. There were two buttons that his thumb could easily reach, and several others along the bottom of the shaft that were almost inaccessible without using two hands. Obviously, the two buttons near his thumb were meant to be instantly usable.

He aimed the gun at the floor and pulled back on the trigger. He felt the gun grow instantly warm; when he let go of the trigger, it cooled at once. Also, a tiny circle of light appeared on the floor where he was aiming.

He thumbed the red button at the top of the gun, and pulled the trigger again. Same thing.

Then he pushed the white button. It gave a bright flash of light that illuminated a wide area, but not as intensely. The gun was quite cold when the button was pressed.

The red button makes it like a laser—but it is not a laser, Dap had said—while the white button makes it a lamp. Neither will be much help when it comes to maneuvering.

So everything depends on how you push off, the course you set when you start. It means we're going to have to get very good at controlling our launches and rebounds or we're all going to end up floating around in the middle of nowhere. Ender looked around the room. A few of the boys were drifting close to walls now, flailing their arms to catch a handhold. Most were bumping into each other and laughing; some were holding hands and going around in circles. Only a few, like Ender, were calmly holding onto the walls and watching.

One of them, he saw, was Alai. He had ended up on another wall not too far from Ender. On impulse, Ender pushed off and moved quickly toward Alai. Once in the air, he wondered what he would say. Alai was Bernard's friend. What did Ender have to say to him?

Still, there was no changing course now. So he watched straight ahead, and practiced making tiny leg and hand movements to control which way he was facing as he drifted.

Too late, he realized that he had aimed too well. He was not going to land *near* Alai—he was going to hit him.

"Here, snag my hand!" Alai called.

Ender held out his hand. Alai took the shock of impact and helped Ender make a fairly gentle landing against the wall.

"That's good," Ender said. "We ought to practice that kind of thing."

"That's what I thought, only everybody's turning to butter out there," Alai said. "What happens if we get out there together? We should be able to shove each other in opposite directions."

"Yeah."

"OK?"

It was an admission that all might not be right between them. Is it OK for us to do something together? Ender's answer was to take Alai by the wrist and get ready to push off.

"Ready?" said Alai. "Go."

Since they pushed off with different amounts of force, they began to circle each other. Ender made some small hand movements, then shifted a leg. They slowed. He did it again. They stopped orbiting. Now they were drifting evenly.

"Packed head, Ender," Alai said. It was high praise. "Let's push off before we run into that bunch."

"And then let's meet over in that corner." Ender did not want this bridge into the enemy camp to fail.

"Last one there saves farts in a milk bottle," Alai said.

Then, slowly, steadily, they maneuvered until they faced each other, spread-eagled, hand to hand, knee to knee.

"And then we just scrunch?" asked Alai.

"I've never done this before either," said Ender.

They pushed off. It propelled them faster than they expected. Ender ran into a couple of boys and ended up on a wall that he hadn't expected. It took him a moment to reorient and find the corner where he and Alai were to meet.

Alai was already headed toward it. Ender plotted a course that would include two rebounds, to avoid the largest clusters of boys.

When Ender reached the corner, Alai had hooked his arms through two adjacent handholds and was pretending to doze.

"You win."

"I want to see your fart collection," Alai said.

"I stored it in your locker. Didn't you notice?"

"I thought it was my socks."

"We don't wear socks anymore."

"Oh yeah." A reminder that they were both far from home. It took some of the fun out of having mastered a bit of navigation.

Ender took his pistol and demonstrated what he had learned about the two thumb buttons.

"What does it do when you aim at a person?" asked Alai.

"I don't know."

"Why don't we find out?"

Ender shook his head. "We might hurt somebody."

"I meant why don't we shoot each other in the foot or something. I'm not Bernard, I never tortured cats for fun."

"Oh."

"It can't be too dangerous, or they wouldn't give these guns to kids."

"We're soldiers now."

"Shoot me in the foot."

"No, you shoot me."

Let's shoot each other."

They did. Immediately Ender felt the leg of the suit grow stiff, immobile at the knee and ankle joints.

"You frozen?" asked Alai.

"Stiff as a board."

"Let's freeze a few," Alai said. "Let's have our first war. Us against them."

They grinned. Then Ender said, "Better invite Bernard."

Alai cocked an eyebrow. "Oh?"

"And Shen."

"That little butt-wiggler?"

Ender decided that Alai was joking. "If you didn't hold yours so tight it would wiggle, too."

Alai grinned. "Let's go get Bernard and Shen and freeze these bugger-lovers."

In twenty minutes, everyone in the room was frozen except Ender, Bernard, Shen, and Alai. The four of them sat there whooping and laughing until Dap came in.

"I see you've learned how to use your equipment," he said. Then he did something to a control he held in his hand. Everybody drifted slowly toward the wall he was standing on. He went among the frozen boys, touching them and thawing their suits. There was a tumult of complaint that it wasn't fair how Bernard and Alai had shot them all when they weren't ready.

"Why weren't you ready?" asked Dap. "You had your suits just as long as they did. You had just as many minutes flapping around like drunken ducks. Stop moaning and we'll begin."

Ender noticed that it was assumed that Bernard and Alai were the leaders of the battle. Well, that was fine. Bernard knew that Ender and Alai had learned to use the guns together. And Ender and Alai were friends. Now others might believe that Ender had joined his group, but it wasn't so. Ender had joined a new group. Alai's group. Bernard had joined it too.

It wasn't obvious to everyone; Bernard still blustered and sent his cronies on errands. But Alai now moved freely through the whole room, and when Bernard was crazy, Alai could joke a little and calm him down. When it came time to choose their launch leader, Alai was the almost unanimous choice. Bernard sulked for a few days and then he was fine, and everyone settled into the new pattern. The launch was no longer divided into Bernard's in-group and Ender's outcasts. Alai was the bridge.

—

Ender sat on his bed with his desk on his knees. It was private study time, and Ender was doing Free Play. It was a shifting, crazy kind of game in which the school computer kept bringing up new things, building a maze that you could explore. You could go back to events that you liked, for a while; if you left one alone too long, it disappeared and something else took its place.

Sometimes they were funny things. Sometimes exciting ones, and he had to be quick to stay alive. He had lots of deaths, but that was OK, games were like that, you died a lot until you got the hang of it.

His figure on the screen had started out as a little boy. For a while it had changed into a bear. Now it was a large mouse, with long and delicate hands. He ran his figure under a lot of large items of furniture depicted on the screen. He had played with the cat a lot, but now it was boring—too easy to dodge, he knew all the furniture.

Not through the mousehole this time, he told himself. I'm sick of the Giant. It's a dumb game and I can't ever win. Whatever I choose is wrong.

But he went through the mousehole anyway, and over the small bridge in the garden. He avoided the ducks and the divebombing mosquitoes—he had tried playing with them but they were too easy, and if he played with the ducks too long he turned into a fish, which he didn't like. Being a fish reminded him too much of being frozen in the battleroom, his whole body rigid, waiting for the practice to end so Dap would thaw him. So, as usual, he found himself going up the rolling hills.

The landslides began. At first he had got caught again and again, crushed in an exaggerated blot of gore oozing out from under a rockpile. Now, though, he had mastered the skill of running up the slopes at an angle to avoid the crush, always seeking higher ground.

And, as always, the landslides finally stopped being jumbles of rock. The face of the hill broke open and instead of shale it was white bread, puffy, rising like dough as the crust broke away and fell. It was soft and spongy; his figure moved more slowly. And when he jumped down off the bread, he was standing on a table. Giant loaf of bread behind him; giant stick of butter beside him. And the Giant himself leaning his chin in his hands, looking at him. Ender's figure was about as tall as the Giant's head from chin to brow.

"I think I'll bite your head off," said the Giant, as he always did.

This time, instead of running away or standing there, Ender walked his figure up to the Giant's face and kicked him in the chin.

The Giant stuck out his tongue and Ender fell to the ground.

"How about a guessing game?" asked the Giant. So it didn't make any difference—the Giant only played the guessing game. Stupid computer. Millions of possible scenarios in its memory, and the Giant could only play one stupid game.

The Giant, as always, set two huge shot glasses, as tall as Ender's knees, on the table in front of him. As always, the two were filled with different liquids. The computer was good enough that the liquids had never repeated, not that he could remember. This time the one had a thick, creamy looking liquid. The other hissed and foamed.

"One is poison and one is not," said the Giant. "Guess right and I'll take you into Fairyland."

Guessing meant sticking his head into one of the glasses to drink. He never guessed right. Sometimes his head was dissolved. Sometimes he caught on fire. Sometimes he fell in and drowned. Sometimes he fell out, turned green, and rotted away. It was always ghastly, and the Giant always laughed.

Ender knew that whatever he chose he would die. The game was rigged. On the first death, his figure would reappear on the Giant's table, to play again. On the second death, he'd come back to the landslides. Then to the garden bridge. Then to the mousehole. And then, if he still went back to the Giant and played again, and died again, his desk would go dark, "Free Play Over" would march around the desk, and Ender would lie back on his bed and tremble until he could finally go to sleep. The game was rigged but still the Giant talked about Fairyland, some stupid childish three-year-old's Fairyland that probably had some stupid Mother Goose or Pac-Man or Peter Pan, it wasn't even worth getting to, but he had to find some way of beating the Giant to get there.

He drank the creamy liquid. Immediately he began to inflate and rise like a balloon. The Giant laughed. He was dead again.

He played again, and this time the liquid set, like concrete, and held his head down while the Giant cut him open along the spine, deboned him like a fish, and began to eat while his arms and legs quivered.

He reappeared at the landslides and decided not to go on. He even let the landslides cover him once. But even though he was sweating and he felt cold, with his next life he went back up the hills till they turned into bread, and stood on the Giant's table as the shot glasses were set before him.

He stared at the two liquids. The one foaming, the other with waves in it like the sea. He tried to guess what kind of death each one held. Probably a fish will come out of the ocean one and eat me. The foamy one will probably asphyxiate me. I hate this game. It isn't fair. It's stupid. It's rotten.

And instead of pushing his face into one of the liquids, he kicked one over, then the other, and dodged the Giant's huge hands as the Giant shouted, "Cheater, cheater!" He jumped at the Giant's face, clambered up his lip and nose, and began to dig in the Giant's eye. The stuff came away like cottage cheese, and as the Giant screamed, Ender's figure burrowed into the eye, climbed right in, burrowed in and in.

The Giant fell over backward. The view shifted as he fell, and when the Giant came to rest on the ground, there were intricate, lacy trees all around. A bat flew up and landed on the dead Giant's nose. Ender brought his figure up out of the Giant's eye.

"How did you get here?" the bat asked. "Nobody ever comes here."

Ender could not answer, of course. So he reached down, took a handful of the Giant's eyestuff, and offered it to the bat.

The bat took it and flew off, shouting as it went, "Welcome to Fairyland."

He had made it. He ought to explore. He ought to climb down from the Giant's face and see what he had finally achieved.

Instead he signed off, put his desk in his locker, stripped off his clothes and pulled his blanket over him. He hadn't meant to kill the Giant. This was supposed to be a game. Not a choice between his own grisly death and an even worse murder. I'm a murderer, even when I play. Peter would be proud of me.

7

Salamander

"Isn't it nice to know that Ender can do the impossible?"

"The player's deaths have always been sickening, I've always thought the Giant's Drink was the most perverted part of the whole mind game, but going for the eye like that—this is the one we want to put in command of our fleet?"

"What matters is that he won the game that couldn't be won."

"I suppose you'll move him now."

"We were waiting to see how he handled the thing with Bernard. He handled it perfectly."

"So as soon as he can cope with a situation, you move him to one he can't cope with. Doesn't he get any rest?"

"He'll have a month or two, maybe three, with his launch group. That's really quite a long time in a child's life."

"Does it ever seem to you that these boys aren't children? I look at what they do, the way they talk, and they don't seem like little kids."

"They're the most brilliant children in the world, each in his own way."

"But shouldn't they still act like children? They aren't *normal.* They act like—history. Napoleon and Wellington. Caesar and Brutus."

"We're trying to save the world, not heal the wounded heart. You're too compassionate."

"General Levy has no pity for anyone. All the videos say so. But don't hurt this boy."

"Are you joking?"

"I mean, don't hurt him more than you have to."

Alai sat across from Ender at dinner. "I finally figured out how you sent that message. Using Bernard's name."

"Me?" asked Ender.

"Come on, who else? It sure wasn't Bernard. And Shen isn't too hot on the computer. And I know it wasn't me. Who else? Doesn't matter. I figured out how to fake a new student entry. You just created a student named Bernard-blank, B-E-R-N-A-R-D-space, so the computer didn't kick it out as a repeat of another student."

"Sounds like that might work," said Ender.

"OK, OK. It *does* work. But you did that practically on the first day."

"Or somebody. Maybe Dap did it, to keep Bernard from getting too much control."

"I found something else. I can't do it with your name."

"Oh?"

"Anything with *Ender* in it gets kicked out. I can't get inside your files at all, either. You made your own security system."

"Maybe."

Alai grinned. "I just got in and trashed somebody's files. He's right behind me on cracking the system. I need protection, Ender. I need your system."

"If I give you my system, you'll know how I do it and you'll get in and trash *me*."

"You say *me*?" Alai asked. "I the sweetest friend you got!"

Ender laughed. "I'll set up a system for you."

"Now?"

"Can I finish eating?"

"You never finish eating."

It was true. Ender's tray always had food on it after a meal. Ender looked at the plate and decided he was through. "Let's go then."

When they got to the barracks, Ender squatted down by his bed and said, "Get your desk and bring it over here, I'll show you how." But when Alai brought his desk to Ender's bed, Ender was just sitting there, his lockers still closed.

"What up?" asked Alai.

In answer, Ender palmed his locker. "Unauthorized Access Attempt," it said. It didn't open.

"Somebody done a dance on your head, mama," Alai said. "Somebody eated your face."

"You sure you want my security system now?" Ender got up and walked away from his bed.

"Ender," said Alai.

Ender turned around. Alai was holding a little piece of paper.

"What is it?"

Alai looked up at him. "Don't you know? This was on your bed. You must have sat on it."

Ender took it from him.

ENDER WIGGIN
ASSIGNED SALAMANDER ARMY
COMMANDER BONZO MADRID
EFFECTIVE IMMEDIATELY
CODE GREEN GREEN BROWN
NO POSSESSIONS TRANSFERRED

"You're smart, Ender, but you don't do the battleroom any better than me."

Ender shook his head. It was the stupidest thing he could think of, to promote him now. Nobody got promoted before they were eight years old. Ender wasn't even seven yet. And launches usually moved into the armies together, with most armies getting a new kid at the same time. There were no transfer slips on any of the other beds.

Just when things were finally coming together. Just when Bernard was getting along with everybody, even Ender. Just when Ender was beginning to make a real friend out of Alai. Just when his life was finally getting livable.

Ender reached down to pull Alai up from the bed.

"Salamander Army's in contention, anyway," Alai said.

Ender was so angry at the unfairness of the transfer that tears were coming to his eyes. Mustn't cry, he told himself.

Alai saw the tears but had the grace not to say so. "They're fartheads, Ender, they won't even let you take anything you *own*."

Ender grinned and didn't cry after all. "Think I should strip and go naked?"

Alai laughed, too.

On impulse Ender hugged him, tight, almost as if he were Valentine. He even thought of Valentine then and wanted to go home. "I don't want to go," he said.

Alai hugged him back. "I understand them, Ender. You *are* the best of us. Maybe they in a hurry to teach you everything."

"They don't want to teach me *everything*," Ender said. "I wanted to learn what it was like to have a friend."

Alai nodded soberly. "Always my friend, always the best of my friends," he said. Then he grinned. "Go slice up the buggers."

"Yeah." Ender smiled back.

Alai suddenly kissed Ender on the cheek and whispered in his ear, "Salaam." Then, red-faced, he turned away and walked to his own bed at the back of the barracks. Ender guessed that the kiss and the word were somehow forbidden. A suppressed religion, perhaps. Or maybe the word had some private and powerful meaning for Alai alone. Whatever it meant to Alai, Ender knew that it was sacred; that he had uncovered himself for Ender, as once Ender's mother had done, when he was very young, before they put the monitor in his neck, and she had put her hands on his head when she thought he was asleep, and prayed over him. Ender had never spoken of that to anyone, not even to Mother, but had kept it as a memory of holiness, of how his mother loved him when she thought that no one, not even he, could see or hear. That was what Alai had given him; a gift so sacred that even Ender could not be allowed to understand what it meant.

After such a thing nothing could be said. Alai reached his bed and turned around to see Ender. Their eyes held for only a moment, locked in understanding. Then Ender left.

There would be no green green brown in this part of the school; he would have to pick up the colors in one of the public areas. The others would be finished with dinner very soon; he didn't want to go near the mess hall. The game room would be nearly empty.

None of the games appealed to him, the way he felt now. So he went to the bank of public desks at the back of the room and signed on to his own private game. He went quickly to Fairyland. The Giant was dead when he arrived now; he had to climb carefully down the table, jump to the leg of the Giant's overturned chair, and then make the drop to the ground. For a while there had been rats gnawing at the Giant's body, but Ender had killed one with a pin from the Giant's ragged shirt, and they had left him alone after that.

The Giant's corpse had essentially finished its decay. What could be torn by the small scavengers was torn; the maggots had done their work on the organs; now it was a desiccated mummy, hollowed-out, teeth in a rigid grin, eyes empty, fingers curled. Ender remembered burrowing through the eye when it had been alive and malicious and intelligent. Angry and frustrated as he was, Ender wished to do such violence again. But the Giant had become part of the landscape now, and so there could be no rage against him.

Ender had always gone over the bridge to the castle of the Queen of Hearts, where there were games enough for him; but none of those appealed to him now. He went around the giant's corpse and followed the brook upstream, to where it emerged from the forest. There was a playground there, slides and monkeybars, teeter-totters and merry-go-rounds, with a dozen children laughing as they played. Ender came and found that in the game he had become a child, though usually his figure in the games was adult. In fact, he was smaller than the other children.

He got in line for the slide. The other children ignored him. He climbed up to the top, watched the boy before him whirl down the long spiral to the ground. Then he sat and began to slide.

He had not slid for a moment when he fell right through the slide and landed on the ground under the ladder. The slide would not hold him.

Neither would the monkey bars. He could climb a ways, but then at random a bar seemed to be insubstantial and he fell. He could sit on the see-saw until he rose to the apex; then he fell. When the merry-go-round went fast, he could not hold onto any of the bars, and centrifugal force hurled him off.

And the other children: their laughter was raucous, offensive. They circled around him and pointed and laughed for many seconds before they went back to their play.

Ender wanted to hit them, to throw them in the brook. Instead he walked into the forest. He found a path, which soon became an ancient brick road, much overgrown with weeds but still usable. There were hints of possible games off to either side, but Ender followed none of them. He wanted to see where the path led.

It led to a clearing, with a well in the middle, and a sign that said, "Drink, Traveler." Ender went forward and looked at the well. Almost at once, he heard a snarl. Out of the woods emerged a dozen slavering wolves with human faces. Ender recognized them—they were the children from the playground. Only now their teeth could tear; Ender, weaponless, was quickly devoured.

His next figure appeared, as usual, in the same spot, and was eaten again, though Ender tried to climb down into the well.

The next appearance, though, was at the playground. Again the children laughed at him. Laugh all you like, Ender thought. I know what you are. He pushed one of them. She followed him, angry. Ender led her up the slide. Of course he fell through; but this time, following so closely behind him, she also fell through. When she hit the ground, she turned into a wolf and lay there, dead or stunned.

One by one Ender led each of the others into a trap. But before he had finished off the last of them, the wolves began reviving, and were no longer children. Ender was torn apart again.

This time, shaking and sweating, Ender found his figure revived on the Giant's table. I should quit, he told himself. I should go to my new army.

But instead he made his figure drop down from the table and walk around the Giant's body to the playground.

This time, as soon as the child hit the ground and turned into a wolf, Ender dragged the body to the brook and pulled it in. Each time, the body sizzled as though the water were acid; the wolf was consumed, and a dark cloud of smoke arose and drifted away. The children were easily dispatched, though they began following him in twos and threes at the end. Ender found no wolves waiting for him in the clearing, and he lowered himself into the well on the bucket rope.

The light in the cavern was dim, but he could see piles of jewels. He passed them by, noting that, behind him, eyes glinted among the gems. A table covered with food did not interest him. He passed through a group of cages hanging from the ceiling of the cave, each containing some exotic, friendly-looking creature. I'll play with you later, Ender thought. At last he came to a door, with these words in glowing emeralds:

THE END OF THE WORLD

He did not hesitate. He opened the door and stepped through.

He stood on a small ledge, high on a cliff overlooking a terrain of bright and deep green forest with dashes of autumn color and patches here and there of cleared land, with ox-drawn plows and small villages, a castle on a rise in the distance, and clouds riding currents of air below him. Above him, the sky was the ceiling of a vast cavern, with crystals dangling in bright stalactites.

The door closed behind him; Ender studied the scene intently. With the beauty of it, he cared less for survival than usual. He cared little, at the moment, what the game of this place might be. He had found it, and seeing it was its own reward. And so, with no thought of consequences, he jumped from the ledge.

Now he plummeted downward toward a roiling river and savage rocks; but a cloud came between him and the ground as he fell, and caught him, and carried him away. It took him to the tower of the castle, and through the open window, bearing him in. There it left him, in a room with no apparent door in floor or ceiling, and windows looking out over a certainly fatal fall.

A moment ago he had thrown himself from a ledge carelessly; this time he hesitated.

The small rug before the fire unraveled itself into a long, slender serpent with wicked teeth.

"I am your only escape," it said. "Death is your only escape."

Ender looked around the room for a weapon, when suddenly the screen went dark. Words flashed around the rim of the desk.

REPORT TO COMMANDER IMMEDIATELY.
YOU ARE LATE.
GREEN GREEN BROWN.

Furious, Ender snapped off the desk and went to the color wall, where he found the ribbon of green green brown, touched it, and followed it as it lit up before him. The dark green, light green, and brown of the ribbon reminded him of the early autumn kingdom he had found in the game. I must go back there, he told himself. The serpent is a long thread; I can let myself down from the tower and find my way through that place. Perhaps it's called the end of the world because it's the end of the games, because I can go to one of the villages and become one of the little boys working and playing there, with nothing to kill and nothing to kill me, just living there.

As he thought of it, though, he could not imagine what "just living" might actually be. He had never done it in his life. But he wanted to do it anyway.

—

Armies were larger than launch groups, and the army barracks room was larger, too. It was long and narrow, with bunks on both sides; so long, in fact, that you could see the curvature of the floor as the far end bent upward, part of the wheel of the Battle School.

Ender stood at the door. A few boys near the door glanced at him, but they were older, and it seemed as though they hadn't even seen him. They went on with their conversations, lying and leaning on bunks. They were discussing battles, of course—the older boys always did. They were all much larger than Ender. The ten- and eleven-year-olds towered over him; even the youngest were eight, and Ender was not large for his age.

He tried to see which of the boys was the commander, but most were somewhere between battle dress and what the soldiers always called their sleep uniform—skin from head to toe. Many of them had desks out, but few were studying.

Ender stepped into the room. The moment he did, he was noticed.

"What do you want?" demanded the boy who had the upper bunk by the door. He was the largest of them. Ender had noticed him before, a young giant who had whiskers growing raggedly on his chin. "You're not a Salamander."

"I'm supposed to be, I think," Ender said. "Green green brown, right? I was transferred." He showed the boy, obviously the doorguard, his paper.

The doorguard reached for it. Ender withdrew it, just out of reach. "I'm supposed to give it to Bonzo Madrid."

Now another boy joined the conversation, a smaller boy, but still larger than Ender. "Not bahn-zoe, pisshead. Bone-So. The name's Spanish. Bonzo Madrid. Aqui nosotros hablamos español, Señor Gran Fedor."

"You must be Bonzo, then?" Ender asked, pronouncing the name correctly.

"No, just a brilliant and talented polyglot. Petra Arkanian. The only girl in Salamander Army. With more balls than anybody else in the room."

"Mother Petra she talking," said one of the boys, "she talking, she talking."

Another one chimed in. "Shit talking, shit talking, shit talking!"

Quite a few laughed.

"Just between you and me," Petra said, "if they gave the Battle School an enema, they'd stick it in at green green brown."

Ender despaired. He already had nothing going for him—grossly undertrained, small, inexperienced, doomed to be resented for early advancement. And now, by chance, he had made exactly the wrong friend. An outcast in Salamander Army, and she had just linked him with her in the minds of the rest of the army. A good day's work. For a moment, as Ender looked around at the laughing, jeering faces, he imagined their bodies covered with hair, their teeth pointed for tearing. Am I the only human being in this place? Are all the others animals, waiting only to devour?

Then he remembered Alai. In every army, surely, there was at least one worth knowing.

Suddenly, though no one said to be quiet, the laughter stopped and the group fell silent. Ender turned to the door. A boy stood there, tall and slender, with beautiful black eyes and slender lips that hinted at refinement. I would follow such beauty, said something inside Ender. I would see as those eyes see.

"Who are you?" asked the boy quietly.

"Ender Wiggin, sir," Ender said. "Reassigned from launch to Salamander Army." He held out the orders.

The boy took the paper in a swift, sure movement, without touching Ender's hand. "How old are you, Wiggin?" he asked.

"Almost seven."

Still quietly, he said, "I asked how old you are, not how old you almost are."

"I am six years, nine months, and twelve days old."

"How long have you been working in the battleroom?"

"A few months, now. My aim is better."

"Any training in battle maneuvers? Have you ever been part of a toon? Have you ever carried out a joint exercise?"

Ender had never heard of such things. He shook his head.

Madrid looked at him steadily. "I see. As you will quickly learn, the officers in command of this school, most notably Major Anderson, who runs the game, are fond of playing tricks. Salamander Army is just beginning to emerge from indecent obscurity. We have won twelve of our last twenty games. We have surprised Rat and Scorpion and Hound, and we are ready to play for leadership in the game. So of course, of course I am given such a useless, untrained, hopeless specimen of underdevelopment as yourself."

Petra said, quietly, "He isn't glad to meet you."

"Shut up, Arkanian," Madrid said. "To one trial, we

now add another. But whatever obstacles our officers choose to fling in our path, we are still—''

''Salamander!'' cried the soldiers, in one voice.

Instinctively, Ender's perception of these events changed. It was a pattern, a ritual. Madrid was not trying to hurt him, merely taking control of a surprising event and using it to strengthen his control of his army.

''We are the fire that will consume them, belly and bowel, head and heart, many flames of us, but one fire.''

''Salamander!'' they cried again.

''Even this one will not weaken us.''

For a moment, Ender allowed himself to hope. ''I'll work hard and learn quickly,'' he said.

''I didn't give you permission to speak,'' Madrid answered. ''I intend to trade you away as quickly as I can. I'll probably have to give up someone valuable along with you, but as small as you are you are worse than useless. One more frozen, inevitably, in every battle, that's all you are, and we're now at a point where every frozen soldier makes a difference in the standings. Nothing personal, Wiggin, but I'm sure you can get your training at someone else's expense.''

''He's all heart,'' Petra said.

Madrid stepped closer to the girl and slapped her across the face with the back of his hand. It made little sound, for only his fingernails had hit her. But there were bright red marks, four of them, on her cheek, and little pricks of blood marked where the tips of his fingernails had struck.

''Here are your instructions, Wiggin. I expect that it is the last time I'll need to speak to you. You will stay out of the way when we're training in the battleroom. You have to be there, of course, but you will not belong to any toon and you will not take part in any maneuvers. When we're called to battle, you will dress quickly and present yourself at the gate with everyone else. But you will not pass through the gate until four full minutes after the beginning of the game, and then you will remain at the gate, with your weapons undrawn and unfired, until such time as the game ends."

Ender nodded. So he was to be a nothing. He hoped the trade happened soon.

He also noticed that Petra did not so much as cry out in pain, or touch her cheek, though one spot of blood had beaded and run, making a streak down to her jaw. Outcast she may be, but since Bonzo Madrid was not going to be Ender's friend, no matter what, he might as well make friends with Petra.

He was assigned a bunk at the far end of the room. The upper bunk, so that when he lay on his bed he couldn't even see the door: The curve of the ceiling blocked it. There were other boys near him, tired-looking boys, sullen, the ones least valued. They had nothing of welcome to say to Ender.

Ender tried to palm his locker open, but nothing happened. Then he realized the lockers were not secured. All four of them had rings on them, to pull them open. Nothing would be private, then, now that he was in an army.

There was a uniform in the locker. Not the pale green of the Launchies, but the orange-trimmed dark green of Salamander Army. It did not fit well. But then, they had probably never had to provide such a uniform for a boy so young.

He was starting to take it off when he noticed Petra walking down the aisle toward his bed. He slid off the bunk and stood on the floor to greet her.

"Relax," she said. "I'm not an officer."

"You're a toon leader, aren't you?"

Someone nearby snickered.

"Whatever gave you that idea, Wiggin?"

"You have a bunk in the front."

"I bunk in the front because I'm the best sharpshooter in Salamander Army, and because Bonzo is afraid I'll start a revolution if the toon leaders don't keep an eye on me. As if I could start anything with boys like *these*." She indicated the sullen-faced boys on the nearby bunks.

What was she trying to do, make it worse than it already was? "Everybody's better than I am," Ender said, trying to dissociate himself from her contempt for the boys who would, after all, be his near bunkmates.

"I'm a girl," she said, "and you're a pissant of a six-year-old. We have so much in common, why don't we be friends?"

"I won't do your deskwork for you," he said.

In a moment she realized it was a joke. "Ha," she said. "It's all so military, when you're in the game. School for us isn't like it is for Launchies. History and strategy and tactics and buggers and math and stars, things you'll need as a pilot or a commander. You'll see."

"So you're my friend. Do I get a prize?" Ender asked. He was imitating her swaggering way of speaking, as if she cared about nothing.

"Bonzo isn't going to let you practice. He's going to make you take your desk to the battleroom and study. He's right, in a way—he don't want a totally untrained little kid to screw up his precision maneuvers." She lapsed into giria, the slangy talk that imitated the pidgin English of uneducated people. "Bonzo, he pre-*cise*. He so *careful*, he piss on a plate and never splash."

Ender grinned.

"The battleroom is open all the time. If you want, I'll take you in the off hours and show you some of the things I know. I'm not a great soldier, but I'm pretty good, and I sure know more than you."

"If you want," Ender said.

"Starting tomorrow morning after breakfast."

"What if somebody's using the room? We always went right after breakfast, in my launch."

"No problem. There are really nine battlerooms."

"I never heard of any others."

"They all have the same entrance. The whole center of the battle school, the hub of the wheel, is battlerooms. They don't rotate with the rest of the station. That's how they do the nullo, the no-gravity—it just holds still. No spin, no down. But they can set it up so that any one of the rooms is at the battleroom entrance corridor that we all use. Once you're inside, they move it along and another battleroom's in position."

"Oh."

"Like I said. Right after breakfast."

"Right," Ender said.

She started to walk away.

"Petra," he said.

She turned back.

"Thanks."

She said nothing, just turned around again and walked down the aisle.

Ender climbed back up on his bunk and finished taking off his uniform. He lay naked on the bed, doodling with his new desk, trying to decide if they had done anything to his access codes. Sure enough, they had wiped out his security system. He couldn't own anything here, not even his desk.

The lights dimmed a little. Getting toward bedtime. Ender didn't know which bathroom to use.

"Go left out of the door," said the boy on the next bunk. "We share it with Rat, Condor, and Squirrel."

Ender thanked him and started to walk on past.

"Hey," said the boy. "You can't go like that. Uniforms at all times out of this room."

"Even going to the toilet?"

"Especially. And you're forbidden to speak to anyone from any other army. At meals or in the toilet. You can get away with it sometimes in the game room, and of course whenever a teacher tells you to. But if Bonzo catch you, you dead, eh?"

"Thanks."

"And, uh, Bonzo get mad if you skin by Petra."

"She was naked when I came in, wasn't she?"

"She do what she like, but you keep you clothes on. Bonzo's orders."

That was stupid. Petra still looked like a boy, it was a stupid rule. It set her apart, made her different, split the army. Stupid stupid. How did Bonzo get to be a commander, if he didn't know better than that? Alai would be a better commander than Bonzo. He knew how to bring a group together.

I know to bring a group together, too, thought Ender. Maybe I'll be commander someday.

In the bathroom, he was washing his hands when somebody spoke to him. "Hey, they putting babies in Salamander uniforms now?"

Ender didn't answer. Just dried off his hands.

"Hey, look! Salamander's getting babies now! Look at this! He could walk between my legs without touching my balls!"

"Cause you got none, Dink, that's why," somebody answered.

As Ender left the room, he heard somebody else say, "It's Wiggin. You know, the smartass Launchie from the game room."

He walked down the corridor smiling. He may be short, but they knew his name. From the game room, of course, so it meant nothing. But they'd see. He'd be a good soldier, too. They'd all know his name soon enough. Not in Salamander Army, maybe, but soon enough.

—

Petra was waiting in the corridor that led to the battleroom. "Wait a minute," she said to Ender. "Rabbit Army just went in, and it takes a few minutes to change to the next battleroom."

Ender sat down beside her. "There's more to the battleroom than just switching from one to the next," he said. "For instance, why is there gravity in the corridor outside the room, just before we go in?"

Petra closed her eyes. "And if the battlerooms are really free-floating, what happens when one is connected?

Why doesn't it start to move with the rotation of the school?''

Ender nodded.

''These are the mysteries,'' Petra said in a deep whisper. ''Do not pry into them. Terrible things happened to the last soldier who tried. He was discovered hanging by his feet from the ceiling of the bathroom, with his head stuffed in the toilet.''

Of course she was joking, but the message was clear. ''So I'm not the first person to ask the question.''

''You remember this, little boy.'' When she said *little boy* it sounded friendly, not contemptuous. ''They never tell you any more truth than they have to. But any kid with brains knows that there've been some changes in science since the days of old Mazer Rackham and the Victorious Fleet. Obviously we can now control gravity. Turn it on and off, change the direction, maybe reflect it—I've thought of lots of neat things you could do with gravity weapons and gravity drives on starships. And think how starships could move near planets. Maybe tear big chunks out of them by reflecting the planet's own gravity back on itself, only from another direction, and focused down to a smaller point. But they say nothing.''

Ender understood more than she said. Manipulation of gravity was one thing; deception by the officers was another; but the most important message was this: the adults are the enemy, not the other armies. They do not tell us the truth.

''Come, little boy,'' she said. ''The battleroom is ready. Petra's hands are steady. The enemy is deadly.'' She giggled. ''Petra the poet, they call me.''

''They also say you're crazy as a loon.''

''Better believe it, baby butt.'' She had ten target balls in a bag. Ender held onto her suit with one hand and the wall with the other, to steady her as she threw them, hard, in different directions. In the null gravity, they bounced every which way. ''Let go of me,'' she said. She shoved off, spinning deliberately; with a few deft hand moves she steadied herself, and began aiming carefully at ball after ball. When she shot one, its glow changed from white to red. Ender knew that the color change lasted less than two minutes. Only one ball had changed back to white when she got the last one.

She rebounded accurately from a wall and came at high speed back to Ender. He caught her and held her against her own rebound—one of the first techniques they had taught him as a Launchy.

"You're good," he said.

"None better. And you're going to learn how to do it."

Petra taught him to hold his arm straight, to aim with the whole arm. "Something most soldiers don't realize is that the farther away your target is, the longer you have to hold the beam within about a two-centimeter circle. It's the difference between a tenth of a second and a half a second, but in battle that's a long time. A lot of soldiers think they missed when they were right on target, but they moved away too fast. So you can't use your gun like a sword, swish swish slice-em-in-half. You got to aim."

She used the ballcaller to bring the targets back, then launched them slowly, one by one. Ender fired at them. He missed every one.

"Good," she said. "You don't have any bad habits."

"I don't have any good ones, either," he pointed out.

"I give you those."

They didn't accomplish much that first morning. Mostly talk. How to think while you were aiming. You've got to hold your own motion and your enemy's motion in your mind at the same time. You've got to hold your arm straight out and aim with your body, so in case your arm is frozen you can still shoot. Learn where your trigger actually fires and ride the edge, so you don't have to pull so far each time you fire. Relax your body, don't tense up, it makes you tremble.

It was the only practice Ender got that day. During the army's drills in the afternoon, Ender was ordered to bring his desk and do his schoolwork, sitting in a corner of the room. Bonzo had to bring all his soldiers to the battleroom, but he didn't have to use them.

Ender did not do his schoolwork, however. If he couldn't drill as a soldier, he could study Bonzo as a tactician. Salamander Army was divided into the standard four toons of ten soldiers each. Some commanders set up their toons so that A toon consisted of the best soldiers, and D toon had the worst. Bonzo had mixed them, so that each consisted of good soldiers and weaker ones.

Except that B toon had only nine boys. Ender wondered who had been transferred to make room for him. It soon became plain that the leader of toon B was new. No wonder Bonzo was so disgusted—he had lost a toon leader to get Ender.

And Bonzo was right about another thing. Ender was not ready. All the practice time was spent working on maneuvers. Toons that couldn't see each other practiced performing precision operations together with exact timing; toons practiced using each other to make sudden changes of direction without losing formation. All these soldiers took for granted skills that Ender didn't have. The ability to make a soft landing and absorb most of the shock. Accurate flight. Course adjustment using the frozen soldiers floating randomly through the room. Rolls, spins, dodges. Sliding along the walls—a very difficult maneuver and yet one of the most valuable, since the enemy couldn't get behind you.

Even as Ender learned how much he did not know, he also saw things that he could improve on. The well-rehearsed formations were a mistake. It allowed the soldiers to obey shouted orders instantly, but it also meant they were predictable. Also, the individual soldiers were given little initiative. Once a pattern was set, they were to follow it through. There was no room for adjustment to what the enemy did against the formation. Ender studied Bonzo's formations like an enemy commander would, noting ways to disrupt the formation.

During free play that night, Ender asked Petra to practice with him.

"No," she said. "I want to be a commander someday, so I've got to play the game room." It was a common belief that the teachers monitored the games and spotted potential commanders there. Ender doubted it, though. Toon leaders had a better chance to show what they might do as commanders than any video player.

But he didn't argue with Petra. The after-breakfast practice was generous enough. Still, he had to practice. And he couldn't practice alone, except a few of the basic skills. Most of the hard things required partners or teams. If only he still had Alai or Shen to practice with.

Well, why *shouldn't* he practice with them? He had never heard of a soldier practicing with Launchies, but there was no rule against it. It just wasn't done; Launchies were held in too much contempt. Well, Ender was still being treated like a Launchy anyway. He needed someone to practice with, and in return he could help them learn some of the things he saw the older boys doing.

"Hey, the great soldier returns!" said Bernard. Ender stood in the doorway of his old barracks. He'd only been away for a day, but already it seemed like an alien place, and the others of his launch group were strangers. Almost he turned around and left. But there was Alai, who had made their friendship sacred. Alai was not a stranger.

Ender made no effort to conceal how he was treated in Salamander Army. "And they're right. I'm about as useful as a sneeze in a spacesuit." Alai laughed, and other Launchies started to gather around. Ender proposed his bargain. Free play, every day, working hard in the battleroom, under Ender's direction. They would learn things from the armies, from the battles Ender would see; he would get the practice he needed in developing soldier skills. "We'll get ready together."

A lot of boys wanted to come, too. "Sure," Ender said.

"If you're coming to work. If you're just farting around, you're out. I don't have any time to waste."

They didn't waste any time. Ender was clumsy, trying to describe what he had seen, working out ways to do it. But by the time free play ended, they had learned some things. They were tired, but they were getting the knack of a few techniques.

"Where were you?" asked Bonzo.

Ender stood stiffly by his commander's bunk. "Practicing in a battleroom."

"I hear you had some of your old Launchy group with you."

"I couldn't practice alone."

"I won't have any soldiers in Salamander Army hanging around with Launchies. You're a soldier now."

Ender regarded him in silence.

"Did you hear me, Wiggin?"

"Yes, sir."

"No more practicing with those little farts."

"May I speak to you privately?" asked Ender.

It was a request that commanders were required to allow. Bonzo's face went angry, and he led Ender out into the corridor. "Listen, Wiggin, I don't want you, I'm trying to get rid of you, but don't give me any problems or I'll paste you to the wall."

A good commander, thought Ender, doesn't have to make stupid threats.

Bonzo grew annoyed at Ender's silence. "Look, you asked me to come out here, now talk."

"Sir, you were correct not to place me in a toon. I don't know how to do anything."

"I don't need you to tell me when I'm correct."

"But I'm going to become a good soldier. I won't screw up your regular drill, but I'm going to practice, and I'm going to practice with the only people who will practice with me, and that's my Launchies."

"You'll do what I tell you, you little bastard."

"That's right, sir. I'll follow all the orders that you're authorized to give. But free play is free. No assignments can be given. None. By anyone."

He could see Bonzo's anger growing hot. Hot anger was bad. Ender's anger was cold, and he could use it. Bonzo's was hot, and so it used him.

"Sir, I've got my own career to think of. I won't interfere in your training and your battles, but I've got to learn sometime. I didn't ask to be put into your army, you're trying to trade me as soon as you can. But nobody will take me if I don't know anything, will they? Let me learn something, and then you can get rid of me all the sooner and get a soldier you can really use."

Bonzo was not such a fool that anger kept him from recognizing good sense when he heard it. Still, he couldn't let go of his anger immediately.

"While you're in Salamander Army, you'll obey me."

"If you try to control my free play, I can get you iced."

It probably wasn't true. But it was possible. Certainly if Ender made a fuss about it, interfering with free play could conceivably get Bonzo removed from command. Also, there was the fact that the officers obviously saw something in Ender, since they had promoted him. Maybe Ender *did* have influence enough with the teachers to ice somebody.

"Bastard," said Bonzo.

"It isn't my fault you gave me that order in front of everybody," Ender said. "But if you want, I'll pretend you won this argument. Then tomorrow you can tell me you changed your mind."

"I don't need you to tell me what to do."

"I don't want the other guys to think you backed down. You wouldn't be able to command as well."

Bonzo hated him for it, for the kindness. Ender tried to understand why. Maybe it seemed to Bonzo as if Ender were granting him his command as a favor. Galling, and yet he had no choice. No choice about anything. Well it was Bonzo's own fault, for giving Ender an unreasonable order. Still, he would only know that Ender had beaten him, and then rubbed his nose in it by being magnanimous.

"I'll have your ass someday," Bonzo said.

"Probably," said Ender. The lights out buzzer sounded. Ender walked back into the room, looking dejected. Beaten. Angry. The other boys drew the obvious conclusion.

And in the morning, as Ender was leaving for breakfast, Bonzo stopped him and spoke loudly. "I changed my mind, pinprick. Maybe by practicing with your Launchies you'll learn something, and I can trade you easier. Anything to get rid of you faster."

"Thank you, sir," Ender said.

"Anything," whispered Bonzo. "I hope you're iced."

Ender smiled gratefully and left the room. After breakfast he practiced again with Petra. All afternoon he watched Bonzo drill and figured out ways to destroy his army. During free play he and Alai and the others worked themselves to exhaustion. I can do this, thought Ender as he lay in his bed, his muscles throbbing, unknotting themselves. I can handle it.

—

Salamander Army had a battle four days later. Ender followed behind the real soldiers as they jogged along the corridors to the battleroom. There were two ribbons along the walls, the green green brown of Salamander and the black white black of Condor. When they came to the place where the battleroom had always been, the corridor split instead, with green green brown leading to the left and black white black to the right. Around another turn to the right, and the army stopped in front of a blank wall.

The toons formed up in silence. Ender stayed behind them all. Bonzo was giving his instructions. "A take the handles and go up. B left, C right, D down." He saw that the toons were oriented to follow instructions, then added, "And you, pinprick, wait four minutes, then come just inside the door. Don't even take your gun off your suit."

Ender nodded. Suddenly the wall behind Bonzo became transparent. Not a wall at all, then, but a forcefield. The battleroom was different, too. Huge brown boxes were suspended in midair, partially obstructing the view. So these were the obstacles that the soldiers called *stars*. They were distributed seemingly at random. Bonzo seemed not to care where they were. Apparently the soldiers already knew how to handle the stars.

But it soon became clear to Ender, as he sat and watched the battle from the corridor, that they did not know how to handle the stars. They did know how to softland on one and use it for cover, the tactics of assaulting the enemy's position on a star. They showed no sense at all of *which* stars mattered. They persisted in assaulting stars that could have been bypassed by wallsliding to a more advanced position.

The other commander was taking advantage of Bonzo's neglect of strategy. Condor Army forced the Salamanders into costly assaults. Fewer and fewer Salamanders were unfrozen for the attack on the next star. It was clear, after only four minutes, that Salamander Army could not defeat the enemy by attacking.

Ender stepped through the gate. He drifted slightly downward. The battlerooms he had practiced in always had their doors at floor level. For real battles, however, the door was set in the middle of the wall, as far from the floor as from the ceiling.

Abruptly he felt himself reorient, as he had in the shuttle. What had been down was now up, and now sideways. In nullo, there was no reason to stay oriented the way he had been in the corridor. It was impossible to tell, looking at the perfectly square doors, which way had been up. And it didn't matter. For now Ender had found the orientation that made sense. The enemy's gate was down. The object of the game was to fall toward the enemy's home.

Ender made the motions that oriented himself in his new direction. Instead of being spread out, his whole body presented to the enemy, now Ender's legs pointed toward them. He was a much smaller target.

Someone saw him. He was, after all, drifting aimlessly in the open. Instinctively he pulled his legs up under him. At that moment he was flashed, and the legs of his suit froze in position. His arms remained unfrozen, for without a direct body hit, only the limbs that were shot froze up. It occurred to Ender that if he had not been presenting his legs to the enemy, it would have been his body they hit. He would have been immobilized.

Since Bonzo had ordered him not to draw his weapon, Ender continued to drift, not moving his head or arms, as if they had been frozen, too. The enemy ignored him and concentrated their fire on the soldiers who were firing at them. It was a bitter battle. Outnumbered now, Salamander Army gave ground stubbornly. The battle disintegrated into a dozen individual shootouts. Bonzo's discipline paid off now, for each Salamander that froze took at least one enemy with him. No one ran or panicked, everyone remained calm and aimed carefully.

Petra was especially deadly. Condor Army noticed it and took great effort to freeze her. They froze her shooting arm first, and her stream of curses was only interrupted when they froze her completely and the helmet clamped down on her jaw. In a few minutes it was over. Salamander Army offered no more resistance.

Ender noted with pleasure that Condor could only muster the minimal five soldiers necessary to open the gate to victory. Four of them touched their helmets to the lighted spots at the four corners of Salamander's door, while the fifth passed through the forcefield. That ended the game. The lights came back on to their full brightness, and Anderson came out of the teacher door.

I could have drawn my gun, thought Ender, as the enemy approached the door. I could have drawn my gun and shot just one of them, and they would have been too few. The game would have been a draw. Without four men to touch the four corners and a fifth man to pass through the gate, Condor would have had no victory. Bonzo, you ass, I could have saved you from this defeat. Maybe even turned it to victory, since they were sitting there, easy targets, and they wouldn't have known at first where the shots were coming from. I'm a good enough shot for that.

But orders were orders, and Ender had promised to obey. He did get some satisfaction out of the fact that on the official tally Salamander Army recorded, not the expected forty-one disabled or eliminated, but rather forty eliminated and one damaged. Bonzo couldn't understand it, until he consulted Anderson's book and realized who it was. I was only damaged, Bonzo, thought Ender. I could still shoot.

He expected Bonzo to come to him and say, "Next time, when it's like that, you can shoot." But Bonzo didn't say anything to him at all until the next morning after breakfast. Of course, Bonzo ate in the commanders' mess, but Ender was pretty sure the odd score would cause as much stir there as it did in the soldiers' dining hall. In every other game that wasn't a draw, every member of the losing team was either eliminated—totally frozen—or disabled, which meant they had some body parts still unfrozen, but were unable to shoot or inflict damage on the enemy. Salamander was the only losing army with one man in the Damaged but Active category.

Ender volunteered no explanation, but the other members of Salamander Army let it be known why it had happened. And when other boys asked him why he hadn't disobeyed orders and fired, he calmly answered, "I obey orders."

After breakfast, Bonzo looked for him. "The order still stands," he said, "and don't you forget it."

It will cost you, you fool. I may not be a good soldier, but I can still help and there's no reason you shouldn't let me.

Ender said nothing.

An interesting side effect of the battle was that Ender emerged at the top of the soldier efficiency list. Since he hadn't fired a shot, he had a perfect record on shooting—no misses at all. And since he had never been eliminated or disabled, his percentage there was excellent. No one else came close. It made a lot of boys laugh, and others were angry, but on the prized efficiency list, Ender was now the leader.

He kept sitting out the army practice sessions, and kept working hard on his own, with Petra in the mornings and his friends at night. More Launchies were joining them now, not on a lark but because they could see results—they were getting better and better. Ender and Alai stayed ahead of them, though. In part, it was because Alai kept trying new things, which forced Ender to think of new tactics to cope with them. In part it was because they kept making stupid mistakes, which suggested things to do that no self-respecting, well-trained soldier would even have tried. Many of the things they attempted turned out to be useless. But it was always fun, always exciting, and enough things worked that they knew it was helping them. Evening was the best time of the day.

The next two battles were easy Salamander victories; Ender came in after four minutes and remained untouched by the defeated enemy. Ender began to realize that Condor Army, which had beaten them, was unusually good; Salamander, weak as Bonzo's grasp of strategy might be, was one of the better teams, climbing steadily in the ratings, clawing for fourth place with Rat Army.

Ender turned seven. They weren't much for dates and calendars at the Battle School, but Ender had found out how to bring up the date on his desk, and he noticed his birthday. The school noticed it, too; they took his measurements and issued him a new Salamander uniform and a new flash suit for the battleroom. He went back to the barracks with the new clothing on. It felt strange and loose, like his skin no longer fit properly.

He wanted to stop at Petra's bunk and tell her about his home, about what his birthdays were usually like, just tell her it was his birthday so she'd say something about it being a happy one. But nobody told birthdays. It was childish. It was what landsiders did. Cakes and silly customs. Valentine baked him his cake on his sixth birthday. It fell and it was terrible. Nobody knew how to cook anymore, it was the kind of crazy thing Valentine would do. Everybody teased Valentine about it, but Ender saved a little bit of it in his cupboard. Then they took out his monitor and he left and for all he knew, it was still there, a little piece of greasy yellow dust. Nobody talked about home, not among the soldiers; there had been no life before Battle School. Nobody got letters, and nobody wrote any. Everybody pretended that they didn't care.

But I do care, thought Ender. The only reason I'm here is so that a bugger won't shoot out Valentine's eye, won't blast her head open like the soldiers in the videos of the first battles with the buggers. Won't split her head with a beam so hot that her brains burst the skull and spill out like rising bread dough, the way it happens in my worst nightmares, in my worst nights, when I wake up trembling but silent, must keep silent or they'll hear that I miss my family, I want to go home.

It was better in the morning. Home was merely a dull ache in the back of his memory. A tiredness in his eyes. That morning Bonzo came in as they were dressing. "Flash suits!" he called. It was a battle. Ender's fourth game.

The enemy was Leopard Army. It would be easy. Leopard was new, and it was always in the bottom quarter in the standings. It had been organized only six months ago, with Pol Slattery as its commander. Ender put on his new battle suit and got into line; Bonzo pulled him roughly out of line and made him march at the end. You didn't need to do that, Ender said silently. You could have let me stay in line.

Ender watched from the corridor. Pol Slattery was young, but he was sharp, he had some new ideas. He kept his soldiers moving, darting from star to star, wallsliding to get behind and above the stolid Salamanders. Ender smiled.

Bonzo was hopelessly confused, and so were his men. Leopard seemed to have men in every direction. However, the battle was not as lopsided as it seemed. Ender noticed that Leopard was losing a lot of men, too—their reckless tactics exposed them too much. What mattered, however, was that Salamander *felt* defeated. They had surrendered the initiative completely. Though they were still fairly evenly matched with the enemy, they huddled together like the last survivors of a massacre, as if they hoped the enemy would overlook them in the carnage.

Ender slipped slowly through the gate, oriented himself so the enemy's gate was down, and drifted slowly eastward to a corner where he wouldn't be noticed. He even fired at his own legs, to hold them in the kneeling position that offered him the best protection. He looked to any casual glance like another frozen soldier who had drifted helplessly out of the battle.

With Salamander Army waiting abjectly for destruction, Leopard obligingly destroyed them. When Salamander finally stopped firing, Leopard had nine boys left. They formed up and started to open the Salamander gate.

Ender aimed carefully with a straight arm, as Petra had taught him. Before anyone knew what was happening, he froze three of the soldiers who were about to press their helmets against the lighted corners of the door. Then some of the others spotted him and fired—but at first they hit only his already-frozen legs. It gave him time to get the last two men at the gate. Leopard had only four men left unfrozen when Ender was finally hit in the arm and disabled. The game was a draw, and they never had hit him in the body.

Pol Slattery was furious, but there had been nothing unfair about it. Everyone in Leopard Army assumed that it had been a strategy of Bonzo's, to leave a man till the last minute. It didn't occur to them that little Ender had fired against orders. But Salamander Army knew. Bonzo knew, and Ender could see from the way his commander looked at him that Bonzo hated him for rescuing him from total defeat. I don't care, Ender told himself. It will just make me easier to trade away, and in the meantime you won't drop so far in the standings. Just trade me. I've learned all I'm ever going to learn from *you*. How to fail with style, that's all you know, Bonzo.

What *have* I learned so far? Ender listed things in his mind as he undressed by his bunk. The enemy's gate is down. Use my legs as a shield in battle. A small reserve, held back until the end of the game, can be decisive. And soldiers can sometimes make decisions that are smarter than the orders they've been given.

Naked, he was about to climb into bed when Bonzo came toward him, his face hard and set. I have seen Peter like this, thought Ender, silent with murder in his eye. But Bonzo is not Peter. Bonzo has more fear.

"Wiggin, I finally traded you. I was able to persuade Rat Army that your incredible place on the efficiency list is more than an accident. You go over there tomorrow."

"Thank you, sir," Ender said.

Perhaps he sounded too grateful. Suddenly Bonzo swung at him, caught his jaw with a vicious open-handed slap. It knocked Ender sideways, into his bunk, and he almost fell. Then Bonzo slugged him, hard, in the stomach. Ender dropped to his knees.

"You disobeyed me," Bonzo said. Loudly, for all to hear. "No good soldier ever disobeys."

Even as he cried from the pain, Ender could not help but take vengeful pleasure in the murmurs he heard rising through the barracks. You fool, Bonzo. You aren't enforcing discipline, you're destroying it. They know I turned defeat into a draw. And now they see how you repay me. You made yourself look stupid in front of everyone. What is your discipline worth now?

The next day, Ender told Petra that for her sake the shooting practice in the morning would have to end. Bonzo didn't need anything that looked like a challenge now, and so she'd better stay clear of Ender for a while. She understood perfectly. "Besides," she said, "you're as close to being a good shot as you'll ever be."

He left his desk and flash suit in the locker. He would wear his Salamander uniform until he could get to the commissary and change it for the brown and black of Rat. He had brought no possessions with him; he would take none away. There were none to have—everything of value was in the school computer or his own head and hands.

He used one of the public desks in the game room to register for an earth-gravity personal combat course during the hour immediately after breakfast. He didn't plan to get vengeance on Bonzo for hitting him. But he did intend that no one would be able to do that to him again.

8

Rat

"Colonel Graff, the games have always been run fairly before. Either random distribution of stars, or symmetrical."

"Fairness is a wonderful attribute, Major Anderson. It has nothing to do with war."

"The game will be compromised. The comparative standings will become meaningless."

"Alas."

"It will take months. Years, to develop the new battlerooms and run the simulations."

"That's why I'm asking you now. To begin. Be creative. Think of every stacked, impossible, unfair star arrangement you can. Think of other ways to bend the rules. Late notification. Unequal forces. Then run the simulations and see which ones are hardest, which easiest. We want an intelligent progression here. We want to bring him along."

"When do you plan to make him a commander? When he's eight?"

"Of course not. I haven't assembled his army yet."

"Oh, so you're stacking it that way, too?"

"You're getting too close to the game, Anderson. You're forgetting that it is merely a training exercise."

"It's also status, identity, purpose, name; all that makes these children who they are comes out of this game. When it becomes known that the game can be manipulated, weighted, *cheated*, it will undo this whole school. I'm not exaggerating."

"I know."

"So I hope Ender Wiggin truly is the one, because you'll have degraded the effectiveness of our training method for a long time to come."

"If Ender isn't the one, if his peak of military brilliance does not coincide with the arrival of our fleet at the bugger homeworlds, then it doesn't really matter what our training method is or isn't."

"I hope you will forgive me, Colonel Graff, but I feel that I must report your orders and my opinion of their consequences to the Strategos and the Hegemon."

"Why not our dear Polemarch?"

"Everybody knows you have him in your pocket."

"Such hostility, Major Anderson. And I thought we were friends."

"We are. And I think you may be right about Ender. I just don't believe you, and you alone, should decide the fate of the world."

"I don't even think it's right for me to decide the fate of Ender Wiggin."

"So you won't mind if I notify them?"

"Of course I mind, you meddlesome ass. This is something to be decided by people who know what they're doing, not these frightened politicians who got their office because they happen to be politically potent in the country they come from."

"But you understand why I'm doing it."

"Because you're such a short-sighted little bureaucratic

bastard that you think you need to cover yourself in case things go wrong. Well, if things go wrong we'll all be bugger meat. So trust me now, Anderson, and don't bring the whole damn Hegemony down on my neck. What I'm doing is hard enough without them."

"Oh, is it unfair? Are things stacked against you? You can do it to Ender, but you can't take it, is that it?"

"Ender Wiggin is ten times smarter and stronger than I am. What I'm doing to him will bring out his genius. If I had to go through it myself, it would crush me. Major Anderson, I know I'm wrecking the game, and I know you love it better than any of the boys who play. Hate me if you like, but don't stop me."

"I reserve the right to communicate with the Hegemony and the Strategoi at any time. But for now—do what you want."

"Thank you so very kindly."

"Ender Wiggin, the little farthead who leads the standings, what a pleasure to have you with us." The commander of Rat Army lay sprawled on a lower bunk wearing only his desk. "With you around, how can any army lose?" Several of the boys nearby laughed.

There could not have been two more opposite armies than Salamander and Rat. The room was rumpled, cluttered, noisy. After Bonzo, Ender had thought that undiscipline would be a welcome relief. Instead, he found that he had come to expect quiet and order, and the disorder here made him uncomfortable.

"We doing OK, Ender Bender. I Rose de Nose, Jewboy extraordinaire, and you ain't nothin but a pinheaded pinprick of a goy. Don't you forget it."

Since the I.F. was formed, the Strategos of the military forces had always been a Jew. There was a myth that Jewish generals didn't lose wars. And so far it was still true. It made any Jew in the Battle School dream of being Strategos, and conferred prestige on him from the start. It also caused resentment. Rat Army was often called the Kike Force, half in praise, half in parody of Mazer Rackham's Strike Force. There were many who liked to remember that during the Second Invasion, even though an American Jew, as President, was Hegemon of the alliance, an Israeli Jew was Strategos in overall command of I.F. defense, and a Russian Jew was Polemarch of the fleet, it was Mazer Rackham, a little-known, twice-court-martialled, half-Maori New Zealander whose Strike Force broke up and finally destroyed the bugger fleet in the action around Saturn.

If Mazer Rackham could save the world, then it didn't matter a bit whether you were a Jew or not, people said.

But it did matter, and Rose the Nose knew it. He mocked himself to forestall the mocking comments of anti-semites—almost everyone he defeated in battle became, at least for a time, a Jew-hater—but he also made sure everyone knew what he was. His army was in second place, bucking for first.

"I took you on, goy, because I didn't want people to think I only win because I got great soldiers. I want them to know that even with a little puke of a soldier like you I can still win. We only got three rules here. Do what I tell you and don't piss in the bed."

Ender nodded. He knew that Rose wanted him to ask what the third rule was. So he did.

"That *was* three rules. We don't do too good in math, here."

The message was clear. Winning is more important than anything.

"Your practice sessions with half-assed little Launchies are over, Wiggin. Done. You're in a big boys' army now. I'm putting you in Dink Meeker's toon. From now on, as far as you're concerned, Dink Meeker is God."

"Then who are you?"

"The personnel officer who hired God." Rose grinned.

"And you are forbidden to use your desk again until you've frozen two enemy soldiers in the same battle. This order is out of self-defense. I hear you're a genius programmer. I don't want you screwing around with my desk."

Everybody erupted in laughter. It took Ender a moment to understand why. Rose had programmed his desk to display and animate a bigger-than-lifesize picture of male genitals, which waggled back and forth as Rose held the desk on his naked lap. This is just the sort of commander Bonzo would trade me to, thought Ender. How does a boy who spends his time like this win battles?

Ender found Dink Meeker in the game room, not playing, just sitting and watching. "A guy pointed you out," Ender said. "I'm Ender Wiggin."

"I know," said Meeker.

"I'm in your toon."

"I know," he said again.

"I'm pretty inexperienced."

Dink looked up at him. "Look, Wiggin, I know all this. Why do you think I asked Rose to get you for me?"

He had not been dumped, he had been picked up, he had been asked for. Meeker wanted him. "Why?" asked Ender.

"I've watched your practice sessions with the Launchies. I think you show some promise. Bonzo is stupid and I wanted you to get better training than Petra could give you. All she can do is shoot."

"I needed to learn that."

"You still move like you were afraid to wet your pants."

"So teach me."

"So learn."

"I'm not going to quit my freetime practice sessions."

"I don't want you to quit them."

"Rose the Nose does."

"Rose the Nose can't stop you. Likewise, he can't stop you from using your desk."

"So why did he order it?"

"Listen, Ender, commanders have just as much authority as you let them have. The more you obey them, the more power they have over you."

"What's to stop them from hurting me?" Ender remembered Bonzo's blow.

"I thought that was why you were taking personal attack classes."

"You've really been watching me, haven't you?"

Dink didn't answer.

"I don't want to get Rose mad at me. I want to be part of the battles now, I'm tired of sitting out till the end."

"Your standings will go down."

This time Ender didn't answer.

"Listen, Ender, as long as you're part of my toon, you're part of the battle."

Ender soon learned why. Dink trained his toon independently from the rest of Rat Army, with discipline and vigor; he never consulted with Rose, and only rarely did the whole army maneuver together. It was as if Rose commanded one army, and Dink commanded a much smaller one that happened to practice in the battleroom at the same time.

Dink started out the first practice by asking Ender to demonstrate his feet-first attack position. The other boys didn't like it. "How can we attack lying on our backs?" they asked.

To Ender's surprise, Dink didn't correct them, didn't say, "You aren't attacking on your back, you're dropping downward toward them." He had seen what Ender was doing, but he had not understood the orientation that it implied. It soon became clear to Ender that even though Dink was very, very good, his persistence in holding onto the corridor gravity orientation instead of thinking of the enemy gate as downward was limiting his thinking.

They practiced attacking an enemy-held star. Before trying Ender's feet-first method, they had always gone in standing up, their whole bodies available as a target. Even now, though, they reached the star and then assaulted the enemy from one direction only; "Over the top," cried Dink, and over they went. To his credit, he then repeated the exercise, calling, "Again, upside down," but because of their insistence on a gravity that didn't exist, the boys became awkward when the maneuver was under, as if vertigo seized them.

They hated the feet-first attack. Dink insisted that they use it. As a result, they hated Ender. "Do we have to learn how to fight from a Launchy?" one of them muttered, making sure Ender could hear. "Yes," answered Dink. They kept working.

And they learned it. In practice skirmishes, they began to realize how much harder it was to shoot an enemy who is attacking feet first. As soon as they were convinced of that, they practiced the maneuver more willingly.

That night was the first time Ender had come to one of his launchy practice sessions after a whole afternoon of work. He was tired.

"Now you're really in an army," said Alai, "you don't have to keep practicing with us."

"From you I can learn things that nobody knows," said Ender.

"Dink Meeker is the best. I hear he's your toon leader."

"Then let's get busy. I'll teach you what I learned from him today."

He put Alai and two dozen others through the same exercises that had worn him out all afternoon. But he put new touches on the patterns, made the boys try the maneuvers with one leg frozen, with both legs frozen, or using frozen boys for leverage to change directions.

Halfway through the practice, Ender noticed Petra and Dink together, standing in the doorway, watching. Later, when he looked again, they were gone.

So they're watching me, and what we're doing is known. He did not know whether Dink was his friend; he believed that Petra was, but nothing could be sure. They might be angry that he was doing what only commanders and toon leaders were supposed to do—drilling and training soldiers. They might be offended that a soldier would associate so closely with Launchies. It made him uneasy, to have older children watching.

"I thought I told you not to use your desk." Rose the Nose stood by Ender's bunk.

Ender did not look up. "I'm completing the trigonometry assignment for tomorrow."

Rose bumped his knee into Ender's desk. "I said not to use it."

Ender set the desk on his bunk and stood up. "I need trigonometry more than I need you."

Rose was taller than Ender by at least forty centimeters. But Ender was not particularly worried. It would not come to physical violence, and if it did, Ender thought he could hold his own. Rose was lazy and didn't know personal combat.

"You're going down in the standings, boy," said Rose.

"I expect to. I was only leading the list because of the stupid way Salamander Army was using me."

"Stupid? Bonzo's strategy won a couple of key games."

"Bonzo's strategy wouldn't win a salad fight. I was violating orders every time I fired my gun."

Rose hadn't known that. It made him angry. "So everything Bonzo said about you was a lie. You're not only short and incompetent, you're insubordinate, too."

"But I turned defeat into stalemate, all by myself."

"We'll see how you do all by yourself next time." Rose went away.

One of Ender's toonmates shook his head. "You dumb as a thumb."

Ender looked at Dink, who was doodling on his desk. Dink looked up, noticed Ender watching him, and gazed steadily back at him. No expression. Nothing. OK, thought Ender, I can take care of myself.

Battle came two days later. It was Ender's first time fighting as part of a toon; he was nervous. Dink's toon lined up against the right-hand wall of the corridor and Ender was very careful not to lean, not to let his weight slip to either side. Stay balanced.

"Wiggin!" called Rose the Nose.

Ender felt dread come over him from throat to groin, a tingle of fear that made him shudder. Rose saw it.

"Shivering? Trembling? Don't wet your pants, little Launchy." Rose hooked a finger over the butt of Ender's gun and pulled him to the forcefield that hid the battleroom from view. "We'll see how well you do *now*, Ender. As soon as that door opens, you jump through, go straight ahead toward the enemy's door."

Suicide. Pointless, meaningless self-destruction. But he had to follow orders now, this was battle, not school. For a moment Ender raged silently; then he calmed himself. "Excellent, sir," he said. "The direction I fire my gun is the direction of their main contingent."

Rose laughed. "You won't have time to fire anything, pinprick."

The wall vanished. Ender jumped up, took hold of the ceiling handholds, and threw himself out and down, speeding toward the enemy door.

It was Centipede Army, and they only began to emerge from their door when Ender was halfway across the battleroom. Many of them were able to get under cover of stars quickly, but Ender had doubled up his legs under him and, holding his pistol at his crotch, he was firing between his legs and freezing many of them as they emerged.

They flashed his legs, but he had three precious seconds before they could hit his body and put him out of action. He froze several more, then flung out his arms in equal and opposite directions. The hand that held his gun ended up pointing toward the main body of Centipede Army. He fired into the mass of the enemy, and then they froze him.

A second later he smashed into the forcefield of the enemy's door and rebounded with a crazy spin. He landed in a group of enemy soldiers behind a star; they shoved him off and spun him even more rapidly. He rebounded out of control through the rest of the battle, though gradually friction with the air slowed him down. He had no way of knowing how many men he had frozen before getting iced himself, but he did get the general idea that Rat Army won again, as usual.

After the battle Rose didn't speak to him. Ender was still first in the standings, since he had frozen three, disabled two, and damaged seven. There was no more talk about insubordination and whether Ender could use his desk. Rose stayed in his part of the barracks, and left Ender alone.

Dink Meeker began to practice instant emergence from the corridor—Ender's attack on the enemy while they were still coming out of the door had been devastating. "If one man can do that much damage, think what a toon can do." Dink got Major Anderson to open a door in the middle of a wall, even during practice sessions, instead of just the floor-level door, so they could practice launching under battle conditions. Word got around. From now on no one could take five or ten or fifteen seconds in the corridor to size things up. The game had changed.

More battles. This time Ender played a proper role within a toon. He made mistakes. Skirmishes were lost. He dropped from first to second in the standings, then to fourth. Then he made fewer mistakes, and began to feel comfortable within the framework of the toon, and he went back up to third, then second, then first.

—

After practice one afternoon, Ender stayed in the battleroom. He had noticed that Dink Meeker usually came late to dinner, and he assumed it was for extra practice. Ender wasn't very hungry, and he wanted to see what it was Dink practiced when no one else could see.

But Dink didn't practice. He stood near the door, watching Ender.

Ender stood across the room, watching Dink.

Neither spoke. It was plain Dink expected Ender to leave. It was just as plain that Ender was saying no.

Dink turned his back on Ender, methodically took off his flash suit, and gently pushed off from the floor. He drifted slowly toward the center of the room, very slowly, his body relaxing almost completely, so that his hands and arms seemed to be caught by almost nonexistent air currents in the room.

After the speed and tension of practice, the exhaustion, the alertness, it was restful just to watch him drift. He did it for ten minutes or so before he reached another wall. Then he pushed off rather sharply, returned to his flash suit, and pulled it on.

"Come on," he said to Ender.

They went to the barracks. The room was empty, since all the boys were at dinner. Each went to his own bunk and changed into regular uniforms. Ender walked to Dink's bunk and waited for a moment till Dink was ready to go.

"Why did you wait?" asked Dink.

"Wasn't hungry."

"Well, now you know why I'm not a commander."

Ender had wondered.

"Actually, they promoted me twice, and I refused."

Refused?

"The second time they took away my old locker and bunk and desk, assigned me to a commander's cabin, and gave me an army. But I just stayed in the cabin until they gave in and put me back into somebody else's army."

"Why?"

"Because I won't let them do it to me. I can't believe you haven't seen through all this crap yet, Ender. But I guess you're young. These other armies, they aren't the enemy. It's the teachers, they're the enemy. They get us to fight each other, to hate each other. The game is everything. Win win win. It amounts to nothing. We kill ourselves, go crazy trying to beat each other, and all the time the old bastards are watching us, studying us, discovering our weak points, deciding whether we're *good enough* or not. Well, good enough for what? I was six years old when they brought me here. What the hell did I know? *They* decided I was right for the program, but nobody ever asked me if the program was right for me."

"So why don't you go home?"

Dink smiled crookedly. "Because I can't give up the game." He tugged at the fabric of his flash suit, which lay on the bunk beside him. "Because I love this."

"So why not be a commander?"

Dink shook his head. "Never. Look what it does to Rosen. The boy's crazy. Rose de Nose. Sleeps in here with us instead of in his cabin. Why? Because he's scared to be alone, Ender. Scared of the dark."

"Rose?"

"But they made him a commander and so he has to act like one. He doesn't know what he's doing. He's winning, but that scares him worst of all, because he doesn't know *why* he's winning, except that I have something to do with it. Any minute somebody could find out that Rosen isn't some magic Israeli general who can win no matter what. He doesn't know why anybody wins or loses. Nobody does."

"It doesn't mean he's crazy, Dink."

"I know, you've been here a year, you think these people are normal. Well, they're not. *We're* not. I look in the library, I call up books on my desk. Old ones, because they won't let us have anything new, but I've got a pretty good idea what children are, and we're not children. Children can lose sometimes, and nobody cares. Children aren't in armies, they aren't *commanders*, they don't rule over forty other kids, it's more than anybody can take and not get crazy."

Ender tried to remember what other children were like, in his class at school, back in the city. But all he could think of was Stilson.

"I had a brother. Just a normal guy. All he cared about was girls. And flying. He wanted to fly. He used to play ball with the guys. A pickup game, shooting balls at a hoop, dribbling down the corridors until the peace officers confiscated your ball. We had a great time. He was teaching me how to dribble when I was taken."

Ender remembered his own brother, and the memory was not fond.

Dink misunderstood the expression on Ender's face. "Hey, I know, nobody's supposed to talk about home. But we came from *somewhere*. The Battle School didn't create us, you know. The Battle School doesn't create *anything*. It just destroys. And we all remember things from home. Maybe not good things, but we remember and then we lie and pretend that—look, Ender, why is it that *nobody* talks about home, *ever*? Doesn't that tell you how important it is? That nobody even admits that—oh hell."

"No, it's all right," Ender said. "I was just thinking about Valentine. My sister."

"I wasn't trying to make you upset."

"It's OK. I don't think of her very much, because I always get—like this."

"That's right, we never cry. I never thought of that. Nobody ever cries. We really are trying to be adults. Just like our fathers. I bet your father was like you. I bet he was quiet and took it, and then busted out and—"

"I'm not like my father."

"So maybe I'm wrong. But look at Bonzo, your old commander. He's got an advanced case of Spanish honor. He can't allow himself to have weaknesses. To be better than him, that's an insult. To be stronger, that's like cutting off his balls. That's why he hates you, because you didn't suffer when he tried to punish you. He hates you for that, he honestly wants to kill you. He's crazy. They're all crazy."

"And you aren't?"

"I be crazy too, little buddy, but at least when I be craziest, I be floating all alone in space and the crazy, she float out of me, she soak into the walls, and she don't come out till there be battles and little boys bump into the walls and squish out de crazy."

Ender smiled.

"And you be crazy too," said Dink. "Come on, let's go eat."

"Maybe you can be a commander and not be crazy. Maybe knowing about craziness means you don't have to fall for it."

"I'm not going to let the bastards run me, Ender. They've got you pegged, too, and they don't plan to treat you kindly. Look what they've done to you so far."

"They haven't done anything except promote me."

"And she make you life so easy, neh?"

Ender laughed and shook his head. "So maybe you're right."

"They think they got you on ice. Don't let them."

"But that's what I came for," Ender said. "For them to make me into a tool. To save the world."

"I can't believe you still believe it."

"Believe what?"

"The bugger menace. Save the world. Listen, Ender, if the buggers were coming back to get us, they'd *be here*. They aren't invading again. We beat them and they're gone."

"But the videos—"

"All from the First and Second Invasions. Your grandparents weren't born yet when Mazer Rackham wiped them out. You watch. It's all a fake. There *is* no war, and they're just screwing around with us."

"But why?"

"Because as long as people are afraid of the buggers, the I.F. can stay in power, and as long as the I.F. is in power, certain countries can keep their hegemony. But keep watching the vids, Ender. People will catch onto this game pretty soon, and there'll be a civil war to end all wars. *That's* the menace, Ender, not the buggers. And in *that* war, when it comes, you and I won't be friends. Because you're American, just like our dear teachers. And *I* am not."

They went to the mess hall and ate, talking about other things. But Ender could not stop thinking about what Dink had said. The Battle School was so enclosed, the game so important in the minds of the children, that Ender had forgotten there was a world outside. Spanish honor. Civil war. Politics. The Battle School was really a very small place, wasn't it?

But Ender did not reach Dink's conclusions. The buggers were real. The threat was real. The I.F. controlled a lot of things, but it didn't control the videos and the nets. Not where Ender had grown up. In Dink's home in the Netherlands, with three generations under Russian hegemony, perhaps it was all controlled, but Ender knew that lies could not last long in America. So he believed.

Believed, but the seed of doubt was there, and it stayed, and every now and then sent out a little root. It changed everything, to have that seed growing. It made Ender listen more carefully to what people meant, instead of what they said. It made him wise.

There weren't as many boys at the evening practice, not by half.

"Where's Bernard?" asked Ender.

Alai grinned. Shen closed his eyes and assumed a look of blissful meditation.

"Haven't you heard?" said another boy, a Launchy from a younger group. "Word's out that any Launchy who comes to your practice sessions won't ever amount to anything in anybody's army. Word's out that the commanders don't want any soldiers who've been damaged by your training."

Ender nodded.

"But the way I brain it," said the Launchy, "I be the best soldier I can, and any commander worth a damn, he take me. Neh?"

"Eh," said Ender, with finality.

They went on with practice. About a half hour into it, when they were practicing throwing off collisions with frozen soldiers, several commanders in different uniforms came in. They ostentatiously took down names.

"Hey," shouted Alai. "Make sure you spell my name right!"

The next night there were even fewer boys. Now Ender was hearing the stories—little Launchies getting slapped around in the bathrooms, or having accidents in the mess hall and the game room, or getting their files trashed by older boys who had broken the primitive security system that guarded the Launchies' desks.

"No practice tonight," Ender said.

"The hell there's not," said Alai.

"Give it a few days. I don't want any of the little kids getting hurt."

"If you stop, even one night, they'll figure it works to do this kind of thing. Just like if you'd ever backed down to Bernard back when he was being a swine."

"Besides," said Shen, "we aren't scared and we don't care, so you owe it to us to go on. We need the practice and so do you."

Ender remembered what Dink had said. The game was trivial, compared to the whole world. Why should anybody give every night of his life to this stupid, stupid game?

"We don't accomplish that much anyway," Ender said. He started to leave.

Alai stopped him. "They scare you, too? They slap you up in the bathroom? Stick you head in the pissah? Somebody gots a gun up you bung?"

"No," Ender said.

"You still my friend?" asked Alai, more quietly.

"Yes."

"Then I still you friend, Ender, and I stay here and practice with you."

The older boys came again, but fewer of them were commanders. Most were members of a couple of armies. Ender recognized Salamander uniforms. Even a couple of Rats. They didn't take names this time. Instead, they mocked and shouted and ridiculed as the Launchies tried to master difficult skills with untrained muscles. It began to get to a few of the boys.

"Listen to them," Ender said to the other boys. "Remember the words. If you ever want to make your enemy crazy, shout that kind of stuff at them. It makes them do dumb things, to be mad. But *we* don't get mad."

Shen took the idea to heart, and after each jibe from the older boys, he had a group of four Launchies recite the words, loudly, five or six times. When they started singing the taunts like nursery rhymes, some of the older boys launched themselves from the wall and came out for a fight.

The flash suits were designed for wars fought with harmless light; they offered little protection and seriously hampered movement if it came to hand-to-hand fighting in nullo. Half the boys were flashed, anyway, and couldn't fight; but the stiffness of their suits made them potentially useful. Ender quickly ordered his Launchies to gather in one corner of the room. The older boys laughed at them even more, and some who had waited by the wall came forward to join in the attack, seeing Ender's group in retreat.

Ender and Alai decided to throw a frozen soldier in the face of an enemy. The frozen Launchy struck helmet first, and the two caromed off each other. The older boy clutched his chest where the helmet had hit him, and screamed in pain.

The mockery was over. The rest of the older boys launched themselves to enter the battle. Ender didn't really have much hope of any of the boys getting away without some injury. But the enemy was coming haphazardly, uncoordinatedly; they had never worked together before, while

Ender's little practice army, though there were only a dozen of them now, knew each other well and knew how to work together.

"Go nova!" shouted Ender. The other boys laughed. They gathered into three groups, feet together, squatting, holding hands so they formed small stars against the back wall. "We'll go around them and make for the door. Now!"

At his signal, the three stars burst apart, each boy launching in a different direction, but angled so he could rebound off a wall and head for the door. Since all of the enemy were in the middle of the room, where course changes were far more difficult, it was an easy maneuver to carry out.

Ender had positioned himself so that when he launched, he would rendezvous with the frozen soldier he had just used as a missile. The boy wasn't frozen now, and he let Ender catch him, whirl him around and send him toward the door. Unfortunately, the necessary result of the action was for Ender to head in the opposite direction, and at a reduced speed. Alone of all his soldiers, he was drifting fairly slowly, and at the end of the battleroom where the older boys were gathered. He shifted himself so he could see that all his soldiers were safely gathered at the far wall.

In the meantime, the furious and disorganized enemy had just spotted him. Ender calculated how soon he would reach the wall so he could launch again. Not soon enough. Several enemies had already rebounded toward him. Ender was startled to see Stilson's face among them. Then he shuddered and realized he had been wrong. Still, it was the same situation, and this time they wouldn't sit still for a single combat settlement. There was no leader, as far as Ender knew, and these boys were a lot bigger than him.

Still, he had learned some things about weight-shifting in personal combat class, and about the physics of moving objects. Game battles almost never got to hand-to-hand combat—you never bumped into an enemy that wasn't frozen unless *you* were frozen yourself. So in the few seconds he had, Ender tried to position himself to receive his guests.

Fortunately, they knew as little about nullo fighting as he did, and the few who tried to punch him found that throwing a punch was pretty ineffective when their bodies moved backward just as quickly as their fists moved forward. But there were some in the group who had bone-breaking on their minds, as Ender quickly saw. He didn't plan to be there for it, though.

He caught one of the punchers by the arm and threw him as hard as he could. It hurled Ender out of the way of the rest of the first onslaught, though he still wasn't getting any closer to the door. "Stay there!" he shouted at his friends, who obviously were forming up to come and rescue him. "Just stay there!"

Someone caught Ender by the foot. The tight grip gave Ender some leverage; he was able to stamp firmly on the other boy's ear and shoulder, making him cry out and let go. If the boy had let go just as Ender kicked downward, it would have hurt him much less and allowed Ender to use the maneuver as a launch. Instead, the boy had hung on too well; his ear was torn and scattering blood in the air, and Ender was drifting even more slowly.

I'm doing it again, thought Ender. I'm hurting people again, just to save myself. Why don't they leave me alone, so I don't have to hurt them?

Three more boys were converging on him now, and this time they were acting together. Still, they had to grab him before they could hurt him. Ender positioned himself quickly so that two of them would take his feet, leaving his hands free to deal with the third.

Sure enough, they took the bait. Ender grasped the shoulders of the third boy's shirt and pulled him up sharply, butting him in the face with his helmet. Again a scream and a shower of blood. The two boys who had his legs were wrenching at them, twisting him. Ender threw the boy with the bleeding nose at one of them; they entangled, and Ender's leg came free. It was a simple matter then to use the other boy's hold for leverage to kick him firmly in the groin, then shove off him in the direction of the door. He didn't get that good a launch, so that his speed was nothing special, but it didn't matter. No one was following him.

He got to his friends at the door. They caught him and handed him along to the door. They were laughing and slapping him playfully. "You bad!" they said. "You scary! You flame!"

"Practice is over for the day," Ender said.

"They'll be back tomorrow," said Shen.

"Won't do them any good," said Ender. "If they come without suits, we'll do this again. If they come *with* suits, we can flash them."

"Besides," said Alai, "the teachers won't let it happen."

Ender remembered what Dink had told him, and wondered if Alai was right.

"Hey Ender!" shouted one of the older boys, as Ender left the battleroom. "You nothing, man! You be nothing!"

"My old commander Bonzo," said Ender. "I think he doesn't like me."

Ender checked the rosters on his desk that night. Four boys turned up on medical report. One with bruised ribs, one with a bruised testicle, one with a torn ear, and one with a broken nose and a loose tooth. The cause of injury was the same in all cases:

ACCIDENTAL COLLISION IN NULL G

If the teachers were allowing that to turn up on the official report, it was obvious they didn't intend to punish anyone for the nasty little skirmish in the battleroom. Aren't they going to do anything? Don't they care what goes on in this school?

Since he was back to the barracks earlier than usual,

Ender called up the fantasy game on his desk. It had been a while since he last used it. Long enough that it didn't start him where he had left off. Instead, he began by the Giant's corpse. Only now, it was hardly identifiable as a corpse at all, unless you stood off a ways and studied it. The body had eroded into a hill, entwined with grass and vines. Only the crest of the Giant's face was still visible, and it was white bone, like limestone protruding from a discouraged, withering mountain.

Ender did not look forward to fighting with the wolf-children again, but to his surprise they weren't there. Perhaps, killed once, they were gone forever. It made him a little sad.

He made his way down underground, through the tunnels, to the cliff ledge overlooking the beautiful forest. Again he threw himself down, and again a cloud caught him and carried him into the castle turret room.

The snake began to unweave itself from the rug again, only this time Ender did not hesitate. He stepped on the head of the snake and crushed it under his foot. It writhed and twisted under him, and in response he twisted and ground it deeper into the stone floor. Finally it was still. Ender picked it up and shook it, until it unwove itself and the pattern in the rug was gone. Then, still dragging the snake behind him, he began to look for a way out.

Instead, he found a mirror. And in the mirror he saw a face that he easily recognized. It was Peter, with blood dripping down his chin and a snake's tail protruding from a corner of his mouth.

Ender shouted and thrust his desk from him. The few boys in the barracks were alarmed at the noise, but he apologized and told them it was nothing. They went away. He looked again into his desk. His figure was still there, staring into the mirror. He tried to pick up some of the furniture, to break the mirror, but it could not be moved. The mirror would not come off the wall, either. Finally

Ender threw the snake at it. The mirror shattered, leaving a hole in the wall behind it. Out of the hole came dozens of tiny snakes, which quickly bit Ender's figure again and again. Tearing the snakes frantically from itself, the figure collapsed and died in a writhing heap of small serpents.

The screen went blank, and words appeared.

PLAY AGAIN?

Ender signed off and put the desk away.

The next day, several commanders came to Ender or sent soldiers to tell him not to worry, most of them thought the extra practice sessions were a good idea, he should keep it up. And to make sure nobody bothered him, they were sending a few of their older soldiers who needed extra practice to come join him. "They're as big as most of the buggers who attacked you last night. They'll think twice."

Instead of a dozen boys, there were forty-five that night, more than an army, and whether it was because of the presence of older boys on Ender's side or because they had had enough the night before, none of their enemies came.

Ender didn't go back to the fantasy game. But it lived in his dreams. He kept remembering how it felt to kill the snake, grinding it in, the way he tore the ear off that boy, the way he destroyed Stilson, the way he broke Bernard's arm. And then to stand up, holding the corpse of his enemy, and find Peter's face looking out at him from the mirror. This game knows too much about me. This game tells filthy lies. I am not Peter. I don't have murder in my heart.

And then a worse fear, that he *was* a killer, only better at it than Peter ever was; that it was this very trait that pleased the teachers. It's killers they need for the bugger wars. It's people who can grind the enemy's face into the dust and spatter their blood all over space.

Well, I'm your man. I'm the bloody bastard you wanted

when you had me spawned. I'm your tool, and what difference does it make if I hate the part of me that you most need? What difference does it make that when the little serpents killed me in the game, I agreed with them, and was glad.

9

Locke and Demosthenes

"I didn't call you in here to waste time. How in hell did the computer do that?"

"I don't know."

"How could it pick up a picture of Ender's brother and put it into the graphics in this Fairyland routine?"

"Colonel Graff, I wasn't there when it was programmed. All I know is that the computer's never taken anyone to this place before. Fairyland was strange enough, but this isn't Fairyland anymore. It's beyond the End of the World, and—"

"I know the names of the places, I just don't know what they mean."

"Fairyland was programmed in. It's mentioned in a few other places. But nothing talks about the End of the World. We don't have any experience with it."

"I don't like having the computer screw around with Ender's mind that way. Peter Wiggin is the most potent person in his life, except maybe his sister Valentine."

"And the mind game is designed to help shape them, help them find worlds they can be comfortable in."

"You don't get it, do you, Major Imbu? I don't want Ender being comfortable with the end of the world. Our business here is not to be comfortable with the end of the world!"

"The End of the World in the game isn't necessarily the end of humanity in the bugger wars. It has a private meaning to Ender."

"Good. What meaning?"

"I don't know, sir. I'm not the kid. Ask him."

"Major Imbu, I'm asking *you.*"

"There could be a thousand meanings."

"Try one."

"You've been isolating the boy. Maybe he's wishing for the end of *this* world, the Battle School. Or maybe it's about the end of the world he grew up with as a little boy, his home, coming here. Or maybe it's his way of coping with having broken up so many other kids here. Ender's a sensitive kid, you know, and he's done some pretty bad things to people's bodies, he might be wishing for the end of *that* world."

"Or none of the above."

"The mind game is a relationship between the child and the computer. Together they create stories. The stories are true, in the sense that they reflect the reality of the child's life. That's all I *know.*"

"And I'll tell you what *I* know, Major Imbu. That picture of Peter Wiggin was not one that could have been taken from our files here at the school. We have nothing on him, electronically or otherwise, since Ender came here. And that picture is more recent."

"It's only been a year and a half, sir, how much can the boy change?"

"He's wearing his hair completely differently now. His mouth was redone with orthodontia. I got a recent photograph from landside and compared. The only way the computer here in the Battle School could have got that picture was by requisitioning it from a landside computer. And not even one connected with the I.F. That takes requisitionary powers. We can't just go into Guilford County North Carolina and pluck a picture out of school files. Did anyone at this school authorize getting this?"

"You don't understand, sir. Our Battle School computer is only a part of the I.F. network. If *we* want a picture, *we* have to get a requisition, but if the mind game program determines that the picture is necessary—"

"It can just go take it."

"Not just every day. Only when it's for the child's own good."

"OK, it's for his good. But *why*. His brother is dangerous, his brother was rejected for this program because he's one of the most ruthless and unreliable human beings we've laid hands on. Why is he so important to Ender? Why, after all this time?"

"Honestly, sir, I don't know. And the mind game program is designed so that it can't tell us. It may not know itself, actually. This is uncharted territory."

"You mean the computer's making this up as it goes along?"

"You might put it that way."

"Well, that does make me feel a little better. I thought I was the only one."

Valentine celebrated Ender's eighth birthday alone, in the wooded back yard of their new home in Greensboro. She scraped a patch of ground bare of pine needles and leaves, and there scratched his name in the dirt with a twig. Then she made a small teepee of twigs and needles and lit a small fire. It made smoke that interwove with the branches and needles of the pine overhead. All the way into space, she said silently. All the way to the Battle School.

No letters had ever come, and as far as they knew their own letters had never reached him. When he first was taken,

Father and Mother sat at the table and keyed in long letters to him every few days. Soon, though, it was once a week, and when no answers came, once a month. Now it had been two years since he went, and there were no letters, none at all, and no remembrance on his birthday. He is dead, she thought bitterly, because we have forgotten him.

But Valentine had not forgotten him. She did not let her parents know, and above all never hinted to Peter how often she thought about Ender, how often she wrote him letters that she knew he would not answer. And when Mother and Father had announced to them that they were leaving the city to move to North Carolina, of all places, Valentine knew that they never expected to see Ender again. They were leaving the only place where he knew to find them. How would Ender find them here, among these trees, under this changeable and heavy sky? He had lived deep in corridors all his life, and if he was still in the Battle School, there was less of nature there. What would he make of this?

Valentine knew why they had moved here. It was for Peter, so that living among trees and small animals, so that nature, in as raw a form as Mother and Father could conceive of it, might have a softening influence on their strange and frightening son. And, in a way, it had. Peter took to it right away. Long walks out in the open, cutting through woods and out into the open country—going sometimes for a whole day, with only a sandwich or two sharing space with his desk in the pack on his back, with only a small pocket knife in his pocket.

But Valentine knew. She had seen a squirrel half-skinned, spiked by its little hands and feet with twigs pushed into the dirt. She pictured Peter trapping it, staking it, then carefully parting and peeling back the skin without breaking into the abdomen, watching the muscles twist and ripple. How long had it taken the squirrel to die? And all the while Peter had sat nearby, leaning against the tree where perhaps the squirrel had nested, playing with his desk while the squirrel's life seeped away.

At first she was horrified, and nearly threw up at dinner, watching how Peter ate so vigorously, talked so cheerfully. But later she thought about it and realized that perhaps, for Peter, it was a kind of magic, like her little fires; a sacrifice that somehow stilled the dark gods that hunted for his soul. Better to torture squirrels than other children. Peter has always been a husbandman of pain, planting it, nurturing it, devouring it greedily when it was ripe; better he should take it in these small, sharp doses than with dull cruelty to children in the school.

"A model student," said his teachers. "I wish we had a hundred others in the school just like him. Studies all the time, turns in all his work on time. He loves to learn."

But Valentine knew it was a fraud. Peter loved to learn, all right, but the teachers hadn't taught him anything, ever. He did his learning through his desk at home, tapping into libraries and databases, studying and thinking and, above all, talking to Valentine. Yet at school he acted as though he were excited about the puerile lesson of the day. Oh, wow, I never knew that frogs looked like *this* inside, he'd say, and then at home he studied the binding of cells into organisms through the philotic collation of DNA. Peter was a master of flattery, and all his teachers bought it.

Still, it was good. Peter never fought anymore. Never bullied. Got along well with everybody. It was a new Peter.

Everyone believed it. Father and Mother said it, so often it made Valentine want to scream at them. It isn't the new Peter! It's the old Peter, only smarter!

How smart? Smarter than *you*, Father. Smarter than *you*. Mother. Smarter than anybody you have ever met.

But not smarter than me.

"I've been deciding," said Peter, "whether to kill you or what."

Valentine leaned against the trunk of the pine tree, her little fire a few smoldering ashes. "I love you, too, Peter."

"It would be so easy. You always make these stupid little

fires. It's just a matter of knocking you out and burning you up. You're such a firebug."

"I've been thinking of castrating you in your sleep."

"No you haven't. You only think of things like that when I'm with you. I bring out the best in you. No, Valentine, I've decided not to kill you. I've decided that you're going to help me."

"I am?" A few years ago, Valentine would have been terrified at Peter's threats. Now, though, she was not so afraid. Not that she doubted that he was capable of killing her. She couldn't think of anything so terrible that she didn't believe Peter might do it. She also knew, though, that Peter was not insane, not in the sense that he wasn't in control of himself. He was in better control of himself than anyone she knew. Except perhaps herself. Peter could delay any desire as long as he needed to; he could conceal any emotion. And so Valentine knew that he would never hurt her in a fit of rage. He would only do it if the advantages outweighed the risks. And they did not. In a way, she actually preferred Peter to other people because of this. He always, always acted out of intelligent self-interest. And so, to keep herself safe, all she had to do was make sure it was more in Peter's interest to keep her alive than to have her dead.

"Valentine, things are coming to a head. I've been tracking troop movements in Russia."

"What are we talking about?"

"The world, Val. You know Russia? Big Empire? The Second Warsaw Pact? Rulers of Eurasia from the Netherlands to Pakistan?"

"They don't publish their troop movements, Peter."

"Of course not. But they do publish their passenger and freight train schedules. I've had my desk analyzing those schedules and figuring out when the secret troop trains are moving over the same tracks. Done it backward over the past three years. In the last six months, they've stepped up, they're getting ready for war. Land war."

"But what about the League? What about the buggers?" Valentine didn't know what Peter was getting at, but he often launched discussions like this, practical discussions of world events. He used her to test his ideas, to refine them. In the process, she also refined her own thinking. She found that while she rarely agreed with Peter about what the world *ought* to be, they rarely disagreed about what the world actually *was*. They had become quite deft at sifting accurate information out of the stories of the hopelessly ignorant, gullible news writers. The news herd, as Peter called them.

"The Polemarch is Russian, isn't he? And he knows what's happening with the fleet. Either they've found out the buggers aren't a threat after all, or we're about to have a big battle. One way or another, the bugger war is about to be over. They're getting ready for after the war."

"If they're moving troops, it must be under the direction of the Strategos."

"It's all internal, within the Warsaw Pact."

This was troubling. The facade of peace and cooperation had been undisturbed almost since the bugger wars began. What Peter had detected was a fundamental shift in the world order. She had a mental picture, as clear as memory, of the way the world had been before the buggers forced peace upon them. "So it's back to the way it was before."

"A few changes. The shields make it so nobody bothers with nuclear weapons anymore. We have to kill each other thousands at a time instead of millions." Peter grinned. "Val, it was bound to happen. Right now there's a vast international fleet and army in existence, with North American hegemony. When the bugger wars are over, all that power will vanish, because it's all built on fear of the buggers. And suddenly we'll look around and discover that all the old alliances are gone, dead and gone, except one, the Warsaw Pact. And it'll be the dollar against five million lasers. We'll have the asteroid belt, but they'll have Earth, and you run out of raisins and celery kind of fast out there, without Earth."

What disturbed Valentine most of all was that Peter did not seem at all worried. "Peter, why do I get the idea that you are thinking of this as a golden opportunity for Peter Wiggin?"

"For both of us, Val."

"Peter, you're twelve years old. I'm ten. They have a word for people our age. They call us children and they treat us like mice."

"But we don't *think* like other children, do we, Val? We don't *talk* like other children. And above all, we don't *write* like other children."

"For a discussion that began with death threats, Peter, we've strayed from the topic, I think." Still, Valentine found herself getting excited. Writing was something Val did better than Peter. They both knew it. Peter had even named it once, when he said that he could always see what other people hated most about themselves, and bully them, while Val could always see what other people liked best about themselves, and flatter them. It was a cynical way of putting it, but it was true. Valentine could persuade other people to her point of view—she could convince them that they wanted what she wanted them to want. Peter, on the other hand, could only make them fear what he wanted them to fear. When he first pointed this out to Val, she resented it. She had wanted to believe she was good at persuading people because she was right, not because she was clever. But no matter how much she told herself that she didn't ever want to exploit people the way Peter did, she enjoyed knowing that she could, in her way, control other people. And not just control what they did. She could control, in a way, what they wanted to do. She was ashamed that she took pleasure in this power, and yet she found herself using it sometimes. To get teachers to do what she wanted, and other students. To get Mother and Father to see things her way. Sometimes, she was able to persuade even Peter. That was the most frightening thing of all—that she could understand Peter well enough, could empathize with him enough to get inside him that way. There was more Peter in her than she could bear to admit, though sometimes she dared to think about it anyway. This is what she thought as Peter spoke: You dream of power, Peter, but in my own way I am more powerful than you.

"I've been studying history," Peter said. "I've been learning things about patterns in human behavior. There are times when the world is rearranging itself, and at times like that, the right words can change the world. Think what Pericles did in Athens, and Demosthenes—"

"Yes, they managed to wreck Athens twice."

"Pericles, yes, but Demosthenes was right about Philip—"

"Or provoked him—"

"See? This is what historians usually do, quibble about cause and effect when the point is, there are times when the world is in flux and the right voice in the right place can move the world. Thomas Paine and Ben Franklin, for instance. Bismarck. Lenin."

"Not exactly parallel cases, Peter." Now she was disagreeing with him out of habit; she saw what he was getting at, and she thought it might just be possible.

"I didn't expect *you* to understand. *You* still believe that teachers know something worth learning."

I understand more than you think, Peter. "So you see yourself as Bismarck?"

"I see myself as knowing how to insert ideas into the public mind. Haven't you ever thought of a phrase, Val, a clever thing to say, and said it, and then two weeks or a month later you hear some adult saying it to another adult, both of them strangers? Or you see it on a video or pick it up on a net?"

"I always figured I heard it before and only thought I was making it up."

"You were wrong. There are maybe two or three thousand people in the world as smart as us, little sister. Most of them are making a living somewhere. Teaching, the poor bastards, or doing research. Precious few of them are actually in positions of power."

"I guess we're the lucky few."

"Funny as a one-legged rabbit, Val."

"Of which there are no doubt several in these woods."

"Hopping in neat little circles."

Valentine laughed at the gruesome image and hated herself for thinking it was funny.

"Val, *we* can say the words that everyone else will be saying two weeks later. We can do that. We don't have to wait until we're grown up and safely put away in some career."

"Peter, you're *twelve*."

"Not on the nets I'm not. On the nets I can name myself anything I want, and so can you."

"On the nets we are clearly identified as students, and we can't even get into the real discussions except in audience mode, which means we can't *say* anything anyway."

"I have a plan."

"You always do." She pretended nonchalance, but she listened eagerly.

"We can get on the nets as full-fledged adults, with whatever net names we want to adopt, *if* Father gets us onto his citizen's access."

"And why would he do that? We already have student access. What do you tell him, I need citizen's access so I can take over the world?"

"No, Val. *I* won't tell him anything. *You'll* tell him how you're worried about me. How I'm trying so very hard to do well at school, but you know it's driving me crazy because I can never talk to anybody intelligent, everybody always talks down to me because I'm young, I never get to converse with my *peers*. You can prove that the stress is getting to me. There's even evidence."

Valentine thought of the corpse of the squirrel in the woods and realized that even that discovery was part of

Peter's plan. Or at least he had *made* it part of his plan, after it happened.

"So you get him to authorize us to share his citizen's access. To adopt our own identities there, to conceal who we are so people will give us the intellectual respect we deserve."

Valentine could challenge him on ideas, but never on things like this. She could not say, What makes you think you deserve respect? She had read about Adolf Hitler. She wondered what he was like at the age of twelve. Not this smart, not like Peter that way, but craving honor, probably that. And what would it have meant to the world if in childhood he had been caught in a thresher or trampled by a horse?

"Val," Peter said. "I know what you think of me. I'm not a nice person, you think."

Valentine threw a pine needle at him. "An arrow through your heart."

"I've been planning to come talk to you for a long time. But I kept being afraid."

She put a pine needle in her mouth and blew it at him. It dropped almost straight down. "Another failed launch." Why was he pretending to be weak?

"Val, I was afraid you wouldn't believe me. That you wouldn't believe I could do it."

"Peter, I believe you could do anything, and probably will."

"But I was even more afraid that you'd believe me and try to stop me."

"Come on, threaten to kill me again, Peter." Did he actually believe *she* could be fooled by his nice-and-humble-kid act?

"So I've got a sick sense of humor. I'm sorry. You know I was teasing. I need your help."

"You're just what the world needs. A twelve-year-old to solve all our problems."

"It's not my fault I'm twelve right now. And it's not my

fault that right now is when the opportunity is open. Right now is the time when I can shape events. The world is always a democracy in times of flux, and the man with the best voice will win. Everybody thinks Hitler got to power because of his armies, because they were willing to kill, and that's partly true, because in the real world power is always built on the threat of death and dishonor. But mostly he got to power on words, on the right words at the right time."

"I was just thinking of comparing you to him."

"I don't hate Jews, Val. I don't want to destroy anybody. And I don't want war, either. I want the world to hold together. Is that so bad? I don't want us to go back to the old way. Have you read about the world wars?"

"Yes."

"We can go back to that again. Or worse. We could find ourselves locked into the Warsaw Pact. Now, there's a cheerful thought."

"Peter, we're children, don't you understand that? We're going to school, we're growing up—" But even as she resisted, she wanted him to persuade her. She had wanted him to persuade her from the beginning.

But Peter didn't know that he had already won. "If I believe that, if I accept that, then I've got to sit back and watch while all the opportunities vanish, and then when I'm old enough it's too late. Val, listen to me. I know how you feel about me, you always have. I was a vicious, nasty brother. I was cruel to you and crueler to Ender before they took him. But I didn't hate you. I loved you both, I just had to be—had to have *control*, do you understand that? It's the most important thing to me, it's my greatest gift, I can see where the weak points are, I can see how to get in and use them, I just *see* those things without even trying. I could become a businessman and run some big corporation, I'd scramble and maneuver until I was at the top of everything and what would I have? Nothing. I'm going to rule, Val, I'm going to have control of something. But I want it to be something worth ruling. I want to accomplish something worthwhile. A Pax Americana through the whole world. So that when somebody else comes, after we beat the buggers, when somebody else comes here to defeat us, they'll find we've already spread over a thousand worlds, we're at peace with ourselves and impossible to destroy. Do you understand? I want to save mankind from self-destruction."

She had never seen him speak with such sincerity. With no hint of mockery, no trace of a lie in his voice. He was getting better at this. Or maybe he was actually touching on the truth. "So a twelve-year-old boy and his kid sister are going to save the world?"

"How old was Alexander? I'm not going to do it overnight. I'm just going to start now. If you'll help me."

"I don't believe what you did to those squirrels was part of an act. I think you did it because you love to do it."

Suddenly Peter wept into his hands. Val assumed that he was pretending, but then she wondered. It was possible, wasn't it, that he loved her, and that in this time of terrifying opportunity he was willing to weaken himself before her in order to win her love. He's manipulating me, she thought, but that doesn't mean he isn't sincere. His cheeks were wet when he took his hands away, his eyes rimmed in red. "I know," he said. "It's what I'm most afraid of. That I really am a monster. I don't want to be a killer but I just can't help it."

She had never seen him show such weakness. You're so clever, Peter. You saved your weakness so you could use it to move me now.

And yet it did move her. Because if it were true, even partly true, then Peter was not a monster, and so she could satisfy her Peter-like love of power without fear of becoming monstrous herself. She knew that Peter was calculating even now, but she believed that under the calculations he was telling the truth. It had been hidden layers deep, but he had probed her until he found her trust.

"Val, if you don't help me, I don't know what I'll become. But if you're there, my partner in everything, you can keep me from becoming—like that. Like the bad ones.''

She nodded. You are only pretending to share power with me, she thought, but in fact I have power over you, even though you don't know it. ''I will. I'll help you.''

—

As soon as Father got them both onto his citizen's access, they began testing the waters. They stayed away from the nets that required use of a real name. That wasn't hard because real names only had to do with money. They didn't need money. They needed respect, and that they could earn. With false names, on the right nets, they could be anybody. Old men, middle-aged women, anybody, as long as they were careful about the way they wrote. All that anyone would see were their words, their ideas. Every citizen started equal, on the nets.

They used throwaway names with their early efforts, not the identities that Peter planned to make famous and influential. Of course they were not invited to take part in the great national and international political forums—they could only be audiences there until they were invited or elected to take part. But they signed on and watched, reading some of the essays published by the great names, witnessing the debates that played across their desks.

And in the lesser conferences, where common people commented about the great debates, they began to insert their comments. At first Peter insisted that they be deliberately inflammatory. ''We can't learn how our style of writing is working unless we get responses—and if we're bland, no one will answer.''

They were not bland, and people answered. The responses that got posted on the public nets were vinegar; the responses that were sent as mail, for Peter and Valentine to read privately, were poisonous. But they did learn what attributes of their writing were seized upon as childish and immature. And they got better.

When Peter was satisfied that they knew how to sound adult, he killed the old identities and they began to prepare to attract real attention.

"We have to seem completely separate. We'll write about different things at different times. We'll never refer to each other. You'll mostly work on the west coast nets, and I'll mostly work in the south. Regional issues, too. So do your homework."

They did their homework. Mother and Father worried sometimes, with Peter and Valentine constantly together, their desks tucked under their arms. But they couldn't complain—their grades were good, and Valentine was such a good influence on Peter. She had changed his whole attitude toward everything. And Peter and Valentine sat together in the woods, in good weather, and in pocket restaurants and indoor parks when it rained, and they composed their political commentaries. Peter carefully designed both characters so neither one had all of his ideas; there were even some spare identities that they used to drop in third party opinions. "Let both of them find a following as they can," said Peter.

Once, tired of writing and rewriting until Peter was satisfied, Val despaired and said, "Write it yourself, then!"

"I can't," he answered. "They can't both sound alike. Ever. You forget that someday we'll be famous enough that somebody will start running analyses. We have to come up as different people every time."

So she wrote on. Her main identity on the nets was Demosthenes—Peter chose the name. He called himself Locke. They were obvious pseudonyms, but that was part of the plan. "With any luck, they'll start trying to guess who we are."

"If we get famous enough, the government can always get access and find out who we really are."

"When that happens, we'll be too entrenched to suffer much loss. People might be shocked that Demosthenes and Locke are two kids, but they'll already be used to listening to us."

They began composing debates for their characters. Valentine would prepare an opening statement, and Peter would invent a throwaway name to answer her. His answer would be intelligent, and the debate would be lively, lots of clever invective and good political rhetoric. Valentine had a knack for alliteration that made her phrases memorable. Then they would enter the debate into the network, separated by a reasonable amount of time, as if they were actually making them up on the spot. Sometimes a few other netters would interpose comments, but Peter and Val would usually ignore them or change their own comments only slightly to accommodate what had been said.

Peter took careful note of all their most memorable phrases and then did searches from time to time to find those phrases cropping up in other places. Not all of them did, but most of them were repeated here and there, and some of them even showed up in the major debates on the prestige nets. "We're being read," Peter said. "The ideas are seeping out."

"The phrases, anyway."

"That's just the measure. Look, we're having some influence. Nobody quotes us by name, yet, but they're discussing the points we raise. We're helping set the agenda. We're getting there."

"Should we try to get into the main debates?"

"No. We'll wait until they ask us."

They had been doing it only seven months when one of the west coast nets sent Demosthenes a message. An offer for a weekly column in a pretty good newsnet.

"I can't do a weekly column," Valentine said. "I don't even have a monthly period yet."

"The two aren't related," Peter said.

"They are to me. I'm still a kid."

"Tell them yes, but since you prefer not to have your true identity revealed, you want them to pay you in network time. A new access code through their corporate identity."

"So when the government traces me—"

"You'll just be a person who can sign on through CalNet. Father's citizen's access doesn't get involved. What I can't figure out is why they wanted Demosthenes before Locke."

"Talent rises to the top."

As a game, it was fun. But Valentine didn't like some of the positions Peter made Demosthenes take. Demosthenes began to develop as a fairly paranoid anti-Russian writer. It bothered her because Peter was the one who knew how to exploit fear in his writing—she had to keep coming to him for ideas on how to do it. Meanwhile, his Locke followed her moderate, empathic strategies. It made sense, in a way. By having her write Demosthenes, it meant he also had some empathy, just as Locke also could play on others' fears. But the main effect was to keep her inextricably tied to Peter. She couldn't go off and use Demosthenes for her own purposes. She wouldn't know how to use him. Still, it worked both ways. He couldn't write Locke without her. Or could he?

"I thought the idea was to unify the world. If I write this like you say I should, Peter, I'm pretty much calling for war to break up the Warsaw Pact."

"Not war, just open nets and prohibition of interception. Free flow of information. Compliance with the League rules, for heaven's sake."

Without meaning to, Valentine started talking in Demosthenes' voice, even though she certainly wasn't speaking Demosthenes' opinions. "Everyone knows that from the beginning of the League the Second Warsaw Pact was to be regarded as a single entity where those rules were concerned. International free flow is still open. But between the Warsaw Pact nations these things are internal matters. That was why they were willing to allow American hegemony in the League."

"You're arguing Locke's part, Val. Trust me. You have to call for the Warsaw Pact to lose official status. You have to get a lot of people really angry. Then, later, when you begin to recognize the need for compromise—"

"Then they stop listening to me and go off and fight a war."

"Val, trust me. I know what I'm doing."

"How do you know? You're not any smarter than me, and you've never done this before either."

"I'm thirteen and you're ten."

"Almost eleven."

"And I know how these things work."

"All right, I'll do it your way. But I won't do any of these liberty or death things."

"You will too."

"And someday when they catch us and they wonder why your sister was such a warmonger, I can just bet you'll tell them that you told me to do it."

"Are you *sure* you're not having a period, little woman?"

"I hate you, Peter Wiggin."

What bothered Valentine most was when her column got syndicated into several other regional newsnets, and Father started reading it and quoting from it at table. "Finally, a man with some sense," he said. Then he quoted some of the passages Valentine hated worst in her own work. "It's fine to work with these hegemonist Russians with the buggers out there, but after we win, I can't see leaving half the civilized world as virtual serfs in the Russian Empire, can you, dear?"

"I think you're taking this all too seriously," said Mother.

"I like this Demosthenes. I like the way he thinks. I'm surprised he isn't in the major nets—I looked for him in the international relations debates and you know, he's never taken part in any of them."

Valentine lost her appetite and left the table. Peter followed her after a respectable interval.

"So you don't like lying to Father," he said. "So what? You're *not* lying to him. He doesn't think that you're really Demosthenes, and Demosthenes isn't saying things you really believe. They cancel each other out, they amount to nothing."

"That's the kind of reasoning that makes Locke such an ass." But what really bothered her was not that she was lying to Father—it was the fact that Father actually agreed with Demosthenes. She had thought that only fools would follow him.

A few days later Locke got picked up for a column in a New England newsnet, specifically to provide a contrasting view for their popular column from Demosthenes. "Not bad for two kids who've only got about eight pubic hairs between them," Peter said.

"It's a long way between writing a newsnet column and ruling the world," Valentine reminded him. "It's such a long way that no one has ever done it."

"They have, though. Or the moral equivalent. I'm going to say snide things about Demosthenes in my first column."

"Well, Demosthenes isn't even going to notice that Locke exists. Ever."

"For now."

With their identities now fully supported by their income from writing columns, they used Father's access now only for the throwaway identities. Mother commented that they were spending too much time on the nets. "All work and no play makes Jack a dull boy," she reminded Peter.

Peter let his hand tremble a little, and he said, "If you think I should stop, I think I might be able to keep things under control this time, I really do."

"No, no," Mother said. "I don't want you to *stop*. Just—be careful, that's all."

"I'm careful, Mom."

—

Nothing was different, nothing had changed in a year. Ender was sure of it, and yet it all seemed to have gone sour. He was still the leading soldier in the standings, and no one doubted that he deserved it now. At the age of nine he was a toon leader in Phoenix Army, with Petra Arkanian as his commander. He still led his evening practice sessions, and now they were attended by an elite group of soldiers nominated by their commanders, though any Launchy who wanted to could still come. Alai was also a toon leader, in another army, and they were still good friends; Shen was not a leader, but that was no barrier. Dink Meeker had finally accepted command and succeeded Rose the Nose in Rat Army's command. All is going well, *very* well, I couldn't ask for anything better—

So why do I hate my life?

He went through the paces of the practices and games. He liked teaching the boys in his toon, and they followed him loyally. He had the respect of everyone, and he was treated with deference in his evening practices. Commanders came to study what he did. Other soldiers approached his table at mess and asked permission to sit down. Even the teachers were respectful.

He had so much damn respect he wanted to scream.

He watched the young kids in Petra's army, fresh out of their launch groups, watched how they played, how they made fun of their leaders when they thought no one was looking. He watched the camaraderie of old friends who had known each other in the Battle School for years, who talked and laughed about old battles and long-graduated soldiers and commanders.

But with *his* old friends there was no laughter, no remembering. Just work. Just intelligence and excitement about the game, but nothing beyond that. Tonight it had come to a head in the evening practice. Ender and Alai were discussing the nuances of open-space maneuvers when Shen came up and listened for a few moments, then suddenly took Alai by the shoulders and shouted, "Nova! Nova! Nova!" Alai burst out laughing, and for a moment or two Ender watched them remember together the battle where openroom maneuvering had been for real, and they had dodged past the older boys and—

Suddenly they remembered that Ender was there. "Sorry, Ender," Shen said.

Sorry. For what? For being friends? "I was there, too, you know," Ender said.

And they apologized again. Back to business. Back to *respect*. And Ender realized that in their laughter, in their friendship, it had not occurred to them that he could have been included.

How could they think I was part of it? Did I laugh? Did I join in? Just stood there, watching, like a teacher.

That's how they think of me, too. Teacher. Legendary soldier. Not one of *them*. Not someone that you embrace and whisper Salaam in his ear. That only lasted while Ender still seemed a victim. Still seemed vulnerable. Now he was the master soldier, and he was completely, utterly alone.

Feel sorry for yourself, Ender. He typed the words on his desk as he lay on his bunk. POOR ENDER. Then he laughed at himself and cleared away the words. Not a boy or girl in this school who wouldn't be glad to trade places with me.

He called up the fantasy game. He walked as he often did through the village that the dwarves had built in the hill made by the Giant's corpse. It was easy to build sturdy walls, with the ribs already curved just right, just enough space between them to leave windows. The whole corpse was cut into apartments, opening onto the path down the Giant's spine. The public amphitheatre was carved into the pelvic bowl, and the common herd of ponies was pastured between the Giant's legs. Ender was never sure what the dwarves were doing as they went about their business, but they left him alone as he picked his way through the village, and in return he did them no harm either.

He vaulted the pelvic bone at the base of the public square, and walked through the pasture. The ponies shied away from him. He did not pursue them. Ender did not understand how the game functioned anymore. In the old days, before he had first gone to the End of the World, everything was combat and puzzles to solve—defeat the enemy before he kills you, or figure out how to get past the obstacle. Now, though, no one attacked, there was no war, and wherever he went, there was no obstacle at all.

Except, of course, in the room in the castle at the End of the World. It was the one dangerous place left. And Ender, however often he vowed that he would not, always went back there, always killed the snake, always looked his brother in the face, and always, no matter what he did next, died.

It was no different this time. He tried to use the knife on the table to pry through the mortar and pull out a stone from the wall. As soon as he breached the seal of the mortar, water began to gush in through the crack, and Ender watched his desk as his figure, now out of his control, struggled madly to stay alive, to keep from drowning. The windows of his room were gone, the water rose, and his figure drowned. All the while, the face of Peter Wiggin in the mirror stayed and looked at him.

I'm trapped here, Ender thought, trapped at the End of the World with no way out. And he knew at last the sour taste that had come to him, despite all his successes in the Battle School. It was despair.

—

There were uniformed men at the entrances to the school when Valentine arrived. They weren't standing like guards, but rather slouched around as if they were waiting for someone inside to finish his business. They wore the uniforms of I.F. Marines, the same uniforms that everyone saw in bloody combat on the videos. It lent an air of romance to this day at school; all the other kids were excited about it.

Valentine was not. It made her think of Ender, for one thing. And for another, it made her afraid. Someone had recently published a savage commentary on Demosthenes' collected writings. The commentary, and therefore her work, had been discussed in the open conference of the international relations net, with some of the most important people of the day attacking and defending Demosthenes. What worried her most was the comment of an Englishman: "Whether he likes it or not, Demosthenes cannot remain incognito forever. He has outraged too many wise men and pleased too many fools to hide behind his too-appropriate pseudonym much longer. Either he will unmask himself in order to assume leadership of the forces of stupidity he has marshalled, or his enemies will unmask him in order to better understand the disease that has produced such a warped and twisted mind."

Peter had been delighted, but then he would be. Valentine was afraid that enough powerful people had been annoyed by the vicious persona of Demosthenes that she would indeed be tracked down. The I.F. could do it, even if the American government was constitutionally bound not to. And here were I.F. troops gathered at Western Guilford Middle School, of all places. Not exactly the regular recruiting grounds for the I.F. Marines.

So she was not surprised to find a message marching around her desk as soon as she logged in.

PLEASE LOG OFF AND GO TO DR.
LINEBERRY'S OFFICE AT ONCE.

Valentine waited nervously outside the principal's office until Dr. Lineberry opened the door and beckoned her inside. Her last doubt was removed when she saw the soft-bellied man in the uniform of an I.F. colonel sitting in the one comfortable chair in the room.

"You're Valentine Wiggin," he said.

"Yes," she whispered.

"I'm Colonel Graff. We've met before."

Before? When had she had any dealings with the I.F.?

"I've come to talk to you in confidence, about your brother."

It's not just me, then, she thought. They have Peter. Or

is this something new? Has he done something crazy? I thought he stopped doing crazy things.

"Valentine, you seem frightened. There's no need to be. Please, sit down. I assure you that your brother is well. He has more than fulfilled our expectations."

And now, with a great inward gush of relief, she realized that it was Ender they had come about. This must be the officer who had taken him away. Ender. It wasn't punishment at all, it was little Ender, who had disappeared so long ago, who was no part of Peter's plots now. You were the lucky one, Ender. You got away before Peter could trap you into his conspiracy.

"How do you feel about your brother, Valentine?"

"Ender?"

"Of course."

"How can I feel about him? I haven't seen him or heard from him since I was eight."

"Dr. Lineberry, will you excuse us?"

Lineberry was annoyed.

"On second thought, Dr. Lineberry, I think Valentine and I will have a much more productive conversation if we walk. Outside. Away from the recording devices that your assistant principal has placed in this room."

It was the first time Valentine had seen Dr. Lineberry speechless. Colonel Graff lifted a picture out from the wall and peeled a sound-sensitive membrane from the wall, along with its small broadcast unit. "Cheap," said Graff, "but effective. I thought you knew."

Lineberry took the device and sat down heavily at her desk. Graff led Valentine outside.

They walked out into the football field. The soldiers followed at a discreet distance; they split up and formed a large circle, to guard them from the widest possible perimeter.

"Valentine, we need your help for Ender."

"What kind of help?"

"We aren't even sure of that. We need you to help us figure out how you can help us."

"Well, what's wrong?"

"That's part of the problem. We don't know."

Valentine couldn't help but laugh. "I haven't seen him in three years! You've got him up there with you all the time!"

"Valentine, it costs more money than your father will make in his lifetime for me to fly to Earth and back to the Battle School again. I don't commute casually."

"The king had a dream," said Valentine, "but he forgot what it was, so he told his wise men to interpret the dream or they'd die. Only Daniel could interpret it, because he was a prophet."

"You read the Bible?"

"We're doing classics this year in advanced English. I'm not a prophet."

"I wish I could tell you everything about Ender's situation. But it would take hours, maybe days, and afterward I'd have to put you in protective confinement because so much of it is strictly confidential. So let's see what we can do with limited information. There's a game that our students play with the computer." And he told her about the End of the World and the closed room and the picture of Peter in the mirror.

"It's the computer that puts the picture there, not Ender. Why not ask the computer?"

"The computer doesn't know."

"*I'm* supposed to know?"

"This is the second time since Ender's been with us that he's taken this game to a dead end. To a game that seems to have no solution."

"Did he solve the first one?"

"Eventually."

"Then give him time, he'll probably solve this one."

"I'm not sure. Valentine, your brother is a very unhappy little boy."

"Why?"

"I don't know."

"You don't know much, do you?"

Valentine thought for a moment that the man might get angry. Instead, though, he decided to laugh. "No, not much. Valentine, why would Ender keep seeing your brother Peter in the mirror?"

"He shouldn't. It's stupid."

"Why is it stupid?"

"Because if there's ever anybody who was the opposite of Ender, it's Peter."

"How?"

Valentine could not think of a way to answer him that wasn't dangerous. Too much questioning about Peter could lead to real trouble. Valentine knew enough about the world to know that no one would take Peter's plans for world domination seriously, as a danger to existing governments. But they might well decide he was insane and needed treatment for his megalomania.

"You're preparing to lie to me," Graff said.

"I'm preparing not to talk to you anymore," Valentine answered.

"And you're afraid. Why are you afraid?"

"I don't like questions about my family. Just leave my family out of this."

"Valentine, I'm *trying* to leave your family out of this. I'm coming to you so I don't have to start a battery of tests on Peter and question your parents. I'm trying to solve this problem now, with the person Ender loves and trusts most in the world, perhaps the only person he loves and trusts at all. If we can't solve it this way, then we'll sequester your family and do as we like from then on. This is not a trivial matter, and I won't just go away."

The only person Ender loves and trusts at all. She felt a deep stab of pain, of regret, of shame that now it was Peter she was close to, Peter who was the center of her life. For you, Ender, I light fires on your birthday. For Peter I help fulfil all his dreams. "I never thought you were a nice man. Not when you came to take Ender away, and not now."

"Don't pretend to be an ignorant little girl. I saw your tests when you were little, and at the present moment there aren't very many college professors who could keep up with you."

"Ender and Peter hate each other."

"I knew that. You said they were opposites. Why?"

"Peter—can be hateful sometimes."

"Hateful in what way?"

"Mean. Just mean, that's all."

"Valentine, for Ender's sake, tell me what he does when he's being mean."

"He threatens to kill people a lot. He doesn't mean it. But when we were little, Ender and I were both afraid of him. He told us he'd kill us. Actually, he told us he'd kill Ender."

"We monitored some of that."

"It was because of the monitor."

"Is that all? Tell me more about Peter."

So she told him about the children in every school that Peter attended. He never hit them, but he tortured them just the same. Found what they were most ashamed of and told it to the person whose respect they most wanted. Found what they most feared and made sure they faced it often.

"Did he do this with Ender?"

Valentine shook her head.

"Are you sure? Didn't Ender have a weak place? A thing he feared most, or that he was ashamed of?"

"Ender never did anything to be ashamed of." And suddenly, deep in her own shame for having forgotten and betrayed Ender, she started to cry.

"Why are you crying?"

She shook her head. She couldn't explain what it was like to think of her little brother, who was so good, whom she had protected for so long, and then remember that now she was Peter's ally, Peter's helper, Peter's slave in a scheme that was completely out of her control. Ender never surrendered to Peter, but I have turned, I've become part of him, as Ender never was. "Ender never gave in," she said.

"To what?"

"To Peter. To being like Peter."

They walked in silence along the goal line.

"How would Ender ever be like Peter?"

Valentine shuddered. "I already told you."

"But Ender never did that kind of thing. He was just a little boy."

"We both wanted to, though. We both wanted to—to kill Peter."

"Ah."

"No, that isn't true. We never said it. Ender never said that he wanted to do that. I just—*thought* it. It was me, not Ender. He never said that he wanted to kill him."

"What *did* he want?"

"He just didn't want to be—"

"To be what?"

"Peter tortures squirrels. He stakes them out on the ground and skins them alive and sits and watches them until they die. He did that for a while, after Ender left; he doesn't do it now. But he did it. If Ender knew that, if Ender saw him, I think that he'd—"

"He'd what? Rescue the squirrels? Try to heal them?"

"No, in those days you didn't—undo what Peter did. You didn't cross him. But Ender would be kind to squirrels. Do you understand? He'd feed them."

"But if he fed them, they'd become tame, and that much easier for Peter to catch."

Valentine began to cry again. "No matter what you do, it always helps Peter. Everything helps Peter, everything, you just can't get away, no matter what."

"Are you helping Peter?" asked Graff.

She didn't answer.

"Is Peter such a very bad person, Valentine?"

She nodded.

"Is Peter the worst person in the world?"

"How can he be? I don't know. He's the worst person I know."

"And yet you and Ender are his brother and sister. You have the same genes, the same parents, how can he be so bad if—"

Valentine turned and screamed at him, screamed as if he were killing her. "Ender is not like Peter! He is not like Peter in any way! Except that he's smart, that's all—in every other way a person could possibly be like Peter he is nothing nothing nothing like Peter! Nothing!"

"I see," said Graff.

"I know what you're thinking, you bastard, you're thinking that I'm wrong, that Ender's like Peter. Well maybe *I'm* like Peter, but Ender isn't, he isn't at all, I used to tell him that when he cried, I told him that lots of times, you're not like Peter, you never like to hurt people, you're kind and good and not like Peter at all!"

"And it's true."

His acquiescence calmed her. "Damn right it's true. It's true."

"Valentine, will you help Ender?"

"I can't do anything for him now."

"It's really the same thing you always did for him before. Just comfort him and tell him that he never likes to hurt people, that he's good and kind and not like Peter at all. That's the most important thing. That he's not like Peter at all."

"I can see him?"

"No. I want you to write a letter."

"What good does that do? Ender never answered a single letter I sent."

Graff sighed. "He answered every letter he got."

It took only a second for her to understand. "You really stink."

"Isolation is—the optimum environment for creativity. It was *his* ideas we wanted, not the—never mind, I don't have to defend myself to you."

Then why are you doing it, she did not ask.

"But he's slacking off. He's coasting. We want to push him forward, and he won't go."

"Maybe I'd be doing Ender a favor if I told you to go stuff yourself."

"You've already helped me. You can help me more. Write to him."

"Promise you won't cut out anything I write."

"I won't promise any such thing."

"Then forget it."

"No problem. I'll write your letter myself. We can use your other letters to reconcile the writing styles. Simple matter."

"I want to see him."

"He gets his first leave when he's eighteen."

"You told him it would be when he was twelve."

"We changed the rules."

"Why should I help you!"

"Don't help me. Help Ender. What does it matter if that helps us, too?"

"What kind of terrible things are you doing to him up there?"

Graff chuckled. "Valentine, my dear little girl, the terrible things are only about to begin."

Ender was four lines into the letter before he realized that it wasn't from one of the other soldiers in the Battle School. It had come in the regular way—a MAIL WAITING message when he signed into his desk. He read four lines into it, then skipped to the end and read the signature. Then he went back to the beginning, and curled up on his bed to read the words over and over again.

ENDER,
THE BASTARDS WOULDN'T PUT ANY OF
MY LETTERS THROUGH TILL NOW. I
MUST HAVE WRITTEN A HUNDRED TIMES
BUT YOU MUST HAVE THOUGHT I NEVER
DID. WELL I DID. I HAVEN'T
FORGOTTEN YOU. I REMEMBER YOUR
BIRTHDAY. I REMEMBER EVERYTHING.
SOME PEOPLE MIGHT THINK THAT
BECAUSE YOU'RE BEING A SOLDIER
YOU ARE NOW A CRUEL AND HARD
PERSON WHO LIKES TO HURT PEOPLE,
LIKE THE MARINES IN THE VIDEOS,
BUT I KNOW THAT ISN'T TRUE. YOU
ARE NOTHING LIKE YOU-KNOW-WHO.
HE'S NICER-SEEMING BUT HE'S
STILL A SLUMBITCH INSIDE.
MAYBE YOU SEEM MEAN, BUT IT
WON'T FOOL ME. STILL PADDLING
THE OLD KNEW,
ALL MY LOVE TURKEY LIPS,
VAL
DON'T WRITE BACK THEY'LL PROBLY
SIKOWANALIZE YOUR LETTER.

Obviously it was written with the full approval of the teachers. But there was no doubt it was written by Val. The spelling of *psychoanalyze*, the epithet *slumbitch* for Peter, the joke about pronouncing *knew* like *canoe* were all things that no one could know but Val.

And yet they came pretty thick, as though someone wanted to make very sure that Ender believed that the letter was genuine. Why should they be so eager if it's the real thing?

It isn't the real thing anyway. Even if she wrote it in her own blood, it isn't the real thing because they made her write it. She'd written before, and they didn't let any of those letters through. Those might have been real, but this was asked for, this was part of their manipulation.

And the despair filled him again. Now he knew why. Now he knew what he hated so much. He had no control over his own life. They ran everything. They made all the choices. Only the game was left to him, that was all, everything else was them and their rules and plans and lessons and programs, and all he could do was go this way or that way in battle. The one real thing, the one precious real thing was his memory of Valentine, the person who loved him before he ever played a game, who loved him whether there was a bugger war or not, and they had taken her and put her on their side. She was one of them now.

He hated them and all their games. Hated them so badly that he cried, reading Val's empty asked-for letter again. The other boys in Phoenix Army noticed and looked away. *Ender Wiggin* crying? That was disturbing. Something terrible was going on. The best soldier in any army, lying on his bunk *crying*. The silence in the room was deep.

Ender deleted the letter, wiped it out of memory and then punched up the fantasy game. He was not sure why he was so eager to play the game, to get to the End of the World, but he wasted no time getting there. Only when he coasted on the cloud, skimming over the autumnal colors of the pastoral world, only then did he realize what he hated most about Val's letter. All that it said was about Peter. About how he was not at all like Peter. The words she had said so often as she held him, comforted him as he trembled in fear and rage and loathing after Peter had tortured him, that was all that the letter had said.

And that was what they had asked for. The bastards knew about *that*, and they knew about Peter in the mirror in the castle room, they knew about everything and to them Val was just one more tool to use to control him, just one more trick to play. Dink was right, they were the enemy, they loved nothing and cared for nothing and he was not going to do what they wanted, he was damn well not going to do anything for them. He had had only one memory that was safe, one good thing, and those bastards had plowed it into him with the rest of the manure—and so he was finished, he wasn't going to play.

As always the serpent waited in the tower room, unraveling itself from the rug on the floor. But this time Ender didn't grind it underfoot. This time he caught it in his hands, knelt before it, and gently, so gently, brought the snake's gaping mouth to his lips.

And kissed.

He had not meant to do that. He had meant to let the snake bite him on the mouth. Or perhaps he had meant to eat the snake alive, as Peter in the mirror had done, with his bloody chin and the snake's tail dangling from his lips. But he kissed it instead.

And the snake in his hands thickened and bent into another shape. A human shape. It was Valentine, and she kissed him again.

The snake could not be Valentine. He had killed it too often for it to be his sister. Peter had devoured it too often for Ender to bear it that it might have been Valentine all along.

Was this what they planned when they let him read her letter? He didn't care.

She arose from the floor of the tower room and walked to the mirror. Ender made his figure also rise and go with her. They stood before the mirror, where instead of Peter's cruel reflection there stood a dragon and a unicorn. Ender reached out his hand and touched the mirror and so did Valentine; the wall fell open and revealed a great stairway downward, carpeted and lined with shouting, cheering multitudes. Together, arm in arm, he and Valentine walked down the stairs. Tears filled his eyes, tears of relief that at last he had broken free of the room at the End of the World. And because of the tears, he didn't notice that every member of the multitude wore Peter's face. He only knew that wherever he went in this world, Valentine was with him.

—

Valentine opened the letter that Dr. Lineberry had given her. "Dear Valentine," it said, "We thank you and commend you for your efforts on behalf of the war effort. You are hereby notified that you have been awarded the Star of the Order of the League of Humanity, First Class, which is the highest military award that can be given to a civilian. Unfortunately, I.F. security forbids us to make this award public until after the successful conclusion of current operations, but we want you to know that your efforts resulted in complete success. Sincerely, General Shimon Levy, Strategos."

When she had read it twice, Dr. Lineberry took it from her hands. "I was instructed to let you read it, and then destroy it." She took a cigarette lighter from a drawer and set the paper afire. It burned brightly in the ashtray. "Was it good or bad news?" she asked.

"I sold my brother," Valentine said, "and they paid me for it."

"That's a bit melodramatic, isn't it, Valentine?"

Valentine went back to class without answering. That night Demosthenes published a scathing denunciation of the population limitation laws. People should be allowed to have as many children as they like, and the surplus population should be sent to other worlds, to spread mankind so far across the galaxy that no disaster, no invasion could ever threaten the human race with annihilation. "The most noble title any child can have," Demosthenes wrote, "is Third."

For you, Ender, she said to herself as she wrote.

Peter laughed in delight when he read it. "That'll make them sit up and take notice. Third! A noble title! Oh, you have a wicked streak."

10

Dragon

"Now?"

"I suppose so."

"It has to be an order, Colonel Graff. Armies don't move because a commander says 'I suppose it's time to attack.' "

"I'm not a commander. I'm a teacher of little children."

"Colonel, sir, I admit I was on you, I admit I was a pain in the ass, but it worked, everything worked just like you wanted it to. The last few weeks Ender's even been, been—"

"Happy."

"Content. He's doing well. His mind is keen, his play is excellent. Young as he is, we've never had a boy better prepared for command. Usually they go at eleven, but at nine and a half he's top flight."

"Well, yes. For a few minutes there, it actually occurred to me to wonder what kind of a man would heal a broken child of some of his hurt, just so he could throw him back into battle again. A little private moral dilemma. Please overlook it. I was tired."

"Saving the world, remember?"

"Call him in."

"We're doing what must be done, Colonel Graff."

"Come on, Anderson, you're just dying to see how he handles all those rigged games I had you work out."

"That's a pretty low thing to—"

"So I'm a low kind of guy. Come on, Major. We're both the scum of the earth. I'm dying to see how he handles them, too. After all, our lives depend on him doing real well. Neh?"

"You're not starting to use the boys' slang, are you?"

"Call him in, Major. I'll dump the rosters into his files and give him his security system. What we're doing to him isn't all bad, you know. He gets his privacy again."

"Isolation, you mean."

"The loneliness of power. Go call him in."

"Yes sir. I'll be back with him in fifteen minutes."

"Good-bye. Yes sir yessir yezzir. I hope you had fun, I hope you had a nice, nice time being happy, Ender. It might be the last time in your life. Welcome, little boy. Your dear Uncle Graff has plans for you."

Ender knew what was happening from the moment they brought him in. Everyone expected him to go commander early. Perhaps not *this* early, but he had topped the standings almost continuously for three years, no one else was remotely close to him, and his evening practices had become the most prestigious group in the school. There were some who wondered why the teachers had waited this long.

He wondered which army they'd give him. Three commanders were graduating soon, including Petra, but it was beyond hope for them to give him Phoenix Army—no one ever succeeded to command of the same army he was in when he was promoted.

Anderson took him first to his new quarters. That sealed it—only commanders had private rooms. Then he had him fitted for new uniforms and a new flash suit. He looked on the forms to discover the name of his army.

Dragon, said the form. There was no Dragon Army.

"I've never heard of Dragon Army," Ender said.

"That's because there hasn't been a Dragon Army in four years. We discontinued the name because there was a superstition about it. No Dragon Army in the history of the Battle School ever won even a third of its games. It got to be a joke."

"Well, why are you reviving it now?"

"We had a lot of extra uniforms to use up."

Graff sat at his desk, looking fatter and wearier than the last time Ender had seen him. He handed Ender his hook, the small box that allowed commanders to go where they wanted in the battleroom during practices. Some said they worked magnetically, some said it was gravity. Many times during his evening practice sessions Ender had wished that he had a hook, instead of having to rebound off walls to get where he wanted to go. Now that he'd got quite deft at maneuvering without one, here it was. "It only works," Anderson pointed out, "during your regularly scheduled practice sessions." Since Ender already planned to have extra practices, it meant the hook would only be useful some of the time. It also explained why so many commanders never held extra practices. They depended on the hook, and it wouldn't do anything for them during the extra times. If they felt that the hook was their authority, their power over the other boys, then they were even less likely to work without it. That's an advantage I'll have over some of my enemies, Ender thought.

Graff's official welcome speech sounded bored and over-rehearsed. Only at the end did he begin to sound interested in his own words. "We're doing something unusual with Dragon Army. I hope you don't mind. We've assembled a new army by advancing the equivalent of an entire launch course early and delaying the graduation of quite a few advanced students. I think you'll be pleased with the quality of your soldiers. I hope you are, because we're forbidding you to transfer any of them."

"No trades?" asked Ender. It was how commanders always shored up their weak points, by trading around.

"None. You see, you've been conducting your extra practice sessions for three years now. You have a following. Many good soldiers would put unfair pressure on their commanders to trade them into your army. We've given you an army that can, in time, be competitive. We have no intention of letting you dominate unfairly."

"What if I've got a soldier I just can't get along with?"

"Get along with him." Graff closed his eyes, Anderson stood up and the interview was over.

Dragon was assigned the colors grey, orange, grey; Ender changed into his flash suit, then followed the ribbons of light until he came to the barracks that contained his army. They were there already, milling around near the entrance. Ender took charge at once. "Bunking will be arranged by seniority. Veterans to the back of the room, newest soldiers to the front."

It was the reverse of the usual pattern, and Ender knew it. He also knew that he didn't intend to be like many commanders, who never even saw the younger boys because they were always in the back.

As they sorted themselves out according to their arrival dates, Ender walked up and down the aisle. Almost thirty of his soldiers were new, straight out of their launch group, completely inexperienced in battle. Some were even underage—the ones nearest the door were pathetically small. Ender reminded himself that that's how he must have looked to Bonzo Madrid when he first arrived. Still, Bonzo had had only one underage soldier to cope with.

Not one of the veterans belonged to Ender's elite practice group. None had ever been a toon leader. None, in fact, was older than Ender himself, which meant that even his veterans didn't have more than eighteen months' experience. Some he didn't even recognize, they had made so little impression.

They recognized Ender, of course, since he was the most celebrated soldier in the school. And some, Ender could see, resented him. At least they did me one favor—none of my soldiers is older than me.

As soon as each soldier had a bunk, Ender ordered them to put on their flash suits and come to practice. "We're on the morning schedule, straight to practice after breakfast. Officially you have a free hour between breakfast and practice. We'll see what happens after I find out how good you are." After three minutes, though many of them still weren't dressed, he ordered them out of the room.

"But I'm naked!" said one boy.

"Dress faster next time. Three minutes from first call to running out the door—that's the rule this week. Next week the rule is two minutes. Move!" It would soon be a joke in the rest of the school that Dragon Army was so dumb they had to practice getting dressed.

Five of the boys were completely naked, carrying their flash suits as they ran through the corridors; few were fully dressed. They attracted a lot of attention as they passed open classroom doors. No one would be late again if he could help it.

In the corridors leading to the battleroom, Ender made them run back and forth in the halls, fast, so they were sweating a little, while the naked ones got dressed. Then he led them to the upper door, the one that opened into the middle of the battleroom just like the doors in the actual games. Then he made them jump up and use the ceiling handholds to hurl themselves into the room. "Assemble on the far wall," he said. "As if you were going for the enemy's gate."

They revealed themselves as they jumped, four at a time, through the door. Almost none of them knew how to establish a direct line to the target, and when they reached the far wall few of the new ones had any idea how to catch on or even control their rebounds.

The last boy out was a small kid, obviously underage. There was no way he was going to reach the ceiling handhold.

"You can use a side handhold if you want," Ender said.

"Go suck on it," said the boy. He took a flying leap, touched the ceiling handhold with a finger tip, and hurtled through the door with no control at all, spinning in three directions at once. Ender tried to decide whether to like the little kid for refusing to take a concession or to be annoyed at his insubordinate attitude.

They finally got themselves together along the wall. Ender noticed that without exception they had lined up with their heads still in the direction that had been up in the corridor. So Ender deliberately took hold of what they were treating as a floor and dangled from it upside down. "Why are you upside down, soldier?" he demanded.

Some of them started to turn the other way.

"Attention!" They held still. "I said why are you upside down!"

No one answered. They didn't know what he expected.

"I said why does every one of you have his feet in the air and his head toward the ground!"

Finally one of them spoke. "Sir, this is the direction we were in coming out of the door."

"Well what difference is that supposed to make! What difference does it make what the gravity was back in the corridor! Are we going to fight in the corridor? Is there any gravity here?"

No sir. No *sir*.

"From now on, you forget about gravity before you go through that door. The old gravity is gone, erased. Understand me? Whatever your gravity is when you get to the door, remember—the enemy's gate is *down*. Your feet are toward the enemy gate. Up is toward your own gate. North is that way, south is that way, east is that way, west is—what way?''

They pointed.

''That's what I expected. The only process you've mastered is the process of elimination, and the only reason you've mastered that is because you can do it in the toilet. What was the circus I saw out here! Did you call that forming up? Did you call that flying? Now everybody, launch and form up on the ceiling! Right now! Move!''

As Ender expected, a good number of them instinctively launched, not toward the wall with the door in it, but toward the wall that Ender had called *north*, the direction that had been up when they were in the corridor. Of course they quickly realized their mistake, but too late—they had to wait to change things until they had rebounded off the north wall.

In the meantime, Ender was mentally grouping them into slow learners and fast learners. The littlest kid, the one who had been last out of the door, was the first to arrive at the correct wall, and he caught himself adroitly. They had been right to advance him. He'd do well. He was also cocky and rebellious, and probably resented the fact that he had been one of the ones Ender had sent naked through the corridors.

''You!'' Ender said, pointing at the small one. ''Which way is down?''

''Toward the enemy door.'' The answer was quick. It was also surly, as if to say, OK, OK, now get on with the important stuff.

''Name, kid?''

''This soldier's name is Bean, sir.''

''Get that for size or for brains?'' The other boys laughed a little. ''Well, Bean, you're right onto things. Now listen to me, because this matters. Nobody's going to get through that door without a good chance of getting hit. In the old days, you had ten, twenty seconds before you even had to move. Now if you aren't already streaming out of the door when the enemy comes out, you're frozen. Now, what happens when you're frozen?''

''Can't move,'' one of the boys said.

''That's what frozen *means*,'' Ender said. ''But what *happens* to you?''

It was Bean, not intimidated at all, who answered intelligently. ''You keep going in the direction you started in. At the speed you were going when you were flashed.''

''That's true. You five, there on the end, move!'' Startled, the boys looked at each other. Ender flashed them all. ''The next five, move!''

They moved. Ender flashed them, too, but they kept moving, heading toward the walls. The first five, though, were drifting uselessly near the main group.

''Look at these so-called soldiers,'' Ender said. ''Their commander ordered them to move, and now look at them. Not only are they frozen, they're frozen right here, where they can get in the way. While the others, because they moved when they were ordered, are frozen down there, plugging up the enemy's lanes, blocking the enemy's vision. I imagine that about five of you have understood the point of this. And no doubt Bean is one of them. Right, Bean?''

He didn't answer at first. Ender looked at him until he said, ''Right, sir.''

''Then what is the point?''

''When you are ordered to move, move fast, so if you get iced you'll bounce around instead of getting in the way of your own army's operations.''

''Excellent. At least I have one soldier who can figure things out.'' Ender could see resentment growing in the way the other soldiers shifted their weight and glanced at each other, the way they avoided looking at Bean. Why am I doing this? What does this have to do with being a good commander, making one boy the target of all the others? Just because they did it to me, why should I do it to him? Ender wanted to undo his taunting of the boy, wanted to tell the others that the little one needed their help and friendship more than anyone else. But of course Ender couldn't do that. Not on the first day. On the first day even his mistakes had to look like part of a brilliant plan.

Ender hooked himself nearer the wall and pulled one of the boys away from the others. ''Keep your body straight,'' said Ender. He rotated the boy in midair so his feet pointed toward the others. When the boy kept moving his body, Ender flashed him. The others laughed. ''How much of his body could you shoot?'' Ender asked a boy directly under the frozen soldier's feet.

''Mostly all I can hit is his feet.''

Ender turned to the boy next to him. ''What about you?''

''I can see his body.''

''And you?''

A boy a little farther down the wall answered. ''All of him.''

''Feet aren't very big. Not much protection.'' Ender pushed the frozen soldier out of the way. Then he doubled his legs under him, as if he were kneeling in midair, and flashed his own legs. Immediately the legs of his suit went rigid, holding them in that position.

Ender twisted himself in the air, so that he knelt above the other boys.

''What do you see?'' he asked.

A lot less, they said.

Ender thrust his gun between his legs. ''I can see fine,'' he said, and proceeded to flash the boys directly under him. ''Stop me!'' he shouted. ''Try and flash me!''

They finally did, but not until he had flashed more than a third of them. He thumbed his hook and thawed himself and every other frozen soldier. ''Now,'' he said, ''which way is the enemy's gate?''

''Down!''

''And what is our attack position?''

Some started to answer with words, but Bean answered by flipping himself away from the wall with his legs doubled under him, straight toward the opposite wall, flashing between his legs all the way.

For a moment Ender wanted to shout at him, to punish him; then he caught himself, rejected the ungenerous impulse. Why should I be so angry at this little boy? "Is Bean the only one who knows how?" Ender shouted.

Immediately the entire army pushed off toward the opposite wall, kneeling in the air, firing between their legs, shouting at the top of their lungs. There may be a time, thought Ender, when this is exactly the strategy I'll need—forty screaming boys in an unbalancing attack.

When they were all at the other side, Ender called for them to attack him, all at once. Yes, thought Ender. Not bad. They gave me an untrained army, with no excellent veterans, but at least it isn't a crop of fools. I can work with this.

When they were assembled again, laughing and exhilarated, Ender began the real work. He had them freeze their legs in the kneeling position. "Now, what are your legs good for, in combat?"

Nothing, said some boys.

"Bean doesn't think so," said Ender.

"They're the best way to push off walls."

"Right," Ender said.

The other boys started to complain that pushing off walls was movement, not combat.

"There is no combat without movement," Ender said. They fell silent and hated Bean a little more. "Now, with your legs frozen like this, can you push off walls?"

No one dared answer, for fear they'd be wrong.

"Bean?" asked Ender.

"I've never tried it, but maybe if you faced the wall and doubled over at the waist—"

"Right but wrong. Watch me. My back's to the wall, legs are frozen. Since I'm kneeling, my feet are against the wall. Usually, when you push off you have to push downward, so you string out your body behind you like a string *bean*, right?''

Laughter.

''But with my legs frozen, I use pretty much the same force, pushing downward from the hips and thighs, only now it pushes my shoulders and my feet backward, shoots out my hips, and when I come loose my body's tight, nothing stringing out behind me. Watch this.''

Ender forced his hips forward, which shot him away from the wall; in a moment he readjusted his position and was kneeling, legs downward, rushing toward the opposite wall. He landed on his knees, flipped over on his back, and jackknifed off the wall in another direction. ''Shoot me!'' he shouted. Then he set himself spinning in the air as he took a course roughly parallel to the boys along the far wall. Because he was spinning, they couldn't get a continuous beam on him.

He thawed his suit and hooked himself back to them. ''That's what we're working on for the first half hour today. Build up some muscles you didn't know you had. Learn to use your legs as a shield and control your movements so you can get that spin. Spinning doesn't do any good up close, but far away, they can't hurt you if you're spinning—at that distance the beam has to hit the same spot for a couple of moments, and if you're spinning it can't happen. Now freeze yourself and get started.''

''Aren't you going to assign lanes?'' asked a boy.

''No I'm not going to assign lanes. I want you bumping into each other and learning how to deal with it all the time, except when we're practicing formations, and then I'll usually have you bump into each other on purpose. Now move!''

When he said *move*, they moved.

Ender was the last one out after practice, since he stayed to help some of the slower ones improve on technique. They'd had good teachers, but the inexperienced soldiers fresh out of their launch groups were completely helpless when it came to doing two or three things at the same time. It was fine to practice jackknifing with frozen legs, they had no trouble maneuvering in midair, but to launch in one direction, fire in another, spin twice, rebound with a jackknife off a wall, and come out firing, facing the right direction—that was way beyond them. Drill drill drill, that was all Ender would be able to do with them for a while. Strategies and formations were nice, but they were nothing if the soldiers didn't know how to handle themselves in battle.

He had to get this army ready *now*. He was early at being a commander, and the teachers were changing the rules now, not letting him trade, giving him no top-notch veterans. There was no guarantee that they'd give him the usual three months to get his army together before sending them into battle.

At least in the evenings he'd have Alai and Shen to help him train his new boys.

He was still in the corridor leading out of the battleroom when he found himself face to face with little Bean. Bean looked angry. Ender didn't want problems right now.

"Ho, Bean."

"Ho, Ender."

Pause.

"*Sir*," Ender said softly.

"I know what you're doing, Ender, sir, and I'm warning you."

"Warning me?"

"I can be the best man you've got, but don't play games with me."

"Or what?"

"Or I'll be the worst man you've got. One or the other."

"And what do you want, love and kisses?" Ender was getting angry now.

Bean looked unworried. "I want a toon."

Ender walked back to him and stood looking down into his eyes. "Why should you get a toon?"

"Because I'd know what to do with it."

"Knowing what to do with a toon is easy," Ender said. "It's getting them to do it that's hard. Why would any soldier want to follow a little pinprick like you?"

"They used to call *you* that, I hear. I hear Bonzo Madrid still does."

"I asked you a question, soldier."

"I'll earn their respect, sir, if you don't stop me."

Ender grinned. "I'm helping you."

"Like hell," said Bean.

"Nobody would notice you, except to feel sorry for the little kid. But I made sure they *all* noticed you today. They'll be watching every move you make. All you have to do to earn their respect now is be perfect."

"So I don't even get a chance to learn before I'm being judged."

"Poor kid. Nobody's treatin' him fair." Ender gently pushed Bean back against the wall. "I'll tell you how to get a toon. Prove to me you know what you're doing as a soldier. Prove to me you know how to use other soldiers. And then prove to me that somebody's willing to follow you into battle. Then you'll get your toon. But not bloody well until."

Bean smiled. "That's fair. *If* you actually work that way, I'll be a toon leader in a month."

Ender reached down and grabbed the front of his uniform and shoved him into the wall. "When I say I work a certain way, Bean, then that's the way I work."

Bean just smiled. Ender let go of him and walked away. When he got to his room he lay down on his bed and trembled. What am I doing? My first practice session, and I'm already bullying people the way Bonzo did. And Peter. Shoving people around. Picking on some poor little kid so the others'll have somebody they all hate. Sickening. Everything I hated in a commander, and I'm doing it.

Is it some law of human nature that you inevitably become whatever your first commander was? I can quit right now, if that's so.

Over and over he thought of the things he did and said in his first practice with his new army. Why couldn't he talk like he always did in his evening practice group? No authority except excellence. Never had to give orders, just made suggestions. But that wouldn't work, not with an army. His informal practice group didn't have to learn to do things together. They didn't have to develop a group feeling; they never had to learn how to hold together and trust each other in battle. They didn't have to respond instantly to commands.

And he could go to the other extreme, too. He could be as lax and incompetent as Rose the Nose, if he wanted. He could make stupid mistakes no matter what he did. He had to have discipline, and that meant demanding—and getting—quick, decisive obedience. He had to have a well-trained army, and that meant drilling the soldiers over and over again, long after they thought they had mastered a technique, until it was so natural to them that they didn't have to think about it anymore.

But what was this thing with Bean? Why had he gone for the smallest, weakest, and possibly the brightest of the boys? Why had he done to Bean what had been done to Ender by commanders that he despised?

Then he remembered that it hadn't begun with his commanders. Before Rose and Bonzo treated him with contempt, he had been isolated in his launch group. And it wasn't Bernard who began that, either. It was Graff.

It was the teachers who had done it. And it wasn't an accident. Ender realized that now. It was a strategy. Graff had deliberately set him up to be separate from the other boys, made it impossible for him to be close to them. And he began now to suspect the reasons behind it. It wasn't to unify the rest of the group—in fact, it was divisive. Graff had isolated Ender to make him struggle. To make him prove, not that he was competent, but that he was far better than everyone else. That was the only way he could win respect and friendship. It made him a better soldier than he would ever have been otherwise. It also made him lonely, afraid, angry, untrusting. And maybe those traits, too, made him a better soldier.

That's what I'm doing to you, Bean. I'm hurting you to make you a better soldier in every way. To sharpen your wit. To intensify your effort. To keep you off balance, never sure what's going to happen next, so you always have to be ready for anything, ready to improvise, determined to win no matter what. I'm also making you miserable. That's why they brought you to me, Bean. So you could be just like me. So you could grow up to be just like the old man.

And me—am I supposed to grow up like Graff? Fat and sour and unfeeling, manipulating the lives of little boys so they turn out factory perfect, generals and admirals ready to lead the fleet in defense of the homeland? You get all the pleasures of the puppeteer. Until you get a soldier who can do more than anyone else. You can't have that. It spoils the symmetry. You must get him in line, break him down, isolate him, beat him until he gets in line with everyone else.

Well, what I've done to you this day, Bean, I've done. But I'll be watching you, more compassionately than you know, and when the time is right you'll find that I'm your friend, and you are the soldier you want to be.

Ender did not go to classes that afternoon. He lay on his bunk and wrote down his impressions of each of the boys in his army, the things he noticed right about them, the things that needed more work. In practice tonight, he would talk with Alai and they'd figure out ways to teach small groups the things they needed to know. At least he wouldn't be in this thing alone.

But when Ender got to the battleroom that night, while most others were still eating, he found Major Anderson waiting for him. "There has been a rule change, Ender. From now on, only members of the same army may work together in a battleroom during freetime. And, therefore, battlerooms are available only on a scheduled basis. After tonight, your next turn is in four days."

"Nobody else is holding extra practices."

"They are now, Ender. Now that you command another army, they don't want their boys practicing with you. Surely you can understand that. So they'll conduct their own practices."

"I've always been in another army from them. They still sent their soldiers to me for training."

"You weren't commander then."

"You gave me a completely green army, Major Anderson, sir—"

"You have quite a few veterans."

"They aren't any good."

"Nobody gets here without being brilliant, Ender. Make them good."

"I needed Alai and Shen to—"

"It's about time you grew up and did some things on your own, Ender. You don't need these other boys to hold your hand. You're a commander now. So kindly act like it, Ender."

Ender walked past Anderson toward the battleroom. Then he stopped, turned, asked a question. "Since these evening practices are now regularly scheduled, does it mean I can use the hook?"

Did Anderson almost smile? No. Not a chance of that. "We'll see," he said.

Ender turned his back and went on into the battleroom. Soon his army arrived, and no one else; either Anderson waited around to intercept anyone coming to Ender's practice group, or word had already passed through the whole school that Ender's informal evenings were through.

It was a good practice, they accomplished a lot, but at the end of it Ender was tired and lonely. There was a half hour before bedtime. He couldn't go into his army's barracks—he had long since learned that the best commanders stay away unless they have some reason to visit. The boys have to have a chance to be at peace, at rest, without someone listening, to favor or despise them depending on the way they talk and act and think.

So he wandered to the game room, where a few other boys were using the last half hour before final bell to settle bets or beat their previous scores on the games. None of the games looked interesting, but he played one anyway, an easy animated game designed for Launchies. Bored, he ignored the objectives of the game and used the little player-figure, a bear, to explore the animated scenery around him.

"You'll never win that way."

Ender smiled, "Missed you at practice, Alai."

"*I* was there. But they had your army in a separate place. Looks like you're big time now, can't play with the little boys anymore."

"You're a full cubit taller than I am."

"Cubit! Has God been telling you to build a boat or something? Or are you in an archaic mood?"

"Not archaic, just arcane. Secret, subtle, roundabout. I miss you already, you circumcised dog."

"Don't you know? We're enemies now. Next time I meet you in battle, I'll whip your ass."

It was banter, as always, but now there was too much truth behind it. Now when Ender heard Alai talk as if it were all a joke, he felt the pain of losing his friend, and the worse pain of wondering if Alai really felt as little pain as he showed.

"You can try," said Ender. "I taught you everything you know. But I didn't teach you everything *I* know."

"I knew all along that you were holding something back, Ender."

A pause. Ender's bear was in trouble on the screen. He climbed a tree. "I wasn't, Alai. Holding anything back."

"I know," said Alai. "Neither was I."

"Salaam, Alai."

"Alas, it is not to be."

"What isn't?"

"Peace. It's what *salaam* means. Peace be unto you."

The words brought forth an echo from Ender's memory. His mother's voice reading to him softly, when he was very young. Think not that I am come to bring peace on earth. I came not to bring peace, but a sword. Ender had pictured his mother piercing Peter the Terrible with a bloody rapier, and the words had stayed in his mind along with the image.

In the silence, the bear died. It was a cute death, with funny music. Ender turned around. Alai was already gone. Ender felt as if part of himself had been taken away, an inward prop that was holding up his courage and confidence. With Alai, to a degree impossible even with Shen, Ender had come to feel a unity so strong that the word *we* came to his lips much more easily than *I*.

But Alai had left something behind. Ender lay in bed, dozing into the night, and felt Alai's lips on his cheek as he muttered the word *peace*. The kiss, the word, the peace were with him still. I am only what I remember, and Alai is my friend in a memory so intense that they can't tear him out. Like Valentine, the strongest memory of all.

The next day he passed Alai in the corridor, and they greeted each other, touched hands, talked, but they both knew that there was a wall now. It might be breached, that wall, sometime in the future, but for now the only real conversation between them was the roots that had already grown low and deep, under the wall, where they could not be broken.

The most terrible thing, though, was the fear that the wall could never be breached, that in his heart Alai was glad of the separation, and was ready to be Ender's enemy. For now that they could not be together, they must be infinitely apart, and what had been sure and unshakable was now fragile and insubstantial; from the moment we are not together, Alai is a stranger, for he has a life now that will be no part of mine, and that means that when I see him we will not know each other.

It made him sorrowful, but Ender did not weep. He was done with that. When they had turned Valentine into a stranger, when they had used her as a tool to work on Ender, from that day forward they could never hurt him deep enough to make him cry again. Ender was certain of that.

And with that anger, he decided he was strong enough to defeat them—the teachers, his enemies.

11

Veni Vidi Vici

"You can't be serious about this schedule of battles."

"Yes I can."

"He's only had his army three and a half weeks."

"I told you. We did computer simulations on probable results. And here is what the computer estimated Ender would do."

"We want to teach him, not give him a nervous breakdown."

"The computer knows him better than we do."

"The computer is also not famous for having mercy."

"If you wanted to be merciful, you should have gone to a monastery."

"You mean this *isn't* a monastery?"

"This is best for Ender, too. We're bringing him to his full potential."

"I thought we'd give him two years as commander. We usually give them a battle every two weeks, starting after three months. This is a little extreme."

"Do we *have* two years to spare?"

"I know. I just have this picture of Ender a year from now. Completely useless, worn out, because he was pushed farther than he or any living person could go."

"We told the computer that our highest priority was having the subject remain useful after the training program."

"Well, as long as he's useful—"

"Look, Colonel Graff, you're the one who made me prepare this, over my protests, if you'll remember."

"I know, you're right, I shouldn't burden you with my conscience. But my eagerness to sacrifice little children in order to save mankind is wearing thin. The Polemarch has been to see the Hegemon. It seems Russian intelligence is concerned that some of the active citizens on the nets are already figuring how America ought to use the I.F. to destroy the Warsaw Pact as soon as the buggers are destroyed."

"Seems premature."

"It seems insane. Free speech is one thing, but to jeopardize the League over nationalistic rivalries—and it's for people like that, short-sighted, suicidal people, that we're pushing Ender to the edge of human endurance."

"I think you underestimate Ender."

"But I fear that I also underestimate the stupidity of the rest of mankind. Are we absolutely sure that we ought to win this war?"

"Sir, those words sound like treason."

"It was black humor."

"It wasn't funny. When it comes to the buggers, nothing—"

"Nothing is funny, I know."

Ender Wiggin lay on his bed staring at the ceiling. Since becoming commander, he never slept more than five hours a night. But the lights went off at 2200 and didn't come on again until 0600. Sometimes he worked at his desk, anyway, straining his eyes to use the dim display. Usually, though, he stared at the invisible ceiling and thought.

Either the teachers had been kind to him after all, or he was a better commander than he thought. His ragged little group of veterans, utterly without honor in their previous armies, were blossoming into capable leaders. So much so that instead of the usual four toons, he had created five, each with a toon leader and a second; every veteran had a position. He had the army drill in eight-man toon maneuvers and four-man half-toons, so that at a single command, his army could be assigned as many as ten separate maneuvers and carry them out at once. No army had ever fragmented itself like that before, but Ender was not planning to do anything that had been done before, either. Most armies practiced mass maneuvers, preformed strategies. Ender had none. Instead he trained his toon leaders to use their small units effectively in achieving limited goals. Unsupported, alone, on their own initiative. He staged mock wars after the first week, savage affairs in the practice room that left everybody exhausted. But he knew, with less than a month of training, that his army had the potential of being the best fighting group ever to play the game.

How much of this did the teachers plan? Did they know they were giving him obscure but excellent boys? Did they give him thirty Launchies, many of them underage, because they knew the little boys were quick learners, quick thinkers? Or was this what any similar group could become under a commander who knew what he wanted his army to do, and knew how to teach them to do it?

The question bothered him, because he wasn't sure whether he was confounding or fulfilling their expectations.

All he was sure of was that he was eager for battle. Most armies needed three months because they had to memorize dozens of elaborate formations. We're ready now. Get us into battle.

The door opened in darkness. Ender listened. A shuffling step. The door closed.

He rolled off his bunk and crawled in the darkness the

two meters to the door. There was a slip of paper there. He couldn't read it, of course, but he knew what it was. Battle. How kind of them. I wish, and they deliver.

—

Ender was already dressed in his Dragon Army flash suit when the lights came on. He ran down the corridor at once, and by 0601 he was at the door of his army's barracks.

"We have a battle with Rabbit Army at 0700. I want us warmed up in gravity and ready to go. Strip down and get to the gym. Bring your flash suits and we'll go to the battleroom from there."

What about breakfast?

"I don't want anybody throwing up in the battleroom."

Can we at least take a leak first?

"No more than a decaliter."

They laughed. The ones who didn't sleep naked stripped down; everyone bundled up their flash suits and followed Ender at a jog through the corridors to the gym. He put them through the obstacle course twice, then split them into rotations on the tramp, the mat, and the bench. "Don't wear yourselves out, just wake yourselves up." He didn't need to worry about exhaustion. They were in good shape, light and agile, and above all excited about the battle to come. A few of them spontaneously began to wrestle—the gym, instead of being tedious, was suddenly fun, because of the battle to come. Their confidence was the supreme confidence of those who have never been in the contest, and think they are ready. Well, why shouldn't they think so? They are. And so am I.

At 0640 he had them dress out. He talked to the toon leaders and their seconds while they dressed. "Rabbit Army is mostly veterans, but Carn Carby was made their commander only five months ago, and I never fought them under him. He was a pretty good soldier, and Rabbit has done fairly well in the standings over the years. But I expect to see formations, and so I'm not worried."

At 0650 he made them all lie down on the mats and relax. Then, at 0656, he ordered them up and they jogged along the corridor to the battleroom. Ender occasionally leaped up to touch the ceiling. The boys all jumped to touch the same spot on the ceiling. Their ribbon of color led to the left; Rabbit Army had already passed through to the right. And at 0658 they reached their gate to the battleroom.

The toons lined up in five columns. A and E were ready to grab the side handholds and flip themselves out toward the sides. B and D lined up to catch the two parallel ceiling holds and flip upward into null gravity. C toon were ready to slap the sill of the doorway and flip downward.

Up, down, left, right; Ender stood at the front, between columns so he'd be out of the way, and reoriented them. "Which way is the enemy's gate?"

Down, they all said, laughing. And in that moment *up* became north, *down* became south, and *left* and *right* became east and west.

The grey wall in front of them disappeared, and the battleroom was visible. It wasn't a dark game, but it wasn't a bright one either—the lights were about half, like dusk. In the distance, in the dim light, he could see the enemy door, their lighted flash suits already pouring out. Ender knew a moment's pleasure. Everyone had learned the wrong lesson from Bonzo's misuse of Ender Wiggin. They all dumped through the door immediately, so that there was no chance to do anything other than name the formation they would use. Commanders didn't have time to think. Well, Ender would take the time, and trust his soldiers' ability to fight with flashed legs to keep them intact as they came late through the door.

Ender sized up the shape of the battleroom. The familiar open grid of most early games, like the monkey bars at the park, with seven or eight stars scattered through the grid. There were enough of them, and in forward enough positions, that they were worth going for. "Spread to the near stars," Ender said. "C try to slide the wall. If it works, A and E will follow. If it doesn't, I'll decide from there. I'll be with D. Move."

All the soldiers knew what was happening, but tactical decisions were entirely up to the toon leaders. Even with Ender's instructions, they were only ten seconds late getting through the gate. Rabbit Army was already doing some elaborate dance down at the end of the room. In all the other armies Ender had fought in, he would have been worrying right now about making sure he and his toon were in their proper place in their own formation. Instead, he and all his men were only thinking of ways to slip around past the formation, control the stars and the corners of the room, and then break the enemy formation into meaningless chunks that didn't know what they were doing. Even with less than four weeks together, the way they fought already seemed like the only intelligent way, the only *possible* way. Ender was almost surprised that Rabbit Army didn't know already that they were hopelessly out of date.

C toon slipped along the wall, coasting with their bent knees facing the enemy. Crazy Tom, the leader of C toon, had apparently ordered his men to flash their own legs already. It was a pretty good idea in this dim light, since the lighted flash suits went dark wherever they were frozen. It made them less easily visible. Ender would commend him for that.

Rabbit Army was able to drive back C toon's attack, but not until Crazy Tom and his boys had carved them up, freezing a dozen Rabbits before retreating to the safety of a star. But it was a star behind the Rabbit formation, which meant they were going to be easy pickings now.

Han Tzu, commonly called Hot Soup, was the leader of D toon. He slid quickly along the lip of the star to where Ender knelt. "How about flipping off the north wall and kneeling on their faces?"

"Do it," Ender said. "I'll take B south to get behind them." Then he shouted, "A and E slow on the walls!" He slid footward along the star, hooked his feet on the lip, and flipped himself up to the top wall, then rebounded down to E toon's star. In a moment he was leading them down against the south wall. They rebounded in near perfect unison and came up behind the two stars that Carn Carby's soldiers were defending. It was like cutting butter with a hot knife. Rabbit Army was gone, just a little cleanup left to do. Ender broke his toons up into half-toons to scour the corners for any enemy soldiers who were whole or merely damaged. In three minutes his toon leaders reported the room clean. Only one of Ender's boys was completely frozen—one of C toon, which had borne the brunt of the assault—and only five were disabled. Most were damaged, but those were leg shots and many of them were self-inflicted. All in all, it had gone even better than Ender expected.

Ender had his toon leaders do the honors at the gate—four helmets at the corners, and Crazy Tom to pass through the gate. Most commanders took whoever was left alive to pass the gate; Ender could have picked practically anyone. A good battle.

The lights went full, and Major Anderson himself came through the teachergate at the south end of the battleroom. He looked very solemn as he offered Ender the teacher hook that was ritually given to the victor in the game. Ender used it to thaw his own army's flash suits, of course, and he assembled them in toons before thawing the enemy. Crisp, military appearance, that's what he wanted when Carby and Rabbit Army got their bodies under control again. They may curse us and lie about us, but they'll remember that we destroyed them, and no matter what they say other soldiers and other commanders will see that in their eyes; in those Rabbit eyes, they'll see us in neat formation, victorious and almost undamaged in our first battle. Dragon Army isn't going to be an obscure name for long.

Carn Carby came to Ender as soon as he was unfrozen. He was a twelve-year-old, who had apparently made commander only in his last year at the school. So he wasn't cocky, like the ones who made it at eleven. I will remember this, thought Ender, when I am defeated. To keep dignity, and give honor where it's due, so that defeat is not disgrace. And I hope I don't have to do it often.

Anderson dismissed Dragon Army last, after Rabbit Army had straggled through the door that Ender's boys had come through. Then Ender led his army through the enemy's door. The light along the bottom of the door reminded them of which way was down once they got back to gravity. They all landed lightly on their feet, running. They assembled in the corridor. "It's 0715," Ender said, "and that means you have fifteen minutes for breakfast before I see you all in the battleroom for the morning practice." He could hear them silently saying, Come on, we won, let us celebrate. All right, Ender answered, you may. "And you have your commander's permission to throw food at each other during breakfast."

They laughed, they cheered, and then he dismissed them and sent them jogging on to the barracks. He caught his toon leaders on the way out and told them that he wouldn't expect anyone to come to practice till 0745, and that practice would be over early so the boys could shower. Half an hour for breakfast, and no shower right after a battle—it was still stingy, but it would look lenient compared to fifteen minutes. And Ender liked having the announcement of the extra fifteen minutes come from the toon leaders. Let the boys learn that leniency comes from their toon leaders, and harshness from their commander—it will bind them better in the small, tight knots of this fabric.

Ender ate no breakfast. He wasn't hungry. Instead he went to the bathroom and showered, putting his flash suit in the cleaner so it would be ready when he was dried off. He washed himself twice and let the water run and run on him. It would all be recycled. Let everybody drink some of my sweat today. They had given him an untrained army, and he had won, and not just nip and tuck, either. He had won with only six frozen or disabled. Let's see how long other commanders keep using their formations now that they've seen what a flexible strategy can do.

He was floating in the middle of the battleroom when his soldiers began to arrive. No one spoke to him, of course. He would speak, they knew, when he was ready, and not before.

When all were there, Ender hooked himself near them and looked at them, one by one. "Good first battle," he said, which was excuse enough for a cheer, and an attempt to start a chant of Dragon, Dragon, which he quickly stopped. "Dragon Army did all right against Rabbits. But the enemy isn't always going to be that bad. If that had been a good army, C toon, your approach was so slow they would have had you from the flanks before you got into good position. You should have split and angled in from two directions, so they couldn't flank you. A and E, your aim was wretched. The tallies show that you averaged only one hit for every two soldiers. That means most of the hits were made by attacking soldiers close in. That can't go on—a competent enemy would cut up the assault force unless they have much better cover from the soldiers at a distance. I want every toon to work on distance marksmanship at moving and unmoving targets. Half-toons take turns being targets. I'll thaw the flash suits every three minutes. Now move."

"Will we have any stars to work with?" asked Hot Soup. "To steady our aim?"

"I don't want you to get used to having something to steady your arms. If your arm isn't steady, freeze your elbows! Now move!"

The toon leaders quickly got things going, and Ender moved from group to group to make suggestions and help soldiers who were having particular trouble. The soldiers knew by now that Ender could be brutal in the way he talked to groups, but when he worked with an individual he was always patient, explaining as often as necessary, making suggestions quietly, listening to questions and problems and explanations. But he never laughed when they tried to banter with him, and they soon stopped trying. He was commander every moment they were together. He never had to remind them of it; he simply *was*.

They worked all day with the taste of victory in their mouths, and cheered again when they broke half an hour early for lunch. Ender held the toon leaders until the regular lunch hour, to talk about the tactics they had used and evaluate the work of their individual soldiers. Then he went to his own room and methodically changed into his uniform for lunch. He would enter the commanders' mess about ten minutes late. Exactly the timing that he wanted. Since this was his first victory, he had never seen the inside of the commanders' mess hall and had no idea what new commanders were expected to do, but he did know that he wanted to enter last today, when the scores of the morning's battles were already posted. Dragon Army will not be an obscure name now.

There was no great stir when he came in. But when some of them noticed how small he was, and saw the dragons on the sleeves of the uniform, they stared at him openly, and by the time he got his food and sat at a table, the room was silent. Ender began to eat, slowly and carefully, pretending not to notice that he was the center of attention. Gradually conversation and noise started up again, and Ender could relax enough to look around.

One entire wall of the room was a scoreboard. Soldiers were kept aware of an army's overall record for the past two years; in here, however, records were kept for each commander. A new commander couldn't inherit a good standing from his predecessor—he was ranked according to what he had done.

Ender had the best ranking. A perfect won-lost record, of course, but in the other categories he was far ahead. Average soldiers-disabled, average enemy-disabled, average time-elapsed-before-victory—in every category he was ranked first.

When he was nearly through eating, someone came up behind him and touched his shoulder.

"Mind if I sit?" Ender didn't have to turn around to know it was Dink Meeker.

"Ho Dink," said Ender. "Sit."

"You gold-plated fart," said Dink cheerfully. "We're all trying to decide whether your scores up there are a miracle or a mistake."

"A habit," said Ender.

"One victory is not a habit," Dink said. "Don't get cocky. When you're new they seed you against weak commanders."

"Carn Carby isn't exactly on the bottom of the rankings." It was true. Carby was just about in the middle.

"He's OK," Dink said, "considering that he only just started. Shows some promise. You don't show promise. You show threat."

"Threat to what? Do they feed you less if I win? I thought you told me this was all a stupid game and none of it mattered."

Dink didn't like having his words thrown back at him, not under these circumstances. "You were the one who got me playing along with them. But I'm not playing games with you, Ender. You won't beat *me*."

"Probably not," Ender said.

"I taught you," Dink said.

"Everything I know," said Ender. "I'm just playing it by ear right now."

"Congratulations," said Dink.

"It's good to know I have a friend here." But Ender wasn't sure Dink was his friend anymore. Neither was Dink. After a few empty sentences, Dink went back to his table.

Ender looked around when he was through with his meal. There were quite a few small conversations going on. Ender spotted Bonzo, who was now one of the oldest commanders. Rose the Nose had graduated. Petra was with a group in a far corner, and she didn't look at him once. Since most of the others stole glances at him from time to time, including the ones Petra was talking with, Ender was pretty sure she was deliberately avoiding his glance. That's the problem with winning right from the start, thought Ender. You lose friends.

Give them a few weeks to get used to it. By the time I have my next battle, things will have calmed down in here.

Carn Carby made a point of coming to greet Ender before the lunch period ended. It was, again, a gracious gesture, and, unlike Dink, Carby did not seem wary. "Right now I'm in disgrace," he said frankly. "They won't believe me when I tell them you did things that nobody's ever seen before. So I hope you beat the snot out of the next army you fight. As a favor to me."

"As a favor to you," Ender said. "And thanks for talking to me."

"I think they're treating you pretty badly. Usually new commanders are cheered when they first join the mess. But then, usually a new commander has had a few defeats under his belt before he first makes it in here. I only got in here a month ago. If anybody deserves a cheer, it's you. But that's life. Make them eat dust."

"I'll try." Carn Carby left, and Ender mentally added him to his private list of people who also qualified as human beings.

That night, Ender slept better than he had in a long time. Slept so well, in fact, that he didn't wake up until the lights came on. He woke up feeling good, jogged on out to take his shower, and did not notice the piece of paper on his floor until he came back and started dressing in his uniform. He only saw the paper because it moved in the wind as he snapped out the uniform to put it on. He picked up the paper and read it.

PETRA ARKANIAN, PHOENIX ARMY, 0700

It was his old army, the one he had left less than four weeks before, and he knew their formations backward and forward. Partly because of Ender's influence, they were the most flexible of armies, responding relatively quickly to new situations. Phoenix Army would be the best able to cope with Ender's fluid, unpatterned attack. The teachers were determined to make life interesting for him.

0700, said the paper, and it was already 0630. Some of his boys might already be heading for breakfast. Ender tossed his uniform aside, grabbed his flash suit, and in a moment stood in the doorway of his army's barracks.

"Gentlemen, I hope you learned something yesterday, because today we're doing it again."

It took a moment for them to realize that he meant a battle, not a practice. It had to be a mistake, they said. Nobody ever had battles two days in a row.

He handed the paper to Fly Molo, the leader of A toon, who immediately shouted "Flash suits" and started changing clothes.

"Why didn't you tell us earlier?" demanded Hot Soup. Hot had a way of asking Ender questions that nobody else dared ask.

"I thought you needed the shower," Ender said. "Yesterday Rabbit Army claimed we only won because the stink knocked them out."

The soldiers who heard him laughed.

"Didn't find the paper till you got back from the showers, right?"

Ender looked for the source of the voice. It was Bean, already in his flash suit, looking insolent. Time to repay old humiliations, is that it, Bean?

"Of course," Ender said, contemptuously. "I'm not as close to the floor as you are."

More laughter. Bean flushed with anger.

"It's plain we can't count on old ways of doing things," Ender said. "So you'd better plan on battles anytime. And often. I can't pretend I like the way they're screwing around with us, but I do like one thing—that I've got an army that can handle it."

After that, if he had asked them to follow him to the moon without space suits, they would have done it.

Petra was not Carn Carby; she had more flexible patterns and responded much more quickly to Ender's darting, improvised, unpredictable attack. As a result, Ender had three boys flashed and nine disabled at the end of the battle. Petra was not gracious about bowing over his hand at the end, either. The anger in her eyes seemed to say, I was your friend, and you humiliate me like this?

Ender pretended not to notice her fury. He figured that after a few more battles, she'd realize that in fact she had scored more hits against him than he expected anyone ever would again. And he was still learning from her. In practice today he would teach his toon leaders how to counter the tricks Petra had played on them. Soon they would be friends again.

He hoped.

—

At the end of the week Dragon Army had fought seven battles in seven days. The score stood 7 wins and 0 losses. Ender had never had more losses than in the battle with Phoenix Army, and in two battles he had suffered not one soldier frozen or disabled. No one believed anymore that it was a fluke that put him first in the standings. He had beaten top armies by unheard-of margins. It was no longer possible for the other commanders to ignore him. A few of them sat with him at every meal, carefully trying to learn from him how he had defeated his most recent opponents. He told them freely, confident that few of them would know how to train their soldiers and their toon leaders to duplicate what his could do. And while Ender talked with a few commanders, much larger groups gathered around the opponents Ender had defeated, trying to find out how Ender might be beaten.

There were many, too, who hated him. Hated him for being young, for being excellent, for having made their victories look paltry and weak. Ender saw it first in their faces when he passed them in the corridors; then he began to notice that some boys would get up in a group and move to another table if he sat near them in the commanders' mess; and there began to be elbows that accidently jostled him in the game room, feet that got entangled with his when he walked into and out of the gym, spittle and wads of wet paper that struck him from behind as he jogged through the corridors. They couldn't beat him in the battleroom, and knew it—so instead they would attack him where it was safe, where he was not a giant but just a little boy. Ender despised them—but secretly, so secretly that he didn't even know it himself, he feared them. It was just such little torments that Peter had always used, and Ender was beginning to feel far too much at home.

These annoyances were petty, though, and Ender persuaded himself to accept them as another form of praise. Already the other armies were beginning to imitate Ender. Now most soldiers attacked with knees tucked under them; formations were breaking up now, and more commanders were sending out toons to slip along the walls. None had caught on yet to Ender's five-toon organization—it gave him the slight advantage that when they had accounted for the movements of four units, they wouldn't be looking for a fifth.

Ender was teaching them all about null gravity tactics. But where could Ender go to learn new things?

He began to use the video room, filled with propaganda vids about Mazer Rackham and other great commanders of the forces of humanity in the First and Second Invasion. Ender stopped the general practice an hour early, and allowed his toon leaders to conduct their own practice in his absence. Usually they staged skirmishes, toon against toon. Ender stayed long enough to see that things were going well, then left to watch the old battles.

Most of the vids were a waste of time. Heroic music, closeups of commanders and medal-winning soldiers, confused shots of marines invading bugger installations. But here and there he found useful sequences: ships, like points of light, maneuvering in the dark of space, or, better still, the lights on shipboard plotting screens, showing the whole of a battle. It was hard, from the videos, to see all three dimensions, and the scenes were often short and unexplained. But Ender began to see how well the buggers used seemingly random flight paths to create confusion, how they used decoys and false retreats to draw the I.F. ships into traps. Some battles had been cut into many scenes, which were scattered through the various videos; by watching them in sequence, Ender was able to reconstruct whole battles. He began to see things that the official commentators never mentioned. They were always trying to arouse pride in human accomplishments and loathing of the buggers, but Ender began to wonder how humanity had won at all. Human ships were sluggish; fleets responded to new circumstances unbearably slowly, while the bugger fleet seemed to act in perfect unity, responding to each challenge instantly. Of course, in the First Invasion the human ships were completely unsuited to fast combat, but then so were the bugger ships; it was only in the Second Invasion that the ships and weapons were swift and deadly.

So it was from the buggers, not the humans, that Ender learned strategy. He felt ashamed and afraid of learning from them, since they were the most terrible enemy, ugly and murderous and loathsome. But they were also very good at what they did. To a point. They always seemed to follow one basic strategy only—gather the greatest number of ships at the key point of conflict. They never did anything surprising, anything that seemed to show either brilliance or stupidity in a subordinate officer. Discipline was apparently very tight.

And there was one oddity. There was plenty of talk about Mazer Rackham but precious little video of his actual battle. Some scenes from early in the battle, Rackham's tiny force looking pathetic against the vast power of the main bugger fleet. The buggers had already beaten the main human fleet out in the comet shield, wiping out the earliest starships and making a mockery of human attempts at high strategy—that film was often shown, to arouse again and again the agony and terror of bugger victory. Then the fleet coming to Mazer Rackham's little force near Saturn, the hopeless odds, and then—

Then one shot from Mazer Rackham's little cruiser, one enemy ship blowing up. That's all that was ever shown. Lots of film showing marines carving their way into bugger ships. Lots of bugger corpses lying around inside. But no film of buggers killing in personal combat, unless it was spliced in from the First Invasion. It frustrated Ender that Mazer Rackham's victory was so obviously censored. Students in the Battle School had much to learn from Mazer Rackham, and everything about his victory was concealed from view. The passion for secrecy was not very helpful to the children who had to learn to accomplish again what Mazer Rackham had done.

Of course, as soon as word got around that Ender Wiggin was watching the war vids over and over again, the video room began to draw a crowd. Almost all were commanders, watching the same vids Ender watched, pretending they understood why he was watching and what he was getting out of it. Ender never explained anything. Even when he showed seven scenes from the same battle, but from different vids, only one boy asked, tentatively, "Are some of those from the same battle?"

Ender only shrugged, as if it didn't matter.

It was during the last hour of practice on the seventh day, only a few hours after Ender's army had won its seventh battle, that Major Anderson himself came into the video room. He handed a slip of paper to one of the commanders sitting there, and then spoke to Ender. "Colonel Graff wishes to see you in his office immediately."

Ender got up and followed Anderson through the corridors. Anderson palmed the locks that kept students out of the officers' quarters; finally they came to where Graff had taken root on a swivel chair bolted to the steel floor. His belly spilled over both armrests now, even when he sat upright. Ender tried to remember. Graff hadn't seemed particularly fat at all when Ender first met him, only four years ago. Time and tension were not being kind to the administrator of the Battle School.

"Seven days since your first battle, Ender," said Graff.

Ender did not reply.

"And you've won seven battles, once a day."

Ender nodded.

"Your scores are unusually high, too."

Ender blinked.

"To what, commander, do you attribute your remarkable success?"

"You gave me an army that does whatever I can think for it to do."

"And what have you thought for it to do?"

"We orient downward toward the enemy gate and use our lower legs as a shield. We avoid formations and keep our mobility. It helps that I've got five toons of eight instead of four of ten. Also, our enemies haven't the time to respond effectively to our new techniques, so we keep beating them with the same tricks. That won't hold up for long."

"So you don't expect to keep winning."

"Not with the same tricks."

Graff nodded. "Sit down, Ender."

Ender and Anderson both sat. Graff looked at Anderson, and Anderson spoke next. "What condition is your army in, fighting so often?"

"They're all veterans now."

"But how are they doing? Are they tired?"

"If they are, they won't admit it."

"Are they still alert?"

"You're the ones with the computer games that play with people's minds. You tell *me*."

"We know what *we* know. We want to know what *you* know."

"These are very good soldiers, Major Anderson. I'm sure they have limits, but we haven't reached them yet. Some of the newer ones are having trouble because they never really mastered some basic techniques, but they're working hard and improving. What do you want me to say, that they need to rest? Of course they need to rest. They need a couple of weeks off. Their studies are shot to hell, none of us are doing any good in our classes. But you know that, and apparently you don't care, so why should I?"

Graff and Anderson exchanged glances. "Ender, why are you studying the videos of the bugger wars?"

"To learn strategy, of course."

"Those videos were created for propaganda purposes. All our strategies have been edited out."

"I know."

Graff and Anderson exchanged glances again. Graff drummed on his table. "You don't play the fantasy game anymore," he said.

Ender didn't answer.

"Tell me why you don't play it."

"Because I won."

"You never win *everything* in that game. There's always more."

"I won."

"Ender, we want to help you be as happy as possible, but if you—"

"You want to make me the best soldier possible. Go down and look at the standings. Look at the all-time standings. So far you're doing an excellent job with me. Congratulations. Now when are you going to put me up against a good army?"

Graff's set lips turned to a smile, and he shook a little with silent laughter.

Anderson handed Ender a slip of paper. "Now," he said.

"That's ten minutes from now," said Ender. "My army will be in the middle of showering up after practice."

Graff smiled, "Better hurry, then, boy."

—

He got to his army's barracks five minutes later. Most were dressing after their showers; some had already gone to the game room or the video room to wait for lunch. He sent three younger boys to call everyone in, and made everyone else dress for battle as quickly as they could.

"This one's hot and there's no time," Ender said. "They gave Bonzo notice about twenty minutes ago, and by the time we get to the door they'll have been inside for a good five minutes at least."

The boys were outraged, complaining loudly in the slang that they usually avoided around the commander. What they doing to us? They be crazy, neh?

"Forget why, we'll worry about that tonight. Are you tired?"

Fly Molo answered. "We worked our butts off in practice today. Not to mention beating the crap out of Ferret Army this morning."

"Same day nobody ever do two battles!" said Crazy Tom.

Ender answered in the same tone. "Nobody ever beat Dragon Army, either. This be your big chance to lose?" Ender's taunting question was the answer to their complaints. Win first, ask questions later.

All of them were back in the room, and most of them were dressed. "Move!" shouted Ender, and they ran along behind him, some of them still dressing when they reached the corridor outside the battleroom. Many of them were panting, a bad sign; they were too tired for this battle. The door was already open. There were no stars at all. Just empty, empty space in a dazzlingly bright room. Nowhere to hide, not even in darkness.

"My heart," said Crazy Tom, "they haven't come out yet, either."

Ender put his hand across his own mouth, to tell them to be silent. With the door open, of course the enemy could hear every word they said. Ender pointed all around the door, to tell them that Salamander Army was undoubtedly deployed against the wall all around the door, where they couldn't be seen but could easily flash anyone who came out.

Ender motioned for them all to back away from the door. Then he pulled forward a few of the taller boys, including Crazy Tom, and made them kneel, not squatting back to sit on their heels, but fully upright, so they formed an L with their bodies. He flashed them. In silence the army watched him. He selected the smallest boy, Bean, handed him Tom's gun, and made Bean kneel on Tom's frozen legs. Then he pulled Bean's hands, each holding a gun, through Tom's armpits.

Now the boys understood. Tom was a shield, an armored spacecraft, and Bean was hiding inside. He was certainly not invulnerable, but he would have time.

Ender assigned two more boys to throw Tom and Bean through the door, but signalled them to wait. He went on through the army, quickly assigning groups of four—a shield, a shooter, and two throwers. Then, when all were frozen or armed or ready to throw, he signalled the throwers to pick up their burdens, throw them through the door, and then jump through themselves.

"Move!" shouted Ender.

They moved. Two at a time the shield-pairs went through the door, backward so that the shield would be between the shooter and the enemy. The enemy opened fire at once, but they mostly hit the frozen boy in front. In the meantime, with two guns to work with and their targets neatly lined up and spread flat along the wall, the Dragons had an easy time of it. It was almost impossible to miss. And as the throwers also jumped through the door, they got handholds on the same wall with the enemy, shooting at a deadly angle so that the Salamanders couldn't figure out whether to shoot at the shield-pairs slaughtering them from above or the throwers shooting at them from their own level. By the time Ender himself came through the door, the battle was over. It hadn't taken a full minute from the time the first Dragon passed through the door until the shooting stopped. Dragon had lost twenty frozen or disabled, and only twelve boys were undamaged. It was their worst score yet, but they had won.

When Major Anderson came out and gave Ender the hook, Ender could not contain his anger. "I thought you were going to put us against an army that could match us in a fair fight."

"Congratulations on the victory, commander."

"Bean!" shouted Ender. "If you had commanded Salamander Army, what would you have done?"

Bean, disabled but not completely frozen, called out from where he drifted near the enemy door. "Keep a shifting pattern of movement going in front of the door. You never hold still when the enemy knows exactly where you are."

"As long as you're cheating," Ender said to Anderson, "why don't you train the other army to cheat intelligently!"

"I suggest that you remobilize your army," said Anderson.

Ender pressed the buttons to thaw both armies at once. "Dragon Army dismissed!" he shouted immediately. There would be no elaborate formation to accept the surrender of the other army. This had not been a fair fight, even though they had won—the teachers had meant them to lose, and it was only Bonzo's ineptitude that had saved them. There was no glory in *that*.

Only as Ender himself was leaving the battleroom did he realize that Bonzo would not realize that Ender was angry at the teachers. Spanish honor. Bonzo would only know that he had been defeated even when the odds were stacked in his favor; that Ender had had the youngest child in his army publicly state what Bonzo should have done to win; and that Ender had not even stayed to receive Bonzo's dignified surrender. If Bonzo had not already hated Ender, he would surely have begun; and hating him as he did, this would surely turn his rage murderous. Bonzo was the last person to strike me, thought Ender. I'm sure he has not forgotten that.

Nor had he forgotten the bloody affair in the battleroom when the older boys tried to break up Ender's practice session. Nor had many others. They were hungry for blood then; Bonzo will be thirsting for it now. Ender toyed with the idea of taking advanced personal defense; but with battles now possible not only every day, but twice in the same day, Ender knew he could not spare the time. I'll have to take my chances. The teachers got me into this—they can keep me safe.

—

Bean flopped down on his bunk in utter exhaustion—half the boys in the barracks were already asleep, and it was still fifteen minutes before lights out. Wearily he pulled his desk from its locker and signed on. There was a test tomorrow in geometry and Bean was woefully unprepared. He could always reason things out if he had enough time, and he had read Euclid when he was five, but the test had a time limit so there wouldn't be a chance to think. He had to know. And he didn't know. And he would probably do badly on the test. But they had won twice today, and so he felt good.

As soon as he signed on, however, all thoughts of geometry were banished. A message paraded around the desk:

SEE ME AT ONCE—ENDER

The time was 2150, only ten minutes before lights out. How long ago had Ender sent it? Still, he'd better not ignore it. There might be another battle in the morning—the thought made him weary—and whatever Ender wanted to talk to him about, there wouldn't be time then. So Bean rolled off the bunk and walked emptily through the corridor to Ender's room. He knocked.

"Come in," said Ender.

"Just saw your message."

"Fine," said Ender.

"It's near lights out."

"I'll help you find your way in the dark."

"I just didn't know if you knew what time it was—"

"I always know what time it is."

Bean sighed inwardly. It never failed. Whenever he had any conversation with Ender, it turned into an argument. Bean hated it. He recognized Ender's genius and honored him for it. Why couldn't Ender ever see anything good in him?

"Remember four weeks ago, Bean? When you told me to make you a toon leader?"

"Eh."

"I've made five toon leaders and five assistants since then. And none of them was you." Ender raised his eyebrows. "Was I right?"

"Yes, sir."

"So tell me how you've done in these eight battles."

"Today was the first time they disabled me, but the computer listed me as getting eleven hits before I had to stop. I've never had less than five hits in a battle. I've also completed every assignment I've been given."

"Why did they make you a soldier so young, Bean?"

"No younger than you were."

"But why?"

"I don't know."

"Yes you do, and so do I."

"I've tried to guess, but they're just guesses. You're—very good. They knew that, they pushed you ahead—"

"Tell me *why*, Bean."

"Because they need us, that's why." Bean sat down on the floor and stared at Ender's feet. "Because they need somebody to beat the buggers. That's the only thing they care about."

"It's important that you know that, Bean. Because most boys in this school think the game is important *for itself*, but it isn't. It's only important because it helps them find kids who might grow up to be real commanders, in the real war. But as for the game, screw that. That's what they're doing. Screwing up the game."

"Funny. I thought they were just doing it to us."

"A game nine weeks earlier than it should have come. A game every day. And now two games in the same day. Bean, I don't know what the teachers are doing, but my army is getting tired, and I'm getting tired, and they don't care at all about the rules of the game. I've pulled the old charts up from the computer. No one has ever destroyed so many enemies and kept so many of his own soldiers whole in the history of the game."

"You're the best, Ender."

Ender shook his head. "Maybe. But it was no accident that I got the soldiers I got. Launchies, rejects from other armies, but put them together and my worst soldier could be a toon leader in another army. They've loaded things my way, but now they're loading it all against me. Bean, they want to break us down."

"They can't break you."

"You'd be surprised." Ender breathed sharply, suddenly, as if there were a stab of pain, or he had to catch a sudden breath in a wind; Bean looked at him and realized that the impossible was happening. Far from baiting him, Ender Wiggin was actually confiding in him. Not much. But a little. Ender was human and Bean had been allowed to see.

"Maybe you'll be surprised," said Bean.

"There's a limit to how many clever new ideas I can come up with every day. Somebody's going to come up with something to throw at me that I haven't thought of before, and I won't be ready."

"What's the worst that could happen? You lose one game."

"Yes. That's the worst that could happen. I can't lose *any* games. Because if I lose *any*—"

He didn't explain himself, and Bean didn't ask.

"I need you to be clever, Bean. I need you to think of solutions to problems we haven't seen yet. I want you to try things that no one has ever tried because they're absolutely stupid."

"Why me?"

"Because even though there are some better soldiers than you in Dragon Army—not many, but some—there's nobody who can think better and faster than you." Bean said nothing. They both knew it was true.

Ender showed him his desk. On it were twelve names. Two or three from each toon. "Choose five of these," said Ender. "One from each toon. They're a special squad, and you'll train them. Only during the extra practice sessions. Talk to me about what you're training them to do. Don't spend too long on any one thing. Most of the time you and your squad will be part of the whole army, part of your regular toons. But when I need you. When there's something to be done that only you can do."

"These are all new," said Bean. "No veterans."

"After last week, Bean, all our soldiers are veterans. Don't you realize that on the individual soldier standings, all forty of our soldiers are in the top fifty? That you have to go down seventeen places to find a soldier who *isn't* a Dragon?"

"What if I can't think of anything?"

"Then I was wrong about you."

Bean grinned. "You weren't wrong."

The lights went out.

"Can you find your way back, Bean?"

"Probably not."

"Then stay here. If you listen very carefully, you can hear

the good fairy come in the night and leave our assignment for tomorrow."

"They won't give us another battle tomorrow, will they?"

Ender didn't answer. Bean heard him climb into bed. He got up from the floor and did likewise. He thought of a half dozen ideas before he went to sleep. Ender would be pleased—every one of them was stupid.

12

Bonzo

"General Pace, please sit down. I understand you have come to me about a matter of some urgency."

"Ordinarily, Colonel Graff, I would not presume to interfere in the internal workings of the Battle School. Your autonomy is guaranteed, and despite our difference in ranks I am quite aware that it is my authority only to advise, not to order you to take action."

"Action?"

"Do not be disingenuous with me, Colonel Graff. Americans are quite apt at playing stupid when they choose to, but I am not to be deceived. You know why I am here."

"Ah. I guess this means Dap filed a report."

"He feels—paternal toward the students here. He feels your neglect of a potentially lethal situation is more than negligence—that it borders on conspiracy to cause the death or serious injury of one of the students here."

"This is a school for children, General Pace. Hardly a matter to bring the chief of I.F. military police here for."

"Colonel Graff, the name of Ender Wiggin has percolated through the high command. It has even reached my ears. I have heard him described modestly as our only hope of victory in the upcoming invasion. When it is his life or health that is in danger, I do not think it untoward that the military police take some interest in preserving and protecting the boy. Do you?"

"Damn Dap and damn you too, sir, I know what I'm doing."

"Do you?"

"Better than anyone else."

"Oh, that is obvious, since nobody else has the faintest idea what you're doing. You have known for eight days that there is a conspiracy among some of the more vicious of these 'children' to cause the beating of Ender Wiggin, if they can. And that some members of this conspiracy, notably the boy named Bonito de Madrid, commonly called Bonzo, are quite likely to exhibit no self-restraint when this punishment takes place, so that Ender Wiggin, an inestimably important international resource, will be placed in serious danger of having his brains pasted on the walls of your orbiting schoolhouse. And you, fully warned of this danger, propose to do exactly—"

"Nothing."

"You can see how this excites our puzzlement."

"Ender Wiggin has been in this situation before. Back on Earth, the day he lost his monitor, and again when a large group of older boys—"

"I did not come here ignorant of the past. Ender Wiggin has provoked Bonzo Madrid beyond human endurance. And you have no military police standing by to break up disturbances. It is unconscionable."

"When Ender Wiggin holds our fleets in his control, when he must make the decisions that bring us victory or destruction, will there be military police to come save him if things get out of hand?"

"I fail to see the connection."

"Obviously. But the connection is there. Ender Wiggin must believe that no matter what happens, no adult will ever, ever step in to help him in any way. He must believe, to the core of his soul, that he can only do what he and the other children work out for themselves. If he does not believe that, then he will never reach the peak of his abilities."

"He will also not reach the peak of his abilities if he is dead or permanently crippled."

"He won't be."

"Why don't you simply graduate Bonzo? He's old enough."

"Because Ender knows that Bonzo plans to kill him. If we transfer Bonzo ahead of schedule, he'll know that we saved him. Heaven knows Bonzo isn't a good enough commander to be promoted on merit."

"What about the other children? Getting them to help him?"

"We'll see what happens. That is my first, final, and only decision."

"God help you if you're wrong."

"God help us all if I'm wrong."

"I'll have you before a capital court martial. I'll have your name disgraced throughout the world if you're wrong."

"Fair enough. But do remember, if I happen to be right, to make sure I get a few dozen medals."

"For what!"

"For keeping you from meddling."

Ender sat in a corner of the battleroom, his arm hooked through a hand-hold, watching Bean practice with his squad. Yesterday they had worked on attacks without guns, disarming enemies with their feet. Ender had helped them with some techniques from gravity personal combat—many things had to be changed, but inertia in flight was a tool that could be used against the enemy as easily in nullo as in Earth gravity.

Today, though, Bean had a new toy. It was a deadline, one of the thin, almost invisible twines used during construction in space to hold two objects together. Deadlines were sometimes kilometers long. This one was just a bit longer than a wall of the battleroom, and yet it looped easily, almost invisibly, around Bean's waist. He pulled it off like an article of clothing and handed one end to one of his soldiers. "Hook it to a handhold and wind it around a few times." Bean carried the other end across the battleroom.

As a tripwire it wasn't too useful, Bean decided. It was invisible enough, but one strand of twine wouldn't have much chance of stopping an enemy that could easily go above or below it. Then he got the idea of using it to change his direction of movement in midair. He fastened it around his waist, the other end still fastened to a handhold, slipped a few meters away, and launched himself straight out. The twine caught him, changed his direction abruptly, and swung him in an arc that crashed him brutally against the wall.

He screamed and screamed. It took Ender a moment to realize that he wasn't screaming in pain. "Did you see how fast I went! Did you see how I changed direction!"

Soon all of Dragon Army stopped work to watch Bean practice with the twine. The changes in direction were stunning, especially when you didn't know where to look for the twine. When he used the twine to wrap himself around a star, he attained speeds no one had ever seen before.

It was 2140 when Ender dismissed the evening practice. Weary but delighted at having seen something new, his army walked through the corridors back to the barracks. Ender walked among them, not talking, but listening to their talk. They were tired, yes—a battle every day for more than four weeks, often in situations that tested their abilities to the utmost. But they were proud, happy, close—they had never lost, and they had learned to trust each other. They trusted their fellow soldiers to fight hard and well; trusted their leaders to use them rather than waste their efforts; above all trusted Ender to prepare them for anything and everything that might happen.

As they walked the corridor, Ender noticed several older boys seemingly engaged in conversations in branching corridors and ladderways; some were in their corridor, walking slowly in the other direction. It became too much of a coincidence, however, that so many of them were wearing Salamander uniforms, and that those who weren't were often older boys belonging to armies whose commanders most hated Ender Wiggin. A few of them looked at him, and looked away too quickly; others were too tense, too nervous as they pretended to be relaxed. What will I do if they attack my army here in the corridor? My boys are all young, all small, and completely untrained in gravity combat. When would they learn?

"Ho, Ender!" someone called. Ender stopped and looked back. It was Petra. "Ender, can I talk to you."

Ender saw in a moment that if he stopped and talked, his army would quickly pass him by and he would be alone with Petra in the hallway. "Walk with me," Ender said.

"It's just for a moment."

Ender turned around and walked on with his army. He heard Petra running to catch up. "All right, I'll walk with you," Ender tensed when she came near. Was she one of them, one of the ones who hated him enough to hurt him?

"A friend of yours wanted me to warn you. There are some boys who want to kill you."

"Surprise," said Ender. Some of his soldiers seemed to perk up at this. Plots against their commander were interesting news, it seemed.

"Ender, they can do it. He said they've been planning it ever since you went commander—"

"Ever since I beat Salamander, you mean."

"I hated you after you beat Phoenix Army, too, Ender."

"I didn't say I blamed anybody."

"It's true. He told me to take you aside today and warn

you, on the way back from the battleroom, to be careful tomorrow because—''

''Petra, if you had actually taken me aside just now, there are about a dozen boys following along who would have taken me in the corridor. Can you tell me you didn't notice them?''

Suddenly her face flushed. ''No, I didn't. How can you think I did? Don't you know who your friends are?'' She pushed her way through Dragon Army, got ahead of him, and scrambled up a ladderway to a higher deck.

''Is it true?'' asked Crazy Tom.

''Is what true?'' Ender scanned the room and shouted for two roughhousing boys to get to bed.

''That some of the older boys want to kill you?''

''All talk,'' said Ender. But he knew that it wasn't. Petra had known something, and what he saw on the way here tonight wasn't imagination.

''It may be all talk, but I hope you'll understand when I say you've got five toon leaders who are going to escort you to your room tonight.''

''Completely unnecessary.''

''Humor us. You owe us a favor.''

''I owe you nothing.'' He'd be a fool to turn them down. ''Do as you want.'' He turned and left. The toon leaders trotted along with him. One ran ahead and opened his door. They checked the room, made Ender promise to lock it, and left him just before lights out.

There was a message on his desk.

DON'T BE ALONE. EVER.—DINK

Ender grinned. So Dink was still his friend. Don't worry. They won't do anything to me. I have my army.

But in the darkness he did not have his army. He dreamed that night of Stilson, only he saw now how small Stilson was, only six years old, how ridiculous his tough-guy posturing was; and yet in the dream Stilson and his friends tied

Ender so he couldn't fight back, and then everything that Ender had done to Stilson in life, they did to Ender in the dream. And afterward Ender saw himself babbling like an idiot, trying hard to give orders to his army, but all his words came out as nonsense.

He awoke in darkness, and he was afraid. Then he calmed himself by remembering that the teachers obviously valued him, or they wouldn't be putting so much pressure on him; they wouldn't let anything happen to him, nothing bad, anyway. Probably when the older kids attacked him in the battleroom years ago, there were teachers just outside the room, waiting to see what would happen; if things had got out of hand, they would have stepped in and stopped it. I probably could have sat there and done nothing, and they would have seen to it I came through all right. They'll push me as hard as they can in the game, but outside the game they'll keep me safe.

With that assurance, he slept again, until the door opened softly and the morning's war was left on the floor for him to find.

—

They won, of course, but it was a grueling affair, with the battleroom so filled with a labyrinth of stars that hunting down the enemy during mop-up took forty-five minutes. It was Pol Slattery's Badger Army, and they refused to give up. There was a new wrinkle in the game, too—when they disabled or damaged an enemy, he thawed in about five minutes, the way it worked in practice. Only when the enemy was completely frozen did he stay out of action the whole time. But the gradual thawing did not work for Dragon Army. Crazy Tom was the one who realized what was happening, when they started getting hit from behind by people they thought were safely out of the way. And at the end of the battle, Slattery shook Ender's hand and said, "I'm glad you won. If I ever beat you, Ender, I want to do it fair."

"Use what they give you," Ender said. "If you've ever got an advantage over the enemy, use it."

"Oh, I did," said Slattery. He grinned. "I'm only fair-minded before and after battles."

The battle took so long that breakfast was over. Ender looked at his hot, sweating, tired soldiers waiting in the corridor and said, "Today you know everything. No practice. Get some rest. Have some fun. Pass a test." It was a measure of their weariness that they didn't even cheer or laugh or smile, just walked into the barracks and stripped off their clothes. They would have practiced if he had asked them to, but they were reaching the end of their strength, and going without breakfast was one unfairness too many.

Ender meant to shower right away, but he was also tired. He lay down on his bed in his flash suit, just for a moment, and woke up at the beginning of lunchtime. So much for his idea of studying more about the buggers this morning. Just time to clean up, go eat, and head for class.

He peeled off his flash suit, which stank from his sweat. His body felt cold, his joints oddly weak. Shouldn't have slept in the middle of the day. I'm beginning to slack off. I'm beginning to wear down. Can't let it get to me.

So he jogged to the gym and forced himself to climb the rope three times before going to the bathroom to shower. It didn't occur to him that his absence in the commanders' mess would be noticed, that showering during the noon hour, when his own army would be wolfing down their first meal of the day, he would be completely, helplessly alone.

Even when he heard them come into the bathroom he paid no attention. He was letting the water pour over his head, over his body; the muffled sound of footsteps was hardly noticeable. Maybe lunch was over, he thought. He started to soap himself again. Maybe somebody finished practice late.

And maybe not. He turned around. There were seven of them, leaning back against the metal sinks or standing closer to the showers, watching him. Bonzo stood in front of them.

Many were smiling, the condescending leer of the hunter for his cornered victim. Bonzo was not smiling, however.

"Ho," Ender said.

Nobody answered.

So Ender turned off the shower, even though there was still soap on him, and reached for his towel. It wasn't there. One of the boys was holding it. It was Bernard. All it would take for the picture to be complete was for Stilson and Peter to be there, too. They needed Peter's smile; they needed Stilson's obvious stupidity.

Ender recognized the towel as their opening point. Nothing would make him look weaker than to chase naked after the towel. That was what they wanted, to humiliate him, to break him down. He wasn't going to play. He refused to feel weak becausc hc was wet and cold and unclothed. He stood strongly, facing them, his arms at his sides. He fastened his gaze on Bonzo.

"Your move," Ender said.

"This is no game," said Bernard. "We're tired of you, Ender. You graduate today. On ice."

Ender did not look at Bernard. It was Bonzo who hungered for his death, even though he was silent. The others were along for the ride, daring themselves to see how far they might go. Bonzo knew how far he would go.

"Bonzo," Ender said softly. "Your father would be proud of you."

Bonzo stiffened.

"He would love to see you now, come to fight a naked boy in a shower, smaller than you, and you brought six friends. He would say, Oh, what honor."

"Nobody came to fight you," said Bernard. "We just came to talk you into playing fair with the games. Maybe lose a couple now and then."

The others laughed, but Bonzo didn't laugh, and neither did Ender.

"Be proud, Bonito, pretty boy. You can go home and tell your father, Yes, I beat up Ender Wiggin, who was barely ten years old, and I was thirteen. And I had only six of my friends to help me, and somehow we managed to defeat him, even though he was naked and wet and alone—Ender Wiggin is so *dangerous* and *terrifying* it was all we could do not to bring two hundred."

"Shut your mouth, Wiggin," said one of the boys.

"We didn't come to hear the little bastard talk," said another.

"You shut up," said Bonzo. "Shut up and stand out of the way." He began to take off his uniform. "Naked and wet and alone, Ender, so we're even. I can't help that I'm bigger than you. You're such a genius, you figure out how to handle me." He turned to the others. "Watch the door. Don't let anyone else in."

The bathroom wasn't large, and plumbing fixtures protruded everywhere. It had been launched in one piece, as a low-orbit satellite, packed full of the water reclamation equipment; it was designed to have no wasted space. It was obvious what their tactics would have to be. Throw the other boy against fixtures until one of them does enough damage that he stops.

When Ender saw Bonzo's stance, his heart sank. Bonzo had also taken classes. And probably more recently than Ender. His reach was better, he was stronger, and he was full of hate. He would not be gentle. He will go for my head, thought Ender. He will try above all to damage my brain. And if this fight is long, he's bound to win. His strength can control me. If I'm to walk away from here, I have to win quickly, and permanently. He could still feel again the sickening way that Stilson's bones had given way. But this time it will be my body that breaks, unless I can break him first.

Ender stepped back, flipped the showerhead so it turned outward, and turned on pure hot water. Almost at once the steam began to rise. He turned on the next, and the next.

"I'm not afraid of hot water," said Bonzo. His voice was soft.

But it wasn't the hot water that Ender wanted. It was the heat. His body still had soap on it, and his sweat moistened it, made his skin more slippery than Bonzo would expect.

Suddenly there was a voice from the door. "Stop it!" For a moment Ender thought it was a teacher, come to stop the fight, but it was only Dink Meeker. Bonzo's friends caught him at the door, held him. "Stop it, Bonzo!" Dink cried. "Don't hurt him!"

"Why not?" asked Bonzo, and for the first time he smiled. Ah, thought Ender, he loves to have someone recognize that he is the one in control, that he has power.

"Because he's the best, that's why! Who else can fight the buggers! That's what matters, you fool, the buggers!"

Bonzo stopped smiling. It was the thing he hated most about Ender, that Ender really mattered to other people, and, in the end, Bonzo did not. You've killed me with those words, Dink. Bonzo doesn't want to hear that I might save the world.

Where are the teachers? thought Ender. Don't they realize that the first contact between us in this fight might be the end of it? This isn't like the fight in the battleroom, where no one had the leverage to do any terrible damage. There's gravity in here, and the floor and walls are hard and jutted with metal. Stop this now or not at all.

"If you touch him you're a buggerlover!" cried Dink. "You're a traitor, if you touch him you deserve to die!" They jammed Dink's face backward into the door and he was silent.

The mist from the showers dimmed the room, and the sweat was streaming down Ender's body. Now, before the soap is carried off me. Now, while I'm still too slippery to hold.

Ender stepped back, letting the fear he felt show in his face. "Bonzo, don't hurt me," he said. "Please."

It was what Bonzo was waiting for, the confession that he was in power. For other boys it might have been enough that Ender had submitted; for Bonzo, it was only a sign that his victory was sure. He swung his leg as if to kick, but changed it to a leap at the last moment. Ender noticed the shifting weight and stooped lower, so that Bonzo would be more off-balance when he tried to grab Ender and throw him.

Bonzo's tight, hard ribs came against Ender's face, and his hands slapped against his back, trying to grip him. But Ender twisted, and Bonzo's hands slipped. In an instant Ender was completely turned, yet still inside Bonzo's grasp. The classic move at this moment would be to bring up his heel into Bonzo's crotch. But for that move to be effective required too much accuracy, and Bonzo expected it. He was already rising onto his toes, thrusting his hips backward to keep Ender from reaching his groin. Without seeing him, Ender knew it would bring his face closer, almost in Ender's hair; so instead of kicking, he lunged upward off the floor, with the powerful lunge of the soldier bounding from the wall, and jammed his head into Bonzo's face.

Ender whirled in time to see Bonzo stagger backward, his nose bleeding, gasping from surprise and pain. Ender knew that at this moment he might be able to walk out of the room and end the battle. The way he had escaped from the battleroom after drawing blood. But the battle would only be fought again. Again and again until the will to fight was finished. The only way to end things completely was to hurt Bonzo enough that his fear was stronger than his hate.

So Ender leaned back against the wall behind him, then jumped up and pushed off with his arms. His feet landed in Bonzo's belly and chest. Ender spun in the air and landed on his toes and hands; he flipped over, scooted under Bonzo, and this time when he kicked upward into Bonzo's crotch, he connected, hard and sure.

Bonzo did not cry out in pain. He did not react at all, except that his body rose a little in the air. It was as if Ender had kicked a piece of furniture. Bonzo collapsed, fell to the side, and sprawled directly under the spray of steaming water from a shower. He made no movement whatever to escape the murderous heat.

"My God!" someone shouted. Bonzo's friends leaped to turn off the water. Ender slowly rose to his feet. Someone thrust his towel at him. It was Dink. "Come on out of here," Dink said. He led Ender away. Behind them they heard the heavy clatter of adults running down a ladderway. Now the teachers would come. The medical staff. To dress the wounds of Ender's enemy. Where were they before the fight, when there might have been no wounds at all?

There was no doubt now in Ender's mind. There was no help for him. Whatever he faced, now and forever, no one would save him from it. Peter might be scum, but Peter had been right, always right; the power to cause pain is the only power that matters, the power to kill and destroy, because if you can't kill then you are always subject to those who can, and nothing and no one will ever save you.

Dink led him to his room, made him lie on the bed. "Are you hurt anywhere?" he asked.

Ender shook his head.

"You took him apart. I thought you were dead meat, the way he grabbed you. But you took him apart. If he'd stood up longer, you would've killed him."

"He meant to kill me."

"I know it. I know him. Nobody hates like Bonzo. But not anymore. If they don't ice him for this and send him home, he'll never look you in the eye again. You or anybody. He had twenty centimeters on you, and you made him look like a crippled cow standing there chewing her cud."

All Ender could see, though, was the way Bonzo looked as Ender kicked upward into his groin. The empty, dead look in his eyes. He was already finished then. Already unconscious. His eyes were open, but he wasn't thinking or moving anymore, just that dead, stupid look on his face, that terrible look, the way Stilson looked when I finished with him.

"They'll ice him, though," Dink said. "Everybody knows he started it. I saw them get up and leave the commanders' mess. Took me a couple of seconds to realize you weren't there, either, and then a minute more to find out where you had gone. I told you not to be alone."

"Sorry."

"They're bound to ice him. Troublemaker. Him and his stinking honor."

Then, to Dink's surprise, Ender began to cry. Lying on his back, still soaking wet with sweat and water, he gasped his sobs, tears seeping out of his closed eyelids and disappearing in the water on his face.

"Are you all right?"

"I didn't want to hurt him!" Ender cried. "Why didn't he just leave me alone!"

—

He heard his door open softly, then close. He knew at once that it was his battle instructions. He opened his eyes, expecting to find the darkness of early morning, before 0600. Instead, the lights were on. He was naked, and when he moved the bed was soaking wet. His eyes were puffy and painful from crying. He looked at the clock on his desk. 1820, it said. It's the same day. I already had a battle today, I had two battles today—the bastards know what I've been through, and they're doing this to me.

WILLIAM BEE, GRIFFIN ARMY, TALO MOMOE,
TIGER ARMY, 1900

He sat on the edge of the bed. The note trembled in his hand. I can't do this, he said silently. And then not silently. "I can't do this."

He got up, bleary, and looked for his flash suit. Then he remembered—he had put it in the cleaner while he showered. It was still there.

Holding the paper, he walked out of his room. Dinner

was nearly over, and there were a few people in the corridor, but no one spoke to him, just watched him, perhaps in awe of what had happened at noon in the bathroom, perhaps because of the forbidding, terrible look on his face. Most of his boys were in the barracks.

Ho, Ender. There gonna be a practice tonight?

Ender handed the paper to Hot Soup. ''Those sons of bitches,'' he said. ''Two at once?''

''Two armies!'' shouted Crazy Tom.

''They'll just trip over each other,'' said Bean.

''I've got to clean up,'' Ender said. ''Get them ready, get everybody together, I'll meet you there, at the gate.''

He walked out of the barracks. A tumult of conversation rose behind them. He heard Crazy Tom scream, ''Two fart-eating armies! Wc'll whip their butts!''

The bathroom was empty. All cleaned up. None of the blood that poured from Bonzo's nose into the shower water. All gone. Nothing bad ever happened here.

Ender stepped under the water and rinsed himself, took the sweat of combat and let it run down the drain. All gone, except they recycled it and we'll be drinking Bonzo's bloodwater in the morning. All the life gone out of it, but his blood just the same, his blood and my sweat, washed down in their stupidity or cruelty or whatever it was that made them let it happen.

He dried himself, dressed in his flash suit, and walked to the battleroom. His army was waiting in the corridor, the door still not opened. They watched him in silence as he walked to the front to stand by the blank grey forcefield. Of course they all knew about his fight in the bathroom today; that and their own weariness from the battle that morning kept them quiet, while the knowledge that they would be facing two armies filled them with dread.

Everything they can do to beat me, thought Ender. Everything they can think of, change all the rules, they don't care, just so they beat me. Well, I'm sick of the game. No game is worth Bonzo's blood pinking the water on the bathroom floor. Ice me, send me home, I don't want to play anymore.

The door disappeared. Only three meters out there were four stars together, completely blocking the view from the door.

Two armies weren't enough. They had to make Ender deploy his forces blind.

"Bean," said Ender. "Take your boys and tell me what's on the other side of this star."

Bean pulled the coil of twine from his waist, tied one end around him, handed the other end to a boy in his squad, and stepped gently through the door. His squad quickly followed. They had practiced this several times, and it took only a moment before they were braced on the star, holding the end of the twine. Bean pushed off at great speed, in a line almost parallel to the door; when he reached the corner of the room, he pushed off again and rocketed straight out toward the enemy. The spots of light on the wall showed that the enemy was shooting at him. As the rope was stopped by each edge of the star in turn, his arc became tighter, his direction changed, and he became an impossible target to hit. His squad caught him neatly as he came around the star from the other side. He moved all his arms and legs so those waiting inside the door would know that the enemy hadn't flashed him anywhere.

Ender dropped through the gate.

"It's really dim," said Bean, "but light enough you can't follow people easily by the lights on their suits. Worst possible for seeing. It's all open space from this star to the enemy side of the room. They've got eight stars making a square around their door. I didn't see anybody except the ones peeking around the boxes. They're just sitting there waiting for us."

As if to corroborate Bean's statement, the enemy began to call out to them. "Hey! We be hungry, come and feed us! Your ass is draggin'! Your ass is Dragon!"

Ender's mind felt dead. This was stupid. He didn't have a chance, out-numbered two to one and forced to attack a protected enemy. "In a real war, any commander with brains at all would retreat and save this army."

"What the hell," said Bean. "It's only a game."

"It stopped being a game when they threw away the rules."

"So, you throw 'em away, too."

Ender grinned. "OK. Why not. Let's see how they react to a formation."

Bean was appalled. "A formation! We've never done a formation in the whole time we've been an army!"

"We've still got a month to go before our training period is normally supposed to end. About time we started doing formations. Always have to know formations." He formed an A with his fingers, showed it to the blank door, and beckoned. A toon quickly emerged and Ender began arranging them behind the star. Three meters wasn't enough room to work in, the boys were frightened and confused, and it took nearly five minutes just to get them to understand what they were doing.

Tiger and Griffin soldiers were reduced to chanting catcalls, while their commanders argued about whether to try to use their overwhelming force to attack Dragon Army while they were still behind the star. Momoe was all for attacking—"We outnumber him two to one"—while Bee said, "Sit tight and we can't lose, move out and he can figure out a way to beat us."

So they sat tight, until finally in the dusky light they saw a large mass slip out from behind Ender's star. It held its shape, even when it abruptly stopped moving sideways and launched itself toward the dead center of the eight stars where eighty-two soldiers waited.

"Doobie doo," said a Griffin. "They're doing a formation."

"They must have been putting that together for all five

minutes,'' said Momoe. ''If we'd attacked while they were doing it, we could've destroyed them.''

''Eat it, Momoe,'' whispered Bee. ''You saw the way that little kid flew. He went all the way around the star and back behind without ever touching a wall. Maybe they've all got hooks, did you think of that? They've got something new there.''

The formation was a strange one. A square formation of tightly-packed bodies in front, making a wall. Behind it, a cylinder, six boys in circumference and two boys deep, their limbs outstretched and frozen so they couldn't possibly be holding on to each other. Yet they held together as tightly as if they had been tied—which, in fact, they were.

From inside the formation, Dragon Army was firing with deadly accuracy, forcing Griffins and Tigers to stay tightly packed on their stars.

''The back of that sucker is open,'' said Bee. ''As soon as they get between the stars, we can get around behind—''

''Don't talk about it, do it!'' said Momoe. Then he took his own advice and ordered his boys to launch against the wall and rebound out behind the Dragon formation.

In the chaos of their takeoff, while Griffin Army held tight to their stars, the Dragon formation abruptly changed. Both the cylinder and the front wall split in two, as boys inside it pushed off; almost at once, the formations also reversed direction, heading back toward the Dragon gate. Most of the Griffins fired at the formations and the boys moving backward with them; and the Tigers took the survivors of Dragon Army from behind.

But there was something wrong. William Bee thought for a moment and realized what it was. Those formations couldn't have reversed direction in midflight unless someone pushed off in the opposite direction, and if they took off with enough force to make that twenty-man formation move backward, they must be going *fast*.

There they were, six small Dragon soldiers down near

William Bee's own door. From the number of lights showing on their flash suits, Bee could see that three of them were disabled and two of them damaged; only one was whole. Nothing to be frightened of. Bee casually aimed at them, pressed the button, and—

Nothing happened.

The lights went on.

The game was over.

Even though he was looking right at them, it took Bee a moment to realize what had just happened. Four of the Dragon soldiers had their helmets pressed on the corners of the door. And one of them had just passed through. They had just carried out the victory ritual. They were getting destroyed, they had hardly inflicted any casualties, and they had the gall to perform the victory and end the game right under their noses.

Only then did it occur to William Bee that not only had Dragon Army ended the game, it was possible that, under the rules, they had won it. After all, no matter what happened, you were not certified as the winner unless you had enough unfrozen soldiers to touch the corners of the gate and pass someone through into the enemy's corridor. Therefore, by one way of thinking, you could argue that the ending ritual *was* victory. The battleroom certainly recognized it as the end of the game.

The teachergate opened and Major Anderson came into the room. "Ender," he called, looking around.

One of the frozen Dragon soldiers tried to answer him through jaws that were clamped shut by the flash suit. Anderson hooked over to him and thawed him.

Ender was smiling. "I beat you again, sir," he said.

"Nonsense, Ender," Anderson said softly. "Your battle was with Griffin and Tiger."

"How stupid do you think I am?" said Ender.

Loudly, Anderson said, "After that little maneuver, the rules are being revised to require that all of the enemy's soldiers must be frozen or disabled before the gate can be reversed."

"It could only work once anyway," Ender said.

Anderson handed him the hook. Ender unfroze everyone at once. To hell with protocol. To hell with everything. "Hey!" he shouted as Anderson moved away. "What is it next time? My army in a cage without guns, with the rest of the Battle School against them? How about a little equality?"

There was a loud murmur of agreement from the other boys, and not all of it came from Dragon Army. Anderson did not so much as turn around to acknowledge Ender's challenge. Finally, it was William Bee who answered. "Ender, if you're on one side of the battle, it won't be equal no matter what the conditions are."

Right! called the boys. Many of them laughed. Talo Momoe began clapping his hands. "Ender Wiggin!" he shouted. The other boys also clapped and shouted Ender's name.

Ender passed through the enemy gate. His soldiers followed him. The sound of them shouting his name followed him through the corridors.

"Practice tonight?" asked Crazy Tom.

Ender shook his head.

"Tomorrow morning then?"

"No."

"Well, when?"

"Never again, as far as I'm concerned."

He could hear the murmurs behind him.

"Hey, that's not fair," said one of the boys. "It's not our fault the teachers are screwing up the game. You can't just stop teaching us stuff because—"

Ender slammed his open hand against the wall and shouted at the boy. "I don't care about the game anymore!" His voice echoed through the corridor. Boys from other armies came to their doors. He spoke quietly into the silence.

"Do you understand that?" And he whispered. "The game is over."

He walked back to his room alone. He wanted to lie down, but he couldn't because the bed was wet. It reminded him of all that had happened today, and in fury he tore the mattress and blankets from the bedframe and shoved them out into the corridor. Then he wadded up a uniform to serve as a pillow and lay on the fabric of wires strung across the frame. It was uncomfortable, but Ender didn't care enough to get up.

He had only been there a few minutes when someone knocked on the door.

"Go away," he said softly. Whoever was knocking didn't hear him or didn't care. Finally Ender said to come in.

It was Bean.

"Go away, Bean."

Bean nodded but didn't leave. Instead he looked at his shoes. Ender almost yelled at him, cursed at him, screamed at him to leave. Instead he noticed how very tired Bean looked, his whole body bent with weariness, his eyes dark from lack of sleep; and yet his skin was still soft and translucent, the skin of a child, the soft curved cheek, the slender limbs of a little boy. He wasn't eight years old yet. It didn't matter he was brilliant and dedicated and good. He was a child. He was *young*.

No he isn't, thought Ender. Small, yes. But Bean has been through a battle with a whole army depending on him and on the soldiers that he led, and he performed splendidly, and they won. There's no youth in that. No childhood.

Taking Ender's silence and softening expression as permission to stay, Bean took another step into the room. Only then did Ender see the small slip of paper in his hand.

"You're transferred?" asked Ender. He was incredulous, but his voice came out sounding uninterested, dead.

"To Rabbit Army."

Ender nodded. Of course. It was obvious. If I can't be defeated with my army, they'll take my army away. "Carn

Carby's a good man," said Ender. "I hope he recognizes what you're worth."

"Carn Carby was graduated today. He got his notice while we were fighting our battle."

"Well, who's commanding Rabbit then?"

Bean held his hands out helplessly. "Me."

Ender looked at the ceiling and nodded. "Of course. After all, you're only four years younger than the regular age."

"It isn't funny. I don't know what's going on here. All the changes in the game. And now this. I wasn't the only one transferred, you know. They graduated half the commanders, and transferred a lot of our guys to command their armies."

"Which guys?"

"It looks like—every toon leader and every assistant."

"Of course. If they decide to wreck my army, they'll cut it to the ground. Whatever they're doing, they're thorough."

"You'll still win, Ender. We all know that. Crazy Tom, he said, 'You mean I'm supposed to figure out how to beat Dragon Army?' Everybody knows you're the best. They can't break you down, no matter what they—"

"They already have."

"No, Ender, they can't—"

"I don't care about their game anymore, Bean. I'm not going to play it anymore. No more practices. No more battles. They can put their little slips of paper on the floor all they want, but I won't go. I decided that before I went through the door today. That's why I had you go for the gate. I didn't think it would work, but I didn't care. I just wanted to go out in style."

"You should've seen William Bee's face. He just stood there trying to figure out how he had lost when you only had seven boys who could wiggle their toes and he only had three who couldn't."

"Why should I want to see William Bee's face? Why should I want to beat anybody?" Ender pressed his palms against his eyes. "I hurt Bonzo really bad today, Bean. I really hurt him bad."

"He had it coming."

"I knocked him out standing up. It was like he was dead, standing there. And I kept hurting him."

Bean said nothing.

"I just wanted to make sure he never hurt me again."

"He won't," said Bean. "They sent him home."

"Already?"

"The teachers didn't say much, they never do. The official noticc says he was graduated, but where they put the assignment—you know, tactical school, support, precommand, navigation, that kind of thing—it just said Cartagena, Spain. That's his home."

"I'm glad they graduated him."

"Hell, Ender, we're just glad he's gone. If we'd known what he was doing to you, we would've killed him on the spot. Was it true he had a whole bunch of guys gang up on you?"

"No. It was just him and me. He fought with honor." If it weren't for his honor, he and the others would have beaten me together. They might have killed me, then. His sense of honor saved my life. "I didn't fight with honor," Ender added. "I fought to win."

Bean laughed. "And you did. Kicked him right out of orbit."

A knock on the door. Before Ender could answer, the door opened. Ender had been expecting more of his soldiers. Instead it was Major Anderson. And behind him came Colonel Graff.

"Ender Wiggin," said Graff.

Ender got to his fee. "Yes sir."

"Your display of temper in the battleroom today was insubordinate and is not to be repeated."

"Yes sir," said Ender.

Bean was still feeling insubordinate, and he didn't think Ender deserved the rebuke. "I think it was about time somebody told a teacher how we felt about what you've been doing."

The adults ignored him. Anderson handed Ender a sheet of paper. A fullsized sheet. Not one of the little slips of paper that served for internal orders within the Battle School; it was a full-fledged set of orders. Bean knew what it meant. Ender was being transferred out of the school.

"Graduated?" asked Bean. Ender nodded. "What took them so long? You're only two or three years early. You've already learned how to walk and talk and dress yourself. What will they have left to teach you?"

Ender shook his head. "All I know is, the game's over." He folded up the paper. "None too soon. Can I tell my army?"

"There isn't time," said Graff. "Your shuttle leaves in twenty minutes. Besides, it's better not to talk to them after you get your orders. It makes it easier."

"For them or for you?" Ender asked. He didn't wait for an answer. He turned quickly to Bean, took his hand for a moment, and then headed for the door.

"Wait," said Bean. "Where are you going? Tactical? Navigational? Support?"

"Command School," Ender answered.

"*Pre*-command?"

"Command," said Ender, and then he was out the door. Anderson followed him closely. Bean grabbed Colonel Graff by the sleeve. "Nobody goes to Command School until they're sixteen!"

Graff shook off Bean's hand and left, closing the door behind him.

Bean stood alone in the room, trying to grasp what this might mean. Nobody went to Command School without three years of Pre-command in either Tactical or Support. But then, nobody left Battle School without at least six years, and Ender had had only four.

The system is breaking up. No doubt about it. Either somebody at the top is going crazy, or something's gone wrong with the war, the real war, the bugger war. Why else would they break down the training system like this, wreck the game the way they did? Why else would they put a little kid like me in command of an army?

Bean wondered about it as he walked back down the corridor to his own bed. The lights went out just as he reached his bunk. He undressed in darkness, fumbling to put his clothing in a locker he couldn't see. He felt terrible. At first he thought he felt bad because he was afraid of leading an army, but it wasn't true. He knew he'd make a good commander. He felt himself wanting to cry. He hadn't cried since the first few days of homesickness after he got here. He tried to put a name on the feeling that put a lump in his throat and made him sob silently, however much he tried to hold it down. He bit down on his hand to stop the feeling, to replace it with pain. It didn't help. He would never see Ender again.

Once he named the feeling, he could control it. He lay back and forced himself to go through the relaxing routine until he didn't feel like crying anymore. Then he drifted off to sleep. His hand was near his mouth. It lay on his pillow hesitantly, as if Bean couldn't decide whether to bite his nails or suck on his fingertips. His forehead was creased and furrowed. His breathing was quick and light. He was a soldier, and if anyone had asked him what he wanted to be when he grew up, he wouldn't have known what they meant.

—

When he was crossing into the shuttle, Ender noticed for the first time that the insignia on Major Anderson's uniform had changed. "Yes, he's a colonel now," said Graff. "In fact, Major Anderson has been placed in command of the Battle School, as of this afternoon. I have been reassigned to other duties."

Ender did not ask him what they were.

Graff strapped himself into a seat across the aisle from

him. There was only one other passenger, a quiet man in civilian clothes who was introduced as General Pace. Pace was carrying a briefcase, but Graff carried no more luggage than Ender did. Somehow that was comforting to Ender, that Graff also came away empty.

Ender spoke only once on the voyage home. ''Why are we going home?'' he asked. ''I thought Command School was in the asteroids somewhere.''

''It is,'' said Graff. ''But the Battle School has no facilities for docking long-range ships. So you get a short landside leave.''

Ender wanted to ask if that meant he could see his family. But suddenly, at the thought that it might be possible, he was afraid, and so he didn't ask. Just closed his eyes and tried to sleep. Behind him, General Pace was studying him; for what purpose, Ender could not guess.

It was a hot summer afternoon in Florida when they landed. Ender had been so long without sunlight that the light nearly blinded him. He squinted and sneezed and wanted to get back indoors. Everything was far away and flat; the ground, lacking the upward curve of Battle School floors, seemed instead to fall away, so that on level ground Ender felt as though he were on a pinnacle. The pull of real gravity felt different and he scuffed his feet when he walked. He hated it. He wanted to go back home, back to the Battle School, the only place in the universe where he belonged.

"Arrested?"

"Well, it's a natural thought. General Pace *is* the head of the military police. There *was* a death in the Battle School."

"They didn't tell me whether Colonel Graff was being promoted or court-martialed. Just transferred, with orders to report to the Polemarch."

"Is that a good sign or bad?"

"Who knows? On the one hand, Ender Wiggin not only survived, he passed a threshold, he graduated in dazzlingly good shape, you have to give old Graff credit for that. On the other hand, there's the fourth passenger on the shuttle. The one traveling in a bag."

"Only the second death in the history of the school. At least it wasn't a suicide this time."

"How is murder better, Major Imbu?"

"It wasn't murder, Colonel. We have it on video from two angles. No one can blame Ender."

"But they might blame Graff. After all this is over, the civilians can rake over our files and decide what was right and what was not. Give us medals where they think we were right, take away our pensions and put us in jail where they decide we were wrong. At least they had the good sense not to tell Ender that the boy died."

"It's the second time, too."

"They didn't tell him about Stilson, either."

"The kid is scary."

"Ender Wiggin isn't a killer. He just wins—thoroughly. If anybody's going to be scared, let it be the buggers."

"Makes you almost feel sorry for them, knowing Ender's going to be coming after them."

"The only one I feel sorry for is Ender. But not sorry enough to suggest they ought to let up on him. I just got access to the material that Graff's been getting all this time. About fleet movements, that sort of thing. I used to sleep easy at night."

"Time's getting short?"

"I shouldn't have mentioned it. I can't tell you secured information."

"I know."

"Let's leave it at this: they didn't get him to Command School a day too soon. And maybe a couple of years too late."

13

Valentine

"Children?"

"Brother and sister. They'd layered themselves five times through the nets—writing for companies that paid for their memberships, that sort of thing. Devil of a time tracking them down."

"What are they hiding?"

"Could be anything. The most obvious thing to hide, though, is their ages. The boy is fourteen, the girl is twelve."

"Which one is Demosthenes?"

"The girl. The twelve-year-old."

"Pardon me. I don't really think it's funny, but I can't help but laugh. All this time we've been worried, all the time we've been trying to persuade the Russians not to take Demosthenes too seriously, we held up Locke as proof that Americans weren't all crazy warmongers. Brother and sister, pubescent—"

"And their last name is Wiggin."

"Ah. Coincidence?"

"*The* Wiggin is a third. They are one and two."

"Oh, excellent. The Russians will never believe—"

"That Demosthenes and Locke aren't as much under our control as *the* Wiggin."

"*Is* there a conspiracy? Is someone controlling them?"

"We have been able to detect *no* contact between these two children and any adult who might be directing them."

"That is not to say that someone might not have invented some method you can't detect. It's hard to believe that two children—"

"I interviewed Colonel Graff when he arrived from thc Battle School. It is his best judgment that nothing these children have done is out of their reach. Their abilities are virtually identical with—*the* Wiggin. Only their temperaments are different. What surprised him, however, was the orientation of the two personas. Demosthenes is definitely the girl, but Graff says the girl was rejected for Battle School because she was too pacific, too conciliatory, and above all, too empathic."

"Definitely not Demosthenes."

"And the boy has the soul of a jackal."

"Wasn't it Locke that was recently praised as 'The only truly open mind in America'?"

"It's hard to know what's really happening. But Graff recommended, and I agree, that we should leave them alone. Not expose them. Make no report at this time except that we have determined that Locke and Demosthenes have no foreign connections and have no connections with any domestic group, either, except those publicly declared on the nets."

"In other words, give them a clean bill of health."

"I know Demosthenes seems dangerous, in part because he—or she—has such a wide following. But I think it's significant that the one of the two of them who is most ambitious has chosen the moderate, wise persona. And they're still just talking. They have influence, but no power."

"In my experience, influence *is* power."

"If we ever find them getting out of line, we can easily expose them."

"Only in the next few years. The longer we wait, the older they get, and the less shocking it is to discover who they are."

"You know what the Russian troop movements have been. There's always the chance that Demosthenes is *right*. In which case—"

"We'd better have Demosthenes around. All right. We'll show them clean, for now. But watch them. And I, of course, have to find ways of keeping the Russians calm."

In spite of all her misgivings, Valentine was having fun being Demosthenes. Her column was now being carried on practically every newsnet in the country, and it was fun to watch the money pile up in her attorney's accounts. Every now and then she and Peter would, in Demosthenes' name, donate a carefully calculated sum to a particular candidate or cause: enough money that the donation would be noticed, but not so much that the candidate would feel she was trying to buy a vote. She was getting so many letters now that her newsnet had hired a secretary to answer certain classes of routine correspondence for her. The fun letters, from national and international leaders, sometimes hostile, sometimes friendly, always diplomatically trying to pry into Demosthenes' mind—those she and Peter read together, laughing in delight sometimes that people like *this* were writing to children, and didn't know it.

Sometimes, though, she was ashamed. Father was reading Demosthenes regularly; he never read Locke, or if he did, he said nothing about it. At dinner, though, he would often regale them with some telling point Demosthenes had made in that day's column. Peter loved it when Father did that—"See, it shows that the common man is paying attention"—but it made Valentine feel humiliated for Father. If he ever found out that all this time *I* was writing the columns he told us about, and that I didn't even believe half the things I wrote, he would be angry and ashamed.

At school, she once nearly got them in trouble, when her history teacher assigned the class to write a paper contrasting the views of Demosthenes and Locke as expressed in two of their early columns. Valentine was careless, and did a brilliant job of analysis. As a result, she had to work hard to talk the principal out of having her essay published on the very newsnet that carried Demosthenes' column. Peter was savage about it. "You write too much like Demosthenes, you can't get published, I should kill Demosthenes now, you're getting out of control."

If he raged about that blunder, Peter frightened her still more when he went silent. It happened when Demosthenes was invited to take part in the President's Council on Education for the Future, a blue-ribbon panel that was designed to do nothing, but do it splendidly. Valentine thought Peter would take it as a triumph, but he did not. "Turn it down," he said.

"Why should I?" she asked. "It's no work at all, and they even said that because of Demosthenes' well-known desire for privacy, they would net all the meetings. It makes Demosthenes into a respectable person, and—"

"And you love it that you got that before I did."

"Peter, it isn't you and me, it's Demosthenes and Locke. We made them up. They aren't real. Besides, this appointment doesn't mean they like Demosthenes better than Locke, it just means that Demosthenes has a much stronger base of support. You knew he would. Appointing him pleases a large number of Russian-haters and chauvinists."

"It wasn't supposed to work this way. Locke was supposed to be the respected one."

"He is! Real respect takes longer than official respect. Peter, don't be angry at me because I've done well with the things you told me to do."

But he was angry, for days, and ever since then he had left her to think through all her own columns, instead of telling her what to write. He probably assumed that this would make the quality of Demosthenes' columns deteriorate, but if it did no one noticed. Perhaps it made him even angrier that she never came to him weeping for help. She had been Demosthenes too long now to need anyone to tell her what Demosthenes would think about things.

And as her correspondence with other politically active citizens grew, she began to learn things, information that simply wasn't available to the general public. Certain military people who corresponded with her dropped hints about things without meaning to, and she and Peter put them together to build up a fascinating and frightening picture of Warsaw Pact activity. They were indeed preparing for war, a vicious and bloody earthbound war. Demosthenes wasn't wrong to suspect that the Second Warsaw Pact was not abiding by the terms of the League.

And the character of Demosthenes gradually took on a life of his own. At times she found herself thinking like Demosthenes at the end of a writing session, agreeing with ideas that were supposed to be calculated poses. And sometimes she read Peter's Locke essays and found herself annoyed at his obvious blindness to what was really going on.

Perhaps it's impossible to wear an identity without becoming what you pretend to be. She thought of that, worried about it for a few days, and then wrote a column using that as a premise, to show that politicians who toadied to the Russians in order to keep the peace would inevitably end up subservient to them in everything. It was a lovely bite at the party in power, and she got a lot of good mail about it. She also stopped being frightened of the idea of becoming, to a degree, Demosthenes. He's smarter than Peter and I ever gave him credit for, she thought.

Graff was waiting for her after school. He stood leaning on his car. He was in civilian clothes, and he had gained weight, so she didn't recognize him at first. But he beckoned to her, and before he could introduce himself she remembered his name.

"I won't write another letter," she said. "I never should have written that one."

"You don't like medals, then, I guess."

"Not much."

"Come for a ride with me, Valentine."

"I don't ride with strangers."

He handed her a paper. It was a release form, and her parents had signed it.

"I guess you're not a stranger. Where are we going?"

"To see a young soldier who is in Greensboro on leave."

She got in the car. "Ender's only ten years old," she said. "I thought you told me last time he'd be eligible for a leave when he was sixteen."

"He skipped a few grades."

"So he's doing well?"

"Ask him when you see him."

"Why me? Why not the whole family?"

Graff sighed. "Ender sees the world his own way. We had to persuade him to see you. As for Peter and your parents, he was not interested. Life at the Battle School was—intense."

"What do you mean, he's gone crazy?"

"On the contrary, he's the sanest person I know. He's sane enough to know that his parents are not particularly eager to reopen a book of affection that was closed quite tightly four years ago. As for Peter—we didn't even suggest a meeting, and so he didn't have a chance to tell us to go to hell."

They went out Lake Brandt Road and turned off just past the lake, following a road that wound down and up until they came to a white clapboard mansion that sprawled along the top of a hill. It looked over Lake Brandt on one side and a five-acre private lake on the other. "This is the house that Medly's Mist-E-Rub built," said Graff. "The I.F. picked it up in a tax sale about twenty years ago. Ender insisted that his conversation with you should not be bugged. I promised him it wouldn't be, and to help inspire confidence, the two of you are going out on a raft he built himself. I should warn you, though. I intend to ask you questions about your conversation when it is finished. You don't have to answer, but I hope you will."

"I didn't bring a swimming suit."

"We can provide one."

"One that isn't bugged?"

"At some point, there must be trust. For instance, I know who Demosthenes really is."

She felt a thrill of fear run through her, but said nothing.

"I've known since I landed from the Battle School. There are, perhaps, six of us in the world who know his identity. Not counting the Russians—God only knows what they know. But Demosthenes has nothing to fear from us. Demosthenes can trust our discretion. Just as I trust Demosthenes not to tell Locke what's going on here today. Mutual trust. We tell each other things."

Valentine couldn't decide whether it was Demosthenes they approved of, or Valentine Wiggin. If the former, she would not trust them; if the latter, then perhaps she could. The fact that they did not want her to discuss this with Peter suggested that perhaps they knew the difference between them. She did not stop to wonder whether she herself knew the difference anymore.

"You said he built the raft. How long has he been here?"

"Two months. We meant his leave to last only a few days. But you see, he doesn't seem interested in going on with his education."

"Oh. So I'm therapy again."

"This time we can't censor your letter. We're just taking our chances. We need your brother badly. Humanity is on the cusp."

This time Val had grown up enough to know just how much danger the world was in. And she had been Demosthenes long enough that she didn't hesitate to do her duty. "Where is he?"

"Down at the boat slip."

"Where's the swimming suit?"

Ender didn't wave when she walked down the hill toward him, didn't smile when she stepped onto the floating boat slip. But she knew that he was glad to see her, knew it because of the way his eyes never left her face.

"You're bigger than I remembered." she said stupidly.

"You too," he said. "I also remembered that you were beautiful."

"Memory does play tricks on us."

"No. Your face is the same, but I don't remember what beautiful means anymore. Come on. Let's go out into the lake."

She looked at the small raft with misgivings.

"Don't stand up on it, that's all," he said. He got on by crawling, spiderlike, on toes and fingers. "It's the first thing I built with my own hands since you and I used to build with blocks. Peter-proof buildings."

She laughed. They used to take pleasure in building things that would stand up even when a lot of the obvious supports had been removed. Peter, in turn, liked to remove a block here or there, so the structure would be fragile enough that the next person to touch it would knock it down. Peter was an ass, but he did provide some focus to their childhood.

"Peter's changed," she said.

"Let's not talk about him," said Ender.

"All right."

She crawled onto the boat, not as deftly as Ender. He used a paddle to maneuver them slowly toward the center of the private lake. She noticed aloud that he was sun-browned and strong.

"The strong part comes from Battle School. The sun-browning comes from this lake. I spend a lot of time on the water. When I'm swimming, it's like being weightless. I miss being weightless. Also, when I'm here on the lake, the land slopes up in every direction."

"Like living in a bowl."

"I've lived in a bowl for four years."

"So we're strangers now?"

"Aren't we, Valentine?"

"No," she said. She reached out and touched his leg. Then, suddenly, she squeezed his knee, right where he had always been most ticklish.

But almost at the same moment, he caught her wrist in his hand. His grip was very strong, even though his hands were smaller than hers and his own arms were slender and tight. For a moment he looked dangerous; then he relaxed. "Oh, yes," he said. "You used to tickle me."

"Not any more," she said, taking back her hand.

"Want to swim?"

In answer, she dropped herself over the side of the raft. The water was clear and clean, and there was no chlorine in it. She swam for a while, then returned to the raft and lay on it in the hazy sunlight. A wasp circled her, then landed on the raft beside her head. She knew it was there, and ordinarily would have been afraid of it. But not today. Let it walk on this raft, let it bake in the sun as I'm doing.

Then the raft rocked, and she turned to see Ender calmly crushing the life out of the wasp with one finger. "These are a nasty breed," Ender said. "They sting you without waiting to be insulted first." He smiled. "I've been learning about preemptive strategies. I'm very good. No one ever beat me. I'm the best soldier they ever had."

"Who would expect less?" she said. "You're a Wiggin."

"Whatever that means," he said.

"It means that you are going to make a difference in the world." And she told him what she and Peter were doing.

"How old is Peter, fourteen? Already planning to take over the world?"

"He thinks he's Alexander the Great. And why shouldn't he be? Why shouldn't *you* be, too?"

"We can't *both* be Alexander."

"Two faces of the same coin. And I am the metal in between." Even as she said it, she wondered if it was true. She had shared so much with Peter these last few years that even when she thought she despised him, she understood him. While Ender had been only a memory till now. A very small, fragile boy who needed her protection. Not this cold-eyed, dark-skinned manling who kills wasps with his fingers. Maybe he and Peter and I are all the same, and have been all along. Maybe we only thought we were different from each other out of jealousy.

"The trouble with coins is, when one face is up, the other face is down."

And right now you think you're down. "They want me to encourage you to go on with your studies."

"They aren't studies, they're games. All games, from beginning to end, only they change the rules whenever they feel like it." He held up a limp hand. "See the strings?"

"But you can use them, too."

"Only if they want to be used. Only if they think they're using you. No, it's too hard, I don't want to play anymore. Just when I start to be happy, just when I think I can handle things, they stick in another knife. I keep having nightmares, now that I'm here. I dream I'm in the battleroom, only instead of being weightless, they're playing games with gravity. They keep changing its direction. So I never end up on the wall I launched for. I never end up where I meant to go. And I keep pleading with them just to let me get to the door, and they won't let me out, they keep sucking me back in."

She heard the anger in his voice and assumed it was directed at her. "I suppose that's what I'm here for. To suck you back in."

"I didn't want to see you."

"They told me."

"I was afraid that I'd still love you."

"I hoped that you would."

"My fear, your wish—both granted."

"Ender, it really is true. We may be young, but we're not powerless. We play by their rules long enough, and it becomes our game." She giggled. "I'm on a presidential commission. Peter is so angry."

"They don't let me use the nets. There isn't a computer in the place, except the household machines that run the security system and the lighting. Ancient things. Installed back a century ago, when they made computers that didn't hook up with anything. They took away my army, they took away my desk, and you know something? I don't really mind."

"You must be good company for yourself."

"Not me. My memories."

"Maybe that's who you are, what you remember."

"No. My memories of strangers. My memories of the buggers."

Valentine shivered, as if a cold breeze had suddenly passed. "I refuse to watch the bugger vids anymore. They're always the same."

"I used to study them for hours. The way their ships move through space. And something funny, that only occurred to me lying out here on the lake. I realized that all the battles in which buggers and humans fought hand to hand, all those are from the First Invasion. All the scenes from the Second Invasion, when our soldiers are in I.F. uniforms, in those scenes the buggers are always already dead. Lying there, slumped over their controls. Not a sign of struggle or anything. And Mazer Rackham's battle—they never show us any footage from that battle."

"Maybe it's a secret weapon."

"No, no, I don't care about how we killed them. It's the buggers themselves. I don't know anything about them, and yet someday I'm supposed to fight them. I've been through a lot of fights in my life, sometimes games, sometimes—not games. Every time, I've won because I could understand the way my enemy thought. From what they *did*. I could tell what they thought I was doing, how they wanted the battle to take shape. And I played off of that. I'm very good at that. Understanding how other people think."

"The curse of the Wiggin children." She joked, but it frightened her, that Ender might understand her as completely as he did his enemies. Peter always understood her, or at least thought he did, but he was such a moral sinkhole that she never had to feel embarrassed when he guessed even her worst thoughts. But Ender—she did not want him to understand her. It would make her naked before him. She would be ashamed. "You don't think you can beat the buggers unless you know them."

"It goes deeper than that. Being here alone with nothing to do, I've been thinking about myself, too. Trying to understand why I hate myself so badly."

"No, Ender."

"Don't tell me 'No, Ender.' It took me a long time to realize that I did, but believe me, I did. Do. And it came down to this: In the moment when I truly understand my enemy, understand him well enough to defeat him, then in that very moment I also love him. I think it's impossible to really understand somebody, what they want, what they believe, and not love them the way they love themselves. And then, in that very moment when I *love* them—"

"You beat them." For a moment she was not afraid of his understanding.

"No, you don't understand. I *destroy* them. I make it impossible for them to ever hurt me again. I grind them and grind them until they don't *exist*."

"Of course you don't." And now the fear came again, worse than before. Peter has mellowed, but you, they've made you into a killer. Two sides of the same coin, but which side is which?

"I've really hurt some people, Val. I'm not making this up."

"I know, Ender." How will you hurt me?

"See what I'm becoming, Val?" he said softly. "Even you are afraid of me." And he touched her cheek so gently that she wanted to cry. Like the touch of his soft baby hand when he was still an infant. She remembered that, the touch of his soft and innocent hand on her cheek.

"I'm not," she said, and in that moment it was true.

"You should be."

No. I shouldn't. "You're going to shrivel up if you stay in the water. Also, the sharks might get you."

He smiled. "The sharks learned to leave me alone a long time ago." But he pulled himself onto the raft, bringing a wash of water across it as it tipped. It was cold on Valentine's back.

"Ender, Peter's going to do it. He's smart enough to take the time it takes, but he's going to win his way into power—if not right now, then later. I'm not sure yet whether that'll be a good thing or a bad thing. Peter can be cruel, but he knows the getting and keeping of power, and there are signs that once the bugger war is over, and maybe even before it ends, the world will collapse into chaos again. The Russian Empire was on its way to hegemony before the First Invasion. If they try for it afterward—"

"So even Peter might be a better alternative."

"You've been discovering some of the destroyer in yourself, Ender. Well, so have I. Peter didn't have a monopoly on that, whatever the testers thought. And Peter has some of the builder in him. He isn't kind, but he doesn't break every good thing he sees anymore. Once you realize that power will always end up with the sort of people who crave it, I think that there are worse people who could have it than Peter."

"With that strong a recommendation, I could vote for him myself."

"Sometimes it seems absolutely silly. A fourteen-year-old boy and his kid sister plotting to take over the world." She tried to laugh. It wasn't funny. "We aren't just ordinary children, are we. None of us."

"Don't you sometimes wish we were?"

She tried to imagine herself being like the other girls at school. Tried to imagine life if she didn't feel responsible for the future of the world. "It would be so dull."

"I don't think so." And he stretched out on the raft, as if he could lie on the water forever.

It was true. Whatever they did to Ender in the Battle School, they had spent his ambition. He really did not want to leave the sun-warmed waters of this bowl.

No, she realized. No, he *believes* that he doesn't want to leave here, but there is still too much of Peter in him. Or too much of me. None of us could be happy for long, doing nothing. Or perhaps it's just that none of us could be happy living with no other company than ourself.

So she began to prod again. "What is the one name that everyone in the world knows?"

"Mazer Rackham."

"And what if you win the next war, the way Mazer did?"

"Mazer Rackham was a fluke. A reserve. Nobody believed in him. He just happened to be in the right place at the right time."

"But suppose you do it. Suppose you beat the buggers and your name is known the way Mazer Rackham's name is known."

"Let somebody else be famous. Peter wants to be famous. Let him save the world."

"I'm not talking about fame, Ender. I'm not talking about power, either. I'm talking about accidents, just like the accident that Mazer Rackham happened to be the one who was there when somebody had to stop the buggers."

"If I'm here," said Ender, "then I won't be there. Somebody else will. Let them have the accident."

His tone of weary unconcern infuriated her. "I'm talking about *my* life, you self-centered little bastard." If her words bothered him, he didn't show it. Just lay there, eyes closed. "When you were little and Peter tortured you, it's a good thing I didn't lie back and wait for Mom and Dad to save you. They never understood how dangerous Peter was. I knew you had the monitor, but I didn't wait for *them*, either. Do you know what Peter used to do to me because I stopped him from hurting you?"

"Shut up," Ender whispered.

Because she saw that his chest was trembling, because she knew that she had indeed hurt him, because she knew that just like Peter, she had found his weakest place and stabbed him there, she fell silent.

"I can't beat them," Ender said softly. "I'll be out there like Mazer Rackham one day, and everybody will be depending on me, and I won't be able to do it."

"If you can't, Ender, then nobody could. If you can't beat them, then they deserve to win because they're stronger and better than us. It won't be your fault."

"Tell it to the dead."

"If not you, then who?"

"Anybody."

"Nobody, Ender. I'll tell you something. If you try and lose then it isn't your fault. But if you don't try and we lose, then it's all your fault. You killed us all."

"I'm a killer no matter what."

"What else should you be? Human beings didn't evolve brains in order to lie around on lakes. Killing's the first thing we learned. And a good thing we did, or we'd be dead, and the tigers would own the earth."

"I could never beat Peter. No matter what I said or did. I never could."

So it came back to Peter. "He was years older than you. And stronger."

"So are the buggers."

She could see his reasoning. Or rather, his unreasoning. He could win all he wanted, but he knew in his heart that there was always someone who could destroy him. He always knew that he had not really won, because there was Peter, undefeated champion.

"You want to beat Peter?" she asked.

"No," he answered.

"Beat the buggers. Then come home and see who notices Peter Wiggin anymore. Look him in the eye when all the world loves and reveres you. That'll be defeat in his eyes, Ender. That's how you win."

"You don't understand," he said.

"Yes I do."

"No you don't. I don't want to beat Peter."

"Then what do you want?"

"I want him to love me."

She had no answer. As far as she knew, Peter didn't love anybody.

Ender said nothing more. Just lay there. And lay there.

Finally Valentine, the sweat dripping off her, the mosquitos beginning to hover as the dusk came on, took one final dip in the water and then began to push the raft in to shore. Ender showed no sign that he knew what she was doing, but his irregular breathing told her that he was not asleep. When they got to the shore, she climbed onto the dock and said, "*I* love you, Ender. More than ever. No matter what you decide."

He didn't answer. She doubted that he believed her. She walked back up the hill, savagely angry at them for making her come to Ender like this. For she had, after all, done just what they wanted. She had talked Ender into going back into his training, and he wouldn't soon forgive her for that.

Ender came in the door, still wet from his last dip in the lake. It was dark outside, and dark in the room where Graff waited for him.

"Are we going now?" asked Ender.

"If you want to," Graff said.

"When?"

"When you're ready."

Ender showered and dressed. He was finally used to the way civilian clothes fit together, but he still didn't feel right without a uniform or a flash suit. I'll never wear a flash suit again, he thought. That was the Battle School game, and I'm through with that. He heard the crickets chirping madly in the woods; in the near distance he heard the crackling sound of a car driving slowly on gravel.

What else should he take with him? He had read several of the books in the library, but they belonged to the house and he couldn't take them. The only thing he owned was the raft he had made with his own hands. That would stay here, too.

The lights were on now in the room where Graff waited. He, too, had changed clothing. He was back in uniform.

They sat in the back seat of the car together, driving along country roads to come at the airport from the back. "Back when the population was growing," said Graff, "they kept this area in woods and farms. Watershed land. The rainfall here starts a lot of rivers flowing, a lot of underground water moving around. The Earth is deep, and right to the heart it's alive, Ender. We people only live on the top, like the bugs that live on the scum of the still water near the shore."

Ender said nothing.

"We train our commanders the way we do because that's what it takes—they have to think in certain ways, they can't be distracted by a lot of things, so we isolate them. You. Keep you separate. And it works. But it's so easy, when you never meet people, when you never know the Earth itself, when you live with metal walls keeping out the cold of space, it's easy to forget why Earth is worth saving. Why the world of people might be worth the price you pay."

So that's why you brought me here, thought Ender. With all your hurry, that's why you took three months, to make me love Earth. Well, it worked. All your tricks worked.

Valentine, too; she was another one of your tricks, to make me remember that I'm not going to school for myself. Well, I remember.

"I may have used Valentine," said Graff, "and you may hate me for it, Ender, but keep this in mind—it only works because what's between you, that's real, that's what matters. Billions of those connections between human beings. That's what you're fighting to keep alive."

Ender turned his face to the window and watched the helicopters and dirigibles rise and fall.

They took a helicopter to the I.F. spaceport at Stumpy Point. It was officially named for a dead Hegemon, but everybody called it Stumpy Point, after the pitiful little town that had been paved over when they made the approaches to the vast islands of steel and concrete that dotted Pamlico Sound. There were still waterbirds taking their fastidious little steps in the saltwater, where mossy trees dipped down as if to drink. It began to rain lightly, and the concrete was black and slick; it was hard to tell where it left off and the Sound began.

Graff led him through a maze of clearances. Authority was a little plastic ball that Graff carried. He dropped it into chutes, and doors opened and people stood up and saluted and the chutes spat out the ball and Graff went on. Ender noticed that at first everyone watched Graff, but as they penetrated deeper into the spaceport, people began watching Ender. At first it was the man of real authority they noticed, but later, where everyone had authority, it was his cargo they cared to see.

Only when Graff strapped himself into the shuttle seat beside him did Ender realize Graff was going to launch with him.

"How far?" asked Ender. "How far are you going with me?"

Graff smiled thinly. "All the way, Ender."

"Are they making you administrator of Command School?"

"No."

So they had removed Graff from his post at Battle School solely to accompany Ender to his next assignment. How important am I, he wondered. And like a whisper of Peter's voice inside his mind, he heard the question, How can I use this?

He shuddered and tried to think of something else. Peter could have fantasies about ruling the world, but Ender didn't have them. Still, thinking back on his life in Battle School, it occurred to him that although he had never sought power, he had always had it. But he decided that it was a power born of excellence, not manipulation. He had no reason to be ashamed of it. He had never, except perhaps with Bean, used his power to hurt someone. And with Bean, things had worked well after all. Bean had become a friend, finally, to take the place of the lost Alai, who in turn took the place of Valentine. Valentine, who was helping Peter in his plotting. Valentine, who still loved Ender no matter what happened. And following that train of thought led him back to Earth, back to the quiet hours in the center of the clear water ringed by a bowl of tree-covered hills. That is the Earth, he thought. Not a globe thousands of kilometers around, but a forest with a shining lake, a house hidden at the crest of the hill, high in the trees, a grassy slope leading upward from the water, fish leaping and birds strafing to take the bugs that lived at the border between water and sky. Earth was the constant noise of crickets and winds and birds. And the voice of one girl, who spoke to him out of his far-off childhood. The same voice that had once protected him from terror. The same voice that he would do anything to keep alive, even return to school, even leave Earth behind again for another four or forty or four thousand years. Even if she loved Peter more.

His eyes were closed, and he had not made any sound but breathing; still, Graff reached out and touched his hand across the aisle. Ender stiffened in surprise, and Graff soon withdrew, but for a moment Ender was struck with the startling thought that perhaps Graff felt some affection for him. But no, it was just another calculated gesture. Graff was creating a commander out of a little boy. No doubt Unit 17 in the course of studies included an affectionate gesture from the teacher.

The shuttle reached the IPL satellite in only a few hours. Inter-Planetary Launch was a city of three thousand inhabitants, breathing oxygen from the plants that also fed them, drinking water that had already passed through their bodies ten thousand times, living only to service the tugs that did all the oxwork in the solar system and the shuttles that took their cargoes and passengers back to the Earth or the Moon. It was a world where, briefly, Ender felt at home, since its floors sloped upward as they did in the Battle School.

Their tug was fairly new; the I.F. was constantly casting off its old vehicles and purchasing the latest models. It had just brought a vast load of drawn steel processed by a factory ship that was taking apart minor planets in the asteroid belt. The steel would be dropped to the Moon, and now the tug was linked to fourteen barges. Graff dropped his ball into the reader again, however, and the barges were uncoupled from the tug. It would be making a fast run this time, to a destination of Graff's specification, not to be stated until the tug had cut loose from IPL.

"It's no great secret," said the tug's captain. "Whenever the destination is unknown, it's for ISL." By analogy with IPL, Ender decided the letters meant Inter-Stellar Launch.

"This time it isn't," said Graff.

"Where then?"

"I.F. Command."

"I don't have security clearance even to know where that is, sir."

"Your ship knows," said Graff. "Just let the computer have a look at this, and follow the course it plots." He handed the captain the plastic ball.

"And I'm supposed to close my eyes during the whole voyage, so I don't figure out where we are?"

"Oh, no, of course not. I.F. Command is on the minor planet Eros, which should be about three months away from here at the highest possible speed. Which is the speed you'll use, of course."

"Eros? But I thought that the buggers burned that to a radioactive—ah. When did I receive security clearance to know this?"

"You didn't. So when we arrive at Eros, you will undoubtedly be assigned to permanent duty there."

The captain understood immediately, and didn't like it. "I'm a pilot, you son of a bitch, and you got no right to lock me up on a rock!"

"I will overlook your derisive language to a superior officer. I do apologize, but my orders were to take the fastest available military tug. At the moment I arrived, that was you. It isn't as though anyone were out to get you. Cheer up. The war may be over in another fifteen years, and then the location of I.F. Command won't have to be a secret anymore. By the way, you should be aware, in case you're one of those who relies on visuals for docking, that Eros has been blacked out. Its albedo is only slightly brighter than a black hole. You won't see it."

"Thanks," said the captain.

It was nearly a month into the voyage before he managed to speak civilly to Colonel Graff.

The shipboard computer had a limited library—it was geared primarily to entertainment rather than education. So during the voyage, after breakfast and morning exercises, Ender and Graff would usually talk. About Command School. About Earth. About astronomy and physics and whatever Ender wanted to know.

And above all, he wanted to know about the buggers.

"We don't *know* much," said Graff. "We've never had a live one in custody. Even when we caught one unarmed and alive, he died the moment it became obvious he was captured. Even the *he* is uncertain—the most likely thing, in fact, is that most bugger soldiers are females, but with atrophied or vestigial sexual organs. We can't tell. It's their psychology that would be most useful to you, and we haven't exactly had a chance to interview them."

"Tell me what you know, and maybe I'll learn something that I need."

So Graff told him. The buggers were organisms that could conceivably have evolved on Earth, if things had gone a different way a billion years ago. At the molecular level, there were no surprises. Even the genetic material was the same. It was no accident that they looked insectlike to human beings. Though their internal organs were now much more complex and specialized than any insects, and they had evolved an internal skeleton and shed most of the exoskeleton, their physical structure still echoed their ancestors, who could easily have been very much like Earth's ants. "But don't be fooled by that," said Graff. "It's just as meaningful to say that our ancestors could easily have been very much like squirrels."

"If that's all we have to go on, that's *something*," said Ender.

"Squirrels never built starships," said Graff. "There are usually a few changes on the way from gathering nuts and seeds to harvesting asteroids and putting permanent research stations on the moons of Saturn."

The buggers could probably see about the same spectrum of light as human beings, and there was artificial lighting in their ships and ground installations. However, their antennae seemed almost vestigial. There was no evidence from their bodies that smelling, tasting, or hearing were particularly important to them. "Of course, we can't be sure. But we can't see any way that they could have used sound for communication. The oddest thing of all was that they also don't have any communication devices on their ships. No radios, nothing that could transmit or receive any kind of signal."

"They communicate ship to ship. I've seen the videos, they talk to each other."

"True. But body to body, mind to mind. It's the most important thing we learned from them. Their communication, however they do it, is instantaneous. Lightspeed is no barrier. When Mazer Rackham defeated their invasion fleet, they all closed up shop. At once. There was no time for a signal. Everything just stopped."

Ender remembered the videos of uninjured buggers lying dead at their posts.

"We knew then that it was possible. To communicate faster than light. That was seventy years ago, and once we knew what could be done, we did it. Not *me*, mind you, I wasn't born then."

"How is it possible?"

"I can't explain philotic physics to you. Half of it nobody understands anyway. What matters is we built the ansible. The official name is Philotic Parallax Instantaneous Communicator, but somebody dredged the name *ansible* out of an old book somewhere and it caught on. Not that most people even know the machine exists."

"That means that ships could talk to each other even when they're across the solar system," said Ender.

"It means," said Graff, "that ships could talk to each other even when they're across the galaxy. And the buggers can do it without machines."

"So they knew about their defeat the moment it happened," said Ender. "I always figured—everybody always said that they probably only found out they lost the battle twenty-five years ago."

"It keeps people from panicking," said Graff. "I'm telling you things that you can't know, by the way, if you're ever going to leave I.F. Command. Before the war's over."

Ender was angry. "If you know me at all, you know I can keep a secret."

"It's a regulation. People under twenty-five are assumed to be a security risk. It's very unjust to a good many responsible children, but it helps narrow the number of people who might let something slip."

"What's all the secrecy for, anyway?"

"Because we've taken some terrible risks, Ender, and we don't want to have every net on earth second-guessing those decisions. You see, as soon as we had a working ansible, we tucked it into our best starships and launched them to attack the buggers home systems."

"Do we know where they are?"

"Yes."

"So we're not waiting for the Third Invasion."

"We *are* the Third Invasion."

"We're attacking them. Nobody says that. Everybody thinks we have a huge fleet of warships waiting in the comet shield—"

"Not one. We're quite defenseless here."

"What if they've sent a fleet to attack us?"

"Then we're dead. But our ships haven't seen such a fleet, not a sign of one."

"Maybe they gave up and they're planning to leave us alone."

"Maybe. You've seen the videos. Would you bet the human race on the chance of them giving up and leaving us alone?"

Ender tried to grasp the amounts of time that had gone by. "And the ships have been traveling for seventy years—"

"Some of them. And some for thirty years, and some for twenty. We make better ships now. We're learning how to play with space a little better. But every starship that is not still under construction is on its way to a bugger world or outpost. Every starship, with cruisers and fighters tucked into its belly, is out there approaching the buggers. Decelerating. Because they're almost there. The first ships we sent to the most distant objectives, the more recent ships to the closer ones. Our timing was pretty good. They'll all be arriving in combat range within a few months of each other. Unfortunately, our most primitive, outdated equipment will be attacking their homeworld. Still, they're armed well enough—we have some weapons the buggers never saw before."

"When will they arrive?"

"Within the next five years, Ender. Everything is ready at I.F. Command. The master ansible is there, in contact with all our invasion fleet; the ships are all working, ready to fight. All we lack, Ender, is the battle commander. Someone who knows what the hell to do with those ships when they get there."

"And what if no one knows what to do with them?"

"We'll just do our best, with the best commander we can get."

Me, thought Ender. They want me to be ready in five years. "Colonel Graff, there isn't a chance I'll be ready to command a fleet in time."

Graff shrugged. "So. Do your best. If you aren't ready, we'll make do with what we've got."

That eased Ender's mind.

But only for a moment. "Of course, Ender, what we've got right now is nobody."

Ender knew that this was another of Graff's games. Make me believe that it all depends on me, so I can't slack off, so I push myself as hard as possible.

Game or not, though, it might also be true. And so he would work as hard as possible. It was what Val had wanted of him. Five years. Only five years until the fleet arrives, and I don't know anything yet. "I'll only be fifteen in five years," Ender said.

"Going on sixteen," said Graff. "It all depends on what you know."

"Colonel Graff," he said. "I just want to go back and swim in the lake."

"After we win the war," said Graff. "Or lose it. We'll have a few decades before they get back here to finish us off. The house will be there, and I promise you can swim to your heart's content."

"But I'll still be too young for security clearance."

"We'll keep you under armed guard at all times. The military knows how to handle these things."

They both laughed, and Ender had to remind himself that Graff was only acting like a friend, that everything he did was a lie or a cheat calculated to turn Ender into an efficient fighting machine. I'll become exactly the tool you want me to be, said Ender silently, but at least I won't be *fooled* into it. I'll do it because I choose to, not because you tricked me, you sly bastard.

The tug reached Eros before they could see it. The captain showed them the visual scan, then superimposed the heat scan on the same screen. They were practically on top of it—only four thousand kilometers out—but Eros, only twenty-four kilometers long, was invisible if it didn't shine with reflected sunlight.

The captain docked the ship on one of the three landing platforms that circled Eros. It could not land directly because Eros had enhanced gravity, and the tug, designed for towing cargoes, could never escape the gravity well. He bade them an irritable good-bye, but Ender and Graff remained cheerful. The captain was bitter at having to leave his tug; Ender and Graff felt like prisoners finally paroled from jail. When they boarded the shuttle that would take them to the surface of Eros, they repeated perverse misquotations of lines from the videos that the captain had endlessly watched, and laughed like madmen. The captain grew surly and withdrew by pretending to go to sleep. Then, almost as an afterthought, Ender asked Graff one last question.

"Why are we fighting the buggers?"

"I've heard all kinds of reasons," said Graff. "Because they have an overcrowded system and they've got to colonize. Because they can't stand the thought of other intelligent life in the universe. Because they don't think we *are* intelligent life. Because they have some weird religion. Because they watched our old video broadcasts and decided we were hopelessly violent. All kinds of reasons."

"What do you believe?"

"It doesn't matter what I believe."

"I want to know anyway."

"They must talk to each other directly, Ender, mind to mind. What one thinks, another can also think; what one remembers, another can also remember. Why would they ever develop language? Why would they ever learn to read and write? How would they know what reading and writing were if they saw them? Or signals? Or numbers? Or anything that we use to communicate? This isn't just a matter of translating from one language to another. They don't have a language at all. We used every means we could think of to communicate with them, but they don't even have the machinery to know we're signaling. And maybe they've been trying to think to us, and they can't understand why we don't respond."

"So the whole war is because we can't talk to each other."

"If the other fellow can't tell you his story, you can never be sure he isn't trying to kill you."

"What if we just left them alone?"

"Ender, we didn't go to them first, they came to us. If they were going to leave us alone, they could have done it a hundred years ago, before the First Invasion."

"Maybe they didn't know we were intelligent life. Maybe—"

"Ender, believe me, there's a century of discussion on this very subject. Nobody knows the answer. When it comes down to it, though, the real decision is inevitable: If one of us has to be destroyed, let's make damn sure we're the ones alive at the end. Our genes won't let us decide any other way. Nature can't evolve a species that hasn't a will to survive. Individuals might be bred to sacrifice themselves, but the race as a whole can never decide to cease to exist. So if we can we'll kill every last one of the buggers, and if they can they'll kill every last one of us."

"As for me," said Ender, "I'm in favor of surviving."

"I know," said Graff. "That's why you're here."

14

Ender's Teacher

"Took your time, didn't you, Graff? The voyage isn't short, but the three-month vacation seems excessive."

"I prefer not to deliver damaged merchandise."

"Some men simply have no sense of hurry. Oh well, it's only the fate of the world. . . . Never mind me. You must understand our anxiety. We're here with the ansible, receiving constant reports of the progress of our starships. We have to face the coming war every day. If you can call them days. He's such a very *little* boy."

"There's greatness in him. A magnitude of spirit."

"A killer instinct, too, I hope."

"Yes."

"We've planned out an impromptu course of study for him. All subject to your approval, of course."

"I'll look at it. I don't pretend to know the subject matter, Admiral Chamrajnagar. I'm only here because I know Ender. So don't be afraid that I'll try to second-guess the order of your presentation. Only the pace."

"How much can we tell him?"

"Don't waste his time on the physics of interstellar travel."

"What about the ansible?"

"I already told him about that, and the fleets. I said they would arrive at their destination within five years."

"It seems there's very little left for us to tell him."

"You can tell him about the weapons systems. He has to know enough to make intelligent decisions."

"Ah. We can be useful after all, how very kind. We've devoted one of the five simulators to his exclusive use."

"What about the others?"

"The other simulators?"

"The other children."

"You were brought here to take care of Ender Wiggin."

"Just curious. Remember, they were all my students at one time or another."

"And now they are all mine. They are entering into the mysteries of the fleet, Colonel Graff, to which you, as a soldier, have never been introduced."

"You make it sound like a priesthood."

"And a god. And a religion. Even those of us who command by ansible know the majesty of flight among the stars. I can see you find my mysticism distasteful. I assure you that your distaste only reveals your ignorance. Soon enough Ender Wiggin will also know what I know; he will dance the graceful ghost dance through the stars, and whatever greatness there is within him will be unlocked, revealed, set forth before the universe for all to see. You have the soul of a stone, Colonel Graff, but I sing to a stone as easily as to another singer. You may go to your quarters and establish yourself."

"I have nothing to establish except the clothing I'm wearing."

"You own nothing?"

"They keep my salary in an account somewhere on Earth. I've never needed it. Except to buy civilian clothes on my—vacation."

"A non-materialist. And yet you are unpleasantly fat. A gluttonous ascetic? Such a contradiction."

"When I'm tense, I eat. Whereas when you're tense, you spout solid waste."

"I like you, Colonel Graff. I think we shall get along."

"I don't much care, Admiral Chamrajnagar. I came here for Ender. And neither of us came here for you."

Ender hated Eros from the moment he shuttled down from the tug. He had been uncomfortable enough on Earth, where floors were flat; Eros was hopeless. It was a roughly spindle-shaped rock only six and a half kilometers thick at its narrowest point. Since the surface of the planetoid was entirely devoted to absorbing sunlight and converting it to energy, everyone lived in the smooth-walled rooms linked by tunnels that laced the interior of the asteroid. The closed-in space was no problem for Ender—what bothered him was that all the tunnel floors noticeably sloped downward. From the start, Ender was plagued by vertigo as he walked through the tunnels, especially the ones that girdled Eros's narrow circumference. It did not help that gravity was only half of Earth-normal—the illusion of being on the verge of falling was almost complete.

There was also something disturbing about the proportions of the rooms—the ceilings were too low for the width, the tunnels too narrow. It was not a comfortable place.

Worst of all, though, was the number of people. Ender had no important memories of the scale of the cities of Earth. His idea of a comfortable number of people was the Battle School, where he had known by sight every person who dwelt there. Here, though, ten thousand people lived within the rock. There was no crowding, despite the amount of space devoted to life support and other machinery. What bothered Ender was that he was constantly surrounded by strangers.

They never let him come to know anyone. He saw the

other Command School students often, but since he never attended any class regularly, they remained only faces. He would attend a lecture here or there, but usually he was tutored by one teacher after another, or occasionally helped to learn a process by another student, whom he met once and never saw again. He ate alone or with Colonel Graff. His recreation was in a gym, but he rarely saw the same people in it twice.

He recognized that they were isolating him again, this time not by setting the other students to hating him, but rather by giving them no opportunity to become friends. He could hardly have been close to most of them anyway—except for Ender, the other students were all well into adolescence.

So Ender withdrew into his studies and learned quickly and well. Astrogation and military history he absorbed like water; abstract mathematics was more difficult, but whenever he was given a problem that involved patterns in space and time, he found that his intuition was more reliable than his calculation—he often saw at once a solution that he could only prove after minutes or hours of manipulating numbers.

And for pleasure, there was the simulator, the most perfect videogame he had ever played. Teachers and students trained him, step by step, in its use. At first, not knowing the awesome power of the game, he had played only at the tactical level, controlling a single fighter in continuous maneuvers to find and destroy an enemy. The computer-controlled enemy was devious and powerful, and whenever Ender tried a tactic he found the computer using it against him within minutes.

The game was a holographic display, and his fighter was represented only by a tiny light. The enemy was another light of a different color, and they danced and spun and maneuvered through a cube of space that must have been ten meters to a side. The controls were powerful. He could rotate the display in any direction, so he could watch from any angle, and he could move the center so that the duel took place nearer or farther from him.

Gradually, as he became more adept at controlling the fighter's speed, direction of movement, orientation, and weapons, the game was made more complex. He might have two enemy ships at once; there might be obstacles, the debris of space; he began to have to worry about fuel and limited weapons; the computer began to assign him particular things to destroy or accomplish, so that he had to avoid distractions and achieve an objective in order to win.

When he had mastered the one-fighter game, they allowed him to step back into the four-fighter squadron. He spoke commands to simulated pilots of four fighters, and instead of merely carrying out the computer's instructions, he was allowed to determine tactics himself, deciding which of several objectives was the most valuable and directing his squadron accordingly. At any time he could take personal command of one of the fighters for a short time, and at first he did this often; when he did, however, the other three fighters in his squadron were soon destroyed, and as the games became harder and harder he had to spend more and more of his time commanding the squadron. When he did, he won more and more often.

By the time he had been at Command School for a year, he was adept at running the simulator at any of fifteen levels, from controlling an individual fighter to commanding a fleet. He had long since realized that as the battleroom was to Battle School, so the simulator was to Command School. The classes were valuable, but the real education was the game. People dropped in from time to time to watch him play. They never spoke—hardly anyone ever did, unless they had something specific to teach him. The watchers would stay, silently watching him run through a difficult simulation, and then leave just as he finished. What are you doing, he wanted to ask. Judging me? Determining whether you want to trust the fleet to me? Just remember that I didn't ask for it.

He found that a great deal of what he had learned at Battle School transferred to the simulator. He would routinely reorient the simulator every few minutes, rotating it so that he didn't get trapped into an up-down orientation, constantly reviewing his position from the enemy point of view. It was exhilarating at last to have such control over the battle, to be able to see every point of it.

It was also frustrating to have so little control, too, for the computer-controlled fighters were only as good as the computer allowed. They took no initiative. They had no intelligence. He began to wish for his toon leaders, so that he could count on some of the squadrons doing well without having his constant supervision.

At the end of his first year he was winning every battle on the simulator, and played the game as if the machine were a natural part of his body. One day, eating a meal with Graff, he asked, "Is that all the simulator does?"

"Is what all?"

"The way it plays now. It's easy, and it hasn't got any harder for a while."

"Oh."

Graff seemed unconcerned. But then, Graff always seemed unconcerned. The next day everything changed. Graff went away, and in his place they gave Ender a companion.

He was in the room when Ender awoke in the morning. He was an old man, sitting cross-legged on the floor. Ender looked at him expectantly, waiting for the man to speak. He said nothing. Ender got up and showered and dressed, content to let the man keep his silence if he wanted. He had long since learned that when something unusual was going on, something that was part of someone else's plan and not his own, he would find out more information by waiting than by asking. Adults almost always lost their patience before Ender did.

The man still hadn't spoken when Ender was ready and went to the door to leave the room. The door didn't open. Ender turned to face the man sitting on the floor. He looked to be about sixty, by far the oldest man Ender had seen on Eros. He had a day's growth of white whiskers that grizzled his face only slightly less than his close-cut hair. His face sagged a little and his eyes were surrounded by creases and lines. He looked at Ender with an expression that bespoke only apathy.

Ender turned back to the door and tried again to open it.

"All right," he said, giving up. "Why's the door locked?"

The old man continued to look at him blankly.

So this is a game, thought Ender. Well, if they want me to go to class, they'll unlock the door. If they don't, they won't. I don't care.

Ender didn't like games where the rules could be anything and the objective was known to them alone. So he wouldn't play. He also refused to get angry. He went through a relaxing exercise as he leaned on the door, and soon he was calm again. The old man continued to watch him impassively.

It seemed to go on for hours, Ender refusing to speak, the old man seeming to be a mindless mute. Sometimes Ender wondered if he were mentally ill, escaped from some medical ward somewhere in Eros, living out some insane fantasy here in Ender's room. But the longer it went on, with no one coming to the door, no one looking for him, the more certain he became that this was something deliberate, meant to disconcert him. Ender did not want to give the old man the victory. To pass the time he began to do exercises. Some were impossible without the gym equipment, but others, especially from his personal defense class, he could do without any aids.

The exercises moved him around the room. He was practicing lunges and kicks. One move took him near the old man, as he had come near him before, but this time the old claw shot out and seized Ender's left leg in the middle of a kick. It pulled Ender off his feet and landed him heavily on the floor.

Ender leapt to his feet immediately, furious. He found the old man sitting calmly, cross-legged, not breathing heavily, as if he had never moved. Ender stood poised to fight, but the other's immobility made it impossible for Ender to attack. What, kick the old man's head off? And then explain it to Graff—oh, the old man kicked me, and I had to get even.

He went back to his exercises; the old man kept watching.

Finally, tired and angry at this wasted day, a prisoner in his room, Ender went back to his bed to get his desk. As he leaned over to pick up the desk, he felt a hand jab roughly between his thighs and another hand grab his hair. In a moment he had been turned upside down. His face and shoulders were being pressed into the floor by the old man's knee, while his back was excruciatingly bent and his legs were pinioned by the old man's arm. Ender was helpless to use his arms, he couldn't bend his back to gain slack so he could use his legs. In less than two seconds the old man had completely defeated Ender Wiggin.

"All right," Ender gasped. "You win."

The man's knee thrust painfully downward. "Since when," asked the man, his voice soft and rasping, "do you have to tell the enemy when he has won?"

Ender remained silent.

"I surprised you once, Ender Wiggin. Why didn't you destroy me immediately afterward? Just because I looked peaceful? You turned your back on me. Stupid. You have learned nothing. You have never had a teacher."

Ender was angry now, and made no attempt to control or conceal it. "I've had too many teachers, how was I supposed to know you'd turn out to be a—"

"An enemy, Ender Wiggin," whispered the old man. "I am your enemy, the first one you've ever had who was smarter than you. There is no teacher but the enemy. No one but the enemy will tell you what the enemy is going to do. No one but the enemy will ever teach you how to destroy and conquer. Only the enemy shows you where you are weak. Only the enemy tells you where he is strong. And the rules of the game are what you can do to him and what you can stop him from doing to you. I am your enemy from now on. From now on I am your teacher."

Then the old man let Ender's legs fall. Because he still held Ender's head to the floor, the boy couldn't use his arms to compensate, and his legs hit the surface with a loud crack and a sickening pain. Then the old man stood and let Ender rise.

Slowly Ender pulled his legs under him, with a faint groan of pain. He knelt on all fours for a moment, recovering. Then his right arm flashed out, reaching for his enemy. The old man quickly danced back and Ender's hand closed on air as his teacher's foot shot forward to catch Ender on the chin.

Ender's chin wasn't there. He was lying flat on his back, spinning on the floor, and during the moment that his teacher was off balance from his kick, Ender's feet smashed into the old man's other leg. He fell in a heap—but close enough to strike out and hit Ender in the face. Ender couldn't find an arm or a leg that held still long enough to be grabbed, and in the meantime blows were landing on his back and arms. Ender was smaller—he couldn't reach past the old man's flailing limbs. Finally he managed to pull away and scramble back near the door.

The old man was sitting cross-legged again, but now the apathy was gone. He was smiling. "Better, this time, boy. But slow. You will have to be better with a fleet than you are with your body or no one will be safe with you in command. Lesson learned?"

Ender nodded slowly. He ached in a hundred places.

"Good," said the old man. "Then we'll never have to have such a battle again. All the rest with the simulator. *I* will program your battles now, not the computer; I will devise the strategy of your enemy, and you will learn to be quick and discover what tricks the enemy has for you. Remember, boy. From now on the enemy is more clever than you. From now on the enemy is stronger than you. From now on you are always about to lose."

The old man's face grew serious again. "You will be about to lose, Ender, but you will win. You will learn to defeat the enemy. He will teach you how."

The teacher got up. "In this school, it has always been the practice for a young student to be chosen by an older student. The two become companions, and the older boy teaches the younger one everything he knows. Always they fight, always they compete, always they are together. I have chosen you."

Ender spoke as the old man walked to the door. "You're too old to be a student."

"One is never too old to be a student of the enemy. I have learned from the buggers. You will learn from me."

As the old man palmed the door open, Ender leaped into the air and kicked him in the small of the back with both feet. He hit hard enough that he rebounded onto his feet, as the old man cried out and collapsed on the floor.

The old man got up slowly, holding onto the door handle, his face contorted with pain. He seemed disabled, but Ender didn't trust him. Yet in spite of his suspicion he was caught off guard by the old man's speed. In a moment he found himself on the floor near the opposite wall, his nose and lip bleeding where his face had hit the bed. He was able to turn enough to see the old man standing in the doorway, wincing and holding his back. The old man grinned.

Ender grinned back. "Teacher," he said. "Do you have a name?"

"Mazer Rackham," said the old man. Then he was gone.

From then on, Ender was either with Mazer Rackham or alone. The old man rarely spoke, but he was there; at meals, at tutorials, at the simulator, in his room at night. Sometimes Mazer would leave, but always, when Mazer wasn't there, the door was locked, and no one came until Mazer returned. Ender went through a week in which he called him Jailor Rackman. Mazer answered to the name as readily as to his own, and showed no sign that it bothered him at all. Ender soon gave it up.

There were compensations. Mazer took Ender through the videos of the old battles from the First Invasion and the disastrous defeats of the I.F. in the Second Invasion. These were not pieced together from the censored public videos, but whole and continuous. Since many videos were working in the major battles, they studied bugger tactics and strategies from many angles. For the first time in his life, a teacher was pointing out things that Ender had not already seen for himself. For the first time, Ender had found a living mind he could admire.

"Why aren't you dead?" Ender asked him. "You fought your battle seventy years ago. I don't think you're even sixty years old."

"The miracle of relativity," said Mazer. "They kept me here for twenty years after the battle, even though I begged them to let me command one of the starships they launched against the bugger home planet and the bugger colonies. Then they—came to understand some things about the way soldiers behave in the stress of battle."

"What things?"

"You've never been taught enough psychology to understand. Enough to say that they realized that even though I would never be able to command the fleet—I'd be dead before the fleet even arrived—I was still the only person able to understand the things I understood about the buggers. I was, they realized, the only person who had ever defeated the buggers by intelligence rather than luck. They needed me here to—teach the person who *would* command the fleet."

"So they sent you out in a starship, got you up to a relativistic speed—"

"And then I turned around and came home. A very dull voyage, Ender. Fifty years in space. Officially, only eight years passed for me, but it felt like five hundred. All so I could teach the next commander everything I knew."

"Am I to be the commander, then?"

"Let's say that you're our best bet at present."

"There are others being prepared, too?"

"No."

"That makes me the only choice, then, doesn't it?"

Mazer shrugged.

"Except you. You're still alive, aren't you? Why not you?"

Mazer shook his head.

"Why not? You won before."

"I cannot be the commander for good and sufficient reasons."

"Show me how you beat the buggers, Mazer."

Mazer's face went inscrutable.

"You've shown me every other battle seven times at least. I think I've seen ways to beat what the buggers did before, but you've never shown me how you actually *did* beat them."

"The video is a very tightly kept secret, Ender."

"I know. I've pieced it together, partly. You, with your tiny reserve force, and their armada, those great big heavy-bellied starships launching their swarms of fighters. You dart in at one ship, fire at it, an explosion. That's where they always stop the clips. After that, it's just soldiers going into bugger ships and already finding them dead inside."

Mazer grinned. "So much for tightly kept secrets. Come on, let's watch the video."

They were alone in the video room, and Ender palmed the door locked. "All right, let's watch."

The video showed exactly what Ender had pieced together. Mazer's suicidal plunge into the heart of the enemy formation, the single explosion, and then—

Nothing. Mazer's ship went on, dodged the shock wave, and wove his way among the other bugger ships. They did not fire on him. They did not change course. Two of them crashed into each other and exploded—a needless collision that either pilot could have avoided. Neither made the slightest movement.

Mazer sped up the action. Skipped ahead. "We waited for three hours," he said. "Nobody could believe it." Then the I.F. ships began approaching the bugger starships. Marines began their cutting and boarding operations. The videos showed the buggers already dead at their posts.

"So you see," said Mazer, "you already knew all there was to see."

"Why did it happen?"

"Nobody knows. I have my personal opinions. But there are plenty of scientists who tell me I'm less than qualified to have opinions."

"You're the one who won the battle."

"I thought that qualified me to comment, too, but you know how it is. Xenobiologists and xenopsychologists can't accept the idea that a starpilot scooped them by sheer guesswork. I think they all hate me because, after they saw these videos, they had to live out the rest of their natural lives here on Eros. Security, you know. They weren't happy."

"Tell me."

"The buggers don't talk. They think to each other, and it's instantaneous, like the philotic effect. Like the ansible. But most people always thought that meant a controlled communication, like language—I think you a thought and then you answer me. I never believed that. It's too *immediate*, the way they respond together to things. You've seen the videos. They aren't conversing and deciding among possible courses of action. Every ship acts like part of a single organism. It responds the way your body responds during combat, different parts automatically, thoughtlessly doing everything they're supposed to do. They aren't having a mental conversation between people with different thought processes. *All* their thoughts are present, together, at once."

"A single person, and each bugger is like a hand or a foot?"

"Yes. I wasn't the first person to suggest it, but I was the first person to believe it. And something else. Something so childish and stupid that the xenobiologists laughed me to silence when I said it after the battle. The buggers are *bugs*. They're like ants and bees. A queen, the workers. That was maybe a hundred million years ago, but that's how they started, that kind of pattern. It's a sure thing none of the buggers *we* saw had any way of making more little buggers. So when they evolved this ability to think together, wouldn't they still keep the queen? Wouldn't the queen still be the center of the group? Why would that ever change?"

"So it's the queen who controls the whole group."

"I had evidence, too. Not evidence that any of them could see. It wasn't there in the First Invasion, because that was exploratory. But the Second Invasion was a colony. To set up a new hive, or whatever."

"And so they brought a queen."

"The videos of the Second Invasion, when they were destroying our fleets out in the comet shell." He began to call them up and display the buggers' patterns. "Show me the queen's ship."

It was subtle. Ender couldn't see it for a long time. The bugger ships kept moving, all of them. There was no obvious flagship, no apparent nerve center. But gradually, as Mazer played the videos over and over again, Ender began to see the way that all the movements focused on, radiated from a center point. The center point shifted, but it was obvious, after he looked long enough, that the eyes of the fleet, the *I* of the fleet, the perspective from which all decisions were being made, was one particular ship. He pointed it out.

"You see it. I see it. That makes two people out of all of those who have seen this video. But it's true, isn't it."

"They make that ship move just like any other ship."

"They know it's their weak point."

"But you're right. That's the queen. But then you'd think that when you went for it, they would have immediately focused all their power on you. They could have blown you out of the sky."

"I know. That part I don't understand. Not that they didn't try to stop me—they were firing at me. But it's as if they really couldn't believe, until it was too late, that I would actually *kill* the queen. Maybe in their world, queens are never killed, only captured, only checkmated. I did something they didn't think an enemy would ever do."

"And when she died, the others all died."

"No, they just went stupid. The first ships we boarded, the buggers were still alive. Organically. But they didn't move, didn't respond to anything, even when our scientists vivisected some of them to see if we could learn a few more things about buggers. After a while they all died. No will. There's nothing in those little bodies when the queen is gone."

"Why don't they believe you?"

"Because we didn't find a queen."

"She got blown to pieces."

"Fortunes of war. Biology takes second place to survival. But some of them *are* coming around to my way of thinking. You can't live in this place without the evidence staring you in the face."

"What evidence is there in Eros?"

"Ender, look around you. Human beings didn't carve this place. We like taller ceilings, for one thing. This was the buggers' advance post in the First Invasion. They carved this place out before we even knew they were here. We're living in a bugger hive. But we already paid our rent. It cost the marines a thousand lives to clear them out of these honeycombs, room by room. The buggers fought for every meter of it."

Now Ender understood why the rooms had always felt wrong to him. "I knew this place wasn't a human place."

"This was the treasure trove. If they had known we would win that first war, they probably would never have built this place. We learned gravity manipulation because they enhanced the gravity here. We learned efficient use of stellar energy because they blacked out this planet. In fact, that's how we discovered *them*. In a period of three days, Eros gradually disappeared from telescopes. We sent a tug to find out why. It found out. The tug transmitted its videos, including the buggers boarding and slaughtering the crew. It kept right on transmitting through the entire bugger examination of the boat. Not until they finally dismantled the entire tug did the transmissions stop. It was their blindness—they never had to transmit anything by machine, and so with the crew dead, it didn't occur to them that anybody could be watching."

"Why did they kill the crew?"

"Why not? To them, losing a few crew members would be like clipping your nails. Nothing to get upset about. They probably thought they were routinely shutting down our communications by turning off the workers running the tug. Not murdering living, sentient beings with an independent genetic future. Murder's no big deal to them. Only queen-killing, really, is murder, because only queen-killing closes off a genetic path."

"So they didn't know what they were doing."

"Don't start apologizing for them, Ender. Just because they didn't know they were killing human beings doesn't mean they weren't killing human beings. We do have a right to defend ourselves as best we can, and the only way we found that works is killing the buggers before they kill us. Think of it this way. In all the bugger wars so far, they've killed thousands and thousands of living, thinking beings. And in all those wars, we've killed only one."

"If you hadn't killed the queen, Mazer, would we have lost the war?"

"I'd say the odds would have been three to two against us. I still think I could have trashed their fleet pretty badly before they burned us out. They have great response time and a lot of firepower, but we have a few advantages, too. Every single one of our ships contains an intelligent human being who's thinking on his own. Every one of us is capable of coming up with a brilliant solution to a problem. They can only come up with one brilliant solution at a time. The buggers think fast, but they aren't smart all over. But on *our* side, even when some incredibly timid and stupid commanders lost the major battles of the Second Invasion, some of their subordinates were able to do real damage to the bugger fleet."

"What about when our invasion reaches them? Will we just get the queen again?"

"The buggers didn't learn interstellar travel by being dumb. That was a strategy that could work only once. I suspect that we'll never get near a queen unless we actually make it to their home planet. After all, the queen doesn't have to be *with* them to direct a battle. The queen only has to be present to have little baby buggers. The Second Invasion was a colony—the queen was coming to populate the Earth. But this time—no, that won't work. We'll have to beat them fleet by fleet. And because they have the resources of dozens of star systems to draw on, my guess is they'll outnumber us by a lot, in every battle."

Ender remembered his battle against two armies at once. And I thought they were cheating. When the real war begins, it'll be like that every time. And there won't be any gate I can go for.

"We've only got two things going for us, Ender. We don't have to aim particularly well. Our weapons have great spread."

"Then we are aren't using the nuclear missiles from the First and Second Invasions?"

"Dr. Device is much more powerful. Nuclear weapons, after all, were weak enough to be used on Earth at one time. The Little Doctor could never be used on a planet. Still, I wish I'd had one during the Second Invasion."

"How does it work?"

"I don't know, not well enough to build one. At the focal point of two beams, it sets up a field in which molecules can't hold together anymore. Electrons can't be shared. How much physics do you know, at that level?"

"We spend most of our time on astrophysics, but I know enough to get the idea."

"The field spreads out in a sphere, but it gets weaker the farther it spreads. Except that where it actually runs into a lot of molecules, it gets stronger and starts over. The bigger the ship, the stronger the new field."

"So each time the field hits a ship, it sends out a new sphere—"

"And if their ships are too close together, it can set up a chain that wipes them all out. Then the field dies down, the molecules come back together, and where you had a ship, you now have a lump of dirt with a lot of iron molecules in it. No radioactivity, no mess. Just dirt. We may be able to trap them close together on the first battle, but they learn fast. They'll keep their distance from each other."

"So Dr. Device isn't a missile—I can't shoot around corners."

"That's right. Missiles wouldn't do any good now. We learned a lot from them in the First Invasion, but they also learned from us—how to set up the Ecstatic Shield, for instance."

"The Little Doctor penetrates the shield?"

"As if it weren't there. You can't *see* through the shield to aim and focus the beams, but since the generator of the Ecstatic Shield is always in the exact center, it isn't hard to figure it out."

"Why haven't I ever been trained with this?"

"You always have. We just let the computer tend to it

for you. Your job is to get into a superior strategic position and choose a target. The shipboard computers are much better at aiming the Doctor than you are."

"Why is it called Dr. Device?"

"When it was developed, it was called a Molecular Detachment Device. M.D. Device."

Ender still didn't understand.

"M.D. The initials stand for Medical Doctor, too. M.D. Device, therefore Dr. Device. It was a joke." Ender didn't see what was funny about it.

—

They had changed the simulator. He could still control the perspective and the degree of detail, but there were no ship's controls anymore. Instead, it was a new panel of levers, and a small headset with earphones and a small microphone.

The technician who was waiting there quickly explained how to wear the headset.

"But how do I control the ships?" asked Ender.

Mazer explained. He wasn't going to control ships anymore. "You've reached the next phase of your training. You have experience in every level of strategy, but now it's time for you to concentrate on commanding an entire fleet. As you worked with toon leaders in Battle School, so now you will work with squadron leaders. You have been assigned three dozen such leaders to train. You must teach them intelligent tactics; you must learn their strengths and limitations; you must make them into a whole."

"When will they come here?"

"They're already in place in their own simulators. You will speak to them through the headset. The new levers on your control panel enable you to see from the perspective of any of your squadron leaders. This more closely duplicates the conditions you might encounter in a real battle, where you will know only what your ships can see."

"How can I work with squadron leaders I never see?"

"And why would you need to see them?"

"To know who they are, how they think—"

"You'll learn who they are and how they think from the way they work with the simulator. But even so, I think you won't be concerned. They're listening to you right now. Put on the headset so you can hear them."

Ender put on the headset.

"Salaam," said a whisper in his ears.

"Alai," said Ender.

"And me, the dwarf."

"Bean."

And Petra, and Dink; Crazy Tom, Shen, Hot Soup, Fly Molo, Carn Carby, all the best students Ender had fought with or fought against, everyone that Ender had trusted in Battle School. "I didn't know you were here," he said. "I didn't know you were coming."

"They've been flogging us through the simulator for three months now," said Dink.

"You'll find that I'm by far the best tactician," said Petra. "Dink tries, but he has the mind of a child."

So they began working together, each squadron leader commanding individual pilots, and Ender commanding the squadron leaders. They learned many ways of working together, as the simulator forced them to try different situations. Sometimes the simulator gave them a larger fleet to work with; Ender set them up then in three or four toons that consisted of three or four squadrons each. Sometimes the simulator gave them a single starship with its twelve fighters, and he chose three squadron leaders with four fighters each.

It was pleasure; it was play. The computer-controlled enemy was none too bright, and they always won despite their mistakes, their miscommunications. But in the three weeks they practiced together, Ender came to know them very well. Dink, who deftly carried out instructions but was slow to improvise; Bean, who couldn't control large groups of ships effectively but could use a few like a scalpel, reacting beautifully to anything the computer threw at him; Alai, who was almost as good a strategist as Ender and could be entrusted to do well with half a fleet and only vague instructions.

The better Ender knew them, the faster he could deploy them, the better he could use them. The simulator would display the situation on the screen. In that moment Ender learned for the first time what his own fleet would consist of and how the enemy fleet was deployed. It took him only a few minutes now to call the squadron leaders that he needed, assign them to certain ships or groups of ships, and give them their assignments. Then, as the battle progressed, he would skip from one leader's point of view to another's, making suggestions and, occasionally, giving orders as the need arose. Since the others could see only their own battle perspective, he would sometimes give them orders that made no sense to them; but they, too, learned to trust Ender. If he told them to withdraw, they withdrew, knowing that either they were in an exposed position, or their withdrawal might entice the enemy into a weakened posture. They also knew that Ender trusted them to do as they judged best when he gave them no orders. If their style of fighting were not right for the situation they were placed in, Ender would not have chosen them for that assignment.

The trust was complete, the working of the fleet quick and responsive. And at the end of three weeks, Mazer showed him a replay of their most recent battle, only this time from the enemy's point of view.

"This is what he saw as you attacked. What does it remind you of? The quickness of response, for instance?"

"We look like a bugger fleet."

"You match them, Ender. You're as fast as they are. And here—look at this."

Ender watched as all his squadrons moved at once, each responding to its own situation, all guided by Ender's overall command, but daring, improvising, feinting, attacking with an independence no bugger fleet had ever shown.

"The bugger hive-mind is very good, but it can only concentrate on a few things at once. All your squadrons can concentrate a keen intelligence on what they're doing, and what they've been assigned to do is also guided by a clever mind. So you see that you do have some advantages. Superior, though not irresistible, weaponry; comparable speed and greater available intelligence. These are your advantages. Your disadvantage is that you will always, always be outnumbered, and after each battle your enemy will learn more about you, how to fight you, and those changes will be put into effect instantly."

Ender waited for his conclusion.

"So Ender, we will now begin your education. We have programmed the computer to simulate the kinds of situations we might expect in encounters with the enemy. We are using the movement patterns we saw in the Second Invasion. But instead of mindlessly following these same patterns, I will be controlling the enemy simulation. At first you will see easy situations that you are expected to win handily. Learn from them, because I will always be there, one step ahead of you, programming more difficult and advanced patterns into the computer so that your next battle is more difficult, so that you are pushed to the limit of your abilities."

"And beyond?"

"The time is short. You must learn as quickly as you can. When I gave myself to starship travel, just so I would still be alive when you appeared, my wife and children all died, and my grandchildren were my own age when I came back. I had nothing to say to them. I was cut off from all the people that I loved, everything I knew, living in this alien catacomb and forced to do nothing of importance but teach student after student, each one so hopeful, each one, ultimately, a weakling, a failure. I teach, I teach, but no one learns. You, too, have great promise, like so many students before you, but the seeds of failure may be in you, too. It's my job to find them, to destroy you if I can, and believe me, Ender, if you can be destroyed I can do it."

"So I'm not the first."

"No, of course you're not. But you're the last. If you don't learn, there'll be no time to find anyone else. So I have hope for you, if only because you are the only one left to hope for."

"What about the others? My squadron leaders?"

"Which of them is fit to take your place?"

"Alai."

"Be honest."

Ender had no answer, then.

"I am not a happy man, Ender. Humanity does not ask us to be happy. It merely asks us to be brilliant on its behalf. Survival first, then happiness as we can manage it. So, Ender, I hope you do not bore me during your training with complaints that you are not having fun. Take what pleasure you can in the interstices of your work, but your work is first, learning is first, winning is everything because without it there is nothing. When you can give me back my dead wife, Ender, then you can complain to me about what this education costs you."

"I wasn't trying to get out of anything."

"But you will, Ender. Because I am going to grind you down to dust, if I can. I'm going to hit you with everything I can imagine, and I will have no mercy, because when you face the buggers they will think of things I *can't* imagine, and compassion for human beings is impossible for them."

"You can't grind me down, Mazer."

"Oh, can't I?"

"Because I'm stronger than you."

Mazer smiled. "We'll see about that, Ender."

Mazer wakened him before morning; the clock said 0340, and Ender felt groggy as he padded along the corridor behind

Mazer. "Early to bed and early to rise," Mazer intoned, "makes a man stupid and blind in the eyes."

He had been dreaming that buggers were vivisecting him. Only instead of cutting open his body, they were cutting up his memories and displaying them like holographs and trying to make sense of them. It was a very odd dream, and Ender couldn't easily shake loose of it, even as he walked through the tunnels to the simulator room. The buggers tormented him in his sleep, and Mazer wouldn't leave him alone when he was awake. Between the two of them he had no rest. Ender forced himself awake. Apparently Mazer meant it when he said he meant to break Ender down—and forcing him to play when tired and sleepy was just the sort of cheap and easy trick Ender should have expected. Well, today, it wouldn't work.

He got to the simulator and found his squadron leaders already on the wire, waiting for him. There was no enemy yet, so he divided them into two armies and began a mock battle, commanding both sides so he could control the test that each of his leaders was going through. They began slowly, but soon were vigorous and alert.

Then the simulator field went blank, the ships disappeared, and everything changed at once. At the near edge of the simulator field they could see the shapes, drawn in holographic light, of three starships from the human fleet. Each would have twelve fighters. The enemy, obviously aware of the human presence, had formed a globe with a single ship at the center. Ender was not fooled—it would not be a queen ship. The buggers outnumbered Ender's fighter force by two to one, but they were also grouped much closer together than they should have been—Dr. Device would be able to do much more damage than the enemy expected.

Ender selected one starship, made it blink in the simulator field, and spoke into the microphone. "Alai, this is yours; assign Petra and Vlad to the fighters as you wish." He assigned the other two starships with their fighter forces, except for one fighter from each starship that he reserved for Bean. "Slip the wall and get below them, Bean, unless they start chasing you—then run back to the reserves for safety. Otherwise, get in a place where I can call on you for quick results. Alai, form your force into a compact assault at one point in their globe. Don't fire until I tell you. This is maneuver only."

"This one's easy, Ender," Alai said.

"It's easy, so why not be careful? I'd like to do this without the loss of a single ship."

Ender grouped his reserves in two forces that shadowed Alai at a distance; Bean was already off the simulator, though Ender occasionally flipped to Bean's point of view to keep track of where he was.

It was Alai, however, who played the delicate game with the enemy. He was in a bullet-shaped formation, and probed the enemy globe. Wherever he came near, the bugger ships pulled back, as if to draw him in toward the ship in the center. Alai skimmed to the side; the bugger ships kept up with him, withdrawing wherever he was close, returning to the sphere pattern when he had passed.

Feint, withdraw, skim the globe to another point, withdraw again, feint again; and then Ender said, "Go on in, Alai."

His bullet started in, while he said to Ender, "You know they'll just let me through and surround me and eat me alive."

"Just ignore that ship in the middle."

"Whatever you say, boss."

Sure enough, the globe began to contract. Ender brought the reserves forward; the enemy ships concentrated on the side of the globe nearer the reserves. "Attack them there, where they're most concentrated," Ender said.

"This defies four thousand years of military history," said Alai, moving his fighters forward. "We're supposed to attack where we outnumber them."

"In this simulation they obviously don't know what our

weapons can do. It'll only work once, but let's make it spectacular. Fire at will."

Alai did. The simulation responded beautifully: first one or two, then a dozen, then most of the enemy ships exploded in dazzling light as the field leapt from ship to ship in the tight formation. "Stay out of the way," Ender said.

The ships on the far side of the globe formation were not affected by the chain reaction, but it was a simple matter to hunt them down and destroy them. Bean took care of stragglers that tried to escape toward his end of space. The battle was over. It had been easier than most of their recent exercises.

Mazer shrugged when Ender told him so. "This is a simulation of a real invasion. There had to be one battle in which they didn't know what we could do. Now your work begins. Try not to be too arrogant about the victory. I'll give you the real challenges soon enough."

Ender practiced ten hours a day with his squadron leaders, but not all at once; he gave them a few hours in the afternoon to rest. Simulated battles under Mazer's supervision came every two or three days, and as Mazer had promised, they were never so easy again. The enemy quickly abandoned its attempt to surround Ender, and never again grouped its forces closely enough to allow a chain reaction. There was something new every time, something harder. Sometimes Ender had only a single starship and eight fighters; once the enemy dodged through an asteroid belt; sometimes the enemy left stationary traps, large installations that blew up if Ender brought one of his squadrons too close, often crippling or destroying some of Ender's ships. "You cannot absorb losses!" Mazer shouted at him after one battle. "When you get into a *real* battle you won't have the luxury of an infinite supply of computer-generated fighters. You'll have what you brought with you and *nothing more*. Now get used to fighting without unnecessary waste."

"It wasn't unnecessary waste," Ender said. "I can't win

battles if I'm so terrified of losing a ship that I never take any risks."

Mazer smiled. "Excellent, Ender. You're beginning to learn. But in a real battle, you would have superior officers and, worst of all, civilians shouting those things at you. Now, if the enemy had been at all bright, they would have caught you *here*, and taken Tom's squadron." Together they went over the battle; in the next practice, Ender would show his leaders what Mazer had shown him, and they'd learn to cope with it the next time they saw it.

They thought they had been ready before, that they had worked smoothly together as a team. Now, though, having fought through real challenges together, they all began to trust each other more than ever, and battles became exhilarating. They told Ender that the ones who weren't actually playing would come into the simulator rooms and watch. Ender imagined what it would be like to have his friends there with him, cheering or laughing or gasping with apprehension; sometimes he thought it would be a great distraction, but other times he wished for it with all his heart. Even when he had spent his days lying out in the sunlight on a raft in a lake, he had not been so lonely. Mazer Rackham was his companion, was his teacher, but was not his friend.

He made no complaint, though. Mazer had told him there would be no pity, and his private unhappiness meant nothing to anyone. Most of the time it meant nothing even to Ender. He kept his mind on the game, trying to learn from the battles. And not just the particular lessons of that battle, but what the buggers might have done if they had been more clever, and how Ender would react if they did it in the future. He lived with past battles and future battles both, waking and sleeping, and he drove his squadron leaders with an intensity that occasionally provoked rebelliousness.

"You're too kind to us," said Alai one day. "Why don't you get annoyed with us for not being brilliant *every* moment of *every* practice. If you keep coddling us like this we'll think you like us."

Some of the others laughed into their microphones. Ender recognized the irony, of course, and answered with a long silence. When he finally spoke, he ignored Alai's complaint. "Again," he said, "and this time without self-pity." They did it again, and did it right.

But as their trust in Ender as a commander grew, their friendship, remembered from the Battle School days, gradually disappeared. It was to each other that they became close; it was with each other that they exchanged confidences. Ender was their teacher and commander, as distant from them as Mazer was from him, and as demanding.

They fought all the better for it. And Ender was not distracted from his work.

At least, not while he was awake. As he drifted off to sleep each night, it was with thoughts of the simulator playing through his mind. But in the night he thought of other things. Often he remembered the corpse of the Giant, decaying steadily; he did not remember it, though, in the pixels of the picture on his desk. Instead it was real, the faint odor of death still lingering near it. Things were changed in his dreams. The little village that had grown up between the Giant's ribs was composed of buggers now, and they saluted him gravely, like gladiators greeting Caesar before they died for his entertainment. He did not hate the buggers in his dream; and even though he knew that they had hidden their queen from him, he did not try to search for her. He always left the Giant's body quickly, and when he got to the playground, the children were always there, wolven and mocking; they wore faces that he knew. Sometimes Peter and sometimes Bonzo, sometimes Stilson and Bernard; just as often, though, the savage creatures were Alai and Shen, Dink and Petra; sometimes one of them would be Valentine, and in his dream he also shoved her under the water and waited for her to drown. She writhed in his hands, fought to come up, but at last was still. He dragged her out of the lake and onto the raft, where she lay with her face in the rictus of death. He screamed and wept over her, crying again and again that it was a game, a game, he was only playing!—

Then Mazer Rackham shook him awake. "You were calling out in your sleep," he said.

"Sorry," Ender said.

"Never mind. It's time for another battle."

Steadily the pace increased. There were usually two battles a day now, and Ender held practices to a minimum. He would use the time while the others rested to pore over the replays of past games, trying to spot his own weaknesses, trying to guess what would happen next. Sometimes he was fully prepared for the enemy's innovations; sometimes he was not.

"I think you're cheating," Ender told Mazer one day.

"Oh?"

"You can observe my practice sessions. You can see what I'm working on. You seem to be ready for everything I do."

"Most of what you see is computer simulations," Mazer said. "The computer is programmed to respond to your innovations only after you use them once in battle."

"Then the computer is cheating."

"You need to get more sleep, Ender."

But he could not sleep. He lay awake longer and longer each night, and his sleep was less restful. He woke too often in the night. Whether he was waking up to think more about the game or to escape from his dreams, he wasn't sure. It was as if someone rode him in his sleep, forcing him to wander through his worst memories, to live in them again as if they were real. Nights were so real that days began to seem dreamlike to him. He began to worry that he would not think clearly enough, that he would be too tired when he played. Always when the game began, the intensity of it awoke him, but if his mental abilities began to slip, he wondered, would he notice it?

And he seemed to be slipping. He never had a battle anymore in which he did not lose at least a few fighters.

Several times the enemy was able to trick him into exposing more weakness than he meant to; other times the enemy was able to wear him down by attrition until his victory was as much a matter of luck as strategy. Mazer would go over the game with a look of contempt on his face. "Look at this," he would say. "You didn't have to do this." And Ender would return to practice with his leaders, trying to keep up their morale, but sometimes letting slip his disappointment with their weaknesses, the fact that they made mistakes.

"Sometimes we make mistakes," Petra whispered to him once. It was a plea for help.

"And sometimes we don't," Ender answered her. If she got help, it would not be from him. He would teach; let her find her friends among the others.

Then came a battle that nearly ended in disaster. Petra led her force too far; they were exposed, and she discovered it in a moment when Ender wasn't with her. In only a few moments she had lost all but two of her ships. Ender found her then, ordered her to move them in a certain direction; she didn't answer. There was no movement. And in a moment those two fighters, too, would be lost.

Ender knew at once that he had pushed her too hard—because of her brilliance he had called on her to play far more often and under much more demanding circumstances than all but a few of the others. But he had no time now to worry about Petra, or to feel guilty about what he had done to her. He called on Crazy Tom to command the two remaining fighters, then went on, trying to salvage the battle; Petra had occupied a key position, and now all of Ender's strategy came apart. If the enemy had not been too eager and clumsy in exploiting their advantage, Ender would have lost. But Shen was able to catch a group of the enemy in too tight a formation and took them out with a single chain reaction. Crazy Tom brought his two surviving fighters in through the gap and caused havoc with the enemy, and though his ships and Shen's as well were finally destroyed, Fly Molo was able to mop up and complete the victory.

At the end of the battle, he could hear Petra crying out, trying to get a microphone, "Tell him I'm sorry, I was just so tired, I couldn't think, that was all, tell Ender I'm sorry."

She was not there for the next few practices, and when she did come back she was not as quick as she had been, not as daring. Much of what had made her a good commander was lost. Ender couldn't use her anymore, except in routine, closely supervised assignments. She was no fool. She knew what had happened. But she also knew that Ender had no other choice, and told him so.

The fact remained that she had broken, and she was far from being the weakest of his squad leaders. It was a warning—he could not press his commanders more than they could bear. Now, instead of using his leaders whenever he needed their skills, he had to keep in mind how often they had fought. He had to spell them off, which meant that sometimes he went into battle with commanders he trusted a little less. As he eased the pressure on them, he increased the pressure on himself.

Late one night he woke up in pain. There was blood on his pillow, the taste of blood in his mouth. His fingers were throbbing. He saw that in his sleep he had been gnawing on his own fist. The blood was still flowing smoothly. "Mazer!" he called. Rackham woke up and called at once for a doctor.

As the doctor treated the wound, Mazer said, "I don't care how much you eat, Ender, self-cannibalism won't get you out of this school."

"I was asleep," Ender said. "I don't want to get out of Command School."

"Good."

"The others. The ones who didn't make it."

"What are you talking about?"

"Before me. Your other students, who didn't make it through the training. What happened to them?"

"They didn't make it. That's all. We don't punish the ones who fail. They just—don't go on."

"Like Bonzo."

"Bonzo?"

"He went home."

"Not like Bonzo."

"*What*, then? What happened to them? When they failed?"

"Why does it matter, Ender?"

Ender didn't answer.

"None of them failed at *this* point in their course, Ender. You made a mistake with Petra. She'll recover. But Petra is Petra, and you are you."

"Part of what I am is her. Is what she made me."

"You won't fail, Ender. Not this early in the course. You've had some tight ones, but you've always won. You don't know what your limits are yet, but if you've reached them already you're a good deal feebler than I thought."

"Do they die?"

"Who?"

"The ones who fail."

"No, they don't die. Good heavens, boy, you're playing games."

"I think that Bonzo died. I dreamed about it last night. I remembered the way he looked after I jammed his face with my head. I think I must have pushed his nose back into his brain. The blood was coming out of his eyes. I think he was dead right then."

"It was just a dream."

"Mazer, I don't want to keep dreaming these things. I'm afraid to sleep. I keep thinking of things that I don't want to remember. My whole life keeps playing out as if I were a recorder and someone else wanted to watch the most terrible parts of my life."

"We can't drug you if that's what you're hoping for. I'm sorry if you have bad dreams. Should we leave the light on at night?"

"Don't make fun of me!" Ender said. "I'm afraid I'm going crazy."

The doctor was finished with the bandage. Mazer told him he could go. He went.

"Are you really afraid of that?" Mazer asked.

Ender thought about it and wasn't sure.

"In my dreams," said Ender, "I'm never sure whether I'm really me."

"Strange dreams are a safety valve, Ender. I'm putting you under a little pressure for the first time in your life. Your body is finding ways to compensate, that's all. You're a big boy now. It's time to stop being afraid of the night."

"All right," Ender said. He decided then that he would never tell Mazer about his dreams again.

The days wore on, with battles every day, until at last Ender settled into the routine of the destruction of himself. He began to have pains in his stomach. They put him on a bland diet, but soon he didn't have an appetite for anything at all. "Eat," Mazer said, and Ender would mechanically put food in his mouth. But if nobody told him to eat, he didn't eat.

Two more of his squadron leaders collapsed the way that Petra had; the pressure on the rest became all the greater. The enemy outnumbered them by three or four to one in every battle now; the enemy also retreated more readily when things went badly, regrouping to keep the battle going longer and longer. Sometimes battles lasted for hours before they finally destroyed the last enemy ship. Ender began rotating his squadron leaders within the same battle, bringing in fresh and rested ones to take the place of those who were beginning to get sluggish.

"You know," said Bean one time, as he took over command of Hot Soup's four remaining fighters, "this game isn't quite as fun as it used to be."

Then one day in practice, as Ender was drilling his squadron leaders, the room went black and he woke up on the floor with his face bloody where he had hit the controls.

They put him to bed then, and for three days he was very ill. He remembered seeing faces in his dreams, but they weren't real faces, and he knew it even while he thought he saw them. He thought he saw Valentine sometimes, and sometimes Peter; sometimes his friends from the Battle School, and sometimes the buggers vivisecting him. Once it seemed very real when he saw Colonel Graff bending over him, speaking softly to him, like a kind father. But then he woke up and found only his enemy, Mazer Rackham.

"I'm awake," said Ender.

"So I see," Mazer answered. "Took you long enough. You have a battle today."

So Ender got up and fought the battle and won it. But there was no second battle that day, and they let him go to bed earlier. His hands were shaking as he undressed.

During the night he thought he felt hands touching him gently. Hands with affection in them, and gentleness. He dreamed he heard voices.

"You haven't been kind to him."

"That wasn't the assignment."

"How long can he go on? He's breaking down."

"Long enough. It's nearly finished."

"So soon?"

"A few days, and then he's through."

"How will he do, when he's already like this?"

"Fine. Even today, he fought better than ever."

In his dream, the voices sounded like Colonel Graff and Mazer Rackham. But that was the way dreams were, the craziest things could happen, because he dreamed he heard one of the voices saying, "I can't bear to see what this is doing to him." And the other voice answered, "I know. I love him too." And then they changed into Valentine and Alai, and in his dream they were burying him, only a hill grew up where they laid his body down, and he dried out and became a home for buggers, like the Giant was.

All dreams. If there was love or pity for him, it was only in his dreams.

He woke up and fought another battle and won. Then he went to bed and slept again and dreamed again and then he woke up and won again and slept again and he hardly noticed when waking became sleeping. Nor did he care.

The next day was his last day in Command School, though he didn't know it. Mazer Rackham was not in the room with him when he woke up. He showered and dressed and waited for Mazer to come unlock the door. He didn't come. Ender tried the door. It was open.

Was it an accident that Mazer had let him be free this morning? No one with him to tell him he must eat, he must go to practice, he must sleep. Freedom. The trouble was, he didn't know what to do. He thought for a moment that he might find his squadron leaders, talk to them face to face, but he didn't know where they were. They could be twenty kilometers away, for all he knew. So, after wandering through the tunnels for a little while, he went to the mess hall and ate breakfast near a few marines who were telling dirty jokes that Ender could not begin to understand. Then he went to the simulator room for practice. Even though he was free, he could not think of anything else to do.

Mazer was waiting for him. Ender walked slowly into the room. His step was slightly shuffling, and he felt tired and dull.

Mazer frowned. "Are you awake, Ender?"

There were other people in the simulator room. Ender wondered why they were there, but didn't bother to ask. It wasn't worth asking; no one would tell him anyway. He walked to the simulator controls and sat down, ready to start.

"Ender Wiggin," said Mazer. "Please turn around. Today's game needs a little explanation."

Ender turned around. He glanced at the men gathered at the back of the room. Most of them he had never seen before. Some were even dressed in civilian clothes. He saw Anderson and wondered what he was doing there, who was taking care of the Battle School if he was gone. He saw Graff and remembered the lake in the woods outside Greensboro, and wanted to go home. Take me home, he said silently to Graff. In my dream you said you loved me. Take me home.

But Graff only nodded to him, a greeting, not a promise, and Anderson acted as though he didn't know him at all.

"Pay attention, please, Ender. Today is your final examination in Command School. These observers are here to evaluate what you have learned. If you prefer not to have them in the room, we'll have them watch on another simulator."

"They can stay." Final examination. After today, perhaps he could rest.

"For this to be a fair test of your ability, not just to do what you have practiced many times, but also to meet challenges you have never seen before, today's battle introduces a new element. It is staged around a planet. This will affect the enemy's strategy, and will force you to improvise. Please concentrate on the game today."

Ender beckoned Mazer closer, and asked him quietly, "Am I the first student to make it this far?"

"If you win today, Ender, you will be the first student to do so. More than that I'm not at liberty to say."

"Well, I'm at liberty to hear it."

"You can be as petulant as you want, tomorrow. Today, though, I'd appreciate it if you would keep your mind on the examination. Let's not waste all that you've already done. Now, how will you deal with the planet?"

"I have to get someone behind it, or it's a blind spot."

"True."

"And the gravity is going to affect fuel levels—cheaper to go down than up."

"Yes."

"Does the Little Doctor work against a planet?"

Mazer's face went rigid. "Ender, the buggers never deliberately attacked a civilian population in either invasion. You decide whether it would be wise to adopt a strategy that would invite reprisals."

"Is the planet the only new thing?"

"Can you remember the last time I've given you a battle with only one new thing? Let me assure you, Ender, that I will not be kind to you today. I have a responsibility to the fleet not to let a second-rate student graduate. I will do my best against you, Ender, and I have no desire to coddle you. Just keep in mind everything you know about yourself and everything you know about the buggers, and you have a fair chance of amounting to something."

Mazer left the room.

Ender spoke into the microphone. "Are you there?"

"All of us," said Bean. "Kind of late for practice this morning, aren't you?"

So they hadn't told the squadron leaders. Ender toyed with the idea of telling them how important this battle was to him, but decided it would not help them to have an extraneous concern on their minds. "Sorry," he said. "I overslept."

They laughed. They didn't believe him.

He led them through maneuvers, warming up for the battle ahead. It took him longer than usual to clear his mind, to concentrate on command, but soon enough he was up to speed, responding quickly, thinking well. Or at least, he told himself, I think that I'm thinking well.

The simulator field cleared. Ender waited for the game to appear. What will happen if I pass the test today? Is there another school? Another year or two of grueling training, another year of isolation, another year of people pushing me this way and that way, another year without any control over my own life? He tried to remember how old he was. Eleven. How many years ago did he turn eleven? How many days? It must have happened here at the Command School, but he couldn't remember the day. Maybe he didn't even notice it at the time. Nobody noticed it, except perhaps Valentine.

And as he waited for the game to appear, he wished he could simply lose it, lose the battle badly and completely so that they would remove him from training, like Bonzo, and let him go home. Bonzo had been assigned to Cartagena. He wanted to see travel orders that said Greensboro. Success meant it would go on. Failure meant he could go home.

No, that isn't true, he told himself. They need me, and if I fail, there might not be any home to return to.

But he did not believe it. In his conscious mind he knew it was true, but in other places, deeper places, he doubted that they needed him. Mazer's urgency was just another trick. Just another way to make me do what they want me to do. Another way to keep me from resting. From doing nothing, for a long, long time.

Then the enemy formation appeared, and Ender's weariness turned to despair.

The enemy outnumbered him a thousand to one; the simulator glowed green with them. They were grouped in a dozen different formations, shifting positions, changing shapes, moving in seemingly random patterns through the simulator field. He could not find a path through them—a space that seemed open would close suddenly, and another appear, and a formation that seemed penetrable would suddenly change and be forbidding. The planet was at the far edge of the field, and for all Ender knew there were just as many enemy ships beyond it, out of the simulator's range.

As for his own fleet, it consisted of twenty starships, each with only four fighters. He knew the four-fighter starships—they were old-fashioned, sluggish, and the range of their Little Doctors was half that of the newer ones. Eighty fighters, against at least five thousand, perhaps ten thousand enemy ships.

He heard his squadron leaders breathing heavily; he could also hear, from the observers behind him, a quiet curse. It was nice to know that one of the adults noticed that it wasn't a fair test. Not that it made any difference. Fairness wasn't part of the game, that was plain. There was no attempt to give him even a remote chance at success. All that I've been through, and they never meant to let me pass at all.

He saw in his mind Bonzo and his vicious little knot of

friends, confronting him, threatening him; he had been able to shame Bonzo into fighting him alone. That would hardly work here. And he could not surprise the enemy with his ability as he had done with the older boys in the battleroom. Mazer knew Ender's abilities inside and out.

The observers behind him began to cough, to move nervously. They were beginning to realize that Ender didn't know what to do.

I don't care anymore, thought Ender. You can keep your game. If you won't even give me a chance, why should I play?

Like his last game in Battle School, when they put two armies against him.

And just as he remembered that game, apparently Bean remembered it, too, for his voice came over the headset, saying, "Remember, the enemy's gate is *down*."

Molo, Soup, Vlad, Dumper, and Crazy Tom all laughed. They remembered, too.

And Ender also laughed. It *was* funny. The adults taking all this so seriously, and the children playing along, playing along, believing it too until suddenly the adults went too far, tried too hard, and the children could see through their game. Forget it, Mazer. I don't care if I pass your test, I don't care if I follow your rules. If you can cheat, so can I. I won't let you beat me unfairly—I'll beat you unfairly first.

In that final battle in Battle School, he had won by ignoring the enemy, ignoring his own losses; he had moved against the enemy's gate.

And the enemy's gate was down.

If I break this rule, they'll never let me be a commander. It would be too dangerous. I'll never have to play a game again. And that is victory.

He whispered quickly into the microphone. His commanders took their parts of the fleet and grouped themselves into a thick projectile, a cylinder aimed at the nearest of the enemy formations. The enemy, far from trying to repel him, welcomed him in, so he could be thoroughly entrapped before they destroyed him. Mazer is at least taking into account the fact that by now they would have learned to respect me, thought Ender. And that does buy me time.

Ender dodged downward, north, east, and down again, not seeming to follow any plan, but always ending up a little closer to the enemy planet. Finally the enemy began to close in on him too tightly. Then, suddenly, Ender's formation burst. His fleet seemed to melt into chaos. The eighty fighters seemed to follow no plan at all, firing at enemy ships at random, working their way into hopeless individual paths among the bugger craft.

After a few minutes of battle, however, Ender whispered to his squadron leaders once more, and suddenly a dozen of the remaining fighters formed again into a formation. But now they were on the far side of one of the enemy's most formidable groups; they had, with terrible losses, passed through—and now they had covered more than half the distance to the enemy's planet.

The enemy sees now, thought Ender. Surely Mazer sees what I'm doing.

Or perhaps Mazer cannot believe that I would do it. Well, so much the better for me.

Ender's tiny fleet darted this way and that, sending two or three fighters out as if to attack, then bringing them back. The enemy closed in, drawing in ships and formations that had been widely scattered, bringing them in for the kill. The enemy was most concentrated beyond Ender, so he could not escape back into open space, closing him in. Excellent, thought Ender. Closer. Come closer.

Then he whispered a command and the ships dropped like rocks toward the planet's surface. They were starships and fighters, completely unequipped to handle the heat of passage through an atmosphere. But Ender never intended them to reach the atmosphere. Almost from the moment they began to drop, they were focusing their Little Doctors on one thing only. The planet itself.

One, two, four, seven of his fighters were blown away.

It was all a gamble now, whether any of his ships would survive long enough to get in range. It would not take long, once they could focus on the planet's surface. Just a moment with Dr. Device, that's all I want. It occurred to Ender that perhaps the computer wasn't even equipped to show what would happen to a planet if the Little Doctor attacked it. What will I do then, shout Bang, you're dead?

Ender took his hands off the controls and leaned in to watch what happened. The perspective was close to the enemy planet now, as the ship hurtled into its well of gravity. Surely it's in range now, thought Ender. It must be in range and the computer can't handle it.

Then the surface of the planet, which filled half the simulator field now, began to bubble; there was a gout of explosion, hurling debris out toward Ender's fighters. Ender tried to imagine what was happening inside the planet. The field growing and growing, the molecules bursting apart but finding nowhere for the separate atoms to go.

Within three seconds the entire planet burst apart, becoming a sphere of bright dust, hurtling outward. Ender's fighters were among the first to go; their perspective suddenly vanished, and now the simulator could only display the perspective of the starships waiting beyond the edges of the battle. It was as close as Ender wanted to be. The sphere of the exploding planet grew outward faster than the enemy ships could avoid it. And it carried with it the Little Doctor, not so little anymore, the field taking apart every ship in its path, erupting each one into a dot of light before it went on.

Only at the very periphery of the simulator did the M.D. field weaken. Two or three enemy ships were drifting away. Ender's own starships did not explode. But where the vast enemy fleet had been, and the planet they protected, there was nothing meaningful. A lump of dirt was growing as gravity drew much of the debris downward again. It was glowing hot and spinning visibly; it was also much smaller than the world had been before. Much of its mass was now a cloud still flowing outward.

Ender took off his headphones, filled with the cheers of his squadron leaders, and only then realized that there was just as much noise in the room with him. Men in uniform were hugging each other, laughing, shouting; others were weeping; some knelt or lay prostrate, and Ender knew they were caught up in prayer. Ender didn't understand. It seemed all wrong. They were supposed to be angry.

Colonel Graff detached himself from the others and came to Ender. Tears streamed down his face, but he was smiling. He bent over, reached out his arms, and to Ender's surprise he embraced him, held him tightly, and whispered, "Thank you, thank you, Ender. Thank God for you, Ender."

The others soon came, too, shaking his hand, congratulating him. He tried to make sense of this. Had he passed the test after all? It was *his* victory, not theirs, and a hollow one at that, a cheat; why did they act as if he had won with honor?

The crowd parted and Mazer Rackham walked through. He came straight to Ender and held out his hand.

"You made the hard choice, boy. All or nothing. End them or end us. But heaven knows there was no other way you could have done it. Congratulations. You beat them, and it's all over."

All over. Beat them. Ender didn't understand. "I beat *you*."

Mazer laughed, a loud laugh that filled the room. "Ender, you never played *me*. You never played a *game* since I became your enemy."

Ender didn't get the joke. He had played a great many games, at a terrible cost to himself. He began to get angry.

Mazer reached out and touched his shoulder. Ender shrugged him off. Mazer then grew serious and said, "Ender, for the past few months you have been the battle commander of our fleets. This was the Third Invasion. There were no games, the battles were real, and the only enemy you fought was the buggers. You won every battle, and today you finally fought them at their home world, where the queen was, all the queens from all their colonies, they all were there and you destroyed them completely. They'll never attack us again. You did it. You."

Real. Not a game. Ender's mind was too tired to cope with it all. They weren't just points of light in the air, they were real ships that he had fought with and real ships he had destroyed. And a real world that he had blasted into oblivion. He walked through the crowd, dodging their congratulations, ignoring their hands, their words, their rejoicing. When he got to his own room he stripped off his clothes, climbed into bed, and slept.

Ender awoke when they shook him. It took a moment to recognize them. Graff and Rackham. He turned his back on them. Let me sleep.

"Ender, we need to talk to you," said Graff.

Ender rolled back to face them.

"They've been playing out the videos on Earth all day, all night since the battle yesterday."

"Yesterday?" He had slept through until the next day.

"You're a hero, Ender. They've seen what you did, you and the others. I don't think there's a government on Earth that hasn't voted you their highest medal."

"I killed them all, didn't I?" Ender asked.

"All who?" asked Graff. "The buggers? That was the idea."

Mazer leaned in close. "That's what the war was for."

"All their queens. So I killed all their children, all of everything."

"*They* decided that when they attacked us. It wasn't your fault. It's what had to happen."

Ender grabbed Mazer's uniform and hung onto it, pulling him down so they were face to face. "I didn't want to kill them all. I didn't want to kill anybody! I'm not a killer! You didn't want me, you bastards, you wanted Peter, but you made me do it, you tricked me into it!" He was crying. He was out of control.

"Of course we tricked you into it. That's the whole point," said Graff. "It had to be a trick or you couldn't have done it. It's the bind we were in. We had to have a commander with so much empathy that he would think like the buggers, understand them and anticipate them. So much compassion that he could win the love of his underlings and work with them like a perfect machine, as perfect as the buggers. But somebody with that much compassion could never be the killer we needed. Could never go into battle willing to win at all costs. If you knew, you couldn't do it. If you were the kind of person who would do it even if you knew, you could never have understood the buggers well enough."

"And it had to be a child, Ender," said Mazer. "You were faster than me. Better than me. I was too old and cautious. Any decent person who knows what warfare is can never go into battle with a whole heart. But you didn't know. We made sure you didn't know. You were reckless and brilliant and young. It's what you were born for."

"We had pilots with our ships, didn't we."

"Yes."

"I was ordering pilots to go in and die and I didn't even know it."

"*They* knew it, Ender, and they went anyway. They knew what it was for."

"You never asked me! You never told me the truth about anything!"

"You had to be a weapon, Ender. Like a gun, like the Little Doctor, functioning perfectly but not knowing what you were aimed at. *We* aimed you. We're responsible. If there was something wrong, we did it."

"Tell me later," Ender said. His eyes closed.

Mazer Rackham shook him. "Don't go to sleep, Ender," he said. "It's very important."

"You're finished with me," Ender said. "Now leave me alone."

"That's why we're here," Mazer said. "We're trying to tell you. They're not through with you, not at all. It's crazy down there. They're going to start a war. Americans claiming the Warsaw Pact is about to attack, and the Russians are saying the same thing about the Hegemon. The bugger war isn't twenty-four hours dead and the world down there is back to fighting again, as bad as ever. And all of them are worried about you. All of them want you. The greatest military leader in history, they want you to lead their armies. The Americans. The Hegemon. Everybody but the Warsaw Pact, and they want you dead."

"Fine with me," said Ender.

"We have to take you away from here. There are Russian marines all over Eros, and the Polemarch is Russian. It could turn to bloodshed at any time."

Ender turned his back on them again. This time they let him. He did not sleep, though. He listened to them.

"I was afraid of this, Rackham. You pushed him too hard. Some of those lesser outposts could have waited until after. You could have given him some days to rest."

"Are you doing it, too, Graff? Trying to decide how I could have done it better? You don't know what would have happened if I hadn't pushed. Nobody knows. I did it the way I did it, and it worked. Above all, it worked. Memorize that defense, Graff. You may have to use it, too."

"Sorry."

"I can see what it's done to him. Colonel Liki says there's a good chance he'll be permanently damaged, but I don't believe it. He's too strong. Winning meant a lot to him, and he won."

"Don't tell me about strong. The kid's eleven. Give him some rest, Rackham. Things haven't exploded yet. We can post a guard outside his door."

"Or post a guard outside another door and pretend that it's his."

"Whatever."

They went away. Ender slept again.

—

Time passed without touching Ender, except with glancing blows. Once he awoke for a few minutes with something pressing his hand, pushing downward on it, with a dull, insistent pain. He reached over and touched it; it was a needle passing into a vein. He tried to pull it out, but it was taped on and he was too weak. Another time he awoke in darkness to hear people near him murmuring and cursing. His ears were ringing with the loud noise that had awakened him; he did not remember the noise. "Get the lights on," someone said. And another time he thought he heard someone crying softly near him.

It might have been a single day; it might have been a week; from his dreams, it could have been months. He seemed to pass through lifetimes in his dreams. Through the Giant's Drink again, past the wolf-children, reliving the terrible deaths, the constant murders; he heard a voice whispering in the forest, You had to kill the children to get to the End of the World. And he tried to answer, I never wanted to kill anybody. Nobody ever asked me if I wanted to kill anybody. But the forest laughed at him. And when he leapt from the cliff at the End of the World, sometimes it was not clouds that caught him, but a fighter that carried him to a vantage point near the surface of the buggers' world, so he could watch, over and over, the eruption of death when Dr. Device set off a reaction on the planet's face; then closer and closer, until he could watch individual buggers explode, turn to light, then collapse into a pile of dirt before his eyes. And the queen, surrounded by infants; only the queen was Mother, and the infants were Valentine and all the children he had known in Battle School. One of them had Bonzo's face, and he lay there bleeding through the eyes and nose, saying, You have no honor. And always the dream ended with a mirror or a pool of water or the metal surface of a ship, something that would reflect his face back to him. At first it was always Peter's face, with blood and a snake's tail coming from the mouth. After a while, though, it began to be his own face, old and sad, with eyes that grieved for a billion, billion murders—but they were his own eyes, and he was content to wear them.

That was the world Ender lived in for many lifetimes during the five days of the League War.

When he awoke again he was lying in darkness. In the distance he could hear the thump, thump of explosions. He listened for a while. Then he heard a soft footstep.

He turned over and flung out a hand, to grasp whoever was sneaking up on him. Sure enough, he caught someone's clothing and pulled him down toward his knees, ready to kill him if need be.

"Ender, it's me, it's me!"

He knew the voice. It came out of his memory as if it were a million years ago.

"Alai."

"Salaam, pinprick. What were you trying to do, kill me?"

"Yes. I thought you were trying to kill *me*."

"I was trying not to wake you up. Well, at least you have some survival instinct left. The way Mazer talks about it, you were becoming a vegetable."

"I was trying to. What's the thumping?"

"There's a war going on here. Our section is blacked out to keep us safe."

Ender swung his legs out to sit up. He couldn't do it, though. His head hurt too bad. He winced in pain.

"Don't sit up, Ender. It's all right. It looks like we might win it. Not all the Warsaw Pact people went with the Polemarch. A lot of them came over when the Strategos told them you were loyal to the I.F."

"I was asleep."

"So he lied. You weren't plotting treason in your dreams, were you? Some of the Russians who came in told us that when the Polemarch ordered them to find you and kill you, they almost killed *him*. Whatever they may feel about other people, Ender, they love you. The whole world watched our battles. Videos, day and night. I've seen some. Complete with your voice giving the orders. It's all there, nothing censored. Good stuff. You've got a career in the vids."

"I don't think so," said Ender.

"I was joking. Hey, can you believe it? We won the war. We were so eager to grow up so we could fight in it, and it was us all the time. I mean, we're kids, Ender. And it was us." Alai laughed. "It was you, anyway. You were good, bosh. I didn't know how you'd get us out of that last one. But you did. You were good."

Ender noticed the way he spoke in the past. I *was* good. "What am I *now*, Alai?"

"Still good."

"At what?"

"At—anything. There's a million soldiers who'd follow you to the end of the universe."

"I don't want to go to the end of the universe."

"So where do you want to go? They'll follow you."

I want to go home, thought Ender, but I don't know where it is.

The thumping went silent.

"Listen to that," said Alai.

They listened. The door opened. Someone stood there. Someone small. "It's over," he said. It was Bean. As if to prove it, the lights went on.

"Ho, Bean," Ender said.

"Ho, Ender."

Petra followed him in, with Dink holding her hand. They came to Ender's bed. "Hey, the hero's awake," said Dink.

"Who won?" asked Ender.

"We did, Ender," said Bean. "You were there."

"He's not *that* crazy, Bean. He meant who won just now." Petra took Ender's hand. "There was a truce on

Earth. They've been negotiating for days. They finally agreed to accept the Locke Proposal."

"He doesn't know about the Locke Proposal—"

"It's very complicated, but what it means here is that the I.F. will stay in existence, but without the Warsaw Pact in it. So the Warsaw Pact marines are going home. I think Russia agreed to it because they're facing a revolt of the Islamic States. Everybody's got troubles. About five hundred died here, but it was worse on Earth."

"The Hegemon resigned," said Dink. "It's crazy down there. Who cares."

"You OK?" Petra asked him, touching his head. "You scared us. They said you were crazy, and we said *they* were crazy."

"I'm crazy," said Ender. "But I think I'm OK."

"When did you decide that?" asked Alai.

"When I thought you were about to kill me, and I decided to kill you first. I guess I'm just a killer to the core. But I'd rather be alive than dead."

They laughed and agreed with him. Then Ender began to cry and embraced Bean and Petra, who were closest. "I missed you," he said. "I wanted to see you so bad."

"You saw us pretty bad," Petra answered. She kissed his cheek.

"I saw you magnificent," said Ender. "The ones I needed most, I used up soonest. Bad planning on my part."

"Everybody's OK now," said Dink. "Nothing was wrong with any of us that five days of cowering in blacked-out rooms in the middle of a war couldn't cure."

"I don't have to be your commander anymore, do I?" asked Ender. "I don't want to command anybody again."

"You don't have to command anybody," said Dink, "but you're always our commander."

Then they were silent for a while.

"So what do we do now?" asked Alai. "The bugger war's over, and so's the war down there on Earth, and even the war here. What do we do now?"

"We're kids," said Petra. "They'll probably make us go to school. It's a law. You have to go to school till you're seventeen."

They all laughed at that. Laughed until tears streamed down their faces.

15

Speaker for the Dead

The lake was still; there was no breeze. The two men sat together in chairs on the floating dock. A small wooden raft was tied up at the dock; Graff hooked his foot in the rope and pulled the raft in, then let it drift out, then pulled it in again.

"You've lost weight."

"One kind of stress puts it on, another takes it off. I am a creature of chemicals."

"It must have been hard."

Graff shrugged. "Not really. I knew I'd be acquitted."

"Some of us weren't so sure. People were crazy for a while there. Mistreatment of children, negligent homicide—those videos of Bonzo's and Stilson's deaths were pretty gruesome. To watch one child do that to another."

"As much as anything, I think the videos saved me. The prosecution edited them, but we showed the whole thing. It was plain that Ender was not the provocateur. After that, it was just a second-guessing game. I said I did what I believed was necessary for the preservation of the human race, and it worked; we got the judges to agree that the prosecution had to prove beyond doubt that Ender would have won the war *without* the training we gave him. After that, it was simple. The exigencies of war."

"Anyway, Graff, it was a great relief to us. I know we quarreled, and I know the prosecution used tapes of our conversations against you. But by then I knew that you were right, and I offered to testify for you."

"I know, Anderson. My lawyers told me."

"So what will you do now?"

"I don't know. I'm still relaxing. I have a few years of leave accrued. Enough to take me to retirement, and I have plenty of salary that I never used, sitting around in banks. I could live on the interest. Maybe I'll do nothing."

"It sounds nice. But I couldn't stand it. I've been offered the presidency of three different universities, on the theory that I'm an educator. They don't believe me when I say that all I ever cared about at the Battle School was the game. I think I'll go with the other offer."

"Commissioner?"

"Now that the wars are over, it's time to play games again. It'll be almost like vacation, anyway. Only twenty-eight teams in the league. Though after years of watching those children flying, football is like watching slugs bash into each other."

They laughed. Graff sighed and pushed the raft with his foot.

"That raft. Surely you can't float on it."

Graff shook his head. "Ender built it."

"That's right. This is where you took him."

"It's even been deeded over to him. I saw to it that he was amply rewarded. He'll have all the money he ever needs."

"If they ever let him come back to use it."

"They never will."

"With Demosthenes agitating for him to come home?"

"Demosthenes isn't on the nets anymore."

Anderson raised an eyebrow. "What does *that* mean?"

"Demosthenes has retired. Permanently."

"You know something, you old farteater. You know who Demosthenes is."

"Was."

"Well, tell me!"

"No."

"You're no fun anymore, Graff."

"I never was."

"At least you can tell me *why*. There were a lot of us who thought Demosthenes would be Hegemon someday."

"There was never a chance of that. No, even Demosthenes' mob of political cretins couldn't persuade the Hegemon to bring Ender back to Earth. Ender is far too dangerous."

"He's only eleven. Twelve, now."

"All the more dangerous because he could so easily be controlled. In all the world, the name of Ender is one to conjure with. The child-god, the miracle worker, with life and death in his hands. Every petty tyrant-to-be would like to have the boy, to set him in front of an army and watch the world either flock to join or cower in fear. If Ender came to Earth, he'd want to come here, to rest, to salvage what he can of his childhood. But they'd never let him rest."

"I see. Someone explained that to Demosthenes?"

Graff smiled. "Demosthenes explained it to someone else. Someone who could have used Ender as no one else could have, to rule the world and make the world like it."

"Who?"

"Locke."

"Locke is the one who argued for Ender to stay on Eros."

"All is not always as it seems."

"It's too deep for me, Graff. Give me the game. Nice, neat rules. Referees. Beginnings and endings. Winners and losers and then everybody goes home to their families."

"Get me tickets to some games now and then, all right?"

"You won't really stay here and retire, will you?"

"No."

"You're going into the Hegemony, aren't you?"

"I'm the new Minister of Colonization."

"So they're doing it."

"As soon as we get the reports back on the bugger colony worlds. I mean, there they are, already fertile, with housing and industry in place, and all the buggers dead. Very convenient. We'll repeal the population limitation laws—"

"Which everybody hates—"

"And all those thirds and fourths and fifths will get on starships and head out for worlds known and unknown."

"Will people really go?"

"People always go. Always. They always believe they can make a better life than in the old world."

"What the hell, maybe they can."

At first Ender believed that they would bring him back to Earth as soon as things quieted down. But things were quiet now, had been quiet for a year, and it was plain to him now that they would not bring him back at all, that he was much more useful as a name and a story than he would ever be as an inconvenient flesh-and-blood person.

And there was the matter of the court martial on the crimes of Colonel Graff. Admiral Chamrajnagar tried to keep Ender from watching it, but failed; Ender had been awarded the rank of admiral, too, and this was one of the few times he asserted the privileges the rank implied. So he watched the videos of the fights with Stilson and Bonzo, watched as the photographs of the corpses were displayed, listened as the psychologists and lawyers argued whether murder had been committed or the killing was in self-defense. Ender had his own opinion, but no one asked him. Throughout the trial, it was really Ender himself under attack. The prosecution was too clever to charge him directly, but there were attempts to make him look sick, perverted, criminally insane.

"Never mind," said Mazer Rackham. "The politicians are afraid of you, but they can't destroy your reputation yet. That won't be done until the historians get at you in thirty years."

Ender didn't care about his reputation. He watched the videos impassively, but in fact he was amused. In battle I killed ten billion buggers, whose queens, at least, were as alive and wise as any man, who had not even launched a third attack against us, and no one thinks to call it a crime.

All his crimes weighed heavy on him, the deaths of Stilson and Bonzo no heavier and no lighter than the rest.

And so, with that burden, he waited through the empty months until the world that he had saved decided he could come home.

One by one, his friends reluctantly left him, called home to their families, to be received with heroes' welcomes in hometowns they barely remembered. Ender watched the videos of their homecomings, and was touched when they spent much of their time praising Ender Wiggin, who taught them everything, they said, who taught them and led them into victory. But if they called for him to be brought home, the words were censored from the videos and no one heard the plea.

For a time, the only work in Eros was cleaning up after the bloody League War and receiving the reports of the starships, once warships, that were now exploring the bugger colony worlds.

But now Eros was busier than ever, more crowded than it had ever been during the war, as colonists were brought here to prepare for their voyages to the empty bugger worlds. Ender took part in the work, as much as they would let him; it did not occur to them that this twelve-year-old boy might be as gifted at peace as he was at war. But he was patient with their tendency to ignore him, and learned to make his proposals and suggest his plans through the few adults who listened to him, and let them present them as their own. He was concerned, not about getting credit, but about getting the job done.

The one thing he could not bear was the worship of the colonists. He learned to avoid the tunnels where they lived, because they would always recognize him—the world had memorized his face—and then they would scream and shout and embrace him and congratulate him and show him the children they had named after him and tell him how he was so young it broke their hearts and *they* didn't blame him for any of his murders because it wasn't his fault he was just a *child*—

He hid from them as best he could.

There was one colonist, though, he couldn't hide from.

He wasn't inside Eros that day. He had gone up with the shuttle to the new ISL, where he had been learning to do surface work on the starships; it was unbecoming to an officer to do mechanical labor, Chamrajnagar told him, but Ender answered that since the trade he had mastered wasn't much called for now, it was about time he learned another skill.

They spoke to him through his helmet radio and told him that someone was waiting to see him as soon as he could come in. Ender couldn't think of anyone he wanted to see, and so he didn't hurry. He finished installing the shield for the ship's ansible and then hooked his way across the face of the ship and pulled himself up into the airlock.

She was waiting for him outside the changing room. For a moment he was annoyed that they would let a colonist come to bother him here, where he came to be alone; then he looked again, and realized that if the young woman were a little girl, he would know her.

"Valentine," he said.

"Hi, Ender."

"What are you doing here?"

"Demosthenes retired. Now I'm going with the first colony."

"It's fifty years to get there—"

"Only two years if you're aboard the ship."

"But if you ever came back, everybody you knew on Earth would be dead—"

"That was what I had in mind. I was hoping, though, that someone I knew on Eros might come with me."

"I don't want to go to a world we stole from the buggers. I just want to go home."

"Ender, you're never going back to Earth. I saw to that before I left."

He looked at her in silence.

"I tell you that now, so that if you want to hate me, you can hate me from the beginning."

They went to Ender's tiny compartment in the ISL and she explained. Peter wanted Ender back on Earth, under the protection of the Hegemon's Council. "The way things are right now, Ender, that would put you effectively under Peter's control, since half the council now does just what Peter wants. The ones that aren't Locke's lapdogs are under his thumb in other ways."

"Do they know who he really is?"

"Yes. He isn't publicly known, but people in high places know him. It doesn't matter any more. He has too much power for them to worry about his age. He's done incredible things, Ender."

"I noticed the treaty a year ago was named for Locke."

"That was his breakthrough. He proposed it through his friends from the public policy nets, and then Demosthenes got behind it, too. It was the moment he had been waiting for, to use Demosthenes' influence with the mob and Locke's influence with the intelligentsia to accomplish something noteworthy. It forestalled a really vicious war that could have lasted for decades."

"He decided to be a statesman?"

"I think so. But in his cynical moments, of which there are many, he pointed out to me that if he had allowed the

League to fall apart completely, he'd have had to conquer the world piece by piece. As long as the Hegemony existed, he could do it in one lump."

Ender nodded. "That's the Peter that I knew."

"Funny, isn't it? That Peter would save millions of lives."

"While I killed billions."

"I wasn't going to say that."

"So he wanted to use me?"

"He had plans for you, Ender. He would publicly reveal himself when you arrived, going to meet you in front of all the videos. Ender Wiggin's older brother, who also happened to be the great Locke, the architect of peace. Standing next to you, he would look quite mature. And the physical resemblance between you is stronger than ever. It would be quite simple for him, then, to take over."

"Why did you stop him?"

"Ender, you wouldn't be happy spending the rest of your life as Peter's pawn."

"Why not? I've spent my life as someone's pawn."

"Me too. I showed Peter all the evidence that I had assembled, enough to prove in the eyes of the public that he was a psychotic killer. It included full-color pictures of tortured squirrels and some of the monitor videos of the way he treated you. It took some work to get it all together, but by the time he saw it, he was willing to give me what I wanted. What I wanted was your freedom and mine."

"It's not my idea of freedom to go live in the house of the people that I killed."

"Ender, what's done is done. Their worlds are empty now, and ours is full. And we can take with us what their worlds have never known—cities full of people who live private, individual lives, who love and hate each other for their own reasons. In all the bugger worlds, there was never more than a single story to be told; when we're there, the world will be full of stories, and we'll improvise their endings day by day. Ender, Earth belongs to Peter. And if you don't go with me now, he'll have you there, and use you up until you wish you'd never been born. Now is the only chance you'll get to get away."

Ender said nothing.

"I know what you're thinking, Ender. You're thinking that I'm trying to control you just as much as Peter or Graff or any of the others."

"It crossed my mind."

"Welcome to the human race. Nobody controls his own life, Ender. The best you can do is choose to fill the roles given you by good people, by people who love you. I didn't come here because I wanted to be a colonist. I came because I've spent my whole life in the company of the brother that I hated. Now I want a chance to know the brother that I love, before it's too late, before we're not children anymore."

"It's already too late for that."

"You're wrong, Ender. You think you're grown up and tired and jaded with everything, but in your heart you're just as much a kid as I am. We can keep it secret from everybody else. While you're governing the colony and I'm writing political philosophy, they'll never guess that in the darkness of night we sneak into each other's room and play checkers and have pillowfights."

Ender laughed, but he had noticed some things she dropped too casually for them to be accidental. "Governing?"

"I'm Demosthenes, Ender. I went out with a bang. A public announcement that I believed so much in the colonization movement that I was going in the first ship myself. At the same time, the Minister of Colonization, a former colonel named Graff, announced that the pilot of the colony ship would be the great Mazer Rackham, and the governor of the first colony it established would be Ender Wiggin."

"They might have asked *me*."

"I wanted to ask you myself."

"But it's already announced."

"No. They'll be announcing it tomorrow, if you accept. Mazer accepted a few hours ago, back in Eros."

"You're telling everyone that you're Demosthenes? A fourteen-year-old girl?"

"We're only telling them that Demosthenes is going with the colony. Let them spend the next fifty years poring over the passenger list, trying to figure out which one of them is the great demagogue of the Age of Locke."

Ender laughed and shook his head. "You're actually having fun, Val."

"I can't think why I shouldn't."

"All right," said Ender. "I'll go. Maybe even as governor, as long as you and Mazer are there to help me. My abilities are a little underused at present."

She squealed and hugged him, for all the world like a typical teenage girl who just got the present that she wanted from her little brother.

"Val," he said. "I just want one thing clear. I'm not going for you. I'm not going in order to be governor, or because I'm bored here. I'm going because I know the buggers better than any other living soul, and maybe if I go there I can understand them better. I stole their future from them; I can only begin to repay by seeing what I can learn from their past."

—

The voyage was long. By the end of it, Val had finished the first volume of her history of the bugger wars and transmitted it by ansible, under Demosthenes' name, back to Earth, and Ender had won something better than the adulation of the passengers. They knew him now, and he had won their love and their respect.

He worked hard on the new world. He quickly understood the differences between military and civilian leadership, and governed by persuasion rather than fiat, and by working as hard as anyone at the tasks involved in setting up a self-sustaining economy. But his most important work, as everyone agreed, was exploring what the buggers had left behind, trying to find among structures, machinery, and fields long untended some things that human beings could use, could learn from. There were no books to read—the buggers never needed them. With all things present in their memories, all things spoken as they were thought, when the buggers died their knowledge died with them.

And yet. From the sturdiness of the roofs that covered their animal sheds and their food supplies, Ender learned that winter would be hard, with heavy snows. From fences with sharpened stakes that pointed outward he learned that there were marauding animals that were a danger to the crops or the herds. From the mill he learned that the long, foul-tasting fruits that grew in the overgrown orchards were dried and ground into meal. And from the slings that once were used to carry infants along with adults into the fields, he learned that even though the buggers were not much for individuality, they did care for their young.

Life settled down, and years passed. The colony lived in wooden houses and used the tunnels of the bugger city for storage and manufactories. They were governed by a council now, and administrators were elected, so that Ender, though they still called him governor, was in fact only a judge. There were crimes and quarrels, alongside kindness and cooperation; there were people who loved each other and people who did not; it was a human world. They did not wait so eagerly for each new transmission from the ansible; the names that were famous on Earth meant little to them now. The only name they knew was that of Peter Wiggin, the Hegemon of Earth; the only news that came was news of peace, of prosperity, of great ships leaving the littoral of Earth's solar system, passing the comet shield and filling up the bugger worlds. Soon there would be other colonies on this world, Ender's World; soon there would be neighbors; already they were halfway here; but no one cared. They would help the newcomers when they came, teach them what they had learned, but what mattered in life now was who would marry whom, and who was sick, and when was planting time, and why should I pay him when the calf died three weeks after I got it.

"They've become people of the land," said Valentine. "No one cares now that Demosthenes is sending the seventh volume of his history today. No one here will read it."

Ender pressed a button and his desk showed him the next page. "Very insightful, Valentine. How many more volumes until you're through?"

"Just one. The story of Ender Wiggin."

"What will you do, wait to write it until I'm dead?"

"No. Just write it, and when I've brought it up to the present day, I'll stop."

"I have a better idea. Take it up to the day we won the final battle. Stop it there. Nothing that I've done since then is worth writing down."

"Maybe," said Valentine. "And maybe not."

—

The ansible had brought them word that the new colony ship was only a year away. They asked Ender to find a place for them to settle in, near enough to Ender's colony that the two colonies could trade, but far enough apart that they could be governed separately. Ender used the helicopter and began to explore. He took one of the children along, an eleven-year-old boy named Abra; he had been only three when the colony was founded, and he remembered no other world than this. He and Ender flew as far away as Ender thought the new colony should be, then camped for the night and got a feel for the land on foot the next morning.

It was on the third morning that Ender suddenly began to feel an uneasy sense that he had been in this place before. He looked around; it was new land, he had never seen it. He called out to Abra.

"Ho, Ender!" Abra called. He was on top of a steep low hill. "Come up!"

Ender scrambled up, the turves coming away from his feet in the soft ground. Abra was pointing downward. "Can you believe this?" he asked.

The hill was hollow. A deep depression in the middle, partially filled with water, was ringed by concave slopes that cantilevered dangerously over the water. In one direction the hill gave way to two long ridges that made a V-shaped valley; in the other direction the hill rose to a piece of white rock, grinning like a skull with a tree growing out of its mouth.

"It's like a giant died here," said Abra, "and the Earth grew up to cover his carcass."

Now Ender knew why it had looked familiar. The Giant's corpse. He had played here too many times as a child not to know this place. But it was not possible. The computer in the Battle School could not possibly have seen this place. He looked through his binoculars in a direction he knew well, fearing and hoping that he would see what belonged in that place.

Swings and slides. Monkey bars. Now overgrown, but the shapes still unmistakable.

"Somebody had to have built this," Abra said. "Look, this skull place, it's not rock, look at it. This is concrete."

"I know," said Ender. "They built it for me."

"What?"

"I know this place, Abra. The buggers built it for me."

"The buggers were all dead fifty years before we got here."

"You're right, it's impossible, but I know what I know. Abra, I shouldn't take you with me. It might be dangerous. If they knew me well enough to build this place, they might be planning to—"

"To get even with you."

"For killing them."

"So don't go, Ender. Don't do what they want you to do."

"If they want to get revenge, Abra, I don't mind. But

perhaps they don't. Perhaps this is the closest they could come to talking. To writing me a note."

"They didn't know how to read and write."

"Maybe they were learning when they died."

"Well, I'm sure as hell not sticking around here if you're taking off somewhere. I'm going with you."

"No. You're too young to take the risk of—"

"Come on! You're Ender *Wiggin*. Don't tell me what eleven-year-old kids can do!"

Together they flew in the copter, over the playground, over the woods, over the well in the forest clearing. Then out to where there was, indeed, a cliff, with a cave in the cliff wall and a ledge right where the End of the World should be. And there in the distance, just where it should be in the fantasy game, was the castle tower.

He left Abra with the copter. "Don't come after me, and go home in an hour if I don't come back."

"Eat it, Ender, I'm coming with you."

"Eat it yourself, Abra, or I'll stuff you with mud."

Abra could tell, despite Ender's joking tone, that he meant it, and so he stayed.

The walls of the tower were notched and ledged for easy climbing. They meant him to get in.

The room was as it had always been. Ender remembered well enough to look for a snake on the floor, but there was only a rug with a carved snake's head at one corner. Imitation, not duplication; for a people who made no art, they had done well. They must have dragged these images from Ender's own mind, finding him and learning his darkest dreams across the lightyears. But why? To bring him to this room, of course. To leave a message for him. But where was the message, and how would he understand it?

The mirror was waiting for him on the wall. It was a dull sheet of metal, in which the rough shape of a human face had been scratched. They tried to draw the image I should see in the picture.

And looking at the mirror he could remember breaking

it, pulling it from the wall, and snakes leaping out of the hidden place, attacking him, biting him wherever their poisonous fangs could find purchase.

How well do they know me, wondered Ender. Well enough to know how often I have thought of death, to know that I am not afraid of it. Well enough to know that even if I feared death, it would not stop me from taking that mirror from the wall.

He walked to the mirror, lifted, pulled away. Nothing jumped from the space behind it. Instead, in a hollowed-out place, there was a white ball of silk with a few frayed strands sticking out here and there. An egg? No. The pupa of a queen bugger, already fertilized by the larval males, ready, out of her own body, to hatch a hundred thousand buggers, including a few queens and males. Ender could see in his mind the slug-like males clinging to the walls of a dark tunnel, and the large adults carrying the infant queen to the mating room; each male in turn penetrated the larval queen, shuddered in ecstasy, and died, dropping to the tunnel floor and shriveling. Then the new queen was laid before the old, a magnificent creature clad in soft and shimmering wings, which had long since lost the power of flight but still contained the power of majesty. The old queen kissed her to sleep with the gentle poison in her lips, then wrapped her in threads from her belly, and commanded her to become herself, to become a new city, a new world, to give birth to many queens and many worlds—

How do I know this, thought Ender. How can I see these things, like memories in my own mind.

As if in answer, he saw the first of all his battles with the bugger fleets. He had seen it before on the simulator; now he saw it as the hive-queen saw it, through many different eyes. The buggers formed their globe of ships, and then the terrible fighters came out of the darkness and the Little Doctor destroyed them in a blaze of light. He felt then what the hive-queen felt, watching through her workers' eyes as death came to them too quickly to avoid, but not too quickly to be anticipated. There was no memory of pain or fear, though. What the hive-queen felt was sadness, a sense of resignation. She had not thought these words as she saw the humans coming to kill, but it was in words that Ender understood her: The humans did not forgive us, she thought. We will surely die.

"How can you live again?" he asked.

The queen in her silken cocoon had no words to give back; but when he closed his eyes and tried to remember, instead of memory came new images. Putting the cocoon in a cool place, a dark place, but with water, so she wasn't dry, so that certain reactions could take place in the cocoon. Then time. Days and weeks, for the pupa inside to change. And then, when the cocoon had changed to a dusty brown color, Ender saw himself splitting open the cocoon, and helping the small and fragile queen emerge. He saw himself taking her by the forelimb and helping her walk from her birthwater to a nesting place, soft with dried leaves on sand. Then I am alive, came the thought in his mind. Then I am awake. Then I make my ten thousand children.

"No," said Ender. "I can't."

Anguish.

"Your children are the monsters of our nightmares now. If I awoke you, we would only kill you again."

There flashed through his mind a dozen images of human beings being killed by buggers, but with the image came a grief so powerful he could not bear it, and he wept their tears for them.

"If you could make them feel as you can make me feel, then perhaps they could forgive you."

Only me, he realized. They found me through the ansible, followed it and dwelt in my mind. In the agony of my tortured dreams they came to know me, even as I spent my days destroying them; they found my fear of them, and found also that I had no knowledge I was killing them. In the few weeks they had, they built this place for me, and the Giant's corpse and the playground and the ledge at the End of the World, so I would find this place by the evidence of my eyes. I am the only one they know, and so they can only talk to me, and through me. We are like you; the thought pressed into his mind. We did not mean to murder, and when we understood, we never came again. We thought we were the only thinking beings in the universe, until we met you, but never did we dream that thought could arise from the lonely animals who cannot dream each other's dreams. How were we to know? We could live with you in peace. Believe us, believe us, believe us.

He reached into the cavity and took out the cocoon. It was astonishingly light, to hold all the hope and future of a great race within it.

"I'll carry you," said Ender, "I'll go from world to world until I find a time and a place where you can come awake in safety. And I'll tell your story to my people, so that perhaps in time they can forgive you, too. The way that you've forgiven me."

He wrapped the queen's cocoon in his jacket and carried her from the tower.

"What was in there?" asked Abra.

"The answer," said Ender.

"To what?"

"My question." And that was all he said of the matter; they searched for five more days and chose a site for the colony far to the east and south of the tower.

Weeks later he came to Valentine and told her to read something he had written; she pulled the file he named from the ship's computer, and read it.

It was written as if the hive-queen spoke, telling all that they had meant to do, and all that they had done. Here are our failures, and here is our greatness; we did not mean to hurt you, and we forgive you for our death. From their earliest awareness to the great wars that swept across their home world, Ender told the story quickly, as if it were an ancient memory. When he came to the tale of the great mother, the queen of all, who first learned to keep and teach the new queen instead of killing her or driving her away, then he lingered, telling how many times she had finally to destroy the child of her body, the new self that was not herself, until she bore one who understood her quest for harmony. This was a new thing in the world, two queens that loved and helped each other instead of battling, and together they were stronger than any other hive. They prospered; they had more daughters who joined them in peace; it was the beginning of wisdom.

If only we could have talked to you, the hive-queen said in Ender's words. But since it could not be, we ask only this: that you remember us, not as enemies, but as tragic sisters, changed into a foul shape by fate or God or evolution. If we had kissed, it would have been the miracle to make us human in each other's eyes. Instead we killed each other. But still we welcome you now as guestfriends. Come into our home, daughters of Earth; dwell in our tunnels, harvest our fields; what we cannot do, you are now our hands to do for us. Blossom, trees; ripen, fields; be warm for them, suns; be fertile for them, planets: they are our adopted daughters, and they have come home.

The book that Ender wrote was not long, but in it was all the good and all the evil that the hive-queen knew. And he signed it, not with his name, but with a title:

SPEAKER FOR THE DEAD

On Earth, the book was published quietly, and quietly it was passed from hand to hand, until it was hard to believe that anyone on Earth might not have read it. Most who read it found it interesting; some who read it refused to set it aside. They began to live by it as best they could, and when their loved ones died, a believer would arise beside the grave to be the Speaker for the Dead, and say what the dead one would have said, but with full candor, hiding no faults and pretending no virtues. Those who came to such services sometimes found them painful and disturbing, but there were many who decided that their life was worthwhile enough, despite their errors, that when they died a Speaker should tell the truth for them.

On Earth it remained a religion among many religions. But for those who traveled the great cave of space and lived their lives in the hive-queen's tunnels and harvested the hive-queen's fields, it was the only religion. There was no colony without its Speaker for the Dead.

No one knew and no one really wanted to know who was the original Speaker. Ender was not inclined to tell them.

When Valentine was twenty-five years old, she finished the last volume of her history of the bugger wars. She included at the end the complete text of Ender's little book, but did not say that Ender wrote it.

By ansible she got an answer from the ancient Hegemon, Peter Wiggin, seventy-seven years old with a failing heart.

"I know who wrote it," he said. "If he can speak for the buggers, surely he can speak for me."

Back and forth across the ansible Ender and Peter spoke, with Peter pouring out the story of his days and years, his crimes and his kindnesses. And when he died, Ender wrote a second volume, again signed by the Speaker for the Dead. Together, his two books were called the Hive-Queen and the Hegemon, and they were holy writ.

"Come on," he said to Valentine one day. "Let's fly away and live forever."

"We can't," she said. "There are miracles even relativity can't pull off, Ender."

"We have to go. I'm almost happy here."

"So stay."

"I've lived too long with pain. I won't know who I am without it."

So they boarded a starship and went from world to world. Wherever they stopped, he was always Andrew Wiggin, itinerant speaker for the dead, and she was always Valentine, historian errant, writing down the stories of the living while Ender spoke the stories of the dead. And always Ender carried with him a dry white cocoon, looking for the world where the hive-queen could awaken and thrive in peace. He looked a long time.